EIRELAN

LIAM O'SHIEL

ISBN: 1463569327
ISBN-13: 9781463569327

Strike me, ye winds of a frightful black night,
Bend, all ye boughs till your limbs touch the Earth.
Rain in great torrents, blind my pale eyes,
I fear not the rage of the storm.
Thunder, ye waves of the sea on the shore,
Crack, ye hard stones and fall into the foam.
Bolts of fierce lightning, strike where ye will,
I stand on the edge of the cliff.
Howl on, ye wolves of the forest together,
Rend the night's calm with your heart-chilling song.
Shriek, ye great owl, and hunt as you will,
I stride through the deep woods alone.
Touch me, sweet dawn with your rain-scented mist,
Call to me, larks and ye sea-hunting birds.
Zephyr of morning, caress my fair hair,
I rejoice to be part of it all.

Liadan Conmaicne Laigain
PY 962

On the shores of Lough Ennell, toward early evening on the winter solstice, in the old calendar year 2954 A.D., the Twenty Clans gathered, not all of the people to be sure, but the leaders and elders and scholars and the ordinary folk who farmed and fished and made things with their skilled hands. As the sun set over the lake, a solemn song was sung while twenty great stones were set in a circle, one for each clan. This circle of stones was ever after venerated as marking the time and place of our joining together, to live as we wished to live, speaking the ancient tongue of the Celts, and forsaking forever after the machines which had brought mankind low and torn the beautiful earth asunder. On that day near a thousand years ago at Lough Ennell, we became the Province of the Twenty Clans.

Seanlaoch Osraige, Historian of the Province

Chapter 1
October 8, Province Year 999

The Harvest Fair at Wicklow was by no means the largest in the Province, yet no other fair east or west surpassed the joy of its music, the riot of its colors, the variety of its foods and ales, and the artistry of its crafts. Today the fair had been blessed with a balmy early autumn day of gentle sun and cool breeze from the sea.

People came from as far as Ballycanew to the south and Athy to the west, in creaking, thick-axled farm wagons drawn by snorting teams, bearing fathers and mothers and infants on the buckboard and the older children crowded in amid tubs of grain, strings of cured sausages, wheels of aged cheese, crocks overtopped with fresh butter, kegs of strong ale, boxes of potatoes and tomatoes and carrots, cartons of herbs for curing and herbs for cooking, and every other item large and small that might be bartered or sold for Province coin.

In smaller wagons or on horseback came the vendors of fine metalwork, jewelry, pottery, glassware, clothing for every purpose, shoes, caps, hats, tools, cookware, wood carvings, paintings, wall coverings, carpets, weapons, and armor. Musicians, drama troupes, storytellers, mystics, bards and singers had been working the rolling fields since dawn, their cups and baskets filling fast with coin. The innocent laughter of children mingled with shouts of greeting, the banter of bartering, guffaws at a joke, the sweet lilt of a fine soprano lifted in song. Clans scattered over the land gathered to exchange the news of births and deaths and weddings and seamy tales of family intrigue, jealousy and secret grudges.

Conor Laigain, son of Domnall and Liadan, strolled among the booths and tables, smiling and greeting friends. Among the men at the fair he stood neither tall nor short and was perhaps slenderer at the waist than most. Chestnut hair evenly blended his father's black and his mother's blond, but the gray-green color of his eyes drifted back a generation to his grandfather Uinseann. His hands bore the heavy calluses of ten years' army service. A long scar from left ear to jaw hardened fine-drawn features that suggested melancholy.

That he was a soldier was obvious to those who passed him. Though he wore no armor and carried no weapons, a captain's cape the color of polished copper billowed in the breeze, and on his shoulders glinted the crossed silver swords of a senior captain in the Line of Blades. Rowdy bands of younger soldiers quieted at his approach, and he was not allowed to pay for any morsel of food or cup of stout.

After a half hour of pleasured wandering, Conor found himself gazing up at the tall, ornate clock that marked the fairgrounds' center and melodiously chimed the time on the hour. Its scrolled hands now read three minutes past noon, the time when he had agreed to meet Mairin. He looked about but could not see far along the visitor-choked aisles. Wicklow being a port of call for the Province Squadron, there were plenty of sailors in view, young women roving about with the swaying gait of those used to the pitching deck of a ship, attired in pale green woolen tunics drawn tight at the waist by white sash-belts, round white tams fitted over short-cut hair and set at a jaunty slant, shiny brass pins of service time and rank that glinted in the brilliant sunshine. Here and there he spotted an ensign or lieutenant clad in forest green tunic and black sash, tri-corner black hat squarely set, shoulders bearing silver medallions of rank and stitched with the name of the ship. Each sighting raised his hope that it was Mairin; none were. Not that her being late was unusual, in fact it was what he expected. Today he wanted all the time he could have with her. Her ship waited for her in Wicklow Harbor.

"Conor."

A woman's voice behind him. It was not someone he wished to see at the moment.

"Aideen," he said, turning. "Good to see you, sister."

Aideen Laigain, older than Conor by four years, was no amalgam of her parents: she was their father Domnall in lanky female form. Shiny black hair flecked with gray, penetrating dark brown eyes, angular face, and a certain arch of her back and high cast of her chin all bespoke of their long-since-fallen father. Where Domnall always seemed ready to laugh, his eldest daughter's face rather gave the expectation of a command that was to be obeyed. It was this stern face that she wore now, reinforced by her Commodore's uniform, alike in color and style to the other officers but festooned with polished gold captain's anchors on each shoulder and ornate gold Celtic crosses pinned on each side of her chest, the sign of her supreme rank in the Squadron. Seeing her, sailors and officers alike drifted away from the great clock.

She managed a wan smile and touched him on the arm. "She's on her way, Conor."

"I'm sure," he said, edging his arm away. "Let's walk and let your sailors have their fun."

He led Aideen though the throngs of fairgoers to the north end of the grounds, taking some pleasure in the thought that she would resent following him. When they passed the last booth of cabinet makers, the meadow gave way to a thin stand of trees. A shallow, rocky stream, well-filled and gurgling with the waters of a damp, cool summer, wound its way through the wood. Conor took them into the woods far enough so they could not be overheard. He rested his back upon the gnarled trunk of a giant oak.

She stopped a few paces from him, spread her boots to shoulder-width and clasped her hands behind her back, a pose he assumed she adopted on the quarterdeck of her flagship. Her face was cool and unreadable as ever.

"You didn't come on me by accident, Aideen."

"No, I suppose I didn't. I didn't have you followed if that's what you're implying. I hazarded a guess that you would see Captain Fotharta here today and checked the most logical meeting place."

"And delayed her arrival, no doubt." He gave her a look of pure frustration. "Can't you call her by her name? We're not on a ship here."

"Whatever you like. Her name and rank are not the issue. Mairin has said nothing to me directly, though our mother seems to think you have marriage plans."

"I've made no secret of my hope for that. I haven't proposed to her, if that's what you're probing for."

"I suppose it is. And you know my views on that, I've told you more than once."

He straightened up and met her cold stare with one of his own. "And I've told you what I think of your views."

"Fine. Let me repeat my objections. First, there is bad blood between our two families and this will only serve to increase it. Second, at the moment and for the foreseeable future I need my senior captain at sea, not home nursing babies. And three, the marriage will never work because you don't know Mairin as I do. Like me, she'll never be content puttering around an idyllic cottage. Is that clear enough?"

Conor held on to an angry face, while his heart cringed at his sister's unfeeling assessment.

"Oh, it's clear enough. Just let me correct one thing. You and Mairin are nothing alike. If you were, I would hardly be interested in her at all."

"I am stating honest facts that I wish you would face."

"I don't suppose any human emotions might creep into your analysis?"

"I don't have that luxury."

"You're as cold as winter's ice," he said, shaking his head in dismay. "Aideen, I've sacrificed a lot for the Province. I am not going to sacrifice bringing children into the world. What you can't seem to understand is that fighting for the survival of our people has no meaning unless there is someone to come after us." He reached down and pulled up a clump of grass and earth, then let it tumble through his fingers. "This is just dirt. Our father did not lay down his life to protect dirt."

Her features darkened with rage. "Don't presume to tell me what our father fought for. Keep in mind that without that dirt, brother, your children would have nowhere to live."

"I've defended our right to that dirt as long and hard as you have."

In spite of the cool breeze, sweat trickled down his sides and stung its way into a wound on his right hip where an enemy lance had sliced under his cuirass. He stalked past Aideen to the brook, pulled a small white towel from his belt pouch and dipped it into the stream. He slipped it under his shirt and blotted the wound. The fresh, cool water eased the sting of the sweat. When he brought the towel out it was stained pink, so he rinsed it in the stream and wrung it out.

"You might have told me you were wounded, Conor," Aideen said with less rancor.

"Funny that would concern you." He pulled up his shirt to expose the full length of the wound. "An inch or two deeper and you'd have no worries about losing your senior captain to marriage and children. I'm on duty again tonight, so who knows?"

"You have your own brand of cruelty, brother," she said, turning away.

He dropped his shirt. "You bring out the worst in me."

"I'm not asking that much, Conor. Marry if you must, just no children, not now. Mairin stays at sea."

"How many years?"

"I don't know. Until we and Kernow get the upper hand again."

"Two?"

"At least."

"Ten?"

"It's possible, yes. How can I tell you that?"

"Mairin agrees with your opinion?"

"She knows our situation and how much she's needed."

"Then she'll refuse me if I ask her. Which I intend to do."

Aideen pulled off her hat and snapped it against her leg in frustration.

"All right, let me put it to you this way. I command twenty warships and two dozen more service craft, give or take. Kernow's Admiralty is pressing me constantly to accept more ships and crew them because every year there are more raiders, they have bigger ships, and they attack more often. Every warship needs a captain who can lead and inspire junior officers, command the respect of eighty sailors, take the ship to sea and bring it back safely, not to mention engaging and destroying enemy ships. Anything less in a captain and every sailor and officer aboard is put at terrible risk. Captains of that quality do not automatically spring from ensigns and lieutenants like apples on a tree, Conor. I have on the roster twenty-eight captains capable of commanding a warship. Four are not in the best of health and would like to retire, two are new and inexperienced, and two others are laid up with injuries. And of all twenty-eight on the list, Mairin is the best I have. Whether she and I like each other is utterly beside the point. Taking her from the Squadron now would be very damaging. I mean it."

She was about to go on, but he broke in.

"Stop, Aideen. I know the numbers. The army is no better off and you know it. By your logic every able-bodied citizen would serve from eighteen to forty and we'd be the last generation of the Twenty Clans."

"We might be that anyway!"

Faces in the crowd a hundred feet away turned to see what the argument was about. She lowered her voice. "You have no idea the kind of pressure I am under. No idea of what our real situation is. You live in a dream world, brother."

He abandoned trying to hold in what he felt.

"Let me tell you about my dream world," he said, standing so close to her that his sweat-soaked shirt brushed against her spotless uniform. "Three nights ago, when I got this," he touched his wounded side, "we fought for forty long minutes with midland raiders who broke through the Rampart near Ballynamult. When it was over, it seemed like everyone was walking back to the field hospital alone or with help. Then I saw a surgeon bending over someone near the gate. I knelt down and I found a young Blade, blood pouring from a huge wound in his neck. The surgeon whispered in my ear that he would not live. When I saw him, this boy was alive and awake and staring up at me with terror in his eyes. I cradled his head in my hands and leaned over his face and told him it was all right, as his lifeblood poured out on the earth around my knees. It was not long before his eyes closed and he died, his blood leaking through my fingers and my mouth breathing in his last breath. That's my dream world, Commodore. That's the real situation I face every day."

He turned and pressed his hand against the tree. He fought back tears of rage and anguish because he knew Aideen would see them as mere weakness.

She said nothing for a long moment. He took a deep breath and faced her.

"Conor, we simply don't see things the same way," she said, donning her hat. "We never have. Next time you see Mairin, ask her how she feels about quitting. Now, or two or four years from now. You'll see I'm right."

She turned and strode away.

When she had blended into the crowd, he sank to his knees on the stream bank and splashed cold water over his face. His thoughts turned to Domnall, whom Aideen so much resembled in appearance and so little in spirit. She remembered only his ability to lead, to decide, to act, and not his endless capacity to love and laugh and maybe, in private moments, to cry. They remembered a different father. And what of Liadan, their mother? So different from Domnall, cool and contained at times yet filled with great reserves of love for her children and for her people. Much as he wanted to, he could not bring her into this argument. Liadan had enough worries pressing down on her and she had long since grown weary of the struggles between her two older children.

He headed back for the clock, and when the crowd momentarily thinned he spotted Mairin. *So beautiful*, he thought: lean muscular body, deeply-tanned skin, auburn hair trimmed close, a face that fused the legendary beauty of her mother Etain and the strength of her now-dissipated father Gorman. She was talking and laughing with another uniformed officer, a lieutenant by her insignia. Mairin was in uniform too, her gold anchors sparkling as a ray of sun caught them.

Much as he hated to admit it, Aideen was partly right, there was a side of the woman he loved that his imagination could hardly conjure. A few times he had gone aboard her ship and seen her transform from a warm and introspective woman with an easy laugh to a woman who commanded respect and admiration from those around her, whose stern roving eye missed nothing awry. Even her voice changed, the soft alto replaced by an edgy insistence, nothing so cold as Aideen yet still the voice of authority. Each time, he left the ship wondering who it was he said goodbye to.

She hadn't seen him yet. *Should I walk away now and concede defeat? Is that what she truly wants me to do and can't bring herself to tell me? Am I setting myself up for heartbreak?*

Laughter burst from the puppet-show booth behind him, drawing Mairin's attention. She smiled and waved and now it was too late to walk away. He approached her, halted a few strides away.

"I'll take my leave," Mairin's companion said. "You have company."

"Wait, Sinea," said Mairin. "Conor, let me present my first officer, Lieutenant Sinea Danaan."

"Lieutenant, you look ..." he began.

"Familiar?" Sinea broke in. She let him struggle for a moment. "Ballyhale Fort, seven years ago?"

He searched his memory. A lonesome place, Ballyhale ... and there had been a blizzard that year, stranded the garrison for over a month on short rations. His eyes widened as the memory of her finally surfaced.

"You were the card shark!"

"I was." She extended her hand and Conor took it. "I left the Bows that spring for the Squadron," she explained to Mairin. "Conor was a regular in the card game. His problem was that he had too honest a face."

"Only too true," he admitted. "But you cleaned out everyone!"

"It's funny, I remember your honest face like it was yesterday but your name, not a whit. Captain Fotharta has told me all about you and I never made the connection."

"You remember the faces you took hard-earned coins from," he said with mock dismay. "Names don't matter in a card game."

"I'll give you a chance at revenge this winter. Now I'll take my leave so you two can enjoy the fair. Captain, see you on the ship."

She saluted Mairin and disappeared into the milling crowd. Conor linked his arm with Mairin's and they strolled down the aisle of food vendors.

"What was Sinea like then?" Mairin asked him.

"Funny. Overconfident, maybe. Very smart and ..."

"Sexy?"

"I suppose."

"You don't remember?"

He saw she was teasing him. "She remembers faces, I remember—"

She whacked his shoulder with an open hand. "You'd better not finish that sentence! You've never seen her on the *Caillech*? I guess not. She's been my first for over a year."

"You've spoken highly of her. You said she's due for promotion."

"She is," Mairin said as they entered a food vendor's booth. "Aideen would promote her if I suggested it. I just hate to lose her ... but I'll have to. And soon."

They stopped in front of the vendor's massive cast iron frying pans, filled to the rim with plump chicken breasts browned to a turn.

"Hungry?"

"Famished, not a morsel since breakfast at sunrise and that was cold oatmeal."

"And they say navy food is better than army food!" he scoffed. "Sir, two sandwiches with extra sauce."

The vendor handed over two buns stuffed with hot chicken and oozing with butter-herb sauce. They carried their repast down the aisle until they reached the edge of the woods, where benches and tables had been set out for eating and relaxing. Conor found an open bench and they sat down together. A vendor passed by with a cart and sold them two bottles of ice-cold stout to wash down the sandwiches. When they finished, Conor leaned back and laid his arm on the bench behind her. His other hand rested on his belt pouch. After a moment's hesitation, he made a decision.

He reached into the pocket. "I have something for you."

In his hand he held a three-pointed Celtic Knot, fashioned of leather and decorated in silver. It was the symbol of proposed union: two points for a man and a woman, one for their children to come. He took hold of her right wrist and laid the amulet in the palm of her hand.

"Mairin, I love you," he said, and then the words of sacred ritual, "and I ask you to join with me in a union of heart, mind and spirit."

She stared down in amazement at the symbolic ornament. Her trembling hand closed around it and with her left land she took hold of his.

"Conor, I love you," she said, "and I *will* join with you in a union of heart, mind and spirit."

He wrapped his arms around her and whispered in her ear, "I was so afraid."

At that moment his eyes settled on the gold anchors adorning her shoulder.

"That I'd say no?" she whispered back. "You know my heart."

He released her to arm's length. She ran her fingers over the amulet and then tucked it gently into her own belt-purse.

"It would mean leaving the sea, when we start our family."

She reached out and brushed errant hair from his forehead. "I know that, love. Two years more, that would be all right? Retire when I'm thirty?"

"Of course," he said. He kissed her cheek. "I need some time to build our home!"

Her gaze wandered over the fairground.

"You know, it will be a strange ceremony. My mother and father will not be there."

"Kellen will be. And there must be cousins and aunts and uncles who would come. You know my whole family adores you."

"I know. Kellen will be happy about it, certain sure."

Tears started to pour down her cheeks and a sob escaped. Conor put his arms around her again. He felt her body trembling against him.

"Are you all right?"

"Yes," she said after drawing a deep breath. "Just a little overwhelmed."

Conor offered her a leftover napkin from their lunch. She mopped away the tears and managed a smile.

"You must think I'm sad," she said. "I'm not, Conor. I love you so much. It's that, well, I never thought I'd be part of a real family, have children of my own. It's a lot to think about. Not simple and clean like being on my ship."

"I understand." He thought a moment. "Let's announce our betrothal together, when you get back. I won't even tell Kellen tonight."

"You're both at the fort?"

"Yes, I think he's commanding the Blades there all week."

She took hold of his hands and intertwined their fingers.

"Watch out for him."

Conor smiled and leaned close to her face. "He's a Blade Captain, Mairin, one of the best. I don't think he needs watching out for."

"Promise," she insisted, her eyes searching his.

"Sure I will," he said. "Now, can I kiss you?"

"Any sailors around?" she said, scanning the other benches.

"None that I can see."

"All right, then."

He kissed her long and tenderly, luxuriating in the softness of her lips pressing against his, the hard suppleness of her body, the strength of her hands on his shoulders. After what seemed like a long time, he reluctantly let go and they both peered about to see if anyone was staring. At the very next bench, two teen-aged lovers were putting them to shame.

They both laughed. The kissing youngsters broke their embrace and glared at them, thinking they were the subject of the old-timers' mirth.

Mairin stood and drew Conor to his feet.

"I have about two hours," she said, "and I want us to enjoy every second."

"Then let's go!"

They linked arms and plunged into the mob.

They spent the two precious hours as ordinary fair-goers, laughing at the joke tellers, applauding the bands, *oohing* at the end of a story-teller's heroic tale, rewarding jugglers and knife throwers with coins tossed in a basket, munching on pastries and eating tidbits that did not go well together, trying their hand at target games, buying each other silly gifts.

As the last chord of a madrigal choir's concert faded out, the fair's clock chimed three times. They strolled arm in arm to the shady corral at the south end of the park where the horses waited patiently amid bales of hay and tubs of fresh water. Mairin handed in the chit for her military mount, and moments later a stablehand led her horse out of the grassy paddock and quickly saddled him.

They held hands at arms' length.

"I should be back in two weeks," she said. "A quick cargo run to Falmouth, then two weeks guarding the Welsh coast."

"We'll have a party when you return, at Laigain House, and we'll tell everyone then."

She kissed him and turned to mount. He laid a restraining hand on her arm.

"One last thing. Before I found you at the clock ... Aideen found me."

Her smile faded. "What did she have to say?"

"Mainly that I was fooling myself to think you'd give up the sea to marry me and raise children."

Mairin cursed under her breath, then drew the Celtic Knot from her pouch.

"I would never have accepted this from you if I felt that way. I wish she'd mind her own business."

Conor took hold of the hand that held his gift. "She imagines it is her business. I didn't want to spoil our afternoon by saying anything earlier. Still I thought you should know."

"Now I know," she said with an angry edge. "She commands me at sea, Conor, and that's the end of it."

She replaced the amulet in her pouch and swung easily into the saddle.

"Give my best to your mother," she said, struggling to regain a cheerful smile. "Plan a good party, love."

"I will."

She clicked her tongue and rode off towards the port of Wicklow. Conor leaned against the paddock fence until Treasach spotted him and trotted over. Conor fed him an apple he had saved.

"Maybe I shouldn't have told her about Aideen," he said, stroking the stallion's long snout. "It seemed like she deserved to know. So, did I do the right thing in proposing?"

Treasach finished off the apple in two bites and snorted.

"Not sure how to take that."

Conor saddled Treasach himself and headed north on the sandy road that ran along the western shore of Broad Lough. Elation and worry struggled in his mind. Mairin had accepted, sure that was cause enough for joy? And she denied what Aideen said about her. Yet, was the denial too quick, too easy, too expected? Did she say what she did because she believed it, or because it was what he wanted to hear?

Other worries surfaced as he neared the fort he would command that night. The harvest was in, the warehouses full, and attacks had broken out all along the Rampart. Almost always the attacks came under cover of darkness—it would be a long and tense night at Wicklow Fort. And where was his friend Oran Osraige, who was supposed to have reported back a week ago? Perhaps there was no cause for worry yet. Oran was not one to keep to a schedule if he still had scouting work to do. Still, as the sun sank below the purple-hued Wicklow Mountains and deep shadows stretched across the silent land, he dearly wished his friend was on this side of the Rampart.

By a tally of eighteen to two, the Council of Twenty orders the construction of a rampart of wood posts, at least fifteen feet high, a foot or more in thickness, sharpened at the top, fronted by a ditch, with a well-maintained road on the Province side. This barrier will begin in the east where the River Vartry enters Broad Lough north of Wicklow, and end on the west side of the port of Dungarvan, swinging inland as far as possible while taking advantage of natural barriers as mountains and rivers. A large, manned fort with tower will be built every five miles. Watchtowers will be erected between the forts no further than two miles apart, terrain permitting. Every resource of the Province shall be bent to this task. When it is completed, all citizens of the Province will be urged, but not forced, to move behind this barrier. Work to commence tomorrow.

Official Minutes, Council of the Twenty Clans
April 7, Province Year 953

Chapter 2

October 8, 999, Wicklow Fort. All quiet at 8:00 pm. Watch complement of 40 Blades, 40 in barracks reserve, Kellen Fotharta, Cpt., 40 Bows, 40 in barracks, Duann Loigde, Cpt. Mounted scouts report signs that an attack is imminent. Morale is high, though everyone is on edge.

Conor Laigain, Fort Captain, First Rank

Conor replaced the logbook on its stand next to the telescope, then took a few steps to the railing and scanned the countryside from the Ballinalea Watchtower two miles west to the placid waters of Broad Lough a mile east of the fort. He saw nothing amiss in the grassy fields or in the waters of the River Vartry which flowed past the fort. He pushed the telescope aside and turned his poet's eye on a blood-red sun sinking beneath the Wicklow Mountains. The last rays skimming past the peaks caught the top of the Rampart's posts and for a brief time gave the illusion that the sharp tips were suspended in midair. Then all fell into shadow.

In his mind's eye he traveled the full hundred and twenty miles along those pillars, all the way from Broad Lough to the seaport of Dungarvan. South and east of that wooden wall lay the fertile coastal plains and thriving port cities that made up the lifeblood of the Province. Ten years in the army had seen him posted in every one of the Rampart's twenty-four major forts and forty watchtowers. He had marched or ridden a hundred times over every mile of the military road that ran behind the wall, blistered his hands deepening the ditch on its exposed side, drilled troops in the reserve camps at Ballyduff, Cameross, and Gorey, and fought five score desperate battles to stave off attacks or destroy raiders who managed to breach the barrier.

For over four decades, the Rampart had been the dike holding back the flood waters of chaos. Four thousand men and women guarded it day and night—more than enough in summer and mid-winter. In autumn after the harvest, attacks were frequent and bloody and each year more desperate than the last. Then, the Rampart more resembled a picket fence expected to stand against a charging bull.

A picket fence: Conor shook his head to clear the gloomy simile from his mind. The itch and sting from the wound in his side reminded him that attacks had started earlier this year, and the results bloodier than last year, and last year was worse than the year before. Was Aideen right after all? Why plan for a wife and a home and children when the next fight might find him staring at the sky with lifeless eyes? Why build his cherished cottage only to see it overrun and his children put to the sword?

A low conversation of youthful voices reminded him that he was by no means alone on the tower's high watch platform. Three sharp-eyed sentries of the night watch had climbed the staircase and now waited at the far side of the platform for him to address them first. Two boys and a girl tonight, he noted, the girl holding the hand of the larger boy.

"Take your posts," he ordered mildly, "and I'll serve out tea. You can join me one at a time."

The tall boy posted himself at the telescope while the other boy took the east side of the platform and the girl the west. Conor sat down at a corner table and poured out two cups of hot tea from a flask he had carried up from the fort's kitchen, three stories below.

"You first, young lady," he said to the girl.

She walked over to him, brushed back honey-colored hair that tumbled over bright hazel eyes, and offered a shy smile. Conor handed her a cup which she took gratefully in hands callused by hard work.

"Thank you, Captain Laigain," she said in a soft voice.

"What's your name?"

"Liadan Cumain."

"My mother's name is Liadan," he said, "so I'm very fond of that name. Do you live near the fortress?"

"At Glenealy, sir, where we farm. I ride here on a horse with my brother." She nodded in the direction of the tall boy at the telescope.

"How old are you, Liadan?"

"Twelve, sir."

"What's your brother's name?"

"Bradaigh."

"Take your tea with you, Liadan, and watch through the telescope for your brother. Bradaigh?"

The boy straightened, tugged his pale blue homespun shirt down through his belt, and marched over to Conor with a long, confident stride. He was a fairer version of his sister: tousled straw-colored hair, bright blue eyes, a solid frame and big hands that suggested size and power yet to come.

"Bradaigh Cumain, sir, senior sentry tonight."

"Tea?" Conor offered him a filled cup.

"Thank you, sir."

"How old are you, Bradaigh?"

"Just turned fifteen, sir."

"It's all right if you sit," Conor said, waving his hand at a chair.

Bradaigh glanced at his sister and the other boy. Satisfied that they were alert and watching, he settled into the offered chair with a tired sigh.

"Just for a moment, thank you, sir. T'will be a long night after a heavy day."

Bradaigh took a long draft of his tea.

"Your sister tells me your family has a farm."

"Yes, sir, I baled hay this whole day. We all have to work, at harvest time."

"How many are you?"

"Eight. Oh, I mean seven, now."

"Did someone move away?"

Bradaigh shook his head and looked down.

"There's been a loss, then?"

Bradaigh turned his head in his sister's direction. Liadan had her eye glued to the telescope's eyepiece and was slowly sweeping it back and forth as she'd been taught. Bradaigh leaned over the table towards Conor.

"Our brother Driscol," he whispered. "Last week at Ballynamult. We're ... having a hard time with it, Captain. Liadan loved him dearly. So did I."

Tears dripped onto the table.

Ballynamult. Last week. A dying boy. Only one soldier had died at Ballynamult, the young Blade who died in his arms. *Oh, sweet heaven, it was this boy's brother.*

"I was there, Bradaigh. I was there with your brother."

Bradaigh swiped the tears away and looked up wide-eyed.

"You were? When he died?"

Conor clamped his hand on Bradaigh's rock-hard forearm. "Yes. But this is not the place or time to tell you about it. It would upset Liadan. And me too, I guess."

"I understand, Captain." He gulped his tea and struggled for composure. "Maybe in a few weeks?"

"You come and see me," Conor said, "at my home if you like. Any time."

Bradaigh nodded his thanks, then turned his eyes on Conor's sword, which lay in its sheath on the table. "Won't be long till I take up a sword like that, Captain, and make someone pay for Driscol."

Conor slid the sword out of its sheath and handed it to him. "See how it feels in your hand."

Bradaigh gripped the hilt, got to his feet and stepped away from the table. He made four quick thrusts and parries.

"You've been instructed already."

"Yes, sir," he said. He slid the sword back into the sheath. "By Driscol."

Conor tapped a finger on the sheath. "This sword belonged to my father, Domnall. He fought with it the day he died. When I was about your age, he told me it was forged by a blacksmith in the remotest mountains of Wales. Said it takes the sharpest edge and will never shatter in battle. So far he's been right. I've fought with it a hundred times and not a dent nor chip in the blade."

Bradaigh stared at the sword a moment more, then said, "best I go back to the scope, sir. A dangerous time, it is."

He walked over to his sister and kissed her on the forehead. Liadan whispered in her brother's ear and returned to her own post. All the while, the third boy faced east, hands clasped behind his back, humming to himself.

"Sentry?" Conor called him. "Join me for tea?"

The boy turned and approached with a measured step. Tall and slender with roan hair and delicate features, he sported a blue-and-green tartan cap cocked to one side.

"My name is Trev Fiachrach, Captain," he said in an alto voice that seemed on the verge of cracking. "Your piper for tonight."

"Trev, some tea for you," Conor said. He refilled the cup with steaming brew.

The boy nodded his thanks and wrapped the cup in long, sinewy fingers. He held his meadow-green eyes steady on Conor's face as he sipped his tea. *How strange*, Conor thought. *I feel as if he's looking inside me.*

"Do you live near the fort, Trev?"

"Not far, sir, in Avoca, near Meeting of the Waters. My mother serves at sea in the Squadron and my father crafts cuirasses like the one you're wearing at the Wicklow Armory."

"I saw your instrument," Conor said. He glanced towards the sentries' table in the opposite corner of the platform. "It doesn't look like standard army-issue pipes."

"It is not, sir," the boy said with obvious pride. "That is a full set of great warpipes and it's my own. My father made them special for me. I can play for battle, sure enough. I also play my own music."

"*Your* music?"

"Yes, Captain," he said. "I'm a composer."

"If we have a quiet night, you can play a tune for us?"

"Of course, sir. My uillean pipes are in the Common Room."

Conor turned his gaze on the boy's tartan cap. "The plaid must mean something to you, Trev."

"My mother is Scottish, sir," he said. " 'Tis the tartan of Clan Carmichael."

"Glad to have the Scots with us tonight."

Trev smiled at the remark, finished his tea, and returned to his post. *An unusual boy*, Conor pondered. *Can't be more than thirteen yet he has an unsettling maturity about him.*

The sun had now set, and as twilight descended on the tower, Bradaigh and Trev climbed short staircases at the tower's north-facing corners where they fired four powerful lanterns, each a multi-wicked oil lamp encased in lenses and reflectors made by Kernow's Guild of Glass. On this clear, moonless night, the beacons shed pale white light half a mile. This task done, Bradaigh took up a signal trumpet and at Conor's order, blew a single long note towards the Ballinalea Watchtower. Moments later, a sentry in that tower repeated the signal to the next tower. In thirty minutes, the signal would be passed a hundred and twenty miles west and south to Dungarvan, and as each tower received the signal, sentries fired the lanterns. The horns signaled the formal start of the night watch, and reminded soldiers in more isolated parts of the Rampart that they were not alone.

From the open staircase wafted the tempting smell of frying sausage and onions. In the Common Room at the fort's ground level, Blades and Bows mixed together at long tables and devoured their evening meal. An occasional burst of laughter lifted above the low buzz of conversation, a sign of high morale among nervous troops. Conor could have gone down to join them, and he often did. Tonight, a sense of foreboding held him in the tower.

Footsteps echoed up the staircase. A moment later, Kellen Fotharta emerged in full battle armor to report. Even in armor, the twenty-four-year-old fighter's appearance was not impressive. Yet Conor had fought often enough beside Mairin's younger brother to know that his size made little difference. A slender frame and delicate, pale features, copied from his mother, belied a fierce fighter and clear-eyed battle-field commander who inspired confidence in his men and kept his head when the going got rough. Such were the men Padraic Conmaicne promoted to officers over those who could merely stab and pound and hammer at the enemy.

Kellen had thoughtfully brought with him a platter loaded with sausage and onions and a slice of bread. He laid the platter in front of Conor and eased himself into the chair opposite him.

"Many thanks, my friend," said Conor. "A long night ahead."

Kellen smiled. "My pleasure."

"Duann could join us if she likes."

"She's having a talk with an archer who showed up late for duty and out of uniform. God help the poor girl." Kellen let his eyes drift towards the fading violet glow in the west. "I heard that Mairin's ship is in Wicklow Harbor."

Conor grinned and answered between bites. "We spent the after-noon together at the Fair. She made me promise to watch out for you."

"Watch out for me!"

"Just sisterly affection. I promised, she insisted on it. You should be thankful for such a sister. Aideen was there too, beforehand."

"Unpleasant?"

"You could say that."

Kellen thought for a moment. "You and Mairin will marry, do you think?"

"Yes, I think we will."

"I hope you do, truly, Conor. She's had a lonely life and nothing but the service for a long time. At least so far as I know. She needs a good man to be with."

"We need each other, I'd say. And I'd gain a brother in the bargain! On the other hand, Gorman and Etain will not be so happy about it."

"They don't care a whit about Mairin," Kellen snapped with sud-den ferocity.

"I already know that. And seem to hate me and my whole family, exactly why I know not. Bram despises me too but at least there I know his reason."

"Not important," Kellen said in a quieter voice. "Bram won't be there either."

"Mairin almost gets sick if I mention his name."

"My brother was as cruel to her—"

Kellen broke off and swallowed hard. He turned his face away from Conor.

"Are you all right?" Conor asked him. "We don't need to talk about this. Forget I asked."

Kellen took a deep breath. "I'm okay. Sometimes the anger gets the better of me." He rubbed his hands over his face. "Mairin has never told you the whole story?"

"About your life as children? No. If I bring the subject up she gets uneasy and defensive. I don't press her about it."

"She'll tell you in her own time, I guess."

"Maybe it would be easier if I heard it from you?"

Kellen stared upward at the friendly stars beginning to show themselves.

"We're friends, Conor, and I trust you with my life. You know that. If Mairin weren't involved I *would* tell you everything, gladly. She is involved and it's best you hear it from her."

"She doesn't have to tell me anything. What's past is past."

"Not always," Kellen said, meeting Conor's eyes. "Parts of our past are not so easy to lay aside. Not so easy at all."

He fell silent, lost in his thoughts.

"Captain Laigain."

Liadan's high-pitched voice startled both of them.

"Yes, what is it?

The girl's eyes were fixed on Ballinalea Watchtower.

"Silent signal, sir, please wait," she replied, holding up her hand. The watchtower's beacon two miles away was flashing long and short. "I have it, Captain," she said, turning to Conor. "Boats in the river, twenty counted, more coming."

Kellen leaped up and flung himself onto the staircase. Conor strapped on his sword and pulled on his helmet.

"Trev, signal the Squadron, *attack coming down the river.*"

Trev bounded up the right-hand staircase to signal with a lantern. Seeing the blinking pattern, the Squadron's Harbor Patrol would launch fighting boats into Broad Lough. Any raider boat portaged past the fort would get a warm reception when it reached the lake.

"Bradaigh?"

The boy had the telescope trained on the Vartry. "Not good, Captain."

He shifted aside so Conor could get to the eyepiece. Dozens of boats were poling down the river towards them, each one crammed with Dublin raiders.

"They know they've been seen by now," Conor said. "Bradaigh, sound the trumpet alarm, watch me for signals. Trev, you know where to go?"

The boy, his cap now on straight, pulled tight the leather straps holding his warpipes and battle drum. "On the bridge with the Bows, Captain."

"Right. Let's go. Bradaigh, bolt the hatch after us."

Conor sprinted down the stairs with Trev a stair behind. In the empty Common Room he grabbed a shield. Together they plunged down the sloping riverbank.

Directly in front of the fort, a stone bridge arched over the Vartry's hundred-foot span. Duann Loigde's archers reached the bridge first and released pins holding up a massive iron grate. The grate crashed into the river directly below the bridge, blocking passage to boats but not water. The land on the bridge's far side was a soggy bog at any time save the dead of winter. The only sure-footed path for the Dublin fighters to reach the fort was a two hundred-foot strip of dry land between the river's edge and the steeper part of the southern bank. This strip was fast being blocked by Kellen's massing Bladesmen.

The bridge's span was packed from end to end with Duann Loigde's archers. Crowded among them at the span's center was Trev Fiachrach, the blowstick of his warpipes touching his lips and his battle drum hanging at his side. In the fort's tower, Bradaigh leaned over the balustrade, signal trumpet ready, with a worried Liadan at his elbow. The barracks reserve troops sprinted down the bank, some still tugging on armor and helmets, and joined the forces already assembled.

Conor lowered his faceguard and took a position next to Kellen a few strides behind the battle line. Two hundred yards upstream, boats glided onto the river's sandy banks and disgorged twenty fighters each.

"How many do you think?" Kellen asked.

"At least twenty boats. Four hundred fighters, even five."

Kellen barked out an order to extend the left flank another two paces.

"They haven't tried a direct assault here for two years," Kellen observed. "Why now?"

"Padraic thinks they plan to wear us down before attacking with a big army." Shouting broke out upriver. "Here they come."

"Javelins up!" Kellen shouted.

Eighty Bladesman lifted their weapons to shoulder height. Behind them Duann Loigde's voice called out "knock arrows, ready fire." Her archers raised longbows to firing position.

Conor swept his eyes over his force. With such experienced fighting captains there was no adjustment he could make that would matter.

He pointed his sword at Trev. "Sound the pipes."

Trev unleashed the full power of his warpipes. Conor felt a chill run up his back at the astonishing sound. Never had he heard the warpipes played this way. It seemed as if five thousand years of the Celts at war were cascading over the battlefield.

He turned back, pulled the straps of his cuirass tight, and waited. Upstream, hundreds of Dubliner fighters pounded towards them, their screams and bellows clashing strangely with the melodious battle anthem. When the vanguard of the fighters came in range, the Line of Bows launched a first volley, then a second, and a third, not two seconds apart. Dozens of fighters crashed face first into the damp sands.

At fifty yards, Kellen cried "Blades, launch!"

Two dense ranks of heavy-armored infantry hurled javelins in a broad arc. More screams and death-gurgles erupted from the charging mass of warriors.

Kellen cried out again, "Swords up, brace and hold the line!"

Conor tightened his grip on his father's sword. *Father, protect all of us.* He took two steps backward and signaled upward to Bradaigh with his sword. The boy blew three long blasts on the trumpet, alerting Ballinalea and the Harbor Patrol that battle had commenced.

Then came the familiar crunch of body against body, sword and pike against shield and armor, the grunting and cursing and anguished cries of mortal combat. Blood-smell mingled with the sweet scent of wet grass. The massed double-rank of Blades bent and wavered yet held firm against the first rush of four or five times its number. Duann's archers poured fire over the heads of the Blades into the swelling rear ranks of the enemy's force.

From long experience Conor was certain the Dubliners would use sheer weight of numbers and ferocity of attack to break them. A steep, muddy bank made an attack on the left flank virtually impossible. An attack in the shallows of the river on the right would bring their fighters under withering fire from the archers on the bridge, yet the Dubliners lacked for nothing in courage and audacity, and less than a minute into the furious fight, the attack on the right was on its way. Enemy fighters splashed forward in the shallows, instantly drawing the concentrated fire of the Line of Bows. Conor had to admire the raw courage of warriors protected only by circular shields plunging ahead into a blizzard of longbow fire. Come on they did, and in great enough numbers to threaten the flank and the entire battle line.

Kellen saw it too and blew two short blasts on his signal trumpet, followed by two more, the signal for the second rank to shift right and take on the assault. This meant the front rank bore the full weight of the main assault.

"I'll lead the flank," Conor shouted to Kellen. "Hold the center!"

Conor sprinted to the point where the bridge intersected the river. The archers were directly over his head and the blast from Trev's pipes was deafening. Kellen's second rank ran to new positions in the shallows facing outward, forming a line bent at an angle to the main battle line. Into this thin line the attackers splashed ahead, and as they came close, the archers had to stop firing into them for fear of hitting their own soldiers.

Conor posted himself at the end of the line where the cool river water overtopped his boots. The soldier on his left had just butted shields with him when the full force of the assault struck their line.

Conor knew in an instant it would be a close fight: the attackers were two and three deep, big men, wild with battle fury, swinging heavy swords and hammers and maces. The single line of Blades slowly gave ground, stabbing and killing as they bent further backward. The Blade on Conor's left took a direct hit with a hammer on his chest and fell with a muffled cry into the shallow water. Conor found himself facing five men, alone. Only for a second: Kellen took the fallen man's place and together they attacked, stabbing and slashing while taking heavy blows on armor and shield.

Conor slashed open the throat of the man in front of him. The man splashed face down into the swirling water and drifted away. Kellen deflected a hammer strike with his shield and then gutted the hammer's wielder. A tall, heavy man lunged toward Conor and whirled a spiked iron mace straight at his head. Conor raised his shield and absorbed the shattering blow, but the sheer force of it drove him sideways, his boots slipped in the muddy ooze and he fell onto his knees. He hacked at his attacker's shins and the man roared with pain, yet stayed on his feet and whirled the heavy mace again, driving it straight into Kellen's undefended right side with a sickening thud. In a frozen instant of time, Conor saw the mace stove in Kellen's cuirass as if it were made of paper. Kellen sank to his knees. Another blow would mean his death.

There would be no next blow. Still on his knees, Conor drove his father's sword full through the man's belly. The Dubliner stumbled backward, slid off the bloody blade and splashed into the blood-tinged waters. Conor no sooner regained his footing than a hammer wielded by yet another attacker glanced off his helmet. Thick steel saved his life but did not spare him a stunning shock that grayed his vision and brought him again to his knees. In the brief seconds that passed until he could see again, some part of his mind waited for the death-blow. It never came. When his eyes focused he saw his attacker floating downstream with an arrow in his side. Duann had led half of her archers into the river where they gained an open line of fire past the hard-pressed Line of Blades.

Conor plunged back into the fray and slowly the bent flank straightened. When he was convinced the line was no longer in danger of collapse, he stepped backward to see what had happened to Kellen. Medics had carried him onto the sandy shore, where he lay on his back. Blood leaked from the corners of his mouth. His face was bleach-white and his features frozen into a mask of pain. Seeing Conor kneeling beside him, he seized hold of Conor's blood-spattered bracer.

"Get the bastards," he said. "All of them."

Conor leaped to his feet and sounded his own signal trumpet. Two long blasts: *attack and destroy*. In response, Trev silenced his warpipes and pounded the battle drum with a steady pulse that gave the Line of Blades their cadence for advance. Conor wedged himself into the center of the line and after that he saw and heard and smelled nothing except fighting. All conscious thought faded into a distant place. Steel-hard muscles and a superbly conditioned body did what they needed to do. Shield up, jab and step, slash and jab, jab and step. Dimly he was aware that Duann's entire archer force had abandoned the bridge and waded upstream past their line. From that position, eighty archers poured relentless, accurate fire into the Dubliners.

It could not go on much longer. After five minutes of the grinding attack, the remaining Dubliners turned and tried to flee back upstream to their boats. It was too late for that now. Archers sprinted up the river bank, shooting as they ran. Arrows found every one of the panicked fighters. Corpses piled up against the iron grating below the bridge, blocking the river's flow and sending pink water pouring over the banks.

Blades sank to their knees in exhaustion and pain. When Conor eased off his own helmet, agony flared from his head as unyielding steel squeezed over the place the hammer struck him. He knew he was bleeding too, though not dangerously.

He made his way back to where Kellen lay on a stretcher carried by two medics. Conor walked alongside until Kellen saw him. Kellen seized hold of Conor's hand.

"Tell Mairin I love her."

He coughed, spewing bright red blood onto the white cloth of the stretcher.

"You can tell her yourself in a few days."

Kellen managed a weak smile. "Sure, Conor." His eyelids fluttered. "Just tell her."

The medics hurried him up the river bank towards the fort's surgery.

Trev Fiachrach approached him, his face shining with sweat, his tartan cap clutched in a trembling hand.

"My first real battle," he said in a quavering voice. "Not like the drills at all, Captain. I wasn't ready for it."

Conor leaned against the cool stone of the bridge, his heart sinking into a black abyss at the moaning of the wounded and the sobbing of comrades bent over lifeless friends.

"Don't concern yourself, Trev," he said. "You did your job very well indeed." He drew the shaking boy under his arm. "Nothing makes a man ready for this."

I must down to the seas again, to the lonely sea and the sky,
And all I ask is a tall ship and a star to steer her by, And the
wheel's kick and the wind's song and the white sail's shaking,
And a grey mist on the sea's face, and a grey dawn breaking. I
must down to the seas again, for the call of the running tide Is a
wild call and a clear call that may not be denied; And all I ask
is a windy day with the white clouds flying, And the flung spray
and the blown spume, and the sea-gulls crying. I must down to
the seas again, to the vagrant gypsy life, To the gull's way and the
whale's way where the wind's like a whetted knife; And all I ask
is a merry yarn from a laughing fellow-rover And quiet sleep and
a sweet dream when the long trick's over.
John Masefield, poet of ancient England
(Gaelic trans. Myghal Keigwin)

Chapter 3

A splendid sight greeted Mairin Fotharta at Wicklow Harbor. She halted her horse in a clearing along the road a half mile south of the town. Her vessel, the three-masted warship *Caillech*, four years out of Falmouth's yards, was washed in the orange glow of a late afternoon sun. The ship's bow pointed north into a stiffening cool breeze that shook the furled courses, topsails, and topgallants. Slanting sunbeams glittered from polished side trim and orange-tinted the mainmast's broad white pennant emblazoned with a mint-green Celtic Cross. Sailors propelled by the sharp commands of officers and masters readied the ship for sea. A half mile seaward of *Caillech*, Aideen Laigain's corvette *Leinster* also rode at anchor.

So she's seen Conor and now she plans to see me. I'll have to be very careful what I say. I can't afford a shouting match.

Mairin urged the sorrel mare forward to the Squadron's stable, tethered her in a hay-filled stall, and took her time covering the two hundred paces to the quay. This was always an uneasy time in her mind, a disturbing passage from the world of the Province on land to the world of the Province at sea. No one doubted that the former was the natural element of the clans; they had only taken up seafaring in the last century under the tutelage of Kernow's Admiralty. The Cornish claimed a naval history of twenty-five centuries; whether it was true or not mattered little, weighed against their unquestioned mastery of seagoing.

Watching her gig pull across from the *Caillech*, Mairin felt the two halves of her heart struggle to separate. Fresh in her mind was the man who had proposed to her, the soft-edged poet who dreamed of a family and a cottage in the hills. Yet before her eyes now lay that admirable ship, her dedicated officers and all-volunteer crew, the oak-framed embodiment of the Province's power to intercept and destroy raiding ships threatening the coasts and pirate vessels preying on shipping. Lovely as *Caillech* was now, bathed in sunlight, it was nothing compared to the excitement of sailing her in a steady gale, her bow cleaving the waves, prodigious suit of sails stretched and driving, masts and yards groaning and stays whistling a mournful song.

The gig approached: her thoughts turned at the last to Conor. She had accepted ... her abiding love for him allowed no other answer. Could she give up the life now calling to her, its clear duties and responsibilities, its lines of command and unchanging routines and known dangers? She had told Conor *two years*; the words had escaped her teeth easily enough, but did she truly mean them? Could she overcome the fear that surged from her inmost spirit whenever she pondered the moral weight of raising children in a happy home? What would it be like to abandon the glorious, almost drunken, sensation of taking a ship to sea and bringing her home safely again? To know the sea only from the shore?

"Captain."

Brigid Auteini, *Caillech*'s bosun, touched a hand to her cap.

"Good to see you again, Brigid," Mairin said as she climbed in. "We've missed you!"

The grey-haired woman's heavily-lined face lit up.

"Truth to tell, Captain," she replied, "forty-five is too young to retire from the sea. Vacation has its place but a whole month of it and

I was bored to tears, if I may say so. Pull, youngsters," she ordered the two sixteen-year-olds at the oarlocks.

Oars bit seawater, driving the craft smoothly towards the waiting warship.

"Any visits from *Leinster*?" Mairin asked.

Brigid eyed the elegant two-master. "No visits, sir. Signals an hour ago."

"I've been summoned?"

"No sir, the Commodore plans to come aboard. The crew has been spittin' and polishin' ever since."

Mairin muttered an oath she reserved for special occasions, drawing chortles from the two rowing sailors. Under Brigid's baleful glare they fast regained serious expressions.

"Be that as it may, Captain, she'll be aboard ten minutes after we touch."

Arriving on *Caillech*'s quarterdeck minutes later, Mairin found the ship a very busy place indeed. Both watches swarmed over the ship, tidying up knots, straightening anything that could be straightened, polishing brass and scrubbing coin-sized stains off the deck planks. Her relatively new second officer, Rowenna Briuin, worked the forecastle; two of her three ensigns covered amidships, and Sinea herself managed operations from the quarterdeck aft. No doubt the scene below was much the same.

Sinea, her face coated with a fine sheen of sweat, met her at the top of the ladder and saluted.

"You heard, Captain?" she said.

"I did. And I'm sorry about it, too. It's intentional, of course, the Commodore could have simply ordered me aboard *Leinster*."

"That would have been customary, Captain," Sinea agreed. She pulled a rag from her pocket and mopped her face. "Officer's line?"

"Yes," Mairin said, her eyes sweeping the tops. "Everyone on deck, starboard watch forward, port watch amidships. Make sure Danu leaves his apron below."

"Commodore's gig in the water," the mizzentop lookout sang out.

"Stop what you're doing!" Sinea shouted. "All hands on deck, officers in the line."

Mairin moved back to the taffrail to get out of the way as officers and sailors pounded up staircases and ran to assigned positions on deck. Lookouts slid down stays and joined their watches. Ship's officers assembled on the quarterdeck in a line along the port rail so they would face the starboard-side ladder. Bosun's whistle in hand, Brigid posted herself just aft of the mizzen.

The corvette's gig bumped the side and seconds later Aideen Laigain swung over the rail. Brigid piped the Commodore aboard; hands came to rigid attention. Mairin strode forward and extended her hand.

"Commodore, welcome to the *Caillech*," she said, doing her best to sound truly welcoming.

Aideen accepted her hand. "A proud ship and a fine crew," she responded in a strong voice. Much lower, she said, "I know this is unusual. The corvette is so small, a private conversation is impossible."

"Understood, sir," Mairin said. She turned and waved a hand towards the opposite rail. "May I present my officers?"

"Of course," Aideen said. "Lead on."

Sinea was first in line.

"Lieutenant, good to see you again," Aideen said, shaking her hand.

"And you, sir."

On down the line, Mairin followed her commanding officer. Aideen knew Rowenna Briuin, whose ruddy, freckled face was flushed beet red by her frantic efforts to ready the ship. Aideen easily topped the shorter lieutenant by six inches.

"Rowenna, you look warm," Aideen commented.

Rowenna forced a smile. "The jacket, Commodore. And a warm day."

"I daresay," said Aideen, shaking her hand. "I didn't sit on your exam for lieutenant, but the reports reaching me were glowing."

"No doubt exaggerated, sir."

"Not by Kennat Gailenga, who chaired the exam. She wanted you for *Morrigan*."

"Kennat's loss is my gain," Mairin intervened to Rowenna's barely-concealed relief.

Aideen eyed Mairin. "So Kennat says too."

Next came the three ensigns, Kensa Velnowarth of Kernow, Brigid's distant cousin Edwina Auteini, and Sithmaith Laigain, whose family only shared the name with Conor's. Aideen was well-acquainted with the ship's two veteran masters, powerfully-built Eavan Sechnaill, Master of Weapons, and Sailing Master Finnsech Cholmain, who had served for years with Aideen before her elevation to commodore. Aideen warmly greeted the ship's medical officer Mor Dal Reti, her surgeon on the *Nore* before his transfer to *Caillech*.

Aideen did not know the two watch chiefs, Ciar Loigde and Lavena Ulaid, and took a minute with each asking about their prior service. Last in line was the ship's portly chef and Chief of Provisions, Danu Eogain. Aideen recognized him instantly as the cook on *Rosc Catha* when she served on it as a lieutenant.

"Danu," she said with genuine warmth, "very good to see you. Didn't you plan to retire and open a restaurant?"

"Tried it," the jovial man said with a chagrined look and forgetting to add a "sir."

"It couldn't have failed!"

"Nay, nay, Commodore," he said, now entirely forgetting his posture, "it did too well. I couldn't stand the long hours!"

Laughter broke out among the crew; even the officers smiled and trembled. To Mairin's astonishment, Aideen laughed along with them.

"Sorry I can't stay for dinner," she said, shaking his hand. "Another time."

Mairin led Aideen below to her cabin, closed the door and threw open the casements.

Aideen laid her jacket over the back of a chair at the chart table and sat down. Mairin did likewise.

From over their heads and the corridor came the sounds of the crew sorting themselves out into sea-going watches.

"The ship looked Admiralty-perfect," Aideen observed. She set her clasped hands on the table. "Not necessary, I know what kind of a ship you keep."

Thinner than last I saw her, Mairin noted, *and more stress-lines in her face. Her voice is ragged, tired.*

"Thank you, Commodore. I have an excellent wardroom and a sharp crew."

The intervening silence went on so long Mairin wondered if Aideen was making her squirm.

"If you think I came to talk about Conor," she said at last, "I did not. You know I saw him today and we'll leave it at that. I came to talk business. Navy business."

"Of course, sir. I made no assumptions."

Aideen sent her a glare that said, *you did make assumptions.*

"What I say next is strictly confidential," she went on in a subdued tone. "I haven't discussed any of this with the Council of Twenty, though I will soon enough. You must have heard I've accepted two more ships from Kernow?"

"I've heard the rumor," Mairin admitted.

"It's fact. Two this winter and they're pressing me to crew six more in the spring."

"Can we crew and officer that many?"

Aideen leaned back in her chair and let her gaze drift out the stern windows.

"Two, yes, six ... I don't see how at the moment. But that's my worry. The immediate issue is our command structure. When I became commodore four years ago we had sixteen capital ships, by spring we may have many as twenty-eight, operating from Brest to Tralee in the west and Wicklow to the Bristol Channel in the east. Even with my staff I can't command that many ships alone. So, I plan to propose some changes to the Council. The Province Squadron would be renamed the Province Battle Fleet, divided into the Atlantic Squadron based in Dungarvan and the Channel Squadron based in Wicklow. If this is sanctioned, I will assume the rank of admiral and name a commodore for each squadron. I am intending to offer Tierney Ulaid's name for the Channel Squadron ... and yours for the Atlantic."

Caught completely by surprise, Mairin felt as if the deck planks had collapsed beneath her.

"You don't have to give me an answer now." Aideen said. "As I told you, it's just a plan and very secret one at that. If you intend to refuse, though, it would be better for me to know now rather than later."

Her mind whirled with conflict. A terrible responsibility ... and a great challenge too.

"You'd expect a long-term commitment?"

"Five years, to get the new system fully established. If you wanted to continue after that, fine, if not, there would be time to work someone new in. The job would be devoted almost entirely to fleet operations at sea. I'd try to take on all the administrative burden at HQ."

Mairin drew in a deep breath and met Aideen's relentless stare.

"I'm honored, Commodore, truly I am. I'd like some time to consider it."

"You're not refusing, is that right?"

"No sir, I am not refusing. I have much to weigh in the balance."

Aideen studied her a moment longer, seemed about to comment, then sighed and rose from her chair. Mairin followed suit and edged around her to open the door.

"One last thing," Aideen said when their faces were scarcely a foot apart. "It should be clear I'm offering this because I believe you're the best for the job, not just as a way to keep you in the service. I would be personally very grateful if you accepted."

She extended her hand. "Good voyage, Captain."

Mairin took her hand, then opened the cabin door and followed her onto the quarterdeck, where salutes snapped out from nearby officers and crew.

"A good voyage to you all," she said, and clambered over the side to her waiting gig.

Mairin stood at the rail and watched the gig return to the corvette. The small craft was no sooner hauled aboard than *Leinster* weighed anchor and set sail.

Sinea approached her with a cautious look. "Any orders, Captain?"

"What? Oh, sorry," Mairin said, turning to face her first officer. "No, no orders. Early dinner for all hands, then get under way for Wicklow."

"Are you all right, Captain?" Sinea asked softly. "You're as pale as sailcloth."

"I have reason to be," Mairin replied. She idly ran her fingers along *Caillech*'s smooth, freshly-polished rail. "Oh, I wasn't dressed down and we didn't cross swords. Just a lot to think about."

Two hours later as evening settled over a gently-rolling sea, Mairin and Sinea strolled forward along the port rail while twenty-two-year-old Rowenna Briuin conned the ship. Mairin was well pleased with Rowenna's speedy efficiency in weighing anchor and shaking our full sail. Sharp orders, no nonsense, and no mistakes. In three months as *Caillech*'s second officer, the stocky, red-haired officer had given Mairin ample proof of her qualities.

"What's your impression so far of Lieutenant Briuin?" Mairin asked Sinea when they reached an isolated spot.

"A bit curt at times but she knows what she's doing. So far as I can see, she deserved the stellar rating she got from the Admiralty. Didn't you tell me the Commodore commended her?"

"She wrote a very complimentary note about Ensign Briuin while she served on the *Nore*. Needless to say, almost unheard of. I begged on my hands and knees to get her. As you heard earlier, the Commodore almost gave her to Kennat Gailenga."

"A good way to ruin a young officer."

"You only served under her a few months, I was stuck for almost a year! If it hadn't been for Finnsech," Mairin said, nodding aft towards the Sailing Master who conned the ship at the moment, "I might have jumped overboard. I don't know why Aideen ... ah, not worth discussing, it depresses me. We have new sailors?"

"Changed out ten altogether. Six of the replacements are not very experienced. This should be a quiet voyage, we'll break them in."

They headed aft along the starboard rail, talking over crew changes and sailing plans for the upcoming Channel patrol. From the taffrail they had a lovely view of Wicklow's twinkling street lanterns and house lights spread out along the shoreline. North of the harbor blazed the brilliant lanterns of Wicklow Fort. Mairin wondered absently if Conor or her brother might be looking in her direction from the fort's tower.

"I'm going below," she said to Sinea. "Have the officers gather for dinner at eight."

"Aye, sir."

Mairin set her boot on the top step of the staircase ... and froze. "What was that sound?"

"Silence on deck!" Sinea's commanding voice rang out.

All talk and movement ceased.

"I heard it clearly, sir," Rowenna said. "Signal trumpets, alarm at the fort."

Mairin strode aft and clamped her hands on the taffrail. Possibly it was nothing more than a nervous sentry spotting a herd of deer through the telescope. Or else the tough and violent Dubliners had come down the Vartry to attack the fort and Wicklow itself.

She turned to Ciar Loigde, port watch chief. "Signal the Harbor Squadron by lantern: *is an attack underway?*"

The chief scampered up the ratlines past the maintop to the crosstrees where the mainmast lantern hung. Flashing the lantern's shades, she sent the signal. Mairin trained her pocket telescope on the signal tower in the harbor. It flashed a return message: *attack in progress, boats launched.*

"Captain," said Rowenna, "should we come about? We're not on a tight schedule."

Mairin hesitated in answering. If the fort were overwhelmed—meaning both Conor and Kellen might well be dead—her crew and officers could land and assist in protecting the town and launching a counterattack. The timing would be doubtful at best: to return to the harbor they would have to beat to weather, fighting the north wind the entire way. The half hour they had sailed southwest would expand to two hours sailing back, and by that time the army's mobile reserves would have reached the area in force. Turning back would serve only the personal interest of knowing the fate of two men she happened to love.

It would not answer.

"We have a fine wind for Wexford, Lieutenant," she said in a tight voice. "No change."

"Aye, aye, sir, Wexford it is."

Mairin retreated below to her cabin and sat before the open windows, listening. Sinea followed and took a chair at the chart table. They both heard it, faint yet clear and unmistakable over ten miles of open water: the cry of the warpipes. After five long minutes the sound faded out, whether because the battle was over or *Caillech* was now too far away was impossible to tell.

Mairin doffed her jacket and took a chair across from Sinea. She rested her head on her hands and closed her eyes.

"Captain Laigain is at the fort tonight, sir?" Sinea asked.

"Yes. My brother too."

Laughter erupted from the main cabin. Sinea got up and shut the cabin door.

Mairin lifted her head at the sound. "Best I get myself together, Sinea. Nothing I can do now but worry. What's happened has happened."

"I can have a private dinner sent in, Captain."

"No."

She got to her feet, combed her hair in the mirror, and put her jacket back on.

"I said we'll have an officers' meal and we will." She glanced at the bulkhead chronometer. "It's six now. I'll work on the manifests until dinner."

"Would you like help?"

"Not needed. Rest and relax, you have the next watch."

Sinea moved to the door, paused before opening it. "You know my beliefs encompass prayer, Captain. I'll offer one for Conor and Kellen."

"Thank you, Sinea, I'd like that. I don't pray myself, I just hope. Leave the door open."

Mairin was grateful for the mindless work of the manifests, which forced her to concentrate on mundane drudgery. Generally a warship did not carry cargo, but arms and armor and naval supplies and equipment were a different matter; they could not be allowed to fall into the hands of pirates. On this trip, *Caillech*'s capacious holds were crammed with the output of the sprawling armory near Gorey: body armor (plate, mail, and leather), longbows, arrows, crossbows, ballistae, ammunition, swords, shields, and boots. The holds would be topped off at Wexford with a modest consignment of merchant goods, offered by the Squadron to the Admiralty as a gesture of good will and fellowship. The gift list included brooches, earrings, pendants, wrist bands, rings, and buttons, oil lamps and candelabra, ornate metal platters, plates, silverware, cups, glasses, tankards, and teapots; and last but not least, fifty-pound wheels of Province cheese and hundred-gallon kegs of Province stout.

Caillech would return after the Channel patrol carrying an array of critical naval supplies: chronometers, barometers, charts, chart tools, sand glass timers, sextants, lead lines, log lines, lanterns, telescopes, pumps, blocks, tackle, capstan bars, ropes (seven sizes), anchors, and marlin spikes. In exchange for the Squadron's goodwill offerings, the Kernow Admiralty would send back salt, pepper and other spices; fine-spun dresses and scarves; leather jerkins, caps, belts, jackets and shoes; fifty pounds of precious coffee; and last but not least, fifty-pound wheels of Cornish cheese and hundred-gallon kegs of Cornish stout.

Mairin finished a last check of the lists by seven-thirty and had a thought to catch a short nap before dinner when a frazzled-looking young sailor rapped on her cabin door to report: "Master Sechnaill requests your presence on deck, sir, to witness arms drill."

"Now?"

"I believe she said now, Captain. She tells us drills work up an appetite for our supper."

"Yes, I guess she does say that."

The sailor saluted and hurried off. With a tired sigh, Mairin donned her hat, straightened her uniform, and arrived on the lantern-lit quarterdeck to find Eavan Sechnaill pacing anxiously. The thickset veteran gave every impression of a hard task master—which indeed she was. Yet Mairin had seen the fierce fighter also console homesick youngsters and show great patience with anyone who worked hard and needed help.

Sinea, Rowenna and the three ensigns had gathered along the quarterdeck's portside rail. Every sailor on deck, knowing what was afoot, had her eyes on Sechnaill.

"Captain," Sechnaill said when Mairin joined her officers, "ready for arms drill."

"You may begin," Mairin said in formal reply.

Sechnaill raised a trumpet to her lips, pointed it forward, blew three high-pitched blasts, then turned over a sandglass timed for three minutes. At the signal, the port watch on deck scrambled down the forecastle hatch to don armor below, while the starboard watch below threw on armor and came up through the quarterdeck hatch. Mail-clad archers climbed into the three fighting tops, each large enough to hold ten archers, and drew longbows from bow-holsters. Behind them, eight four-person ballistae crews wearing similar flexible armor threw open big lockers in the waist, hoisted out heavy bolt-throwers that they swung into iron swivels bolted to the deck. On the heels of the ballistae crews, four steel-armored sailors toting axes and sledgehammers posted themselves at the fore and aft rails, their task to cut loose or smash boarding grapples and lines. At the two-minute mark, a leather-armored port watch re-emerged from both hatches and swarmed upward into the rigging.

With thirty seconds left on the sandglass, ballistae crews cranked the cords tight, set firing pins, and loaded dummy bolts into firing trays. Archers in the tops knocked cheap practice arrows and raised bows to firing position. When the last grain of sand dropped through the sandglass's neck, Sechnaill scanned the ship and then shouted, "attack on the port side, ballistae shoot!"

The four portside ballistae fired into an imaginary enemy ship.

"Tops, shoot!"

The archers loosed a barrage of arrows, filling the air with a peculiar hissing sound punctuated by the thunderclaps of the ballistae.

"Attack on the starboard side!"

The starboard ballistae crews fired their killing machines at the first sound of Sechnaill's "starboard." As one body the archers in the tops swung about, all turning clockwise with bows lowered, then opened a second volley of arrows.

"Continuous fire, both sides. Boarders forward."

The heavy-armored sailors with axes charged into the forecastle, followed close by sailors sliding down ratlines to defend the ship. On the portside, a long-legged young woman tripped over a ballistae mount and fell heavily, her already-drawn sword clattering along the deck. A charging sailor on the starboard side found no sword in the sheath when she reached to draw. The archers in the tops poured a steady fire of practice arrows, though three found themselves empty-quivered well before the drill was over. Sweating, gasping ballistae crews cranked, loaded, fired, and cranked again. The portside forward machine jammed soon after the drill started and did not fire another bolt, despite much shouting and cursing from its crew.

Sechnaill bellowed "end drill," followed by the order to stow arms and armor. The master turned to Mairin. Her expression was grim.

"Drill complete, sir. Timing was acceptable at three minutes even. Two ballistae did not maintain rate of fire, one jammed. Three archers did not carry a full quiver of arrows, one sail-tender could not find her helmet, another had no sword. And so on. Deficiencies will be remedied, sir."

Oh, I bet they will, Mairin said to herself. Out loud, she said, "Not bad for so many new sailors, Master. We'll drill again tomorrow, weather permitting."

"Aye, aye, sir," Sechnaill said. "We will that."

She saluted and heading down the stairs.

"T'will be hell to pay come the morning," Sinea commented.

Rowenna nodded. "With good reason."

"I agree," Mairin said, "only let's not hammer the fresh crew too hard."

She thought back to when she was fifteen, a raw recruit with a whole month of basic training under her belt. "My first drill, I was posted to the foretop. I got there on time with my bow, armor, and arrows ... alas, no string on the bow."

"May I ask the outcome, sir?" asking a grinning Rowenna.

"The other archers blocked the view of the officers and one told me to pretend I was shooting. I never forgot that act of kindness. I was scared they would throw me out right there." *The worst fate I could imagine at the time.* "Let's get our dinner."

Mor Dal Reti joined Mairin, her two lieutenants and three ensigns at the wardroom table. Eyes widened with delight when Danu Eogain squeezed through the doorway from the main cabin carrying a cauldron of his Squadron-famous ham and pea soup and a basket of hot biscuits. Normally Mairin would have dove in with the rest. Tonight her stomach rebelled at the idea of food. Yet she dared not disappoint Danu, who had worked so hard to serve a fine meal on their first night out of port. She forced down a cup of the soup, sampled roast pork and seasoned fried potatoes, and nibbled at a thick-crusted cherry pie he served up for dessert. She did her best to join in the friendly banter and ordered Danu's mate to fetch two of her best bottles of port to serve out after the pie was demolished. Her mind never drifted far from the chilling sound of the warpipes at the fort. A half-bottle of port still remained when she rose from her chair and bade the others to finish it without her. She caught Mor's inquiring glance, *want company?* She answered with a furtive shake of the head and retreated to her cabin.

There she sought relief from aching worry in a book of sea-poems in Old English that took a great deal of concentration to comprehend in the original language. An hour passed, the watch changed and she read on. What little she had eaten sat like a rock in her stomach. And every time she took note of the barometer mounted above her cabin door, its pointer had dipped lower. When exhaustion finally overcame tension, she made the final entry in the ship's log for the day:

> *Departed Wicklow Sept. 8, 999, 9:30 pm port tack, course SbW, wind N, speed 6 knots. Barometer falling slowly. Destination Wexford to take on final cargo for exchange with Kernow. Caillech company: 10 officers, 64 sailors, all fit for duty at sailing. Weapons drill at 7:30, minor problems to be remedied.*
> *Mairin Fotharta, Senior Captain, Province Squadron*

She pulled off her boots, put out the lantern, and settled into her hammock. Sleep did not come immediately. Her mind ran in circles from the attack at the fort to the falling barometer over her head to the difficult choices she faced between her life at sea and her life on land. Another hour passed. Cabin doors opened and closed in the corridor, the ship's motion increased with a rising wind that sang a low note in the stays. An hour before first light she dozed off and entered the strange dream-world of exhausted sleep. In this world she was eight years old, Kellen four ...

She awoke to the sound of angry voices. Downstairs. Oh not again. Please not again. She stared across the dark room and saw her brother sitting up in bed, sobbing. She went over to him and gathered him in her arms, whispered "it's all right Kellen, adults have arguments, it's all right," but he kept sobbing. She left him and stole down the hallway to the balustrade overlooking the great room. She crouched and edged her face forward. Her father Gorman swayed unsteadily directly beneath her. Etain her mother wearing a white robe leaned on the frame of the kitchen door to the right. Etain's eyes showed no fear, only derision.

"You had that young bastard again, don't tell me you haven't!"

Gorman Fotharta, drunk and dangerous, tried to run at her and stumbled forward, catching himself on the back of a high-backed chair near the hearth. Etain remained still, a smirk creeping over her face.

"Whether I have or haven't is not your concern," she said as if commenting on the weather. "If I have, it's the price you pay for thirteen years of hell. Look at yourself, drunk, smelling of sweat and bad ale, face torn with scars, you expect me to make love to you? The night we made Kellen was your last time in my bed, I told you that."

His left hand seized an iron poker which he held over the flames until it glowed dull red.

"For that your face will have a scar too."

He pulled the hot poker out of the fire and took a step forward. Her hand reached under her robe and withdrew a long, straight blade that glinted in the firelight.

"Try it," she said.

Mairin leaped up and ran down the long, curving staircase.

"Father, please no!" she begged. She seized hold of the powerful arm that held the poker.

Then she was flying through the air, free as a bird, until she crashed into the edge of the oak table. Pain exploded from her forehead and her vision blurred. When she could see again it was only from her left eye; blood leaked into the right. Gorman was gone and Etain lounged in the doorway, calmly putting the knife away.

"You should have stayed in your room," she said.

From above, she saw Kellen's face peeking through the bars of the balustrade. He was crying hard. And next to him stood Bram, twelve years old, unnaturally tall and strong. Bram shook his head and laughed harshly.

"It would have been such a great show," he said to Mairin with a sneer. "Next time let them have their fun."

Her heart thudded in her chest, her breath came in gasps as if she had run up to the crosstrees a dozen times. Sweat beaded on her chest, her night-tunic was drenched, her fingers ached from seizing the edge of the hammock. Tears had poured down her face onto the pillow. She hoped desperately that she had not cried out.

The visions lingered in her mind, agonizing feelings at war with rational thought. Only the ship's bell tolling the hour and the shuffling sounds of a watch change overhead fully broke the nightmare's spell. She rolled bare feet onto the deck and reached for a towel to dry her face and her chest, threw open the stern windows and shivered at the cold, damp wind that blew in.

Minute by minute her head cleared and her heartbeat steadied. Faint light glowed in the east, where heavy overcast was about to erase the last sliver of clear sky. Porch lanterns of cottages shone along the shoreline north of Wexford. The barometer continued its descent to a range that signaled an oncoming storm.

Conor, I should have told you before now what damaged goods you want to take into your life.

With a heavy sigh she rose and lit the cabin lantern, splashed cold water on her face and dared a peek in a small hand mirror to comb her hair. Circles darker than usual beneath her eyes, she noticed, and lines creeping into her forehead. Was the slight downturn at the corners of her mouth a visible sign of the weight of those memories? Or just plain age?

A tap sounded on the door.

"Captain? Lieutenant Briuin reports we will be approaching the harbor in one hour" came a soft voice from the other side of the door.

"Please tell her I'll be on deck in a moment."

"Aye, sir."

Ofttimes, Mor Dal Reti had told her: *"Dreams are merely wishes and reminders."* So she repeated her litany: *I am Mairin Fotharta, Captain of the three-masted warship Caillech and Senior Captain of the Province Squadron. I love and will marry a gentle man from an honored family. Gorman and Etain and Bram can no longer hurt me.*

She straightened up and stripped off the soaked nightshirt, mopped sweat from her body with the towel, donned a fresh tunic and leggings, wiped sea salt off her leather boots, brushed the dust off her hat, and polished the gold anchors on her epaulets. A full-length mirror on the back of the armoire door revealed, she thought, at least a dignified officer if not a cheerful one. At the moment, dignified would have to do.

Sinea had the watch; she supervised a crew of sailors working in the forecastle. Rowenna, looking fresh and alert after four hours' sleep, approached Mairin as she reached the quarterdeck.

"Good morning, sir," she said, touching her hat. "Starboard watch on deck, course now south-southwest, speed five knots, Wexford Harbor an hour ahead if the wind holds."

"Very good, Lieutenant," Mairin replied. "We can send the watch to early breakfast. Your thoughts on the weather?"

Rowenna turned to look east at the threatening sky. "I would say, sir, that we will be in dirty weather after we touch at Wexford. It's early fall by the calendar but the signs point toward a winter-style storm. Red sky at morning, sailor take warning."

Mairin watched as the helmswoman swung the wheel to compensate for a sudden puff of wind more westerly than the steady breeze. "I agree, it smells like it too, for whatever that's worth. We'll need to take on the cargo as fast as we can and get out of the harbor, or we may not get out at all. I don't want to get stuck here if I can help it. Get the cargo hatches open and rig the cranes before we reach the pier. Use all the crew you need."

"I have it, sir."

"A private word, Lieutenant." Mairin led her to the starboard rail and faced towards the shoreline.

"Sir."

"You will receive a formal rating in a few days, based on my own observations and those of Lieutenant Danaan."

"Yes, sir, I'm aware of that."

"It will be a rating of 'outstanding.' I could not be more pleased with your work on this ship."

Mairin heard the exhale of held breath. "Thank you, Captain. I've already learned a great deal serving under you."

"Anything in particular?"

Rowenna paused in thought before answering. "Mainly how to maintain discipline and morale without taking on an air of authority.

And how to keep a sense of humor as a senior officer. I find those very valuable lessons, Captain."

Mairin turned to her. "As nice a compliment as anyone has ever paid to me, Lieutenant. An officer can't afford to be made a fool of, but we're all human too. I learned that from serving under Captain Dowlyn as an ensign."

"An Admiralty captain?"

"Indeed. Isn't that strange? He's gone now, I heard, he was never in good health. I'd served on two ships with hard-fisted captains before that, and for the first month under him I couldn't figure out what he expected of me or anyone else, for that matter. He gave very few direct orders and those he did give were stated in a rather thready voice. One day, I asked him straight out what his theory of command was. Imagine asking that! He laughed for about a whole minute, and then he said, 'Ensign Fotharta, I have no *theory*. I expect every sailor and officer to do his best every day, that's what you owe yourself and your shipmates. If you can't give me that of your own accord, I can't force it out of you by shouting or the cat.' I've lived by that statement ever since."

"Thank you for telling me that story," Rowenna said after a long silence. "Time for our turn to the harbor, Captain."

Events now moved apace. The watch changed, Rowenna gathered a crew to open the cargo hatches in the waist and rig heavy cranes for loading operations. For a few minutes, weak sunlight streamed over the sea until the deepening overcast smothered it completely. *Caillech* came about and beat close-hauled under reefed topsails into Wexford Harbor. Sinea conned the ship along the deep-water channel leading to the long piers. With a backed topsail the ship halted her way, sailors heaved mooring cables caught by dockhands and secured to bollards, and the gangplanks slammed down. Rowenna wasted no time getting the loading operation underway.

Squadron Headquarters' weather flags signaled "storm approaching, small craft remain in port." Mairin fought the urge to run to the two-story brick building, where news of the battle surely had arrived overnight by fast-courier. The fresh-faced ensign on duty at the operations desk accepted Mairin's fair copy of the log.

"Captain Fotharta, the weather forecasters are advising caution even for warships," the ensign said as she stamped the log sheets. "A major storm is moving in."

"I'll try to get ahead of it. Ensign, was there an attack at Wicklow Fort last night?"

"There was, Captain. We know the fort held."

"Casualty report?"

"Not in yet, sir, expected within the hour. If you can delay that long, I will—"

"Thank you, Ensign, we'll be hull down by then."

Mairin left the building and walked without hurry back to *Caillech*, where the last of the crates hung in mid-air from a crane. Sinea on the quarterdeck spread her arms in an "any news?" gesture. Mairin shook her head and started up the forward ramp but halted at the sound of hooves thundering on the pier. She turned to see a cloaked rider draw up a horse sharply, dismount, and run towards her. The cloak's hood flew back, revealing the ivory skin and gray-blond hair of Liadan Laigain.

Liadan hugged her briefly, then clasped Mairin's forearms in a fierce grip. "Do you know about the battle last night? At Wicklow?"

"Yes, we were already at sea when we heard the alarm. Conor was—"

"Conor is fine," Liadan broke in. "He sent special word to me last night by courier. An ugly welt on his forehead and a few minor wounds, no more."

"And Kellen?"

Liadan searched for words. "He's alive, badly hurt. They have him at the army hospital at Gorey. I am so sorry. Conor wanted you to know. He also apologized for breaking his promise to you. What did that mean?"

Anguish spread like wildfire in Mairin's mind, consuming her ability to think or speak. But speak she must: behind her the cargo hatches banged shut and dockhands had hold of the mooring cables.

"I said something very foolish to him," she told Liadan with infinite regret. "Tell Conor I love him."

"I will." Liadan leaned towards her and whispered in her ear. "*Take heart, my child, for love is near, do not despair, and do not fear, take heart, my child, nor shed a tear, for I am with you always.* We love you at Laigain House. I know in my heart Kellen will live."

It was more compassion than she could now bear. She kissed Liadan on the cheek, took a deep breath to cover a sob, and climbed the boarding ramp which swung upwards the instant she reached the quarterdeck.

"Take us to sea, Lieutenant," Mairin ordered Sinea, sounding harsher than she intended. "Course for Falmouth."

Dockhands slipped the cables, *Caillech*'s topsails backed, the bow swung round, and the warship gathered way into the rising gale.

Three days ago I turned eighteen years old. I burned my old diary that I kept since I was eight. This new journal will carry my story to my children and to their children too. It is hard to tell how long any of us will live and I would want them to know who I was and how I thought about things. Of my father Domnall who died when I was six I remember mostly that he laughed at dinner and liked to raise me high over his head. From my mother Liadan I have learned how to love my family and my friends and be loyal to them, for that is what she does every day. From my sister Aideen I have learned to keep a cool head no matter what is happening around me, and not to be afraid of the sea. My brother Conor I love very much because he has watched out for me ever since our father was killed. From him I have learned that it is possible to be a fighter and not hate your enemy. I have trained for six long years to serve in the Line of Bows and now I am posted. I understand why Mother is afraid because now all her children will be fighters, but that's not my fault really. My friend Ewan's father says, we live on the edge of a knife. We all have to do what we can.
Journal of Fethnaid Conmaicne Laigain

Chapter 4

The transport bound for Dungarvan sailed from Rosslare at dawn and now cleaved through mounting, foam-tipped waves at eight knots. Feth had sailed often enough with Aideen to know that the captain of the schooner-rigged craft was struggling to guide his ship between shoals and reefs near shore and open water where wind and waves would pummel it and turn the stomachs of his passengers. Even so, the ship was rolling and pitching and a dozen passengers, civilian and military, hung over the lee side.

Feth relaxed on a bench in the ship's plunging bow where she had no company save for two burly sailors working the jib. At a steady count of five seconds the bow cut through another wave and a thin spray of cold water raked her face. It was easy for her to grasp what Aideen loved about the sea: there was freedom here, and danger, and beauty. Aideen had long encouraged her to join the Squadron, begged her at times, and she had been tempted. Certainly Liadan wanted her to do it, yet somehow it did not seem right. Aideen sailed the fighting ships; Conor was a Bladesman; and her place was with the Line of Bows.

She held her longbow in her hand now and ran her fingers along its smooth, varnished length. It had not been made in the Province's armories, though there was nothing wrong with the bows they made. She had constructed it herself in the barn, carefully and lovingly, with help from a local bowyer who, though blind, knew by touch alone what needed to be done. She tried dozens of different designs and draw weights until she had it right. It was one of her few prized possessions.

The night before, she was too excited to sleep, and spent the long hours after sunset reading a book of poems Conor had given her and wondering what her new life would be like. A few hours past midnight, a horse thundered into the yard beneath her window. Its rider, a military courier from Wicklow, had stopped by on Conor's special orders to tell Liadan the news of himself and of Mairin's brother Kellen. After that, she stayed up with her mother in the great room, drinking tea and passing the time telling old family stories and reading aloud from a popular play.

At dawn, Feth had watched her sad-faced mother mount and ride off for Wexford, where Mairin's ship would touch-and-go on its way to Falmouth. Her mother gone and the old farmhouse empty and silent, she took a last look at her secure little room, packed the last of her belongings, kissed her father's portrait hanging near the front door, and walked the mile to Rosslare quay in the fresh, cool air of early morning. In the harbor, as she boarded the packet for Dungarvan, she saw a warship approaching, her sister's pennant streaming from the mainmast.

These and other thoughts of home drifted through her mind as the vessel plunged along past Tramore Bay. For a time the gusting wind eased and the plunging and spray subsided. She slid the longbow back into its protective leather case and reached into a canvas duffel bag stuffed to bursting with her clothes, boots, books, toothbrush, comb, mirror, pencil, and journal and one other item, a small leather pouch. She glanced around and seeing no one nearby but the busy sailors, emptied the pouch into her lap. One by one, she took up the keepsakes. A silver brooch given to her by Domnall on her sixth birthday, the only remembrance she had of him; a centuries-old gold bracelet from grandmother Rionach; and an ornate silk ribbon, a gift from Aideen that she had often used to tie back her flaxen hair. With her locks now trimmed to fit under her helmet—though she left them as long as the rules allowed—there was not enough hair left for the ribbon to hold onto. Last, a bronze locket from her friend Ewan, her first love and now a valued friend. Poor Ewan with his crippled leg had cried when she told him of her posting.

Out of the corner of her eye, she saw someone approaching along the rail from the stern. She stuffed her treasures in the pouch and restowed it in the duffel. Her new companion was a tall, broad-shouldered young Blade, with a pleasant face and an exaggerated swagger. He carried two duffel bags twice the size of hers and even at that he was wearing most of his body armor. *Doesn't travel light*, she observed. He dropped his bags and sat down on the bench a few feet forward of her, otherwise paying no attention.

"Hello," she said, stretching out her hand. "I'm Feth, from Rosslare."

He gazed down at her face and then down at her hand, which he wrapped inside his own.

"Keegan Cholmain," he said without much warmth.

"You're going to the Dungarvan Fort?"

"Very observant."

She struggled to maintain her smile. "There are other postings in the west."

"I'm going to Dungarvan Fort!"

"Where does your family live?"

He gave her an irritated look. "Wexford, if you must know." His eyes drifted to her longbow. "You're going to the fort too?"

Her smile faded. "That's where a bow like this is usually used, yes," she said, resting her hand on the case.

Keegan nodded, seemed about to offer a remark, then turned his eyes towards the sea.

"You're not very friendly," she said. "I could use a friend just now. This is my first posting."

Keegan sighed and rubbed his eyes.

"I'm sorry," he said, offering a tired smile. "Feth, was it? I was out of line. I'm exhausted, two hours sleep in three days, and my body hurts everywhere. But that's no excuse."

"Let's start over." She put out her hand again. "Fethnaid Conmaicne Laigain, I'm glad to know you, Keegan."

He took her hand. Then a look of horror spread over his face. "Conor is your brother?"

"Yes, do you know him?"

Keegan ran a scarred hand through black, curly hair.

"Know him? We've been in a dozen fights together, not to mention plenty of off-duty adventures in pubs. Please don't tell him Keegan Cholmain was rude to you."

"I won't, I promise."

"How is he? Haven't seen him this past year, luck of the draw, I guess."

"He's fought twice in the last two weeks, at Ballynamult and Wicklow. I bet he feels no better than you."

Keegan stretched his back and winced. "Lots of attacks, all along the Rampart. We're all hurting. Does he still plan to leave the army and get married? Last time I saw him he had a sweetheart he talked about, someone from the navy."

"He still hopes for it. His girlfriend is a captain, actually. How about you? Do you want a family?"

"Doesn't everyone?" he said with a surprised look. "Three or four years from now, or when my body wears out, whichever comes first. I just wish ...". Keegan pressed his lips together and his eyes turned sad. "Never mind."

"What were you going to say?"

"Ah, I wish my father could have lived to see my children."

"Oh. Sorry."

He turned to her. "I know you lost your father too, Feth. It's just that my father died not long ago."

"In battle?"

Keegan rested his hands on the ship's rail and set his chin on his hands.

"In battle, yes, if you can call a silly little skirmish near Clonmel a battle. Band of raiders attacked farms north of the Rampart, three months ago. My Dad led a century out, caught up with them, and killed most of them. A couple of the raiders were archers, not very good ones. A lucky shot went right between his cuirass and pauldron. Cut the artery and he died."

The anguish in his voice touched her heart. She reached out and took hold of his callused hand.

"He didn't need to be out there, he was almost fifty. With the children grown he re-enlisted to help out since we're stretched so thin."

Feth squeezed his hand. "How about your mother?"

A smile crossed his face. "An artist. Paints mostly, sometimes sculpture too. Everyone buys from her at the market fairs."

"And you?"

"What do you mean?"

"What do you do besides fight?"

Keegan seemed surprised by the question. "You won't laugh?"

"Why should I?"

"I'm a potter. You know, vases, pitchers, plates, everything. My father got me started when I was a little boy."

"Make me something this winter?"

Keegan laughed and laid a gentle hand on her shoulder. "Of course I will. Anyway, if you write to Conor, please say hello for me. And you might mention my father, his name was Tomaisin. I'm sure Conor knew him."

"I will."

"When do you report?" he asked.

"Tomorrow night. I'll spend tonight with a friend of our family's in Dungarvan."

"I have to report today," he said. "Be posted there long?"

"I don't know. My orders just said to be there tomorrow."

He stood and gathered up his travel bags. "We're almost in, I'd better get back with the other Blades. Look me up at the fort?"

"I will. I'm glad I have a friend there."

He smiled down at her and shook his head. "Conor's kid sister! First chance we get, I'll buy you dinner in the town to make up for my sullen attitude."

"I'd like that, Keegan. See you soon."

As he strode back to the vessel's stern, Feth pondered what just happened. She was hopeful about Seanlaoch ... if that didn't work out, Keegan was a fine-looking man, and he seemed to like her.

"Dungarvan Harbor, ten minutes!" brayed the ship's master. "Get your junk together, folks!"

Feth grabbed her own bag and hustled aft since a flapping jib now became the center of frantic attention. Following an extraordinary range of curses bellowed by the master, the streamlined packet came about well enough and then struggled to maintain headway into Dungarvan's cozy harbor while the pernicious gods of weather added driving rain to a cold wind. Feth snatched a heavy sweater and oilcloth cloak from her duffel and tried to shelter herself on the lee side of bigger passengers. She searched for Keegan but he was sandwiched in the midst of twenty or so Blades all packed together at the taffrail.

After much additional cursing and one tack, the coaster bumped roughly against the pier, cables encircled bollards, and the gangplank crashed to the dock. Horses, wagons and carts waited at the pier and the ship emptied fast. Feth stayed aboard as long as she could, using the height of the deck to look for Seanlaoch. She did not see him anywhere. Finally she drew a scowl from the master, who had incoming passengers waiting in line on the pier. She headed down the gangplank and wondered where she would go if he had forgotten her.

Now fully exposed on the pier, the fiercely-gusting wind blew rain inside her hood until her hair was plastered to her skull and cold water ran down inside her sweater. Carts and wagons and horses scurried off into the rainstorm, the outgoing passengers clambered aboard, and the coaster cast off its lines for a wild return run to Rosslare. She felt especially despondent when the covered wagon carrying the contingent of Blades rumbled away, with Keegan waving from a rear seat and looking concerned for her welfare.

She was about to give up and find shelter in a pub or rooming house when she spotted a lone figure bolt from an inn across the square and splash his way towards her. Seanlaoch to be sure: slender, average height, wearing no cloak and struggling to keep spectacles on his nose. He skidded up to her, apologizing at every step.

"Feth, I am so sorry," he said with water streaming down his face. "I didn't forget about you. I was working in my room, paid no attention to the clock."

"Don't worry about it, let's get out of the rain!"

"Right, come on," he said.

He seized her cold hand and they ran together across the square to the door he came out of. A wood sign over the door flapped in the wind: "Inn of the Laughing Gael, Naomham Monaig, Proprietor."

They plunged into a dark room which turned out to be the anteroom for a friendly-looking pub, with a fire blazing in a big hearth and plenty of empty tables and chairs. She hung her dripping oilcloth on a peg, kept her bow and satchel with her. Seanlaoch's tan sweater and black wool trousers were soaked yet he could hardly take them off. Naomham the innkeeper gave them a disapproving scowl as he led them to a table near the fire. Seanlaoch ordered two mulled ciders and a loaf of hot bread with cheese.

"Feth, I apologize again, I can't believe I lost track of the time."

He used a rather shabby napkin to mop water from his face. His long, dark brown hair dripped water as fast as he mopped it. Seeing his genuine distress at being late, Feth remembered why it was she liked him so much. There was a sweetness about his face and manner that had attracted her since she was old enough to notice the opposite sex. Seanlaoch looked the part of scholar and historian. The spectacles made necessary by countless hours of reading in bad light gave his face a serious cast and aged him more than his twenty-four years. She especially liked his unusual gray eyes that never seemed to blink.

His face is not so much handsome as it is warm and friendly and intelligent. And that's exactly what he is.

She laughed and fished a comb out of her bag. "I was only there fifteen minutes, Sean," she said, using a nickname that she wasn't absolutely sure he liked. "But it was raining so hard!"

She had to lean over the floor to comb out the rain from her hair. Naomham arrived with the bread, his mood not improved by the sight of water flecking from her comb onto his hardwood floor.

"Cider and bread," he said curtly, "with cheese. Ten farthings, that'll be."

Sean searched two damp pockets to come up with the coins. After Naomham retreated to the kitchen, she handed Sean her comb. He took it hesitantly and combed his own drenched hair.

"Thanks for this," she said, nibbling on a slice of cheese. "I'm starved, I had to leave early and I was so nervous I couldn't eat. The coaster's sandwiches smelled of old socks and seawater."

He cut off two slices of bread and laid them on her plate. Feth made a sandwich and dove in.

"This isn't a bad place," Sean said while sawing himself a slice. "I live on the third floor, off the front where I can see the square. Naomham isn't a bad sort. He gets testy with me because I forget to pay the rent on time, and his wife is ... a difficult woman, from what I can see."

Feth washed down the bread with cider before answering. "My mother says to say hello and wonders why you never visit."

"I was there not too long ago," he said. "Wasn't I?"

"Over a year," she replied. She started on a second slice. "I remember because you showed up late for my birthday party."

"Did I? A whole year? It doesn't seem that long. I guess I'm obsessive about my research and my writing. I forget to eat, to pay my rent, to meet friends on the pier. To be honest, I'm something of a mess, Feth."

He seemed so upset with himself that her hand shot out of its own accord and took hold of his. He looked up in surprise.

"Sean, stop that! My mother wasn't scolding you, she misses you. We all do. Conor always asks Oran how you are and Oran doesn't seem to know."

His expression brightened marginally. She eased her hand away.
"How is Conor?"

"A little battered up at the moment."

"Relentless attacks this year, I knew there would be." He tossed his spectacles on the table. "I should be out there on the line."

"Why do you say that?"

"I'm twenty-four, in good health, why shouldn't I be?"

"How well do you see without glasses?"

"Well enough."

"What time does the clock over the bar say?"

He twisted in his chair. The pendulum clock on a shelf had a face a foot across with bold numbers and was well-lit by an overhead lantern.

"You can't read it."

He turned back to her. "I could fight with glasses on."

Feth set her food aside and fixed her eyes on his. "Sean, don't be ridiculous. You could serve in the army, sure, as a cook or a medic or a supply clerk. But those jobs can be done by anyone! You're a writer and a historian. That's important."

"To whom?"

"To me, for one. To a lot of people. Your first book is already required reading in the schools. I read it, three times."

He smiled at that. "Come on, Feth, I appreciate what you're saying but—"

"You think I'm making it up?" She seized hold of her satchel and rummaged in it.

"Here," she said. She laid a small, leather-bound book on the table and opened it to the title page. "That says, *History of the Province of the Twenty Clans, Volume I, The Early Years*. Does it look brand new and fresh?"

He touched the page with his fingertips. "No, I guess it doesn't."

She replaced the book in her satchel.

"We lost most of our books fifty years ago, didn't we?"

"In the panic when the Rampart was being built, yes."

"So we need to put everything back together. Not just our history, everyone's history."

He stared at her. "Why do you want to know about history?"

"Because I want my children to know where we came from and I want them to understand what their mother fought to preserve for them."

He clamped his hands on her forearms. "That's why I write it, Feth. That's exactly why I work so hard on it."

She enjoyed the feeling of his hands on her arms. "Then you're defending our people as much as me or Conor or anyone. Who are we without our past?"

He put his spectacles back on and tilted his head to one side, studying her.

"This may sound odd to you, Feth, but I don't think I knew you at all before today."

"And I don't care that I got wet. I'm glad I'm here, with you. Can I make a small confession?"

"Confession?"

"I've had a crush on you for a long time."

"Me? Now you *are* telling a fib."

"I am not. Ever since I got my orders, I wondered how it would be to see you."

He leaned back in his chair, still puzzled.

"I always liked you, but being six years apart—"

"I was Conor's little sister."

"Well, yes."

"And now? What do you see now?"

"A woman I would like to know better. Starting now."

She felt her face flush hot. *Well, in for a penny in for a pound, isn't that the old saying?*

"Do you have a ... a ... "

"Girlfriend? No, I don't. Most women don't find scholars a great catch. You have a boyfriend back in Rosslare?"

"I've had a couple, none recently. I was training all the time the past year."

Naomham returned to clear the table. "Will there be anything else?" he said with obvious sarcasm.

"No," Sean told him. "Say, is my rent due yet?"

"Very funny," the man grumbled. Muttering, he clumped back to the kitchen.

Feth stretched and yawned.

"You need rest," said Sean. "Let's go up to my room. We can get dried out and you can catch a nap while I work for a couple of hours. Then we'll go out for dinner and talk about history. How does that sound?"

"It sounds terrific."

"There is one other thing I should tell you."

"What's that?"

He seemed to have a hard time getting started.

"Well, I know you wanted to stay with me tonight. And you are welcome, believe me! It's just that, well, I only have one room and it's pretty cramped. I don't earn much teaching and selling my book."

"Is there anything for me to sleep on besides the floor?"

"I have an extra bed, yes, sometimes Oran stops by, my father too now and then."

"You won't hang a curtain across the middle of the room?"

"Of course not!"

Her laugh told him he was being put on.

"Okay then," he said, taking hold of her bag. "I should warn you, it's a little cluttered."

They retrieved Feth's cloak from the entryway and climbed the two flights to his room. In spite of his preparing her, she was taken aback when they entered. At twenty feet square the room was not so small by its gross dimensions; it was made closet-like by the fact that not much of the floor was left exposed to view. Floor-to-ceiling shelves crowded in from all sides. Unfinished pine boards bowed under the weight of books and journals and boxes of papers and manuscripts. Ink pots, quill pens, sheafs of blank paper, and empty bottles of stout and wine had been abandoned on top of papers or tucked into shelf corners.

In the room's center, a single round table surrounded by four chairs was obviously his working space. Three of the chairs and the tabletop were piled high with books and sheets of paper. Beneath the table, a wicker wastebasket overflowed with pages crunched into a ball. A nearly-full ink pot perched precariously close to one edge of the table; a quill pen lay across a sheet of paper half-filled with fine, clear script. An extra pair of spectacles with badly bent bows kept the quill pen company.

Ignoring the clutter, Feth found the modest flat cheerful. A single large bay window with hinged casements on either side overlooked the town's well-kept square and spacious, busy harbor. To the right of the door, a small cookstove rested on a stone base; the vent pipe disappeared into the rough-plastered wall. Two single beds had been squeezed in between bookcases on opposing walls; one bed had obviously been slept in recently, the other was buried in clothes that might have been freshly washed or were awaiting it. A tall, battered armoire, its doors hanging open, revealed the sum total of his limited wardrobe.

"I'm not much of a housekeeper," he said. He gazed about as if seeing the condition of the room for the first time. "Sorry, I should have cleaned up."

Feth set down her bag and laid her bow on top of it.

"I love it," she said. "I really love it, Sean."

Feth awoke early the next morning. Gray pre-dawn light bathed the room. The square below was silent; Sean's deep, soft breathing was the only sound she heard. Though the room was cold, her wool nightshirt and winter-weight socks kept her warm when she peeled back the covers. She sat up, stretched muscles built up over six years of hard training, and eyed the table with its paper and pens and ink. Would he mind if she used a spot of ink and one sheet? She did not think so.

She arose from the cot silently and padded to the table, wincing when the chair creaked under her weight. Sean did not stir. She located a clean sheet of paper, dipped the pen in the ink pot, and wrote:

> *Dear Mother, I am with Seanlaoch now. I report for duty at the fort this morning. I met a Blade named Keegan on the packet coming here, a friend of Conor's! He will be at the fort with me. Did you see Mairin at Wexford? If you did, it must have been very hard to tell her what happened to Kellen. Don't worry about me too much, I am well-trained and the army watches out for newcomers. Make sure to visit the barn cats and don't rent out my room. Your loving daughter, Feth. p.s. I am still taken with Seanlaoch and I think he likes me too.*

She waited for the ink to dry, then folded the paper in thirds and left it on the table. When she stood the chair creaked again and Sean sat up, rubbing his eyes.

"Feth ... you're up. Not even dawn yet."

"You don't need to get up, Sean," she said. "I love to watch the dawn."

"I do too," he said, struggling out of the cot. "I usually see it after working all night."

He got to his feet, yawned hugely, and padded to her side. His hair tumbled around his face and his loose woolen nightshirt was well-worn. When he reached her and laid a gentle hand on her shoulder, she felt a certain thrill emanating from her thighs and belly. *Without the spectacles*, she thought, *it is a sweet and tender face, and his touch is filled with true affection.*

"Do you mind that I call you Sean?"

"Not at all."

She turned and laid her head against his chest. Slowly his arms encircled her waist.

"I had a great time last night, Sean. I'd like to come again."

"I'd be very sad if you didn't. How often will you get leave?"

"I don't know. Maybe a day a week, if things are quiet. Schedules tend to be irregular, I may be on duty three days straight and then get two days off. Depends how much they are moving people around and how many Bows they assign at the fort."

He stroked her hair, a sensation she savored.

"I'm not going anywhere. I'll worry like crazy, though."

She ran her hands up between his shoulder blades. They were both trembling slightly and perilously close to making love. *Not yet,* she told herself. *Another time when I don't have to rush off. If he really wants me.*

"You think anyone will be using the bath this early?"

"Probably not. There might be hot water if the cheapskate land-lord kept the hearth downstairs going late and the piping isn't blocked up again."

She backed out of his arms, picked up her bag, and headed down the silent hallway.

The water oozing from the bathtub's faucet could not have been called hot but she was satisfied with lukewarm. Ten minutes later she felt free of sweat, sea salt and rainwater. A cracked mirror on the wall allowed her to comb her hair and check that her teeth gleamed after brushing. She was pleased to see summer freckles fading out, they made her look fifteen instead of eighteen.

Sean left for the men's bath when she returned to his room. She proudly donned her uniform: a cobalt blue tunic bearing a white Celtic Cross on the chest and cinched at the waist by a sky-blue belt. Silver crossed arrows on her shoulders marked her service in the Line of Bows. With cold weather coming on fast, she added slate-gray leggings. She tucked her sky-blue tam into her belt. Last but not least, she slid her feet into soft, black leather boots, a prized birthday present from Aideen.

Belongings fully packed, she took in the fine view from his window. It was obvious the day would not be much of an improvement over yesterday: heavy gray overcast left not a patch of blue sky showing. No rain, though, the cobblestone streets were dry. Flags and banners near the pier stretched taut in a stiff wind from the north.

For a brief moment, she felt a touch of homesickness. At this hour in Laigain House, old and drafty and damp as it was, the huge hearth would be ablaze, Mother would have hot tea on the table and oatmeal bubbling on the stove. She saw no sign of food in Sean's room, nor did a single cooking pot hang near the wood stove.

He returned from the men's bath with washed and combed hair and a face reddened and nicked from a close shave.

"Any warm water?" he asked.

"Enough. You?"

"Alas, only cold." He tugged on clean trousers and then tossed aside his well-worn bathrobe. "You used every drop and left me nothing." With his sweater over his head he went on in a muffled voice, "I should punish you for that."

She seized the sweater before he could get it past his face. "Oh, really? And how are you going to do that?"

They wrestled around the room, laughing and stumbling until they fell onto his bed. She let him pull the sweater on and then kissed him. His eyes opened wide in surprise. Then he drew her hard against him and kissed her until they both had to surface for air.

He grinned at her. "Uniforms always do to that to me."

"Seanlaoch Osraige!"

She kissed him until he begged mercy.

"You better let me up," he said, his breath coming in deep gasps, "or you will never report on time."

She got to her feet, straightened her uniform, and tried to ignore the desire that made her fingertips tingle.

"Right. Bad to show up late your first day."

He got up, found a comb and straightened out his still-wet hair.

"If you attack me again," he said with a grave expression, "I will not be responsible for what happens."

She took the comb from him and fixed her own mussed hair.

"You put on something in the bath. The scent was what did it."

"You're blaming my shave tonic?"

"You blamed my uniform."

They kissed again, gently this time. When their lips parted, she said, "So, how about breakfast?"

"I figured that out in the bath," he said. "Get the stove going. You saw the wood and turf in the hall? I'll be right back."

He ran out the door. Feth fetched some small logs and turf kindling from a communal supply at the end of the hall—leaving a coin in the cup as a hand-lettered sign requested—and started a fire is Sean's stove. By the time it was throwing heat he was back with a basket of warm buttered rolls and pot of hot tea purchased at the diner next door, which opened at dawn for sailors and dockworkers. He set his heavy metal teapot on the hot stove top and laid the rolls down in a hastily-cleared space on the table. She poured out the tea and they sat together once he cleared off a second chair.

"You don't know how much easier it is for me today, knowing you're here." She picked up the letter she had written. "Can you mail this to Liadan for me?"

"Of course. Right after I drop you off. Where do you need to go?"

"My orders said they'll pick us up at the carriage station. Is that far?"

"Four blocks. It's across from the town hospital."

The chilly wind buffeted them as soon as they stepped into the street. Turning the last corner onto the station's block, they both saw it at the same time: a big covered wagon bearing army insignia lumbering its way under the long portico in front of the hospital, where four orderlies waited. As soon as the ambulance halted, the orderlies took hold of stretchers and carried them inside.

"I don't like the looks of that," Feth said, breaking into a run.

By the time they reached the hospital entrance, all the stretchers had been unloaded. The teamster, a rheumy-eyed man clad in dirty clothes and a motley cap, leaned against a post and swilled from a flask.

"Why are you bringing in wounded?" Feth asked him.

"Now why would you think, little lady?" he said, capping his flask. "There was a fight there was, plenty of dead and wounded."

"At the fort?"

"Right. Close to a breakthrough, I heard."

She pulled at Sean's sleeve. "Come on, I need to go inside."

In the anteroom they were promptly intercepted by a woman wearing a surgeon's white robe. In one hand she held a clipboard, in the other a bloody towel.

"Hold it," she said, blocking their way. "Who are you?"

Feth pulled back her cloak to show her uniform. "Feth Laigain, Line of Bows, this is my friend Sean. Can you tell me if you brought in a Blade named Keegan?"

She glanced down at the list. "Yes ... Cholmain. Came in two hours ago. You know him?"

"Yes."

The surgeon seemed anxious to get moving. "All right, go in, he's in the fourth row on the right."

"Feth," Sean whispered as he trailed behind her, "you know someone already?"

"Met him on the packet," she whispered over her shoulder. "I forgot to tell you."

Keegan lay on a cot with his head propped up by two pillows. A blanket covered him to the waist, leaving his scarred torso bare. Bloodstained bandages covered his upper right arm and shoulder. A long, shallow slash, stitched at the widest point, ran along his face from his temple to the edge of his mouth on the left. His rib cage and stomach were turning shades of yellow and purple. Seeing her, he forced a weak smile.

"Well, we meet again," he said with effort. "A good thing you didn't report yesterday." He waved his right hand towards the wall. "Stools there, if you want to sit."

Sean retrieved two folding stools and they sat on opposite sides of his cot.

"My friend Sean Osraige," she said to Keegan.

Sean reached out and took Keegan's right hand. "Can we do anything for you?"

"I'll be all right, used to this," he said. "You know Conor too?"

"I do," Sean replied. "We were all friends growing up."

"What happened?" Feth asked. "And when?"

"Past midnight. Very clever attack east of the fort. Three, maybe four hundred threw scaling ladders over, very quick at it too. By the time we attacked they were all on our side of the Rampart. Wild scene, total darkness, so confused the Bows couldn't help us much at first. We just slugged it out."

Ten feet away, the surgeon who had stopped them pulled the blankets over the face of a soldier.

"If it hadn't been for my friend Ionhar, I'd be like that poor soldier. We held our own, formed something of a battle line, then the Bows charged in behind them and opened fire. Saved our ... well, saved us." He closed his eyes and took a slow, deep breath. "Second fight for me in a week. It's going to be a long two months to winter if this keeps up."

Feth held his left hand in both of hers.

"What did the doctors say?"

"Two weeks no fighting," he replied. "Cracked ribs from four or five hammer strikes. I don't mind the cuts but gods above the rib blows hurt."

A male surgeon drew blankets over a face near the window.

"How many?" she whispered, her vision starting to cloud over.

"About thirty," Keegan said. "I knew that man. He has a family." Seeing Feth's expression, he said, "best you get out of here, Feth. This is hard to look at any time, it's worse when you're new. I'll see you at the barracks soon, they won't keep me here very long."

She squeezed his hand gently. "See you there, Keegan."

"Thanks for coming in, both of you," he said. "Sean, I hope we get to meet again when I'm vertical."

"I do too, Keegan. If you need anything, send me a note at the Inn of the Laughing Gael."

"I will. Thanks again."

Outside they found the teamster in the same position, but now his wagon was nearly filled with Blades and Bows and their kits.

"I have to go, Sean."

"I know."

He hovered over her awkwardly, then drew her tight against him. "Be careful, Feth," he whispered into her ear. "Come back as soon as you can."

"I will."

She kissed him on the cheek, then climbed into the wagon and squeezed into last open space. The teamster grunted, jumped up on the buckboard in front, and barked an order to his two-horse team. The wagon turned sharply and rumbled down the cobblestone street. Sean watched her and just before the wagon turned a corner, held up his hand in farewell. A surprising stab of regret and loneliness passed through her.

Feth nodded politely to her companions but said nothing. Though the wagon now passed through a pleasant forest of pine and birch and maple, she saw only Keegan's battered body and blankets being drawn up over silent faces.

Sept. 10, 999, 8:30am, course due south, speed 9+ knots. Gale NNW, storm gathering to the north. Courses and topsails full-reefed. Barometer 29.35 falling, heavy following sea, temp. 44 deg. Will try to clear Land's End before worst of it.
Mairin Fotharta, Sr. Captain, Province Squadron
Captain's Official Log

Chapter 5

The *Caillech* pitched heavily, sailing large with a following sea. Mairin hovered over the chart table with her two lieutenants, all three rocking in time with the ship's motion.

"Where do you have us now?" Mairin asked Rowenna.

"Here, sir," she pointed, "eighty-five miles northwest of Land's End."

"Plenty of sea-room, sir," Sinea commented. "We need to head southeast soon."

Mairin nodded towards Rowenna. "Your evaluation, Lieutenant?"

Rowenna straightened up and thought carefully before answering.

"I estimate, sir, that the storm will overtake us late afternoon. By that time we could be within an hour's sail of Land's End if we make our turn now. I see two hazards. One, the Scilly Isles. The passage between them and Land's End is only twenty-five miles. We need to clear that passage before nightfall. Two, if the wind backs to the north-west or west, we'll be driven hard towards the point or towards the Isles if we decide to clear them to the west."

Mairin glanced up at Sinea, who added nothing. It was a sound evaluation.

"In my position, what would you do?"

Again, Mairin noted the pause, longer this time.

"I believe we can clear the point before nightfall if we turn now. There is the chance of a westerly gale. If that occurs earlier than I expect, we can go to a starboard tack, round the Isles well to the west, run with the wind past the point and into Falmouth."

Mairin signaled Sinea with a raised eyebrow for her opinion. "I agree, Captain. Storm sails and harnesses may be a good idea as well."

Without warning the ship pitched more sharply, forcing all three of them to seize hold of the table.

"Right," Mairin said. "Get all the officers and chiefs down here now, except for those needed on deck. I'm going up for a moment, then we'll meet in the wardroom. Stow the table."

Reaching the quarterdeck, Mairin struggled to conceal uneasiness at the look of sea and sky as the storm gathered strength. A deck of clouds nearer to black than gray rolled and boiled across the sky from north to south, seemingly low enough to touch from the crosstrees. The wind blew steady at gale force. Every sail was reefed to the last point and yet stretched as tight as the backstays. What worried her most was the following sea, which had taken on a confused look as if waves were being piled up to the north in random fashion and then driven to grow and clash on their way south.

I could have held us in Wexford, she reflected. *Why didn't I? Afraid to look timid in the eyes of the Commodore, or the crew? Or was I fleeing the bad news brought to me by Liadan? Too late to second guess now, we have to ride it out as best we can.*

For the moment, *Caillech* rode the crests and troughs well enough, though Brigid at the helm was fighting hard to keep the ship's yaw under control. Sailing Master Cholmain, posted a step forward of the wheel, wore a tense expression that confirmed Mairin's assessment of their predicament.

"Finnsech," Mairin said, "we'll rig for a major storm. I'll be giving out orders below, meanwhile clear the tops and have the watch on deck double-bind all sails. Haul in the courses and break out storm topsails."

"Aye, sir," said Cholmain. She lifted her trumpet and set the hands to work.

Below, the wardroom table had been folded away and all of the remaining officers and chiefs crowded into the room. Mairin edged her way to the doorway leading to the main cabin.

"My guess," she said to the group, "is that we are in for it. Once the storm sails are up and the yards double-lashed I want no one in the rigging except as specifically ordered. All hands to wear safety harnesses at all times, below decks and above. Rig safety lines fore and aft, if I give the order to attach, I want everyone on deck hooked on unless you're moving. Very soon we will not be able to heave to if someone pitches overboard. Watch below will check and secure our cargo and everything else that can move. All hands to don heavy weather clothes and have oilskins ready to hand. Officers and chiefs will carry speaking trumpets. Storm lanterns at the wheel and in the tops. Station an experienced hand in the well, man the pumps if the level is over a foot. Danu, galley fires out and doused. Mor, do your best to be ready for injuries."

She scanned the roomful of swaying figures. Confident faces, mostly, a few worried ones among the newcomers.

"Most you have come through storms before, we'll be fine if we keep our heads and stay alert. Questions?"

There were none.

"Let's get to work. Dismissed."

The room emptied except for the two lieutenants. Mairin turned to Rowenna first.

"Lieutenant, I'm counting on you to keep us on a heading between the Isles and the Point. You know as well as I do that if the wind shifts we'll need to make quick changes and we may not be able to use the charts. Can you do it?"

"I can, sir."

"Very well, on deck then."

Rowenna touched her hat and climbed to the quarterdeck.

"As always," Mairin said to Sinea, "don't wait to ask me if something needs doing. I trust your judgment."

"Thank you, sir. Captain ... at Wexford, I saw you talking to someone on the pier. Would it be out of line to ask if it was news of the battle?"

Mairin swore a quiet oath and laid a hand to her forehead. "I should have said something to the crew. I got word at Squadron HQ that the fort held. Make sure the word is passed around."

"Conor? And your brother?"

"Conor is fine, that was his mother on the pier. Kellen isn't."

"Alive?"

"Yes. Not by much, I think."

"I'm very sorry, Captain. The army surgeons work miracles, he's in the best hands. We'll get some word at Falmouth, I'm sure Conor will see to that."

"Yes, he will." *Caillech*'s plunging motion moved up yet another notch. "Time we got to work. I'll be on deck in a few minutes."

In her cabin, Mairin opened a cupboard to retrieve her own safety harness. Her hand strayed to the top shelf where a waterproof box nestled among sweaters and sox. She took it down and slid open the lid. Familiar documents lay on top: citations she had received over the years, her captain's commission, the deed to her rarely-used cottage in Killinick, letters and poems from Conor, and beneath them, letters from Richard she had never answered. At the bottom of the box lay two pictures she had saved from an anguished childhood. One was a drawing of her at age nine, inked by a talented artist at a fair. Though he made her rather prettier than she had been then, he captured the apprehensive expression she wore until the day she signed up for the Squadron. The other was her only picture of Kellen, a finely-drawn likeness she had taken from home the day she left forever. He was nine years old in the image, small for his age yet already handsome, wearing a rare smile. Neither of them smiled much in those years.

She studied his child's face and recalled events that she wished could be erased from her memory. Thirteen years she had been at sea, since the day she first stuffed this picture into her duffle and ran away from that evil place, not stopping until her lungs ached and her knees trembled. Now the young lad in the picture was beyond her protection. How she wished she had not asked Conor to watch out for him! When the warpipes sound, everyone watches out for everyone else. At this moment Conor would be suffering too.

She set Kellen's picture on top of the pile, slid the lid shut and re-stowed the box. Following her own orders, she donned a thick wool sweater, heavy trousers, and a sturdy leather safety belt equipped with a spring-loaded hook. Though it was not yet raining, she added the oil-skin over the sweater; it would be pouring soon enough. She hesitated a moment before opening the cabin door. It was time now to clear her mind of sadness and distraction. Seventy-one women and two men trusted her to bring them through the storm alive. Let the sea have at them, the *Caillech* would anchor at Falmouth tonight.

On deck she found matters well in hand: fair weather sails lashed hard to the yards, tough, gray-canvas storm sails snapping from the topmast yards and the forestays of the mainmast. Though driven by reduced sail, *Caillech* raced ahead at eleven knots measured by cast of the log-line. The frothy following sea towered thirty feet high at the stern. Brigid worked a crew to double lash all boats and set up the safety lines; Eavan Sechnaill had taken over the griping wheel.

"How is it?" Mairin asked the Weapons Master.

"Still answers, sir. In the troughs we're starting to lose a bit of rudder."

Mairin nodded and scanned the angry northern sky. The cloud deck seemed to skim the masts; a squall line laced with lightning swept towards them from the northwest.

Mairin lifted the trumpet. "Hook on, fore and aft!"

Sinea ran forward to make sure everyone was clipped to an anchor point. Rowenna scribbled notes on a pad, checked the compass in the binnacle and again ordered the ensigns to cast the log-line. Mairin took a second to focus on the barometer. Its ornate red needle pointed to 29.10, down three-tenths in less than an hour.

She had just closed the binnacle cover when the squall line blasted over the ship, bringing with it blinding lightning, deafening thunder, and a wildly choppy sea. Simple breathing became a chore in the spray-filled gale. Mairin clamped her hands onto the wheel next to Sechnaill and together they fought to hold the ship steady before the wind. When the worst of the squall passed, she was able to breathe a sigh of relief. The storm sails held and the ship raced downwind again. Now the wind bit hard with cold and the following sea piled itself into foamy, spray-capped mountains.

Sinea returned from the bow, hooked her belt to the starboard safety line and patted the railing. Catching Mairin's eye, she gave her the thumbs-up signal. Mairin knew what she was saying: *trust the ship and the craftsmen who built her.* Mairin answered in kind.

Rowenna shouted to Mairin over the howl of the rigging, "Sixty miles to Land's End on this heading."

Sixty miles, Mairin thought. About the distance from Rosslare to Dungarvan by horse, an easy days' ride with a stop for lunch at Waterford. Or, six squall-plagued hours of wild sailing with the ocean bottom waiting if the ship should broach to but once. Sixty miles.

"Ten miles northeast of the isles," Rowenna reported. "We need to start watching for St. Martin's."

The squalls abated at last. Wind and rain pounded the ship steadily from the northwest and it grew ever colder, the cold of premature winter. The thermometer inside the binnacle hovered at thirty-six. Wet hands and feet stiffened into useless lumps at that temperature in a gale. Mairin cycled the watches every thirty minutes. Though it was only slightly warmer below, it was dry and sheltered from the biting wind.

Towering waves lifted *Caillech*'s stern into the air while rollers from the west heaved the starboard side, giving the vessel a corkscrew motion that made handling her a second-by-second trial. Mairin kept her eye on the masts, for it was this kind of motion that strained the finest oak and ash and maple to the limits of tolerance. The light press of storm sails gave them plenty of headway and stabilized the masts to a degree, yet the topmasts swayed side to side with each corkscrew. The turn to the southeast would bring the sea directly onto the stern again. With as much leeway as they were making, she had to be sure they were not too far east of St. Martin's. They needed to spot the island's lighthouse as soon as they possibly could despite the awful conditions. If they were not as far east as Rowenna estimated, a sudden shift of wind could force them onto the island's ship-destroying reefs.

Rowenna said into her ear, "Captain, best I replace Lieutenant Danaan in the foretop, she's been there an hour."

"No, I'll go. Stay here and navigate as best you can."

Mairin unclipped from the binnacle post and clambered forward hand over hand to the bow, then into the foretop where Sinea scanned ahead with her glass, watching for reefs and for the St. Martin's lighthouse.

"Very close to freezing," Mairin said into her first officer's blood-red ear. "We may have ice soon."

"Already started, Captain," Sinea said, pointing towards glistening forestays.

Caillech buried her bow into roiling green ocean. In spite of their position forty feet over the deck, icy spray blew over them both.

"What a profession!" Mairin shouted with a grin.

Sinea answered with a grin of her own. "None better, sir!"

"I'll take over here. Take the quarterdeck."

Sinea nodded, unclipped her harness and descended through the lubber's hole. Mairin secured her own harness, then pulled out from under her flapping oilskin the powerful glass given her by Richard. A memory flashed through her mind as she focused the prized instrument. Her twenty-sixth birthday ... Tredinnick House north of Falmouth. Opening an ornate box, she found the beautiful naval telescope, her name engraved on the gleaming brass tube. She shed tears and Richard kissed her. *More than two years ago. Where is he now?*

She divided each wild, pitching minute of the next thirty into two halves: one to wipe the lens of the glass, train it in the direction of St. Martin's, and steady it enough to see, the other to sweep her eyes over the fast-icing *Caillech* and take a quick glance at the quarterdeck. Cholmain and Auteini, two of the strongest sailors on the ship, now gripped the wheel together, with equally strong Sechnaill posted close by. Rowenna Briuin was in constant motion, checking their compass heading, calling for the log-line, scribbling figures with a wax pencil on a slate and then rubbing them off with her sleeve. Overhead, the storm sails held together so far, it was the yards and the topmasts that worried Mairin. *Caillech* continued to corkscrew in the tumultuous sea, and every violent twist threw terrific strain on masts that grew heavier by the minute with thickening ice. Snow mixed in with the rain but it did not signify except to worsen visibility. Anxiety began to gnaw at her stomach: the shoals extended out from the island at least three miles. Surely they would see the lighthouse beacon before then?

She was one last telescope search away from chancing a new heading when she caught a flash of faint light in the glass. She swept it back and forth. Imagination? Wishful thinking? No, the welcome blaze of St. Martin's Lighthouse, about six miles off the starboard bow. Under the worst imaginable conditions, Rowenna Briuin had brought them right where they needed to be. For an extra second, Mairin focused on that lovely rotating beacon and called up from memory the ancient stone tower that held it ten stories aloft.

"On deck," she cried aft, "St. Martin's light, six miles off the starboard bow. Hold your course, I'm coming down."

Frozen hands and feet made the descent painful and awkward and she nearly fell flat when her boots touched the ice-coated deck. Two sailors grabbed hold of her and seconds later she clipped her harness to the binnacle post next to Rowenna Briuin.

"Fine navigating, Lieutenant, very fine indeed," she said into Rowenna's ear.

"Thank you, sir," Rowenna said, blue-faced with cold but smiling nonetheless.

To Sinea she shouted, "all hands below ready with tools, we may have damage when we come about."

Sinea disappeared down the quarterdeck hatch.

With miles to spare to the reefs, Mairin bided her time for the maneuver. *Caillech* labored under tons of ice and would respond sluggishly to the rudder. The new heading would be a safer point of sail, a beam reach off the starboard quarter. Speed would increase and the rudder would bite more securely. The catch: during the maneuver the ship's pitching and rolling would increase, subjecting ice-laden masts and yards to even greater stress.

She waited for the ship to mount the top of a wave, when the wind was strongest in the topsails, then gave the order to bring the bow to port. Cholmain and Auteini together eased the wheel counterclockwise two full turns. For several seconds the ship did not respond and Mairin wondered in horror if rudder cables had parted. Not so: the bow reluctantly turned from south-southeast to east-southeast, a course that would bring them safely past St. Martin's reefs and then under the welcome protection of Land's End. Sailors clumsily worked the topmast yards to accommodate the new wind direction.

Mairin opened her mouth to order "hold this course" when a *crack-splinter* sound overhead made her pause and look up. The mizzen topmast had snapped off at the lower cap. The mast, yard, and now-flapping sail toppled into the stays and shrouds feet above the mizzen-top. For a moment Mairin had hopes it would lodge there, giving deck hands time to scramble aloft and secure it. It was not to be. The raging wind forced the tangled mass free of the rigging and down it came. Fifteen feet above the wheel, the massive wooden cross snagged on mizzen backstays and twisted upside down. The point of the mast itself slammed through the deckplates a foot in front of the wheel and the yard crashed flat into the deck with a thunderclap, taking two mizzen backstays with it.

Under enormous tension, one backstay whipped loose and struck Mairin across the shoulder blades. She fell forward, getting her gloved hands out in time to keep her face from striking the deckplates. Pain intense enough to gray her vision flared from her back. Struggling to her feet, she found Cholmain and Auteini motionless on the deck. Rowenna was pinned beneath the wreckage yet judging from the stream of obscenities as she fought to get free, she was not badly hurt. The ship itself was in terrible danger of broaching. The sheered-off mast and rigging and sails covered the wheel and interlaced with its spokes. Meanwhile the following sea hammered on *Caillech*'s stern, slowly swinging her broadside to mountainous waves.

Sinea and a dozen hands leaped up from the hatchway and attacked the tangled, ice-coated wreckage with hatchets and sledges. Mairin clamped her own hands on the jammed wheel. A moment later Rowenna squirmed free and joined in the frantic effort to free the wheel. No shouting and no orders: everyone knew what had to be done. Hatchets and saws and hammers cut and splintered, and after thirty agonizing seconds, Sinea heaved the last jagged splinter free from the wheel's spokes. Rowenna leaped up and seized hold of the damaged wheel at Mairin's side.

"Here we go!" Mairin called out.

Hand over hand they eased the bucking wheel to starboard. Point by point the bow swung out of danger and *Caillech* gathered way again, driven hard by the two surviving topsails. The immediate danger to the ship passed, but not the danger to the work crew whose harnesses were not secured. Halfway through the gentle turn, an enormous wave slipped under *Caillech* and pitched the deck forty degrees to port. Sinea and the more experienced sailors caught hold of rigging or wreckage. One tall, slender newcomer skidded full speed into the port rail and toppled over. Her body disappeared—leaving one blue-cold hand clamped onto the safety line secured to the railing.

"Sinea!" Mairin screamed.

Sinea had seen it too. The hapless sailor was hanging over the side, in danger of being dragged into the sea or dashed to pieces against the ship's hull. Sinea boot-skated across the deck, leaned over the rail and seized hold of the sailor's wrist. Before help could reach her, a monstrous wave forced the portside into the churning cold waters. Sinea disappeared from sight, and Mairin's heart sank. Unsecured, she would surely be lost. With seemingly infinite slowness, the water subsided. Sinea hung half over the side herself, legs wrapped around the safety cable and hands still clamped onto the invisible sailor's forearm. Nearby sailors slid across to help while Mairin and Rowenna fought for control of the ship.

Yet another towering whitecap blasted the portside with water and spray, obscuring vision. When it cleared, Sinea and the near-drowned young woman had been hauled back over the side. *Gods of the sea, thank you*, Mairin prayed silently.

"Get them below!" Mairin shouted.

Auteini was on her feet again, a lump on her right temple and blood oozing from her mouth.

"I can take the wheel, sir," she said, spitting blood. "Master Cholmain's in a bad way."

Mairin and Rowenna moved aside and let her take hold. On this point of sail, the ship was handling well and the violence of her motion diminished. Fresh hands led by Mor Dal Reti flooded up through the quarterdeck hatch and helped all of the injured below. An unconscious Cholmain had to be carried and Mairin did not like the anxious look on

Mor's face as he followed the stretcher. Sinea made it with help, her left shoulder clearly dislocated and her face white with pain.

In short order the wreckage obstructing the quarterdeck was chopped, sawed and heaved over the side. *Caillech* now raced on a beam reach for the lee of Land's End.

"I'm going below," Mairin said to Rowenna. "Can you manage until I get back?"

"I'm all right, sir, I was very lucky. I saw you knocked down by something."

"Loose stay. First time I've been lashed!"

In spite of pain that flared from her back, Mairin pasted on a smile and made her way through a main cabin filled with dripping sailors trembling with cold, some bleeding, many still gripping hatchets and hammers and saws. In the surgery she found Mor bending over Cholmain, who was strapped tight to an anchored table and buried in heavy blankets. His fingers were gently probing her temple on the left side.

"How is she?" Mairin asked him.

"Not good," he said, straightening up. "Depressed fracture, bleeding inside her skull. In a moment I'll drill a small hole to release the blood. That's the most I can do under these conditions. Just get us into Falmouth as fast as you can."

Mairin pulled a towel from a hamper and mopped her face and hair.

"You were very close to her," Mor said, "and not a scratch?"

"Nothing visible," she replied. "A broken stay whipped my back."

"Hurts?"

"Like sin."

"I'll look at it as soon as I take care of Sinea's wrist." He nodded towards the first officer who lay in a hammock under blankets, talking with one of Mor's assistants. "Her shoulder was dislocated too, I've already dealt with that. The sailor she saved is conscious again, bruised and cold is all, frightened to death of course. Nothing else serious among the crew, some frostbite and hypothermia."

Mairin handed him the towel. "Do what you can for Cholmain. We should reach Falmouth in four or five hours."

She headed back up the stairs through the quarterdeck hatch. The rain and sleet had abated to a cold, freezing mist though the storm-wind still blasted over the portside. Auteini managed the wheel alone and Rowenna was staring into the binnacle.

"Course east southeast and steady, sir," she reported, "temperature down to twenty-eight. I'm going forward with my glass, we should have Land's End lighthouse in sight soon off the port bow."

"How's she handling, Brigid?" Mairin asked her bosun.

"Tolerable, sir, heavy but the rudder answers well."

"Go below and get warm, I'll take the wheel. Once we reach the lee of Lands End, we'll bring up all able hands to work the ice."

"Aye, aye, sir," said the rugged woman. "Captain, I've been at sea since afore you were born, never seen ice in October."

She disappeared down the hatch shaking her head and muttering. Mairin took a position by Rowenna's side at the wheel.

"You sure you weren't hurt, Lieutenant?"

"A few cuts and bruises, nothing more, sir. My hands are losing feeling."

"Go below, get dry clothes for yourself, gloves for both of us. Lanterns fore and aft. Make sure everyone uses a harness, I'll be damned if we lose anyone now. Let the watch chiefs know, reefed courses as soon as we clear Land's End. We need all possible speed for Falmouth."

An hour later, *Caillech* raced past the Land's End lighthouse. The towering storm-driven rollers barreling down the Channel could no longer reach them and the ship steadied herself. Driven by reefed courses and topsails, *Caillech* plunged ahead swiftly through a calming sea. When they cleared the next lighthouse at Lizard Point, Mairin swung the ship further to port. Next they raised the lighthouse at Coverack, a mere ten miles out from Falmouth.

Sinea returned to the deck, her left arm in a sling.

"Strange," she said, "now all we hear is the water and the creaking of the ice. I thought I'd lost my hearing entirely back there." She gazed up into the darkness above the masts and pointed. "Look, Captain. We have stars ... and moonlight too."

"What's the time, Lieutenant?" Mairin asked Rowenna.

"About eleven-thirty, sir, Kernow time." She raised her glass. "I have the light at Pendennis Castle, sir. And the castle itself ... the Admiralty is working late as usual."

"How many injuries?" Mairin asked Sinea.

"About twenty, sir, none serious except Cholmain."

"Unconscious?"

"Yes, sir."

"None lost, Lieutenant. That's what counts."

"Indeed, sir. That is what counts."

Caillech sailed into the familiar and friendly waters of Falmouth Harbor. The shoreline on either side was dotted with porch lanterns of cottages and illuminated signs of inns and pubs. Ship's lanterns hanging from the tops spread a warm, yellow light over sailors chipping and hammering the ice away from lines and braces and blocks. Mairin ordered the courses struck as they glided past the hulking mass of Pendennis Castle, headquarters of the Kernow Admiralty for many centuries. As Rowenna reported, light glowed at most of the six-over-six windows though it was now near to midnight. The strangely-deserted warship pier a mile ahead was dark and silent.

"Make our distress signal, Lieutenant," Mairin ordered Rowenna, who passed the order forward to a sailor posted in the foretop. "Let's hope they're paying attention."

The sailor worked the lantern's signal shades. No sooner had she completed one full pattern than alarm trumpets blared from Pendennis Castle's central tower. In immediate answer to the alarm, lanterns blazed up along the entire quay, doors to barracks flew open, and barefooted men by the dozen sprinted towards the Pier Number One where *Caillech* would tie up. Pier lanterns ignited and Admiralty sailors manned the docking bollards. Further ahead, Mairin spied the lights of the port hospital flare up and heard its own low-pitched horn call for medical personnel to report from the town.

Rowenna handed off the wheel to Brigid Auteini for the last maneuver. *Caillech* flew up into the wind, glided a few yards ahead and sideways until her starboard planking thudded gently against the pier's bumpers. Docking cables sailed to willing hands, the planks slammed down, and sailors and officers swarmed aboard. A young ensign with his shirt hanging out over his trousers presented himself to Mairin with a sharp salute.

"Ensign James Lethlean, Captain, what do you need?"

"My sailing master is below with a skull fracture, get her to the hospital fast as possible. We've attended the rest of the injuries. My crew could use some hot tea and warm quarters for the night if it's not too much trouble. As you can see, the ship has taken a beating."

"I'll be about it," he said, snapping another salute. "Welcome to Falmouth, Captain."

Mairin retreated alone to the aft rail. In a moment, Sinea joined her.

"A hard day, Captain," Sinea said.

Mairin nodded, her eyes following the stretcher bearing Finnsech Cholmain down the aft ramp. She smiled at the shivering, bare-chested sailors who carried it.

"I was never so happy to hear the Pendennis trumpets."

She turned to face her first officer. "Sinea, when I saw the sea wash over you and that poor sailor, I thought ... " she swallowed hard, "well, I thought Davy Jones had you."

Sinea shook her head. "Not finished with living yet, Captain. T'will take more than that to send me to his locker. I'm going below to collect a bag. See you ashore, sir."

Mairin waited alone a bit longer, reveling in the friendly banter and jokes hurled back and forth between her crew and the half-dressed Kernow sailors. *A hard day indeed. But we made it through. Poseidon, we beat you again.*

81

Atop a hill, surrounded by tall oaks,
A cottage stands alone in ruinèd state.
No roof to hold out rain, no chimney tall,
Nor any window holding out the wind.
What is there after all to call a home?
Four thick walls, a door, and brickèd hearth.
The stones beneath my boots, who carried here?
Did laughter once pour out this aged door?
Did turf fire scent the air and warm the folk,
Who gathered here when snows of winter fell?
My heart's dream is to make this lonely place,
A home again where love and kindness dwell.
I'll fill the hilltop's air with music's grace,
And whisper wondrous tales by fire's light.
I'll hang great lanterns telling all below,
That here, atop the mount, does friendship flow.
Conor Laigain (998)

Chapter 6

Conor's thoughts drifted away from the vicious fight at the fort to a whitewashed stone cottage atop a wooded hill. He did not actually own that cottage, or any cottage for that matter, yet it was as clear in his mind's eye as the old family home in Rosslare. Though not a remarkable cottage in appearance, its stones were ancient as the land and its lofty position gave it a clear view of sunrise and sunset and the stars. Here he and Mairin would raise their children. On special days they would heap food onto a long table crowded about by friends and kin. The big stone hearth he would build with his own hands would keep them warm when winter's winds blew and snow piled high in the yard.

The vision had been with him since his teens, sometimes waking and sometimes sleeping. Lately, in dreams, he came upon his cottage and found it dark and cold and empty.

He left Gorey's military hospital at dawn. Kellen was alive yet, and for that he was thankful. The surgeons opened his side, drained a dangerous blood clot, repaired fractured ribs and done what they could for a bruised lung. When Conor left him, Kellen was pale, clammy, and breathing with effort. The surgeons believed he might survive if he could live to see another day.

The road to Rosslare on which he now rode first headed east to the coast, and there he stopped along a sandy beach that was mostly free of old ruins. He dismounted and let Treasach wander—he would never stray far—while he strolled along the water's edge. There was no one in sight. Even in summer this beach was not much used except by travelers on the road stopping for a picnic.

His head throbbed fiercely. The hammer blow had raised a lump and deep purple bruise from his right temple to his forehead. The wound in his side throbbed. His stomach was empty and rebelled at the idea of food. The gathering wind from the north and steadily lowering sky promised a northern storm by nightfall. *So little true autumn we have now, compared with the days of my own youth. And I am only twenty-eight!*

The sudden cry of petrels hunting along the shore brought Feth to mind. After Domnall died she begged him to take her to the shore to watch the birds. *Oh my dear sister, how I remember your tears of confusion when our father was brought home by Padraic!* Now the crying little girl wore the cobalt-and-white uniform of the Line of Bows and would very soon find use for her handmade longbow.

A sigh escaped him. Kittiwakes mocked his melancholy with their manic calls.

Two sisters so very different, he pondered. One ice: Aideen, cool and calculating, supremely competent, a born leader like their father had been, yet seeming to lack his compassion and humanity. The other fire: Fethnaid, passionate, outgoing, loving, vulnerable, given to flights of fancy and sometimes foolishness. He could not help but admire Aideen, envy her seemingly endless capacity to face adversity and death without flinching. He loved Feth, there was not much else to say.

Treasach whinnied nervously. Conor looked about and spotted a lone figure on a horse a half mile north, riding slowly towards him. The ponderous weight on his heart lifted. The small, dapple-gray mare with an odd rolling gait was Seara, and her rider was Oran Osraige, returned at last. Relief spread over him like sudden sunshine after a storm. *Today of all days, I need his friendship.*

Seara trotted to a halt and whinnied a greeting to Treasach. Oran slid off, a bit stiffly. His eyes drifted to Conor's livid forehead.

"Ye gods, you look terrible!" he cried.

"No worse than you!"

They embraced hard. Conor felt his friend's gaunt frame through the cloak.

"You came on a good day, brother," said Conor, releasing Oran and grasping his forearms. "Did you come through Wicklow?"

"Late last night ... you'd left with the ambulances for Gorey. I rested poor Seara and grabbed a few hours sleep at the fort, then went on to Gorey myself. Missed you there by half an hour, sentry told me you'd headed for the coast road. Sorry to see Kellen like that."

"Not half as sorry as me. Mairin asked me to look out for him and I promised I would."

Oran clamped a hand on his shoulder. "She's not going to blame you, Conor, you know that."

Conor whistled sharply at Treasach, who was showing too much interest in Oran's weary mare. "Let's ride and talk," he said, glancing up at the threatening sky. "We might make Rosslare before this storm hits."

They mounted and rode at a gentle pace down the winding coast road towards Wexford.

"How did it happen, to Kellen?" Oran asked.

"We were fighting together in the shallows, I was on his right. I took a blow on my shield and slipped in the mud, left him exposed. A mace went straight into his side."

Oran looked over at him. "I can hear in your voice that you're blaming yourself, as usual. You would have taken the blow for him if you could've, and he for you."

Conor gave no answer.

"Well, am I right?"

"I suppose you are."

Oran cursed in a low voice.

"What was that for?"

"Because you are determined to feel it's somehow your fault. As if the man who swung the mace had nothing to with it. Or the fact that the Dubliners attacked in the first place. There are times when your determination to find fault with yourself wearies even me."

"Ride alone, then."

Oran reined in Seara, turned his eyes towards the sea and drew in a deep breath of sea-fresh air. "Sorry Conor, I'm exhausted beyond belief. I've seen a world of suffering in the last three months and it's weakened me somehow. As hard as things may be for us, they're worse for folks across the country we never see."

Conor edged Treasach until his mammoth flanks touched Seara's.

"I'd rather not ride alone."

"I know. We're both tired."

"And I know you're right about Kellen. My mind knows you're right, on all counts. My heart still aches for him, and for Mairin."

They turned their horses and continued down the deserted sandy road side by side.

"She's at sea?" Oran asked. "I heard at the fort that *Caillech* was in Wexford Harbor until yesterday."

"On her way to Falmouth as far as I know."

"Did you see her in Wicklow?"

"We went to Harvest Fair together. Breathe no word of this ... I proposed to her sitting on a bench with people all around. Can you believe it?"

Oran turned towards him, eyes wide. "You didn't!"

"I did. Gave her the amulet right there. Stupid to do it that way I guess but I didn't want to wait any longer."

"Not stupid at all," said Oran. "Have I retained my post as best man?"

"Who else? No bawdy stories at the dance."

"I make no promises."

"I had another visitor at the fair, before Mairin."

"An old flame?"

"I should be so lucky," Conor said with frown. "My sister, the one with dark hair."

Conor recounted the confrontation in the woods.

"That must have hurt," Oran commented when he finished.

"Hurt? I suppose it did," Conor said with a shrug. "Truth to tell I don't care anymore. Mairin accepted the amulet and said yes. I'll leave it at that. Now, tell me what you saw these past three months."

Oran began an account of his travels, and from that their conversation drifted to mutual friends and ordinary events and then, inevitably, to the past. They recalled with laughter the time they were both five and set the Osraige barn on fire—extinguished before total destruction by a raging Hagan, Oran's usually affable father; poking innocent fun at Seanlaoch's bookish habits and oversized vocabulary; drinking bouts in taverns east and west; and past loves and romantic exploits.

By noon they reached the halfway point at Ballyvaldon, where they stopped at Blackwater Tavern, an old haunt. Aichlinn Loigde, owner from time immemorial, spied them and barreled up, his huge belly knocking aside tables, chairs, and patrons.

"By all that's holy, my two bad boys!" he roared. His broad grin faded at the sight of Conor's bruised forehead and Oran's sunken cheeks. "Greaves and bucklers, you two look worse than old Aichlinn. By the big fire come and sit. Tanks of stout will I bring."

The kindly old man rumbled off, leaving more destruction in his broad wake. They took a table near the peat fire which he kept going on all save the warmest summer days. He brought the promised stout, a basket of dense dark bread and a half-pound of butter.

"Why *are* you so thin?" Conor asked with his mouth full. "You've never come back looking this way."

"There's no food to be had," Oran replied. "Three years of failed crops everywhere except the south. People are starving and they're desperate. Sean carries on about a 'Great Famine' that overtook Éirelan in the dim past. Maybe this is what it was like. I couldn't buy or steal anything except stale bread for the last week."

"Then we can expect more attacks."

"No doubt of it. Desperation breeds desperate acts. I'm sure the Dubliners will be coming in force when they stop arguing with each other."

"So we reinforce the forts on this end of the line?"

Oran took a long draft of his stout and edged his chair closer to the fire.

"Not that simple. The Ghaoth Aduaidh out of Belfast are gathering a big army. They won't be ready for another month but when they are, we can expect a major attack in the west. Meanwhile the aggressive clans closer to our western border may try raids any time. Cork and Kerry are fighting back harder and that may put more pressure on the Rampart near Dungarvan. I swung through that area two weeks ago and my guess is they are going to try it, so we can't afford to weaken those forts. Maybe we can thin out the central forts some, the terrain alone there makes it a more difficult place to assault." Oran paused and gave Conor a quizzical stare. "You look like I just stabbed you with a knife. What's wrong?"

"Feth is what's wrong."

"What about her?"

"She posted to the Line of Bows on her eighteenth birthday. To ease my mother's worries Padraic sent her off to the west. To Dungarvan Fort to be exact."

"Is she already gone?"

"By packet yesterday. She planned to spend a night with Sean in town then report to the fort."

"I don't suppose Padraic could recall her?"

Conor shook his head sadly. "I don't suppose he could. It's her right to be posted, she has the training and skills to prove it. And I wouldn't want to be in my uncle's boots if he tried."

Oran stared up at the pub's smoky-dark rafters. "The towheaded girl who followed us everywhere, what a nuisance she was! Now ... can she take care of herself?"

"Yes, I would say she can take care of herself. Deadly with the bow, anyway, and she's quick-witted. I've never seen anyone train so hard. How long since you've seen her?"

"How long? Why I guess over a year, she was off at training every time I stopped in Rosslare."

"Nothing to be done now."

Conor stretched his arms overhead and winced as the wound in his side complained.

"From last night?" Oran asked.

"No, at Ballynamult, last week. Fighter on the ground stabbed upward, right underneath my armor. Last act of his life, mind you."

"One of these days you're going to get killed."

"You're one to talk."

"You have a point," Oran said with a hand to his left ear. "About two inches separated me from sitting here or lying by the roadside near Galway."

"Do I want to know the details?"

"I doubt it."

Conor sighed and gazed at window behind Oran. "Best we ride. If we're going to get wet I'd as soon it be now than after dark."

Outside, cold rain slanted from the north. They threw woolen blankets over the horses and oilskin cloaks over themselves. Two hours of steady riding along the muddy road brought them across the River Slaney bridge, and soon thereafter among the log and stone buildings of the Province's army headquarters. From here, Padraic Conmaicne commanded the defense of the Rampart. Under the protected canopy of the main building, a three-story hulk of blue granite, two fresh-faced army sentries in light armor chatted more than amiably with two equally fresh-faced Squadron sailors, one of whom gripped a flagstaff.

Conor halted Treasach fifty yards away.

"Aideen is here, that's her pennant. My head won't take another argument tonight."

"Why don't you go home? I'll report to Padraic and join you later tonight. In the morning I'll head on to Kilmore Quay if the general gives me a breather."

"I'd like to see my uncle, but my head is splitting and I can't face Aideen."

"Go," Oran said. He dismounted and tapped Seara, who made a beeline for the big army stable with its warm stalls and fresh bales of hay.

Conor waited until Oran passed the sentries, then touched Treasach's flanks with his heels. It was nearly dark now and the wind-driven rain fell in sheets. Two miles down the road, he glimpsed the bright lanterns swinging beneath the front porch of Laigain House. Welcoming light streamed from its windows and smoke from its hearth scented the air.

Treasach needed no urging to step lively into the barn. Conor toweled him dry, petted two of the barn cats who came to investigate the newcomers, then braved one last bout of pelting rain to cross the broad yard, vault the porch steps, and burst dripping into the great room. Its warmth washed over him. Liadan, surprised, jumped out of a chair and helped him pull off the heavy oilskin and the soaked wool cape beneath it.

"Before you sit," she said, "I have cheering news for you."

He held his frozen hands to the blazing fire. "I've had one piece of good news already today: Oran is back. We rode together as far as army headquarters."

She smiled. "That is good news for certain. Let me add to it. A courier from Gorey passed by an hour ago. Kellen is awake and they think he'll pull through."

Conor leaned on the mantle and closed his eyes in relief. Liadan stroked his back gently, saying nothing. Between them, words were not needed.

Conor awoke to the sound of voices, one a raspy basso and the other a deep alto, echoing up the staircase of Laigain House. He could not catch the exact words, but the distress in his mother's voice was unmistakable. Last night, tired and careworn as he was, he had not passed on to her Oran's warning about Dungarvan. Padraic, owner of the bass voice, must have told her with as much reassurance as he could muster. Apparently his brotherly soft-sell had not assuaged a mother's abiding worry for her youngest child.

He experimented with sitting up and paid the price of a thudding pain in his head. Without making any quick motions he got to his feet and splashed cool water on his face. Then he dared a look in the mirror above the basin. The bruise's colors had spread to his eye on the right side and the lump on his forehead had not shrunk at all. He shivered; it was cold in the upper-floor room with the door closed. He rummaged in his closet for a sweater and wool trousers.

A tap on his door was followed by Oran's sotto voce "Conor, you up?"

"Sure, come in."

He'd heard Oran come into the house well past midnight and enter Feth's room as the note he'd left on the door instructed. Oran was dressed and from his wet hair had taken a bath that he no doubt desperately needed. He closed the door quietly and eased into a worn wicker chair near the window.

"Padraic gave my mother the news about Feth?"

"Not just that. We have word that Dungarvan Fort was attacked last night. And I don't mean a feint. A full-scale assault that cost us many lives."

Conor halted in his attempt to comb tangled hair.

"It's started already then."

"Yes. Feth would not have been on duty yet, from what you told me."

Conor gave up on his hair and sagged onto his bed. "Any chance that we'll get a breather after an attack like that?"

"Possible ... though I wouldn't count on it. Not this year."

"Don't complain about my mood, then." He listened a moment. "Voices stopped."

"Your mother said she was going out for a ride to clear her head. Padraic is waiting to talk to you."

"What about?"

"I don't know, but I can tell you Aideen got him aside last night at HQ."

"I'm going back to bed." Conor tumbled back on the pillow and pulled a blanket over his chest.

Oran reached over and stripped the blanket away. "Can't keep the general waiting. How's your head feel?"

"It feels like a hammer hit my helmet, what do you think?"

"Testy, aren't we?" Oran shoved himself to his feet. "Look, Conor, I'm going to ride home and spend one day with Mom and Dad. Then I have to be off again."

Conor stood and embraced his friend. "Come back in one piece."

"To be honest, brother," said Oran with a grin, "anyone seeing us together would give that advice to you first! And by the way, take that depressed look off your face. Padraic won't care, but if your mother comes back she doesn't need to see you wearing your melancholy mask."

Oran blocked the doorway and waited.

"All right!" Conor offered his best forced smile. "Better?"

Oran shook his head and cursed mildly. "Not convincing, but it'll have to do."

In the great room they found Padraic leaning back in a chair, his oversized boots on the table and his enormous hands clasped around a mug of tea. He raised bushy gray eyebrows and smiled at the sight of Conor's livid forehead.

"That must hurt," he remarked. "I must have forgotten to teach you how to duck."

"I did duck, Uncle," said Conor. "If I hadn't, my head would have come off entirely."

Oran offered a casual salute. "I'm off, General. You know where I'll be."

"I wish I could give you more rest," Padraic said with a concerned look. "But we need your eyes now more than ever. Report when you can."

Oran left by the veranda doors. A moment later they heard Seara's hooves thumping down the road.

"He's worn down, Uncle," Conor said as he poured himself tea. "I've never seen him this thin. No food to be had, he says."

Padraic nodded but said nothing. *This morning,* Conor thought, *he looks every year of his age, and more.* It was not the long, clubbed hair gone gray; like most of the Conmaicnes, Padraic had grayed early. No doubt his physical power was not much diminished, coming as it did from such tremendous breadth and height and never-neglected training. This morning, though, Conor was struck by deep furrows in his fifty-four-year-old face and anxious weariness about his eyes, the price paid for thirty-five years of heavy fighting, the last twelve of it commanding the army.

"Oran filled you in?" Padraic asked after a minute of thought.

Conor took a chair opposite his uncle. "Yes. Only bad news, it seems."

"Not entirely, we're lucky about Kellen Fotharta."

"Very lucky. I wish I could get word to Mairin."

Padraic fingered the empty mug absently. "One of the best young captains we have, sure he is."

"So what do we do now?" Conor asked. "Oran told me yesterday the Dubliners will come in force soon, and we don't dare strip the central forts after the attack at Ballynamult. And now Dungarvan for all love."

"I don't intend to wait for the big attacks to come. I'm building two field armies, one in the east and one in the west, using all our reserves and every soldier we can spare from the Rampart. We'll go on the offensive, and soon. As to Dungarvan ... I wish I could do something to make it easier on your mother. I can't. Feth wears the cross now and she'll fight like the rest of us. It's what she wanted and it's her right."

Conor pushed hair away from his face, carefully skirting the bruise. "Oran ordered me to wear a pleasant face. You're not helping."

His uncle's great fist struck the table, rattling the teacups. "You think I don't know that?"

"Yes, of course, Uncle, I'm sorry," Conor said, startled at his uncle's reaction and appalled at his own flippant remark. "My head isn't so clear this morning."

"Nor mine," rumbled the older man. "I didn't get much sleep, makes me cranky." He stared across the table at Conor. "Aideen and I had a long talk about you."

"Did you now?"

His cutting tone drew a surprised glance from Padraic.

"I mean no offense, I just wish Aideen would leave me alone."

"I know all about your differences, son. And I certainly don't take every suggestion your sister makes to heart. Yet I value her opinion, both as a strategist and as a member of this family."

"She's fighting me on marrying Mairin."

"The subject did come up, and she has her reasons, harsh though they may seem to you."

Padraic got to his feet with effort and walked to the veranda windows.

"Clearing up, it seems. Let's take our tea outside, I need fresh air and I think you do too."

Conor followed his uncle through the double-doors onto the stone veranda which offered a panoramic view of the town below, and beyond it, the harbor and the open ocean. Though the town was a mile away, its sounds carried up the hill: the clanking of wagons, shouts of vendors, laughter of children playing in a schoolyard. A three-masted warship flying the Squadron ensign flashed out a full suit of alabaster sails on its way out of the harbor. Aideen's flagship? From this distance, he couldn't tell.

Padraic leaned on the stone wall fronting the veranda and sniffed the cool, rain-fresh air.

"A fine day to go fishing in a mountain stream," he said.

"Indeed it would," Conor agreed. "We haven't had the chance to do that together in a long time. Maybe we can before the snows come?"

"I'd like that, son. Still, 'tis sad that we can't go today. I miss fishing very much. Mostly the quiet of it, watching the end of a pole and not having to think too hard about anything."

Padraic fell silent then for a full minute. *I've never seen him quite like this*, Conor thought. *Tired, yes, but more than that, subdued, distant.*

"Uncle," Conor broke the silence, "what exactly did you want to talk about?"

Padraic turned his deeply-lined face toward Conor. "I want to talk about your father."

Conor felt a cold chill run up his back. Twelve years had passed since his father died, yet the heartache remained fresh and the memories all too clear.

"I know you remember him with reverence," Padraic went on, "and that is well because he was a marvel of a man. The finest I have ever known."

"I miss him still," Conor said, his throat closing with upwelling grief. "Especially when I face battle and my heart flies into my mouth, I pray to him. I know that must sound odd ... it helps me somehow."

"More times than I can count," said Padraic, "I've turned to my right in battle and imagined he was there, protecting me." He turned back towards the sea and fell silent again.

At last he sighed and went on. "It's not his memory I have in mind today, Conor. Your father was a great fighter, but no greater than me or you if it's only the sword and the shield in question. There was much more to him than that as well you know. The years leading up to his death were a dark time, you were old enough to understand."

"The Rampart was overrun three times," said Conor. "I laid awake at night wondering if the next day we would lose everything."

"Oh, yes," Padraic said, "blood ran in the streets of Wexford and Waterford and Clonmel too. The worst of it was that the clans had split apart. The Council of Twenty was a roomful of shouting maniacs. I was there, I know. We were disintegrating as a people."

"I sometimes heard father and mother talking, late at night." *I haven't thought of this in a long time.* "I didn't understand all they said, but I think at times my father was very discouraged."

"He was, because he saw so clearly what was happening. What was so remarkable is that in two years, he had done it."

"I've lost you, Uncle. Done what?"

Padraic turned and leaned his back against the wall. He fixed his gaze on a meadowlark perched on the edge of the chimney and again, a long pause.

"Done? He glued us back together. To this day I truly don't know how he did it. Maybe it was the force of his personality. Maybe his brilliance. I do know that in the six months leading up to his death, we became the Twenty Clans of the Province again, as much united in thought and purpose as we were at Lough Ennell, a thousand years ago. United, our enemies could not stand against us." Padraic stopped and Conor saw a tear leak from his eye. "Would that he had lived on, Conor. Twelve years we've held together now, and it's because of him."

"I never thought of it that way, Uncle. Thank you."

"Oh, don't thank me, son, until we're finished."

I was hoping we were finished. He has something to say I'm not going to like. That's why he hesitates, talks about the past.

The meadowlark launched into song, bringing a faint smile to Padraic's face.

"Anyway," he went on, "we're not in danger of flying apart now, at least I don't think so. Tensions in the Council are building all the same. Yet there is another danger, and you know exactly what I am talking about."

"I'm not sure—"

Bright blue eyes bored into him from above without mercy. He did know.

"We could be overrun again," Conor admitted. "I didn't hear all of the details from Oran, but that much is clear."

"The details aren't important at the moment," Padraic said with an impatient wave of his hand. "The plain facts are enough. Attacks all along the Rampart, and two major armies to face, possibly at the same time. I'm going to need your help, Conor."

"I'll go wherever you send me, of course. I've never done otherwise."

That drew a laugh from Padraic. "Go where I send you? As Blade Captain of the First Rank?"

"That's what I am, Uncle. Senior to some, junior to others."

"I know what you see in your own future, Conor," Padraic said, laying a heavy hand on Conor's shoulder. "You'll serve as a captain till you're thirty and then hang your sword on the wall. Marry, raise children in a cottage on a hilltop. Write your poems and tell stories of your fighting youth and live out a happy life. I've heard you speak of this often enough, so has your mother, and Aideen too."

Conor spun out from under his uncle's hand.

"Yes, I don't deny it. Why should I? As I told Aideen, we have to bring children into the world or we'll have nothing to fight for. Of course I want a family and a home! My father had that much, if he hadn't you'd be standing out here talking to yourself."

"I understand that, Conor, believe me I do," Padraic said, his voice filled with sympathy. "And if it was in my power to give you what you want, I would. I would give it to all the young men and women out there along the Rampart and on the ships at sea. The sad fact is that none of us get to live exactly the life we dream of. I had the same dream as you, once. It's too late for me now. You still have a chance, it just won't be soon, son. It can't be."

"Aideen—"

"This has nothing to do with your sister! She's made her own choices and she tries to live with the consequences. This has to do with you, and what Domnall would have expected of you had he lived."

"Uncle, I am not him. I try to act as I think he would have wanted me to. I try to live up to the ideals he taught me. It's the best I can do. It's not fair for you to compare me to him."

"I'm not comparing you to him," Padraic disagreed gently. "There was only one Domnall Laigain and none of us would do well held up to his example. The problem we face is that he is gone yet his people live on and they need leaders."

Padraic set his cup on the stone wall and rested his hands on the ancient, cool stones.

"The time is dangerous, Conor, easily as dangerous as when your father led us. Maybe in ten years it will not be so, who can say? My task is to think of this year, and the next, and the next after that." Padraic looked down at his hands, then held them up in front of Conor. "These hands have killed a thousand men, maybe more. I can break a man's neck, or cut him through with my sword. But look at me! You think I'm young? I'm fifty-four, soon to be fifty-five. My steps are slower, my wounds bother me day and night, and I don't go without sleep so well any more. How much longer do you think I can keep this up?"

"Uncle, what do you want of me?" Conor walked a few steps away, tried and failed to keep frustration and anger out of his voice. "I'm not a natural leader like my father, you must know that. I'm a poet like my mother, a dreamer, a man who wants a family and a life. I do the best I can in the army because it's my duty. I have no special talent for it. Yes, I'll serve two more years, then I want to marry Mairin and have a son or daughter to come home to. I want the life my father had, while I'm young enough to have it. While I'm still alive."

Padraic thought a moment, then turned and walked down to the end of the veranda. Conor followed, though he wanted dearly to end the conversation, leap on Treasach, and ride away as fast as the stallion could carry him.

Padraic pointed a finger at a small clearing in the autumn-tinged woods fifty yards from the house. There, a rusty iron fence surrounded a white stone marker.

"Do you visit his grave often?" Padraic asked.

"You know I do. You've seen me there."

"Then you know what your grandfather wrote for his son?"

"I know what Uinseann wrote, yes. *Domnall Bairrche Laigain, 946 to 987, son of Uinseann and Meadhbh, leader of his people in time of need.*"

"There's more, Conor, and well you know it. The line beneath the cross."

Yes, there is the last line, beneath the Celtic Cross.

"Take up what I have put down."

Padraic sighed heavily. "Are those Uinseann's words?"

"I know where they came from."

"Best I remind you. Domnall wrote those words to you, in a letter. You showed it to me after he died. He said, 'son, if I should fall, it will be your task to take up what I have put down.' Am I wrong? Is my memory failing?"

"No, he said that to me," Conor admitted in a small voice.

The quiet of the morning was shattered by the laughter and shouts of a red-haired girl and a roan-haired boy, Fianna and Tynan Finguine. They chased each other through the grove of trees, around the gravesite, and back towards their farm.

"All I am asking is that you think on what your father meant when he said those words to you."

Padraic started down the stone stairs leading to the yard, where his stallion Alastair nibbled at the tall grass.

"I have to ride back to headquarters and see if we have a detailed report from Dungarvan. I'm sure Feth is all right. For now. We'll talk again."

He mounted his big stallion and rode off at an easy trot. For a time Conor felt unable to move, paralyzed by a torrent of conflicting memories and thoughts and emotions. Fianna and Tynan. Enemy armies. His cottage. Blood in the streets. Mairin. His father.

A half hour passed. Ships plied the harbor yet he scarcely noticed them. The cheerful and persistent meadowlark had no success in distracting him. Finally and with a reluctant step he wandered out to the gravesite and laid his hands on the rusting iron railing. Though the words at the bottom of the marker were carved no larger than the others, they seemed to cover the whole stone, to shout in his ears with his father's well-remembered voice. Now and then, a tear dripped from his eyes. He did not hear his mother ride into the yard and walk up to him.

"You spoke with Padraic," she said. "I'm sorry, my son, but I believe he's right. Your father would have expected you to do all you can. Domnall and I were lucky in one way, we had you and Aideen years before the worst of the troubles came and by then Feth was growing in my womb. It hurts me beyond measure to say it, but your dream may have to wait awhile. The life our people is at stake."

Conor wrapped his arms around Liadan, and felt hers hold him tightly in return.

"I wish for two things," he whispered into her ear.

"What would those be?"

"That I was a little boy again. And that my father was alive to help me."

This is my first night in the barracks at Dungarvan. There is one building for the Blades and one for the Bows. At this fort we have one big room and it's going to get crowded because of the attack two nights ago. At the moment we only have seventy Bows to fill out three watches at the fort - reinforcements are due in tomorrow. Six years of training has paid off for me even if I hated it at times. Yesterday I passed all the field tests for new postings and made the top rank of archers for both accuracy and rate of fire. I am so glad I spent time with Sean. He is a far more interesting man than my girl's fantasy made him out to be.
Journal of Fethnaid Laigain

Chapter 7

Feth lounged on the hard bunk and surveyed her forty square feet of domain: the bunk itself, open underneath for storage, a plain-wood locker with hundreds of initials carved in it, and a tiny oil lamp to be carried when nature called after lights out. In an adjoining room, a shower of sorts dispensed sometimes warm and usually cold water from a reservoir on the roof. The room had windows enough at either end that it was not gloomy during the day. Four big lanterns resting on shelves in the room's four corners provided light after sunset, and it was that shadowy light that she now used to finish her journal entry. She closed the leather-covered book, a birthday gift from Conor, and tucked it in her kit bag under the bunk. If the clock over the main door was right, supper was still a half hour away.

She was exhausted. The day before, all new postings, Blades and Bows alike, were tested for fighting skills, signal recognition, maneuvers, and overall fitness. Then she had gone on watch at the fort, where thankfully it had been quiet. Three hours sleep was all she managed before breakfast call, then morning tactics drills and another eight-hour watch. If the room ever quieted down she hoped for six hours of sleep tonight.

So far, she thought, she had been pretty well treated. The food was greasy and over-spiced; she was used to that from the training camps. A handful of other Bows had welcomed her and seemed friendly enough. Yet she also sensed an undercurrent of tension in the barracks, caught anxious looks and heard conversations die out when certain veterans entered the room. Conor had warned her about this and she knew to keep her head down and her mouth shut until she understood the situation better.

Her immediate bunkmates were on watch at the fort and she didn't feel like seeking out anyone. So she laid back on the bunk, closed her eyes, and tried to tune out the steady drone of conversations and incessant clatter of soldiers coming and going and working on their gear.

"Nice bow," commented a heavy voice, close by.

She opened her eyes and sat up. The voice's owner was a tall, muscular woman who casually tossed Feth's custom-made bow from one hand to the other. Two other veterans wearing superior expressions sauntered up. Feth had seen the three of them together on watch the night before. None of them had spoken to her so she didn't know their names.

She didn't like someone grabbing her bow like that. Still, it didn't seem worth a serious confrontation.

"Thanks," she said, getting to her feet. "I made it myself."

"Did you now?" The woman snapped the string a few times. "On the light side."

Feth shrugged. "Seventy pounds. It suits me." She put her hand out. "My name is Feth."

"Steise," she said, ignoring Feth's hand. "Mind if I go out and play with it?"

"I'd rather you didn't," Feth said. She raised her voice to be heard across the room. "Please give it back."

Conversations and clatter came to an abrupt halt.

"Leave her alone, Steise," said a fine-featured woman with a bandage wrapped around her midsection.

"Mind your own business, pretty Polly," said Steise without turning to look. "We have word that *little* Feth here has *big* connections in the army. Isn't that so, *little* Feth?"

Pushing it, isn't she? Conor, I'm doing my best to get along.

"Please call me Feth."

Steise handed the bow to one of her friends. "Oooh, 'please'! How polite."

Everyone in the barracks was watching now. There could be no backing down. Feth took a step forward, within Steise's reach if she chose to fight.

"My full name is Fethnaid Conmaicne Laigain, daughter of Liadan and Domnall. I came here to fight our enemies, not other Bows. Now shut your mouth and return the bow."

A deep flush of anger rose in Steise's face. Knowing her back would be exposed, Feth stepped past her towards the woman holding her bow. She held out her hand palm-up.

Someone in the back of the room called out, "give her back her bow." Another voice said, "yeah, give it back." A third asked, "what are you trying to prove, Steise?"

Then a commanding voice shot from the direction of the entrance. "Return the bow."

Bow-Captain Dunlaith Dal Reti marched toward them. Dal Reti was not much bigger than Feth and appeared to be well into middle age, with graying red hair and a weathered face that now wore a black expression. Dunlaith simply glared at Steise and her two friends. The one holding Feth's bow handed it back. Dal Reti took another step and stopped inches short of Steise's face.

"I've warned you before, Steise, you and your friends. No hazing or bullying in this camp. Three shifts tomorrow, all of you, and no leave for a week. One more offense and you'll get a month of latrine duty. Laigain, come with me please."

Dal Reti spun and charged out with Feth trailing at her heels. Feth caught up with her on the steps leading to the mess hall. Dal Reti halted and turned on her.

"Bow Junior Grade, I overheard the whole incident."

"I'm sorry, sir, I didn't—"

"Never apologize when you're in the right," Dal Reti interrupted. "You handled that well, amazingly well. You turned a bit of stupid and possibly dangerous hazing into a chance to assert leadership and make allies of people who don't know you at all. I've tried to weed out the worst of them but the fact is we're so short-handed I can no longer be picky. After our losses the other night I can't even get rid of Steise and she's the worst."

"I understand, sir."

"I know your background, of course," Dal Reti went on in a low voice. "So I assume you're well trained and know something about command and control of soldiers."

"I've done my best to learn from my family. My Uncle Padraic has taught me about commanding others, but I have no experience in it."

"You'll do well to follow everything your uncle has told you. A great general, Padraic Conmaicne." She paused, seeming to weigh whether to say more. "I served with your father, Feth. Well, I should say he was the army commander when I was a junior captain. He probably didn't know my name. I got to watch him work and I learned a great deal from him. He always found a way to keep people working together, even people who hated each other." She paused again and stared off into the trees. "To this day I have a hard time thinking about his loss. He meant so much to everyone who served under him."

"I was only six when he died, Captain," said Feth, "so I mainly remember him as a father at home."

The mess bells sounded.

"Get your dinner," said Dal Reti. "And welcome to Dungarvan, Feth Laigain. I'll be expecting a great deal from you."

Dal Reti headed off towards the officer's mess, leaving Feth to ponder the multitude of people whose lives her father had touched. Then she joined in the stream of other hungry archers charging out of the dormitory. She heard whispers of "good job, Feth" and "well done" on her way to the mess hall.

The dream was mixed up and vaguely threatening, filled with clashing images and illogical happenings. This much was clear: she was clad in her armor, a battle was raging and she could not find her bow. After much frantic searching she located a bow lying on the floor of a dimly-lit room. It was not her bow, it was too large and when she tried to draw it the limbs snapped off. All the while, someone was screaming "Bows arm!"

She sat bolt upright in her bunk—the shouting was real, it was Captain Dal Reti's stentorian voice. Alarm trumpets blared, lanterns blazed, and after a full minute of cursing and frantic scramble, armed and armored Bows poured out the door. Feth had checked her gear three times before she dozed off, so she found herself running with bow in hand near the front of the crush. Outside, Dal Reti and her junior captain bellowed for them to follow, then everyone plunged off the path and over the hill past the firing range. That meant an attack where the Rampart intersected the River Colligan.

Feth stumbled over tree roots, fell twice headlong, but kept up with the others. She was surrounded by panting, vile curses, and the Dal Reti's incessant "go, go, go." No one could see five feet ahead; they counted on Dal Reti in front and Junior Captain Renny Loigde at the rear to keep them together. They sprinted on, running and falling and running again. Their comrades at the fort would meet the attack first and by now might be fighting for their lives.

The trees thinned out and they crested a hill—the riverbank. Torches flared over the water and on the shore. Boats, scores of boats! The warpipes screamed. Blades and Bows from the fort had already attacked the massing landing parties.

"Form on the ridge," Dal Reti shouted. "Sort targets!"

Along the crest they made a line and tried to steady their breathing. How far were they from the water? Fifty yards? It was so dark except where there were torches. Enough light on the shore to see the Blades engaged in a desperate struggle. Feth swung her quiver to the front and nocked an arrow, lifted the bow, drew back the string. She was near the center of the line so her field of fire would be the center of the enemy's force.

"Shoot!" Dal Reti screamed.

Feth aimed for a man on the shore directly below her and at full draw let an arrow fly. She saw the man fall as she aimed and shot again. Screams and bellows of agony lifted above the warpipes and the shouting of commanders. Seventy archers poured in steady fire and dark shapes fell by the dozen, yet still more torches and boats crowded onto the slender beach. Most of the fighters swung right and attacked the Line of Blades, others formed a line to face the archers and launched well-aimed javelins uphill at their assailants. One lance whizzed by Feth's right ear, another struck the archer to her left full in the chest, punching through her cuirass. The woman fell backward and made no sound.

Distantly, Feth heard Dal Reti screaming "hold the line, keep shooting!" Cries of pain from female throats. A javelin plunged into the turf an inch from Feth's left boot. Nothing to do but stand and shoot now. If they broke, the Blades would be overwhelmed.

The javelin-throwers charged up the hill. She heard Dal Reti call out in a strange, raspy voice, "Bows, stand your ground."

She shot as fast as her hands could work. Men fell as they came at her, three, four, five stumbled backwards down the slope with arrows through the chest. One towering fighter with a torch in one hand and a hammer in the other took her arrow and kept coming. He crashed into her at a stumbling run and knocked her flat on her back. His great weight crushed the air out of her and sent pain blazing through her torso. She was pinned under the huge, writhing body. The stink was terrible, she had no air in her lungs, and he was not yet dead. He roared in pain, sat up on top of her, raised an enormous fist. It thundered down on the left side of her helmeted face. Then he found his hammer, and though his eyes glazed with approaching death, he lifted the hammer high for a death blow.

Her boot-knife slid in beneath his sternum and drove into his heart. The hammer slipped from his upraised hand and crashed into her left bicep. She shoved hard and he fell sideways, dead.

Where was her bow? There, two feet away, and not broken. She scrambled to her feet and opened a steady fire while trying to draw air into starved lungs. Javelins flew at them, one glanced off her thigh guard, another skimmed her helmet's white crest. What was Aideen saying to her? *Keep thinking, Feth, keep clear. In battle you must keep your mind focused to stay alive.*

Screams everywhere. The warpipes wailed on and on. Torches at the water's edge, the Blades holding, stabbing, bellowing in rage and battle fury. Boats and torches going the other way. She ran out of arrows. The poor dead girl on her left still had plenty. She grabbed a handful and fired long-range at the fleeing boats.

Then someone was holding her arm. Another Bow, gasping, half her armor torn away, helmet gone, blood pouring down her face.

"You can stop now. Feth, was it? You can stop."

They both sank to their knees and held each other's shoulders. The warpipes fell silent. All she could hear now was the gentle burble of the river and a hundred throats pouring out agony.

After a gasping minute, she had the strength to look up. Torches in the hands of Blades on the shore illuminated the carnage. Along the ridge to her right and left, no more than half of the Bows stood or knelt, the rest lay still in the wet grass. The Bow she was with fell back onto the turf, holding her head in her hands. Feth heard a moan of pain from her and lifted her to a sitting position. In the faint light she saw it was the woman Steise had given her bow to in the barracks. Feth pulled out a clean cloth from a pocket and pressed it to a gaping wound in the woman's forehead.

So this is battle. I stink of sweat and blood, I hurt so much I can't stop gasping. Half of us on this ridge are dead or dying. Well, Fethnaid, you couldn't wait to get your first posting and now you have it.

Choosing the exact spot she fought from the night before, Feth eased herself onto dry, sun-warmed grass at the top of the riverbank. It was a mild autumn afternoon. The placid River Colligan swirled its way towards Dungarvan Harbor, wrens and sparrows cackled busily in the trees, squirrels ran about hiding nuts for winter, and a fresh breeze rustled leaves painted with autumn's colors.

All the bodies were gone. An hour past dawn, thirty-one Blades and twenty-three Bows had been carried in flag-draped wagons back to Dungarvan for services and burial. A hundred and twenty-two dead raiders were gathered up in carts and buried in a common, unmarked grave on the far side of the river.

Worst of all in Feth's mind, Dunlaith Dal Reti was among the fallen.

Feth counted herself extremely lucky. A continuous bruise and abrasion covered the side of her face where the man's fist had struck her faceguard. Her left bicep was deeply bruised and hurt like sin, though the arm was usable with gritted teeth. Her ribcage was bruised by the weight of the man crashing down on her. No amount of washing could cleanse from her nostrils the stench of the raider who so personally tried to kill her.

She had been given two days' leave to recuperate, subject to emergency recall, and she could have gone straight to Dungarvan where Sean would have taken care of her. He knew she was alive and not seriously hurt: the injury and death lists had been posted in town at dawn. Why then did she come back to this scene of horror? Perhaps it was the need to feel that the battle and its terrible consequences were the exception, that today what she felt and smelled and saw was Nature as it was supposed to be, unspoiled by the violent spilling of blood and cries of the dying.

She heard someone approaching and turned to see a bandaged and pale Keegan Cholmain pause a few steps from her.

"I saw you leaving the camp," he said with a wan smile. "I thought you might need some company."

She patted the grass next to her. "I do."

He folded his big frame down next to her, careful not to put weight on his torn shoulder.

"Should you be out of the hospital?" she asked him.

"They needed space for soldiers a lot worse off. I can rest in the barracks just as well, it's a pretty quiet place just now." She turned her face towards him and he winced when he saw the damage on the left side. "How did that happen?"

She told him. At the end, tears started to flow and he pulled her gently towards him.

"Easy, Feth, easy. I know what you're feeling. You're first real battle tears your heart out. I remember mine like it was yesterday. Your training keeps you alive and fighting but it doesn't protect you from what you see and hear."

"It was like nothing I ever imagined. The girl right next to me took a spear through the chest. I could have been killed four or five times. Captain Dal Reti was killed. So many of us died."

"I know," he said softly. "I know."

Feth wiped tears from her face and tried to remember when she had last cried. *A very long time.*

"Peaceful here today," she said after a long pause. She pulled up a few blades of grass and tossed them into the breeze. "Hard to believe what it was like twelve hours ago."

Keegan swallowed hard. "I lost more friends last night."

He shifted his weight and grimaced with pain.

"You really shouldn't be walking around, Keegan."

"Maybe. It's just that the barracks are so depressing. I had to get away. And I wanted to see you again."

"Keegan, I should tell you—"

"Ah, your friend from the hospital?" he broke in with a half-smile. "More than a friend, is he?"

"I wasn't sure, when we talked on the coaster. Yes, he's more than a friend. That doesn't mean we can't be friends, does it?"

"Not at all. Tell me about him."

"His name is Seanlaoch, Seanlaoch Osraige. His brother Oran is a friend of Conor's."

"I know Oran. He was a Blade for years, now he's our best scout."

"Well, we all grew up together, more or less. Sean's parents and mine were best friends. They still are."

"He's older than you?"

"Twenty-four, yes."

"Same age I am, then. What does he do?"

Feth thought back to two nights ago, when she had talked with Sean for hours about his work.

"He studies history, he writes books, translates sometimes. Teaches school." Keegan made no comment but the unspoken question hung in the air. "He has poor vision so he can't be a fighter."

"We can't all fight," Keegan said. "Though maybe it will come to that some day." He swore a quiet oath. "I'm sorry, Feth, I've had a really bad too weeks. I came out here to see how you were and I'm dragging you down with me. Some friend."

He looked so dejected that Feth reached out and stroked his armor-hard back.

"I'm really glad you're here with me. You've helped me a lot already. Now, how about you? You must have a girlfriend somewhere."

"Ah, well, a few," he said, his mood lifting. "No one really close to my heart, though. Not yet, anyway."

"You'll find someone, sure."

His expression turned sad again and his eyes fixed on the river's edge, where so much blood had been spilled.

"I don't really expect to live that long."

His head sank between his knees and he closed his eyes.

"Don't say that, Keegan. We can't live that way."

He made no answer.

"Help me with something," she said. "What I can't—"

She paused as two Bows walked by headed for the shoreline, one with an arm in a sling and the other using a crutch to support a bandaged leg. When they drifted out of earshot, she went on in a low voice.

"What I can't figure out is this. When I saw that raider lift his hammer, I knew all he wanted in that moment was to kill me. He knew he was dying and still, he wanted to kill me. He looked me straight in the eyes and I saw murder there. Later on, after the battle, I wondered, why was he trying to kill me? He doesn't *know* Feth Laigain. I never did anything to him until I shot him in self-defense. I can't understand why he wanted so much to kill me before he died."

Keegan opened his eyes and brushed his own tears away. "Feth, is it important to know that?"

"It is to me. Did he hate me? Should I hate the people I fight against?"

Keegan thought a moment, then shook his head. "My father never believed in hate, even when he saw people do hateful things. He used to say that hate just breeds hate, and if we go down that path we lose ourselves along the way."

They fell silent again, content to soak in the sunlight. After a few quiet minutes he asked, "you have leave?"

"Two days, subject to recall. Not for my face. My left arm doesn't work too well and everything from my chin to my hips is bruised. That man weighed more than you by far."

Keegan struggled to his feet and pointed across the river. "Big as he was, he's over there in the cold ground and you're here, alive."

He reached down with his left hand and helped her up, for which she was grateful. Her whole torso was beginning to ache more and not less. They strolled together back to the barracks, speaking of hard bunks, watery eggs served at breakfast, vermin skittering around the barracks after lights out.

Where the paths diverged, he said, "see you, Feth. Get some rest."

"You too, Keegan." She gripped his hands. "And thanks for following me. I mean it."

She went inside. As Keegan had said of the Blades' barracks, it was a depressing place to be. All of the reinforcements had been taken up to the fort for duty, and would likely be kept there on watch overnight. The injured who did not need hospital care managed with the help of their friends to eat, dress, bath, and change their own bandages. She noticed Steise's bunk was empty. She felt no joy at that, and yet, it seemed better that someone who divided rather than united them was gone. They didn't have to love each other, yet there had to be respect.

She thought briefly about staying, then decided it would be just as well to get away for a time, see Sean, try to settle her feelings and get ready for the next battle that was sure to come. She packed her bag and boarded the next transport for town.

Dungarvan was strangely quiet for a pleasant autumn afternoon. All but a few vendor stalls were vacant; "Closed" signs hung in many shop windows; and those folks who were out and about wore closed, worried expressions. A glum Naomham Monaig leaned against the doorpost of his empty pub. He nodded to her with an expression that bordered on friendliness.

She climbed the two flights of stairs to Sean's room and knocked lightly. Hearing nothing within, she knocked louder, with the same result. Trying the knob, she found the door unlocked. Sean lay atop his bed, fully dressed, unshaved, eyes closed. His sweater and trousers bore maroon stains that certainly looked like blood. Feth's stomach clenched with fear.

She sat on the edge of the bed and touched the stains on his clothes. Dry. His face was unmarked and his hands, though dirty and seemingly bloodstained, showed no injuries. His breathing was deep and regular.

"Sean," she said, brushing at his tangled hair. "Sean, it's me."

His eyelids fluttered open and he stared up at her with unfocused eyes.

"Oh, Feth," he said, then coughed and struggled to sit up.

She cupped his face in her hands. "Are you hurt?"

"What? No, no. Oh, the bloodstains," he said, rubbing his eyes. "Not my blood. Sorry it scared you. I went in to volunteer at the hospital last night. I was there all night and most of this morning. What time is it?"

"About noon."

He fumbled for his glasses hanging on the bedpost. "When I saw the list come in from the fort and your name wasn't on it ... I've never been so relieved."

He put his arms around her.

"Easy," she said, holding him too. "My ribs took a beating."

"And your face," he said, holding her at arms' length. He touched his fingertips to her livid cheek. "I hope whoever did this paid the price."

"He did," she said, grasping his hand in her own. "I made sure of that."

"You want to tell me what happened?"

"Not now," she said. "I'm hungry and you need a bath. We can talk later."

He got up and walked stiffly over to the window.

"People are scared," he said, looking out over the square, "The road east was jammed with carts and horses this morning, and the line for the morning packet stretched all the way across the square. I stocked up on food yesterday so we can eat here if that's okay. How long can you stay?"

"Till tomorrow evening, unless the recall sounds."

"I'll get cleaned up." He retrieved his robe and a towel from the armoire. "Won't be long."

He kissed her on the way out. While he bathed and dressed, she gazed out over the square and the harbor beyond. The north wind of the early morning had shifted to the southwest, bringing with it the salty smell of the sea and a last hint of summer's warmth. On another such day, when her body did not ache in every bone and cry out for rest, she would have suggested a picnic. In a quiet, shady spot outside of town, they might have enjoyed a bottle of wine together, recalled childhood days, laughed, kissed, and laid in the warm grass beside each other. There would be no alarm to listen for, no pain in her chest nor visions of death and bloodshed crowding into her mind.

So deep was she thought that she did not hear him return. She felt his hands caress her arms and she drank in the clean male scent of his body behind her. He turned her about to face him, laid his hands ever-so-lightly on both sides of her face, then kissed her long and deeply.

"What a world we live in," he said.

She massaged his back. "We have some time, Sean. Let's make the best of it."

He dressed and served out a simple lunch of cheese and fruit. Warm autumn air blowing in the window drew them outside, where they strolled along the waterfront past the docks and into a park that the town lovingly kept planted with colorful flowers and trimmed shrubs.

"On a day like this there would usually be picnics all over here," Sean said of the empty park. "Strange to see it so empty."

He found a big oak and sat with his back against it. Feth laid down in the warm grass and rested her head in his lap. She closed her eyes while he stroked her hair, and then she did relate the story of the battle.

"Funny," she said at the end, "how it seems so isolated in my mind. Like it happened long ago or to someone else."

She heard him answer as sleep overtook her. When she awoke, Sean lay beside her, his hand holding hers, his face almost touching her own.

"Sean. Sean?"

"Uh." He opened his eyes and smiled. "Shouldn't have awakened me. I was dreaming I was lying next to a beautiful woman in a park, on a balmy autumn day."

She mussed his unruly hair. "What color hair did she have?"

"Hmm. Black, I think."

She rolled on top of him and spread her legs around his narrow waist.

"Wrong answer. Are you ticklish?"

She jabbed her fingers under his armpits and then tickled his ribs.

"No ... no ... please ... blond ... green eyes ... I swear."

"Better." She leaned over to kiss him and paid the price of pain as her ribs flexed. *Worth it*, she decided.

She let him up.

"Not fair," he said, massaging his ribs. "I can't retaliate."

He looked back at the quiet town, now swathed in late-afternoon shadow.

"Best we get back, Feth. How does a quiet dinner and reading to each other sound to you?"

"It sounds like the best thing in the world."

He helped her to her feet and they headed back to his room. There he lit a candle lantern and they enjoyed a hot dinner of boiled corn beef, cabbage and potatoes, enlivened by a bottle of wine he found after some searching behind a stack of books. By the candle's flickering light they read aloud poems and stories, none of which Feth had ever read. By the time the town's clock struck nine her head was sagging as Sean began the Legend of Cuchulain.

"You're going to bed," he said, closing the tattered volume. "You take my bed, it's softer than the other one."

She reached out and held his hand. "I'd rather not sleep alone tonight. Will you hold me?"

He looked startled for a moment, then nodded. She retrieved a linen sleeping gown from her bag and laid down, waiting for him. He peeled off his sweater and shirt, doused the candle, then doffed his trousers and stood awkwardly next to the bed. Light filtering from the windows shone on dark-colored drawers.

"Feth, I don't really have, I mean I never needed—"

"Get in, silly," she said, lifting the covers. "Unless you don't want to hold me."

He got in.

I make no pretense to be an historian, yet I believe it to be true that loss and anguish have often hung heavy on our pleasing and harmonious country. Is this the price we pay for living in this blessed place? If there is a balance in the universe, then for every moment of splendid joy in seeing the morning's mist clear over the mountains, we must offer up a toll of heartache. Why this should be so is part of the mystery of our lives. We can wish it to be otherwise but wishing so leads us nowhere. We can only love and care for each other, share the joys and the sorrows as they come upon us. This is our belief, and our way.
Uinseann Laigain, Credo Mysterium

Chapter 8

Conors's hands ached from the effort of reining in Treasach. The big stallion begged to gallop the seven winding miles from Laigain House in Rosslare to the village of Baile Mhurain. Conor kept whispering in the horse's twitching ears, "we can gallop all the way back, boy." Conor wanted the time to think, so Treasach had to walk.

He halted Treasach at the fork in the road a half-mile short of the village. A turn left would take him into the village proper, a turn right onto the ancestral lands of Clan Fotharta. The great manor house, occupied by Gorman's branch of the clan for the past century, would lie a mile past the fork. Conor had not seen it in a dozen years, yet his memory told him this road was once not so quiet. So far as he knew, the ancient house was now home only to Gorman, Etain, and Bram, their oldest son, though it was the childhood home of Mairin and Kellen too. It was Bram he met first, at Blade training camp when he was sixteen and Bram was twenty and Domnall had already perished in battle.

"*Domnall Laigain's brat,*" *Bram repeated.* "*I think it's a good name.*"
"*Do not say that to me again,*" *Conor warned.* "*You'll regret it.*"

"Domnall's brat," Bram said again as other trainees gathered around the two men.

In front of the crowd Conor challenged Bram to a sword duel, completely illegal under training camp regulations yet often permitted by officers as a means to cool overheated tempers. Conor had trained in swordsmanship from an early age under Domnall and Padraic and he was much faster than his taller, stronger opponent, who could have overpowered him in a genuine fight to the death. The fight ended with Bram half torn to ribbons and Conor relatively unmarked. From then on, Bram never missed an opportunity to make his training camp life miserable, though always in ways that could not be detected and punished.

Four years later, Conor was promoted to junior captain, and Bram, who had a reputation for hard drinking and whoring, remained a line soldier. As luck would have it, on Conor's first night commanding Blades at a Rampart fort, Bram served in his unit. Conor did his best, following Padraic's explicit orders, to stay away from him. Late in the night Bram sought him out. Somehow he discovered that Conor was seeing a young woman from Baile Mhurain. Bram claimed he had been with the same girl on many occasions, sometimes right after Conor had. A vicious fight started in the pub where Conor had taken the girl. By the time other soldiers broke it up, both men had suffered broken bones and deep cuts and the pub was a shambles. Had Liadan not prevailed on her brother, an enraged Padraic was of a mind to break Conor back into the ranks or out of the army entirely. As it was, Bram was fined a half-years' pay and Conor confined to military quarters for three months running.

Six more years passed and Bram faded into the recesses of his memory. Aideen hosted an officer's Winter Solstice party at Wexford Naval Headquarters to which he was invited. He was standing in one corner, a glass of wine in his hand, making small talk with a comely, shy ensign when a new arrival entered the room. The forest-green officer's tunic clung tightly to a tall, athletic frame; thick auburn hair was trimmed to her ears; luminous brown eyes scanned the room nervously. Captain's double-anchors gleamed on her shoulders To Conor it seemed she was not happy to be there.

He excused himself and intercepted the captain on her way to the food and drink table.

"*I beg your pardon, my name is Conor Laigain,*" he said, smiling and extending his hand.

"*Mairin Fotharta,*" she replied, taking his hand. "*You're the Commodore's brother?*"

"*Yes. You won't hold that against me?*"

He brought her a glass of wine and they retreated to a quiet corner to talk. Her somber, uneasy expression puzzled him yet he was entranced by the mellow sound of her voice and the strength of personality that emerged at odd moments. Expecting a negative answer, he asked her if she was close kin to Bram. She looked down at her feet and said in a soft, constricted voice that Bram was her older brother. His first impulse was to smile, say "oh, really?" and find an excuse to talk with someone else. Yet he hadn't. Looking back on it later, he knew the hook had already been set and he would not be able to struggle free even if he wanted to. He talked with her until the party broke up and then walked her back to her ship. By the time he left her, he was already starting to fall in love with her.

Two months after the party, Conor, now a Fort Captain, commanded the isolated and lonely Rampart outpost at Graiguenamanagh. His first night at the fort he met a freshly-minted Blade Captain named Kellen Fotharta and knew it had to be the brother of that name Mairin had spoken of. There was much physical resemblance and a similar guarded personality on first meeting in the fort's tower.

"*Good evening, Captain Laigain,*" Kellen said. "*We haven't met but Mairin told me about you last time I saw her.*"

Conor shook his outstretched hand. "*She's talked about you, too. She's very fond of you.*"

"*And I of her,*" Kellen said, staring into Conor's eyes. "*You will be good to her?*"

"*I will. You can be sure of it.*"

Since then, they had become friends and went fishing and hunting together when their leaves and postings coincided. Conor did what he could to maneuver their being posted together, as they had been at Wicklow.

Kellen lived in a small cabin at the outer boundary of Fotharta land, as far from the main house itself as one could get. Conor had gotten word that a cousin was helping Kellen recuperate from his injuries at home, at his own request. Conor had never been here though Kellen had invited him often enough. He worried still that an encounter with Bram on this road could lead to violence. The need to see his friend now outweighed his apprehension.

A narrow dirt path led off to the right, marked by a hand-lettered sign reading "K. Fotharta" nailed to a tree. Conor dismounted and led Treasach through a shallow swale, passing by a stream-fed pond coated with late-blooming water lilies. Perched on the far shore of the pond was a stoutly-built log cabin that seemed to blend into the woods surrounding it. It was unusual only in the large casement windows cut into its timbered sides, as if its builder or possibly Kellen himself wanted a brightly-lit interior. A fishing pole leaned against the porch rail.

Conor led Treasach past the cabin into a modest three-sided stable, where the stallion joined two mares munching contentedly on oats. He climbed the three steps onto the cabin's covered porch and tapped with an ornate brass knocker. A moment later the heavy door swung open and before him appeared a tall, slender young woman whose strikingly beautiful face shocked him into silence. Soft brown hair tumbled over her shoulders, hair matched by gentle amber eyes that bore no hint of wariness.

"Good morning," she said in musical soprano.

"Captain Conor Laigain," he said, too formally. "A friend of Kellen's."

"Of course, he told me to expect you. I'm Triona Bairrche, his second cousin."

He clasped her offered hand; the grip was stronger than he expected.

"Sorry," he said with a nervous laugh, "I'm staring. It's just that I, well—"

"Expected a man?"

"No doubt I did."

"Disappointed?"

"What? No, of course not. I didn't mean—"

She threw her head back and laughed, and he saw she was playing with him.

"All right!" he said, laughing himself. "I expected a big-chested Blade with a two-day stubble."

She took a step back. "I'll have to do as a substitute. Please come in, I know Kellen wants to see you."

He followed her into the cabin's cheerful front room. To his left, the room resembled any other cabin's front room: hearth, kitchen, table and straight-back chairs; three upholstered chairs and one small divan; a shelf holding a scattering of books; brooms, axes, saws, and shovels hanging from pegs; lanterns suspended from ceiling beams.

The other half of the room surprised him. It was a painter's studio, furnished with a large and a small easel, tables littered with tubes of paint, cans, brushes, and palettes, blank canvases leaning against the wall, and one completed painting hanging between two windows. It was a large scenic work, fully five feet wide and three high. He knew the place it depicted: Waterford Harbor. The time was sunset. Orange and pink light swept over the sea. A big cargo ship, its sails barely drawing, edged towards a pier where dockhands and stevedores waited. He felt the serenity of the moment, could hear in his mind the oath-filled banter between the sailors and rough-clothed dockworkers.

Conor tipped his head towards the painting. "Kellen did this?"

"You didn't know he was an artist?"

"I've heard him talk about painting. He claims to be a poor amateur."

Triona moved closer, near enough for him to detect the scent of jasmine.

"Kellen is very talented," Triona said, her voice filled with admiration. "So far he hasn't tried to show or sell any paintings so people don't know about him. I want him to take this one to an art fair."

"He should. How's he doing?"

"Considering his injury, pretty well. He was very lucky that Guinnein MacFhearghuis happened to be at Gorey teaching surgeons in training. Best surgeon in the world, so far as I know. I learned a great deal from watching him."

"You're a surgeon too?"

"Not yet. I have my physician's certificate and I'm in training for surgery. I asked for leave to take care of Kellen, watch for special problems. They needed the beds with so many severe cases coming in, so I was granted two weeks' leave. By then he'll be in fair condition."

"For combat?"

She shook her head. "Two months, minimum. Command, yes, fighting, no." She touched Conor's sleeve. "Let's go wake him, he was dozing when you arrived. You'll find him pale and weak from blood loss, but he's gaining strength back fast."

She led Conor down the short hallway and into the room on the left. Two more exquisite paintings hung there, one a winter scene of moonlight shining on snow-draped mountains, the other of autumn colors decorating the woods around the pond near the cabin. Kellen, dressed in a loose-fitting shirt and trousers, lay on top of the bedcovers. His head was propped up on two pillows and an open book lay near his left hand. Triona spread the heavy curtains, then leaned over the bed and brushed Kellen's hair from his forehead.

"Cousin," she said, "you have a visitor. Remember, you have to lay quiet."

His eyes fluttered open and settled on Conor. "Conor? Welcome. To my cabin. Agh, if I sound a trifle slow ... it's because dear cousin Triona potions my brain. You two have gotten acquainted?"

Triona nodded. "We have. I'll leave you to talk. I need to start some cooking or we'll have nothing decent for lunch."

"Thanks, Triona," Kellen said. "And no more of that gruel, please."

Kellen's eyes followed her out. "Lovely, isn't she? Don't repeat this ... she has three homely sisters!" He waved a hand towards a chair. "Sit if you have time to stay."

"I have plenty of time."

Conor dragged the chair next to the bed and sat on it with his arms across the back.

"Triona's whole family lived near here, once," Kellen went on. "When Mairin and I were kids we played with Triona and her sisters and brothers. Scores of cousins lived here then. Most of them moved away years ago."

"Because?"

"Too much ... ah, not worth going into."

"You look better than I expected," Conor said. His eyes drifted to Kellen's side. " How do you feel?."

"Fine, if I don't move. Hurts like the devil if I do but Triona says that Scottish doctor knew his business." He raised his shirt to expose his right side. A one-foot stitch line ran from his armpit to his waist, and his whole side was colored a lurid mixture of green, purple and yellow.

Conor winced at the sight. The moment it happened flashed vividly through his mind. On his knees in the mud, the whirling mace caving in Kellen's side-armor as if it were sheet metal. And this was the result. He swallowed hard and said nothing.

Kellen lowered his shirt. "Your knuckles are white, my friend. Don't break the chair."

"Sorry." He relaxed his grip.

"Mairin told me once you take on blame for things that aren't your fault."

"Maybe not my best quality," Conor admitted with a sigh.

"On the other hand, you're been a godsend to my sister. I can't believe how much she's changed in the last two years, since she met you. You don't know how good that makes me feel, Conor."

"I love her very much."

"I know that."

Conor turned towards the paintings behind him. "You're a much better artist than you claim to be! I wonder why Mairin never told me how good you are."

"She's never been in this cabin," said Kellen with a downcast look. "It's on Fotharta land and she'll not set foot here, not that I blame her. It's a peaceful, private place to work when I'm off-duty. Gorman and Etain and Bram leave me alone and if I see them by accident now and then it doesn't bother me. Not the same for Mairin. Not the same at all."

Conor rested his chin on his hands. "I know I've asked you before ... I'd really like to understand why Mairin won't talk about her life at home."

Kellen said nothing for a moment. A warm breeze stirred the curtains and carried in the rich smell of damp leaves. From the front room came the sound of chopping and Triona's musical humming.

"She doesn't talk about it," Kellen said, "because the memories hurt her far worse than my side hurts me. Part of the reason she loves being at sea, I think, is that it helps to bury the bad memories."

"Except in dreams, I think."

Kellen eyebrows rose in a silent question.

"We actually slept together one time, a few months after I met her. I mean actually stayed together all night, in the same bed. Towards morning she had a nightmare, screamed in her sleep. I almost had heart failure. It took me a long time to calm her down. Ever since then she seems wary of spending the whole night with me."

Kellen lifted the book from the bed and turned it over in his hands, thinking.

"She didn't tell you what the dream was about?"

"I asked. She claimed she couldn't remember."

"It was about home," Kellen said, his eyes turning sad and inward. "She comes back to Fotharta House in dreams. It worries her no end because the nightmares happen at sea sometimes."

"If I knew more maybe I could—"

"She'll tell you in her own time."

"I feel like she doesn't trust me."

"Of course she does! It's not an issue of trust. Probably she worries you'll walk away from her once you know everything about her life."

"I wouldn't do that!"

Kellen held up his hand. "Conor, I know. She probably does too, in her head. Fear is a powerful force, though. Just give her time. Please."

Conor walked to the open window, which faced the stable. Treasach saw him, whipped his tail back and forth and snorted, as if to say, *I expect the gallop you promised.*

"I do love her," he said. "And I want us to have a family and a happy life together. I can't say I'm getting any help from Aideen who insists Mairin stay at sea and Padraic who's pushing me to ... to do things I really don't want to do."

He heard Kellen sigh.

"Padraic thinks you should be moving up in command, yes?"

Conor turned in surprise. "How did you know?"

Kellen laughed and then grimaced at the pain it cost him. "You think the army doesn't have a rumor mill? You think people don't expect Domnall Laigain's son to command the army some day?"

"It's not funny, Kellen. I'm not cut out for it."

"I don't agree."

Conor returned to the chair and glared at Kellen. "I thought you were my friend."

"I *am* your friend. You *are* cut out for it."

"Everyone's against me, even my mother!"

"No one's *against* you. The point is ... what's that?" he whispered.

A deep male voice echoed down the hall, followed by Triona's voice, hushed, insistent, angry.

"Bram," said Kellen, his pallid face flushing pink. "Stay quiet. She can probably get rid of him."

Triona cried out, "stop it, you're hurting me!"

Conor instinctively reached towards his belt and his hand touched air. His sword hung on Treasach's back.

"There." Kellen pointed to the wall, where his own sword hung on a hook. Conor whipped it out of the sheath and bolted down the hall. Bram, tall as Padraic and nearly as broad, had hold of Triona's wrist.

"Well look at this! If it isn't Domnall's brat once again," he spat out. "I thought that was your horse. Long time no see, Conor."

"Let go of her," Conor said. He raised Kellen's sword to fighting position.

"I'm unarmed," Bram said, "and you're a trespasser here."

"Bram, don't be an idiot," Triona said, her wrist still imprisoned. "Go back to drinking wherever you were drinking."

Bram turned his gaze from Conor to her. Triona's face whitened with pain as his hand squeezed harder. She tried to pull away to no avail. Suddenly he opened his fingers and she stumbled backward. Her legs struck a table and she fell on her back, her head making a sickening thud on the stone slab. She lay still.

Bram tried to use Conor's momentary distraction to attack, but Conor saw it coming. Bram halted his charge with the tip of Kellen's sword an inch from his throat.

"Get out or die," Conor said. "Your choice."

Bram opened his mouth to answer, then shrugged and took a step back.

"You're on our land," he said. "Don't be here when I come back. Armed."

He turned to leave, then whirled with astonishing speed for so big a man. The urge to kill him was overwhelming, yet Conor knew he could not. He sidestepped Bram's drunken charge and slammed the flat of the blade onto the back of Bram's neck. Bram sank to the floor and sprawled out face down.

"You should have killed him," Kellen said. He leaned on the wall, hand clutching his injured side.

"Do not move," Conor ordered. "Please, Kellen, stay where you are."

He laid the sword aside and led Kellen back to his bed.

"I'm all right," Kellen said between gasps of pain. "See to her."

Conor found Triona exactly as she had fallen. Her eyes were closed and her breathing shallow and rapid. He tucked a chair cushion under her head, then dipped a clean towel in a water basin, wrung it out and laid it on her forehead.

"Triona," he said softly, "can you hear me?"

Her answer was a groan of pain. She opened her eyes.

"Lie still," Conor said. "I'll get help from the town."

"Don't order me around, I'm the doctor," she muttered through clenched teeth. She reached around and gently fingered the back of her skull. "Broke the skin, probably no serious damage. Help me up, Conor. Slow and easy."

He lifted her by the waist and eased her into a chair. She lowered her head between her knees and pressed the wet cloth onto the back of her head.

"Is he dead?" she asked of Bram, who had not moved.

"No. I hit him with the sword. The bad news is that Kellen followed me out here. I got him back as carefully—"

"Oh, he didn't!" She lifted her head and sat up. "Gods above, this hurts. Help me in to see him."

He slid an arm around her waist. Despite the circumstances, the press of her body against his and the sweet odor of jasmine set off reactions he did not want yet could not entirely suppress. He led her slowly down the hall. Kellen had lain back on the pillows. His forehead glistened with sweat. Triona set the bloody towel on the nightstand, lifted Kellen's shirt, and carefully probed his side.

"No harm done, I think," she said with relief. "Getting up like that could have cost you your life, cousin."

Kellen reached out for the bloody cloth. "You could have lost *yours*, cousin. You don't know what Bram is capable of, or my father for that matter. It's not safe here for you, I told you that from the start. You insisted! Now you have to get me someone else, or move me back to the hospital."

"There's another alternative," said Conor. "I can take you both in at Laigain House until Kellen is recovered. We have plenty of room, and to be honest my mother is lonely with Feth gone now too."

"You don't owe me that, Conor," Kellen said.

"It's not a question of owing. Triona would be safe there."

"It might be best," Triona said. She pressed the wet towel to her head again. "I think I'll be okay, but sometimes concussions have delayed effects. The question is how. Kellen can't ride."

Conor stepped over to the window. "There's a cart out there in the stable. We could load it with straw and make a stretcher out of a sheet. Kellen, will your mare pull it?"

"Kiara? Sure she will. I use the cart to bring supplies from town."

Triona considered the idea, then nodded assent. "All right, it'll work if we go slow. What about Bram?"

"If he wakes up before we're well away," said Kellen, "he'll come after Conor. And he'll have his sword."

Triona grabbed her medical bag and searched.

"Here," she said, holding up a vial. "A spoonful of this powder under his tongue will keep him out for hours."

She left with the vial in hand.

"I don't believe this happened to her," said Kellen in a voice that shook with anger. "Bram is a damnable animal."

"If I hadn't been here ... "

Kellen squeezed his eyes shut. "I don't want to think about it."

Triona returned. "Done. We have plenty of time to be careful about this. I'll rig the stretcher, Conor, you can fill the wagon with hay and hitch up Kiara."

"Agreed," said Conor. "Once you're well down the road, I'll pay a quick visit to Fotharta House and let them know what happened."

"Find my mother, say what you need to say and get out," Kellen warned. "Bram will have one idea when he wakes up, and you need to be away from here by then."

A half hour later, Kellen rode comfortably on a bed of soft hay and Conor turned back towards Fotharta House. As he turned at the crossroads, Etain came riding towards him, accompanied by a man Conor found vaguely familiar. Conor halted Treasach and bowed slightly when Etain and her companion reached him.

"Conor," she acknowledged him coldly. "My brother-in-law Zephan. May I ask your business on our property?"

"This is a public road," Conor observed with a faint smile. "No matter. I know I'm not welcome here. I came only to see your son Kellen. While I was there, Bram arrived drunk and attacked Triona Bairrche who's caring for Kellen. I think he meant to rape her."

"Possibly," Etain admitted, to Conor's amazement. "And?"

"Bram is unconscious on the floor of the cabin. I leave him in your care."

Etain leaned over her horse to whisper to Zephan, a middle-aged man of dark skin and hair, thick beard, and powerful build. He whispered back with an angry look.

"Bram can shift for himself," Etain said. "My son is thirty, he only lives under my roof."

"As you wish."

"Will he be charged?" asked Zephan.

"He should be hung by the neck," Conor replied to the man. "I'll leave that decision to my mother. Good day to you."

He spun Treasach about and set him loose to run hard again. He caught up with Triona and Kellen five miles down the road to Rosslare. Kellen had drifted off to sleep. Conor hitched an unhappy Treasach to the back of the cart, where he was forced to amble along next to Triona's amiable mare. Conor climbed onto the cart's narrow dickey seat and found himself sandwiched thigh-against-thigh with Triona. Once the trauma of the morning faded and her head ached less, she became a lively and interesting companion, full of stories about her childhood, her seven siblings, her medical training, and her other passion which was cooking. In return, she insisted he recite poems he had written and talk about his father. Though he usually found speaking of Domnall difficult, this time he did not.

When they arrived at Laigain House in late afternoon, Triona supervised getting Kellen into a spare bedroom, then excused herself for a bath. Conor gave her Feth's room, next to his own. Liadan had left him a note saying that she had followed Oran to Kilmore Quay to visit with Hagan and Niamh, then she would go directly to the session of the Council of Twenty in Teach Munna.

It was late afternoon. Conor felt the exhaustion of the past days descending on his spirit and his body alike. While Triona bathed and rested indoors, he sank into a stuffed chair on the front porch and dozed in the warmth of a late afternoon sun. Once he was awakened by the shouts and laughter of children down the road: Fianna and Tynan Finguine and their friends playing a game. When their racket faded he drifted into a light sleep again.

"Conor?"

He opened his eyes and saw Triona standing beside his chair. She had traded the plain working tunic for a close-fitting pale yellow sweater and a short, dark brown skirt.

Conor straightened in the chair and rubbed his hands over his face.

"Ah, that felt good. Not much sleep the last few days. Sit down," he said, nodding towards another chair. Triona pulled it closer and eased into it, causing the skirt to hike up well over her knees. The jasmine had been traded in for ... what was it? *Lavender*, he decided.

"I feel much better," she said with relief. "I took medication for the headache. You have a much nicer bath than Kellen, though I don't suppose he cares much about bath tubs."

"How is he?"

"He's fine," she replied, sinking further back into the plump cushions. "If he had fallen at the cabin he might have died right there. I'm glad we brought him here. You know that was the second time I had to deal with Bram?"

"No, I didn't."

"He showed up a couple of hours after we arrived yesterday. Maybe he saw the wagons on the road, maybe he saw me, I don't know. Anyway, he barged into the cabin unannounced when I was making dinner. He wasn't drunk, so far as I could tell. He just hung around making suggestive comments, getting a little too close. Didn't touch me. Never once went in to see Kellen, who was asleep anyway. I got pretty nervous about it, he's so big and his eyes seem to carry a threat. He left eventually. I didn't tell Kellen."

"Bram and I have a history going back to training camp. There's more to his hatred than that, though, some connection between our families that I can't seem to find out. Mairin freezes whenever I mention his name, so I don't."

"From what I remember," said Triona, "Bram was wicked with both Mairin and Kellen. I only saw things from the outside as a young girl ... but that household frightened me."

He reached out and touched the back of her head. "Quite a lump."

"Surface fluid, nothing more."

"I should have run him through when I had the chance."

"You say that now. I think you would never have done it."

"Why do you think that?"

"Because of who you are, or at least who I think you are after we talked today. You would never kill an unarmed man. You'd find another way out—like you did today."

Conor sighed. "Taking his worthless life would have helped no one." Domnall's face flashed through his mind. "My father would be disappointed in me if I acted out of rage."

"You speak as if he were alive."

Conor tapped his temple. "He is, in here. I hear his voice often."

"And your mother? How would she have felt?"

"I suppose she'd understand and forgive me. We're very much alike, mother and me. Ever ready to forgive, maybe too unwilling to judge. I should hate Bram for the way he treated me years ago, for the way he treated his kin, for what he did to you today. I don't. I pity him, I guess, knowing who his parents are."

"We all have to be our own people," she stated in a harder tone. "I don't believe we're prisoners of our own past."

"I'd like to think that. I'm not sure."

Triona tilted her head back against the soft chair cushion and closed her eyes.

"What did Domnall want for you? Did he tell you?"

"I was sixteen when he died. I was falling in love with a new girl every week, training for the Blades, and writing sappy poems. I expect he thought it was too early to discuss my future. I think he wanted all of us to be honorable human beings."

Triona opened her eyes and studied her long-fingered hands. "Ever since I was a child, I wanted to be a doctor. I dreamed about caring for ordinary people, the old, the ill, young women bearing children. In the last six months I've spent all my time attending to men and women with terrible wounds. It's not what I wanted to do with my skill. I have to, for now. You have a dream, Conor?"

"Aye, and I've bored my family and friends to tears talking about it."

She took hold of his hand and shook it playfully. "Tell me."

"It starts with a cottage on the top of a hill. I build it myself. My children run in the yard and the woods, and at night we hang lanterns on the porch and tell stories by firelight. My friends and kin come up often and we cook for them and my children play with their cousins. In quiet times, I write poetry." He paused and shook his head. "It's all beginning to sound like a fairy tale to me. Once upon a time there was a man named Conor who built a cottage. It never gets to the happily ever after part."

Her fingers squeezed his. "There's plenty of time, Conor. Life isn't over at twenty-eight."

"I suppose not."

She turned and caught his eyes with hers. "I mean it. Promise me you won't give up on your dream."

Something about the way she said those words lifted his heart.

"Promise. Now enough about me. Do you have someone special?"

"I did, once, his name was Tierney. He died two years ago, on my twenty-fourth birthday."

"I am sorry, Triona. What happened to him?"

She released his hand and walked to the porch rail. "He was a Blade, like you. He took a spear in his thigh. Nasty wound but he was recovering well. Then a deep infection set in that we couldn't stop. I had to watch him die, day by day, in terrible pain at the end." She started to cry. "He died with his hand in mine."

Now she cried hard, uncontrollably. Conor went to her and held her from behind. She turned in his arms, buried her face in his chest and dug her hands into his shoulders. Her whole body shook with sobs. He held her a long time, stroking her forehead and whispering to her. At last she drew in a deep breath and looked up at him.

"I'm so sorry," she said, struggling to catch her breath. "I've held this sadness inside for so long. I can't believe how much it hurts after two years." She wiped her cheeks with the back of her hand. "I must look terrible."

"You look fine," he said. "More than fine."

Their faces were just inches apart and drawing nearer. Tear-filled amber eyes seemed to fill the universe. He felt control slipping away. Danger flared in his mind, moral sense at war with overwhelming passion. Triona sensed it too, broke free from his arms and ran into the house.

He did not follow. Instead he headed out to the stable to groom Treasach. He was angry with himself and ashamed of his flaring reactions to Triona that had started when he first walked into the cabin. As he often did, he related his problems to a contented stallion.

"Treasach, what am I doing? I pledged himself to Mairin not four days ago! I love Mairin. The problem is I can hardly ever see her. I'm crawling the walls when she's away, or she's here and I'm away. Then I spend a whole day with a lovely woman who dashes on jasmine and lavender and who's intelligent and warm and lonely. It's just more than I can handle, boy."

Treasach whinnied softly.

"Thanks. I know it's all just excuses. If something happened with Triona as it almost just did, I'd never forgive myself. I didn't really do anything wrong, did I? I didn't kiss her. I held her when she cried, that's all."

Treasach shook his noble head in irritation.

"All right, all right. Maybe even that was too much. I felt more than pity for a sad woman. I was falling off a cliff, my mouth had that certain taste in it, my ... well, you get the idea. No sympathy from a stallion, I'm sure."

He was not sure how much time passed until Triona called from the porch: "Hungry?"

"Famished," he called back. "Be right there."

As he neared the house he detected the delicious scent of frying meat and baking bread. He followed Triona inside, relieved that for the moment, one kind of appetite distracted him from another.

And when we come to London Wall,
A pleasant sight to view,
Come forth! come forth! ye cowards all:
Here's men as good as you.
'Trelawney he's in keep and hold;
Trelawney he may die:
But twenty thousand Cornish bold
Will know the reason why.
Anthem of Kernow

Chapter 9

Richard Tredinnick eased open the door to Mairin's room in the officer's quarters of Falmouth naval headquarters. The room's single small window cast enough pre-dawn light for him to see her lying asleep in the bunk. He set the door ajar and allowed himself a minute or two to hover over her, and remember.

Two years of separation had done nothing to erase vivid memories stretching back four years. They met on a long convoy to the Atlantic coast of Africa. It was his first major command and he saw to it that *Ajax* was well-prepared to entertain the other captains in the fleet. Their first day out of Plymouth Harbor, the late-afternoon weather favored his plans: a calm sea and gentle summer breeze. Signal flags flashed, boats splashed into the water from warships and cargo ships alike, and captains arrived in dry uniforms and high spirits. *Caillech* was fresh out of Falmouth yards and under the command of a young Province captain named Mairin Fotharta. *Caillech* being the rear guard ship, her gig was the last to arrive. The bosun's whistle screeched once more and Captain Fotharta climbed gracefully over the starboard rail.

Late afternoon sun caught her as she strode towards him, looking a bit stiff and formal yet outrageously attractive for all that. She was strong-featured, lean and muscular, athletic in motion, yet altogether female in the smile she offered when he greeted her. His other officers noticed her too, of course, and he took great pains not to expose his interest by action or word. Yet the time arrived, later, when he asked her to stay a short time for an extra cup of African coffee. Though she seemed puzzled by the invitation, she accepted gracefully. For two years following that first meeting, he quietly moved heaven and earth to arrange *Caillech*'s assignment to joint actions and patrols.

There had been time ashore, too, and those were the memories he treasured above all, for they were the most intense and intimate. He escorted her to the annual Captain's Ball at Pendennis, when she danced with him under the sparkling lanterns and later made love with him for the first time. And he recalled too the time she sat beside him on the banks of a stream in the Lamorna Valley, sobbing about a childhood memory, a memory too painful for her to put into words.

When she was promoted to senior rank, he could no longer maneuver her regular presence in his life and long periods of separation seemed inevitable. He began writing to her, frequently at first but less often as time passed because she answered only the first two of his letters and then fell silent. No final letter, no goodbye or hope for the future. Silence. After a year passed he imagined she no longer wanted to see him, and he stopped writing. He became involved with another woman, a liaison that ended badly indeed. The naval grapevine told him that Mairin had moved on to another man. That information was now six months' stale. It was possible, just possible ...

He dared reach down and touch her hair, ever so lightly, before calling out her name.

"Mairin." She stirred. "Mairin."

Who was calling out to her? A familiar voice. It drew her out of a vague and disorienting dream. She opened her eyes, saw the uniform first, then a handsome, concerned face.

"Oh ... Richard." She levered herself up on one elbow and rubbed her eyes. "You weren't there last night, were you?"

He lit an oil lamp that hung above the room's single table. "No, I got in two hours ago. *Ajax* was further up-harbor getting a new mainmast set at the shipyards. I brought her down before dawn and saw

Cailleach at the pier looking a bit worse for wear." He sat on the edge of the bunk. "Are you all right?"

"No serious damage to my personal hull and planking," she said, flexing stiff fingers. "Big welt and bruise on my back where a stay hit me. One serious injury I have to check on."

"Your Sailing Master? I checked on one of my own crew at the hospital before I came here and saw they had someone there from *Cailleach*. The doctors told me she has a skull fracture but she'll recover in time. Your surgeon saved her life by what he did on board."

"That's a relief." She brought her feet to the floor and carefully stretched her back. "One more piece of good news I could use."

"About?"

She told him of Kellen's injury.

"I'm so sorry, my heart," he said. "I know how worried you must be. I'll give an order to be informed of any news as soon as it comes in." After a pause, he said, "I missed you."

She looked up at him. "I missed you too."

How long had it been since she'd seen him? Two years, sure it was. Had he changed? Faint lines now etched his deeply-tanned face. No trace of gray in thick black hair that waved in every direction. Sea-blue eyes, powerful hands, and a warm smile, these she remembered too. This morning he wore his full captain's uniform: dark blue slacks and long jacket, gold braid and buttons, with the Cross of St. Piran emblazoned on each shoulder and his ship's name *Ajax* stitched on the front of his hat lying on the table.

Oh, I should have written! At least one last letter. I tried and kept throwing them in the waste basket. I felt so sad and lonely, I couldn't find the words. I still can't.

"Fantastic storm for October," she said, changing the subject. "Ice like you wouldn't believe."

"Two merchanters came in during the night, both damaged too." His eyes drifted towards her chest and then her legs. "Very stylish outfit."

She suddenly realized she was not in uniform, nor in any of her own clothes, but rather sported a hastily-assembled version of seaman's pajamas.

"Red with little blue anchors," she said with an amused smile. "I was so tired last night I came straight here, soaked to my, well, soaked.

A kind ensign rounded these up for me." She tugged at the over-generous shirt. "I don't fill it out very well."

"You'd look ravishing in anything, or nothing at all, for that matter."

"Be good," she said, getting to her feet. "I'm ... well, I'm seeing someone."

"I heard that."

"You did? How?"

"I have my spies," he said with an impish grin. "Doesn't stop me from admiring you in baggy pajamas. We're not strangers, for all love."

"No, we're not strangers. And you?"

"Me what?"

"Are you seeing someone?"

He looked away and a shadow passed over his face. "I was, awhile ago. Not now."

"Oh."

"No matter," he said, regaining his smile. "We're still friends, aren't we?"

"Of course we are. That will never change." She walked stiffly to the window, which faced the harbor below. *Caillech* was dark and silent.

"They'll be swarming over her at dawn," Richard said. "No serious damage that I could see. Where were you when the mast came down?"

"A few steps from the wheel."

"Lucky no one was killed."

"Very lucky," she said, heading for the water basin in the corner. She splashed cold water on her face and toweled dry. "Nothing we could do. With the ice so bad we were all clipped on, no time to move before it hit."

She went back to the window and gazed at her ship, rocking gently as the morning tide swept by. "I brought everyone home. We could easily have gone under."

He moved to stand behind her.

"I'd like to hold you," he said softly.

She hesitated, then turned and let him put his arms around her. His body trembled against hers.

"I'm glad you didn't go under," he whispered in her ear.

He took her hands and held her at arms' length.

"It'll take at least a full day, maybe two, to refit *Caillech*. Would you consider staying at Tredinnick House? Your own room, of course. I know my father would love to see you, and Wenna too."

Mairin freed one hand and fingered the baggy pajama shirt uneasily. "Before I answer, you should know I accepted a proposal of marriage. So we're clear."

"Ah."

"I'd understand if you withdrew the offer."

"I wouldn't think of it. Look, I admit my heart did a small leap of expectation when I found out you were here. So I'm a little disappointed. But I value your friendship and your company. The house is depressingly quiet since my mother died. So please come."

"All right," she said, "if you promise to behave yourself."

He spread his arms wide. "Didn't I always?"

"You did not."

He swept one arm across his body and bowed. "Never uninvited."

"True," she admitted. "So I'll come. Business first. I need a bath and a clean uniform and off-duty clothes. Then I'll check on the ship, visit the infirmary and the barracks and send a report to Aideen Laigain. *Then* I can relax."

He touched a finger to his hat. "Yes, Captain, as you wish, sir."

"Shoo," she said, waving a hand at him.

"I am shooed," he said, backing out and closing the door.

She returned to the open window and drank in the cool, sea-scented breeze of morning. Sunlight cascaded over the big harbor, and as she watched, a boisterous crew clambered over *Caillech*. Two berths away from *Caillech*, Richard's own *Ajax* also hosted a crew hard at work with buckets of paint and varnish. No other warships at the docks or in sight. Never had she seen the Kernow Admiralty's main base so deserted. Whatever the reason, it could not spell good news.

They rode horses six miles from Falmouth to the village of Ponsanooth, at a leisurely pace that allowed them to catch up on two years' news and admire the rolling hills and well-tended fields along the road. The ancestral Tredinnick home fronted on the Kennall River two miles west of the village. The true age of the dignified, granite-stoned structure was unknown. It was plain to see that the central two-story section was by far the oldest. At some time in centuries past, wings had been added on both sides, and a long, elevated stone walkway built to connect one end of the house to an arched bridge over the Kennall.

A mast secured to one of the four chimneys displayed the Cornish pennant, the white Cross of St. Piran on a black background; on the opposite chimney hung the blue-and-gold flag of the Admiralty. Stately ancient trees surrounded the house as if to guard it from intruders. Hydrangea, holly, lilac, and honeysuckle battled for space around the house's foundation.

Turning their horses out to pasture, they strolled to the center of the bridge and leaned on its oft-repaired stonework, watching the Kennall's lively waters skip over stones and eddy in quiet pools. A pair of mourning doves perched on a gable called out a melancholy song.

"I'm so glad," Mairin was saying, "that we had word of Kellen." She closed her eyes and took a deep breath. "I haven't had a moment's peace since I left Rosslare."

Richard laid a gentle hand on her back.

"I know how much he means to you," he said. "I haven't forgotten what you told me about your childhood." He pushed back her hair from her forehead. "And how you got that scar."

"I had the dream again, on the ship," she said, closing her eyes. "I was there in that room and father threw me into the table. I don't know why that one memory seems to come back over and over. I have other dreams, vague, weird like everyone else does. This one never seems to change. I wake up and my head hurts as if I had just hit that table again."

"It happened one night we were together. Your body went as rigid as oak and I had a hard time waking you up."

"Sorry."

"I had to work hard to relax you, that morning."

Time for a change of subject. "I wondered about something, Richard. When we came in last night, the Admiralty piers were empty. I've never seen that before."

"In a nutshell, we're stretched to the breaking point," Richard replied in a voice tight with worry. "Every ship we have is at sea, even old-timers that need repairs desperately. Santanders to the south, pirate and coastal raiders everywhere, and bigger ships coming down both channels, not even sure where they're from yet."

"We have our hands full too. Aideen almost let a cargo ship make this weapons run, something we've never done, but in the end decided it was too risky."

"Thank the Commodore for me."

She gave him a puzzled look, then saw what he meant.

"Except for almost being sunk, I'm glad to be here too. I forgot what a lovely place this is."

"I once had hopes you'd spend more time here."

"Please don't, Richard," she said, looking away.

"Sorry. Let's stay with the military situation. The worst of it hit in the last two or three weeks. We had a cool, rainy summer, we think food is short in many places to the north, and another cold winter is surely coming. Hence everyone with a boat or ship is trying to get their hands on food, or on hostages to trade for food." He sagged over the stone rail and closed his eyes. "I am *tired*, Mairin. And my father is working himself to death."

"I've never seen you like this," she said, touching his shoulder. "You've always seen the bright side of things."

He straightened up and faced her. "There is no damned bright side! We're hanging on by a thread. On the other hand, we're not sitting still, my father has a plan to go on the offensive."

"What kind of offensive?"

"Maybe best I not say yet," he said, looking uneasy. "Not that I don't trust you! It's just that my father asked for complete secrecy until he has approval, and I should respect that."

"I'd expect no less."

"You'll see him tonight and he may want to get your opinion." He arched his back, a gesture she always found a touch erotic. "I'm dead on my feet, can we go inside? I've got to catch an hour or two of rest before dinner or my face will fall into my food."

They strolled side-by-side along the stone path leading to the front door of the house. He opened one of the heavy double doors and led her inside. The great room of the house brought back warm memories. Every wall and corner was filled with the paraphernalia of naval life and history. A large-faced barometer hung over the hearth, with a chronometer on one side and on the other, a wind direction indicator connected to a vane on the roof. Polished oak shelves along the walls held journals and logs with year-dates stretching back over a century. Delicate ship models rested on corner shelves, a weathered ship's wheel hung on pegs, and nearly every square inch of leftover wall space was occupied by a painting of a ship: sailing vessels of all kinds, warships and yachts, as well as steel-hulled ships dating back to the Age of Machines. Only the presence of overstuffed chairs and sofas reaffirmed that this was a home and not a naval museum.

"I hope you still feel at home here," said Richard, leaning his hip against a well-worn leather chair. "We had lively evenings here, did we not?"

"We did indeed." Mairin wandered along the book-laden shelves. "I don't remember these," she said, running her hand over a set of faded red and silver bindings. "Were they here before?"

"No, they weren't." He pulled one of the fragile volumes out and opened it carefully. "My father got hold of these last year at an auction in Liskeard. Exact reprints of sailing logs from over two thousand years ago, and the books themselves date back two centuries. They make great reading on a cold, rainy night."

She took the open book from him and turned the pages. "Look at this! Not much different from our own logs. Wind direction, ship speed, repairs ... on and on. Imagine reading the thoughts of someone at sea in the first age of sail!"

"Almost twenty-five hundred years ago in some of those volumes."

"Maybe I can read these day."

"You're always welcome," he said, with a wistful glance quickly suppressed. He eased the volume back into its slot. "Let me show you something else my father acquired since you were here last."

He led her under an archway into the dining room, then through a small study, and finally into a room Mairin remembered as having a billiards table and bar. The table and bar were gone, replaced by a single square table twenty feet on a side bearing a relief map of the Celtic world: Eirelan, England from barren Scotland to rocky Wales to still-fertile Kernow, the coast of Europe from the Bretan Peninsula to the north coast of Spain. Palm-sized ship models plied the painted blue seas singly and in squadrons. Twenty ships carried a tiny Province flag, the rest the flag of Kernow.

Richard lifted a long pole with a hook at one end and pointed with it as he spoke. "You wondered why Falmouth is empty. Eleven ships here, guarding the English Channel, eight in St. George's Channel, twenty-two patrolling the south end of the Celtic Sea. Twelve on convoy duty, returning from Africa. Six in the Brest Squadron. *Ajax* is in port for emergency repairs, which believe me it needs. Your twenty are here, here, and here," he pointed to the west, south and east coasts of Eirelan and the coast of Wales, "except for *Caillech*, which is here," he finished, the hook resting on Falmouth. "There's a bigger, more elaborate version of this layout in the operations room at Pendennis, but my father likes to keep one here too. An ensign rides up from Pendennis every morning and moves ships around."

"I never visualized it so clearly," said Mairin. "It doesn't look the same on small-scale charts. So much area to cover, so many ports and sea lanes. " She shook her head. "Twice as many ships wouldn't be too many."

"And the threat is growing steadily," said Richard, pointing with the pole. "More and more ships pouring down from the north, from Denmark maybe or possibly old Germany, attacking our eastern coastal towns and shipping, not to mention shadowing our Africa-bound convoys. And then there are the damnable raiders from Santander, whom you certainly know." He laid the fork of the pole on a big harbor on the north coast of Spain.

"Oh, we know them well enough," she said, setting her eyes on the Spanish city. "Not such great sailors or ships when I was a youngster. Year by year they've gotten better and tougher."

"They're building ships faster than we are, and good ships at that. They've copied our designs down to the knees and the keelson." He turned his gaze back towards Kernow. "Fifty-four capital ships," he went on, "not counting ten more a-building in Falmouth and Plymouth. You have twenty at sea. With these seventy-four three-masters and an assortment of smaller vessels we are trying to protect twenty-six major harbors, more than a hundred coastal towns, and all the shipping lanes in between. At a guess, a hundred raider ships are prowling the coasts at any given time, and thirty or forty pirate ships are working the open seas. Last month we drove off a squadron of nine ships trying to slip down the Channel past Calais, and at the same time one of your battle groups fought six Santanders off Cork."

Mairin nodded, her face grim. "I lost two friends in that battle."

"If we can't control the seas," Richard went on with rising frustration, "we lose the ability to trade among each other and with North Africa. What would you do without our barometers and compasses? What would we do without your armor and swords and precision steel fittings?" He allowed himself a bleak smile. "What would any of us do without coffee?"

"I only wish we could get more of it."

Richard tapped the table with tip of the pole.

"Maybe the biggest problem is that our ships, and some of yours too, are wearing out faster than we can maintain them. *Caillech* is new, so you don't worry much about rotten timbers. Every time *Ajax* weathers a heavy gale I wonder which mast or yard might come down. Yet we don't dare cut our numbers at sea. So we man the pumps day and night in heavy weather and barely keep up in the well."

He laid down the pole and rubbed his face with both hands.

"Ach, I'm just worn out," he said. "I turn morose when I can't stand up anymore."

Mairin slipped an arm around his waist and they out walked together. *Thinner than he was*, she said to herself. *And he's changed in other ways. He hasn't laughed once today.* As they passed through the dining room, which appeared dusty and unused, she asked, "Didn't you say Wenna would be around?"

"Oh, yes, she should be back from town soon. She took over a pub since you were here last, she usually brings dinner home for us. Unless her unreliable bartender shows up late for the night shift. My father should be along too, he knows you're here."

Richard started a fire to ward off the evening chill creeping into the drafty old house. The sun had set and a gentle rain began to tap on the tin roof. When the fire crackled and the chimney hooted with the draft, Richard collapsed onto a big sofa. Mairin stayed on her feet a moment longer, pondering her options: a chair ten feet away? Too far for quiet talk. She opted for a compromise: the far end of the sofa. He sent her an amused smile.

"I did bathe this morning."

"Richard—"

He waved his hand. "Relax. Even if I wanted to be a naughty boy, I don't have the energy. You have your end, I have mine."

Richard fell speedily into an exhausted sleep, and as the heat of the fire filled the room, Mairin found her own eyelids drooping. How much had she slept the night before? A couple of hours at most, and the night before that, none at all. She dozed off and on, stoking the fire when it needed wood and pondering Richard's gloomy summary of what lay ahead. He slept on, snoring softly. Two hours passed. Where were his sister and father? Three hours. She fell into a deeper sleep, and when she next awoke, rain beat hard on the roof and fire was nearly out. She stoked it with fresh logs, one of which tumbled from the grate and thudded to the stone floor. Richard stirred.

"God, what time is it?" he asked, struggling to sit up.

"Clock on the mantle says past midnight."

"Dirty night," he said, listening to the pounding rain. "My father must've stayed at Pendennis, and Wenna has a pubful of sailors and no replacement. We're stuck here alone."

"You planned this," she accused.

"What? I did not! Not unless I can order up the weather."

He angled himself so he faced her. He said nothing for awhile, then "you know, you are an extraordinary beauty."

"Never true, Richard, and less now with lines and scars. But thank you for saying so."

"True more than ever."

"And you're still as attractive as they come. Remember I told you—"

"It was just an observation," he snapped. "Nothing more. Don't be so touchy!"

A long silence followed in which the crackling of the fire and the drumming of the rain seemed inordinately loud.

"You're angry," said Mairin after a time.

He sighed and patted the arm of the sofa absently. "No, I'm not angry. Lonely as hell and wishing things had turned out differently." He paused and stared into the fire. "You could have answered my letters."

"I know. I'm so sorry about that."

"Why didn't you?"

She felt his eyes on her, heard the pain in his voice. She turned her back to him, not wanting him to see tears on her face.

"It's not easy for me to explain."

"Just say you lost interest in me, found someone else, whatever."

"No, it wasn't that. I tried to answer. I didn't know what to say. Your letters talked about the future, they were full of hope and optimism and dreams. All I knew was that I missed you. You were the first man who loved me and the first man I ever loved, you know that. I was sure you'd find someone else to fit into your dreams and I'd end up sad and alone anyway. So what was the point of writing? It just postponed the inevitable. Sooner or later I'd get a letter from you telling me it's over."

She felt his hands clasp her arms. She fought down sobs that desperately wanted release.

"I would never have written that letter to you," he said. "Not as long as I thought you still loved me." He sighed and stroked her hair. "I shouldn't have asked you here. I didn't mean to make you feel sad."

"No, don't say that," she said, brushing tears aside with her palms. "I wanted to tell you." She touched his cheek. "And I wanted you to know I still care about you, very much. That will never change."

He took hold of her hand and kissed her fingers. "And I you, love. You'll answer now if I write?"

"Of course," she said. "Just make sure you do."

"I will." He got to his feet and stretched. "I'll dredge us up something from the kitchen. Too bad about Wenna, her lamb stew would go down well tonight."

He returned shortly with a tray piled high with cheese, olives, crackers, apples, and two dusty bottles of wine. While lightning flared through the room and peals of thunder shook the window panes, they spoke of happier times, sang a dozen verses of a bawdy sea-chanty, laughed at time-worn stories, exchanged news of comrades. Over the second bottle of wine, they argued points of seamanship, shared the trials of command, traded favorite places to eat, discussed the history of sailing and tried to list all the different hues of myrtle blossoms.

Two hours past midnight, the storm subsided, the fire died to embers, and they both felt the full effects of the food and wine and lack of sleep. Richard stoked the fire one last time, then stretched out on the sofa and drew Mairin alongside him, her head on his chest. A fleeting pang of guilt crowded her mind before she slept. *What exactly am I doing here?* she asked herself. The only answer she could find was that at this time and in this place and with this honorable man, she felt safe.

Mairin drifted up from a deep, dreamless sleep. Though the room was cold, she felt toasty enough under the blanket with Richard's sleeping form tight against her. It had to be near morning: soft gray light glowed from rain-streaked windows.

Once again she wondered, *was this wrong to do?* They had done nothing intimate. And she felt that she owed Richard a better parting than not answering his letters. He was a good-hearted man who cared about her, and she cared about him. In the end, she concluded with a clearing head, it did not matter much. Today they would sail in opposite directions, and might not see each other again for years.

The sharp clatter of hooves on cobblestones shattered the morning quiet. Mairin tossed the blanket aside and leaped to her feet. Richard reacted nearly as fast, stuffing the blanket under a cushion and moving quickly towards the door.

"Not my father," he whispered. "Too noisy."

The heavy brass knocker snapped down three times. Richard swung the door open to find himself saluted by a gasping, mud-spattered young ensign.

"Ensign Hellier, sir. Fleet emergency, the Admiral requests that you come immediately."

"What emergency, Ensign?" Richard demanded.

"I don't have all the details, sir," the dark-haired officer replied with a curious glance at Mairin, "but I heard that the Brest Squadron is heavily engaged. They sent in a corvette asking for help. That's all I know, sir."

"God be with us," Richard said, hand to his forehead. "Ensign, fly back and tell my father I'm on my way. Sound the recall for *Ajax*."

Hellier saluted and ran towards his panting horse.

"Wait!" Mairin cried from the doorway. "I am Captain Fotharta of the *Caillech*. Sound recall for my ship, if you please."

"Will do, sir."

Hellier leaped on his horse and flew off in a spray of mud.

"Are you sure you want to do that?" Richard asked. "Without orders?"

"I'm sure," she said. She grabbed her travel bag and followed him out the door. "I'll notify Aideen, she may be miffed but from what you said, she knows the situation. *Ajax* will have *Caillech* in her wake."

Their horses pelted down the winding road, through sleepy Ponsanooth and then past the deserted hamlet of Penryn. They crested the top of the last hill from where they had a broad view of the harbor. Signal trumpets blared alternate signals, staccato for *Ajax* and long blasts for *Caillech*.

Richard reined in his horse.

"Before we split up," he said, "one request. Will you carry marines?"

She hesitated.

"This will be a fight with the Santanders, maybe a tough fleet action, and you know their tactics."

"We defend our own ships well enough."

"Don't take offense, I know you do. Please, as a favor to me?"

She knew very well what he meant: he didn't want to see carnage on *Caillech*'s deck.

"All right, as a favor. Send a company."

She kicked her horse and raced towards *Caillech*. There she found a scene of wild activity. Sailors rushed towards the ship from all directions, some uniformed and others in casual clothes, all carrying their kits. Sinea, her wrist encased in a plaster cast, barked out orders to square the yards and set sails. Rowenna met Mairin on the pier.

"Captain, we have no ballast, holds are empty." she reported. "Cargo was to be loaded this afternoon after the repairs were finished. I have the holds open and the hoists rigged, crews out looking for water barrels, sandbags, anything heavy."

Mairin nodded assent. "Right. Try for at least ten tons. When *Ajax* is ready we have to pull out, ballast or no."

Rowenna sprinted down the pier towards the supply warehouse. Mairin joined Sinea on the quarterdeck.

"Lieutenant, we're joining *Ajax* in relief of the Brest Squadron. My personal call, I'll record that in the log."

"Captain, please note my agreement in the log, if you don't mind. The decision is yours of course but I want it on record that I support you."

Now that's loyalty, Mairin thought. *She didn't have to say that.*

"I'll do that, Lieutenant. One more thing. At the request of Captain Tredinnick we'll be taking on marines. A company will be here any minute. I'm going to run into the fleet office and get a note off to the Commodore."

Sinea nodded and went back to shouting orders. Mairin ran all the way to the fleet office, a low-slung stone structure halfway between the pier and the castle. There she scribbled a quick note:

Commodore: Minor ship damage in an ice storm. I am sailing in support of the Kernow squadron at Brest, under heavy Santander attack. My responsibility alone. Will report at my first opportunity. M. F., Capt., Caillech.

She shoved the note across the desk to the waiting ensign. "Get this to Rosslare as soon as possible, if you please."

The young man touched his cap. "It will go out on the morning corvette, sir."

Back at the *Caillech*, Rowenna had most of the crew sweating with fifty water casks. At fifty gallons each it would amount to twelve tons of ballast, less than ideal yet much better than nothing. Mairin was about to cross over the gangplank when she heard a shout. A crimson-coated lieutenant followed by forty marines thundered down the pier double-time. Mairin summoned from memory the ancient English word: *lobsters*. The tall, beefy lieutenant appeared to be about her own age, coal-black hair trimmed short, fully-armored, with a kit slung on his back and two shortswords cinched to his broad leather belt.

He pulled up before her, not even breathing hard, and snapped off a salute.

"Lieutenant Cadan Glyn, Fifth Company, First Devon Regiment, reporting as ordered, sir."

"Welcome to the *Caillech*," Mairin said, returning the salute. "We're not set up to carry passengers, so we'll all have to make do as best we can. For now, settle your men on deck and we'll get berths figured out after we're underway."

"Sir," he said, and started marching his company across the aft gangplank.

Mairin followed them, ran below to don her uniform, then took command of the ship. Two hundred yards away, *Ajax*'s colors flew up her mainmast.

"Brigid, hoist colors," she ordered. "St. Piran below ours."

"Aye, sir," replied the bosun.

Two piers over, *Ajax* set topsails and glided smoothly away from the pier. Rowenna finished loading the last of the water casks, and in another minute she had the hoists stowed and the gangplanks drawn up. The dock crew loosed *Caillech*'s hawsers from the pier's bollards.

"Set topsails," Mairin ordered. To Cholmain's mate Nya Gailenga she said, "When we clear the pier, flash them out, Nya."

"Aye, aye, sir, all she'll bear."

Caillech gathered way in *Ajax*'s wake. Marines scrambled out of the way as sailors worked the main courses. Mairin had to smile: it was an odd spectacle to say the least, her green-tuniced sailors trying to get courses set and red-coated soldiers laden with their kits and weapons jumping back and forth with grins on their amused young faces. No doubt some male-to-male commentary was going on too. After a brief period of chaos *Caillech* was driving hard behind *Ajax*, which soon enough flashed out topgallants and then royals. *A heavy press of sail,* Mairin considered. *Manageable if the wind holds at a fresh breeze.*

Rowenna had taken a place at the lee rail, her work done for the moment. Her tunic was soaked with sweat and her ruddy face flushed.

"Well done with the ballast, Lieutenant," Mairin said with an approving nod. "In the rush there wasn't time to tell you what we're doing."

"Something about the Brest squadron, sir?"

"Right. Corvette came in early this morning asking for help. I'm detaching us on my own authority. I'd like you to handle the marines."

"We can give them the empty forward holds and the head next to the surgery."

"Fine. Make them feel welcome. No separate tables at mess, everyone mixes and acts like one crew. Also, pass the word to the crew chiefs and officers what we're about. It's about fifteen hours to Brest at ten knots if we can maintain that speed. Arms drills start after the noon meal and we'll need to work out how to use the marines."

"Aye, sir, I'll get on it."

Rowenna saluted and headed below. Mairin drew Sinea back to the taffrail where they would not be overheard.

"Any reason not to name Nya Gailenga as Sailing Master?" she asked her first officer.

"None at all, sir. Steady and bright. Cholmain always speaks highly of her."

"Make it so, then. I'll give you the deck, I'm going to mix with our guests. And Sinea, no matter what, keep us in *Ajax*'s wake. I won't have us falling back."

"No, sir," Sinea said with a knowing smile. "We'll keep station, Captain."

Mairin made her way towards the bow, greeting and chatting with the marines on the way. Young, mostly, only a couple appearing to be over thirty. Hard, lean bodies, spotless uniforms and weapons; lightweight leather-and-mail body armor that gave them speed in action; black-crested steel helmets etched with their unit's name. Each soldier carried and fought with two shortswords, using a lightning-fast stab-and-slash technique suited for close quarters. Mairin had seem them

in actual battle twice while serving on Admiralty ships: superbly disciplined and incredibly aggressive. Considering the unusual situation,
they seemed at ease and eager to get into a fight.

After speaking briefly with Cadan Glyn, who watched over his
men from the forecastle, she reached the bow. Two hundred yards
ahead, Richard leaned over *Ajax*'s taffrail. Seeing her, he lifted his hat
in greeting. She responded in kind.

Mairin lingered in the bow, which quickly became deserted as Glyn led
his men below. Thirteen years at sea had not faded the memory of the first
time she stood in this exact place, on her first ship, a midshipman on paper
only with no experience and a store of painful memories. The salty taste
of sea-spray, the trembling of the planks beneath the soles of her feet, the
whine of the wind in the stays and shrouds, the occasional snap of a taut
sail, the thunderous crash of the bow meeting the whitecaps, never failed
to free her mind and her heart of past anguish and present worries.

For more than an hour, she allowed the sea and the ship take over
her thoughts. At the watch change she reluctantly retreated to her
cabin to attend to the daily business of running a warship. Her first
task was the official log entry.

> *Departed Falmouth 7:42 am, course due south, speed 10 knots,
> in company with Kernow ship Ajax to assist Admiralty squad-
> ron under attack at Brest. Forty marines aboard, anticipate pos-
> sible boarding actions. Ship is under my orders alone; note sent
> to Cmmdr. Laigain in Rosslare. First Officer Sinea Danaan
> requested that her agreement with my decision be noted in this log.*

In her personal log, she wrote:

> *I am sailing this ship into combat on my own order. Would I have
> done it for anyone but Richard? I like to think so, though I'm not
> sure. And what of him? What does he represent to me? Seeing
> him again has surfaced feelings I'd rather not deal with now. But
> I'm glad we had the time together. I felt so guilty about the letters.*

She closed the journal and opened the note Richard sent aboard
moments before they sailed from Falmouth. It read:

M: Brest squadron of six ships and corvette patrolling the coast, spotted force of ten Santander three-masters attempting to make Brest Harbor from the south. Intercepted near Il-de-Sein, followed and engaged south of Cape Finestere, corvette sent during action to notify Admiralty. Outcome of engagement is not known. I would never have asked it, but I am grateful for your help. R.

Ten ships! If each one carried a hundred fighters, a fleet of that size could land a force large enough to overwhelm Bretan's local militia, seize hostages and raid warehouses bulging with food and wine awaiting shipment. And more than enough fighting power to take on the Brest Squadron ship-to-ship. Now she was certain her choice was right, whatever Aideen Laigain might say.

A tap on the door. "Yes, enter."

Cadan Glyn stuck his head around the door. "Captain, time to see me for a moment?"

"Of course, Lieutenant."

The young officer wedged his massive shoulders through the narrow doorframe. His short-sleeved white linen shirt left exposed thickly-muscled arms laced with scars. He shook his head when she motioned to a chair.

"Only be a moment, Captain," he said with a warm smile. "I wanted to say your officers and sailors have been most welcoming. We'll all mess together?"

"Yes, unless you object. You and your second will join us in the wardroom?"

"Honored," he said with a slight bow. "Later on, we need to discuss business if you take my meaning."

Mairin nodded. "I do indeed. I'll gather all my officers after the mid-day mess, we'll lay plans then. Drills after that."

"Thank you, Captain, see you at dinner." He saluted her and squeezed back through the doorway.

Mairin returned to the quarterdeck. Sinea rested her elbows on the starboard rail, her eyes constantly shifting from sails to sea to the *Ajax* two hundred yards off the bow. The morning's overcast had cleared and in its place, a brilliant azure sky stretched from horizon to horizon.

More important for their mission, the fresh northerly held, driving the two ships hard towards Brest over a rolling, shining sea.

The marines relaxed on deck, situating themselves in places they knew from long experience would be out of the sailors' way. Those in the more sheltered spots stripped off their shirts to soak up the sun. Mairin took note that bare male torsos rippling with muscle garnered furtive, admiring looks from her sailors.

"Captain," said Sinea, touching her hat. "Speed nine knots, barometer steady."

"Interesting view," said Mairin, "if you like lean, powerful men."

"Yes, sir," Sinea agreed. "Should I say anything?"

"No," said Mairin, "let it go. We're under enough pressure as it is. I forbid sex on deck, though."

"Aye, sir," Sinea acknowledged with a grin. "First time I've been given that particular order."

Mairin strolled aft past the ensigns, busily taking their mid-day sightings, and took up a solitary place at the taffrail where she liked to watch the ship's churning wake. She let her mind drift again, soothed by the warmth of the sun and the regularity of the ship's routine carrying on behind her. Only the occasional burst of deep-voiced male laughter was out of place ... yet oddly reassuring too.

I was born to this life, to be at sea on a day such as this, in a sound ship served by a spirited and loyal crew, every sail set and drawing. Would that I were sailing not to fight but to explore! My orders? To wander at my discretion, find out what has become of the vast world these many long centuries.

The fantasy, one she indulged in often, was interrupted by an ominous rasping sound of stone on metal. For a moment she puzzled over it. Then she spotted the source, a shirtless young man with long blond hair, his back resting against the mizzen, patiently sharpening his swords for battle.

Dear Oran, I am relieved beyond measure to hear that you have returned from your long journeys to the north and midlands. When time allows (probably winter as things now stand) I would like to have our annual talk where I pester you with questions for many hours about what you have seen and heard. I am hoping that you have been able to collect some written evidence concerning the immigration of non-Celtic peoples into the northlands. It is possible that I can identify them by their language. As for me ... Fethnaid Laigain is here and I suppose there is no point in my concealing from you my feelings for her. She is posted to the Line of Bows at a dangerous time; I live in fear that she will lose her life before it is hardly begun. Please visit me if you can, even if it is only for a short time.

Your devoted brother, Seanlaoch

Chapter 10

Sean pulled on the halyard to lower the skiff's single sail. The little craft glided to a stop a few hundred yards off Dungarvan Harbor's southern point, from where they could see all of the harbor's autumn-colored coastline. To the east lay the open ocean, shimmering in bright sunlight.

Feth lounged on the boat's forward bench, eyes closed and head tilted upward, soaking up warm sun on her forehead. *A bit of tan to cover the bruises,* she thought. It was a perfect early autumn day, in contrast to the cold, wintry storm two days ago. She opened her eyes at the sound of the sail flapping as it collapsed at their feet.

"Oh, Sean, what a beautiful view!" she cried.

"It is, isn't it?"

Her smile faded to a puzzled frown. "Strange we're the only ones out here, though."

"Normally we wouldn't be alone out here on a fine day like this. You saw the glum look on man who rented us this boat? I've gone to his slip before and found all twenty boats out. People are frightened and I don't blame them. If they haven't left town already, they're home packing."

"Would you be gone too if it weren't for me?"

He shaded his eyes with his hand so he could look straight at her. "No, I wouldn't."

"Why not?"

"You may find this odd ... I would not leave my books and papers unguarded. My life's work, paltry as it is, lies on those shelves. Some of the books and manuscripts are the only copies we have."

"I don't think it's odd. And your work is not paltry. You're just getting started."

He changed seats to sit next to her. She didn't mind at all when his left arm slid around her waist. She covered his hand with one of her own. Guillemots, puffins, and storm-petrels circled overhead, their discordant calls echoing across the water.

"Feth," he said in a deeply serious tone, "I don't know how to tell you this exactly, so I'll just come right out and say it."

Her stomach floated with anxiety. "What? What is it?"

He paused for several seconds as if reluctant to go on.

"You ... you are ruining my work."

She stared at him but he would not look up at her.

"How? I mean, you know I value your work. I don't—"

He waved a hand in the air. "No, that's not the point. The point is ..."

Again he hesitated.

"Tell me!"

"The point is you are too attractive and too desirable and you are making me insane."

With that he seized hold of her arms and kissed her until she struggled for air. He laughed and held up his arms while she pummeled him.

"You and Oran are more alike than you think!" she cried. "I should dunk you for scaring me like that!"

"I planned it out this morning in bed, watching you sleep," he admitted when her attack subsided. "I just couldn't resist." He put his arms around her. "It's true in a way. You're in my thoughts all the time. I've never been so happy in my life."

She pushed errant hair off his forehead. "And I like everything about you. You're so much more than my fantasies."

"Why you would have fantasies about a scholar with spectacles, I can't imagine. Why not Oran instead, a dashing scout with male charm to burn?"

"Your brother is dashing, true enough," she admitted. "You were the quiet one of the group, it seemed to me you were forever thinking hard about something. I hated the way Conor and Oran used to tease you! I thought you were mysterious and exotic."

"So am I?" he teased.

"In a way you are, yes. I like the fact that we're so different, that we don't think the same thoughts. You make my world a different place to live in."

"You make my world a wonderful place to live in."

A full half hour passed in which they embraced and kissed and shared the glory of the day and the sights about them. Pausing to drink from a water flask, Feth looked out to the open ocean and spotted a dark shadow. She shaded her eyes and squinted. "A warship in the offing, headed in," she said, pointing. "I heard a rumor Uncle Padraic may be coming here."

He followed the line of her finger. "I see it."

"He must be coming to start work on the field army and—"

"Feth," he cut her off, "let's not talk about war and fighting right now. It depresses me no end."

"Sure, okay." She eyed a wicker hamper stowed under the rear seat. "Any food in there?"

"Wait till you see. I shopped while you slept in this morning."

He pulled out the hamper and lifted the lid. Feth's eyes widened at the sight and scent of smoked trout, fresh soda bread, blazing red tomatoes, stuffed olives, ripe Welsh cheese, and most astonishing of all, a large bottle of fine Bretan champagne.

"Where did you get all this? You must have spent all your savings."

"Not so." From the hamper he drew out a plaid tablecloth, laid it at their feet, and began to unload the feast. "The food shops are desperate with so few people in town. The champagne was a gift from my parents when I published my first book. I told myself I would open it only for a truly special occasion." He kissed her and said, "which this occasion is."

She kissed him back. "For me too."

For the next two hours, as the tide floated the skiff back to the inner harbor at a leisurely pace, they polished off every last morsel and savored the final drops of champagne cooled by hanging it over the side. Soon they were within sight of the rental docks and Sean unshipped the oars to row them in. Feth closed the hamper lid and knew it was time to ask him.

"Sean, before we go ashore, I need to ask you a favor."

He lifted the oars above the water. "Sure, anything."

"The other night ... I was almost killed."

"I know," he said, eyes turning sad.

"Twice a spear went by my head so close I could feel the wind. The girl next to me took one in the chest, and died."

He stared at the floor of the boat and made no answer.

"Sean, I might not make it out alive the next time."

"I know that too. So what's the favor?"

"So I need you to promise that if ... if I'm killed, you'll make sure I get back to Rosslare? Take me home?"

He slid the oars in and leaned over them. She reached over and touched his arm. He shook off her hand.

"I'm afraid too," she said. "I need you to promise."

He looked up at her, tears filling his eyes.

"I don't want to talk about taking you back to Rosslare in a box! I want time for us, time to get to know each other, to share the beauty of the world. It's heartbreaking enough that I've lost a dozen friends and cousins in the last three years, and who knows how many times Oran escaped dying by a thread? Please don't ask me to plan for your death too. I'm sick of thinking about death."

The anguish is his voice and the tears in his eyes overwhelmed her and she started to cry.

"Who else could I ask?"

He reached out for her and took her into his arms, held her fiercely.

"It's a hard time we live in," he said, stroking her hair. "I'll make sure you get home, Feth. By all I hold sacred I hope it's something I never have to do."

"Thanks," she said in a small voice, he head on his shoulder. "I didn't mean to spoil our day."

He cupped her face between his hands. "You didn't, love. Believe me, you didn't."

The barracks were crowded again, in fact overcrowded. More bunks had been stuffed in the room till there was barely space to walk between them. Padraic had shifted his forces all along the Rampart, brought up reserves, posted recruits close to finishing their training, called back to service as many older fighters as were willing and able to put on the armor again. Feth saw women twice her age and others that looked even younger than her.

She sat cross-legged on her bunk, her journal balanced on her knees and a sheet of paper on top of the journal. The drone of conversation was making it hard to concentrate on the letter she was writing to Conor.

"Feth?"

She looked up and saw an archer close to her own age standing at the foot of her bed. Feth had noticed her before: blazing red hair, rampant freckles, sparkling green eyes. At the moment the girl wore a somber expression.

"That's me," said Feth. She extended her hand. "Feth Laigain."

"Derdre Dal Reti." She took Feth's hand in a strong grasp.

Feth cleared a spot on the bunk and patted it. "Sit."

Derdre accepted the invitation and cast a curious glance at the half-finished letter.

"To my brother," said Feth. "We're from Rosslare. How about you?"

"Dungarvan."

"I like Dungarvan, what I've seen of it so far. Much bigger than Rosslare, busier too."

Derdre nodded. "It's a good place to live."

Feth found her manner curious. She seemed to speak mechanically, as if part of her mind were elsewhere.

"Your father was really Domnall?" Derdre asked.

"He was. My mother is Liadan, the poet. She holds the Laigain chair on the Council of Twenty. How about your family?"

Derdre hesitated, drew patterns on the blanket with her finger.

"My father's a surgeon on a warship, the *Caillech*."

Isn't that Mairin's ship? I'll ask Conor in the letter.

Feth waited ... but Derdre did not go on. And in an instant Feth understood why. The resemblance was too strong.

"Captain Dunlaith was your mother?"

"Yes."

Derdre's right hand twisted the coverlet aimlessly. Feth reached over and laid a hand on her shoulder.

"You don't need to be here," she said. "They'd give you leave."

Derdre shook her head. "No. Mother would not want that, especially not now."

Feth struggled with what to say. *The agony she must be feeling!*

"She talked to me outside after the Steise incident."

"Yes, I saw that."

"She said she served with my father."

Feth saw tears dripping onto the bunk. She took hold of Derdre's hand.

"Where's your father now? Is he at sea?"

"Yes."

"You have other relatives?"

"In Waterford, mostly. The army notified them."

Laughter erupted from a rowdy group halfway across the room. Feth waited till it died down.

"When will the service be?"

"When my father returns, in a week, maybe more. They've already sealed her coffin."

Feth handed Derdre a towel to mop her face, then fetched her a glass of water.

"Thanks," Derdre said. She sipped at the water. "I just feel so empty inside."

Feth looked around the room. "You must have other friends here. Why did you come to me?"

"I overheard you talking with one of the wounded girls earlier. I liked what I heard."

"I could really use a friend here," Feth said. "This is my first posting, I don't know anybody."

Derdre took a deep breath and looked up at Feth.

"Then you have a friend," she said. "And so do I."

"Where's your bunk?"

"There," Derdre pointed, "next to that window."

"How about moving next door?"

"Aren't both of those bunks taken?"

"Regeen, wake up!" Feth said to the girl snoozing on the next bunk. The girl opened her eyes and mumbled "what?"

"Want a window bunk?"

"Sure," said the sleepy girl. "Where?"

Derdre showed her, and in a ten minutes they had swapped all their belongings.

"Thanks, Feth," Derdre said, sitting on her new bunk. "I feel a little better. I'm going to rest a few minutes, I haven't slept at all since the battle." She laid back and closed her eyes.

Feth tried to go back to her letter and found her hand shaking too much to write. She slid the journal back into her bag and sat with her back against the headboard.

She had been only six when Padraic brought her father home, and death was not so easy for her to comprehend then. She tried to imagine what she would feel like now, to find out her mother had died. *Like a lance going through my heart,* she told herself, *yet living on to feel the agony*. Her image of Dunlaith Dal Reti was so clear; her words rang in Feth's ears, "I'll be expecting a great deal from you."

She had just closed her eyes when all conversations in the room ceased. She sat up and saw Bows leaping to their feet, some pulling on clothes as they did so. All eyes were aimed towards the room's entrance which was completely blocked by an enormous man wearing a gold cape. The top of his head brushed against the lintel. Though his face was in shadow, Feth knew perfectly well who it was. Her uncle Padraic, known to the rest as General in Chief of the Army, stepped into the room.

"I apologize to all," he said, his voice a mixture of thunder and the scraping of metal on metal. "I should have had your captain come in first. Please continue doing what you were doing."

After a moment of uncertainty, Feth's comrades relaxed and went back to talking, reading, writing, cleaning armor. Padraic scanned the room, spotted her, winked, then drifted among the bunks taking extended hands, laughing, asking questions, admiring bits of craftwork hanging on the walls, leaning over injured Bows to see how they did, patting the foreheads of those in pain, hefting bows in his gigantic hands, telling brief, funny stories, and never once failing to sound upbeat.

Now I see, Feth told herself, *why he leads the army, why he has led it since the day my father died, why Bows and Blades alike will fight so hard for him. I've never seen him at work, only at home with our family. This is leadership, Fethnaid, take a long, hard look at it.*

Padraic arranged his visits so that he came to her bunk after covering most of the room. She got to her feet and waited in the narrow gap between the bunks until he towered over her. She looked up twelve inches to his battered, smiling face with its familiar grizzled beard and oft-broken nose.

"Bow Junior Grade," he said, "how goes it with you?"

"It goes fine, General," she said, acutely conscious that others were listening.

"You might say your mother is worried about you," he said with a wry grin.

"She would have worried wherever I was posted."

Padraic nodded. "Sure it's true. If you write her, you would do me a favor by not giving too many details."

"I won't."

He reached down and touched the bruise on her forehead. "Bright color. Glad you didn't wreck this fine, straight Conmaicne nose," he said, tapping it lightly.

"It was close, General. Just between us."

He frowned briefly, then brightened and looked across to Derdre.

"My friend Derdre Dal Reti," Feth said.

Feth saw a flicker of understanding pass over her uncle's face at the mention of the name. He stepped over to Derdre and shook her hand.

Then he leaned far down and whispered for a full minute into Derdre's ear, while his hand rested on her shoulder. Derdre whispered back several times and when he straightened up again, she spoke a thready "thank you, General." Padraic reached out and tenderly brushed tears from Derdre's cheeks. To Feth he said in an undertone, "After I leave, come outside and bring your bow." Then he moved on.

Derdre sank onto her bunk and shook her head in bewilderment. "How did he know so much about my mother?"

"My brother Conor told me he reads every casualty report himself, " said Feth. "Every name, and the record that goes with it."

"He said wonderful things about her. I guess he knew her years ago. It was so good of him to talk to me. He must be a quite an uncle to have."

"He is."

Padraic continued chatting, joking, and spending extra time with Bows who were hurt or looked like they needed cheering up. Finally his form again blocked the doorway momentarily and then he was gone. Feth waited a minute, lifted her bow off the wall peg and strolled out as if to practice. Padraic had stopped a couple of paces down the walk and was conferring with two officers. At her approach he thanked them and they moved off.

"Walk with me," he said, heading up the hill towards the practice range. "We can talk more freely now. The battle the other night was a hard one?"

"The Blades were outnumbered, it was totally dark, and they used javelins against us. That's how Captain Dal Reti was killed."

"There will be no more attacks by boat," he said, puffing slightly as they continued up the steep slope. "I've barricaded the river north of the fort and mounted ballistae. Should have done it sooner, perhaps, but we've never been attacked that hard out here."

He stopped momentarily and looked down at her. "It looks like you had a tough fight of your own."

"He was almost as big as you." She fingered her multi-hued forehead. "I killed him all the same."

"Did you now? How?"

"Knife under the sternum."

"Good. *Never* forget your knife."

Feth smiled at him. "You may have told me that before, Uncle."

"Have I?" He laughed and clumped up the hill again.

A moment later they crested the hill and started down a gentle slope into the broad, flat meadow used for arms practice. Far to the right, Blade drills were in full swing: instructors bellowed, swords flashed in the sun and clanged off shields and armor. The archery range was empty; drills were over for the day. Padraic walked towards a man standing beside a rather small, dark brown horse. The man was short, deeply tanned, heavily bearded, and wore high-top black boots. The horse seemed to mimic him: short, thickly-muscled legs, broad chest, and short snout. The saddle on the horse's back was sewn of shiny, butter-colored leather, and was a design Feth had never seen.

"Niece, meet Arvel Rhydderch, Horse-Master of Wales. Arvel, my niece Fethnaid Conmaicne Laigain."

The man bowed slightly.

"Your acquaintance," he said. "My mountain Welsh Gaelic may be hard on your ears, but we will understand each other well enough. Padraic tells me you ride well."

"I started riding when I was four," Feth said proudly.

"And also shoot well," Arvel added with a faint smile towards Padraic.

"Well enough," she said, wary of her uncle's strong distaste for boasting.

"Now the main question," said Arvel. "Can you ride and shoot?"

"You mean, shoot from horseback? I've never tried that."

"Today you try. Sling your bow here."

He held up a leather holster attached to the front of the saddle. Feth slid her bow in as he asked.

"Quiver is here on the other side. Mount up."

Feth had no trouble mounting the horse, whose back was easily a foot lower than an ordinary mare or gelding. The saddle was broader than she was used to, though not uncomfortable. The stirrups were also unusual, having a loop for the toe and a strap on the heel. There were no reins or bit.

"Now," he said, "get used to the horse and let him get used to you. His name is Ioan. He will do anything you ask by the pressure of your knees on his flanks. Left is left knee, right is right, harder with both knees is faster, lighter is slower. Try it."

Arvel drew Padraic back a few paces. Feth leaned forward in the saddle, spoke softly into Ioan's ear and stroked his hard-muscled neck.

"She bonds with him first, Padraic," Arvel said quietly to Padraic. "She does know horses."

Sensing that Ioan was relaxed beneath her, Feth gently pressed her knees inward. Ioan promptly moved out at a gentle trot. It took her four full circles of the field to adjust her posting to his shorter gait and unfamiliar canter. Then she urged him to gallop ... and was astonished at his speed. Though his legs were short, Ioan seemed to have unlimited power in his flanks and chest. She galloped the field twice, circling the targets, then brought Ioan down to an easy trot.

Not like any horse I have ever ridden, she thought with exhilaration.

When she reached Arvel and Padraic she released all pressure in her legs and Ioan stopped instantly. She swung down from the saddle.

"What do you think?" Arvel asked her.

Feth stroked Ioan's neck. "I've heard about your horses, read about them too. I'm really glad I got to ride one."

"This wasn't just for your enjoyment," said Padraic.

"No indeed," Arvel concurred. "Now you try shooting. Mount again, circle the targets at a trot, try a dozen shots."

Feth swung into the saddle, pulled her bow from the holster and set Ioan to a slow trot. At a distance of forty yards out, she let fly an arrow when she was opposite the target. It missed by three yards. *I'm not used to that*, she thought. *It looks like it curves away from the target.* She tried again. A two-yard miss. On the next try, one yard wide. The next arrow struck the target near the edge. Ioan circled patiently as she continued to shoot. The last three arrows hit closer to the bullseye, though none struck dead center.

"Not easy," she said, dismounting with her bow in hand. "Not easy at all, and that was at a trot in a constant circle."

"You did well," said Arvel, "for your first try. At full gallop, moving past the target at an angle, it is a difficult skill. You must learn a new method of aiming. Observe."

Arvel pulled his recurve bow from his back, strung it, and shoved a fistful of arrows into the saddle quiver. He set the horse off at an easy trot.

"Now you will see something," Padraic said to her. "More than twenty years ago, I served a few months with the Welsh when they needed our help in bad terrain, where the horses couldn't be used. Your father was there too. That's when I met Arvel."

Arvel gradually brought Ioan to full gallop. In the next two minutes, he and Ioan were a blur on the field, crossing in front of the targets at every possible angle. At each pass, Arvel drew an arrow and fired ... and each arrow struck near the center of the target. Arrows piled up in the bullseyes.

"Now think of hundreds of Arvels coming at you," said Padraic. "On level ground, the Welsh horse-archers can defeat much larger forces on foot, even those with armor. The horses are fearless in battle. Bred for it for twenty centuries."

"I see that," Feth said, "but why are you showing me this?"

"Because in two or three days, two hundred such horses will begin arriving here on cargo ships escorted from Wales. Every Bow we can find who's a solid rider will be assigned to a new horse-archer corps. Arvel will train them as fast as humanly possible. He believes that three weeks will be enough for effectiveness in battle."

"And then?"

"And then, niece, the western field army will march out of here to meet the Ghaoth Aduiadh. The new cavalry will be used to strike them hard and fast, confuse them, hurry their attack, compress their lines, flank them, and chase them if they retreat."

Arvel dismounted and spoke softly to Ioan, then rejoined them.

"Can you learn to do that in three weeks, Fethnaid?" he asked her.

"I think so," she answered. "My uncle will tell you I train hard."

That brought a smile to Padraic's battle-scarred face. "Yes, I think that would be fair to say, niece. You can go back to the barracks. Please say nothing of this for now."

"Thank you, Uncle," she said. "There are others you could have asked."

She saluted him and headed back to the barracks. It was much quieter than before. Feth could feel the tension level rising as late afternoon faded towards sunset. Derdre lay on her bunk, staring at the ceiling. She looked over as Feth hung up her bow.

"What did he want?"

"Not supposed to say," Feth replied. "I'd tell you if I could."

"What's he like, Feth? I mean, as a person, not as a general."

Feth sat on the edge of her bunk. "He's my mother's sister ... but they aren't really very much alike. Not that they fight or anything. My mother loves him dearly and he loves her. He was around our house a lot when my father was alive. I think the walls shook when he laughed at my father's jokes. After my father died, he wasn't there as much since he took over command, and when he did come he was much quieter. In the last couple of years I haven't seen him much at all, just a dinner now and then. I've been away at training and, well, you know what he's been doing."

"Does he have a wife, children?"

"He had a wife, once," said Feth, thinking back. "My mother told me she died having their first child, and he never married again. He tried to help mother with us when my father was killed, so he's more like a father to me than an uncle."

"I wouldn't want his responsibility," said Derdre. "Especially not now."

"No one would."

"Bows, listen up!"

The voice belonged to Renny Loigde, their new captain.

"Night shift to the fort," she said. "Check your gear, don't leave anything behind."

She waited while fifty-six women donned armor, strapped on quivers and slid bows into holsters.

"One word," Renny said from the doorway. "We all miss Captain Dal Reti. I hope I can be half as good an officer as she was." She stopped and swallowed hard. "Right. A long night ahead, archers. Campfires in the northwest."

A veteran archer a few bunks away cursed under her breath.

"Not good news?" Feth whispered as they queued up.

Derdre gave her cuirass straps a hard tug. "No, not good news at all."

Dear Conor, my first night in battle, I ended up underneath a man almost as big as our uncle. I'd already shot him but he tackled me anyway. He hit me hard and would have killed me with his hammer except I got my knife into him first. I'm OK, just bruised. I made friends here with a Blade named Keegan Cholmain who knows you and a Bow named Derdre Dal Reti. Her mother was our captain and was killed in the battle. Derdre's father is a surgeon on the warship Caillech, isn't that Mairin's ship? I have spent time with Seanlaoch, and I guess you could say we're a couple. Uncle Padraic came to town while I was writing this, he has interesting plans for the western field army. Please don't worry about me, you have enough on your mind as it is. Say hello to my Rosslare friends for me if you see them.

Your loving sister, Feth.

Chapter 11

Conor sat alone in the great room of Laigain House, fingering the letter he'd already read twice by the light of the hearth. He realized now what a welcome and bright presence Feth had been in the house, and how much he missed her smiling face and unrestrained affection. Her short letter unleashed a flood of memories of her, as a tiny baby in his ten-year-old's arms, as a tearful and bewildered six-year-old when their father died, as a sharp-tongued youngster who tried Liadan's reserve of patience at every turn, as the warm and engaging young woman who never failed to raise his spirits. Now, he shook his head to think of her posted on a hillside at night, in the thick of a desperate battle, crushed beneath a massive, wounded man wielding a battle hammer.

He and Triona had eaten with Kellen, though Conor was appalled by the lack of decent food in the house. His mother and Feth had always done the marketing and he paid no attention to the near-empty larder. Still, a resourceful Triona managed a decent ham and potato soup that softened up stale bread. A steady flow of dark ale—which thankfully was not in short supply—and Kellen's surprising stock of funny stories kept the three of them laughing hours after the meal ended. Triona had her own surprise: she carried in memory lengthy passages of poetry that she could recite at will and with feeling. In the hallway outside Kellen's room, Conor felt a guilty flash of desire as he bade her goodnight. He returned to the great room to think and read for a time.

From a shelf he withdrew a favorite volume of poems, written in old Welsh Gaelic. He found the linguistic struggle engrossing and well worthwhile. He did not notice the sound of Aideen's horse pounding across the yard. When she entered the room, he looked up, startled. She tossed her hat on the table and threw herself into a chair across from him.

"You look tired," he said, laying the book aside.

"At sea since we spoke last, trying to get this transport fleet together. I hope Padraic knows what he's doing. I can't spare these ships for long."

Conor passed over the remark about Padraic; a clash lurked there. "Any more word of Mairin and the *Caillech*?"

He caught her irritated look, but she kept her voice even. "I had a report, yes. A falling topmast missed her by inches and punched a hole in the deck, gave her sailing master a serious skull fracture. She's at Falmouth now, probably sail for the Bristol Channel station tomorrow. That's the last word I have."

"Thanks for telling me." *Such a matter-of-fact report of a near-death!* "You should know," he went on, "that we have guests tonight."

"Guests?"

He briefly related the events that brought Kellen and Triona to the house. When he finished, she shoved herself out of her chair and circled behind it so she could stare balefully down at him.

"What were you thinking going onto their land uninvited? Sometimes I despair over your common sense. Now who knows what will happen? Someone could end up dead over this."

"First of all, I was not uninvited. Kellen invited me. And second, if anyone ends up dead it will be me, so stop worrying."

She flung herself away from the chair and paced the room, fuming.

"I don't suppose you considered that Etain sits on the Council of Twenty, along with our mother, and that at times mother might want or need her support? Or that an incident like this can be gossiped about to make you look like a trespasser beating up on a drunken, helpless man?"

"Bram, helpless? Who would believe that? If I hadn't gone, Triona might have been raped by that bastard. As for Etain, she does whatever she pleases anyway."

"And if Bram is here at the crack of dawn wanting your blood? What then?"

Conor jumped out of his own chair. "He can have all—"

"*Stop it!*"

Triona's urgent whisper came from the head of the staircase. She descended quickly and silently on bare feet and took a position between them.

"What is the *matter* with you two? Are you going to take up swords next?"

"Triona Bairrche, I take it?" said Aideen with acid in her voice.

"Yes, Commodore," Triona answered, "and I do realize I'm a guest here. I'm trying to take care of a badly injured man upstairs who needs rest and who would benefit from feeling welcome. Have some regard for a wounded soldier."

"I'm sorry, Triona," Conor said, hanging his head. "I wasn't thinking."

"You have a point about his being a soldier," said Aideen coldly. "I'll say goodnight."

She walked around Triona and ascended the stairs. A moment later came the soft thud of her bedroom door closing. Conor fell back into the chair, rubbing his face with his hands.

"Do you always tear at each other that way?" asked Triona, appalled.

"Oh, since we were eight and four, I guess," he said with a mirthless laugh. "She thinks I'm a soft-hearted fool, and I think she's cold and harsh. Other than that, we get along fine."

"Hard to believe," Triona said, shaking her head. "I have a brother and three sisters and we would all die for each other."

"I have Feth," he said, waving the folded letter.

"A letter from her?"

"Yes. Nearly killed in her first battle. I planned to tell Aideen. As you can see, I never got the chance."

"Would she care?"

"I think she does care, about Feth." He picked up a poker and stirred the embers. "Aideen is hard to fathom. We're so opposite we'll never truly understand each other."

"You take the fighting to heart in a way she doesn't."

"I suppose I do. That's my weakness, as she often tells me."

Triona walked behind his chair and laid her hands on his shoulders. He was uncomfortably aware of her closeness, the sympathy and warmth she emanated, the soft touch of her hands, the faint scent of jasmine again.

"I would not think of a tender heart as a weakness, Conor."

She padded across the room and up the staircase. He stretched out in the battered old chair, thought briefly of going up to his room, and fell asleep before he could reach a decision. When he awoke, gray light filtered in through the veranda windows and doors. He sat up and groaned with stiffness—going up to bed would have been a better idea. He was still tired, but by dawn Aideen would be in his face again. And no food at all left in the kitchen. No markets would be open so early; he would have to beg from the Finguine farm a half mile down the road.

He set off on foot. The morning air was cool, not cold, and a clear sky stretched from horizon to horizon. It was the kind of air to drink in, and he savored every breath. As he approached the last bend in the road, he stroked his chin absently and felt the stubble. He was unshaven and unwashed ... and too tired to turn back.

Dawn broke over fresh-harvested fields as the Finguine farmstead came into view. A brazen rooster's insistent cries shattered the morning's stillness. In a fenced, rolling pasture, cows and sheep intermixed bass and tenor conversations of contentment. The sweet scent of freshly-mowed hay carried on the breeze and mixed with the perfume of dew-drenched grass and fallen leaves. Looking over the peaceful, prosperous farm, it seemed *right* to him, human beings working the fields with their hands, living close to the earth, building of wood and planting trees, sowing crops and caring for the soil. The great cycle of life and death played out over the centuries. How was it Uinseann put it, *we give and take in equal measure.*

He approached the heavy oak door. No chance of being too early: he could hear Shelagh Finguine's sharp voice shepherding five-year-old Fianna and seven-year-old Tynan to breakfast, supported by an occasional bass command from Aonghas. He rapped three times.

The door rasped on rusty hinges. "Conor!" boomed Aonghas, a tall, powerful man in middle age. "Shelagh, we have a guest!"

The children sprang up from the table and stood before Conor expectantly. He lifted each in turn high overhead, as he had done since they were infants, touching their heads to the ceiling beams. They shouted with delight. Aonghas's wife, a strongly-built woman of forty with a broad face and deeply-tanned skin, turned from the massive black stove and came over to hug him.

"We see you so rarely these days," she said. "You look tired, dear. Come and sit down with us."

"Yes, sit," said Aonghas, his cast-iron fingers seizing Conor's arm. "Children, back to your porridge."

Conor squeezed in between Fianna and Tynan.

"A quick cup of tea," he said, wishing it were otherwise. "I have guests at the house and not so much as an egg in the larder. So I come as a beggar."

Aonghas settled his big frame on the bench across from Conor.

"No one from your family comes here as a beggar," he said firmly. "What is ours is yours. Now I will charge you for some news! How are you? Feth and Aideen? And your good mother?"

Shelagh set a steaming mug of tea in front of him and sat next to her husband.

After a long welcome sip of the spiced tea, Conor said, "Feth was posted last week to the Line of Bows. Alas, to Dungarvan Fort."

"Two attacks already," Aonghas said with a worried frown. "She's not injured?"

"No, not seriously anyway."

"Feth is most dear to us," said Shelagh. She anxiously twisted a dish towel in work-worn hands.

"Yes, she is," agreed Aonghas. "And Aideen?"

"At the house last night. I expect she'll be off to the harbor soon."

"We never see her. Please say hello for us," said Shelagh. "And tell Liadan she's always welcome here. That big old house must be lonely with all her children gone so much."

"It is," Conor said. "She looks forward to winter."

"And you, Conor, how are you?" Aonghas asked.

He glanced at the children and shook his head.

"Fianna, Tynan, you're finished!" Aonghas decided. "Time for chores, out to the barn!"

The fidgety pair needed no second command. They leaped up and ran through the open door in a race to the barn. Conor gave a short version of the events of the past week, leaving out his proposal to Mairin and the clashes with Aideen.

"Not good about Bram," said Aonghas as he cleared the children's dishes from the table. "A wild one, given to drink like his father, it sounds."

"A strange family," Shelagh remarked. "So many tales of evil about that house, going back decades. Yet Mairin and Kellen seem to have escaped the curse. It was right of you to take him to your home. Now, let me put together something for your starving friends!"

While Shelagh gathered up eggs, bread, jam, cheese, sausages, bacon, fresh potatoes and apples, her husband leaned on the door jamb listening to the shouts and giggles issuing from the barn. Conor joined him and said, "You have a wonderful home, Aonghas. And children. I hope it's not too long ... well, someday—"

"There's plenty of time for you, Conor," said the big farmer. "You have someone in mind, yes?"

"I do. It's complicated, not like you and Shelagh."

Aonghas downed the last of his tea. "Life can't be forced, son, and we don't always have the choices we like. I didn't marry until I was past forty, after twenty years in the Line of Blades. I might not live long enough to enjoy my grandchildren. Take what life offers, spend no time worrying about what it does not. That's what my father told me, and I believe it."

The children burst from the barn, chasing each other in circles.

"Chores!" Aonghas roared. "Back in the barn!"

More giggles and feigned fear, but they did as he ordered.

"Your father was a wise man," Conor said. "Patience is a virtue, my mother puts it. Just not one of my virtues."

Aonghas gripped his shoulder. "You're tired, man, and hurt too. I know what it feels like, believe me I do. If you love this woman and she loves you, you'll be happy together. And have naughty ones like this!"

Fianna and Tynan passed by the barn door, screeching and laughing. Aonghas marched towards them to restore order. Shelagh handed Conor the overstuffed satchel and called out to Aonghas, "husband, give him a ride back home."

"Thanks, I'll walk," Conor told her. "Not often I get to enjoy the lane between our houses."

"Come back soon then," she said, "and stay longer!"

Aonghas met him halfway across the yard and shook his hand. "My best to Padraic too, if you see him. Tell him I can still down a quart faster than he can."

"I'll do that," Conor said. "He may challenge you yet again."

Aonghas grinned. "That he may."

Aonghas followed him as far as the barn; a moment later Conor heard "Tynan, that's not the way to do it!" booming from inside. On the walk back he did not hurry, instead pausing often to admire late-blooming indigo bellflowers accompanied by the rising chorus of blackbirds, robins and magpies. Visits to the Finguines always lifted his spirits, and he resolved to do it more often.

One unpleasant task lay before him. Aideen, fully outfitted in a fresh uniform, leaned on the front porch railing with a steaming mug in her hand. She glanced at him briefly and then resumed her middle-distance gaze. He ascended the steps, set the satchel on a chair, and joined her. His eyes found the focus of her gaze: the gravesite where Domnall lay.

"I need a word with you."

She turned her head towards him. "About?"

"About last night."

"You'll get no apology from me," she said, turning away again.

"You made a major mistake and I'm sure there'll be consequences."

He sighed inwardly. *I did not expect an apology, dear sister.*

"That's was not what I had in mind. There is one thing I will not take from you, and that is the rudeness you showed to a guest in this house. Triona—"

Aideen moved to leave, and reluctantly he clamped his hand on her wrist, hard enough to see pain flash across her face.

"You will stay here till I'm finished. I mean it, Aideen."

She stared down at his hand in disbelief, then shook it free. "All right, say your piece, I have things to do."

"Triona Bairrche is here by my invitation. You treated her with disrespect, something that we were taught is never, *ever* to happen in this house. Whatever else you may remember of our father, you surely remember that."

She said nothing in response, though her eyes narrowed at the mentioned of Domnall.

"I ask in the name of our clan and our family that you beg Triona's pardon. Use whatever excuse you will, but there must be an apology, a genuine one. Tell her she is welcome here, and Kellen too."

As he finished, he saw Triona come through the open front door and halt a few steps away. She gave him a look that said, *you don't have to do this, it isn't necessary.* A moment of silence passed, broken only by the chattering of birds and rustle of leaves in the morning breeze. Aideen nodded to Conor and turned to Triona.

"My brother is right," she said without a hint of sarcasm. "I was rude and I do ask your pardon. I have no excuse except to say I was tired and caught by surprise of the situation. Still, that does not justify treating a guest as I did."

Conor leaned back against the porch rail, hardly able to believe his ears. Triona cast him a surprised look and then offered her hand to Aideen.

"I did not take offense," she said. "I know the strain you're under."

Conor fully expected a *satisfied?* look from his sister but did not get it. Without a further word Aideen's boots clacked down the steps; moments later she was mounted and riding towards Rosslare.

"I've never seen her apologize to anyone," Conor said, "least of all because I asked her to. How much did you overhear?"

"The last part. I was afraid it was going to be another shouting match."

"So was I," he admitted. "I can take a lot from her. I could not take her making you feel like something a cat dragged in from the barn."

Triona's eyes followed Aideen's horse till it disappeared around a bend in the road. "She's under terrible stress, Conor. I can see it even if you can't."

"So are we all," Conor retorted. "That doesn't mean we act like barbarians."

"No. I didn't mean that."

"Let's forget it." He lifted the satchel. "We have food! Courtesy of friends up the road. Is Kellen awake?"

"Yes," she said, taking the bag from him. "Maybe you could help him clean up while I put a breakfast together?"

"And clean myself up at the same time?"

"That goes without saying," she said with a grin.

An hour later, the three of them feasted on breakfast in Kellen's room. Conor wore his full Blade Captain uniform: crimson tunic emblazoned with a black Celtic cross and cinched with a black belt; a First Rank Fort Captain's silver crossed swords pinned to both shoulders; copper-hued cape trimmed in black Celtic endless knots.

"You need to leave soon?" Kellen asked Conor.

Conor nodded. "Padraic returns on the morning packet from Dungarvan, wind permitting. He wants my help getting the army assembled."

"And then?" asked Triona.

"I'm not sure. He hasn't told me what he has in mind, exactly. My guess is a surprise attack before the Dubliners reach the border."

"I've got to get out of this bed," Kellen said. He levered himself up on his elbows.

"Stop." Conor laid a gentle hand on his chest. "Please, Kellen, wait. We need you, yes, we need all of our best captains. If you get up now you could hurt yourself and you'd be lost to us for months. Am I right?" he asked Triona.

"Right."

Kellen's frustrated curse raised Triona's eyebrows.

"Sorry, Triona."

"No need to apologize. You'd be surprised what I hear during birthings."

Conor helped Triona carry the trays back to the kitchen.

"Back tonight?" she asked. Her eyes added, *I hope you will be.*

"Probably very late."

"It's lonely here at night when Kellen is asleep. So quiet."

She took his hand. Large amber eyes rooted him to the spot. Blood rushed in his ears.

He squeezed her fingers gently, turned away and fled through the house. In the yard he paused at the well to splash cold water on his face. "More than a man should have to bear," he murmured to himself. "And well she knows it."

Treasach clearly hoped for a long run. His ears sagged when Conor pointed him on the short route to the harbor instead of the unlimited road north. While Treasach ambled at an unhappy canter, Conor let his mind drift. The warm, damp autumn day was very much like the day he met his first love, what was her name? *Lasair.* Fourteen he was at the time, so was she. She came into school on a day just like this, a few weeks after the term started, a new girl looking friendless and out-of-place. Lovely she was too, or so she appeared to his youth's eyes: black hair that fairly gleamed in the sun, brilliant blue eyes, flashing smile, musical laugh. How taken he had been with her! Not a night passed for two months that he didn't walk her home from school, though she lived three miles in the wrong direction. His imagination ran wild when he laid on his bed at home thinking of her. And one warm summer day, Lasair became his first lover, and he was hers. Where could she be now?

A horse thundered up behind him. Treasach instinctively shifted to one side, barely in time to avoid a collision with Bram Fotharta's massive black stallion. The stallion wheeled around and came to a halt virtually nose to nose with Treasach. Bram seemed as big in a shirt and trousers as other men in full armor: long, powerful arms held the reins, massive thighs bestrode the saddle. He made no move to draw a sword, in fact he seemed to be unarmed. If he had a bruise on his neck from Conor's blow, it was concealed by his shirt and his long dark hair.

"Conor," he said with a faint, false smile, "I should issue a challenge for what you did."

"For defending myself and a woman against a drunk?"

"That's your story."

"Triona saw what happened. Kellen too. You almost killed him by what you did."

Bram let his nervous horse caper in a circle, then reined him still. He remained silent as a troop wagon loaded with Blades passed between them.

"You'd like to kill me, wouldn't you?"

"The thought occurs to me, yes."

Bram let go the reins and spread his arms wide. "Here's my chest. You have a sword with you. One thrust."

"Don't tempt me," Conor said with a thin smile. "I'd just as soon let an enemy fighter do it for me."

Bram took hold of the reins again. "Never happen, and you know it." He twisted in the saddle to look at the harbor. "I don't see my dear sister's ship. How is she?"

Careful, Conor warned himself. *He's baiting you, looking for a fight that you start in front of witnesses. He did it once, don't let him do it again. Not now.*

"Well enough. Not that you care."

"I wonder why you took Kellen to your house, along with that comely little tart Triona. I had a thought that maybe you're a lonely with dear Mairin at sea. My cuz would make interesting company, yes?"

Conor's hand slid onto the grip of his sword.

"You start that rumor and I *will* kill you."

Bram laughed. "Too close to home, eh? One last thing before you ride off in a snit. Ask Mairin about Fotharta House. Ask her about fathers having their daughters."

He laughed again, swung his horse past Conor and galloped north towards Rosslare.

Conor felt the blood drain from his face and his stomach rebel. Treasach, sensing Conor's cold sweat and fierce tension, edged further off the road and lowered his head.

It could not possibly be true. Bram lied. He had the lie all prepared to use in that way. But what about the dreams?

He felt desperately sick and started to dismount. Then his name was shouted from the field where the troops were assembling. He swallowed acid-tasting saliva, ran a hand over his mouth, and tapped Treasach's flanks. He was needed, and there was much to do. Better now to do, than to think.

My husband, how I do miss thee!
At dawn, your voice into my ear.
At table, laughter, song and verse,
In sadness, tears to mingle mine.
Why does my heart refuse to heal?
Why cannot memory fade with time?
Why does your voice still linger on?
Why does your hand still lie in mine?
My Domnall, you were made for me.
My half was full with you to share.
Yes, I go on, as you would wish,
Look down on me, and know my love.
Liadan Laigain

Chapter 12

Liadan leaned against a massive gnarled oak and read the brief note from Conor delivered by courier from Rosslare. Rionach, her mother-in-law and Speaker of the Council for the past year, sat in a portable chair nearby, writing in a notebook and occasionally brushing wisps of gray hair from her face.

"What news?" she asked when Liadan looked up.

"Nothing happy," said Liadan with a tired sigh. She read the note aloud.

"Never an end to troubles with that family," Rionach commented bitterly. "I love my grandson dearly but I would have advised against setting foot on Fotharta land."

"He went out of concern for his friend, Mother, and may have prevented an assault on the young doctor."

"Yes, yes," Rionach said with an impatient wave of her hand. "I cannot fault him for that. The question is what will happen now. Maybe nothing. Maybe Bram will look for revenge."

"Strange that Etain said nothing today about the incident."

"Not strange at all. She knows Conor's word would be taken over Bram's. And there are two others of her own family who would back him up. Bram and Gorman both are liabilities to her, especially now that she's pushing cousin Zephan's case before the Council."

Liadan let her eyes drift across the broad meadow to the cluster of multi-colored tents, one for each of the Twenty Clans. As if symbolic of the current power division in the Council, the tents of Clans Laigain, Bairrche, Osraige and Conmaicne gathered on the far right, while those of Clans Fotharta, Cumain, Monaig and Gailenga occupied the far left; between them, the tents of twelve nonaligned clans whose votes swung back and forth.

"Not so long ago," Liadan mused, "Clan Fotharta and Clan Laigain were allies. One generation can do so much damage. Even Domnall gave up trying to heal the breach."

"We must be careful," Rionach cautioned, "not to attribute Etain's maneuvers to her entire faction, or even to all of Clan Fotharta. Many disagree with her privately but vote with her publicly. The key is to break her hold over her coalition, possibly get her unseated from Clan Fotharta's chair."

"Five years you've been trying, with my help, and where have we gotten?"

"Not far, 'tis true." Rionach allowed herself a wan smile. "I should be proud of my first child for her tenacity, if only it would be put to a sensible purpose."

Liadan held up the note from Conor. "Part of the problem with Conor is that he knows so little. Maybe it's time for the whole story to be told to him."

Rionach considered a moment before answering.

"Perhaps. My worry is that once the thread is pulled, there is no end to the unraveling. I'm not thinking only of Padraic, who must be given a say in the matter, but of Conor too. From what you told me, he plans to marry Mairin Fotharta. There are things we suspect but cannot prove. What is the old tale, Pandora's Box? Lives and dreams could be destroyed if buried secrets come to light."

"You mean Conor and Mairin's lives?"

"I do."

Liadan recalled the sadness and loneliness she had seen in Mairin's eyes.

"You may be right."

"None of us knows what Mairin may have suffered in that house. It's her place to tell Conor, if she wants to. Our meddling could make matters worse."

Rionach made to rise and welcomed Liadan's help.

"Knees with so much wear no longer like outdoor life," Rionach commented with a grimace.

"You could take an indoor room."

"Next month. I love the evening air for sleeping this time of year."

Liadan folded up Rionach's chair and walked with her arm in arm back to the camp. Rionach opened the flap to her tent and chuckled. "No husband yet!"

"Where is he?"

"Fishing, where else?" Rionach pointed east. "The usual place."

"Alone?"

"Hardly! With three cronies from his service days. I'm going to rest an hour until we have to don our best faces for dinner."

"And on the matter we were discussing?"

"For now, I suggest we say nothing. When the autumn is ended, if we still have homes to live in, we can decide what to do. Much as I care about my grandson, our task here is to hold the Council together and gain the alliance with Cork and Kerry. We *must* have that alliance."

Rionach disappeared inside. With a fast stride Liadan escaped the campground. She was not in a mood to chat with other delegates, indeed she was already weary of the gathering. This first day was mostly ceremonial and dealt with non-controversial matters. At nine sharp tomorrow morning, the Province's administrators would besiege the clan delegates with details of needs, wants, budgets, trade, shortages, and disputes. By early afternoon these reports would come to an end and then they would hear the all-important strategic proposals from Padraic—who would not be present—and from Aideen, who would. Late in the day, by which time nerves would be frayed and tempers short, Rionach would bring up urgent requests from Kernow and Wales and Bretan, all seeking an increasing level of military alliance.

During these debates in the main hall, the maneuvers would continue in side rooms and out in the yard, alliances forming and dissolving, each of the ancestral clans struggling to protect its own interests yet seeking to do what was best for the whole.

She offered a friendly wave to delegates and administrators who called out to her, but did not slacken her pace along the bricked pathway. The walk passed Bluestone, a four-story ornate structure serving as the Province's administrative and judicial center, then the Great Hall, a marble-faced, circular building where the Council of Twenty met. She kept up a vigorous stride as the walk wove among the residence halls used by the Province's permanent staff. When the bricks gave way to gravel she slowed to a stroll. The trail led through sparse woods over a gentle rise and descended into the Meadow of the Sacred Circle.

Here rested the twenty foundation stones of the Province, carved and dedicated a millennium ago on the shores of Lough Ennell. Each granite block, once smooth, now weathered and cracked, took the shape of a chair without arms, its round-topped back inscribed with the name and symbol of a clan. At the center of the circle, a Celtic Cross carved out of marble rose forty feet into the air, its crossed bars symbolizing sacrifice and its circle symbolizing the unity of the clans. At dawn on the first day of a Council meeting, each clan representative garbed in ceremonial robes was seated on the stone chair of his or her clan. The Chief Elder of the Province led the delegates in the service of Blessing and Harmony. Next, all present joined in singing the ancient Gaelic songs first sung at Lough Ennell. The ceremony concluded with an hour of total silence. So it had been for almost ten centuries.

Breathing her own silent prayer of thanks and remembrance, Liadan entered the circle, grateful that there was no one else present. After a long day of constant talking and listening and a night ahead that promised the same, Liadan needed time alone. She rested her hands on the back of the cool stone chair of Clan Laigain that Domnall held prior to his death. Though Liadan was of Clan Conmaicne by birth, by tradition she could also be chosen to hold the chair of her husband's clan. Clan Laigain offered it to her after Domnall's death, and she accepted, reluctantly, because she was certain that would have been his wish. Twelve years of service had worn her out and soon, she had decided, she would give it up. Not just yet.

Confident that she was likely to be alone here, she sat down on the great stone chair, closed her eyes, and tried to imagine what it had been like at Lough Ennell so many centuries ago. Artists had painted the scene, and now Seanlaoch Osraige was writing about it again ... but what had it *felt* like to be there? What did those folks imagine they were doing? Did they intend something as modest as a loose association for mutual benefit? Or did they believe that the bonding of the Twenty Clans under the Celtic Cross would form a people strong enough to survive trial after trial for centuries to come?

It had been a dream of her childhood to see the lake once, before she died. The year of her own birth, 947, marked the beginning of the Five Long Winters that shattered agriculture, destroyed ancient clan loyalties and bonds of friendship, and spread chaos and violence to every part of Eirelan. In 955, the Year of Flight as it was called, the Rampart was completed, the one-ton stones uprooted and carried in heavy wagons under close guard from the shores of the lake to safety at Teach Munna. Her dream of seeing the lake rarely occurred to her now, yet it was never entirely forgotten.

Her fingers touched the crumpled note in her pocket. She sensed Conor's regret—how well she knew her son!—when he wrote the note to her. Often she wished he did not have so much of her in him. He was a dreamer like she was, a poet who sweated blood to be a leader, a man of sensitive feeling who absorbed the full agony of warfare in his heart. Her thoughts drifted backwards, to the years when Aideen and Conor were young, the Rampart secure, the Province thriving in its confined yet bountiful home. She was tired of being worried, tired of facing a new threat each day, tired of fearing a messenger announcing the death of a child in battle.

She dozed lightly for a time and then was awakened by a sudden gust of wind that scattered fallen leaves among the stones. Though she could not see the sun hidden behind hills to the west, the steady darkening of the woods forced her to look at her timepiece. Her brief respite had to come to an end.

With a sigh she arose from the ancient chair, brushed her hand lightly over its carvings, and headed back with reluctant step towards her tent. She did not find it empty: Aideen must have arrived after she left to walk with Rionach. Her eldest daughter lay asleep on the spare cot, in full dress uniform down to her shiny boots. Only her hat had been tossed onto a table. Aideen's black hair was streaked with gray, and Liadan saw with surprise that deep lines spread from the corners of her daughter's eyes. Liadan pictured in her mind's eye the frigid, snowy day thirty-two years ago when, after nine hours of punishing labor, she had given birth. *My first-born! How thrilled we were with her!*

Always a solemn little girl, Liadan remembered, ever a challenge for Domnall to get a laugh out of. At sea by twelve years old, captain at twenty-two, commodore at twenty-eight, decorated a dozen times by the Province and Kernow alike, Aideen was respected throughout the Celtic world. Liadan loved her first-born as much as she loved Conor and Feth, and had spent a lifetime trying to be a friend to her. The problem was, they were so different! At times Liadan felt she did not understand Aideen at all. Domnall's death had struck Aideen the hardest, and perhaps no amount of time would heal the deep wound in her daughter's heart.

Liadan took a few silent steps across the tent and sat down at her writing desk. Even with the tent flap open, the waning light of day was not enough to write by. She lit a small oil lamp on the table and wrote first to Conor, doing her best not to sound upset with him but warning him to be very careful for a time and avoid Bram at all costs. Then she dashed off a lighthearted note to Feth, telling her to watch her brash tongue and brush her teeth—a longstanding joke between them since Feth obsessed over her sparkling-white teeth. No use in warning *her* to be careful: she might as well save the ink and paper. She had just sealed the envelopes with hot wax when the evening horn sounded, calling everyone in the camp to a ceremonial feast in the Great Hall. Much as she would have preferred a quiet gathering of family and friends around a campfire, there could be no bypassing this political event.

Aideen stirred at the sound of the horn. She sat up slowly with a muffled groan, ran her hands through her hair.

"Mother ... sorry, I didn't hear you come in," she mumbled in a husky voice. "No sleep these past two nights."

"I thought as much. You can sleep well tonight, if you can hold up for another two hours at the banquet."

"I shouldn't have left my ship," Aideen said, getting to her feet. "With Padraic not here, someone had to lay out the full military picture. He could have come, Mother."

Liadan heard the barely-hidden anger in the last sentence.

"You know why he doesn't. He draws Etain's sarcasm and loses his temper. Let's not go over that again, please."

While Aideen splashed water on her face, Liadan mentioned the note from Conor.

"Oh, I was there," Aideen said, drying her face with a towel. "Heavens above, he does some foolish things, mother."

"He felt responsible for Kellen and wanted to see him. They're friends and on top of that, he's Mairin's brother."

Aideen tossed the towel down on the cot, straightened her tunic and combed her hair.

"He couldn't have picked a different family to be involved with?"

Liadan stood and put out the lantern. "Aideen, this is old territory and I've had a long and trying day. You and he have always clashed, I accept that. But it's well you remember," she said in a sharper tone, "that Conor would give up his life for you without a second thought."

Aideen froze for a moment, her eyes locked with Liadan's. Then she turned away and moved past Liadan towards the entrance. Liadan donned her own formal cloak and followed her out.

"Let's go to dinner, mother," Aideen said quietly. "I don't want to argue now."

Outside the tent, Liadan wrapped her arm around her daughter's shoulders. "We don't get to dine together often, let's enjoy ourselves."

"I'll do my best." Aideen smiled and laid a hand over her mother's. "You don't know how tired I get of stringy beef and deferential nods from officers afraid to offend me."

"You won't get either one of those tonight," said Liadan. "Fresh pork and politics are on the menu."

Liadan awoke at first light, puzzled momentarily by the sound of someone else's deep breathing in the tent. *Aideen is here.* She lifted herself on one elbow and made out her daughter's form beneath blankets on the other cot. She was happy for the time they spent together, both at the dinner and later that evening in front of a campfire that sizzled in the cool mist. Between them there would never be the free, intuitive connection she had with Conor, yet they spoke frankly of many things personal and political. By evening's end Liadan realized she did not appreciate the immense weight of responsibility her daughter carried, the mounting pressure on ships and officers and sailors, the thin line between holding control of the seas and losing it entirely to brigandage and the growing power of well-organized naval opponents. Aideen had never been given to exaggeration, and she believed that the combined fighting power of the Province Squadron and Kernow's Admiralty was near to giving way.

Liadan arose from her cot and silently made her way outside the tent. She savored the softness of the still, damp morning air, scented by dewy grass and fresh-fallen leaves. How wonderful it would be if this Gathering of the Clans had as its main purpose the planning of the Centennial Festival! If her son was at home caring for his children, if her youngest daughter lay asleep in her bed in Rosslare, dreaming of handsome young men, if her husband ...

She brushed away tears that fell at these longing thoughts. She recalled a time soon after Feth was born, a time of relative peace and bountiful harvests. Domnall was at home enough to raise a great garden of vegetables and teach the children and make love to her in the quiet hours of the night. How brief that time now seemed, and how long ago. She could barely picture her younger self, a woman happy in her home, a home filled with love and laughter and long evenings of stories and poetry and songs. What was the favorite song she sang to the children at night? The lullaby? She hummed softly and called up in her mind the ancient Welsh Gaelic words:

Sleep my child and peace attend thee, all through the night
Guardian angels God will send thee, all through the night
Soft the drowsy hours are creeping, hill and vale in slumber sleeping,
I my loving vigil keeping, all through the night.
While the moon her watch is keeping, all through the night
While the weary world is sleeping, all through the night
O'er thy spirit gently stealing, visions of delight revealing
Breathes a pure and holy feeling, all through the night.

As she hummed, a whisper of morning air ruffled the tent's canvas. Far off in the woods, a pair of nuthatches called to each other.

"I remember that song," said Aideen, who had crept up behind her. "I used to sing it for Feth sometimes, when you were away or feeling ill."

"I didn't know that."

"Didn't sing it as well as you, just well enough to put her to sleep."

"Feth thinks the world of you," said Liadan. "How often I've heard her say, 'Aideen told me that.'"

"I tried to tell her things she'd need to know. She's not like any of us, mother. She has father's outgoing spirit and your compassion, harder than Conor yet softer than me. I do miss her so."

Liadan ran her hand affectionately through Aideen's tangled hair. "Perhaps this winter we can all have more time together in Rosslare?"

"I hope so, Mother. I'd like nothing better."

They fell silent a moment. A soft murmuring came from the campground, the sound of dozens of low-voiced conversations muffled inside tents. Liadan hummed the last two bars of the lullaby again.

"How many nights I sang that to you, and Conor, and Feth," she said. "I was thinking this morning how distant that time of my life now seems. I had a routine for this time of the morning. I'd get up alone before dawn, while everyone else was still asleep, start a fire in the stove, then go out on the porch to think and write. I always did love the hour before dawn."

"At sea as well," said Aideen. She drew in a deep breath of the cool, damp air. "The ship is usually quiet at dawn, before the shift change. It draws comments from the crew, but often I climb high into the rigging, alone, and watch the sun break over the ocean."

How strange she would say that, this hard-nosed daughter of mine! So there is a bit of me in her after all.

Forty feet away, the flap of a tent flying the Bairrche crest flew open and the tall, elegant figure of Uinseann Laigain stepped out. A ceremonial band confined his flowing white hair; the Elder robes of blue and tan draped over a lean, straight-backed frame. It was said that in his day, no man on earth could match Uinseann Laigain in the Duel of Blades. Now, only the arthritic bend of his fingers and deep-etched lines in his forehead suggested his seventy years. He caught sight of Liadan and Aideen, waved and smiled. Liadan's heart skipped: the smile was the same as her late husband's. He covered the distance to them in long, graceful strides.

He embraced Liadan and then Aideen. "Not dressed yet, you sleepy-heads!"

"We're not as young as you," Aideen retorted. "It's so good to see you, grandfather."

"It's good to see you both!" he said, his voice octaves below Aideen's. "My apologies, daughter, I know I've been remiss in visiting Rosslare. Writing at a furious pace and when I'm not writing I try to help Rionach. I'll do better ... if you promise to come to Duncormick. How about a private dinner tonight in our tent?"

Liadan nodded assent. Aideen said with regret, "I can't, grand-father. I would dearly like to but I have to get back to Dungarvan tonight."

"We'll miss you," Uinseann said, looking down at her. "Are you sure?"

Liadan saw a flash of uncertainty on her daughter's face, then a frown of resignation. Uinseann turned back to Liadan; his smile vanished.

"Rionach asked me to tell you something—she's already gone to the hall. Etain will force the question of leadership today, she has the votes to get it on the table ahead of other business. She'll push to have Zephan named Chief of Clans for one year."

"Surely she doesn't have the votes for that?"

"Not yet, but there are wavering clans and Rionach has enemies as well as friends. Worst of all, we expect the delegates from the western clans tonight. I have a note from them sent ahead, they want to appear before the Council tomorrow."

Liadan muttered a curse so vile it raised Uinseann's thick eyebrows and drew a smile from Aideen. "Just in time to witness a bitter debate that will split the clans and make treaty approval all but impossible."

"That's how it looks."

"Padraic would resign before he'd serve under Zephan," Aideen said in a despondent tone. "Army morale would collapse and I'd have a decision to make myself. Gods above, it would be a mess."

"Let's not get ahead of ourselves," Liadan cautioned. "There is much we can do. I suggest we sleepy-heads dress and then we all walk together, if you have time, father."

"I'm not due till you are. We can take the path by the stream."

Minutes later, as sun crept over the campground, Uinseann led them on a path through woods to the broad, rushing stream that provided water to the camp. He halted in a small grove of trees where a chorus of meadowlarks sang on despite the arrival of strangers in their arboreal home. With surprising ease Uinseann knelt and dipped his mouth in the cold water.

"Best-tasting water," he said, wiping his mouth. "We can talk privately here." He reached up and tugged free a blazing orange leaf from a maple branch. "Aideen, what say you about my news?"

Aideen sat on a log and dangled a hand in the water. "I don't remember much about Zephan except that he held a high rank in the army years ago. I haven't heard Padraic mention his name in a long time. Why did he leave the army?"

"Forced out by Padraic," said Liadan. She took a seat next to Aideen. "Not that he's a drunkard like Gorman ... far from it. Smart and well-connected among the clans, and he controls a sizable chunk of the export trade. He would not be easy to oppose, Etain knows that."

"Why did Padraic get rid of him?" Aideen asked.

"Because," said Uinseann, the color in his face rising, "he encouraged wanton killing in the army. And was not above getting his hands on women prisoners we took in the battles Domnall won. Despicable.

No one doubted his courage, though, and there were those in the army who felt he'd been ill-treated for personal reasons."

"How widely is all this known?" Aideen asked.

"Not widely enough now," said Liadan with a grim look. "It was twenty years ago. People come and go, memories get cloudy, details are forgotten."

"Not by Padraic ... or by me," said Uinseann, his hands clasping into fists. "The problem is that bringing all that up again would look like a personal vendetta." He gathered up his robes and sat on a boulder. "Rionach will use other means to block it, if Etain goes ahead. Zephan wants nothing to do with the clans of Cork and Kerry, and they know it. If he's given the high post now, any chance we have of gaining their help is lost. One more thing. Rionach's last resort is to propose someone else in Zephan's place if the Council insists on a Chief of Clans. Ideas?"

"Why not you, grandfather?" said Aideen.

Uinseann smiled. "There was a time when that might have made sense. Now I'm seventy and if I'm honest about it, I can't do without sleep as I once could. A Chief of Clans in this insane time needs the energy of youth. Actually, Rionach and I had thought to propose *you.*"

Liadan saw shock spread over her daughter's face. Aideen stared wide-eyed at Uinseann.

"Does that surprise you?"

"I don't think surprise captures it, grandfather."

"Of course Etain would fight it. That doesn't change the fact that you have every quality we need. Will you consent to your name being offered?"

"I am honored," Aideen said, "but I think the answer has to be no. I simply can't leave the Squadron now, any more than Padraic can leave the army."

Uinseann frowned and thought a moment.

"We have to respect your judgment, of course. There are other names we can propose, the problem is none of them would be strong enough to force Zephan aside. In that case, the best we may be able to do is delay the decision for a few more sessions."

"Father, I need not remind you," said Liadan, "that if the Council meets again next month, Etain will have the Speaker's chair."

"Yes, she will," Uinseann said with a sigh. He got up and brushed off his robes. "We can speak further tonight at dinner in our tent. I'll take the long way back. Stay and enjoy this beautiful place as long as you can."

"I'll say goodbye now, grandfather," Aideen said.

Uinseann embraced her warmly and whispered words in her ear Liadan did not catch. Aideen's eyes glistened with tears as the elder Laigain strode gracefully away. For a short while neither of them spoke. Aideen walked a few paces away, her back to Liadan.

"You're not disappointed in me for refusing Uinseann's offer?"

Liadan looked at her in surprise. "I've *never* been disappointed in you, and certainly not now. You'd be a fine Chief of Clans, I have no doubt of that, yet your judgment is undoubtedly right."

"There's more to it than my being needed at sea, and we both know it," Aideen said, turning to face Liadan. "I do my job well, I work hard, and I'm respected. My officers and sailors trust me to do the right thing and protect them. A Chief of Clans like my father must inspire people to believe they can survive in their darkest hour. I don't think I could do that."

Would that I could say she is wrong, Liadan thought, *but I cannot.*

Liadan rose and took her daughter's hands in her own. "You are loved and admired by me, and by many others. By Conor too, though you may not think so. We can't forever wish that Domnall was here ... he is not. We must look to ourselves, Aideen. Now," she said, kissing her daughter's cheek, "fare you well. We can pass notes during the day, or just wink. You'll be in Rosslare again soon?"

"I don't honestly know." She returned her mother's kiss. "Good luck today, Mother. I'll do everything I can for you and Rionach when it's my turn to speak. And thank you ... for what you said. Walk with me?"

"I'll stay here a short time more and collect my thoughts."

Aideen nodded. She straightened her hat and as she did so her expression shifted from daughter to commodore. And then she was gone.

A single, ornate lantern hung in the center of Uinseann and Rionach's tent, which was half again as large as Liadan's. The three of them sat around a folding wooden table positioned beneath the lamp, nibbling at the remains of cheese and fruit and sipping spiced apple cider that Uinseann kept hot on a campfire. In a nearby tent, a wistful melody was being played on uillean pipes.

Rionach, her long silver hair now loosed around her shoulders, fingered her mug in bony, veined hands, her eyes closed in weariness and thought. Uinseann leaned back in his chair, humming in a deep baritone the melody sung by the pipes. Liadan pulled her Councillor's robe more closely around her as chilly night air seeped into the tent.

"It was a very close thing," Rionach said, "as I knew it would be. We have a reprieve of one month and my daughter will use every day of it to promote Zephan's case."

"She has your talents," said Liadan with a rueful smile, "though I wish she didn't."

"If we're lucky," Uinseann mused, "in a month we may have success in the field and we can argue that a Chief of Clans is not needed. Or we'll have found another candidate. The question is, who?"

"I've racked my brains," said Rionach. She opened her eyes and leaned forward. "The Council might accept Clodagh Sechnaill as a compromise, she could handle the job and she's young enough."

"Though hardly charismatic," Liadan added unnecessarily.

"No," Rionach agreed. "For charisma we could push Garban Briuin. In his forties, tough, a soldier Padraic respects."

"Etain loathes him," Uinseann commented. "And to me her hatred smells personal. Something passed between them beyond politics."

"I agree," said Rionach. "Even if we gathered the votes for him, Etain's faction would tie his hands. Too bad, he's a very competent man and inspires people. So much for our short list of candidates, after these two the pickings are slim."

"So ... ?" Liadan inquired.

"So, we push the issue back." Rionach refilled her mug from the pitcher. "I can't stand another moment of politics. Let's enjoy our cider and talk of something else." She sent a friendly glare to her husband. "And *not* philosophy, my love."

Liadan thought a moment. "Would you like to tell me about Etain's father?"

Rionach eyebrows rose in surprise. "I've never told you?"

"No, and I've never asked. Nothing I need to know if you'd rather not speak of it. Just curious."

"It may be hard to speak of, because it's a sad story. Yet it may be well to tell it again, for my own sake. Husband, fill up the pitcher and add some brandy to it."

Uinseann complied, Rionach took a long sip of the spiked cider and began her story.

"Etain's father was a fine young man, Kerrill Cumain was his name. He grew up on a farm in the Ring of Kerry, with a small group of Cumain families that chose to remain outside the Rampart. I met him on a market day in Dungarvan." Her eyes filled with sweet remembrance. "I was eighteen and quite pretty I like to think—beauty does run in the Bairrche clan! He was handsome and strong and set his sights on me. We were married three months later and settled in his town of Ballynoe, where Etain was born. She was a beautiful child and we doted on her. We planned on more children, of course."

Rionach paused for a draft of cider, sighed and went on.

"When Etain was two, a raiding party from the north struck our town and Kerrill fought alongside the other farmers to drive them off. He was badly wounded and died a week later."

Tears ran down her cheeks. Uinseann reached out and enclosed her hands in his.

"After so long," she said, shaking her head in surprise. "Well, when Kerrill died I left Ballynoe and returned to my family in Dungarvan and raised Etain there. Ever a difficult child, yet brilliant and prized by men for her extraordinary beauty. She had many consorts, some worthy men like Padraic, others not so worthy. I had hopes she would settle on Padraic, who was a bit wild in those days. Still, I could see what kind of a man he was. When that went awry—you know that part of the story—she fixed on Gorman Fotharta. Mind you, Gorman then was nothing like the drunken sot he became later. He was a fair-looking man, strong, danced well, and was respectful enough towards me. Yet there was something about the look in his eyes that made my heart cringe, and he was already given to drink. I considered opposing that marriage ... but a mother's intuition about a daughter's choice is hardly infallible, is it? And by then there was no telling Etain what to do or not do. Etain married at sixteen and moved with Gorman to the Fotharta lands. Perhaps because he knew I didn't like him, I was rarely invited to visit. After Bram's birth the stories began and I did not go there at all. By that time I'd met Uinseann," she squeezed her husband's hand, "and got to know his son Domnall. As Gorman had no love for Uinseann because of their clashes in the army, I saw nothing of Etain after that.'"

She turned to Liadan. "That was more than you asked. Some of it you already knew."

"Some," Liadan admitted. "I wanted to know about Kerrill."

"I'd like to visit his grave again," Rionach said. "Maybe in the spring."

With that, Uinseann got up and took the cider pot outside to refill. A moment later Liadan heard his voice in an urgent, low-toned conversation with a man and then a woman. When he returned carrying the pot, the owners of the voices followed, one a man much shorter than Uinseann, with black, wavy hair streaked with gray, the other a woman of similar height with deep red hair draped around her shoulders.

"May I present," said Uinseann, standing to one side, "Gilvarry Muiredarg of Enniskean and Rainait Phelan of Coumduffmore. You know Rionach, of course. This is my daughter-in-law Liadan who holds the chair of Clan Laigain."

Liadan rose from her chair, bowed slightly and shook each of their hands. Rionach did likewise while Liadan unfolded two more chairs.

"Please sit," said Rionach. "You must be tired."

"Exhausted," Rainait said.

"Cider with a spot of brandy?"

"Most welcome," said Gilvarry.

Uinseann filled two mugs with warm cider and brandy. Gilvarry and Rainait took long draughts.

"Riding almost nonstop for two weeks," said Gilvarry in a hoarse voice. "Forty-two towns and clans we have spoken with. Even Macroom, those ... well, they were difficult."

Uinseann drew up a chair for himself. "What can you tell us?"

Rainait withdrew a folded sheet of paper from her pocket, unfolded it carefully, and smoothed it out on the table.

"All those signing offer a pledge to forget old grievances," she said, "and make alliance with the Province of the Twenty Clans. Provided, first, that your army does its utmost to defend us this fall, and second, that in the spring we combine our efforts to extend the Rampart from Clonmel to Tralee and station joint forces to stop incursions until it is finished."

Gilvarry tapped the rumpled sheet. "We delivered what you asked of us."

"How will we be received?" asked Rainait. "Is there enough support for the alliance?"

Liadan ran her fingers lightly over the historic document.

"Best you get comfortable," she said to them. "We have some planning to do."

Some ancient philosophers we read in school tell us that life is chance, and others say that all things happen for a reason. This is too big a question for a sea captain to answer. I do wonder all the same. Mairin passed out of my life more than two years ago, and though I thought of her often, I gave up hope that we would be together again. Now I have seen her and held her and wanted her and all the old feelings flame in my heart, yet I have no desire to force her into a hard choice. The superb fighting captain overlays an anguished young girl who lives on in her dreams and, at times, in her waking eyes. On the deck of a ship, she is the image of moral authority. In matters of the heart, she is more vulnerable than most.

Private log of Richard Tredinnick

Chapter 13

A dirty night. Mairin smiled at the quaint Admiralty phrase for what *Caillech* had passed through in the night. After a warm, breezy day of sailing towards Brest in company with *Ajax*, sunset brought low overcast and then heavy rain, punctuated by the occasional unseen squall that forced the two ships to fly much reduced storm canvas at a sacrifice of speed they so dearly needed. Rain continued to patter on the deck as a glowing eastern sky signaled a hidden sunrise. The barometer crept up a couple of notches. Mairin felt confident, as Richard obviously did, in setting courses and shaking out reefs in the topsails. *Caillech*'s bow again cleaved *Ajax*'s wake with authority.

"Position?" she inquired of Rowenna, who had just returned from a visit to the chart table.

"I put us eighteen miles northwest of Oessant Island. With no sightings these past twelve hours, I could be off five miles. We should raise the island from the tops soon if this rain would let up."

"Anything hot below?"

"Danu has burgoo up, Captain. Lieutenant Danaan is eating with the port watch and the marines."

"The deck is yours, Lieutenant. Advise all lookouts to watch for the island."

"Aye, sir."

On deck the past six hours, Mairin had almost forgotten about her forty extra passengers. Below decks, she found these brawny lads scattered at the long benches amidst the sailors of the port watch, and judging by the spirited conversations underway, no one seemed to mind the close quarters. At the wardroom table, Sinea Danaan sat with the two off-duty ensigns, Cadan Glyn and his sergeant. Mor Dal Reti, cradling in his hands a bowl of steaming burgoo, leaned on the bulkhead behind Ensign Laigain. Meanwhile, portly ship's cook Danu Eogain strolled along the tables cradling a huge pot in his arms, doling out seconds of the oatmeal-sugar-butter mixture.

Mairin took the last seat at the wardroom table. "Good morning, all."

Her greeting was answered with muffled and distorted "good morning sirs," drawing a grin from Mor who merely nodded his own answer. Danu arrived with a deep wood bowl and a spoon, and she wedged herself in next to Mor. The first hot spoonful of burgoo struck her wet, chilled bones like a warm burst of sunshine.

"Sleep much?" Mor asked her between mouthfuls.

"Napped on and off," she answered truthfully. "Any problems you know of?"

He swallowed and shook his head. "Remarkable how well it's worked, given the crowding. Of course it would be different on a longer voyage, we'd need to figure out better sleeping arrangements and more space for recreation."

"We usually don't fill the forward holds. Some extra bulkheads, bunking, another head."

"Something like that. There's also novelty here: most of our sailors have never seen Kernow and likewise the marines haven't seen the Province, so they have plenty to talk about. I'm sure libidos are raging too. That would also be a problem over a longer time." He scraped out his bowl and gave her a quizzical look. "You think we might have to do this more often? Carry heavy fighters?"

"I don't know. We generally stay away from deck fights and boardings, use our firepower to get results. In bigger actions it may be harder to avoid, ships get packed in with each other and you get too close for the incendiaries. And we may want to start seizing ships, when we can, and to do that you need a boarding force. I've heard Aideen say in strategy meetings ashore that the Admiralty is pushing her in that direction. So far she's said no."

Mor glanced down the long tables.

"The main problem is mixing young men and women," he said. His gaze settled on one obvious flirtation underway at the starboard table. "The Admiralty would never mix their crews, would they?"

Mairin polished off her first serving and waved to Danu for seconds.

"They have women aboard most warships," she reminded him, "just not many. Surgeons to be sure, sometimes navigators and chartmakers. No more than can be given their own cabins. Even so it must get a bit interesting. I've never thought to ask if they have problems."

Cadan Glyn arose from the table and approached Mairin.

"Captain, could you shift some of your people topside for awhile? I hate to ask with the rain, but we could use extra space to arm ourselves."

"You'll have it," Mairin replied. "We'll take the ship to arms, that'll put both watches on deck. Sorry about the crowding and lack of hammocks."

"We're used to far worse," Cadan said with a grin. "We were warm and dry and your cook makes a fine burgoo. No complaints, sir."

"Captain?"

Ensign Auteini paused halfway down the stairs from the quarterdeck.

"Yes?"

"Brest Squadron sighted, sir. Weather clearing."

"On my way." To Sinea she said, "take the ship to arms."

Mairin heard the room behind her erupt into action as she headed for her own cabin to don armor. Five minutes later she found all of her officers and chiefs on deck and in position, while crew continued to cycle through the fore and aft hatches to arm and return.

Rowenna aimed a finger towards the southeast. "Lookouts spotted three ships of the Brest Squadron rounding Oessant, beating up in our direction, six Santander ships in full pursuit."

"Message from *Ajax*," Ensign Velnowarth called out from the port rail. "*Believe Brest Squadron is drawing pursuit by intention.*"

"Yes, that's likely," Mairin said, using her own glass to scan the positions. The three ships of the Brest Squadron were now hull-up and silhouetted against the dark background of Oessant Island. The pursuing ships' masts bobbed above the waves, perhaps four miles aft of the Kernow warships they chased.

"Why only three ships?" she wondered aloud. "Did Brest Squadron lose three? And where are the other four Santanders? The corvette's report said they started with ten."

Sinea bounded up through the hatch in full armor, helmet in hand.

"Almost set below," she reported. "Marines arming, galley fire out."

Above their heads, longbow-armed sailors crowded into the tops. On deck, ballistae crews threw open lockers mounted aft of the mainmast and heaved out their heavy weapons, mounted them in the deck swivels port and starboard, four to a side, and readied their ammunition.

Mairin spent no time watching these actions: she knew Master Sechnaill would have the ship ready to fight. Then one additional thought occurred to her.

"Master," she said to Sechnaill once the bedlam of arming quieted down, "let's have the ballistae crews ready to send over grapplers."

"Begging your pardon, Captain, but I've done that. Captain Glyn and I came up with the option this morning over our burgoo."

She waved a heavily-muscled arm at the nearest portside ballista. Under it lay a four-pronged grappling hook connected to a coiled line, the end of led to a deck-mounted windlass.

Mairin smiled at her long-time weapons master. "And I suppose you've greased the lines to make them slippery as a fresh-caught fish."

"That we have, Captain, the last ten feet are more goose grease than rope."

"Brest is signaling," the mizzentop lookout called down. "*Three ships guarding the harbor, sunk four Santanders.*"

"There's our answer then," Mairin said. "They gambled help was on the way and drew the Santanders out, for what appeared to be a five-to-three fight."

Sinea had her glass trained from the port rail.

"Santanders hull up and they see us," she reported. "They're putting about, Captain."

"Message from *Ajax*," Rowenna called out, "*all ships pursue and destroy*."

As Rowenna's voice died, the *Ajax*'s battle ensign flew to the top of her mainmast below the Cross of St. Piran. Seconds later, *Ajax* set her topgallants and then her royals.

"Flash them out, Master," Mairin ordered Nya Gailenga. "Lieutenant," she said to Sinea, "our battle flag if you would."

Caillech's battle ensign, white ballistae bolts crossed on a crimson background, flew up the mainmast. The warship's full suit of sails matched *Ajax*'s, and with a strong steady wind out of the northwest, every sail to the royals stretched taut and drew hard. *Caillech* leaped ahead to chase the fast-sailing *Ajax*.

Sithmaith Laigain, posted in the starboard chains, tossed out the log line while Kensa Velnowarth watched the twenty-eight-second sandglass. When Kensa called out "time," Sithmaith seized the line, counted, and reported "twelve knots, one quarter, Captain."

Mairin scanned the horizon and checked the barometer, which was still rising. The sky was solid slate-gray from horizon to horizon, wind out of the northwest at fifteen knots and climbing, no sign of squalls so far. It would likely get colder as the day wore on, but for the moment, the conditions couldn't be better for an all-out chase.

"Light on ballast isn't helping, Captain," Nya reported, the wheel in her own skilled hands. "We're shallow in the keel, lots of leeway with this much sail pressure."

"Understood. We're lighter than usual too, on this point of sail the two might cancel."

"They might at that," the Master agreed. She bellowed a sharp command to sailors trimming the royals high over their heads.

"Thirteen, one quarter," Ensign Laigain sang out from the chains.

Mairin walked forward into the bow with Sinea. They leaned together over the rail as *Caillech*'s sharp prow carved aside *Ajax*'s swirling wake. Spray flew over them each time the bow plunged through the rising sea. Two hundred yards ahead, Richard had set every stitch of canvas that could be employed on a broad reach.

"By the stars this is the life!" Mairin cried out between blasts of salty spray. "Is it not?"

"It is!" Sinea yelled back. "Nothing ashore touches it. Five of us chasing six of them, and we'll have them, by my grandmother's shawl and apron we will!"

Mairin sent her a raised-eyebrows question.

"Local phrase, Captain!"

They both laughed and then slid out their telescopes to gauge their progress.

"Brest ships are letting us catch up," Sinea said. "We'll join them in thirty minutes."

"Or less. What would you do if you commanded the enemy fleet?"

Sinea lowered her glass and weighed the options. "If I thought I could keep this up until nightfall, I'd do it. They must see we'll be in position to attack hours before that. I might lighten ship for more speed ... still may not be enough. The options are to risk a fleet action, or scatter my six ships in all directions."

Mairin tucked the scope into a pouch and rested her gloved hands on the rail.

"My guess is the last one," she said. She craned her neck towards the foretop, now crowded with archers. One of them held signal flags. "Foretop there ... signal question to *Ajax, your plan if they scatter?*"

The sailor flashed the flags; two minutes later *Ajax*'s mizzentop answered.

"*Pursue one on one,*" Sinea read off.

"Richard means to have them," Mairin muttered.

"Sir?"

"I said Captain Tredinnick wants them sunk or burned if it means chasing them all the way across the Bay of Biscay."

"The Brest Squadron must've taken losses," Sinea said, "and he means to spill their blood for it."

Sinea raised her glass again. "There they go, Captain."

Mairin pulled out her scope and focused. In a well-disciplined maneuver, the six enemy ships fanned out over a hundred and eighty degrees of the compass, taking on six different downwind points of sail. *Ajax* signaled again: *Caillech* to the far right.

Mairin sprinted aft with Sinea on her heals. Rowenna had already ordered the change of heading to the southeast, while overhead the sail crew furiously shifted yards and trimmed up for a broad reach into the open Atlantic. Their prey: a single three-master that flew every sail they did and seemed more anxious to get home than to fight.

"We're gaining," Rowenna observed, "but look there."

On the horizon in the direction they now sailed, storm clouds piled up and lightning flickered.

Mairin swore the foulest oath that came to mind. "Rain and squalls, a storm from the west for all love. It's a wonder they didn't all head for it."

"Storm is heading this way," Nya Gailenga observed from the wheel. "They're betting it will cover this whole area of the sea by the time we reach them."

"It'll be close," Sinea said. "Very close."

An hour later, the sky overhead turned black and thunder rumbled over a troubled sea. The steady northwest wind began to gust unreliably and back into the west. They lost speed—but so did their prey, now only five hundred yards off *Caillech*'s bow. Mairin searched the Santander ship's quarterdeck and saw no one with a speaking trumpet giving the orders. Either their captain was below, which seemed unlikely, or else he eschewed the trumpet that most Santanders used.

A flash of lightning burst through the heavy clouds, followed by a crack of thunder that shook *Caillech*'s deck planks. At the same time, Rowenna shouted "she's turning!"

The enemy ship swung south as far as she could without tacking. *Caillech* followed smoothly in her wake while storm-sails luffed and sailors flew into action overhead. *Caillech*'s speed fell off further as her bow neared the eye of the wind.

"Nya," Mairin said, but the warning was unnecessary. The sailing master would never let them cross the wind without tacking.

"He's gambling on the storm over his speed," Sinea said, her hands clamped white-knuckled on the port rail. "And he might make it."

Nya Gailenga struggled to hold the weather gauge on the new heading. Sails shuddered and steadied. The Santander ship bent its course further west into the wind.

"He has zero margin," Sinea said, her eyes on their own trembling sails. "One gust and he's finished."

"His boarding planks are raised, he's set to fight," Sechnaill observed. "I hope we can give him one."

Three things happened at once. A blinding burst of lightning and clap of thunder presaged a torrential cloudburst; the squall line veered the wind to the west another point; and the enemy ship was caught in irons, wind square on her bow. Nya managed to spin the wheel fast enough to avoid the same fate. *Caillech* barreled ahead and in seconds closed to within two hundred yards of the struggling warship.

"Grapples away!" Mairin shouted over the roar of the storm.

The two forward ballistae fired at high elevation. Both grapples cleared the Santander ship's taffrail and snagged against the inside of the hull. *Caillech*'s sailors cranked furiously on the windlasses, drawing the lines taut, while foretop archers bombarded enemy sailors trying to saw through the tough, greased cables. The distance closed to a hundred yards. Nya Gailenga swung the ship's bow north, giving the portside ballistae a clear line of fire; three more grapples sailed over the Santander's rails and stuck fast amidst a blizzard of arrows fired from the fighting tops. Sailors drove the heavy windlass bars, yard-by-yard drawing the ships alongside each other.

Mairin at last spotted the enemy captain: he used no speaking trumpet because his clarion voice easily carried over din of the storm breaking over their heads. She could not understand his words though the actions he ordered were clear enough. His crews abandoned the effort to cut the grapples. Instead they let fly their sails. Sixty heavy-armed fighters crowded around the fore and aft boarding ramps.

He means to board us, Mairin exulted. *Just what I had in mind.*

Cadan Glyn lifted the quarterdeck hatch a foot.

"Ramps down any second, ready assault," Mairin told him.

Sinea pounded down the starboard rail to take command of the forecastle. Rowenna screamed encouragement at the windlass crews, which had to fight for footing on slick planking. Thirty yards. Sechnaill's ballistae crews battled the deluge to fire cutter bolts at rigging and fighters, while archers in the tops poured a continuous rain of arrows on the enemy's quarterdeck. At fifteen yards' separation the ponderous boarding ramps smashed down on *Caillech*'s portside rail fore and aft. Steel spikes dug deep into the deckplates, enemy fighters leaped up from protected positions behind the gunwales and piled onto the ramps. Each fighter carried a small round shield over his head to ward off arrows as he ran across the ramp. Reaching a Province warship, the warriors would toss the shields aside and fight with a pike in one hand and a sword in the other. And that was exactly what they planned to do now.

Except that Cadan Glyn and his marines had a different outcome in mind. The instant the planks struck the *Caillech*'s hull, Glyn and his fighters poured up the hatches and slammed into Santanders at *Caillech*'s end of the ramps. Glyn, recognizable by his height and black-crested helmet, led the aft assault himself. Astonished Santander fighters, expecting to be confronted by *Caillech*'s armored officers and sailors, found themselves engaging an entirely different force, powerful men trained and armed for exactly this kind of fighting. Mairin was astonished how quickly Glyn and his men cleared the heaving ramps and carried their attack onto the Santander's deck. The last few marines leaped on the Santander ship an instant before the forward ramp broke loose and tumbled into the warring waves between the two ships, followed seconds later by the aft ramp. Sechnaill ordered the tops and ballistae to stop firing—too much risk of hitting a marine.

"Sorry, Captain," Nya yelled over the thunder, "had to get some distance in this storm."

"Understand," Mairin yelled back. "Try to keep us fifty yards apart."

Glyn's marines now fought against the Santander ship's remaining boarders and crew. Mairin swept the enemy's deck with her telescope, saw little more than whirling swords gleaming in lightning-light. Shouts and screams carried over the continuous thunder and howl of the storm. Nya and her first mate battled the wheel to keep the ship from broaching.

"How will we get them off, Captain?" Sinea shouted. "That ship may overset any time."

Mairin's mind raced to answer Sinea's question. Surely the marines would prevail. Santanders still alive would retreat below dogged hatches and the ship would be completely at the mercy of the storm. The marines would drop incendiaries down air vents and then they needed to get off, fast. Not enough time to launch and crew the big boats. They would have to lay alongside.

"Fenders out," she ordered. "Gig on the starboard davits."

Rowenna gathered a crew to lower fenders along *Caillech*'s portside. Sinea rounded up Brigid Auteini and two strong sailors; together they hoisted the high-freeboard gig onto the davits and swung it out over the starboard side.

Cadan Glyn waved from the Santander ship's rail; the fight was over. His marines, some wounded, gathered along the rail on either side of their commanding officer.

"Nya, bring us alongside," Mairin ordered. "Easy as you can."

The enemy ship scudded downwind, driven by pressure of the storm-wind on her masts and yards and hull. Nya swung *Caillech*'s bow around to parallel the helpless ship's course. Sailors hanging on for dear life in the rigging trimmed the topsail yards.

Mairin saw Rowenna strip off her armor and she quickly followed suit. The marines would have only seconds to climb onto *Caillech* or leap across to the heaving deck. Every plank of both ships was rain-slick and the wind gusted at full storm force. Sechnaill ordered everyone to doff armor and be ready to help at the rail.

Nya brought them closer and closer to the wildly-slewing vessel. A sudden gust closed the last ten feet in a split second. Fenders splintered; the ships' hulls bumped and ground against each other. Marines leaped over by the dozen. Cadan Glyn hung back with three wounded men. Two of them he helped across before a furious gust drove the ships two yards apart. Mairin could only watch in horror as Glyn pitched forward. His height and long arms saved him: his hands caught hold of *Caillech*'s rail and half a dozen sailors hauled him aboard. The last injured marine, blood pouring down his face and legs, made a desperate leap. His fingers lightly brushed the hands reaching out for him and he tumbled headfirst into the whitecaps.

Rowenna launched herself over the side.

"I'll go, Captain," yelled Sinea.

"No, get the gig in the water."

With that order Mairin stepped to the rail and screamed out, "no one else!"

Then she leaped over and plunged into the icy, foam-filled sea. Water boiled up over her head and underwater currents sucked at her. She kicked herself to the surface and found she could see: sailors held lanterns over the side.

"Captain!" Rowenna surfaced five feet from her. "I had him, couldn't hold on."

Rowenna dove again; Mairin flipped upside down and kicked herself under. She searched until her lungs cried out for air, all the while knowing that the rolling, pitching ship threatened to strike her any second and send her to the bottom. She burst the surface, sucked in air, and plunged down again into the murky, swirling waters ... and instantly had to dodge the ship's rolling hull. Then her left foot struck something soft. She twisted and reached out blindly with both hands. Her right hand touched cloth and she seized hold of the unconscious soldier's shirt and then his belt. She drove upward dragging the limp body and surfaced next to Rowenna who had just filled her lungs for another dive. Together they lifted the man's head free of the churning water.

"Captain, we're coming!"

Sinea, Brigid and two sailors forced the gig through the waves, hauled the limp body out of the water, then dragged Rowenna and Mairin over the gunwales. The sailors rowed hard for davit lines hanging down *Caillech*'s starboard. Brigid hooked the lines on and the water-logged gig flew upward out of the deadly sea.

Five minutes later Mairin dripped seawater into a spreading puddle in the doorway of the surgery, watching Mor and two assistants struggle to save the dark-haired soldier's life.

"Come on, come on," Mairin said under her breath. "Breathe."

"Yes!" Mor shouted. The man on the table vomited sea water, choked, vomited again, and then began sucking in huge, rattling breaths. Mor covered him with heavy blankets, waited till his breathing steadied, and then left him to the care of his assistants.

"He'll recover," Mor said to Mairin. He turned to the anxious marines. "His wounds are not that serious and I'm pretty sure we got him out in time."

Mairin felt her hands grasped by much larger, harder ones. Cadan Glyn towered over her.

"Our thanks, Captain. To you and Lieutenant Briuin and your crew."

A murmur of agreement spread among the marines pressing around the surgery door.

Mairin cast an admiring look at the marines, whose soaked, torn shirts and breeches clung tight to hard-muscled bodies.

"All I can say in reply," she said with a broad grin, "is that I will never forget this sight."

The marines and *Caillech*'s crew roared with laughter.

Admiralty Headquarters in Brest Harbor occupied a three-story, somewhat disheveled brick building set back less than a block from the wharf, where five battle-scarred ships floated safely at mooring lines. The first and second floor of the stone structure were given over to fleet operations and shipping management, the third floor to sleeping rooms for in-port officers. Half of the musty basement was used for storage, the other half for a modest, wood-paneled officers' dining room dominated by a massive stone hearth in one corner. That hearth blazed with flame and threw welcome heat on five tired yet cheerful captains seated at a cloth-covered round table.

Presiding over the late-evening meal, Captain Matthews of the Victory was a portly man in his fifties with a ruddy, freckled face that radiated cheer and goodwill. To his right was Captain Odger of the Athenian, tall and slender with thinning black hair and a somber countenance that tended to conceal a finely-polished wit. Richard sat to the left of Matthews, and to his left was towering Captain Innes of the Endymion, not much older than Richard and given to great outbursts of laughter. The three other captains of the Brest squadron had sailed their heavily-damaged ships up-harbor to a repair dockyard and not yet returned. Mairin sat opposite Matthews, more often than not finding herself the custodian of the current wine bottle.

She came at Richard's polite insistence; her own plan for the day after the engagement was to rest on her own ship and dine with her officers and crew. Having dressed and made her appearance, she was forced to admit the late-evening meal had been enjoyable and relaxing. Now as the ornate grandfather clock in a corner struck eleven, the subduing effects of a heavy meal, frequent glasses of wine, a hot room, and precious little sleep for days weighed like anchors on her eyelids. More than once she caught herself beginning to nod and snapped herself back to a modicum of polite attention. Rivulets of sweat poured down her back even after she stripped off the dress jacket. She resorted to chewing hotly-spiced olives to focus her drifting mind.

A sudden hiatus in the banter made her wonder if she'd been spoken to and a response was awaited. Thankfully it was just a natural lull—everyone was beginning to sag in their chairs. Next to her, Innes filled his glass and hers and passed the bottle. *Another glass and I'll slide under the table*, she moaned silently. Innes shifted his big frame sideways and raised his glass towards her. His deeply-tanned face, so often twisted with mirth throughout the evening, was now grave and sincere.

"Gentlemen, I drink to Captain Fotharta and the *Caillech*, whose freely-offered help was vital to our success."

All the glasses were raised and voices joined: "to the *Caillech*."

She was caught utterly off guard. She lowered her own glass, nodded to each of them and muttered a self-conscious "thank you."

"A dangerous engagement," Matthews said, looking around to all and then at Mairin directly, "and to be honest we worried help would not arrive in time. You can't imagine how each of us felt to see not one but two ships appear, one flying the Celtic Cross."

"I've heard," said Odger, "that you risked your own life to save one of our marines. Dove in after him in the middle of a storm."

Richard's eyebrows went up. "I didn't hear anything about that."

"Sheer impulse," Mairin said. "My first officer dove in first and I followed. I thought we'd lost the young man until my hand touched his shirt."

"Our thanks," said Innes. He raised his glass the others joined him.

There followed a moment of silence which Matthew's heavy voice broke. "Richard, the fleet's rumor mill is buzzing about an attack this fall."

"An attack on Santander itself," Odger put in.

Richard swirled the wine in his glass. "Gentlemen, please don't press me on this. We can't be sure about spies in the merchant fleet, or even in the Admiralty itself."

"True enough," Innes rumbled while emptying the last of the wine into his glass. "Though I hate to admit it."

"Whenever an attack is made—and it will happen, I assure you—it must be a surprise," Richard said, looking at them each in turn. "Then we'll throw everything at them we can. I can say," he said to Mairin, "that the province Squadron will be involved, both in the attack itself and in covering the sea lanes while our ships are committed."

"I've had no word," Mairin said, "either directly or by rumor. I doubt the Council has been told, word leaks out of them like water through a sieve."

"Maybe not," Richard admitted. "I ask you all not to discuss the subject, even among yourselves."

"Agreed" was murmured around the table.

Mairin got to her feet. "Captains, I thank you for this fine meal. My head will fall onto the tablecloth if I don't leave now."

Matthews heaved himself aloft. "I suggest we adjourn to our beds, tomorrow we'll all be hard at work again. Captain Fotharta, there's a comfortable room for you here if you wish to stay ashore tonight."

She caught Richard's fleeting, hopeful glance.

"My thanks," she said with a grateful nod. "I'll have to say no. I expect we'll sail at first light if wind and tide serve. I need to get back to Falmouth and collect our cargo."

The group climbed the stairs to the empty, dark first floor, and the three Brest squadron captains kept climbing. Richard stopped in the hallway and led Mairin out the front door to the building's covered portico. Facing as it did to the south, the swirling wind and spitting rain overhead could not be felt. The harbor was deserted and dark; the quay lanterns' yellow glow reflected from rain-coated bricks. Five moored warships, sails furled tight on the yards, rocked gently from the sheer force of the gale.

Richard leaned against a pillar. "It may be a long time till we see each other again."

"I know," she said, "but then again, maybe not. At least let's hope it's not two years."

He turned to face her. "I never realized how much I missed you, until I saw you at Pendennis. I guess I tried to put you out of my mind when you stopped writing."

He reached out to hold her, and she allowed it. His uniform reeked of sea water and sweat. She felt desire rising in her thighs and she had reason to know he felt the same.

He kissed her on the forehead. "Goodbye, love. The fortune of the sea to you."

"And to you, dear Richard."

For a long moment she held his two hands in hers. Then she pulled her cloak over her shoulders and made her way at a fast walk towards her ship. She did not dare turn around.

In the centuries following the founding of the Province in old calendar year 2954, the diverse clans of the southwest of Eirelan had no grievance with the Twenty Clans. This amicable coexistence changed drastically with the decision to build the Rampart in Province Year 953. After much contentious debate, the Province rejected the plea of Cork and Kerry to be included within the defensive perimeter. In my view, this ill-advised decision rested on a prejudice that these clans and peoples , who did not share all of the spiritual and cultural values of the Twenty Clans, did not have a place in our political and social life. The result was bitter resentment by those peoples, only partly mollified in later years by the Province's self-interested decision to defend port cities of the southwest such as Tralee, Cobh and Bantry. To this day, the peoples of Cork and Kerry generally believe they were abandoned to their fate.

Sean Osraige, Historical Musings

Chapter 14

The archery platform at Dungarvan Fort had recently been lengthened from forty to sixty feet, and four additional ballistae mounted. Like all such platforms, it was attached to the second level of the fort and protected the broad gates below which guarded access to the road leading northwest. Attackers trying to force that gate or storm the fort itself would stand under the direct fire of fifty archers and ten heavy bolt-throwers.

It was now an hour past midnight, six full hours from welcome dawn. In the tower, youthful lookouts anxiously scanned the low hills from north to west. The fort's telescope was not needed to see teeming campfires blazing in the distance where the road snaked between high hills on either side. Rather than diminish as night passed, the number of fires steadily increased, lighting the ground-hugging mist with an unearthly, flickering glow.

Feth and Derdre sat side by side on the ammunition crate for the leftmost ballista. They had talked quietly in this private spot for hours. Normally the platform was off-limits, but with so many extra Blades and Bows crowded into the fort, the Fort Captain gave permission for on-duty soldiers to move around the fort or walk outside so long as they took their gear and did not go far.

Feth found herself taking a strong liking to her red-haired companion. Though their childhood lives differed, they found much in common and told each other their hopes and fears for the future.

"I'd like to meet Sean," said Derdre. She pulled out a cloth and wiped her face. "Oh, it's so damp tonight, I'm soaked inside this armor. Do you think you'll marry him?"

Feth smiled as fantasy images flashed through her mind.

"I know he likes me, but marrying and having children? I don't even know if that's something he plans on."

"I liked Finian," said Derdre of her most recent boyfriend. "He's trying to make a go of his smithy in Waterford."

"So you're not still together?"

"Not by my choice," Derdre said with a sigh. "I was away so much, he found someone else, a sailor for all love."

"Sailors are gone alot too."

"Not ones that break their legs and walk with a limp."

"Oh. You'll find someone else."

"Sure."

Feth studied the campfires glowing in the pass. "Who are they? And what do they want?"

Derdre shrugged. "Maybe they're moving and it's just a good place to camp. Or they're gathering slowly to attack. No one really knows."

"I told you about Sean's brother Oran? He's been traveling Éirelan since spring, trying to find out what we're facing."

Feth's mind drifted back to earlier days, when Oran made her laugh until tears ran down her face.

"I can't imagine being outside the Rampart alone," Derdre said with a shudder. "How does Oran stay alive, traveling by himself?"

Feth tried to recall the last time she had seen Oran. Could it be a year ago?

"He says most of the people out there are just like us. Some good, some bad, some frightened, some angry. A great number are starving and desperate. How would we act if our children cried every night because we couldn't give them enough to eat?"

"About the same, maybe. I just can't help hating the people who killed my mother."

Feth shook her head. "We can't let ourselves hate, even when we lose people we love so much. Hate will eat us alive."

Derdre sighed but made no answer. A moment later the sound of footsteps drew their attention to the platform entrance. A tall, hard-muscled archer stepped onto the platform, nodded to them politely, then strolled to the far end and leaned her back against a ballista. The newcomer pushed sweat-soaked black hair from her face, raised a flute to her lips and began to play softly a sweet, mournful melody.

"Do you know her?" whispered Feth. "I'd like to be that tall."

"I'd like to be that strong," replied Derdre. "No, I don't recognize her. She must have come in with the reinforcements today."

"I know the song. It's a lullaby my mother sang to us at night."

"I know it too," Derdre said. "It's Welsh."

They listened as the black-haired girl played the lullaby, first simply, then with extra notes and variations of melody, major to minor key and back again. At the end of a chorus played in a whisper, she lowered the flute from her lips and stared downwards.

"She looks like she could use company," Derdre said.

Feth nodded agreement. She fetched her bow and helmet and walked down the platform with Derdre a step behind. The flutist heard them coming and got to her feet, slipping the flute into her pocket. *A pleasant face*, Feth thought. *The big dark eyes make her look sad, or is it that I see sadness behind them?*

"Did I disturb you?" the young woman asked.

"Just the opposite," Feth said. "We enjoyed it. I'm Feth Laigain and this is Derdre Dal Reti."

"Gwen Cennedi," the flutist said, taking each of their hands in turn. "Of Fahamore Town."

She saw the puzzled looks and added, "in the Dingle Peninsula. Kerry to you."

A moment of awkward silence passed.

"That surprises you?"

"Not at all," Feth said quickly. She sensed Gwen had somehow taken offense. "I trained with folks who came from outside the Province."

"Same for me," said Derdre.

"At least two hundred of us serve in the army," said Gwen, still sounding defensive. "And another hundred at sea." She turned away from them and looked out over the dark landscape. "We bleed and die just like native born citizens."

Feth shot Derdre a puzzled look. Derdre shook her head.

"Gwen, you seem mad about something," Feth tried.

"I am."

"You can tell me it's none of my business," Feth pursued, "but I'd like to know what."

Gwen hesitated, her big hands gripping the platform railing until the knuckles showed white.

"I was down in the Common Room," she said at last, "eating with the second dinner shift. The people I was sitting with were okay, I guess. Then someone at the next table told a 'dumb Kerry farmer' joke and everyone laughed and pounded the table. I'm sitting there, sweating in my armor like everyone else, I've got scars and bruises to show where I've been this past year. I can play the flute and I can read four dialects of Gaelic plus old English and even some old French. And I'm supposed to be ignorant? The bastards, who do they think they are?"

Gwen grabbed her longbow and held it up. "This is a hundred-forty-pound bow, most archers can't get the string halfway back. I've killed scores of enemy fighters with this. And that's the thanks I get? I should just quit and go back home. Now."

Derdre's ruddy face flushed scarlet. "Tell me what they looked like," she said. "I'm going down to straighten things out."

"With me," said Feth. "Give us names if you have them."

Gwen turned, astonishment on her face. "You'd defend me? You don't even know me."

"I know what my father and mother taught me," Derdre said. "To detest ignorance and prejudice."

"Making a scene now wouldn't do any good," Gwen said, hanging her head. "And I suppose they didn't know someone from Kerry was nearby, I mean, they weren't aiming at me."

"Makes no difference," Feth said, her voice trembling with anger. "Those people don't understand what we're fighting for."

Gwen set her bow down and sighed. "Let's let it go, please. It's enough that you'd stand up for me."

The three of them took seats on ammunition boxes. Gwen pulled out the flute again and rubbed its smooth wood absently.

"Sometimes I do wonder why I'm here. Not for the glory of battle, I can tell you. I hate war and fighting."

"Then why do you wear the cross?" Derdre asked. "I'd really like to know."

"Fahamore is not far from Tralee," Gwen began, "and most of my family depends on the port for trade. One day maybe two years ago I was in Tralee with my uncle. A Province warship came into the harbor and tied up at the deep-water pier. They'd been in a fight with raiders who planned to land along the coast, maybe near Fahamore. I saw eleven sailors carried off that ship. Two were dead and the rest were hurt badly. I ran up and took one end of a stretcher. The poor girl on it moaned all the way to the hospital. Afterwards I ran into the weeds and threw up and cried for half an hour."

She paused and swallowed hard. "I remember it like it was yesterday. Anyway, I spent some time thinking about what happened and I got it in my mind to fight. The Tralee militia was out, they take only men. So I thought maybe I'd be a sailor in the Squadron."

"What did your family say?" asked Feth.

Gwen offered a rueful smile. "A few supported me. Others thought I was crazy. I was told over and over that the Province defended ports like Tralee for their own benefit and didn't give a whit about the people of Cork and Kerry."

"So how did you decide what to do?" Derdre asked.

"The last person I talked to," Gwen replied, "was my grandmother Ulicia, my mother's mother. She's blind and confined to bed now. The wisest person I know. I asked her what I should do." Gwen closed her eyes. "She said to me, 'Gwenneth child, there is value in thinking things through and you've done that. Now see what your heart tells you is right.' She wouldn't let me speak right away, she made me come back the next day. By then I knew what I would do."

"I'd like to meet her," Feth murmured.

"Maybe you will," Gwen said. "Anyway, I finished school for the year and took a ship to Dungarvan. I was seasick all the way. The sailors told me I'd get over it and probably they were right. In the end I decided I liked my feet on the solid earth. So, I signed with the Line of Bows. I was already skilled with a longbow, so after three months training I was posted. That was over a year ago now. I was made a citizen after my first battle."

"Have you been home since then?" Feth asked.

"No. No leave more than a week at a time. I may be able to go this winter."

"You must be homesick," said Derdre. "Have you made some friends?"

"I've tried, but to be honest, it's not easy moving around so much. And plenty of native-born citizens still think we're not worth being friends with. Like the people who laughed at the joke."

"I can hardly believe it," Derdre said, angry once more. "Best you not tell me who laughed."

Feth stared straight into Gwen's eyes. "How would you like two new friends? Real friends that will stick by you?"

Gwen looked startled and grateful at the same time. She took Feth's offered hand and then Derdre's.

"I was feeling so down," she said, brushing tears from her dark eyes. "Thanks for coming over. I really was ready to quit and go home. Now the barracks won't seem so lonely."

"Do you have a place to stay when you're off duty?" asked Derdre.

"No. I've been saving my pay to travel back home."

"Then as long as we're stationed here you can come home with me," Derdre said firmly. "My house is in Dungarvan. My father's at sea and we have plenty of room. You too, Feth, if you want."

"I'd like to come," said Feth, "but I'll probably be staying with Sean."

"Boyfriend?" asked Gwen.

"I guess you could say that."

Gwen smiled at Derdre. "That's so nice of you. I didn't expect anyone to welcome me into their home. A bed in a quiet house would be like heaven after the last year. You mentioned your father. Is your mother at home?"

Feth knew Derdre would have a hard time answering, so she spoke for her.

"Derdre's mother Dunlaith was our captain until a couple of nights ago."

Gwen's face registered shock and then dismay. "Dunlaith Dal Reti was killed, I heard it as soon as I got here." She reached out and took hold of Derdre's shoulder. "I am so sorry, Derdre. I served under your mother several times, she was very good to me." She shook her head in disbelief. "It makes me sick to think she's gone."

The three archers sat silently for a time, while the fort itself quieted down for the long night of watching and waiting ahead.

Feth broke the silence. "Play something?" she invited.

Gwen raised the flute to her lips and played a few bars of a song. "You know it?" she asked her companions.

"The Meeting of the Waters," Derdre replied. "One of my favorites. I sang it at a wedding last year."

"You can sing?" asked Feth. "You didn't tell me that!"

"I can carry a tune," Derdre said. "How about you?"

"Not in a basket."

"Should I start again?" Gwen asked. She got to her feet.

Derdre stood beside her. "Yes. Let's try it."

Gwen played one line as an introduction, and then Derdre joined in, singing softly in an old Gaelic dialect with English words mixed in. Feth was glad she had not offered to sing: Derdre possessed a rich alto voice, sweet and plaintive, as fine a voice as Feth had ever heard. Gwen played on, smiling with her eyes. Feth leaned back against the ballista's frame and did her best to let go of the anger she felt over Gwen's experience.

By the time Gwen and Derdre started on a second song together, Blades and Bows began to fill the platform, and overhead, the Fort Captain leaned over the tower's balustrade. Feth wondered if he would order a halt, but he did not. Soon other voices joined in on the familiar songs, basses and tenors among the men, sopranos and altos among the women, the better singers blending harmony lines with the melody. Others simply listened.

Dozens of songs and four hours later, the threatening campfires faded out. Pink-orange light challenged black in the east, the fort's great lanterns were extinguished, and Derdre sang the last words of the last song, the same one they started with:

> *Sweet Vale of Avoca, how calm could I rest,*
> *In thy bosom of shade with the friends I love best.*
> *Where the storms that we feel in this cold world should cease,*
> *And our hearts, like thy waters, be mingled in peace.*
> *And our hearts, like thy waters, be mingled in peace.*

Gwen lowered her flute and the platform slowly emptied. Many of those passing by murmured thanks and compliments. Above their heads, the Fort Captain waved a salute. Gwen and Derdre gathered up their bows and helmets.

"Coming?" Derdre asked Feth.

"You two go ahead, I'll meet you at the barracks."

Left alone, Feth leaned wearily on the wood railing and waited for the first rays of sun to creep over the valleys to the north.

We sing together and listen to this glorious music. We are young and want a future for ourselves. But we are not singing at a fair or a festival, and we are not holding the hands of those we love. We are sweating inside armor, bows and swords and helmets never out of arms' reach, in a place that is not home for most of us, least of all for Gwen. Some of us hold attitudes about others that are wrong and hurtful and damaging to our own future. Much to understand, Fethnaid, and much to do.

Two uneventful days later, Feth, Derdre and Gwen boarded a canvas-roofed transport for the town. Dungarvan appeared livelier than it had after the two battles: most shops were open for business and carts rumbled along the cobblestone streets. The wagon left them by the hospital where Feth hoped to find Sean, but he was not there. So they walked together with arms linked down to the quay, Feth to look in at Sean's room and Derdre to see if her father's ship was expected any time soon. She was told at Squadron Headquarters that *Caillech* was due in that very day.

"He won't know of your mother's death?" Gwen asked Derdre.

"I doubt it. I want to meet him as soon as he gets off the ship."

"You want company?" Feth asked.

Derdre turned to her. "Thank you, friend, but no. Better it's just the two of us. Besides, I have no idea when the ship might come in."

Gwen pointed towards the south arm of the harbor. "It may not be that long."

A three-masted ship, sailing close-hauled into the wind, was rounding the arm of land protecting the bay from the southeast. Moments later, signal horns blared from Squadron Headquarters. The ship cleared the point as they watched, smoothly shifted to the starboard tack and picked up speed.

When the ship was no more than a mile away, Derdre said, "It's the *Caillech*." She put a hand over her eyes and her body trembled. "Oh, I dread this so much!"

Feth embraced her without words. Derdre wiped tears from her cheeks and walked quickly away.

Gwen waited until Derdre was out of earshot. "My heart bleeds for her, Feth. I wish there was more we could do."

Feth stared after her new friend, hurrying down the slip where the *Caillech* would moor.

"Me too, Gwen. I can't even imagine how she must feel."

"My father died when I was six," Feth said as they strolled towards the Inn of the Laughing Gael. "I remember feeling empty and alone. I don't think the permanence of it really sunk in. Conor talked to me about it even though he must have been in agony himself." They stopped under the Inn's sign. "There'll be a service soon, we can help Derdre through that. What's your plan for now?"

"I got paid finally," Gwen said, tapping the leather pouch on her belt. "I'll buy some things I need in the shops. Underwear and sox and winter sweaters. And my dress uniform needs cleaning and mending for the memorial service. Where can I meet you?"

"If I find Sean I may not see you till tomorrow at Derdre's house. Otherwise I'll track you down in the shops."

They clasped hands tightly and Gwen set off towards the town's row of clothiers.

Feth lingered outside to watch *Caillech* swing round on a final tack and glide towards the pier. Sharp orders echoed over the water as the warship covered the last half-mile. Sailors heaved hawsers, waiting dockhands swung them round the bollards, and the warship came to rest. Feth was now certain it was Mairin Fotharta commanding on the quarterdeck. She pondered whether to approach her, but in the end decided it was best not to. Mairin would be busy, and she needed to find Sean.

It did not take long: he was sitting alone alone at a table near the hearth, chin resting on his chest, eyes closed, with a half-full cup of tea on the table in front of him.

She stepped up to his table and leaned over. "Is this chair taken?" she asked politely.

His head came up slowly and his eyes opened. Seeing her, he got to his feet and gathered her in his arms.

"I missed you," he said. "I missed you so much."

"Me too," she spoke into his sweater. "You look more tired than me and I'm ready to fall down."

He held her long enough to draw stares from other patrons. When they at last sat down, a muttering Naomham brought an extra teacup that Sean filled for Feth.

"I worked at the hospital all night," he explained. "I'm learning to be a pretty decent surgical assistant. The blood bothered me at first, now I can handle it on an empty stomach."

She reached out and took one of his hands in her own.

"Sean, I have about twenty-four hours leave. I wish it was more."

He squeezed her hand and smiled warmly. "Then let's make use of every minute."

A half hour and a breakfast later, they climbed wearily up to Sean's apartment. Through the open door, Feth observed startling changes.

The clutter was gone. Even the table was clear of books, replaced by a vase of fresh flowers. A stack of wood had been piled near the stove, bread and cheese and a basket of fruit took up a pantry shelf, and a decent woven rug covered the floor. A larger, solid-looking bed had replaced Sean's single bunk.

"Feth, about the bed," he said as they entered, "if you don't want—"

"Stop," she said, putting a finger to his lips. "I want to be near you, Sean, especially tonight. And thank you for making such an effort. You went to a lot of trouble."

"It was a mess," he said, closing and locking the door. "You deserved better."

She sat on the edge of the new bed, pulled off her boots and eased herself back on the soft, smooth mattress. She wondered sleepily how much he had paid for this luxury.

"What I need," she said, "is three hours' sleep. This afternoon we can do something fun?"

"I have a plan," he said with a knowing look. "Tell you later."

He took off his own boots and sweater and drew a blanket over them. She luxuriated in the sudden warmth, the fresh-smelling pillow, and the safety of his arms around her.

"You know I'm falling in love with you," she whispered drowsily.

"No more than I'm falling in love with you," he said, drawing her closer.

Feth awoke to the clangor of the noonday chimes sounding from the town hall's tower. It had rained for a time: droplets hung on the casement windows. Overhead, a late morning sun's beams slipped through gaps in slow-moving clouds. Sean still slept soundly, his right arm draped over her chest.

She needed desperately to use the bathroom down the hall and managed to extricate herself from the bed without waking him. Being the middle of the day, the hallway was empty and silent, as was the women's bath. She hung her towel on a hook, answered the call of nature, and took a quick glance in the cracked mirror. Her hair was greasy and matted, her skin oily, and though it did not exactly show, she imagined her breath was not pleasant. Thankfully she had taken her kit, and in the space of thirty minutes she remedied the worst problems, despite the sad dribble of tepid water from the bathtub's spigot. She combed her hair straight back, thinking *I look decent, my teeth shine when I smile and my breath won't reek when he kisses me.*

Sean had not awakened. She sat on the edge of the bed and kissed him on the forehead. On the second try he stirred, opened his eyes, and smiled at her sleepily.

"What a nice dream," he said. "I was kissed by a beautiful, alluring young woman." He reached up to stroke her face. "Did the noon chimes ring yet?"

"Yes, that's what woke me up," she said. "Sun is breaking through."

He threw back the blanket and rolled his feet to the floor.

"Let me clean up too, I must smell terrible. Be right back."

While he was gone she fished out of her bag a clean blue sweater that fit a bit more tightly than the rest, gray wool trousers and a jaunty cap. After much searching in the recesses of her satchel, she fished out a tiny fragrance bottle and dabbed some on her neck. Replacing the bottle's stopper drew her attention to her hands: one side smooth, the other hard and calloused. *Nothing to be done there, my caresses will never be soft so long as I serve in the Line of Bows.*

When he returned, he tossed his towel on the bed, pulled her against him, and kissed her deeply until she felt her knees trembling. He held her head against his chest, which smelled clean and male. Desire flooded through her ... tonight, maybe?

He held her at arms' length. "I have a place I want to show you. Not far, a few miles northeast of the city."

"I have to be able to hear a general recall."

"We'll be two miles from the River Glendine Fort, where the river passes between the low hills. You'd hear any alarm from there. Where we're going is outside the Rampart, though."

Her eyes widened at his last statement. "Outside? Is that safe?"

"They patrol the area constantly and they won't let us through the gate if there's been any trouble nearby."

"Okay, as long as we're back before dark."

"We will be."

She nodded assent, turned to the window and threw open the casements. The air was cold and had a delicious rain-washed scent. Half a mile away, *Caillech* rocked at its pier, her ensigns waving proudly in the breeze. Feth's thoughts turned to Derdre and her father, at home perhaps, struggling with the horror of sudden and complete loss.

She felt Sean's arms close around her waist.

"You're thinking of Derdre."

"Yes."

"The service is tomorrow, I saw the posting at the hospital. We'll go together."

She laid her hands over his. "What I can't get into my head is why Derdre had to lose her mother this way. Why is the world punishing us? And why Derdre and her father?"

She turned and gave him a pleading look.

"Oh, dear Feth, I wish I had an answer. I know how we got to where we are, step by step. That's not the same as knowing why we live in such a hard time. I don't think anyone knows that."

"I don't need the answer, Sean. I just need you."

"I need you too," he said, stroking her still-damp hair. "Very much."

He held her awhile longer, then drew the windows shut.

"Let's go," he said. "Six hours till sunset and I don't intend to waste any of them."

Feth gathered up her cloak, a small traveling pouch, and over Sean's objection, took her bow and loaded quiver as a precaution. Minutes later she rode in the saddle behind him on a borrowed, even-tempered gelding named Parlan. The brick-paved streets of Dungarvan gave way to a narrow dirt road winding six miles northeast along the river and through the tiny cluster of houses called An Goirtin. At the foothills a half-mile north of the houses, the Rampart stretched off to the northeast and southwest, while the river and the road crossed underneath the River Glendine fort.

The guard at the fort's gate allowed them through with a stern warning that they had to return before dusk; no one would be sent out to search for them.

"I've been outside the Province before." said Feth. "Always with other soldiers on training patrols."

"Not much to worry about today," Sean said over his shoulder. "Oran showed me this place years ago, and I've come back often. No one lives here because the valley is so narrow. That wasn't always true, though, there are ruins if you look for them."

Thickly-wooded hills rose sharply on either side of the river, which at its widest point was no more than a thirty paces from shore to shore. Wildflowers of varieties Feth had never seen crowded in on the path and lined the river banks. Soon they reached the central point of the pass, with the hills hemming them in on either side. Sean turned Parlan uphill though the trees. Halfway to the top of the rise, the ground leveled out to a broad, grassy meadow. There Sean halted the gelding and they dismounted.

Spread out below them was the meandering river, shining with reflected sunlight that escaped between the clouds. The meadow granted a view of verdant plains to the north and south. Over their heads, a profusion of birds called out over the background rush of the river cascading over a rocky rapids to the north.

"I dream of putting a cabin up here," Sean said. "Not to live all the time ... a place to work away from noise and people. Not that practical, I know. In flood season you'd have to travel along the hillsides unless the river can be navigated then—I've never tried that. And of course it's outside the Rampart. Still, it's close to the fort."

Feth sat cross-legged in the grass and Sean joined her.

"Such a peaceful place," she said. "I see why you like it." She gazed towards fallow, empty fields to the north. "How long since those fields were used?"

"Fifty years probably. They were owned by Province families who moved south behind the Rampart. It's a shame they can't be used for sheep or cattle. Just too many raids in this area over the years."

Feth nodded, trying to imagine what life was like here a century ago.

"What kind of ruins have you found?" she asked him.

Sean brushed a hand over the thick, coarse grass. "Some from not long ago. A cabin once stood at the very top of this hill. Probably from a century or two ago, most of the walls are still standing. If you follow the river north you find much older foundations, some are concrete and not stone. That means at least a thousand years and probably a good deal more."

"So much time," she said with a sigh. "So many people have lived here, walked along that river, maybe sat in the same place as we are now." She paused to listen to a raucous crow soaring over their heads. "I'd like to know more about the people of the west, in Cork and Kerry. I have a feeling what I learned in school is not a fair telling of the story."

Sean laid back on the grass and stared at the clouds.

"Not a fair telling, no," he began. "The true story is not so much in our favor as the lesson books have it. I'll give you the short version, the long one you'll have to read in my next book. When the Province was formed ten centuries ago, the clans holding those regions were invited to be a part of it. If they'd accepted, we'd be something like the Twenty-Eight Clans now. They decided they liked their independent lives the way they were and said no. I don't think it was a big issue at the time, the Twenty Clans was a voluntary association and from what I can tell, relations were always good with those people."

Feth laid back too so her face was close to his. "So what happened?"

"Fifty-some years ago, after the Five Long Winters, we decided to move to the southwest along the coast. At first there was no talk of a defensive barrier, but when starvation spread everywhere, the violence became so terrible we decided to build the Rampart. The clans of Cork and Kerry asked to be included behind the wall and offered to help build it and defend it. You'd think we would have said yes, wouldn't you? That's not what happened. After a bitter fight in the Council of Twenty, the vote was against."

"Why?"

"Ah yes, why? Always the harder question for an historian. The schoolbooks say it was because the Rampart would have been too long to defend, it couldn't have been finished in time, the terrain was unfavorable, all sound tactical and strategic arguments ... if true. The fact is those explanations don't hold water. The real reason was that over the centuries we developed a unique culture and we believed, *still* believe, it was superior to everyone else's. In a few words, Feth, many of our citizens looked down on these people and wanted nothing to do with them. Those attitudes aren't much different today which is why the Council is forever deadlocked on what do do about the west. Your father tried to change things permanently and I think he'd have succeeded, had he lived."

"But now we really need each other," Feth said. "And it's not fair that Gwen and people like her fight for us and we won't help them."

Sean laughed bitterly. "Fair? My love, there is little fairness in this world, except maybe between an honest seller and his customers. Gwen came here by free choice and she's a citizen now."

"So you don't think we should accept their offers of alliance?"

Sean turned to face her. "No, I didn't mean that at all. We should accept. We'd be stronger if we enlisted their help, especially if we have to keep fielding big armies. We're fast running out of people to fight and keep everything else going. You've seen how many shops are empty in the towns, how many farms aren't being worked?"

"Couldn't Padraic try to raise more troops in the west, with or without a formal alliance?"

"He's proposed that at least three times to the Council. Etain Fotharta and her faction block it despite everything your mother and Rionach try."

"It's so complicated," she said, fuming. "There has to be something we can do."

He turned on his side and leaned over to kiss her. "Nothing we can do this afternoon."

He stroked her hair and kissed her again. As if on cue, the sun broke through passing clouds, flooding the meadow with warmth. Was it her imagination, or did the air suddenly seem balmy and fragrant?

They embraced and kissed and before long he pressed her gently back onto the soft carpet of grass. Her mind and body now yielded willingly. *What better place*, came the thought amidst a roar of pleasure and desire, *and what better time than here and now?* And so it was. An hour later, she felt as if her whole body was a fluid. All the aches of her injuries faded away, muscles unknotted, her mind floated free. His face so close to hers was coated with a faint sheen of sweat.

"I love you," he said.

"And I—" A scream shattered the air.

They were no longer alone in the valley of the River Glendine.

Dear Feth, in battle the line between staying alive and dying is often as thin as a blade of grass. You kept your head and your training did the rest. I don't like to agree with Aideen, but she harped on that idea so much it even sank into my poet's brain. Yes, I know Keegan Cholmain well, a fine man and a terrific fighter. I am so glad you met him! Please say hello for me. It's terribly sad what happened to your friend Derdre; it's her good fortune that she now has you for a friend. I know you will help her through the sadness and loss. As for Sean ... I well remember your crush on him though it always puzzled me no end. He is a man of extraordinary talents. His studies and writings will be of great benefit to our people now and long into the future. I hope things work out for the two of you. Lastly, Caillech is Mairin's ship. I miss her and long for the winter when we will have more time together. Make sure you write to your worried mother.

Your loving brother, Conor.

Chapter 15

By late afternoon, twelve centuries of Blades and nine centuries of Bows had set up twenty-one circles of ten tents surrounding a larger captain's tent flying the century's private banner. Century captains walked among the tents, checking off names, inspecting weapons and armor, making sure each soldier had a complete kit for the voyage and march ahead. Off to one side, a mess tent housing the field kitchen belched smoke from its ovens. Fifteen ships crowded the piers: seven warships of the Squadron plus eight large commercial transports.

Conor paced anxiously along the quay, watching for the small vessel that would bring the army commander in from the west. The clear sky and fair north breeze of the morning had given way by late afternoon to a cold blast from the north, the wind rising to gale force making it rough indeed beyond the lee of the shore. Aideen's corvette made it in earlier but Padraic no doubt had been delayed with last-minute work in Dungarvan and suffered the loss of favorable winds.

He had taken it upon himself to assemble the captains and go over Padraic's plans. This task should have been done by Binean Ruairc and Melvina Eogain, Padraic's recently-named Field Army Commanders. Ruairc, a fifty-year-old veteran, had not yet arrived from Waterford, while Bow Commander Melvina Eogain lost her temper entirely in response to a personal affront and stormed out, leaving Conor to exert authority he did not have, a fact he was frequently reminded of over three contentious hours. The task had gotten done, leaving Conor with the feeling he had already fought the main battle itself. He wondered to himself, *how does Padraic stand it?*

Aideen silently observed the long argument in the command tent, sitting in the back row with arms crossed and lips pressed into a disapproving frown. Afterwards she'd left without saying a word. Now she was approaching him from the direction of Squadron Headquarters. No doubt his first batch of criticism was on its way, he imagined. For the twentieth time that day, beginning with the encounter with Bram, he reminded himself to stay calm and say less than came immediately to mind. He physically braced himself as she posted herself a few feet away.

"You did a good job today, brother, in a tough situation."

His eyes widened in astonishment. "Are you serious?"

"Completely."

"You could have helped me instead of just sitting there."

She shook her head. "Not true. With Padraic there I would have contributed, yes. Without him it would have been very impolitic to take over an army staff meeting. And in truth I wanted to see how you'd manage. Your Bow Commander should have held her temper, which you did despite some outrageous provocations. I'd take my hat off if it hadn't already blown overboard."

Conor fought the sensation that he was in a dream. "A compliment from you is a little unexpected, Aideen. I think the last time was maybe twenty years ago."

"I give credit where credit is due. Padraic will be pleased that someone took command of the situation. By the way, the lookouts have spotted his ship, it's beating its way in, he should be here in an hour. I hope our uncle has a strong stomach."

"Binean Ruairc had better get here first," said Conor grimly, "or he'll be cleaning out latrines."

"He's not coming," said Aideen, glancing at a crumpled note in her left hand. "Courier from Waterford brought us a note from the army hospital there. Binean has pneumonia, a bad case. Padraic will need another Blade Commander. He'll ask you to serve, you know."

"At least half the Blade Captains are senior to me, Aideen."

"It's not going to work," she said, clamping a steely hand on his arm. "I know all the captains senior to you and not one of them is fit for that level of command."

"And what makes you think I am?"

Anger flashed over her face. "By all the gods of the sea, you're so infuriating! Of course you're fit for it. Padraic would have promoted you years ago if he didn't worry so much about family favoritism."

He shook free of her hand and turned to face the crowded campground. "Look out there," he said, pointing to the tents. "What do you see?"

"I see an army with excellent discipline and training, the best equipment, high morale and dedication to duty. And well-led."

He nodded. "True enough. Now let me tell you what I see. I see stories and poems never written, songs never sung, children never born, lives snuffed out before they've hardly begun. I see individual soldiers filled with fear yet courageous enough to face death for their people. I see them one at a time and I care about everyone."

"And that," said Aideen, fixing her dark eyes on him, "is exactly why Padraic will ask you to command them. What, do you think he's led the army this long because he's bigger and stronger and has a louder voice than anyone else? Think again, Conor. There isn't a Blade or Bow in the service that doesn't believe he would step in front of them in battle. It was the same with our father. And it's the same with you, I've always known that. You're far more like all those soldiers out there than I am. Plenty of them are just like you, they want families and the peace to raise children in. Why wouldn't they trust you, knowing that's what you want too? This is not a barbarian horde out of the ancient histories, fighting for riches and glory. They need to be led by someone who cares about their lives and wants above all to give them victory over our enemies so their children will have a decent life. Not by someone with an inflated opinion of himself who enjoys giving the orders."

Conor tried to come up with a counter-argument, and failed.

"He will ask me, I know it," he admitted. "He as much as told me so last week at our house."

"You already have responsibility for lives, every time you command a fort. Taking on higher rank is a difference in number but not of kind. Making a mistake can be more costly, I'll grant you that. I've carried that burden around with me for years so I can't feel that sorry for you."

She turned and looked down the pier, where boats were tying up near her corvette. "I've got to get back to my ship and meet with my fleet captains. Believe it or not, I have real martinets in the group, every bit as assertive as your army captains. Good luck, brother."

She turned and headed off at her usual fast pace.

Aideen never said anything like that to me. Why now?

Rain spattered the boards at his feet. He drew his cloak hood over his head and waited for Padraic's ill-fated vessel to dock. The civilian-crewed packet, now a half mile out, struggled against the contrary and gusting wind to reach the fully-protected part of the harbor. Just when it seemed it would have to tack yet once again, the wind shifted slightly and with sails shivering the sloop-rigged craft glided into the slips. The gangplank slammed onto the dock and first off was Padraic himself, general's cloak and a stream of oaths flowing behind him along with his green-faced staff. Conor lowered his hood and saluted as his uncle approached.

"Blast the sea and the winds!" he roared, halting in front of Conor. "Everyone sick and no headway, I should have been here hours ago. Let's get out of this rain."

He stomped off at high speed towards the command tent, Conor at his heels and shaky-legged staff officers trying to keep up. Inside, he ordered the staff to the mess tent for tea to settle their stomachs. When they had all departed, he tugged off his soaked cloak and sank his huge frame into a protesting chair with a sigh of exhaustion. Conor found a pot of lukewarm tea on a sideboard and served Padraic and himself.

"Uncle, after we get business taken care of here you should go to Laigain House and rest," said Conor. "Aideen is certain this gale won't let up till morning and there's no word from Oran yet anyway."

Padraic gulped tea gratefully and nodded. "I may do that, nephew. Much as I hate to admit it, fifty-four is not thirty-four and I am tired. Where may I ask are my Field Commanders?"

"Commander Eogain was meeting with her captains when I saw her last. Binean Ruairc is not coming. Pneumonia."

Padraic stared at his cup. "Pneumonia. Then I have a problem, don't I? Who do you recommend to take his place?"

Conor heard Padraic's subtle challenge: *I dare you to push this onto someone else.*

"Myself, Uncle."

"Agreed," Padraic said with a faint smile. "I'll announce it formally tomorrow morning when we gather all the captains. Find yourself a proper cape and helmet insignia." He stood with a tired grunt. "I think I'll send the staff scurrying around and take up your offer of Laigain House. We'll meet an hour after sunrise tomorrow. You talk to Melvina Eogain. She's new to the job like yourself, but I think you'll be impressed with her. Did she manage the planning session all right on her own?"

"She did fine," he lied. "Everyone is on board with the plan. Before you go ... I need to explain about two guests at our house."

He quickly ran over the events of the day before, finishing with, "I'm sorry about it, Uncle. I had no idea Bram would show up at Kellen's cabin."

"I know you didn't." Padraic sighed heavily, studied his battle-scarred hands. "The time is coming when I will have to deal with him. Is he here?"

"No, I checked. Posted to Ballynamult at the moment."

"All right then, we can let it go for now."

Conor pondered telling Padraic what Bram had said that very morning. Seeing how tired Padraic looked, he decided it was best to wait. Instead, he asked, "Did you happen to see Feth in Dungarvan?"

Padraic smiled. "I did, nephew, I did. She'll be one of our first horse archers. Fifteen minutes' practice and she was getting the hang of it. That pretty face was a bit worse for wear, though," he finished with a frown.

"She's spending time with Sean Osraige."

Padraic's bushy eyebrows lifted. "Really? Now that seems like a strange combination."

"There's more to Feth than sometimes appears, Uncle."

Padraic nodded slowly, thinking. "Yes, I believe you're right about that. Hard for us to see her as an adult instead the pig-tailed young girl."

Staff officers began filing back into the tent.

"General," said Conor formally, "I'll see you later tonight."

Padraic nodded in his direction, already starting to give out orders. Conor headed out into the windy night. The grizzled quartermaster grumbled mightily at being asked to locate a silver cape and Field Commander's insignia. Conor knew the gruff old man and hid his grin at the muttering that accompanied his search in boxes and crates. Then came the expected "very lucky, sir, very lucky indeed" and Conor offered profuse thanks as he donned the items.

He spent the next few minutes transferring his armor and kit from a captain's tent to the larger tent intended for Blade Commander Ruairc. Ten strides away from his new lodgings, he saw Melvina Eogain enter her own tent and close the flap behind her. He decided to look in on her.

"Commander?" he said rather softly to a closed tent flap. "Could I speak with you? It's Captain Laigain."

A moment later the flap parted. "Captain Laigain ... of course, please come in."

He walked in and she quickly offered her hand.

"I'm glad you came," she said, motioning to a chair. "I needed to speak with you."

Conor took the offered chair and she joined him across the table.

"Let me start," she said, "by apologizing for what happened at that session earlier. I was tired and short-fused and I handled it badly."

"Some of the captains were baiting you," Conor said. "Blade Captains are notorious for thinking themselves superior to archers, however senior and competent."

"I knew that," she said with disgust, "and you saw I let it go for awhile? But I got to a point where I couldn't take the jabbing without saying things I would really have regretted."

"Then just as well you left."

"General Conmaicne will be very unhappy when he hears about it."

"He just made me Blade Commander in Ruiarc's absence."

"Congratulations."

He searched for a sign she was offering sarcasm, but saw none. She seemed genuinely pleased at the news.

"So," he went on, "I thought we should get to know each other better. Please call me Conor."

"If you call me Melvina," she replied. "Cider? Still warm, I think."

Conor nodded. She retrieved a spare cup and poured him steaming apple cider. With a quiet moment to study her, he was more certain than ever they had served together in the past. In some ways, she was typical of an archer of thirteen years' service: medium height, slender-waisted, arms and legs thick-corded with muscle and latticed with faint scars. He guessed she was about his own age. Her well-tanned face was friendly if not conventionally pretty. Most unusual were bronze-colored eyes matched to long bronze hair tied into a braid.

"The General did ask about the meeting," he said.

"Ah. What did he say about my abject failure?"

"Nothing."

"He was so angry he was speechless?" she cried.

"No. I told him you did fine."

She set down her cup so hard the cider spilled out. "You lied?"

"I did."

"He may hear the true story from someone else."

Conor nodded while he mopped up the spill. "He might. He'll know why I did it."

"And why did you do it? You don't owe me anything."

"No, I don't," he conceded. "I knew this was your first field command rank, and it's mine too. I had it in mind you could cover for me some time. Beyond that, I don't stand in judgment of others who are doing their best."

Melvina stared at him and shook her head. "Then I owe you, Conor. Not many would have lied to Padraic Conmaicne to cover for someone else." She refilled his cup with cider. "I heard afterward how you handled the situation. I'd like to know how you held your own temper with so much bitching and arguing going on."

"Lose my temper and have it reported to my uncle? I don't think so."

Her eyebrows rose. "Your uncle ... really? I didn't know. Domnall was your father, yes?"

"Yes. Padraic is my mother's brother. No doubt the more senior Blade Captains will have something to say about his naming me to field command."

"No doubt."

Conor leaned back in his chair, cradling his cider. "I'm sure we've served together before but I don't think we've ever talked. You already know about my family, I'd like to hear about yours."

"Nothing quite so glorious," she said with a note of regret. "I grew up in a tiny town called Ballincrea. I went to school like everyone else and enlisted when I turned eighteen. Not much of a story."

Bland words and no inflection, he thought, *but anger and bitterness there.*

"Everyone's story is important," he said aloud, meeting her eyes. "To me, anyway."

The sun sank behind the hills to the west, making the inside of the tent gloomy. Melvina lit the lantern hanging over the table. The tent-walls shook in a gusty wind.

"What do you dream about?" he asked her. "I mean, what do you want for yourself when you don't have to wear this anymore?" He tugged at his uniform tunic.

"Hmm," she said, drumming her fingers on the table. "I guess, being in a real family where people care about me for who I am, not for the amount of work I can do in a day. I didn't have much of that, growing up. I had shoes and enough to eat and all, but no mother and father to love me. How about you? What do you want?"

"A family. A home with children in it. Time enough to write and think and enjoy my friends."

"You don't sound very optimistic about it."

"At the moment, I'm not."

"Why?"

He shrugged. "Complicated. More a topic for a pub conversation. And I didn't mean to be gloomy, it's something of my nature. My sister Feth inherited all of my father's sunny side. My mother and I tend towards melancholy."

"And the Commodore? I saw here here today, someone whispered to me you're brother and sister."

"A bit hard on me, maybe with good reason at times. I tend to go with my heart. Aideen is cool and logical."

"Admirable qualities in a leader," said Melvina, "but we all use what we've been given. Some people say I'm cool too."

"I don't see that at all."

She sighed and offered a tired smile. "Maybe I feel too much inside and don't dare let it show. I don't think on those things much." She reached out her hand. "An honor to serve with you, Conor."

He took her iron-hard hand in his. "The honor is mine, Melvina."

They stood and he drew his cloak around him.

"I'm going to circulate around the camp, see how my Blades are managing."

"I plan to do the same with the Bows," she said. "Goodnight, Conor. And thanks again for saving my ass."

"Any time," he said with a grin. "Goodnight, Melvina."

A cold blast of air struck his face. Overhead he beheld a glorious early twilight, the sky decorated by an burnt-orange moon hanging over the sea and brilliant Venus sinking in the west. He was tired himself, now, and wanted to mount Treasach for a fast ride back to Laigain House and one last night of decent rest. It could not be, yet. His first stop was his new tent, where he donned a sweater under his cloak. When he went back out he nearly collided with a naval courier in Squadron dress. She saluted and handed him a sealed packet.

"For you sir, just came into Rosslare," the young woman said. "I have another for General Conmaicne."

"You know he left for Laigain House?"

The courier nodded. "Yes, sir, I'm on my way."

She saluted again and vanished.

He tore open the packet and found a crumpled, hastily-written note from Oran.

Conor—hope this reaches you. The hurling match is on: I have them located. Not very well organized, slack discipline as usual. But big numbers and plenty of decent weapons. Get ready for a bloody fight. I am in Wicklow, will see you when the fleet is offshore. Stay out of trouble. Oran.

He leaned heavily on the table and breathed deeply with relief. Oran was safe, that was good news. On the less cheerful side, Oran never exaggerated. A bloody fight would be just that.

By now the camp was quiet, though most tents still showed lights inside. He walked among the Blade tents, talking with soldiers, sipping tea, making a list of equipment problems, checking that everyone had a full, hot meal, answering questions as best he could. Two hours later, even the cold north wind in his face was not helping to keep him alert. He headed towards the stable to saddle Treasach. On the way he saw a lone cloaked figure huddling in the lee of a big oak. He made plenty of noise approaching and the figure turned toward him. Pale moonlight outlined a youthful face and straw-colored hair streaming in the wind. The figure snapped straight upright and saluted at the sight of Conor's insignia and cloak.

"Relax," Conor said. "Cold night, eh?"

"Yes, sir," the young soldier said with a nervous edge. "Adrian Loigde, sir, Fifth Century."

The voice was young, too young.

"Conor Laigain." Conor extended his hand. "Now Field Commander of the Blades."

"I knew who you were, Captain," Adrian said as he gripped Conor's hand. "I mean I knew your name anyway. Sorry if I'm out too late, sir."

Conor shook his head. "No formal curfew tonight, Adrian. You do need rest, though. We'll have a long, tough day tomorrow."

"Yes, sir. I was having a hard time sleeping."

In the moonlight it was hard to see the young man's expression, but the tension in his voice was plain enough.

"How long have you served in the Line?"

"Five months, sir."

"And how old are you?"

"Twenty, sir."

"I can check that."

"Ah, eighteen sir, sorry."

Eighteen. And five months service.

"Let me guess, your gut is tied in knots, you can't eat, you're tired and you can't sleep."

Conor saw the young man's eyebrows rise.

"Why, yes sir, I guess that's about it. How did you know?"

"It's the same for me. Ten years in the Line and it's always the same. If I eat before a battle I get sick."

"Really, sir?"

"Sure. I feel that way till the pipes sound. I bet when that happens you're ready to fight, aren't you?"

The handsome young face hardened. "Indeed I am, sir. I cut them down as well as the next man."

"Many fights yet, Adrian?"

"Three so far, the last one at Wicklow last week. You were there too, sir."

"I was. We beat them, didn't we?"

"That we did."

"We're going to do it again, Adrian. You have my word on it."

A broad smile lit up the smooth-skinned, unscarred face.

"We'll have them for breakfast."

"Now get some rest."

The young soldier saluted and walked towards the camp. Conor saddled and mounted a joyful Treasach, then gave him rein to gallop hard through the darkness and cold. The horse knew the road to Rosslare better than he did. In five short minutes the welcoming porch lanterns of Laigain House greeted him. All the bedrooms were dark, save one, Feth's room. Kellen was still up then.

He entered the house without a sound. The clock over the mantle showed midnight and the fire was long out. He pulled off his boots, hung up his cloak, and silently climbed the stairs. He tapped on Kellen's door and heard "come in." He found Kellen propped up with pillows, reading by oil lamp. Conor closed the door and sat on the edge of the bed. Kellen smiled and laid the book aside.

"I was hoping to see you," Kellen said softly. "Padraic told me the news. Congratulations."

He held out his hand which Conor grasped.

"I don't envy you, it's a tremendous responsibility. Wish I was there to help you."

"I wish you were too. How do you feel?"

"Better today. Triona let me walk around, it hurt but not too bad."

Conor traced figures on the bed cover. "I saw your brother today."

"At the camp?"

"No, before, on the road."

"And?"

"No violence. He laughed most of the time."

"Laughed? That's all?" Kellen stared at him intently. "I think there was more than that."

Conor did not answer.

"What did he say?"

"He said ..." Conor swallowed hard. "He implied Mairin was raped by your father."

Kellen sank back into the pillows, eyes closed, breath coming hard.

"Please tell me it's a lie," Conor begged. "If it's the truth ..."

"I don't know," Kellen said. "I was too young to know what was going on most of the time before Mairin left home. Gorman was violent at times, but I never saw him touch Mairin except to belt her. Bram is a vicious liar and he knew telling you that was far worse than using his sword."

"What about her dreams?"

Kellen's eyes widened with fear. "The dreams, yes. It could explain the dreams."

"And Bram could have seen it."

"Yes. He could have."

Conor got up and walked to the window. Below in the lantern-lit yard, a fox strolled in search of prey.

"Gorman would deny it," he said, "and Etain too, if she knows. And I don't dare ask Mairin. Your brother is a very clever man, he stuck a sword in my heart that I can't pull out."

"All you can do is love her, Conor, whether it's true or not. We'll probably never know."

Minutes later in his own room, Conor sat at his writing desk and opened his private journal. He wrote the date and entered one sentence: *I haven't felt so low since my father died.* Then he closed the volume, and slept.

The dominant religions in the Age of Machines insisted on belief in life after death. This belief tended on the one hand to undervalue the life we are given to live on the earth, and on the other encouraged despicable acts to be rewarded in an afterlife. Such faith systems were also characterized by a certainty that seemed to explain nearly every event in life, whether good or evil. The most harmful belief was the notion of mankind's innate superiority over all other creatures. Men were said to have a soul and other living creatures did not. We of the Twenty Clans do not believe in the certainty of an afterlife or in a deity that ultimately rewards certain behaviors. We deny holding a privileged position in the universe of life. We frankly admit that the great cycle of life and death of all living things is a mystery beyond our capacity to penetrate. Whether or not death is an absolute end, none of us can say. Thus when death occurs, we celebrate the life of the deceased and honor his or her memory. We do not expect to see them again.

Uinseann Laigain, Credo Mysterium

Chapter 16

Rowenna Briuin guided the *Caillech* on its final tack around the southern edge of Dungarvan Bay. Mairin and Sinea stood at the taffrail observing the younger officer's crisp handling of the big warship.

"Captain," Sinea said, "why do you think the Commodore ordered us back here instead of the Wales patrol?"

"A very good question," Mairin replied. She pulled out the note that awaited them on their return to Falmouth from Brest. "She didn't waste any words, just load cargo, make all speed for Dungarvan. I expect it's because she plans to be there and wants to see me. Possibly about my taking off to Brest without orders."

Sinea frowned. "Captain, if I may say so, the Commodore can hardly fault your decision. Without us there the Santanders might have taken on the fight and who knows how many lives lost."

Mairin pulled off her hat and absently rubbed salt off the insignia. "She won't do anything drastic, I suppose. I hate taking the dressing down she might offer, even in private. It always seems a bit personal with her. When she says 'Captain Fotharta' it sounds to me like she dislikes something I represent."

Sinea leaned back against the rail and gazed at the fast-approaching pier.

"I think the Commodore envies you, you and Conor, for loving each other and planning a life together."

"Envies me?" Mairin said, a little louder than she intended.

"Yes, sir, envies you. Only my opinion. You assume the Commodore leads the life she wants, but maybe that's not quite the whole story. She may want more, too, or at least did at one time. She sees you finding happiness with Conor and she envies that."

They paused a moment as the last sailing commands were given and *Caillech* glided smoothly toward the pier.

"She doesn't like Conor either."

"Stuff and nonsense," Sinea retorted. "They clash as siblings, sure, but I'll bet my commission she cares about him and wishes she had his capacity for love and friendship."

Mairin replaced her hat and considered. It could be true. Sinea had turned the whole argument around, and it did make sense, strange as it seemed. Never had it occurred to her that anyone would envy her except for purely professional reasons.

"You've given me something to think about, Sinea," she admitted. "Now let me give you something to think about. My report to the Commodore recommends your promotion to captain as soon as a ship is available."

Sinea was stunned into momentary silence.

"You've earned it three times over," Mairin went on, "and much as I'm desperate to keep you here, it isn't fair to you or to the service. We may have as many as ten new ships by spring and we need the best captains to command them."

Sinea swallowed and found her voice at last. "I'd be sorry to leave *Caillech*, and you, Captain. This past year has made a big difference to me. You gave me the chance to grow as an officer, let me make mistakes and correct them on my own. You made me ready for command."

Mairin faced her first officer, met her eyes. "And I've had the luxury of a first officer who never undercut me, never complained, always worked for the good of the ship as a whole, and showed great courage when it was needed. So I think we come out even, Sinea."

Rowenna barked the last few commands, bringing the ship on a parallel course with the pier at the speed of a slow walk. Mairin nodded towards her.

"I plan to ask for Rowenna in your place," she said. "You agree?"

"I do. She's as fine an officer as I've run into, of any age."

"My feeling too," said Mairin. "And that's what I wrote to the Commodore."

The ship slid along the pier and jerked to a halt as cables seized around bollards. A young red-headed woman waited on the pier.

"Captain Fotharta," the woman called out, "could you tell Doctor Dal Reti his daughter Derdre needs to see him?"

"Of course," Mairin called back. "He'll be out in a minute."

She sent Ensign Auteini below to fetch Mor, who generally took his time getting off the ship.

"Something I don't like about this," Mairin said to Sinea. "She doesn't look happy."

"No, she doesn't," Sinea agreed.

Mor emerged from the hatchway carrying his bag and wearing a puzzled look.

"Permission to go ashore," he said to Mairin with a salute.

Mairin read the worry on his face. "Of course, Mor. Let me know if anything's wrong."

"I will," he said over his shoulder.

Her hurried down the ramp and embraced his daughter, who led him down the pier with her arm around her father's waist. Mairin lost sight of them behind a stack of crates. From the same direction an ensign ran towards *Caillech* and bounded onto the quarterdeck.

"Message from Dungarvan Fort, Captain," the ensign said. She handed Mairin a sealed note. "Urgent and confidential."

"Thank you, Ensign," Mairin said, taking the note.

"Sir," the woman said. She saluted and left the ship at a slower pace.

It was unusual to receive a message from the fort. A cold feeling crept into Mairin's stomach as she tore open the seal. A neatly-written note read:

> *Captain Fotharta: I am deeply sorry to inform you that Bow Captain Dunlaith Dal Reti, the wife of your ship's medical officer, has been killed in action. As you may know, his home is here in Dungarvan and his daughter Derdre is currently posted with the Line of Bows at the fort. I thought you would want to know immediately on your arrival.*
>
> *Ft. Cpt. Tearlag Ulaid*

"Bad news?" Sinea asked. With a shaking hand Mairin handed her the note.

"Oh, no. Oh, no," was all Sinea could choke out.

Mairin climbed two flights of stairs to the roof of Squadron Headquarters. She nodded to the sailors manning the powerful telescope and the klaxon; they saluted and paid her no further attention. She wandered to the railing as far from them as possible and gazed out at the harbor, where the Commodore's corvette *Leinster* approached the pier next to *Caillech*. It docked smartly and seconds later the unmistakable figure of the Commodore descended the gangplank and headed towards the headquarters building.

Her heart cringed at the pain Mor must be feeling now. She remembered meeting Dunlaith twice: once here in Dungarvan, and another time in Waterford. The love between them had been so obvious, so natural. On their outward voyage to Falmouth, Mor told her that Dunlaith was about to retire from the Line of Bows. When she did, he planned to leave the Squadron and take up a medical practice in Dungarvan. He said eight months. *And now, she's gone.*

She heard a nervous rustle behind her. Aideen Laigain strode towards her and returned her salute.

"I would have come down, Commodore," Mairin said. "I left word."

"I know," said Aideen with a causal wave of her hand. "I like the view from up here."

Mairin handed over her report, noticing with dismay that she had unconsciously crumpled it.

"Sorry about that, sir," she said, "I had some bad news waiting when we docked. I'll get you a better copy."

Aideen took the report, smoothed it out and glanced quickly at the first page.

"No matter," she said, tucking it away. "What news?"

"Mor Dal Reti's wife was killed in battle."

For the first time in seven years of acquaintance, Mairin saw Aideen's cool composure break and give way to some vestige of sorrow.

"Oh, that is very bad news. Mor knows?"

"His daughter was waiting on the pier. I got a note from a fort captain."

Aideen fell silent and turned away briefly. "Give him my condolences, if you would."

"I will, Commodore."

A long moment of silence intervened. When Aideen turned back, her face had resumed its usual unreadable mask. She pointed towards *Caillech*'s jerry-rigged portside rails.

"You were boarded?"

"The Santanders tried. We were carrying Admiralty marines so I took no casualties. My report gives the details."

"I'm sure it does," Aideen said. "You sailed out with *Ajax*?"

"Yes, sir. I sent a note from Falmouth."

"I believe Captain Tredinnick is a friend of yours, is he not?"

Ye gods, how much does she know?

"Yes, sir, we met on convoy duty several years ago. I'd say we're friends. But I made my decision to depart from orders based on the situation, not on personal feelings."

"I would hope so, Captain. In any event, there's no time for analyzing the matter. I'll have new orders for *Caillech* by late tonight. Where will you be?"

"I'll make sure headquarters knows, sir. I'd like to stay in port long enough to attend the memorial service."

Aideen nodded. "I'll do what I can but I can't promise. Time is short." She turned to leave.

"Commodore, a brief word?"

"Brief, Captain."

"In my report, I recommend Sinea Danaan for promotion to captain and request that my second officer Rowenna Briuin be promoted to first."

"I'll approve it," Aideen said, "but I have no lieutenants to give you."

"I'll promote among the ensigns, sir."

"Usually not a good idea ... but it's your call." She walked two steps away, then paused and looked back.

"I am so sorry about Mor's wife," she said. "Please let him know."

"I will, Commodore."

"He has a daughter, does he not?"

"Yes, Derdre, about twenty I think."

A strange look came over Aideen's face. "I was twenty when my father died. I remember when he ..."

She trailed off, her mind in another place and time entirely. One of the sailors on watch broke into laughter and Aideen's reverie terminated with a snapped, "tend to your duties, sailor." Aideen spun on her heel and vanished down the staircase. Mairin lingered for a time at the railing, pondering what just happened. How unusual to see the Commodore obviously affected by the news about Mor's wife. And could Aideen know that Richard was far more than a casual friend made in the line of duty?

She returned to the ship long enough to change into civilian clothes, then strolled out into Dungarvan's market square. It seemed quieter than usual, fewer vendors crowded the square, and some shops had posted "closed" signs. While glancing at a rack of winter cloaks and sweaters, Mairin saw two figures emerge from an inn across the square and mount a waiting horse. She could not see their faces. From the back one rider appeared to be a broad-shouldered young woman with trimmed blond hair, her companion a slender man who mounted with less grace than the woman. The woman held a bow in her hand; a quiver full of arrows was belted across her back. Was that Fethnaid? Mairin waved and shouted to no avail: the horse trotted down the street away from her and disappeared around the next corner.

She bought a close-knit dark sweater and matching wool trousers, thanked the merchant, and made her way to the inn the two riders had come out of. The Inn of the Laughing Gael brought back memories of her ensign days: she had eaten there often enough with her ship-mates. She went in and took a seat at a small table near the hearth. In one corner she spotted a party of *Caillech*'s sailors and in another, her three ensigns.

The innkeeper, a bulky, bearded man, sauntered over and hovered at her table.

"Spiced wine," she said. "Warm if you have it."

When he returned with her order, she asked him, "Is there a young blond-haired woman staying here, carries archer gear?"

"Not staying here exactly," he grunted, "but she camps out with one of my tenants."

"May I ask which one?"

"Seanlaoch Osraige, usually pays his rent late. Room seven. They just left."

"Yes, thanks, I missed them. Friends of mine. I'll take lunch, whatever you're serving."

Too bad, she thought, it would have been nice to see Feth. Sean too, though she didn't know him well. A few minutes later the inn-keeper delivered a bowl of hot potato soup and a loaf of steaming bread. She took her time with it, in hopes the decent meal would settle her churning emotions. The meal finished, she ordered a flask of tea and did her best to unwind. As she poured her third and last cup, a tall, black-haired young woman carrying a thick-limbed bow and a canvas travel bag entered the pub alone. She glanced around uneasily, as if not certain she would stay. Finally she drifted to an empty table near Mairin's and sat down. The innkeeper asked her what she wanted, and Mairin heard her order lunch and cider in a faint accent Mairin associated with Tralee.

She may well know Feth if she is stationed here, Mairin surmised. *Worth a try.* She turned her chair slightly and leaned in the woman's direction.

"I beg your pardon ... do you happen to know Fethnaid Laigain?"

The archer jumped, not expecting to be spoken to. Uncertainty filled the eyes that met Mairin's.

"Well, yes, I met her last night at the fort," she said as if being challenged.

"Relax," said Mairin. She smiled and reached out with her right hand. "My name is Mairin, a friend of hers. Her brother's girlfriend, actually."

Looking relieved, the archer accepted her hand. "You mean Conor? She talked a lot about him. My name is Gwen Cennedi, from Fahamore Town—near Tralee."

"Oh, I know where Fahamore is," said Mairin. "On the peninsula that guards Tralee Harbor."

Gwen's face took on a look of pure amazement.

"How do you know that? No one here knows my town! Have you been there?"

"Not exactly," Mairin laughed, "but I've been within a mile or two. I serve in the Province Squadron, been to Tralee many times. Join me."

Gwen switched tables just as the innkeeper arrived with her lunch and cider. The man stood by waiting for payment.

"On my bill," Mairin told him. "And bring us some cakes if you have any."

"Thank you," said Gwen, "but you didn't need to do that. I got paid today!"

Mairin waved a hand. "Don't worry about it. A friend of Feth's is a friend of mine."

Gwen dove into her lunch while Mairin sipped tea.

"I'm pretty sure I saw Feth a little while ago, on a horse with a young man."

"Sean," Gwen said between mouthfuls. "We have leave till tomorrow morning, they were probably going on a picnic somewhere. Were you on the *Caillech*?"

"Yes, that's my ship."

"We watched you come in. You have some damage."

"A whopper of a storm, then a battle off the coast of Brest."

"Can you tell me about the battle?"

"I probably shouldn't in a pub," Mairin said. "I can tell you the ship we fought came off the worse."

"I'm sure," Gwen said with a grin. "Tell me, what do you think of Tralee?"

"I like it a great deal," Mairin replied. She summoned up a mental picture of the western port with its clean streets, picturesque shops and lively dockside market. "The people are friendly and the food is excellent. The first time I was there ... "

While Mairin described her first visit to Tralee, the group of sailors quietly made an exit, each one nodding in her direction. Then the three ensigns got up to leave but deliberately walked by the table, as they did so touching their hats and saying "Captain."

Gwen set her spoon down. "You're not a sailor! I'm sorry, I should have, I mean, you don't—"

"Look like a captain?" Mairin said, grinning. "I'm not in uniform. And in any case, what should a captain look like?"

"Older, meaner-looking, you know, pushy or something."

"Sometimes my crew and my officers think I'm pushy," said Mairin, fingering her teacup. "To be honest, most warship captains just look tired, however old they are."

The innkeeper arrived with two frosted honeycakes. Gwen dove into hers and then looked up, embarrassed.

"I'm sorry, I'm eating like a barn animal. I haven't had anything this good in weeks."

"Have at it," said Mairin, taking a big bite out of her own cake. "I am."

The cakes demolished in short order, Mairin asked, "Are you staying in town? Or going back to barracks?"

"I have a friend to stay with, Derdre Dal Reti." Gwen paused and stared down at her empty plate. "Her father lives here. Her mother, well—"

"I know about her death," Mairin broke in. "Mor is my medical officer and a dear friend. I knew Dunlaith too, a little. Sad to say, I've never met Derdre."

"I'm supposed to meet her at the clock in the square around one. I'm sure her father will be with her."

She retrieved her bow from a wall peg.

Mairin laid coins on the table to cover the full tab. "I'll join you there. I'd like to see how Mor is doing. If the pub's clock is right, we have a half-hour. I need to stop by my ship for a moment to check on repairs."

Leaving Gwen to browse the vendors, Mairin walked out onto the pier where *Caillech* was moored. Apparently Aideen had left orders that *Caillech* was to be ready for sea at the earliest possible moment, and by the looks of things, that might be the next day. Mairin chatted briefly with the crew chief and then left him to his work.

She took a room at her favorite inn not far from the quay and returned to the square, where she found Gwen waiting with Mor and Derdre. Derdre's red hair and freckles must have come from her mother, Mairin imagined, but father and daughter shared bright green eyes and a wide mouth that suggested warmth and compassion. Mor looked stunned and hollow-eyed. Derdre had locked her arm tightly around his.

Mairin embraced Mor and whispered in his ear, "I am so sorry, my friend." They parted to arms' length. Mor's hands dug into her arms.

"The service is this evening, Captain," he said in a husky voice. "All are welcome to come. There'll be food and drink at my home later." He seemed at a loss for words for a moment, then released her arms and turned towards Derdre. "Captain, my daughter."

"Derdre, I so wish we'd met under better circumstances," Mairin said, taking Derdre's hands in her own. "Your father never stops talking about you."

"As he does about you," said Derdre. "Maybe tonight, after the service, we can get better acquainted?"

"I'd like nothing better. When and where is the service? I need to get word out to the crew."

"Eight o'clock at the cemetery north of town," Mor said. "Anyone can point you the way."

"What can I do to help?"

Mor smiled in gratitude. "Thanks, Captain, but nothing at the moment. The three of us are going to my home now, prepare for the service and the meal afterwards. We'll be fine." His eyes drifted towards the *Caillech* where the repair crew was finishing up work on the forward rails. "They seem in a hurry, Captain."

"They are. I have a feeling we won't be here long. Let me give you shore leave, at least a week."

Mor shook his head. "I appreciate that, Captain, but I don't think I want leave. Derdre is due back at the fort tomorrow morning, and frankly, sitting around our house alone would be worse than being at sea with friends."

"Then I'll see you at the service. Oh ... Commodore Laigain sends her condolences."

"Tell her thank you, if you see her again."

"I will."

Mairin spent another hour shopping and strolling about the town. For Conor she bought a fine belt of the kind he favored: leather dyed a deep red-brown with a shiny brass buckle ornamented with delicate open whorls. For herself she indulged in decent blouse, dress slacks that fit a body she could not keep weight on, and a heavy tweed cloak for the coming winter. Passing by a bookseller's booth, she thought of Richard and his love of old volumes. When would she see him again? Would he take a gift the wrong way? In the end she passed the booth by, to the obvious disappointment of the hopeful vendor.

Made sleepy by the warm afternoon sun, she returned to her room and slumped into a chair that was well-stuffed if a bit worn. She dozed on and off for an hour, then returned to the ship to collect her dress uniform for the service. On the way back to her room, she stopped at the Inn of the Laughing Gael and climbed the stairs to Sean's apartment. She knocked, and hearing no answer, she found the door unlocked and went in. The room was neat and tidy, though overflowing with books and manuscripts and smelling somewhat of moldy paper. A travel bag lay open in one corner, in it a Line of Bows blue uniform. Using paper and pen she found on the room's single table, she left a note telling Feth where she was staying and the time and place of the service for Dunlaith. Then she returned to her own inn, left word with the innkeeper to be awakened at six o'clock, and sank quickly into sleep.

The innkeeper's pounding on the door forced her upwards from deep, dreamless slumber. For the first time in days she felt able to focus her mind clearly. She went to the window: long, slanting shadows crossed the town square. Vendors were closing their booths, shoppers strolled towards their homes, a few children ran about and shrieked right below her window. What would it be like, she wondered, to live here? To have a house on a quiet street, surrounded a whitewashed fence, with flower boxes in front and a garden in back? Children trudging off to school each morning and returning home each afternoon carrying their drawings and carefully-scripted papers. A husband who worked hard by day and warmed the bed by night. Each day much like the next.

Could I do that? Could I live that way?

One of the children below, a girl no more than six with long black hair and a soiled smock, saw her and waved. She smiled and waved back. Then a little boy pinched the girl, who promptly shrieked and chased him down the block.

Mairin stood there awhile longer, her eyes wandering back and forth from her ship to the restaurant patrons and hand-holding couples out for a stroll. *Maybe*, she answered her own question. *Maybe I could.*

She changed into a robe and indulged herself a full half-hour in the bath down the hall. Returning to her room, she donned a dress uniform that saw so little use. Closely-fitted blouse and slacks shared the forest green color of an officer's working tunic, but were made of a shiny fabric and trimmed with silver piping. Black leather boots reached up to mid-calf. The sea-green formal jacket was curved and open in front, trimmed with silver buttons and triple piping. Her captain's rank was displayed by a pair of large gold anchors, one on each shoulder. The Celtic Cross of the Province, symbolizing sacrifice in its crossed arms and unity in its circle, was embroidered on the left side of her chest; on the right were pinned her numerous service medallions. The formal hat's color matched the jacket's medium green, but unlike the standard tri-corner for everyday use, this hat was round with a small bill in front on which appeared "*Caillech*" in ornate silver letters. Normal dress wear would be completed by a broad white sash worn at the waist; on occasions of mourning the sash was black.

The room's wall-mounted mirror was rather fogged and set too low; she had to bend to comb her hair and square the hat. When she stood erect, her head disappeared. *The uniform is baggy, lost weight again.* Nothing to be done now, it would have to do. She threw a cloak over her arm against the night's chill and headed across the square to see if Feth and Sean had returned.

She found her note untouched. Wherever they had gone for the afternoon, it seemed odd they would stay out past nightfall. The beginnings of uneasiness crept into her mind. Who would know where they were? Surely the scholarly Sean would never take a serious risk?

She left a second note beside the first, then made her way north to the edge of town where she fell in with Sinea and Rowenna. Together they walked the last half-mile to the cemetery. The town's buildings gave way to a quiet country lane canopied by ancient trees. On either side of the lane, ruined buildings overgrown with shrubs and vines created an eerie effect in the deepening gloom. By the time they reached the clearing in front of the cemetery, twilight had vanished entirely. Large lanterns on tall poles burned brightly on either side of the road that bisected the cemetery, the markers of which stretched on into the darkness. Mairin and her crew formed up to the left in two long, plank-straight lines.

A platform of polished bluestone supported the casket. Its dark-stained wood was decorated with intricate carvings of the ancient Celts: knots and open spirals and crosses all linked in complex patterns with no beginning and no end. The top of the coffin was covered with a white linen cloth adorned with the green Celtic Cross of the Province near the head and the crossed golden arrows of the Line of Bows near the foot. Mor in his own dress uniform stood to the left side of the bier with Derdre by his side. Gwen, on the right side of the bier, held her flute ready in her hands.

In response to muted commands from the senior captains present, twenty Blades in full battle armor formed a line leading to the bier on the left, while an equal number of Bows formed a parallel line to the right. When they were all in position, the presiding Elder in robes of blue and tan stepped forward to stand in front of the casket. He was elderly and stooped yet his voice rang out strongly.

"Friends and kin of Dunlaith Ulaid Dal Reti. It is our custom as a people to mourn the loss of our friends, yet also to recognize that all living things come into being and all perish. The ancient Latin has it, *memente, homo, quia pulvis es, et in pulverem reverteris*, remember, Man, that thou are dust, and unto dust thou shalt return. We believe that the cycle of life and death is one of the great mysteries of the world, a mystery we must experience yet not fully understand. Our sister Dunlaith lived among us forty-two years, became a wife to Mor and mother to Derdre. She served in the Line of Bows for twenty years, signified by the twenty Blades and twenty Bows in line of battle before me. She loved her family, was true to her friends, and defended her people bravely without thought of her own life. Greater praise can be given to no person. Her daughter Derdre will now sing the funeral hymn."

Gwen raised the flute and from it poured sweet melody. Mairin shivered as Derdre's clarion alto, on the edge of breaking with sadness, soared out over the people and into the fields beyond.

> *I will arise and go now, and go to Innisfree,*
> *And a small cabin build there of clay and wattles made.*
> *Nine bean rows will I have there, a hive for the honey bee,*
> *And live alone in the bee-loud glade.*
> *And I shall have peace there, for peace comes dropping slow,*
> *Dropping from the veils of the morning to where the cricket sings.*
> *There midnight's all a-glimmer, and noon a purple glow,*
> *And evening full of the linnet's wings.*
> *I will arise and go now, for always night and day*
> *I hear the lake water lapping with low sounds by the shore.*
> *While I stand on the roadway, or on the pavements grey,*
> *I hear it in my deep heart's core.*

A visibly-moved Elder said, "Mor Dal Reti will recite the Litany of Life and Death and all are asked to join him."

Mor stepped in front of the casket, raised his eyes skyward, and intoned the ancient words in a strong voice. Everyone present spoke the words with him.

We are blessed with a beautiful land, for which we are thankful.
We are blessed with brightness of day, for which we are thankful.
We are blessed with the splendor of night, for which we are thankful.
We are blessed with the changing of seasons, for which we are thankful.
We are blessed with the wonder and mystery of living things, for which we are thankful.
We are blessed with the love of friends and family, for which we are thankful.
We are blessed with life and the capacity to know, for which we are thankful.
We are blessed with our unity as a people, for which we are thankful.

Mor stepped back beside the casket. From the left, the senior Blade captain snapped out, "Blades, present." Slowly and in perfect unison, the twenty soldiers drew swords from steel scabbards, the harsh rasp of metal on metal a powerful contrast to the gently song and solemn litany. Each blade was raised upward and held at shoulder height.

Then the senior Bow Captain ordered, "Bows, present." The archers raised their bows in unison to point at a high angle. The Bow Captain strode along the line and with a flaming torch lit the incendiary tar coating the tip of each arrow. When she had lit all twenty, she turned, extinguished her torch, and ordered, "loose arrows." One by one, the flaming arrows soared high into the black sky, disappearing over the line of trees that bordered the clearing. When the last arrow vanished from sight, a long moment of silence was observed.

"Those who wish," the Elder said, breaking the silence, "may come to Mor's home, eat and drink and speak of our sister Dunlaith. The service of remembrance and honor is ended."

Mairin found herself transfixed by the power of the service. In the few extra seconds she remained still, a cloud of thoughts and feelings swirled through her mind. Memories of friends lost in battle, of Conor and Feth and so many others who could easily be lying there in place of Dunlaith, followed by a stunningly clear recollection of her Aunt Mairin for whom she had been named and who was her lifeline to sanity in childhood days. The sudden death of that kind woman drove her to utter despair and thoughts of suicide. Dearest Aunt Mairin ...

"Captain?"

Sinea's hand was on her arm.

"Yes ... yes, Lieutenant, we should go."

She kept silent as she led her two lieutenants along the dark cobblestone path. Reaching the town, they followed other mourners to Mor's home, a modest stone cottage on a street of similar houses. His neighbors had lit porch lanterns and set out tables of food and drinks on the brick sidewalk in front of Mor's home. *This is what it's like,* Mairin thought wistfully, *to be part of a community, to have a place called home where your neighbors are your friends.*

Mairin stayed for a time, spoke again with Mor and Derdre and Gwen, talked over progress on the ship's repairs with her officers, and finally decided it was time to see if Feth had returned. Surely she and Sean had not planned to be away after sunset? She made a short detour along the quay: work on the *Caillech* continued by the light of glaring lanterns. Repairs were complete. Now the dock crew was stuffing *Caillech's* empty holds with food, water, naval supplies, and ammunition.

The pub at the Inn of the Laughing Gael was crowded with dockworkers, merchants, and soldiers on leave. She did not find Feth and Sean there, nor had they returned to his room: both her notes lay on the table where she'd left them. At the window she peered down at the town clock, which read a quarter before nine. Could they have camped somewhere and planned to return at dawn? That did not fit with what she saw earlier in the day: the horse carried no bulging saddlebags. She ran quickly through other possibilities: romantic fun that drove away thoughts of the time; an injured horse; helping someone else along the road.

The surly innkeeper told her where they rented the horse: a stable at the rear of the inn. Mairin found its affable owner mucking out stalls; he too was getting worried. He knew Sean and took him at his word that he would return the horse before sunset.

Mairin trotted back to Mor's house, where she found the outside lights extinguished, guests departed, Gwen and Derdre cleaning up, and an exhausted Mor collapsed in a chair.

"Captain?" said Mor with a questioning look. "We have our orders?"

Derdre and Gwen stopped what they were doing.

"Not yet," Mairin replied. "I'm getting worried about Feth and Sean. They've been gone since noon on horseback and the stable owner says Sean promised to be back by dusk. Any idea where they might've gone?"

"Which road did you see them take?" Derdre asked.

"They were headed northeast, unless they turned when they were out of my sight."

"That's a well-traveled road," Derdre said. "Goes through meadows and farms and eventually reaches the Rampart at the River Glendine Fort. It would be hard to find trouble anywhere along it."

Mor ran a hand through his hair, thinking. "River Glendine. That rings a bell, a vague one. Let me think a minute. I know Sean somewhat, we both belong to a local history club and he's given a lecture or two for us. I haven't seen him in six months. We had a side conversation at the last meeting. He was so enthusiastic we continued it out in the street afterward. He talked about a favorite place of his. I know he mentioned River Glendine."

"Father, can you remember where?" pressed Derdre. "Anything specific?"

Mor paced back and forth. "Wait ... I have it! He talked about the Vale of the Glendine. It's an easy ride, maybe an hour at most. But ..." he trailed off.

"But what?" Mairin demanded.

"It's outside the Rampart, not far to be sure, but outside. A couple of miles north of the fort."

"I don't like the sound of that at all," said Gwen.

Derdre grabbed her bow and quiver and handed Gwen hers.

"Father," said Derdre, throwing on a cloak, "we'll take both our horses and ride hard to the River Glendine fort. If they haven't been seen there we'll ride back and ask at every farm and house along the way."

Seconds later their horses pounded down the road. Mairin lowered herself into a chair and rubbed her hands over her eyes.

"What's the expression, Mor, trouble comes in threes?"

Mor collapsed into a chair opposite her, leaned back and closed his eyes. "Dunlaith, and now this. I shouldn't ask ... what's the third?"

"The orders we'll probably get from the Commodore."

He opened his eyes. "You know what they'll say?"

"Not exactly, no. Aideen said I'd have them tonight. She has every worker in the port repairing and loading *Caillech*. I don't expect a routine patrol off Wales."

Mor nodded, then let his eyes drift toward the fire in the hearth. "I can't begin to comprehend the loss. I'd hate to be alone in this house tonight, Captain."

"Please ... not 'Captain' when we're here alone. I sometimes forget what my given name is. When did you last see Dunlaith?"

"A week ago, at the end of our shore leave. She got leave from the army until the first attack here last week. Derdre was home too, off and on. It was a wonderful time." Tears welled up in his eyes. "I'm glad now we had that time even if it makes the loss all the harder to bear. I told you we had plans?"

"Yes. She was going to retire next spring."

"So close," he whispered to himself. "So very close."

"Derdre—"

"Could have died in the same battle."

Mairin could not find anything to say. Her heart bled at the sight of his anguish.

Mor got up and disappeared down the hall. Mairin heard the sound of splashing water, and when Mor returned, the tears were gone. He rummaged about in a bureau drawer, pulled out a box and set it on a side-table.

"Mairin, I need a distraction. I just can't dwell on the pain, it makes it worse. Chess?"

"Are you sure?"

"Yes. I'll serve coffee."

She sat bolt upright. "You have coffee?"

He went into the kitchen and returned with a small, oil-stained paper bag.

"My one indulgence when we laid over in Falmouth. I traded a surgeon I know there for my best surgical scissors. A full pound of the best African beans, dark-roasted."

Mairin dragged her chair in front of the side-table and began to set up the pieces. "For coffee, you can checkmate me as much as you like."

Mor stoked the hearth-fire and served mug after mug of the precious drink while they maneuvered the pieces. A quiet hour passed, then a soft tap at the door broke their concentration. Knowing Derdre would not knock, Mor took his time answering it. A young sailor stood outside, a packet in her right hand.

"Doctor Dal Reti," she said, "I have orders for Captain Fotharta."

"Yes, come in."

He moved aside so she could deliver the packet into Mairin's hands. Having done so, the sailor saluted crisply and dashed out. Mairin opened the sealed envelope and read the printed text above Aideen's scrawled signature.

"Captain?" said Mor. "Sorry ... slipped out."

"We sail in the morning. As we expected."

"To where?"

"You are ordered," she read aloud, "to proceed offshore of Dungarvan, rendezvous with the *Wexford*, *Morrigan*, and *Rosc Catha*, assume command of the battle group and proceed with all possible speed to Falmouth, there to join in fleet operations to seize the Cantabrian base at Santander Harbor, Spain."

"All-out war," Mor said with resignation. "We knew it had to come."

"You'd better make sure to replace the scissors."

"Already done," he said. "Let's finish our game. And the coffee."

Mairin set the orders aside and tried to focus on the complexity of the middle-game.

"I'm in a difficult situation," she commented, her hands clasped under her chin. "Your rooks are pressing me hard."

"No help from me," he said, taking his own chair. "Your move."

Dear Sean, Your letter found me at Kilmore Quay stuffing myself on our mother's cooking after months of living off the land and not living too well off of it. In the midlands and the north, agriculture as we practice it is virtually destroyed by late springs, early freezes, and torrential rains combined with endless droughts. All the draft animals are gone, not many horses left either. I hoped for a week's rest but it's not possible. Padraic is launching two field armies soon and I have to scout out where our enemies are and how best to attack them. As for your question about non-Celts entering the north of Eirelan, I can't report much detail. I've collected some odd scraps of paper and one small book that I enclose with this letter. I hope you can figure out who these people are and what they might want in our land. I'm happy to hear about Feth, last time I saw her in between her final training sessions, I was astonished how she had changed. Give her my love.

Your devoted brother, Oran.

Chapter 17

The shriek of pain shattered the peaceful calm of the Vale of Glendine. Feth and Sean leaped to their feet. Behind them, Parlan paced nervously and sniffed the air.

"Voices," Sean whispered, "right below us."

"We have to go down," she whispered back. "Armed."

Sean nodded and pulled a sheathed knife from Parlan's saddle. Feth retrieved her bow and strapped on the quiver. Sean tethered Parlan to a tree and they started downhill, moving quietly through thick underbrush. About halfway down, they heard a male voice, hushed and urgent, and a female voice answering in what sounded like painful gasps. They moved on in the direction of the voices. Through the last few yards of forest and underbrush, they spied a woman lying on the ground near the water's edge and a man crouched next to her. Two battered leather packs lay on the ground next to them.

Feth whispered in Sean's ear, "what do you think?"

"I think they need help."

Feth nodded and together they walked out into plain view. The man jumped up and raised his hands in the air.

"We're no threat to you," he said, his eyes fixed on Feth's bow.

"We know that," Feth replied. "Who are you?"

"My name is Vaughn, my wife is Murel. We were running, she fell back there," he gestured upstream, "and hurt herself. I carried her this far but she's in too much pain to carry any further."

Feth walked with Sean to where Murel lay moaning. Her light brown tunic was torn and stained with mud, her face pale and twisted with pain. Feth knelt down and leaned towards her face.

"Murel?" she said. "We'll help you, just lie very still."

"Yes, all right," Murel replied through gritted teeth. "Help us get away, please."

Feth ran her fingers down Murel's leg and felt the ugly break just below her knee. She got to her feet and pulled Sean and Vaughn a few feet away.

"I'm not a doctor," she said, "but I think that's a dangerous kind of break. We'll have to find a way to splint it and then carry her as gently as we can to the fort." She looked at Vaughn. "Before we do that, I'd like to know who you are and why you're running."

"We stole money from Clan Cuirenrige," Vaughn replied, speaking fast. "We planned to bribe our way inside the Rampart. I'll explain everything later. The men chasing us can't be far behind and they mean to kill us. I must ask you to trust me."

Feth glanced at Sean, who gave a slight nod of his head.

"All right," Feth said, "we'll help you to get to the fort. My name is Feth and this is Sean. How many chasing you, how armed?"

"Three, possibly four men, on foot, swords and knives."

Feth pondered the options quickly. "Vaughn, can you tear me some strips of cloth? And I need a straight piece of wood."

"I'll get Parlan," said Sean. He tore uphill into the overgrowth.

Vaughn pulled a piece of clothing from his bag and tore it up, then found a straight fallen limb that he snapped off for the splint. Feth knelt next to Murel, dipped a cloth in the river and handed it to the frightened woman.

"Put this in your mouth and bite on it," she said to her. "As bad as it hurts now, it will get worse."

Murel took the cloth and nodded. "I'll manage. Go ahead."

Vaughn took hold of his wife's hands and Feth did what she had to do. Murel shuddered with pain.

"Done," Feth said, tying off the cloth. "It won't hurt so much now."

Vaughn took the damp cloth from his wife's mouth, dipped it again in the river, and mopped her ashen face.

Sean rode up on Parlan, and together Vaughn and Feth hoisted Murel into the saddle in front of him. Sean brought his arms around Murel, took the reins and started Parlan down the trail towards the fort at an easy pace. Feth slung Murel's pack on her back, Vaughn grabbed his own, and they followed on foot. Feth kept her bow in her left hand with an arrow nocked to the string.

"Are you armed at all?' she asked Vaughn in a low voice.

"A knife is all," he said. "I take it you use that bow for more than hunting."

"Yes," she said, "I fight in the Line of Bows, if that means anything to you."

"More than you might think," he replied. "I lived inside the Province for a year. I had a job in a brewery where they didn't take a big interest in where you came from."

Feth stopped and held up a hand. Over the soft burble of the river and the call of distant larks, male voices echoed along the canyon.

"They're catching up," said Vaughn. "I knew they weren't far back."

Feth looked down the trail towards the fort. Sean was out of sight. Then she studied their immediate surroundings and spotted what she needed: a gnarled oak with a long, thick branch hanging out over the river.

"Quick, help me into that tree."

Vaughn followed her to the base of the tree, where she hid Murel's pack in the underbrush. Vaughn's powerful arms hoisted her up without effort.

"What's your plan?"

"I'll crawl out on this branch, as far as I can. You walk down the trail ten yards or so. They'll focus on you and not see me. How will I know it's the Clan Cuirenrige men?"

"I think that will be obvious." He drew his knife with a frown. "I don't like the idea of you protecting me."

The voices were nearby now, echoing between the valley's high sides.

"Do as I say!" she hissed. "No time for debate."

He hesitated a second more, then did as she ordered. Feth crawled out over the gently-flowing water, turned, set one leg over each side of the limb, and raised her bow to shooting position. She counted the voices—three if everyone was speaking. They were making no attempt at stealth, that was sure. Twigs cracked. Three men passed by, moving fast. By the time they saw Vaughn she had clear line of fire at their backs.

"Caught up with you!" one of the men jeered with a gravelly laugh. He drew his sword. "Now, where's that pretty wife of yours?"

She loosed an arrow at the speaker. The arrow struck him in the center of his back and burrowed through his torso. He gave out a gurgling scream and fell on his face. The other two whirled in her direction, but by then a second arrow flashed out. Her target fell backwards without a sound. The third man spotted her and in one quick motion drew his knife and hurled it. The blade flew straight at her belly. She shifted sideways far enough so the blade slashed through her sweater and the flesh of her left side. The man was reaching for his sword when Vaughn drove his knife into the man's back. He moaned once and toppled forward.

Her side flamed with pain. She slid down the branch to where Vaughn could reach her. When he lifted her down his right hand came away coated with blood. He pulled up the torn sweater to expose the wound.

"Long, not too deep," he said.

"Get something to press on it."

Vaughn retrieved Murel's pack and found a clean white cloth that he folded into a compress. She pressed it to the wound. Pain flared anew and black spots momentarily swam in front of her eyes. Vaughn pulled off his broad leather belt and cinched it snugly around her waist to hold the compress in place. He grabbed Murel's pack in one hand and her bow in the other.

"How far are we from the fort?"

"Maybe two miles. I'll make it all right. If I pass out, carry me, just don't stop."

They walked at the fastest pace Feth could manage. She focused her mind on her training: drink lots of water, keep pressure on the wound, breathe deeply, stay relaxed. Blood was oozing down her leg and it would be best if she didn't arrive at the fort being carried. Poor Sean would have heart failure.

"You're unbelievably fast with this bow," Vaughn commented as he strode along beside her. "Not to mention accurate."

"Keeps us alive in battle."

"They would have killed Murel and me both. We owe you our lives, Feth."

"I don't think much in terms of debts." She stumbled and he caught hold of her hand. "I'll lean on you the last mile, my head is getting a little light."

They kept up a steady pace while Vaughn told her their story. He and Murel were both twenty-five and had grown up together in village called Killaloe on the banks of the Shannon. Vaughn's father, of Clan Maeluidir, worked a modest farm that until ten years ago produced food for his family and enough extra to trade for tools, cloth and what firewood and peat could be had. Murel's father, who died when she was eight, was from Clan Felmeda. Her mother was a seamstress and had a shop in nearby Ballina. By the time Vaughn and Murel reached their teens, drought, flood, and long, severe winters destroyed the last of the farms. The towns began to disintegrate and the midlands clans organized themselves to take food by force wherever they could.

Vaughn and Murel married at age twenty, in the last year Killaloe and Ballina survived. Their first child nearly died of starvation and cold in its first winter. It was that next spring, four years ago, that Vaughn managed to find work in the Wicklow brewery. He settled Murel and their child in abandoned farmhouse a few miles outside the Rampart. That year, they had enough food and fuel for the long winter.

The following spring, a new owner took over the brewery and expelled non-citizen workers. Warfare erupted near Wicklow and the family fled back to the midlands and lived as wanderers, begging charity where they could find it. Next winter, their child died. When Murel became pregnant again, Vaughn vowed to find a way back into the Province. They took temporary refuge with the Province-hating Cuirenrige Clan because they had enough food gained in incessant raids, and frequently traveled close to the Province's borders. One night Vaughn and another man were detailed to guard the clan's cash, also stolen from the Province, and he saw his chance. When his comrade succumbed to a dozen tankards of ale, Vaughn tied and gagged him, took two of the money sacks, collected Murel, and vanished into the forest. They had been on the run for over twenty miles when Murel caught her leg between two rocks.

After pondering his story, Feth said, "I'm curious, Vaughn. What do people like Clan Cuirenrige think of us?"

"As for Clan Cuirenrige itself, they detest the Twenty Clans and are willing to stop at nothing to steal your food, stout, money, anything they can get their hands on. If Éirelan falls to their like, civilized life will be at an end in this land. Otherwise, I guess it depends where you are. People living near the Rampart know quite a bit about life in the Province, some of them may work inside the Rampart like I did for a time. Further away, most folks imagine that you live in great stone houses staffed with servants, stuff yourself with gourmet food and fine wine at nightly banquets. You stole all the best land, the warmest places, and now you refuse to share what you have while other people starve and freeze to death. People from Belfast to Dublin and all through the midlands hate and envy you. And you're none too popular in Cork and Kerry either, though there the reasons may be different."

Feth shook her head sadly. "Servants and great houses! Our house is so cold in winter we have icicles on the inside of the windows and have to thaw our water to drink it in the morning. We have enough to eat, but by spring the larders and the warehouses are empty. As for stealing the land ... that's not true! We lived along the coast before we built the Rampart. We threw no one out."

"I know all that," Vaughn said. "Now let me ask you, why does it hurt to let in people like Murel and me, who will work hard and make good citizens? That brewery I worked in was forever short-handed, with men and women going off to fight all the time."

Feth remembered signs posted in Rosslare and Dungarvan and in other towns, seeking workers of all kinds in shops and factories. And she'd read that more and more farms lay fallow too.

"When things quiet down," Feth said, "I want you to talk with my mother. She sits on the Council of Twenty and maybe she can get some changes made."

"I don't hope for much," Vaughn said with a sigh. "All I want is to work and find a decent place for us to live and have our child."

"How far along is Murel?"

"Four or five months. She has to have decent food or she'll lose this child."

The sun hung low in the sky when they came within sight of the fifteen-foot wall and the massive gates next to River Glendine Fort. Sean could not have been more than a quarter hour ahead, and as there was no sign of him and the gates were ajar, Feth knew he had been allowed through with Murel. They passed through the gates and found themselves face to face with the sentry chief who lectured them that morning. His bearded face wore a deep scowl.

"Your friend is inside," he said curtly to Feth, "and your horse is in the stable. I think the Fort Captain wants to see you." His eyes drifted down to the dark red stain on her trousers below the wound. "Maybe the Captain can wait. You'll find your friend and the injured woman in the infirmary, the doctor will help you there. Use that door," he pointed, "it goes straight into the hospital and you won't have to go through the Common Room."

They did as he directed and found themselves in a storage room with an open doorway into the fort's hospital. There, Murel lay on a table, seemingly comfortable for the moment. Sean, his back to them, was speaking to a tall, white-gowned male doctor who saw them come in.

"Your friends have arrived," the doctor said.

Sean spun around. His face blanched at the sight of Feth's bloody side.

"Feth, what happened?" he cried.

"Looks worse than it is," she replied in a calm voice. "Shallow knife wound that needs stitching."

"Sit down there," the doctor ordered, gesturing towards a chair. "My name is Taicligh Fiachrach. Sean and I were discussing your wife's situation," he said with a nod towards Vaughn. "I gave her a sedative mixture, she's awake but in no pain."

Vaughn took hold of his wife's hand and Murel smiled at him. Taicligh continued talking while he worked on Feth's wound.

"I'm having a bit of trouble with the fort captain," he explained, keeping his voice low. "He claims he's not authorized to take in refugees, let alone offer medical care to them. That young woman needs surgery on her leg and I'm more than willing to do it, but I've been ordered not to. I was explaining that to Sean when you arrived."

Feth started to answer when he dove in with his needle. She uttered a curse that drew a grin from Sean.

"Such language," he commented with mock disapproval.

"Stitch him next," Feth said through gritted teeth. "Devil take it, how many?"

"I'll keep count," Taicligh said. When another curse was about to escape her lips, he tied off the last stitch and snipped the thread. "Twenty-seven. Let me apply antiseptic and a bandage and you're good to go."

"Now let me understand," said Feth, "you're supposed to refuse help to this woman, a *pregnant* woman? Vaughn should sling her over his shoulder and carry her back outside?"

"That's the order I received," Taicligh said with disgust. "I'd disobey in an instant, I don't care a damn about the Fort Captain's say-so. My worry is that he could make a charge of insubordination stick and pack me off to jail for a court martial. Meantime the army has one less experienced surgeon when it needs every one."

"That's insane!" Sean stepped over to Murel and brushed hair back from her clammy forehead. "Can we take her by wagon to Dungarvan, have her treated there?"

"You could," said Taicligh, "but it would be dangerous in her present condition. The jagged edge of the bone could cut an artery and she'd bleed to death."

Feth got to her feet, overcame a brief bout of dizziness, and mopped her sweaty face with a hospital towel.

"I'll see the Fort Captain. What's his name?"

"Ròidh Eogain, and he's not a friendly one, I can tell you."

"Where do I find him?"

Taicligh answered while bending over Murel. "The fort office in back. That's where I saw him last."

"Stay here," she said to Sean and Vaughn. "I won't be long."

The Common Room was noisy and packed with Bows and Blades eating their evening meal. With her bloody side and no uniform, Feth drew curious stares as she passed between the tables. The door to the fort office was ajar, so she rapped and pushed it open. She found Ròidh Eogain sitting at his desk, hunched over a tray of food. An open bottle of wine lay within arm's reach. He was a sour-faced man, middle-aged, with heavy bearded jowels, thick eyebrows, and a well-scarred face. Towards the back of the room, a civilian clerk was filing papers. At a second smaller desk, a partly-armored Blade was filling out the night roster.

She closed the door and approached him. He looked up and sent her an angry glare.

"I suppose you're the one responsible for the situation in the infirmary?"

Feth saluted and he waved a hand in return.

"Bow Junior Grade Fethnaid Laigain, off duty, Captain. I do take responsibility for bringing in two refugees from Clan Cuirenrige. They have money and are willing to pay for any services we offer them. The woman is with child and her leg needs immediate surgery, after that we'll take her to Dungarvan. I ask that you allow the doctor to do the work."

She stayed at attention the whole time and maintained a civil tone.

"Seems to me you've taken a great deal on yourself, Bow Junior Grade. You can take the bastards any place you like, but they get no services here. Not on my watch."

He refilled his mug with wine and waited for her to retreat out the door. Instead, she took a couple of steps forward until her thighs touched the desk.

"Fort Captain Eogain, I would like to ask one more time. You can't refuse aid to a pregnant woman."

"Can't I?" he sneered. "Try me."

I've never yet traded on my family name, she reminded herself, *not once. But Murel could die if I don't do something fast. Sometimes, grandfather Uinseann says, you are forced to choose the lesser of two evils.*

She leaned over the desk until she could smell his stinking breath.

"Captain Eogain, my full name is Fethnaid Conmaicne Laigain, daughter of Domnall who is dead and Liadan who sits on the Council of Twenty. My sister Aideen commands the Province Squadron, and more important from your point of view, my posting papers are signed by my uncle, Padraic Conmaicne, General of the Army. If you don't let your surgeon help that poor suffering woman out there, I will see to it that you are broken from rank, fined every farthing you have ever earned in the service, and chained up in the military prison at Enniscorthy until your bones rot. My charge will be flagrant breaking of the Code of the Twenty Clans which says that mercy and kindness are expected of all. I will also charge you with drinking on duty, for which you could be hung by your miserable neck and tossed into an umarked grave."

The civilian clerk froze in place, his hand halfway into a drawer. The Blade at the desk laid down his pen and fixed his eyes on his desktop. Ròidh Eogain's sneer faded to astonishment and then to anger finally, in the crease of his eyes, to fear. He heaved himself up and stormed past Feth, threw open the door and barreled across the Common Room into the surgery.

"Treat the woman," he snarled at the doctor. "Then get both of them both out of here— tonight."

Feth had barely caught up when Ròidh thumped past her and took the staircase into the tower. Feth closed the surgery door behind her and leaned against it with closed eyes. Her head was spinning and her knees shook. She felt Sean's hands on her and let him ease her into a chair. She lowered her head between her knees.

"Sean, she needs food and fluids right away, no alcohol," Taicligh said. "You can all stay in here if you like. Vaughn, I'll be taking Murel through that door into the operating room and go to work on her leg. I've sent for my assistant from the barracks, she'll be here any minute. I would say Murel will be ready to transport in another hour or so. To get her to Dungarvan Hospital you'll need a regular ambulance or barring that a wagon filled with straw and blankets."

Feth lifted her head to answer. "We'll get everything ready."

Taicligh rolled the cart on which Murel lay towards the operating room door, where he paused with the door half-open.

"Just out of curiosity," he said to Feth, "how did you persuade Ròidh?"

"I threatened to saw off his balls, more or less," she replied. "I knew he'd either hammer me to the floor or give in. He gave in."

Taicligh smiled and departed with Murel.

"You do have a way about you, Fethnaid," said Vaughn. "It's a serious situation, but the look on the captain's face was funny indeed."

"I didn't like what I had to do in there," said Feth. "I'll remember Ròidh Eogain a long time."

"What exactly *did* you say?" Sean asked.

Feth started to answer when the door to the Common Room swung open. The Bow Captain on duty stepped in followed by Derdre and Gwen, both coated in road dust and trailing bits of leaves. The Bow Captain backed out and closed the door.

"We were worried sick!" cried Gwen. "When you didn't get back in time for the funeral service, Captain Fotharta thought—what happened to your side?"

"Sliced by a flying knife," she admitted. She introduced Vaughn and quickly related the day's tale, leaving out details of her confrontation with Ròidh Eogain.

"I missed Dunlaith's funeral?" she finished, shaking her head. "We planned to be back hours ago."

"It was my fault," said Sean. He banged fist on a cabinet. "I had a stupid idea and it nearly cost Feth her life. I'm so sorry, Derdre, we'd never have gone out at all if we knew the service was tonight."

"It's all right," Derdre said. "You were there in spirit ... and you saved two lives." She turned to Vaughn. "My father's a doctor in Dungarvan. He won't be home long but he can make sure Murel gets good care."

Feth nodded towards the surgery.

"The doctor said we have to carry Murel in an ambulance or a wagon. And they'll need somewhere to stay. Any ideas?"

"They can stay with my father and me," said Derdre. "There's plenty of room."

"Let me see about the cart," Gwen put in. "I know this Bow Captain, I think she'll help us."

Gwen left for the Common Room and returned a minute later with the Bow Captain, a short, thickly-built woman whose black hair was streaked with gray. A long scar on the left side of her face disappeared under a patch over her eye.

"Captain Glenna Duncan," said Gwen. "Feth Laigain, Derdre Dal Reti, Sean Osraige, and Vaughn Maeluidir. Captain Duncan was my first battle commander."

The Scotswoman offered a shallow bow to each of them in turn.

"Gwen was an outsider a bit like me," she said in a Scottish brogue, "so we understood each other right from the start." She offered a crooked smile to Gwen. "In our first fight, she didn't shoot that straight but by the spirits o' me ancestors, her arrows went through two at a time."

To Feth, she said, "I hear you need a makeshift ambulance."

Feth stood next to Vaughn and laid a hand on his arm. "We do, but it's a complicated situation. Vaughn and his wife are refugees from Clan Cuirenrige. They have not been given formal asylum and Fort Captain Eogain would not be happy about your helping them."

The rugged archer barked out a laugh. "Piss on him, he's a vile one. I take his orders at the fort and for naught else. Bring the injured woman around to the Common Room doors, I'll handle the rest."

She started to leave, then paused in the doorway and fixed her gaze on Sean.

"By the way, lad, I've read your book. A good start. Just don't leave out the Scots."

She was gone before Sean could answer. True to her word, a half-hour later she had a straw-filled wagon ready, pulled by two horses and driven by a veteran archer from the barracks reserve. Feth thanked Glenne; Sean promised her a monograph on the history of Scotland. Then their little caravan headed off into the cool night. Vaughn sat next to Murel in the back of the cart. Sean and Feth followed on Parlan, then Derdre and Gwen on their horses. A slow ride on the smooth, silent road brought them into Dungarvan in two hours.

Hearing the sound of the horses and the cart, Mor ran out and immediately took charge of bringing Murel inside and easing her onto a bed. When his examination showed that she was recovering well from the surgery, he left the young couple to rest in private.

Derdre laid wood on the fire and boiled water for tea while Gwen went to find Mairin, who had gone to Squadron Headquarters. Sean slumped in a chair looking very unhappy with himself. Feth did her best to convince him he had done nothing wrong.

"If we hadn't gone out there," she pointed out, "Vaughn and Murel would be dead."

His faint smile showed he was unconvinced. "Interesting logic, Feth, but it won't wash. I should not have taken the risk with you. I should have—"

The front door swung open and Mairin followed Gwen into the room. Mairin gave Feth a strong hug and then held onto her arms.

"So good to see you, Feth," she said. "Our paths don't cross very often."

"I'm really glad I didn't miss you," Feth said. "I hear we won't even have time for a meal together."

"I'm sorry, no. Not this time."

Sean took Mairin's hands in his own. "Mairin, it has been too long."

"Far too long," Mairin agreed. She looked at Feth and then back at Sean. "Mor tells me you have something going?"

Feth threw her arm around Sean's waist. "We do."

"Good for you," Mairin said with a warm smile. "In the winter we'll all get together and trade stories."

For a few minutes everyone seemed to talk at once. Then tired goodnights were said and Feth, Sean and Mairin left the house together. They strolled through cold, sea-scented night air into the town, where Sean deposited weary Parlan in his warm stable and went to find his owner. Feth followed Mairin to the lantern-lit pier, where work crews were still loading *Caillech*'s holds with cartons and bags of food, barrels of fresh water, and cases of ballistae and archer ammunition. Mairin leaned back against a stack of sturdy wood boxes labeled "Cutter Bolts - 100 Each." Feth took a spot next to her.

"How bad is that wound, really?" Mairin asked.

"A knife sliced me for about four inches. Flesh only, hurt like the devil."

"What exactly were you doing outside the Rampart?"

"The Vale of the Glendine is a beautiful spot and Sean wanted me to see it. Maybe it was too big a risk. We did save two lives."

Mairin nodded but offered no comment. Her face was set towards the ship, yet it seemed to Feth that the captain's mind was in another time and place entirely. At last Mairin did answer.

"There's nothing wrong in taking a risk for something beautiful, something you'll always remember."

What a strange mood she's in, Feth observed to herself. *Distant though not cold. Vulnerable and lonely?* As if responding to this unspoken thought, Mairin turned to her. Her face was eerily lit from the side by the flickering work lanterns. Her expression was solemn.

"I can't tell you about my orders ... I can say the danger will be extreme. There's a good chance I won't be coming back." Mairin reached into her pocket and brought out the decorated Celtic Knot. Feth stared at it and broke into a smile.

"When did he give it to you?"

"Last week, in Wicklow. Anyway, if I don't make it back, please tell Conor I love him very much."

Feth reached out and closed Mairin's hand over the talisman.

"Oh, Mairin, he knows that," she said, holding on to Mairin's hand. "He knows."

An hour later, Feth lay in Sean's arms. Tired as she was, she could not find sleep.

"Sean?"

"Yes, I'm awake."

"Because I am?"

"Yes."

"Mairin seemed so alone out there."

"Think of the burden she carries when she takes that ship to sea."

Feth shifted her body.

"Your side hurt?"

"Not much. It's hard to be responsible for the lives of other people, isn't it?"

"I think it is, yes. Now try to sleep, love. Morning comes on soon and you have to be off."

She fell silent and soon heard his deep breathing behind her. The last fading thought before sleep was of Mairin's hand in hers.

She was not just going to sea this time. I saw that much in her eyes.

My dearest Liadan, I have been away from you and the children now for two months, longer than we have ever been separated. I should be back in Rosslare soon. The fighting here in Bretan has been fierce as I said in my previous letters. Their eastern border is under heavy pressure and they have no Rampart to make the task more manageable. I am sure our helping them will be repaid some day, we are all Celts after all and speak the Gael ... though the Bretans do have fun with our "accent." I miss you and the children terribly, and I especially miss your warmth at night when I am trying to sleep alone in this cold, wintry land. Is Aideen at sea? Conor sent me poetry, he has your marvelous gift for words. My darling Fethnaid is not causing you fits without me to bellow now and then? It will not be long until I again lie beside you, my beautiful wife.
Your loving and lonely husband, Domnall.
(Redon, Bretan, January 4, 985)

Chapter 18

Liadan had ridden two full hours from Teach Munna by the time sunlight bathed the tower of Rathmacknee Castle in a golden glow. She found nothing so pleasurable and relaxing as riding a familiar road before dawn, when the whole world seemed suspended in anticipation of the coming day. So she had let faithful Joseph amble as he would, pausing now and then for a sip of water at a roadside stream or a nibble at tall, juicy grass. Now she dismounted in the shadow of the ancient castle and led Joseph to the nearby stream.

She came here often as a young girl, played with her friends inside the ancient building, even dared climbing into the still-intact tower to look out over rolling meadows and woods stretching off in all directions. She remembered one particular time when a handsome young lad named Domnall was her companion. They frolicked in the warm summer grass and pledged eternal love to each other. The air this morning, tinged as it was with the early scent of fall, damp and cool and utterly unmoving, brought back the treasured memory of that special day in this place of untold age.

While Joseph drank and grazed contentedly, she sat cross-legged on the grass and pondered the swirling events of the past two days. The proposal of the western clans first stunned the Council of Twenty and then sent it careening into contentious, exhausting debate. The idea of forming a true alliance with these scattered clans had much to recommend it. As she expected, though, the request to extend the Rampart as *quid pro quo* for alliance split the Council into two camps that could not agree. Past grievances and insults rose to the surface, testing the diplomatic patience of Gilvarry and Rainait. They had done well, better than Liadan imagined she would have done in their shoes. By late evening on the second full day of debate, it was obvious that the Council would not take a decision in this session. To demonstrate good faith, Rionach managed to pass—by a slim majority!—a measure increasing the prices the Province would pay for surplus food produced by the farms of Cork and Kerry. That news would sit well with the western clans when word got out into the countryside.

No decision, she sighed inwardly. Twenty clans, large and small, some with extensive landholdings, others with craft businesses, some concentrated in the west, others in the east, old rivalries and grudges, families split among clans: how could it be otherwise? That they shared a thousand years of history, five thousand years of culture, spoke a common tongue, and believed for the most part in the same values and ideals did not in any way guarantee that twenty representatives would agree promptly on a dinner menu. Debate and compromise, debate and compromise. In less dangerous times, this freedom from coercion and restraint was the hallmark of democratic life in the Province, but now, Liadan reflected, could it be their downfall? Decisions had to be made and made without delay. Alliance with the western clans? Extend the Rampart, or abandon it and fight in the field? Launch ever more ships to support Kernow in protecting ports and sea lanes and coastal towns? Resettle non-citizens on the vacant farms, give them jobs in labor-starved factories?

Joseph finished his long drink and came over to nudge her, as if to say, *enjoy yourself, as I am.*

"Ah, you're right, Joseph," she sighed, stroking his wet nose. "It's a delightful place and it holds sweet memories for me. I could stay here all day. Alas, we best be along. I want to see Conor and Padraic and Aideen before they sail today."

She climbed into the saddle and set Joseph back on the road to Rosslare. Two miles further down the winding country lane, she came upon a cemetery perched on a hillside, and set Joseph ambling into it. Dismounting, she picked a bunch of late-blooming wildflowers and approached side-by-side markers beneath a stand of alder trees. She divided the flowers, knelt down and laid half before each stone. One read "Seosaimhthin Conmaicne, 932 - 992" and the other "Blathmac Conmaicne, 930 - 992."

"Hello, Mom, hello Dad," she said. "I miss you."

Tears flowed freely as they always did when she came here.

Seven years since Aideen burst into our home, her face paste-white and her breath coming in great gasps. "The coaster!" she cried out. "It went down. They're lost!"

So few words to announce the death of two marvelous spirits, Liadan and Padraic's parents, grandparents to Aideen and Conor and Feth, friend and kin to so very many from one end of the Province to the other. Blathmac the Poet, he was called, and his dear wife Seosaimhthin the Archer. A gentle poet whose crippled legs never carried him into battle, united in love to a woman who commanded the Line of Bows in twenty battles. Both lost in one terrible moment at sea, their bodies washed ashore five days later.

Two years after I lost Domnall. How terribly unfair. How alone it left me!

She sat cross-legged and pulled weeds for a time, talking quietly, explaining and seeking comfort from them, conjuring in her mind her father's red-faced laughter and her mother's feigned sternness. Sensing her sadness, Joseph ambled to the gravesite and did his best to trim the grass growing at the bottom of the simple bluestone markers.

The bright song of a meadowlark told her it was time to move on. She said goodbye, mounted Joseph and urged him to a fast trot. A mile before she reached Laigain House, she passed through Rosslare's Friday Market, a long chain of stalls crowding both sides of the road leading into town from the west. Though it was not yet eight o'clock, every farmer and craftsman from miles around had erected a booth festooned with signs and colorful pendants. She longed, longed to stop and linger, chat with friends and strangers, buy a trinket or two and the last fresh fruit of the season ... yet in the end she urged a reluctant Joseph along. Soon the welcome sight of Laigain House came into view. At the least, Kellen and Triona would be there. For that she was truly thankful; the big house without people in it was a dreary place.

She unsaddled Joseph, lifted off saddle bags packed with her tent and gear, and left him to wander back to the hay-filled stable on his own. The front door to the house lay ajar and the welcome smell of sausage wafted onto the porch. In the great room, brightly lit by the morning sun, she found Kellen Fotharta with a book in his hands. With a slight grimace Kellen rose from the chair to greet her.

To Liadan's worried look, he said "I'm allowed to stand and walk, thanks be."

She embraced him gingerly. "I'm glad to see it. Conor's letter explained everything to me. Are they gone already?"

"Gone from here, yes," he said. "You won't miss them at the port. The Commodore said they wouldn't sail before mid-morning. Liadan, I regret imposing on you like this."

"Nonsense," Liadan interrupted. "This house is ever open to friends and family alike."

"I only wish I could be at Conor's side."

He eased himself onto a sofa and Liadan joined him, enjoying the soft cushions after four hours in a hard saddle.

"It was *very* interesting," Kellen observed, "seeing Conor with Aideen and Padraic together earlier this morning. Each time the brother-sister sniping started, Padraic intervened or glared at me until I did."

Liadan laughed softly. "Yes, that would be my older two children. Neither I nor Domnall could fathom how those two could be so much oil and water ... yet they are."

Triona appeared at the kitchen door, a wood spatula in one hand and a towel in the other.

"Liadan, I'm so sorry, I didn't hear you come in! That stove roars with a full load of wood."

"I wouldn't know," Liadan said with a sly grin.

"We thank you for taking us in. You must value your privacy here."

Liadan laughed. "Privacy? Why would I want that? You can stay as long as you like. I take it there's been no further trouble?"

"No trouble here," said Kellen cautiously. "I don't expect any."

"I'll be back with breakfast," Triona said. She disappeared into the kitchen.

In a low voice Liadan said to Kellen,"Trouble, wasn't there?"

"Yes, in a way," he said with a heavy sigh, "but best we not discuss it now."

She nodded assent. "How are you doing with your recovery?"

"Well enough, Triona says, for someone whose side was caved in. I hate not being there with the army. It would be an honor to serve under Conor."

"*Under* him?"

Kellen broke into a smile. "Ah, you wouldn't know! Conor is commanding the Blades in the field army. The captain who was supposed to serve is sick and Padraic offered the job to Conor."

"I can imagine how the 'offer' was made," Liadan commented. "He will no doubt be thinking he's not cut out for that level of command."

"You know your son well. We talked long into the night in my room. Liadan, it's not easy to for anyone live up to the memory of Domnall Laigain. I've told Conor over and over that there are many kinds of leaders and that his men love and respect him. You and I both know Padraic would never give him the rank if he didn't believe in him. There's too much at stake."

"Did Aideen comment on it?"

Kellen looked puzzled. "Oddly enough, I don't think she *said* anything. Padraic told her last night, here in this room, before Conor came back. I thought she looked pleased. Maybe it was my imagination."

'Maybe not," said Liadan. "I think Aideen has always wanted Conor to accept leadership. He resists the idea and she can't understand why. It's part of the reason they clash."

Triona entered carrying a tray laden with sausage, hot biscuits, jam, and tea. She laid the tray on a table in front of the sofa and the three of them ate and talked for an hour. Liadan had always liked Kellen, whose temperament seemed—like his sister's—to be such an unexpected product of that unhappy household. Quiet, slightly formal at times, yet capable of telling a self-deprecating story. Though his personality differed drastically from his parents, Kellen's physical resemblance to Etain was striking. Indeed, he looked more like his mother than Mairin did. Liadan found Triona to be extremely bright and possessing of a fine wit. She seemed quite taken with Conor, though well aware of his involvement with Mairin. Only occasionally did the young woman's luminous eyes take on a sad, inward cast.

Liadan went upstairs to take a welcome bath, dress in fresh clothes, and dash off three letters to friends who had written her weeks ago. Then she saddled Joseph and let him gallop the two miles to the harbor. As the road rose and fell, she saw the tops of the masts. She was utterly unprepared for the sight that greeted her eyes when the harbor, ablaze with the slanting light of morning, came into full view. A three-masted ship rocked at every one of the harbor's twelve piers. Six Squadron warships and six broader, deeper commercial cargo ships alternated piers. They were ready for sea: crew and officers on deck, yards crossed, pennants flying, sailors ready to climb the rigging.

Impressive as this sight was, it was matched by the splendor of the field army assembled and ready to embark. In the broad grassy field that bordered the piers, twelve centuries of crimson-clad Blades gathered in three ranks spaced ten feet apart, flanked on either side by nine centuries of Bows clad in cobalt tunics. None wore armor or carried weapons; these would be stored as cargo and given out before landing. Beside each fighter rested a single canvas bag containing keep sakes, pictures of sweethearts, extra socks, perhaps a loaf of barmbrack sent from home. Twenty color bearers were strung out in front of the phalanx, one for each clan, and out in front of them, a single standard bearer holding high the battle flag of the Province, on which the Celtic Cross was formed into a sword.

Liadan thought with anguish, *how vulnerable they look dressed in tunics, cloaks, and camp shoes. The flower of our youth, faces fresh and optimistic, hair shining in the sunlight, bodies lean and hard and so readily destroyed in combat. How many of them will not return, or will return minus an eye or a hand or bearing fearsome scars?*

It took her only seconds to spot gold-caped Padraic, whose massive form towered over the staff officers gathered around him on the pier. Where was Conor? At last she caught sight of him: the copper-colored captain's cape had been replaced by a Field Commander's silver. Wearing a friendly and confident smile, he was strolling up and down the long ranks, stopping now and then to answer a question, laugh at a joke, pat a shoulder, shake a hand, steadying those who seemed nervous.

All the while with his own stomach tied in a knot to the point of nausea. He imagines himself so different from his father, yet in this moment they could hardly be told apart. Domnall loved his fighters, every one of them, and felt his losses in battle cruelly. I remember countless nights when my husband soaked the sheets with sweat, stared at the ceiling, dreaded the pain and death he would soon behold. No one knows this but me, and no one ever will.

She led Joseph off the road and tethered him to a tree in the shade. Minutes later the shrieks of children announced the arrival of her neighbors the Finguines in a hay wagon. Fianna and Tynan leapt down and hugged her; she regretted having no sweets in her pocket to give them. Liadan exchanged warm greetings with Aonghas and Shalagh. Their family and the Laigains and Conmaicnes of Rosslare had been friends for many generations. Liadan was happy for their company at this trying moment.

Over Shalagh's shoulder Liadan was surprised to see her own rarely-used open carriage approaching, pulled by their aging mare Abby and driven by Triona with a Blade-uniformed Kellen sitting next to her. Triona pulled the carriage off the road and helped Kellen down.

"Liadan, I had to see it," Kellen explained. "Triona even agreed to the uniform if I promised not to join the ranks."

"Look," said Liadan. She pointed towards the northern part of the pier, where another road emerged from dense woods.

Uinseann Laigain, as the current High Elder of the Province, led two cerulean-robed columns of children, a boy and a girl from every clan. Each carried the Staff of Life, a simple, rough-hewn pole bearing a banner of green and blue with a single white star, symbolizing Earth, Sea, and Sky, and topped by a carved open spiral of the Celts symbolizing the endless Cycle of Life. After the children marched a hundred-voice chorus of men, woman, and children in the traditional colors and patterns of each clan, followed by the similarly-attired orchestra of twenty-two harps, ten uillean pipes, sixteen viols, and twenty flutes.

Uinseann led the procession to the top of a grassy knoll overlooking Pier Number 1, occupied by Aideen's flagship *Nore*.

"How long has it been since the Blessing has been given?" Triona asked.

"Thirteen years," Liadan answered without hesitation. "The last time was the day my husband led out the great army from Wicklow." She turned to Kellen. "The High Elder that year was your grandfather, Guaire Fotharta, a fine, noble man." She called up the images, still fresh and clear in her mind. "The day was cold and dark, a piecing wind nearly tore the flags from the standards. Not peaceful and warm like today."

By the time all the participants found their positions, thousands of citizens crowded the port. Liadan was surrounded by Rosslare friends and neighbors, most of them having a son or daughter or brother or sister in the assembled ranks of the waiting army. So many like herself, hoping that their loved one would come home again, alive and unharmed.

Uinseann, tall and imposing in his blue-and-tan robes, stepped forward and raised high his own Staff of Life, this one preserved from the earliest days of the Province. Conor and Melvina strode to the front ahead of the standard bearers, taking their place on either side of Padraic and Aideen. The four of them faced the army. Padraic's heavy baritone boomed out, signaling his army to attention. Aideen snapped out a command: the hats of all the sailors and officers on the ships came off in unison. Then, silence.

Uinseann's powerful voice rang out over the assembled throng.

"People of the Twenty Clans of Eirelan, we gather today as we did thirteen years ago for the blessing of our army and navy. I call on all of us here assembled to remember who we are and what we stand for. For the ten centuries that have passed since we joined together at Lough Ennell, we have lived a life of harmony with nature. Our spiritual beliefs demand that we do our best to live in peace with our fellow man. The hard truth is that the world has never been what we might wish it to be. Today, once again, we send out our precious sons and daughters to do battle on land and sea with those who would take what little we have. We dearly wish this were not so. We spare life when we can," and now his voice took on a threatening edge, "but we give no quarter where none is given to us."

"And so we gather, under the glory of the sky and in the warm glow of the sun, to call forth blessings upon our children here gathered. We are believers in mystery. If some higher power directs the cycle of life and death in this world, we hold that it would bless those who love and cherish all living things and honor each other. More than this, we cannot know. This is our belief. This is our way."

A single harp began the melody and Uinseann's rolling baritone intoned the first two lines of the *Blessing of the Nine Elements*, in strange-sounding old Gaelic.

> *May you go forth neath the shelter of heaven,*
> *Under the light of the sun.*

This died away; then all of the instruments poured out their music, the chorus released its harmonized voices, and the gathered thousands joined in the singing of the ancient words:

> *May you go forth neath the shelter of heaven,*
> *Under the light of the sun.*
> *May you go forth under radiance of moon,*
> *Your way lit by splendor of fire.*
> *May you go forth with the swiftness of lightning,*
> *Fleet as the ship-blowing wind.*
> *May you go forth o'er depths of the sea,*
> *Your feet resting on firmed earth.*
> *May you go forth with a will hard as stone,*
> *Never to waver or fade.*
> *May these nine ever surround you, protect you,*
> *And return you to friends, and to home.*

As they sang, Liadan gripped Triona's hand on one side and Kellen's on the other. Three times the blessing was sung; then the orchestra played on while the soldiers marched down the piers in perfect discipline and crossed gangplanks into the waiting ships. A half hour passed before the standard-bearers, their pennants furled, boarded the vessels.

"We'll go back now," said Triona. She had retrieved Abby and was now hitching her to the carriage. "You need to see your family."

Liadan made her way on foot down the hill to where Padraic, Aideen, Conor, and Melvina stood talking among themselves. Uinseann arrived at the same time, his broad, furrowed forehead glistening with sweat under the weight of the robes.

"Mother," Conor said immediately, "this is Melvina Eogain, Bow Commander. Melvina, my mother Liadan Conmaicne Laigain."

Melvina bowed slightly and extended her hand, which Liadan accepted.

"Melvina," said Liadan, "a lovely, poetic name."

"Perhaps, though I can't take any credit for it," Melvina replied. "Conor tells me you're a poet and he promised me one of your books to read when we return."

"What poet doesn't like to be read?" said Liadan, smiling. To Uinseann, she said, "Father, I ask your special blessing on these our brothers and sisters."

Uinseann nodded and bowed his head with closed eyes. Then he gazed up to the sky and spoke in quiet, deep tones.

"We are humble before the mysteries of life and death, we stand in awe of the wonderful world we are given a space of time to live in. Let us today remember all who have gone before us, in the long history of the Twenty Clans and the endless centuries of the Celts whose blood we carry in our veins. It is our task in the present to preserve and protect what has been saved for us, at the price of their blood and sacrifice. To that task we dedicate our minds, our bodies, and our lives."

"So be it," they each said.

"I must be off, Mother," said Aideen. Liadan hugged her and then watched as she strode confidently down the dock to the *Nore*.

Liadan took hold of her brother's hands and stood on tiptoes to whisper in his ear, "come back safe, dear brother."

Conor wrapped his arms around her and said, "I love you, Mother."

She looked into her son's eyes and smiled. "When you were a little boy, I used to tell you not to stay out after dark. It's still sensible advice."

Melvina laughed, shook her hand again and said, "I'm glad we met."

Uinseann offered Liadan his arm and together they strolled up the hill. At the top, the senior Laigain pulled the heavy robes over his head and slung them over an arm.

"You walked from Rosslare?" Liadan asked him.

"Yes," he answered, "my horse is in town."

"Then ride Joseph."

"Daughter," he said, smiling, "my hands do not work so well but my legs are yet strong. We'll walk together and speak of Teach Munna and what we should do next."

Liadan took Joseph's reins and they set off at an easy stroll down the dusty road towards the town. She followed Uinseann to the stable.

"Rionach invited Gilvarry and Rainait to stay with us for a time while the Council sorts out what to do," he said, tightening the saddle straps. "I think we have a great deal to say to each other, much history to understand."

"And I have the task," said Liadan, "of figuring out how to deal with Etain. Any thoughts?"

Uinseann mounted easily for a man of seven decades.

"I'd rather be in Padraic's shoes than yours," he said, offering her a sympathetic smile. "Good luck." He clicked his tongue and the stallion eagerly trotted off onto a country lane.

When she reached Laigain House she found a glum-looking Kellen sitting alone on the sun-warmed front porch. He held in his hands a sheathed battle sword. Liadan deposited Joseph in the stable and joined him.

"Triona's at the Friday market," he greeted her. "I get to sit here and soak up sunlight and listen to the birds."

"Not a terrible fate," Liadan said. She pulled a chair up next to him.

He laid the sword across his knees. "I hope you don't mind that I took this off the wall."

"Of course not," she replied. She ran her fingers along the cool steel of the ornate metal sheath. "It was Domnall's dress sword, he never used it in fighting so far as I know. Immensely old, maybe as old as the Province itself. I suppose Conor told you about it."

"He did." Kellen sighed, laid a hand on his injured side. "He could have used my help on this expedition. You know what he's like, he'll worry himself to death."

"This won't be his last senior command. You'll be there next time for him."

Kellen nodded but said nothing.

"Anything you'd like to tell me about Conor and Bram? Something you didn't want Triona to hear?"

"Ah, yes, that." Kellen turned to face her. "Bram caught up with Conor on the road to Rosslare, taunted him as you might expect."

"And?"

"And he said something that suggested ... "

He trailed off and swallowed hard. Liadan reached out and took hold of his arm.

"Kellen, what is it?"

"You know Mairin and I had a very hard time when we were young," he began in a thready voice.

"Yes, that much I do know. Not much else, except rumors I never trusted."

"Gorman was an abusive drunkard," Kellen struggled on, "and he hurt Mairin and me. He hurt Bram too, until he got too big and strong. Then Bram joined in the fun, he was worse than father most of the time. Mairin tried to protect me, especially from Bram who loved to beat me up. She got hurt plenty of times for that."

Liadan's heart cringed at the idea of children harmed in this way. "What did Bram say to Conor?"

"He said my father ... my father raped Mairin."

"Oh, no." Liadan's hand flew to her mouth. "No, Kellen."

"He said that. Conor was destroyed by it. He had to leave today with that on his mind. I wanted to tell Conor it was just Bram concocting a terrible lie to hurt him, but I had to admit I really don't know."

Kellen wiped away tears and drew in a deep breath. "I hope it's not true," he said in small voice.

Liadan leaned back in her chair and closed her eyes.

"Oh, Kellen, I wish we had known then. We would have done something. I saw your mother often enough, sometimes in the company of another man, but what was I to say? Everyone knew Gorman was a wasted man, ruined by Etain and by his own weaknesses. The rest was mere gossip."

"It's all in the past now, for me," Kellen said. "Not so for Mairin, she has terrible dreams about those days."

Liadan pushed a wisp of grey-blond hair from her eyes. "Some parts of our past seem to fade into the distance, others linger as if no time had passed at all. I sometimes dream of that awful day Padraic returned with my husband's body. Not so often these days, sometimes I go for months and then I awake with that dream flooding my mind. Always so real, so filled with genuine heartache. And yet, a dream and nothing more."

A horse-drawn wagon rounded the bend in the road from town. Triona waved cheerily and snapped the reins. A moment later she drew up in front of the house. The wagon's small bed was filled with sacks and open crates.

"Good prices!" she cried. She reached into the wagon bed and gathered up several items. "For you," she said to Kellen. "A sketch pad and colored pencils."

Kellen broke into a smile, carefully descended the porch steps and kissed Triona on the cheek. "Just what I needed, thank you, cuz. Permission to stroll into the woods and draw?"

Triona nodded. "No bending over and watch your step."

Kellen tapped the pencil on the pad. "Agreed. I'm off, then."

When the wagon was unloaded and the victuals stored, Liadan made tea and served it on the veranda overlooking the ocean. Triona brought out fresh, sticky buns she bought from a bakery vendor.

Liadan bit into one and said, "I know these. A strange-looking old man, cloudy eyes, missing several fingers?"

"The same," Triona managed, her mouth full. "Who is he?"

"Uscias Le Berre, a Bretan native. Came here when he was a child, raised a family and has who-knows-how-many grandchildren. He finally gave up his bakery in Wexford, now he comes to Market Day every week rain or shine. His wife has her own booth of spices and herbs, right next to his."

"Yes, I saw it! I bought fennel and dill from her. Why don't they have one booth?"

Liadan swallowed the remainder of one bun and lifted another. "I asked that once, and Uscias said she ate up his profits!"

Triona laughed till she spilled her tea.

"I did notice," she said, taking a second bun too, "that the spice vendor was a bit portly!"

They laughed together, and for a short time at least, put aside cares and worries and enjoyed the simple pleasures of tea, sweet buns, and the glory of an early autumn day.

I cannot believe it. Sinea Danaan was ordered to stay ashore in Dungarvan and take command of a new ship coming out of the Falmouth yards, so my promotion to First Officer has been confirmed. I owe a debt to Sinea. Though we didn't serve together long she gave me much help and we became friends. Captain Fotharta ... of course I owe her too. She is not easy to grasp, not that understanding her is my job anyway. She is a superb, courageous captain, without question, or she wouldn't be where she is. At times she seems happy and outgoing, so far as a captain can be outgoing among the crew, and at other times she seems withdrawn, oppressed by some secret sadness. Her nightmares must be horrendous. How can I not hear through a thin cabin partition? Now we are taking on an entirely new mission. I am uneasy and wonder what may happen to us.

Private log, Rowenna Briuin

Chapter 19

Mairin had felt on edge all day. It hadn't helped that after the trauma of the funeral and the anxious waiting for Feth and Sean, she slept a bare two hours on the one night she hoped to catch up on rest. An hour before dawn she was so wound up that she abandoned the soft bed, dressed, gathered her gear and headed down to the *Caillech* which was, as she expected, ready for sea duty. Recall horns sounded as she ascended the gangplank.

Among other worries, she had to promote a new second lieutenant from among their three ensigns. It was always far better for ensigns to be promoted to lieutenant rank in a different ship, but Aideen did not have time to offer her that option. Promoting on the same ship often led to resentment from disappointed ensigns and a too-lordly attitude from the new second officer selected from among her recent peers.

To ice the cake, the rendezvous in the offing with *Wexford, Morrigan,* and *Rosc Catha was* delayed when *Morrigan* could not get a favorable wind out of Waterford the day before, and *Rosc Catha's* food and water deliveries in Rosslare were late arriving at the pier. By the time she assembled all four ships, it was mid-day and six hours of fair sailing towards Falmouth were lost. Now the other three ships held close station in *Caillech's* wake. A fair-weather wind blew steady out of the northwest at better than twelve knots.

She stood alone at the taffrail, struggling to relax and wear a less threatening expression. She had already barked at Rowenna twice unnecessarily and dressed down two sailors for minor uniform violations. Now Rowenna was posted next to the wheel, her hands clasped tightly behind her back, scanning constantly for the slightest infraction of discipline or less-than-optimum cast of the sails.

It's not only the rendezvous and lack of sleep, Mairin told herself. *It's the sadness of the funeral and my memories of Aunt Mairin and the extra load of responsibility I feel without Sinea. What a time to recommend her promotion! On top of that, I feel a deep worry about this mission, so unlike anything we've done in the past. All the lives on all four ships are in my hands. Three hundred souls to bring into a battle and bring out alive. How much further can I come from the young ensign I once was, like those three talking quietly among themselves at the port rail? No doubt one is saying "watch your step with the Captain today, mates."*

The ship tacked to maintain a steady heading in a backing wind. *Caillech* came about smartly, as did *Wexford* and *Morrigan. Rosc Catha* was slow and fell off station for at least ten seconds. Mairin felt the surge of irritation and was powerless to contain it.

"Lieutenant," she snapped at Rowenna, who whirled instantly, her face betraying the fact that she expected a tongue-lashing.

"Signal *Rosc Catha, please remain on station during tacks.*"

"Sir, may I point—"

"Send the signal, Lieutenant."

Rowenna frowned faintly but turned and repeated the order to Ensign Velnowarth who ran the signal up the mizzen and then used her glass to await the reply. It came, quickly. The ensign reported the response to Rowenna in a low voice.

"Captain," Rowenna reported, "*Rosc Catha* signals *jib-boom fished, wish to avoid more damage. Tierney.*"

Gods above, I should have known Tierney Ulaid would have a sound reason! Now I look plain churlish, a fate I richly I deserve.

She walked forward and descended two steps onto the quarterdeck.

"Lieutenant," she said to Rowenna, "I assume that's what you tried to say to me?"

"Yes, sir," Rowenna replied with no trace of smugness. "Sorry, sir, I should have reported *Rosc Catha's* condition to you directly. I assumed you knew."

"Signal to *Rosc Catha, my apologies, do the best you can.* Send it twice."

'Aye aye, sir."

The signal flashed up, clearly visible to the other two ships as well as *Rosc Catha.*

"Lieutenant, hand the deck over to the master and join me in my cabin, if you please."

Rowenna followed her below decks and into her cabin. Mairin pulled off her hat and slumped onto the padded bench beneath the windows. Rowenna sat rather rigidly in a chair at the chart table, her hands clasped tightly in front of her.

"Lieutenant," Mairin began, "I'm very tired and edgy, and I do beg your pardon for being testy today."

Rowenna relaxed in the chair and smiled. "Captain, your version of testy hardly compares to some of the captains I served under in the Admiralty. I take no offense at all."

Mairin nodded her appreciation. *She's a steady one, no pouting or gloating there.*

"Then ... we need to appoint a second officer. What are my options?"

From a tunic pocket Rowenna produced a folded sheet of paper and spread it out on the chart table.

"Lieutenant Danaan and I discussed the ensigns on the return trip to Dungarvan. We gave you a report that you probably haven't had time to read."

Mairin ran her fingers through matted hair. "Right, though I should have. I'll catch up tonight, meanwhile we need to make a choice. I'll fetch tea, you talk."

"Yes, sir. All three have completed Admiralty training. Kensa Velnowarth is a Kernow native, born in Plymouth. Her family moved to the Province when she was a young girl. Age twenty-one now, at sea since thirteen. Edwina Auteini is a distant cousin to Brigid, twenty years old, six at sea, from Wicklow. Sithmaith Laigain, nineteen, at sea seven years, from Enniscorthy."

While Rowenna spoke, Mairin poured two mugs of tea half-full and set them in the chart table's holders. She sat down opposite her first officer, took a long sip of tea, and felt some of the tension in her stomach fade.

"You know the problem of appointing in this way," she began. "Much better to bring in a promotion from another ship, but with Sinea already gone we have no choice. In the usual situation we'd rotate an acting assignment for awhile, see how they do. Unfortunately we're in a very *un*usual situation. This mission is a far cry from escort duty, a cargo run, or even chasing a rogue ship or two. We're joining in an attack launched on an immense scale on land and sea. What I need right now is a second officer who can think fast in a totally strange situation and is not afraid to give orders that may send comrades to their death."

Rowenna sipped at her tea and stared for a long time at the sheet of paper.

"For pure seamanship," she said, "you can't touch Kensa Velnowarth. Navigation and ship-handling skills are at the top of any-one's list. Her weakness is that she's a bit overbearing, mentions too often that she's Cornish and possibly born to the sea more than the rest of us. That trait will fade out, I'm sure, but at the moment, it irritates officers and sailors both. Edwina Auteini ... just the oppo-site. Well-liked, takes criticism without batting an eye, works extremely hard. She's a little unsure of herself, maybe underestimates her own abilities. Then there's Sithmaith Laigain."

How many of the crew, Mairin wondered, knew of her personal connection to Clan Laigain? She had no idea how Sithmaith might be related to Conor and his family.

"Go on."

Rowenna drummed her fingers on the table. "Ensign Laigain is the youngest at nineteen, yet she's been at sea since she was twelve which itself is odd. She either lied to get in or had someone help her. Her record shows she had to get a special exception from the Admiralty to begin her three year stint at fifteen. They frown on that as you know, sir. The reports in her Admiralty file are a bit unusual."

Mairin took advantage of Rowenna's pause to glance out the stern windows as *Caillech* swung onto the opposite tack. With the wind gusting harder and coming more across the beam, *Rosc Catha* took even more time to make the tack. She turned back to Rowenna and waited.

"Ensign Laigain gained high marks in all the usual categories, sir, no apparent weaknesses noted by any of her superior officers."

"Good so far."

"Yes, sir. The bad part is that Sithmaith was reported insubordinate on three occasions, by three different captains. In one case, it was deemed serious enough for the lash. I've seen her back, sir, it bears the marks."

"Then you would not recommend her, I take it."

Rowenna seemed in a struggle with herself.

"Neither Sinea nor I would have recommended her for promotion until more service showed she was past that wild tendency. In the current circumstances as you explained them, there's something else in her record that makes me reconsider."

"It had better be pretty important."

"It's the report of her last captain, Miles Endean. You must know him, sir."

Mairin conjured up the image of a man nearing sixty, with bright blue eyes, a steel-hard body, and a sharp voice that commanded instant obedience. *One of their most revered captains*, she recalled, *and a keen judge of character.*

"I do," said Mairin. "He's the best fighting captain Kernow has."

Rowenna nodded. "He was the captain whose cat marked Ensign Laigain's back. Despite that incident, in his report Captain Endean made a remark both Lieutenant Danaan and myself found striking. I can come pretty close from memory. He said, *she steps over the line more than I would like. In a real bloody battle, I would want her on my quarterdeck. She's a born fighter.*"

Rowenna paused; colorful orders echoed from above. Master Gailenga was not happy with someone's performance on the last tack.

"So, Captain, I would have to go with Ensign Laigain when our mission is considered."

"She was steady in the ice-storm and the chase off Brest?"

"Very steady. As were the others for that matter."

Mairin thought a moment, then decided. "Please take the quarter-deck and ask Ensign Laigain to report to me."

Rowenna gathered up her sheet of paper and saluted on her way out. A minute later, a light tap on the cabin door announced the arrival of Ensign Sithmaith Laigain.

"Come," Mairin invited.

The nineteen-year-old ensign who entered was of average height with a broad-shouldered frame, chestnut hair, and unusual dark green eyes. As she saluted and took the proffered chair, Mairin studied her face for a hint of challenge. True, the wide set of her eyes, the straightness of her rather aquiline nose, the high-boned cheeks lacking any layer of fat, and the almost-too-large straight jaw did give her face a certain appearance of arrogance. *Seeing her in a pub*, Mairin reflected, *I might take the same features as pleasantly strong and dignified.*

She took a moment to meet the ensign's steady gaze. *Completely at ease, maybe too much so given the circumstances.*

"Ensign Laigain, I've reviewed your record," she began, mentally observing her slight falsehood, "and I find some disturbing entries from the Admiralty. Would you care to comment?"

Sithmaith smiled faintly. "Not much to comment on, Captain. I argued my point too strongly in each case, it was taken as insubordination, and I paid the price. I meant no disrespect to anyone."

"In these three cases ... you believe you were right?"

"I do ... sir."

Mairin caught the slight delay in "sir."

"Well, Ensign," Mairin said, turning away to watch her squadron, "I have a problem that no doubt you ensigns have discussed among yourselves."

"The ship needs a second officer, Captain."

"Exactly. The ship needs a second officer."

She turned back; the ensign's face bore no readable expression at all.

"Of my three choices, it seems that for pure seamanship I should promote Kensa Velnowarth, and for sheer hard work and ability to take criticism I would choose Edwina Auteini. That would seem to leave you at the bottom of the list."

Sithmaith's eyes flared and a flush rose into her cheeks. Her clasped hands showed white at the knuckles.

"I am the youngest, Captain," she said in a strained voice. "I have time to improve."

"True enough. The fact is I don't have any time at all, Ensign. In less than a week, this ship and the others with us will be engaged in war operations in Santander Bay. I've made no formal announcement of that but I'm sure the rumor mill has done its job. We're going to be fighting for our lives against an extremely tough and skillful enemy. How does that make you feel?"

"May I speak freely, sir?"

"I expect you to."

"Captain," Sithmaith began slowly, "I admit I have a reputation for a big mouth and a bad temper. I'm not the most qualified and I'm still short of twenty. I deserved the scars on my back whether I was right or not. I can tell you this, Captain." She gazed straight into Mairin's eyes. "If we're in a battle, so long as I draw breath, this ship and its crew will be fighting. Sir."

Mairin said nothing in response. Overhead, Rowenna's penetrating voice cracked out orders and *Caillech*'s bow once again swung round to the opposite tack. They were now sailing by the wind; Mairin felt the ship surge ahead as the spanker deployed and royals were set. She saw *Rosc Catha* manage more easily; this point of sail would take strain off the bowsprit and possibly allow her crew to refit the mast before they reached Falmouth—providing they had a spare aboard.

"Ensign," she said after a long pause, "I'm going to make you second officer. There are two conditions I insist on. First, you will carry out all direct orders given by me or the first officer."

"Yes, sir."

"Second, if you have an argument to make, either to me or to Lieutenant Briuin, you will make it privately and out of hearing of the crew and other officers. I welcome frank opinions but we cannot have bickering on the quarterdeck. Understood?"

"Understood, sir."

Mairin stood and rummaged through her cabinet drawers for Lieutenant's insignia. She found none.

"I don't have a silver anchor to give you, perhaps Lieutenant Briuin can spare one."

"I'll ask her, sir."

"Please go on deck and tell Lieutenant Briuin that I'll have a meeting of all officers in the wardroom at the next watch change. I'll formally announce your promotion then. In the meantime, please don't discuss it with anyone except Lieutenant Briuin."

"Yes, sir."

She rose to leave and saluted while opening the cabin door.

"Lieutenant," Mairin said. Sithmaith paused halfway out. "As you well know, there is no lashing in our service. Nor would I use the cat if I could. However, if you violate either of the conditions I set down, I'll break you back to ensign and your next chance at promotion will be a long time coming. Frank opinion honestly expressed is one thing, insubordination is another. Make sure you know the difference."

Laigain nodded and closed the door. Mairin poured another mug of tea and considered her decision. She was taking a chance on Ensign Laigain, and the other two ensigns would not be happy about her promoting the most junior of the group. It would have been so much easier to hold onto Sinea for another few months. Also unfair. Sinea was ready to command a ship and the Squadron needed captains. No doubt she'd have to part with Rowenna in six months or a year.

The cabin warmed in the rays of the early afternoon sun. The ship held a steady, easy point of sail, her companions strung out exactly on station. Two hours to the watch change. She slipped off her boots, stretched out in her hammock and closed her eyes. Sleep came immediately. Her last waking thought was of Conor.

The rap on her cabin door was loud and insistent.

"Captain!"

Mairin reluctantly struggled to consciousness. Why did the sailor have to knock so loud? She swung her feet to the floor, rubbed her eyes, and croaked, "enter."

A darkly-tanned face, one of the topmasters, poked around the door.

"Lieutenant Briuin's compliments, sir, we've sighted a ship. She requests that you come on deck."

"Yes, I'm coming."

She stuffed her feet into her boots, took a second to brush her tangled hair, then sprinted out the door and up the ladder. Rowenna leaned on the port rail, glass in hand, with Ensign Laigain at her elbow.

"What do we have, Lieutenant?"

Rowenna handed her the glass. "Lookout spotted masts and torn sails. Ship does not appear to be underway, sir."

Mairin took the glass and bolted up the mizzen into the top, startling the two lookouts stationed there. Rowenna's description fit what she saw: masts and fragments of sails on a three-master commercial hauler. It had to be dead in the water. Why no signs of life at all, no signals from her crew?

She slid down a backstay to the quarterdeck.

"Lieutenant, signal our consorts, *stay on current heading, Caillech will investigate and catch up later. Do not reduce sail.*"

Ensign Velnowarth worked the flags; seconds later the other ships acknowledged.

"About ship," Mairin ordered. "Ensign Laigain, your promotion is official, I'll make out the papers later. If you have an anchor, you may put it on."

Apparently Rowenna had a spare; Laigain withdrew it from a tunic pocket and carefully pinned it to her left shoulder. Out of the corner of her eye, Mairin watched her other two ensigns for a reaction. They both stood rigidly, eyes fixed straight ahead. Mairin sighed inwardly, *they'll get over it.*

Mairin stepped back to the taffrail and let her officers work. The spanker and royals were hauled in, the ship's head put about and courses set in smooth succession. *Caillech* raced crossways to the waves, her bow crashing through the chop and sending cool, refreshing salt spray along the deck. The new second officer took a place near the wheel, watching with a tightly-buttoned mouth.

Caillech covered the eight miles in less than an hour. By the time they approached the floating hulk, their consorts' masts had sunk below the waves to the south, and the coast of Wales was a thin dark line on the eastern horizon.

"Comment, Lieutenant?" Mairin asked Sithmaith.

The new second officer answered without hesitation. "Falmouth-built, sir, rather old, I'd say at least twenty years. Looks like storm damage."

"Bring us alongside," Mairin said to Rowenna. "Not too close."

"Aye, sir."

Moments later, *Caillech*'s bow swung directly into the wind. Sails were backed and balanced until *Caillech* was brought to, a hundred yards away from the hulk, whose name *Nanscawen* could now be read along her stern. Sithmaith had the *All-Ships Roster* in her hands; she flipped through it rapidly.

"*Nanscawen*, built in the Falmouth commercial yard, launched twenty-three years ago, crew of forty-four, passenger accommodation twenty, cargo capacity three hundred tons," she read. "Last entry indicates she was used mainly between Welsh ports and Plymouth, probably a bit too old for longer runs."

"The question is," Mairin pondered aloud, "was she torn up by the storm and then abandoned, or did something happen to her before the storm?"

"She's yet sailable, Captain," Master Gailenga pointed out. "Masts are sound, she's not low in the water, and sure she'd have spare sails below. Valuable property to leave adrift, even at her age."

Time was wasting. Every minute they waited increased the risk of losing the fine wind for Falmouth. On the other hand, there could be survivors belowdecks, injured or dying.

"Lieutenant," she said to Sithmaith, "take the cutter across with Master Sechnaill and ten sailors, full arms and armor. Go through her and get back as fast as you can."

Caillech rocked easily in the swell as Sithmaith, Weapons Master Sechnaill, and ten armored sailors pulled across to the *Nanscawen*. The boarding party clambered up the ship's side-ladders and then disappeared through the aft hatch.

Mairin paced nervously up and down the starboard rail of the quarterdeck. *Caillech* was unusually quiet: sailors spoke to each other in low voices and whispers. The sight of the wrecked and seemingly abandoned ship, Mairin had to admit, made her skin crawl. No crew of a ship in that condition would leave her adrift unless forced to.

"Captain," Rowenna said, "they're coming up."

Sechnaill's helmet appeared first, followed by Sithmaith and the rest. Five of the sailors ran for the railing and vomited into the sea. After a minute or two the party climbed down the side into the waiting cutter and pulled back to the *Caillech*. Sithmaith was first on deck. She yanked off her helmet, revealing a face that was at the same time composed and ashen. She saluted to Mairin and leaned one hand on the railing.

"Captain." She swallowed and took a breath. "Many bodies belowdecks, at least a week dead. All were killed, most mutilated. Cargo holds broken into, I don't know what was taken."

She leaned over the rail and gasped but did not vomit. She straightened up and continued.

"The Master and I agree she was attacked, boarded, and left adrift. Anyone killed on deck was swept overboard in the storm. Amazing the ship stayed afloat, I guess the sails blew out and she scudded downwind."

She reached underneath the heavy cuirass and pulled out a crumpled piece of brown paper.

"We found this, sir, on the floor of the captain's cabin."

She handed it to Mairin. Parts of the sheet seemed to show navigational information. The text was written in a language unknown to Mairin. She folded it carefully and tucked it in a pocket.

"Master," she said to Sechnaill, who looked disgusted but not sick, "take all the boarders below, get them out of their armor and offer stout if they want it. Lieutenant Laigain, fifteen minutes for yourself, then report back to me. You did well."

"Thank you, sir," the young woman said, her color beginning to return.

"Put us about and flash them out," Mairin ordered Rowenna. "All she will bear, Lieutenant."

"Aye, sir."

In seconds Rowenna had *Caillech's* bow swung round to regain the wind on her stern. Courses were struck, the spanker set, topmast yards swung round, and *Caillech* plunged southward to overtake her sister ships. They had lost about an hour and a half, Mairin estimated.

"Captain," said Rowenna, "what are you thinking about the *Nanscawen?*"

"I think this ship was taken on the high seas a week ago. The attackers, whoever they are, killed the crew and passengers, started to transfer the cargo and then the storm came up. They took what they had and left *Nanscawen* to sink ... which it didn't."

"And that paper, is it any help?"

Mairin pulled it out and handed it to her. "Can you read it? The numbers and symbols look like positions and headings. The letters are clear enough but the words mean nothing to me."

While Rowenna studied the sheet, a memory of more than a week ago edged into Mairin's mind. With Richard at the map in Tredinnick House. He pointed to the area of old Denmark, the Baltic Sea.

"I can visualize the coordinates," Rowenna said. "The positions listed would be northeast of England, on the east coast of the North Sea, roughly."

Mairin did not answer immediately.

"Captain?"

"Yes, you're right about the coordinates, I'm sure. We'll turn this over to the Admiralty. Also report her position so they can salvage her. I don't envy the salvage crew."

She took the paper from Rowenna, folded it carefully and shoved it back in her pocket.

"If I may say, sir, I think Lieutenant Laigain will always remember her first day in rank."

"No doubt," said Mairin with a smile. "No doubt about that at all. I'm going below, I'll see the two ensigns in any order, then we'll have all officers together at the shift change. Let me know if we sight our own squadron."

Despite Rowenna's every attempt to coax more speed out of *Caillech*, they did not catch sight of the *Wexford*'s mast lanterns until well after dark. Mairin had hoped to gather the captains together for an evening meal; reducing sail now and maneuvering boats in the darkness made that unwise. So *Caillech* moved to the front and the four ships sailed through the night on a steady wind veering somewhat east of north. Shortly after midnight they raised the brilliant lighthouse on St. Martins and bore southeast to clear the shoals near the Scilly Isles. No ice storm this time: stars shone brightly overhead.

Mairin napped on and off in her cabin, never for more than an hour. Perhaps it was just as well, she sighed, rolling her feet to the deck after a brief nap. *To sleep is to dream.* Was that the line from the ancient poet? No, it was *to die, to sleep, to sleep, aye, there's the rub.* Yes, the rub indeed. Each time she dozed, she entered a hazy, dark place, awoke in a sweat before the dream turned truly threatening.

What time was it now? The chronometer above her cabin door read a few minutes past four a.m., and in the east, a faint tinge of pink glowed along the horizon. She splashed cold water on her face, toweled off, and changed into a fresh tunic. A soft tap on the cabin door startled her.

"Come," she said, taking a brush to her hair.

Sithmaith Laigain entered and shut the door behind her.

"Sit down, Lieutenant," said Mairin, taking a seat opposite the tired-looking officer. "I wanted a few extra minutes with you before we reach Falmouth."

"Thank you, sir," she said. "Starboard watch on deck, all ships holding station, speed six knots. Lieutenant Briuin estimates we'll make Falmouth in less than two hours, sir."

Not as confident and perky as yesterday, Mairin reflected. *Tired yet still clear-headed.*

"I met with Ensigns Velnowarth and Auteini," Mairin said. "Though I'm sure they were disappointed, they both spoke highly of you. I want you to remember that as you take on your new role."

"I will, sir."

"The other matter is somewhat personal. I have a private connection to Laigains who live in the Rosslare area. To be more specific, I'm involved with the Commodore's brother."

Sithmaith fingered her cap nervously. "My family has no direct connection to Commodore Laigain's family in Rosslare, though we know of them of course. Growing up we spent most of our time with my mother's Loigde and Cumain relatives in Enniscorthy."

"And your father?"

"Ah, yes, my father." Sithmaith paused; a flash of pain crossed her face. "Tomaisin Laigain from Wicklow. Abandoned us when I was eight, never to be seen again. My mother and me and four other children, left to the charity of my mother's relations. I doubt Tomaisin is known to the Laigains of Rosslare."

"I'm sorry, Lieutenant. Not many of us come from perfect families."

Would that my father had left us when I was eight!

"I suppose not, sir."

"About yesterday, Lieutenant … the situation on that ship must have been terrible."

"Yes sir, it was. Never felt that sickened before, by anything."

"Master Sechnaill reported that you kept your head, and your stomach for that matter. Not easy for anyone."

Sithmaith nodded and relaxed her grip on her cap. "I appreciate what the master said."

"One last thing, Lieutenant. I promoted you over the other ensigns because of a remark Miles Endean inserted in your service record. Yes, the very captain who marked your young back. I don't need to repeat it. He's a great sea officer, perhaps the best when it comes to commanding the respect of officers and crew. I ask you to think back on why he commanded that respect. In the end, Lieutenant, you can't demand or order loyalty and devotion from those serving under you. Ours is not an ancient navy that enforces discipline with terror and naked power. You earn respect, day by day. The heavens above know I'm as far from a flawless human being as you can get. I make mistakes and say and do things I regret. You will too. The point is, never be afraid to admit these failures and apologize for them when you need to. That is not weakness, it is strength."

Sithmaith held Mairin's eyes. "I'll remember that. Thank you, sir."

She stood and set her hat back on her head. Mairin held out her hand.

"Congratulations, Lieutenant, and good fortune to all of us."

The hand that grasped hers was cool and strong. When she was gone, Mairin turned towards the stern windows, where the glowing mast lanterns of her squadron no longer seemed so bright against the gathering light of dawn. They could not be far from Falmouth now.

I think she'll do well, she told herself. *She has much to learn ... but so did I at nineteen. She'll begin now to feel the ache of responsibility for so many lives, for bringing home safely officers and sailors whose loved ones wait anxiously during each voyage and dread the sight of the black ensign flying at the main.*

She opened the locker door, withdrew her hat and set it squarely on her head. In the mirror she beheld a tired face that seemed to age by the day.

Loud voices broke out above her head. That could only mean one thing: Falmouth was in sight and the fleet that must lie at anchor there. She pulled the loose fabric of the tunic down through her belt, took a gulp of cold tea, and headed for the quarterdeck. It had been a pleasant sail from Éirelan, now it was time to make war.

Dearest Conor, I can only hope this note reaches you before the field army leaves Rosslare. When we left Wicklow Harbor the day of the fair, we heard the alarm sound at the fort and I was sick with worry, for you and for my brother. Thanks to your mother I learned quickly that you escaped without serious injury, though Kellen did not. We had word at Falmouth that he is recovering. I can't put into words how sorry I am that I made you feel responsible for him. I made that request without thinking and it was foolish. Please forgive me? I've seen Feth, and Seanlaoch too, they look like a couple in love. She's changed a great deal since I last saw her. We sail today back to Falmouth on a major war expedition, best I not give details in the public post. Not a day or a night will pass that I will not wonder how you are. I long to see you again, already the lovely day at the fair seems so far in the past. One last thing: I hope you don't mind that I showed Feth the Celtic Knot you gave me. She can explain why, if you see her.

All my love, Mairin.

Chapter 20

The first six hours out of Rosslare were relatively easy ones, with a southerly wind and low seas that Aideen's flagship *Nore* cleaved straight on. Now as sunset neared, the wind veered into the east and on the new tack the rollers caught the ship at precisely the angle needed to induce roll and pitch and yaw all at once. Virtually every soldier on every ship hung over a leeward rail.

Conor's white-knuckled hands gripped the bow railing as the warship buried its bow sideways in yet another massive wave. Violent as the up and down swinging of the bow seemed to him, it was less nauseating than the corkscrew effect that grew worse towards the ship's waist. He was on the windward side because his vacant stomach did not leap into his mouth, unlike his hapless comrades who had indulged in breakfast. The cool spray on his face eased the nausea, though not by much.

Behind him he heard a sailor say "Commodore" and he turned to see his sister approaching on his side of the ship. She looked quite different from the well-starched officer onshore at Rosslare. She wore a tan canvas jacket over a plain, dark green working tunic, wool leggings, a stocking cap pulled down over her ears, and weather-beaten boots. He did his best to straighten up and hoped that his deep tan would conceal the green tinge of seasickness.

"This would not be a good time to gloat," he warned her.

She shrugged and looked puzzled. "No intention of gloating, Conor. How are you doing?"

"Better than some," he said, "because I couldn't eat anything this morning. I am sick, just not retching like those poor devils. This contrary gale is a piece of bad luck for sure."

Her eyebrows went up. "Contrary gale? Who told you that? This is a 'fresh breeze' off the starboard beam, in sailor's terms, a fine wind for speed without any danger of tearing sails. The problem is the angle of the ship to the waves, but we can't help that. In a few minutes we'll come about and head towards our anchor point south of Dun Laoghaire. The motion will be less awkward then. You need to make sure everyone drinks plenty of water and eats something once they get ashore. I've already told Padraic. By the way, I have something for you."

She reached inside her jacket, withdrew an oiled pouch, and handed it to him.

"Letter for you inside, arrived just before we left Rosslare."

"From Mairin?"

"It's bears the *Caillech* seal."

Conor slid the pouch inside his own damp tunic. "You wouldn't care to say what her orders are?"

Aideen leaned her elbows on the rail, her trim body swaying easily in rhythm with the ship's motion.

"I probably shouldn't."

"I'm not to be trusted, is that it?"

"Not at all," she said. Her gaze was fixed downward on the ship's bow wave. "I can tell you it's dangerous, and if you keep it to yourself, I can also say it's not entirely authorized by the Council."

"Not entirely?"

"Not at all, then."

"That's a little out of character for you, isn't it?"

She straightened up and anger flared in her eyes. Yet it subsided before she spoke.

"Maybe it is. For now, it may be better if we focus on the task at hand."

"Yes, right, if that's what you want."

Orders rang out from the quarterdeck and sailors sprang into action. Conor and Aideen squeezed up against the railing as sailors pounded into the forecastle and scampered up ratlines into the rigging.

"Hold on," Aideen said, "we're coming about."

Seconds later, Conor's thankfully empty stomach did no more than lurch as the *Nore*'s bow flew up into the wind and then swung hard west until it pointed directly at the remnant of the setting sun. Yards came about, slack sails drew taut again, and the *Nore* gathered way towards the Eirelan coast. Aideen silently studied the movements of the other eleven ships. Satisfied her fleet was in good order, she turned back to Conor.

"In two hours, we'll be a mile or so off the coast near Greystones. There's no harbor anywhere on this stretch of coastline, so we'll anchor as close in as high tide allows. That will be about a mile. By then all the soldiers have to be in full gear, on deck, and ready to go. My sailors will boat you ashore in groups of about twenty. This will take overall about two hours. Oran will meet you onshore, he should have returned from his final trip inland. After that, you're on your own."

"What will conditions be like for the boats? My soldiers will sink like stones if a boat overturns in deep water."

"If this mild easterly holds, the landings will be smooth," she assured him. "And even if it doesn't, my sailors know what they're doing."

Melvina approached, strolling comfortably along the port rail.

"May I join you?" she asked.

"By all means," said Aideen. "You don't look sick, Commander."

"I'm not," Melvina admitted. "I sail for recreation when I have time. I feel for all the rest, though, it's a terrible sensation when it first hits you."

"All over soon," said Aideen. "I need to get back to my cabin and go over the landing plans with Padraic and his staff. Good luck to you both."

Conor watched his sister stride quickly aft, along the way snapping out remarks to sailors and deck officers.

"Are you all right?" asked Melvina. "She get after you?"

"She was unusually mild. Strange for her."

"I wouldn't want the responsibility she has," said Melvina. "Not just this mission ... the whole Squadron, every day. Storms, battles, shortages, ships wearing out, cranky captains. Put yourself in her shoes and imagine what your disposition would be." She paused and gazed out over the fleet. "I understand you've never liked each other and that's sad, but I think you're mistaken if you believe she doesn't feel the weight of her position."

"I'm sure she does and I feel for her ... though she never accepts any sympathy from me."

Melvina nodded and leaned back against the rail. The ship drove ahead to the west without much rolling. Blades and Bows no longer hung over the rails; now and then a peal of laughter rang along the decks. A prolonged twilight painted the western sky a spectacular pink. *There's a poem in that sight*, Conor sighed inwardly, *if I had the time and the clear head to write it.*

"What are you thinking?" Melvina asked.

"About that splendid sky. About wanting the time and peace of mind to write a poem about it."

"And instead ... "

"Instead I have all those young lives to think about," he said, waving a hand towards the crowded deck. "I'll tell you something, Melvina, if you keep it to yourself. When I look into the eyes of one of my soldiers, some part of me wants to flee, to go somewhere where there is no fighting, no blood spilled on the ground. A place where I can write the poem about a painted sky and not think about what lies ahead tomorrow. I feel like I was born out of time, a poet who landed in the middle of a war he didn't start and can't finish."

Melvina thought for a moment before answering. Then she pointed to a slender, auburn-haired archer about halfway aft on the opposite railing.

"You see that girl there? Calinda Neill, from Tralee. Her father owns a coaster there. Age nineteen. Bright, funny, full of life. I love her to death. The thought of her lying dead on the field is as terrible an image as I can conjure up. All I can do is remind myself that she's here by choice, that all the young men and women we command are here by choice and know why they're here. They ask us only to lead them, not to mourn for them if they fall."

She paused, then went on. "If you think you're alone in the feeling of wanting to be somewhere else, you're mistaken. Every one of us here would rather be somewhere else, doing *anything* but fighting a battle. I love to sail, not a monster like this ship, just a little boat that I can handle myself. Imagine being right where we are now, sailing along the coast, in no hurry to get anywhere, watching the lights come on in the cottages along the shore, catching the last rays of evening fading to black." She glanced toward the *Nore*'s waist where an especially boisterous mixed group of young Bows and Blades traded loud, innocent taunts. "Maybe when you're that young it's easier to forget where you are and what you're about. For some of those youngsters this is their first major battle. They'd rather be making love in the hayloft or singing bawdy songs in a friendly tavern. We're hardly old but we've already done plenty of that and now we want fuller lives for ourselves, maybe a home, and children. Am I right?"

Conor nodded. "Yes, for me anyway."

Melvina braced a muscular leg on an ammunition locker. "I get the idea you dwell on it, worry it will never happen, that life will slip away from you and there's nothing you can do. That makes you sad, and angry too. You think it will make you bitter with life, in time."

"You seem to know me very well," he said quietly, "for someone who hardly knows me at all."

"I have a confession to make. I asked Padraic if he might have a book of your poetry and he lent me a volume he had with him. I read it last night."

Conor shifted his feet uneasily and stared at the foretop above their heads.

"I hope you liked it."

"I did. It's unfair, I know, because you don't know much about me. Reading it did explain some things to me. You see, you grew up in a loving family and it's natural for you to want the same thing for your-self, except now you would be the parent and not the child. I didn't have what you had. Oh, I wasn't beaten or left outside to freeze. I was my mother's third child and when I was two, my mother died in child-birth with the fourth. My father couldn't raise us alone and work too, so each of us was farmed out to a different relative. I ended up with cousins who really didn't want me. I was fed and clothed and schooled and that was about it."

"I'm sorry," he said, reaching out towards her. He let his hand fall short: they were in clear view of a score of soldiers and sailors.

"Don't feel sorry for me," she said. "I don't. I only told you this to explain why I don't expect too much out of life. My attitude is, do your best, live every day, and accept what life gives you. I won't spend a second being sad about what I didn't have then, or can't have now. It's okay to want, but brooding over what we can't have takes away the joy of life. It would for me, anyway."

When he said nothing in reply, she gave him a worried look. "I hope I didn't overstep, Conor. Please feel free to ignore everything I said."

"You did *not* overstep," he said. "You gave me a lot to think about. Mainly what you did is make me feel less alone up here."

She smiled and laughed lightly. "Your poems gave me plenty to think about too. When we get back to the Province, let's sit down in a dark pub and trade deep insights over cold ale."

"I'm buying," he said, laughing with her.

"I'll drink you under the table."

"I don't think so."

"I know so."

"Now we sound like them," Conor said, nodding towards the merry group in the waist.

"We should," she said. "Nothing depresses an army more than glum-faced commanders."

"Ouch."

"You're not glum-faced now." She reached inside her leather jerkin and pulled out a gold coin worth five crowns. "This says you'll pass out before I do."

Conor fished in his own pockets and came up with no more than a sixpence coin.

"Imagine this is a five-crown," he said, holding it next to her genuine one. "Done."

She replaced the coin in her jerkin. "Time for me set up the plan for the boats."

"I need to read a letter," he said, pulling out the pouch. "Then I'll see to the Blades."

He held out his hand and she took it in a powerful grip.

"Fortune favors the brave," he said.

She gave the ritual Latin reply. "*Fortes fortuna adjuvat.*"

Melvina crossed to the opposite rail and headed aft. Conor pulled out the pouch and opened the note from Mairin. *Written fast in a rough hand.* He frowned at her mention of a "major war expedition." No wonder Aideen was so secretive! He also guessed why Mairin showed the amulet to Feth. *She's thinking she may not come back.*

He dug into his belt pouch, located a pencil, and on the back of her letter scratched an answer. *Nothing to forgive. I love you too. Conor.* He slid the sheet carefully back into the pouch and went aft. He found Aideen on the quarterdeck, talking with her flag captain. At a pause in their conversation he handed Aideen the pouch and leaned close to her ear.

"Please deliver this if I don't make it back," he whispered.

She took it with a troubled frown.

"Of course," she said, and tucked the envelope in her tunic. For a fleeting moment, a hint of fear crossed her face. "Of course," she repeated.

"So much for your mild easterly," Conor observed.

"I don't control the weather," Aideen answered curtly. "And I told you we'd be fine even if the wind came up, which it has. We have a nor'easter building fast, it'll get much worse before it gets better."

They stood side by side on the *Nore*'s quarterdeck, beneath a shaded lantern swinging from the main yard of the mizzen. The launch conveying Padraic and his staff was pulling away towards the invisible shore. In the lantern's glow he could see the boat long enough to watch it tossed about by rolling waves.

"I'm not the best swimmer," he reminded her.

"I did my best to teach you," Aideen retorted, her eyes focused on the next boat lowering away. Melvina waved brightly from the boat's bow. "You never stuck with it. Feth swims like a dolphin."

"In thirty-two pounds of leather and steel armor, not counting weapons, kit, boots, and cape?"

"There'll be no sinkings!" she snapped, loud enough to turn the heads of nearby officers. In a softer hiss, she said, "Listen, it may seem like a devil's night to you, but I assure you, my sailors are trained to handle far worse."

As she finished, a fresh gust blasted through the rigging and drew an angry creak from two anchor cables holding the *Nore* steady.

"I didn't mean it as an insult," Conor said once his stomach stopped trying to climb into his mouth. "I'd never question your seamanship or your crews."

"It's all right, I didn't mean to shout. I know you're worried about your soldiers, not yourself." To his surprise, she took hold of his arm and stared into his eyes. "They'll all be safe, Conor, I promise you. Now get into a boat."

"I'm taking the last one, with the most frightened soldiers." He wondered momentarily at his own sanity. "I thought they might feel better if they saw the Blade Commander looking as nervous as they are."

"You are a piece of work, dear brother," she said in a tone that verged on genuine admiration. "I'll send the *Nore*'s bosun with you, she's the best boat-handler in the fleet. You'll get wet, but you'll get there."

Aideen moved aft to confer with the *Nore*'s captain and first officer. The warship's two largest boats made two more trips each, and then Conor found it was his turn, along with the remaining nine Blades and seven Bows, every one of them sick and near panic. Soldiers were trained to ride in a ship's boat and land on a beach; now he realized those calm-seas, daylight exercises prepared no one for climbing into a pitching boat in the black of night, with wind howling in the rigging and the ship itself rolling and pitching at anchor.

Settled with his gear in the boat's bow, he was promptly greeted by a cold dash of seawater in the face, causing him to wonder why men and women had ever taken to the seas in the first place. When the last soldier half-stumbled in, the lines holding the boat let loose and at the same moment, eight broad-shouldered women at the oars braced their feet and rowed furiously in unison. In seconds the boat turned perpendicular to the *Nore* and plunged into the back of waves that seemed to Conor several feet higher than the boat's gunwales.

Once the bosun set the rowers' cadence, she engaged the soldiers in a salty, comic banter that actually had them laughing instead of puking. Conor peered through the darkness towards the *Nore* and whispered, *thank you, dear sister.*

The sailors rowed even harder as they neared shore, forcing the boat's sharp prow through the breakers at amazing speed.

"Up oars," the bosun barked suddenly, and in perfect unison eight oars tipped high out of the water. The boat scraped onto the sand and the harrowing trip was over.

"Everyone out," the bosun called in a low, urgent voice. "Fast as you can, mates, that nor'easter's about to blow the ship on our heads."

The sailors jumped out first and seized hold of the boat, followed by heavily-laden soldiers who clambered over the gunwales in near-total darkness. Two Blades lost their footing and toppled into shallow water amid a torrent of foul curses.

"Silence there," Conor snapped. "Get moving."

He climbed out himself, thankful even for the squishy sand that greeted his boots. No sooner had he cleared the water than the sailors spun the boat round, leaped back in and began pulling for all they were worth. The bosun called back, "godspeed, all of you."

The shore was dimly lit by two shaded lanterns marking a path into the woods. Conor took a quick head count and then led shaken, relieved fighters between the lanterns. A hundred yards along path brought them to the hidden gathering place for the army. It was a natural clearing, the growth of trees blocked by crumbled concrete and stone ruins that seemed continuous and forced careful walking. *What was this*, Conor wondered? A mansion? A factory? Whatever it had been, it had fallen to ruin at least a millennium ago and now nothing taller than his shins was left standing.

On the left side of the clearing, Bows gathered into their centuries around blue lanterns; on the right side, Blade centuries surrounded red lanterns. The center of the clearing was occupied by a three-sided tent forty feet long, open on the side facing the beach and lit from within by lanterns hanging from poles. At the back of the tent, Padraic's aides had suspended a map twenty feet long and six high, marked by colored lines and dots and arrows. As soon as all the troops were safely gathered in the strange meadow, sixteen century captains drew up in a semicircle around the open side of the command tent. Conor located Melvina and together they waited for Padraic to begin.

A cold hand pressed onto the back of his neck. "What—?"

Oran shoved back the hood of his black cape and grinned at him.

"For once I look better than you!" Oran said in an impish whisper. "Not easy to be pale and green at the same time, brother."

Conor had to admit he was right. "Seafaring does not agree with me. Do you know Melvina Eogain, our Bow Commander?"

Oran bowed slightly towards her and extended his hand. "I haven't had the pleasure."

"The pleasure is mine," said Melvina, taking his hand.

Oran held her hand an extra second, and in that brief space of time Conor spotted a familiar gleam in his friend's eye.

Oran glanced out over the clearing. "An eerie spot I found for us."

"Any idea what this was?" Conor pushed at a shard of concrete with his toe.

"No time to explore," Oran said. "A dwelling of some kind, probably multi-story. This whole beach was covered with them at one time, all the way from Wicklow to Dublin. Resorts, maybe, when people could sit around and do nothing."

"I imagine you know all of Conor's secrets?" Melvina asked Oran, with a sidelong glance at Conor.

"I do."

"You must know about Oran," Conor broke in, "that tall tales come easily to his lips."

"Fah," said Oran. "I never alter the truth one bit."

Conor's rejoinder was cut off by Padraic's usual method for imposing silence: the massive battle sword slid out and thumped down on the table. The low rumble of conversations was replaced by the rumble of the surf and the chirping of crickets. Padraic's eye found Conor, Oran and Melvina and he motioned them to the front.

"My comrades, Bows and Blades all," he said, his heavy voice suppressed so that it just carried to the gathered captains, "this is going to be a tricky and risky attack. So far as we know, we are outnumbered nearly three to one. We have two advantages. First, if we're careful, our attack will be a complete surprise and that lowers three to one to two to one. Second, we have our discipline, our armor, weapons, and tactics, and those bring the odds to even. In an even fight, we'll always prevail."

A quiet murmur of agreement swept through the group.

"You know the plan," he said, stepping to one side to make the map visible to all. "The enemy army is encamped along the eastern shore of Lough Poulaphouca. Their camp is strung out here," he pointed to a red-colored strip along the edge of the blue-colored lake, "very narrow and about half a mile north to south. There's a rise in the terrain a hundred yards or so to the east, so they will not see us coming from that direction. I thank my blessed ancestors for this wind, too, which will rush through the trees and mask any sound we make. Wind or no, once we're within a mile of the camp, there must be no sounds whatsoever. Remind all your fighters of this."

"The Blades will be divided into two forces: one force of eight centuries led by Commander Laigain will form a line of battle on the east side of the ridge. I will lead the other four centuries north and form line of battle in the woods north of the enemy camp to block their escape in that direction. The entire force of Bows under Commander Eogain will move with the larger Blade force and form line of battle interspersed among the Blades, by century."

He paused and wiped a few beads of sweat from his forehead.

"Shortly before dawn, when there is light enough to see clearly, the attack force will form up below the ridgeline. Melvina Eogain and her nine hundred archers will commence the assault. No pipes, no shouts, no warning. They will move silently to the top of the ridge, leaving gaps for the Blades, and pour one minute of rapid fire into the camp. Then the Blades will advance into the gaps of the line and launch a volley of javelins. Bows will drop behind the Blade line, sprint to the flanks and set up enfilading fire. The Blades will of course close up their line as soon as the javelins are in the air. Battle pipes will sound when the Blades close up, signaling the advance into the camp. Where's my lead piper?"

"Here, sir," came the treble voice of Trev Fiachrach, who stepped forward wearing his tartan kilt and cap. Conor had requested the young musician, who was thrilled at the chance to be here. "The pipes will sound, ten of us, never you fear, General."

"I know they will, son," said Padraic. Trev smiled and took a step back.

"The attack must be fierce and relentless," Padraic continued, "and you must drive them hard towards the water. If we gain the surprise I want, the shock will be enough to make most of them run, in the hope of regrouping somewhere else. Instinct will tell them to run north towards Dublin on the road that follows the River Liffey. They could then make a stand in the ruins of Lachan Town, about a half mile away. That's where they'll find me waiting. If they choose to fight in their camp, I will launch a flank assault."

He paused again to quaff stout from his mug. His heavy-lidded gray-green eyes slowly scanned the silent captains. "Questions?"

There were none.

"Captains, form up your fighters for the march. Our scout, Oran Osraige, will lead the column. When he calls for silence down the line, it must be silence. Tomorrow morning, surprise is all."

He picked up his sword and slid it into the sheath. "March in fifteen minutes."

Aides leaped forward to gather in the map and douse the lanterns. Conor and Melvina parted company briefly to make sure all their captains knew the marching order, then rejoined Oran who was to lead the army in total darkness over terrain only he knew.

An old road meandered from the full distance from beachhead to the lake, though it was little more than a trail parting the trees. Conor had no worries about losing their way; Oran seemed to have a compass built into his head. Often when they played in the woods as boys, Conor came to the edge of panic at being lost, only to have Oran laugh and lead him straight back to their starting point.

Voices dropped to whispers and every piece of clanking or squeaking gear was secured or greased. Each soldier carried a small, red-shaded oil lamp to guide his feet, while Oran, at the head of the column, carried a slightly brighter lantern to guide their route. Melvina decided to march partway back at the head of the Bow column, leaving Conor and Oran alone at the front of the army. A moment's reflection told Conor she had moved back to give them that time together.

It was an eerie enough night to make anyone nervous, even an armed soldier in full armor. The nor'easter howled through the black woods, raising an ominous rustling of leaves and creaking of limbs all about the double-file of soldiers. Yet Conor blessed that strong wind, so fearsome when it was rocking the landing boats. Here, it made plenty of background noise that covered the sound of their approach. He prayed it would blow on right to the instant of their attack.

Conor knew that Padraic, for all his outward confidence, had to be thinking that this was a desperate gamble. Being heavily outnumbered defending the Rampart was one thing, but out here in the open, they could be cut to pieces with no way to retreat to safety. He observed as much to Oran, in a low voice that barely carried above the swishing of the trees.

"A gamble? Aye, it is that," his friend said with a shrug. "No other way, my friend. If we wait while they gather strength, they can attack the Rampart at many points, break through somewhere and we'll lose all of the Province north of Wexford, if not more. Padraic tried yet again to bargain, had me carry a note to the Dubliners through an intermediary offering food and medicine to help them through the winter. It led to nothing. They want what we non-believing heathens have, pure and simple. We have to beat the Dubliners now because the Ghaoth Aduaidh will attack in two or three weeks. And they will have a bigger army, better equipped and trained."

"Oh, I don't question what we have to do," said Conor bitterly. "We have to take the chance. Yet so many will die tomorrow, on both sides, and for what? For nothing, brother. For nothing. No principle is served, nothing beautiful is created, at most we gain time at the price of blood."

He felt Oran's hand on his shoulder.

"There is a principle served," Oran countered. "All my travels tell me that we're the last line of defense in this land between order and utter barbarism. If we fall, everybody takes whatever they can get from anybody weaker than themselves. We have to fight on, Conor. We just have to."

They fell silent for a time as the trail twisted and turned sharply. When it straightened out again, Conor edged as close to Oran as he could to speak privately.

"This could be our last time together—no, wait, let me finish. It may be that two weeks from now we'll be hoisting our glasses together in a warm pub, and I truly hope that's what we can do. The stout will be on me. It also may be that one of us doesn't come out alive. If you go back and I don't, I want you to watch out for Mairin."

"I don't get you. She's a senior fleet captain and—"

"I can't go into it all now," Conor broke in. "I can tell you she needs friends she can trust in this world. Be a friend to her."

"I am already."

"Sure, I know, but that's because of my connection to her. If I'm gone, stay in touch with her, when she's ashore. She's had so much to deal with in her life."

"You mean her wicked parents and brutal brother."

"Yes, that's what I mean."

Oran sighed. "All right, Mr. Gloom. Yet I prefer to dwell on being best man at your wedding. And godfather to a squalling child."

The path grew so narrow that two soldiers could barely walk side by side. After a series of low rises and gullies, the trail widened again and the terrain leveled. Oran halted the column.

"We're about three miles out," he said to Conor. "I see a hint of light in the east. We'll take the next two miles at an easy pace. I want us a mile out as the sky brightens."

"We're not lost?"

"Hah!"

Oran led them off again, at a leisurely stroll though a quiet valley filled with wrens and larks anticipating dawn with a raucous chorus.

"Oran," said Conor, "I want to say one more thing in the time we have left. I know I'm dark by nature, sad more often than happy, bleak and withdrawn on a bright summer day. I write poetry that borders on maudlin and often enough I look like I swallowed something sharp and painful. For all of the times you have put up with me, and made me smile and laugh, I thank you. I love you as a brother, but that you know."

"Conor," his friend answered after a moment, "I am flighty by nature, take silly chances, laugh at bad jokes, make up worse jokes, drink too much in pubs, and make light of things that really aren't funny. There have been so many times you said something or wrote something that let me see a truth of the world I had entirely missed. I would be much less a man had I never known you."

The two friends marched on together in the pre-dawn darkness, arms draped over each other's pauldroned shoulders, while slowly the eastern sky behind them turned from coal black to dismal gray. No trace of cheerful lavender and pink and orange, for the overcast was thick and low. At the edge of a broad clearing Oran halted the column and Conor gave hand-signals to douse the lanterns and maintain absolute silence.

On the far side of the clearing, the ground sloped upward. Over the rise lay the lake with the odd name of Poulaphouca, the place where they would fight today.

Other people remember my father as a great man, a leader of our people. I remember him as the man who gave me rides on his horse and took me fishing and showed me when I was six how to shoot a bow. I do have one special memory that sticks in my mind. He took me alone one day on a walk along the coast north of Rosslare. He stopped all of a sudden and looked out over the water, which was calm that day. He said to me, "My precious little Feth, always remember that we are not the most important things in the world. We are no more important than those birds flying over the water, trying to find a meal. We are part of a great cycle of living and dying. When you find yourself feeling too special, too big for your own britches, remember what I have told you." Then he kept on walking. Maybe those aren't the exact words he used but I know I have the idea right. Did he see in me a tendency to think myself important? Thank you, father, for those words. I try to live by them every day.

Journal of Fethnaid Laigain

Chapter 21

Feth edged towards consciousness and for a moment could not remember where she was. Not her room in Rosslare, surely. Then she felt Sean's reassuring arm lying over her. How much she wanted to stay there till bright dawn and then spend the day with him! It could not be.

What time was it? Pale gray light filtered into the window ... not yet daylight. She had a little time to stay warm, to feel his body touching her, to listen to his even, quiet breathing.

Her mind whirled behind closed eyelids. She struggled to sort out the unsettling welter of the past days. Gwen ... born and raised on the far west coast, wearing the uniform of the Line of Bows and risking her life to defend the Province. Vaughn and Murel, who only wished to find a place to live and work and raise children—nearly turned away by a man supposedly taught from childhood to respect the sacred values of the Twenty Clans. And then the rumors, persistent and hard to discount, that the army being raised by the Ghaoth Aduaidh in Belfast would be immense, disciplined and well-armed. How much difference could two hundred new horse archers make in the face of such a Goliath?

An idea drifted up from the tangle of thoughts and feelings. It seemed absurd at first, but the more she considered it, the more sense it seemed to make. Dangerous, yes. Maybe it had to be done.

"Feth ... are you awake?"

"Yes."

Sean tightened his arms around her.

"Thinking?"

"Yes."

She turned in his arms to face him.

"I need a break from thinking."

"I can manage that."

A half hour later, bright pre-dawn light filled the room and she knew they had to get moving.

"Got to get up," she said, swinging her feet to the cool floor. "I have time for breakfast and then I need to report for training with Arvel."

"I have a shift at the hospital this morning," he said while pulling on his trousers. "This afternoon I'm going to write. I haven't done much of that recently."

"Because of me?"

He paused with one sock half on. "Every second I spend with you is precious, love. Writing comes second. Mainly it's been the time at the hospital. They said they won't need me after today." He tugged on his boots and got to his feet. "When will I see you again?"

"Not sure," she replied, her hands on his waist. "I have duty at the fort tonight. By the usual rotation I'd be off in two days. Hard to say now with the horse-archer training."

He brushed errant flaxen hair from her forehead. "You have something on your mind."

"I do," she said. She tugged a sweater over her head. "Tell you over breakfast."

The pub was already bustling when they arrived, and it took a series of glares from Sean to get the attention of Naomham's morning helper, a dour-faced thin man with a pronounced limp. They had to settle for a guttural "here" as he served their tea, oatmeal, and a platter of disappointingly fatty bacon.

"So, what were you thinking about?" Sean asked. He tried an experimental nibble on a rasher of bacon and carefully set it back down on the platter. "I wouldn't eat that if I were you."

Feth took a swallow of tea. "I think we need to try recruiting in the west, Cork and Kerry."

Sean nodded. "Your uncle has proposed that to the Council of Twenty every year for the past three."

"Sure, I know. I meant something different."

"Yesterday's *Daily Bulletin* reported that the western clans proposed a formal alliance. They offered to send soldiers for the army in the spring, in exchange for defense against attacks this fall and a commitment to extend the Rampart to Tralee."

Feth set down her spoon and stared at him. "I hadn't heard that. What did the Council do?"

"Deadlocked," Sean said with a disgusted shake of his head. "As usual. The report said your mother, Rionach and their allies tried for two days to get approval and in the end lost on a tie vote."

"How stupid!" Feth cried, loud enough to draw attention from nearby tables. Lowering her voice, she went on: "What I meant, Sean, was to recruit *now*. We need help right away, the battle can't be more than a month off."

"And who would do this recruiting?"

"I would. Well, me and anyone I could get to come with me."

"You mean recruit on your own, without Padraic's or the Council's approval? That's crazy, Feth, they'll never let you do it."

"Don't be so sure," she retorted, frowning. "I don't need Council approval, because it won't be an official recruiting mission. I do need leave from the service."

"You think any officer here would grant you leave for that without Padraic's okay?"

"I'll send him a note by courier."

"He's commanding the eastern field army, Feth. You can't reach him for at least a week."

"What can I do? Help me instead of being so negative."

Sean drummed his fingers on the table. "You can't go alone."

"Of course not. I'd ask Gwen and Derdre, maybe Keegan too if he's fit enough."

"Then you need to get leave for at least four soldiers, at a time when the army is training for battle. The question is, how? Everyone who could help you is with the field army and out of touch."

"Not everyone."

Sean sent her a questioning look.

"Grandmother Rionach could do it. She's still Speaker and my mother would support her."

Sean cocked an eyebrow. "Your mother would go along with this?"

"Well, maybe not at first," she admitted. "If Rionach agreed my mother would at least not oppose it."

"It would wreck havoc with Council politics if it got out."

"There won't be any Council if we lose this battle."

"Good point," Sean said. He thought for a moment. "Write a note to her—now. I'll pay for the fastest courier I can find."

"So you think it's worth a try?"

He took hold of her hands. "You'll be putting yourself and your friends at terrible risk, if you're allowed to go. Then again, there could be a battle tonight so there's risk any way you turn. Yes, I think it's worth trying. You'll have to move fast."

Feth rummaged in her bag, found her journal and tore out a blank page. Finding a pencil took another few seconds, then she wrote as fast as she could.

"Read it," she said, pushing it across the table.

Her scanned it, then folded it and tossed coins on the table. Outside, he said: "we'll part here. I'm going to the courier station and get this off. What else can I do?"

"Hmmm ... maps. We'll need maps, and any other information you can find on the western regions. Bridges, roads, everything you can think of. How long to get word back?"

"At best, this time tomorrow if I empty my pockets."

"I love you."

She kissed him and set off at a run for the transport station. She turned her head once before passing out of the town square. He was already gone.

The sun blazed a deep orange low in the western sky by the time Feth, Derdre and Gwen dragged their tired bodies into the barracks. Arvel Rhydderch had worked them for twelve straight hours, riding, shooting, maneuvering, every exercise repeated until it was flawless. He wanted to train many more than three horse archers that day, but the ship bringing forty more horses had carried only two extra sets of riding gear. The rest of the horses and saddles were two days behind schedule from Wales.

Derdre tumbled onto her bunk and twisted her torso back and forth, trying to loosen the fierce knots in her back. Gwen, whose long legs had to fold more than the others to fit in the short Welsh stirrups, touched her toes over and over to stretch out cramped hamstrings. Feth tried massaging her own aching shoulders, finally gave up and fell backwards onto the bed.

"I thought I was in top condition," Derdre moaned.

"You are, for running and shooting," said Gwen. "Not for riding a small horse all day and twisting around to hit a moving target. Well, it seems like the target is moving anyway. Ow. I won't be able to walk in the morning."

"Feth, do you think Rionach will go for it?" asked Derdre, her eyes closed. "I know you're excited about it, but it's really a long shot."

"I know that," Feth said with an exhausted sigh. "We should know by tomorrow morning."

More Bows were drifting in from the training fields. They had one hour to rest before dinner and then night duty at the fort. At some point Feth fell into a light sleep, to be awakened with a start. Bow Captain Renny Loigde bent over her, and Feth had the feeling Renny had repeated her name rather sharply.

"Yes, Captain," she said with a thick tongue.

She sat up fast, giving her stitches a yank. Her hand flew to her injured side.

"Fethnaid, are you all right?" Renny asked, staring at her side.

"A scratch I got off duty, sir," she answered while struggling to her feet. "Did you need something, Captain?"

"Arvel asked that you three be released from fort duty tonight, and I agree. We have enough for a full complement without you. I do have a question, though."

Feth's stomach suddenly felt light. *She couldn't know about the note to Rionach, there hasn't been time for an answer yet!*

"Sir?" she inquired cautiously.

"We had an incident report come down the line from River Glendine. You weren't outside the Rampart and take a knife wound, by any chance?"

"That was me, Captain."

"Raise your shirt."

Feth pulled the sweaty shirt out of her riding trousers, revealing a long, neat line of reddened stitches.

"What you do on free time," Renny commented with a frown, "is your own affair, Bow Junior Grade. Keep in mind we need every archer. Please be careful."

"I will, sir."

Renny nodded and made her way out. Feth let out pent up air.

"Heaven above, I thought somehow she knew about my note." She collapsed back onto the bunk.

Derdre peeled off her sweater. "If we have the night off, I need a long shower. Gwen?"

"Me too," the tall girl replied. She sniffed the air. "I think you should come along, Feth."

"I can hardly stand myself. Pray for warm water."

A half hour later, dressed in fresh tunics, the three of them headed for the mess hall. Keegan waved from a nearly-empty table. Next to him sat a massive man with flaming red hair and thick beard to match.

"My friend Ionhar Raithlinn," Keegan said as they approached.

Ionhar rose up and offered a mammoth hand to each of them in turn. *Nearly as tall as Keegan*, Feth said to herself, *and big as my uncle. Padraic must have looked like this, thirty years ago. Ionhar looks strong enough to lift the building off the foundation.*

"Very pleased," Ionhar said quietly, his voice impossibly deep. He eased back down onto the protesting bench and faced Gwen. "We're both from outside the Province, I understand."

"I'm from Fahamore, not far from Tralee."

"Creagh," he replied with a smile of pride, "a tiny town south of Skibbereen. My family has lived there longer than the age of the Twenty Clans. Storytellers from time out of mind."

"I've known Ionhar since my first training camp," said Keegan, smiling at his friend. "We got acquainted because he was the only man who could out-wrestle me."

Ionhar laughed. "True, we met that way. More than that, Keegan was my friend when others would not speak to me."

"I know that feeling," Gwen murmured.

The dinner bell rang and the two Blades volunteered to collect food and stout for their group. The five of them ate together for an hour—both Keegan and Ionhar were on barracks reserve too.

At a pause in the banter, Ionhar said in a low voice, "Feth, I know we cannot speak openly here, but I will tell you what you plan will be dangerous. Maybe not where Gwen comes from, but in other parts of the west, most people would as soon spit at your feet as say hello."

"Then it's time we try to change opinions," Feth insisted. "Will it help that two of us are not born of the Twenty Clans?"

"Matters not, if we're wearing the uniform," Ionhar answered with a frown. "Even in my home town, some people look at me in anger, as if I've betrayed them."

"*If* we get to go," said Derdre to Keegan, "are you sure you're up to it? Feth said you were hurt pretty bad last week."

In answer, he pulled his shirt up to his neck, revealing a chest and belly of rippling muscle and green-yellow bruises. Feth suppressed a grin when Derdre's eyes widened at the enticing sight.

"Colorful, but I can ride and fight," he said. "The arm wounds are almost healed."

"Hurt or no," said Ionhar, "Keegan is the best man with a sword I know."

They left the mess hall together and said friendly farewells where the path split to different barracks.

"I like Ionhar," Gwen said when they were back at their bunks. "Strong, and quiet too. A storyteller!"

"I wouldn't mind getting to know Keegan better," Derdre admitted, her face a bit flushed.

"Is that so?" Feth teased. "I thought your eyes would pop out when he lifted his shirt!"

Derdre laughed. *First time I've ever seen her laugh*, Feth reflected. *I'm glad Keegan showed off!*

That night she dreamt of horses and riding, and of Sean, and once awoke in a sweat from a nightmare of being lost in dense, dark woods. Hours later, dawn arrived unannounced by the friendly rays of the sun. Feth awakened, padded softly to a window, and gazed out at a grey, dreary day. Raindrops streaked the glass and chilly damp air crept around the leaky frame.

Her eyes swept over the shadowy room: half of the hundred-twenty bunks filled, everyone else yet asleep. Her shoulders felt like twisted steel bands. *A night with Sean would have helped*, she mused.

For a time she stared out the window at nothing in particular, turning "ifs" over in her mind. *If grandmother says no, at least I tried. If she says yes ... I'm taking four new friends into peril that everyone has warned me about. If we are killed out there, I may ruin the chances for an alliance that could yet come to pass. If my father were alive to counsel me, what would he say?*

She felt a hand on her shoulder. Gwen stood beside her.

"No sun today," Gwen whispered. She pushed strands of black hair away from her eyes. "My father says dark, rainy days are a blessing because they remind us life is not all sunshine."

"I'd like to know your family. I'd like to see Fahamore Town and look out at the Atlantic from there."

"It's a wonderful place. It sits on the end of a peninsula, all by itself. The houses have to be sturdy because storms blow so hard off the ocean. No thatched roofs, no glass on the ocean side. We have sheep, goats, cows, a big vegetable garden. Our house ... "

Tears streamed down Gwen's cheeks and she muffled a sob with her hand. Her big dark eyes filled with longing and sadness. "I miss it so much, Feth. Gone a full year now, never back once. We write letters but it's not the same."

Feth leaned around to meet Gwen's eyes. "You'll see it soon, I'm sure of it. If we can get through this fall, we'll have plenty of time and we'll go together."

Gwen wiped her eyes with the back of her hands. "You think so?"

"Not think, I know. You can show me everything."

They both heard it at the same time: horse's hooves pounding along the road from town.

"Could be the courier," Feth said.

She headed for the door with Gwen at her heels. Together they walked out and waited under the portico. A liveried express courier barely older than Feth reined in a powerful black stallion, leaped down and tipped his shiny billed cap. Feth quailed at what such premium service must have cost Sean.

"Message for Fethnaid Laigain from Rionach Laigain of Duncormick."

"I am Fethnaid."

He reached into a finely-crafted leather belt pouch and withdrew a plain brown envelope, which he handed to Feth.

"Good day," he said with a slight bow. Seconds later rider and stallion vanished on the road back to town.

Opening the note, Feth found a full page in her grandmother's clear, elegant script. Gwen read over her shoulder.

My dear granddaughter, needless to say your note caught me by surprise. Uinseann and I don't get many liveried couriers here in the country! To the points of your request. It places me in an awkward position with respect to both the Council and your Uncle Padraic. I believe Padraic would approve in principle but might be inclined to say no because of the personal risk involved and because any harm coming to you would make it harder to gain Council approval of alliance with the western clans. We are fortunate that Gilvarry and Rainait, the western clans' official representatives, are staying here with us so I was able to present your idea to them. In general they favor it and give their sanction, though they pointed out that if people in their lands hear of the deadlocked Council vote, they will be angry and could take that anger out on you. Balanced against these hazards is your belief, which I share, that we are in grave peril and everything turns on how great a force we can muster to meet the Ghaoth Aduaidh. As you and I both know, a battle can be decided by a very thin margin indeed. So with a trembling heart I give my permission for you to go. The courier carries a note to your superiors at Dungarvan Fort. They will release you and your comrades for no more than a month. You must return before the main attack comes. I have told your mother in a separate note as you may not have time to write her. Uinseann sends his love, as do I. May a fair wind blow at your back, my child. Love, Rionach.

Feth folded the note. "She said OK. We're going."

"We have to get away today," Gwen said. "Every minute is precious now."

Inside, they found Derdre dressing by her bunk. "I heard the courier's voice. What did your grandmother say?"

Feth waved the note. "Pack your toothbrush. I want to be on the road by noon."

She started throwing on clothes. "I'm going to jump on the next transport to town to see Sean, he's collecting maps and every other scrap of information he can find. You two find the big boys, get our horses together and collect as much food as the commissary will give you. We'll need all our armor and we'll have to take Arvel's recurves, much as we like our longbows. Lots of arrows, too. And make sure Keegan and Ionhar get decent horses."

"Feth." Gwen was pointing towards the door.

Renny Loigde summoned Feth with a curved finger. Feth jammed her legs into trousers and stepped outside with the bow captain.

"I just heard," Renny said. "It sounds like a crazy idea ... but given what we're facing, I think it's worth a try." She extended her hand, which Feth grasped. "Be careful, Fethnaid. All of you."

"We'll do our best, sir. Hold up the battle till we get back."

"I'll try," Renny said with a forced smile. "I'd hate to go into a fight without three of my best archers."

She seemed about to say more, but then merely nodded and walked away. Feth returned to her bunk and yanked on a sweater.

"What did she say?" Derdre asked. "Is she upset with us?"

"No," Feth replied. "More like she was afraid for us."

"Food for at least a week."

Keegan tossed one set of heavy saddlebags to Ionhar and loaded the other on his massive gelding Comhghall. Feth concealed a grin at the sight of Ionhar's horse. To carry his bulk, Ionhar had chosen to rent a farmer's draft horse, an enormously broad-chested dapple gray named Breasal who was more used to pulling a plow than carrying a passenger. He had a habit of eyeing Ionhar with equine derision, and more than once only Ionhar's quick reactions had saved him from a nasty kick in the shins. For the moment, Breasal kept all four iron shoes on the ground.

While they waited for Derdre, Gwen and Arvel to bring the Welsh horses and their armor and weapons, Feth opened the battered leather satchel Sean gave her. It bulged with maps and notes of the country they were about to traverse. She took out one hand-drawn map and struggled to focus on its contents. Her thoughts ran more to the man who drew it than what appeared on the page.

A few hours before, she found Sean in his room, pale, unshaven, exhausted. He had worked ceaselessly through the night, copying maps out of fragile old books and writing up notes on towns and counties and clans and their histories as best he knew them. How her heart soared with love when he looked up from his work, unkempt hair tumbling over bloodshot eyes, and smiled at her. She desperately wanted to stay an hour with him, but it was an hour she did not have to spare. They parted there in his room with a long embrace and kiss, and his whispered "I love you" in her ear.

"He has a polished hand," Keegan said from over her shoulder.

"Yes, he does. He had to hand-copy everything because the books and papers he has are old and precious. He worked twenty hours straight to help us."

"You miss him already."

"I do."

Keegan rested a hand on her shoulder. "Think on how fine it will be when you see him again."

Ionhar erupted in a blast of curses. Breasal objected in his usual way to Ionhar's tightening the cinches, and his huge hoof narrowly missed dealing a blow to Ionhar's right knee.

"The damnable farmer said he rode him all the time," Ionhar growled from a safe distance.

"The farmer was half your weight," Keegan pointed out when he stopped laughing. "If I were Breasal, I'd kick too, seeing who I was going to be carrying!"

"Very funny," Ionhar grumbled. "Maybe Arvel will have a suggestion."

The Welsh fighter had just ridden into view, followed closely by Derdre and Gwen and Feth's gelding Ioan. Derdre's Welsh fighting horse was a leopard-spotted mare answering to Ewerich; Gwen rode a broader, taller chestnut mare named Hunith. Arvel's own black stallion Wledyr was marked by many battle scars and wore a patch over one eye.

Feth quickly donned her armor, loaded Ioan, and slid the short, powerful recurve bow into the saddle holster. Arvel offered suggestions to Ionhar about how to handle Breasal, but Feth could not tell whether the Welshman was being serious or pulling Ionhar's leg.

At last they were all mounted and ready to cross the sturdy plank bridge over the River Colligan, a bridge guarded on the north by the fort itself and along the east bank by twenty heavy ballistae. The day remained as it began: overcast, cool, misty, with wisps of fog drifting along the river. The huge Province flag flying from the fort's high tower drooped against its staff.

Arvel rode up next to Feth and raised his hand over them.

"I will say a Welsh blessing over you," he said, and then spoke in old Welsh; not a word could Feth make out.

"It means this," he said. "*Go forth into the world in peace, be of good courage, hold fast that which is good, render to no one evil for evil, strengthen the faint-hearted, support the weak, help the afflicted, honor all people.*"

He seized each of their hands in a strong grip, tapped his knees to Wledyr's flanks, and thundered back towards the training ground. Derdre drew her horse away a couple of paces and stared at the grass-covered ridge where her mother had fallen. Knowing her thoughts, Feth and the others offered her a minute of silence. Then Feth took from her saddle bag a two-piece staff, extended it fully, and slid it into a holder mounted in front of her left knee. The black banner draped from the staff bore the new insignia designed by Arvel for the horse archers: at the center, a crimson Welsh dragon clutching arrows in its talons, and at the four corners, red Celtic Crosses.

Keegan mounted a similar staff bearing the Province's ensign, a stylized green Celtic Cross set on pure white. The two of them led the way across the bridge; their horses' hooves thudded heavily on rain-dampened planks. Once across, the company rode five abreast over a broad, sweet-smelling meadow. On the far side, a break in the trees marked the beginning of the road towards Cork.

Feth halted them at the road's terminus. From this point, they could see the top of the fort's tower and its sagging pennant. She looked each of her friends in the face, and from each received a nod. She tapped Ioan's flanks gently. The woods quickly enveloped them and all sight of the Province vanished. They rode now in lands where Feth knew they would not be welcome.

It is midnight and I have tried to rest, to sleep, fearing the dreams that may await me. I must be content to watch the ship's iridescent wake and the lanterns of our consorts. It has been a fine sail from Eirelan, a steady wind and easy-rolling sea. My thoughts are of Conor, about to fight a desperate battle in the east. I hope the Book of Fate does not yet have his death written in it. I would be so alone without him to come home to. And what of Richard? In my mind I see him at Brest, on the portico, looking sad and bereft. Oh, why didn't I answer his letters? In his shoes I wouldn't be so forgiving. I would see him often if I accepted the new command Aideen plans to offer me, and when would I see Conor at all? I do so love this life, yet much of the time I am lonely inside. The sea is a silent and unforgiving companion.
Personal log, Mairin Fotharta

Chapter 22

The Squadron ships eased into the wide mouth of Falmouth Harbor. Ahead of them, outlined by rays of sunlight sneaking beneath the lowering overcast, a vast array of tall-masted ships stood to or swung at anchors in the shallow waters of the harbor.

"What's the old word for a giant fleet, Captain?" Rowenna asked.

"*Armada*," Mairin replied. "I'm no scholar but if I remember my Admiralty history class well enough, it's a Spanish word."

"Ironic, then, that we've assembled an *armada* of our own to attack the coast of Spain."

Mairin brushed a hand along the smooth top of the quarterdeck rail. "I may be stretching my memory too far, Lieutenant, but I think the greatest *armada* gathered up by the ancient Spaniards came to grief in its attack on England. Let's hope that won't happen to us."

"Signal flying at Pendennis," the maintop lookout called down. "*Anchor at your discretion. Captains repair to Admiralty.*"

"Cast the lead," Sithmaith ordered. "Signal *Rosc Catha, Morrigan* and *Wexford, anchor four cables behind flag as soundings permit.* Strike the courses, ready to strike topsails at my command."

The lead splashed out from the chains. Moments later Ensign Auteini reported, "ten fathoms, sand and mud, sir."

Sithmaith turned to her superior officers.

"Captain, request permission to heave to and drop anchor."

"Granted," said Mairin. "At your discretion, Lieutenant."

The morning light on Sithmaith's face revealed a brief flash of pride as she turned and called out a series of orders bringing the ship to a smooth halt. Sailors at the bow let go the best bower which splashed into a calm sea trailing its hawser.

"Well done, Lieutenant," said Mairin, walking towards Sithmaith. "Please take charge of the preparations for our passengers."

"Aye, aye, sir."

"*Wexford, Morrigan,* and *Rosc Catha* boats in the water, sir," Ensign Velnowarth reported.

Mairin turned to Rowenna. "We'll take the launch, Lieutenant. I'm going below to dress."

In her cabin, Mairin threw off her working outfit and donned her dress uniform with all the trimmings. As a last touch, she clipped to her chest the Province Cross of Valor, a highly-stylized Celtic Cross inscribed in ancient Gaelic, with a sea-green emerald mounted at the center. So far as she knew, only two others currently serving in the Squadron could claim that honor. *Vain, yes*, she admitted, *but my body and my face bear the scars I got earning this. My left leg aches from the fractures, my back never feels right from being wrenched a dozen times, my right side has a twelve-inch seam in it, and my forehead is marked by two creases that were not there from birth.* As an afterthought, she strapped a watertight leather pouch to her belt; they would be receiving written orders that could not be drenched on the trip back to the *Caillech*.

By the time she returned to the deck, the other three gigs had bumped the side and her fellow captains shifted into *Caillech's* launch. Brigid Auteini gripped the tiller and four of the strongest sailors waited with hands clamped to the oars. Mairin saluted Rowenna, turned over command, and clambered down the rope ladder into the launch. Fore and aft ropes were loosed and Brigid snapped out the command to row.

Mairin took the bow seat so that she faced the other three captains. Nearest her on the right, Tierney Ulaid of *Rosc Catha* smiled and nodded affably despite the incident earlier that day. Ten years Mairin's senior, Tierney's deeply tanned, weathered face bespoke twenty-five years at sea. Mairin resolved to whisper a personal apology in her ear when they had a private moment.

On Mairin's immediate left, twenty-five-year-old Jilleen Conmaicne smiled broadly in her direction. Jilleen, a striking young woman with olive skin and chestnut hair, had been promoted but two months earlier and now commanded the *Wexford*. In the half-year Jilleen served as her first lieutenant in the *Nore*, Mairin found her to be everything a superior officer could want: bright, cheerful, loved by the crew, efficient, respectful but never simpering. More important still, she had proved to be a fierce fighter; her comely face already bore one faint scar. Mairin liked her immensely and had strongly recommended her posting to Aideen.

Morrigan's Kennat Gailenga, a tall, powerful woman of forty, glared at her briefly and then turned away. As a fresh-minted ensign Mairin had served briefly under her and regretted every frightening and disheartening day of it. No one doubted Kennat's seamanship or fighting skills: she could easily have served in the Line of Blades with those corded arms and tree-trunk legs. The problem was her harsh attitude towards discipline. The Squadron forbade the lash and discouraged any form of physical punishment, yet Kennat found ways to make offenders feel pain one way or the other. She had been brought up on charges of brutality twice, and on the second occasion was hauled in front of a three-captain Board of Inquiry. The sentence of formal reprimand and probation was a rarity in the Squadron and through back-channels Mairin got wind of Kennat's angry resentment. *Why did Aideen saddle me with her?* Mairin asked inwardly. *A small reprisal for my attachment to Conor? More likely, she doesn't want Kennat in her own command.*

Small talk seemed like a poor idea in this mixture of company, so Mairin remained silent and the others took their cue from her. For that matter, there was plenty to see. Boats converged on the Pendennis piers from all over the harbor, each craft bearing brightly-uniformed sea officers: the brilliant blue and gold of the Admiralty contrasted with the wildly-mixed colors and insignias of the merchant captains. Brigid had to hold the boat off for several minutes until a gap opened at one of the piers. Then she slid them in smartly and tossed lines to waiting Admiralty sailors on the dock.

As many other boats were waiting, Mairin and her fellow captains jumped out onto the pier and let Brigid cast off. To Mairin's open-mouthed astonishment, Kennat began to walk ahead towards the castle entrance.

"Let it go," Tieney Ulaid whispered in her ear, her hand clamped on Mairin's arm. "We don't want a scene here."

Mairin gritted her teeth and kept moving alongside Tierney, with Jilleen a half step behind.

"Tierney," said Mairin quietly, "my apology. I don't know what I was thinking this morning."

The older woman waved a hand casually. "I knew what happened even before you sent the second signal. You had a rough two weeks, from what I hear. May I ask how your brother is doing?"

"He's all right," said Mairin, "and thank you for asking. I think what hit me hardest was the death of my surgeon's wife. She was a Bow Captain, killed at Dungarvan a week ago. The memorial service was ... hard to handle."

"They do try the spirit," Tierney said with an understanding nod. "We lost two sailors on our last solo voyage, a main yard broke and fell on top of them. One was sixteen, the other seventeen. We all went to the service in a little town near Waterford. Very tough."

They had traveled the full length of a long bricked path from the quay to the castle's main entrance, a towering stone archway that opened onto a grassy field surrounding the central tower. Admiralty offices jammed the higher reaches of that ancient tower. The bottom floor had been left open to create a circular, stone-floored room over a hundred feet across. Mairin remembered being in that vast, cool room twice, the first when she graduated from three years of Admiralty training, the second at Richard's invitation for the Captain's Ball. The latter memory flooded back into her mind: a sultry summer night more than four years ago, a full orchestra playing mellow waltzes, the great room softly lit by sparkling blue-shaded lanterns. Outside in the courtyard, under a brilliant full moon, Richard held her and kissed her in a way she never before experienced.

Her reverie was jolted by the sight that greeted them now. The room was a riot of uniform colors and styles: Admiralty blue and Marines red; green and red plaids for the Scots Guards; Welch Pikemen in somber tan and brown; the ominous black and silver tunics and capes of the huge, silent Bretan Fighters.

They found themselves at the end of a short queue leading up to the great man himself, Admiral Collen Tredinnick. An average-sized man in his middle fifties, he seemed larger than everyone around him. From his mast-straight bearing to his close-trimmed, steel-gray hair to his gleaming blue eyes set against sun-weathered skin, he was a man of the sea, and more than that, a warrior of the sea. Mairin imagined that if they could find pictures of English sea captains of twenty-five centuries ago, they would look like Collen. The chest panels of his dress uniform sagged with the Order of Kernow, the Welsh Medal of Courage, the Province Cross of Valor, the Bretan Black Star, and the Admiralty's own St. George Medallion, given only once in two or three decades. *He has fought for all of us,* Mairin thought, her heart pounding, *for nearly forty years.*

Yet the face remained as Mairin remembered it from meals she enjoyed in his home: suffused with dignity, warmth, and a genuine honesty that defied description. Richard was posted next to his father—younger, taller, ultimately more handsome, but careful to defer to the older man's absolute authority in this gathering. Mairin caught Richard's eye, and also his faint frown and nod towards Kennat, who defiantly remained in front of her in the line. When they reached the head of the queue, Richard immediately greeted Kennat, shook her hand and drew her to one side. Then Collen's hand went out to Mairin and she grasped it. Cool, hard flesh touched hers, and a slight shiver went up her spine.

"Mairin," he said, beaming, "it's wonderful to see you again! Welcome, and my thanks to Commodore Laigain for your help."

"I'm happy to see you as well," she replied, too formally. "We're honored to be here. May I present my fellow captains? I'm sure you've met Tierney Ulaid and Kennat Gailenga? This is Jilleen Conmaicne, the newest posting in our fleet."

Kennat scowled at being mentioned second. The senior Tredinnick inclined his head politely to the two senior captains and extended his hand to Jilleen, who seemed unable to speak.

"Welcome, Captain Conmaicne, to the greatest fellowship on Earth," he said, both his hands wrapped around hers. "I know you'll be of great service to us all."

From other lips, Mairin reflected, *this might sound like overblown platitudes, but not from him. He means it.*

Richard took her hand briefly and leaned to whisper in her ear, "Give me five minutes after we're through." Under close scrutiny, she nodded pleasantly and moved her group ahead, this time making sure Kennat did not force her way to the front.

An enormous table no less than fifty feet on a side was set in the center of the room, lit by six brilliant ship's lanterns hanging from the ceiling. A full-color relief map of Santander Bay and its land environs stretched over the table from edge to edge. No important detail had been omitted; even the town's individual buildings, streets, and lantern poles were skillfully modeled. Sounding flags peppered the blue water of the ocean from the innermost part of the harbor to five miles in the offing, and along the coast to the edges of the map. Elevation flags marked the terrain's hills and valleys. Realistic ship models, at least a hundred in all, clustered in the ocean on the north edge of the map. Mairin spotted *Caillech*, complete with tiny ensign and name imprinted below the taffrail.

As her eyes wandered the impressive display, she noticed in a far corner of the hall a table piled high with thick packets, each one drawn up with red ribbon. Orders for everyone, she realized, complete with maps and charts. Crowded along one wall, ten crisply-uniformed ensigns with tired faces were poised with long poles to move the ship models.

"Astonishing," said Tierney. "Imagine the work this took to build."

Mairin shook her head in admiration. "The Admiral does nothing halfway."

"Do you know him well?" Jilleen asked. "He missed my graduation ceremony so this is the first time I've seen him."

"I do know him, somewhat. Remarkable man, warm and friendly. I'll make sure you get to talk with him when this mission is over."

Out of the corner of her eye, Mairin caught Kennat's smirk. "You have something to add, Captain?"

"I don't engage in hero worship, myself."

Jilleen looked horrified and Mairin felt the flush rise in her face. Her angry response was cut off by Collen Tredinnick's ascending a platform on the far side of the map table. He waited patiently for conversations to cease.

"Welcome, all, to Kernow, to the Admiralty, and to Pendennis Castle," he began, his inflected baritone echoing from the ancient stone walls. "For those of you who have not been here before, you may wish to know that this castle has guarded Falmouth Harbor for twenty-five hundred years. Part of the stonework is original, and what is not was quarried within a three miles of here. That's enough of history for now. Among you are sea captains from the Kernow Fleet, the Province Squadron, and from the merchant service. Also among you are commanders of soldiers from Wales, Bretan, Kernow, and Scotland. We all know each other yet we are different too. We speak different dialects of Gaelic, we have differing beliefs and holy rites ... and we don't all like the same brew of stout!"

Laughter erupted. *He breaks the tension*, Mairin observed. *And laughter draws people together.*

"Be that as it may, we have joined our forces for a very good reason. We are all under threat, and that threat grows larger every year. As we now speak, armies of the Province in Eirelan are about to battle armies brought against them from Dublin and Belfast. The vital ports and coastal towns of Wales are raided despite our best efforts to guard them by land and sea. The Scots, driven from their own northern lands by drought and cold, stand with us today to defend our common heritage. And most recently, the Bretans have been savagely attacked by sea from Santander."

"We have worked hard for over a year to gather intelligence that is reflected in this map. Our best estimate is that in another year, the Santanders will have so many ships raiding our sea lanes and coastal towns that we will begin to lose the battle. Ship for ship, they can neither outfight nor outsail us, but they can outbuild us and that is exactly what they intend to do. So the city and the dockyards of Santander must be taken."

He paused and sipped from a mug in his left hand.

"I want it to be clear: we are not setting out to destroy the city or kill its people. Our objective is to seize it and hold it for ourselves. If our attack succeeds, we will demand their surrender, after which the town itself will be held by Bretan and the shipyards by the Kernow Admiralty. If they refuse to surrender, we will have no choice but to destroy their fighting power, and if need be lay waste to the city. We must try to preserve the docks and warehouses and factories, and all the ships we can. My son Richard, whom most of you know, will now describe the details of the battle plan."

Collen stepped off the platform and Richard took his place. At the same time, the ensigns brought up long poles used to move toy ships over the relief map.

"We will deploy in three battle groups," Richard began. The ensigns on cue slid the ships into three groups but did not move them forward. "On the left is the group of twelve ships to be commanded by Captain Fotharta of the Province Squadron." He offered a shallow bow in her direction. "This group will consist of four Squadron warships and eight heavy transports. It will leave Falmouth empty, break off from the main body of the fleet near Brest, round Cape Finistere, and anchor off the town of Crozon. One thousand Bretan Fighters will board there for transport to Santander for the main attack. The second battle group will be commanded by Captain Miles Endean, and will consist of thirty-six warships carrying no troups. Captain Endean's assignment is to seize or disable all enemy ships that we meet with en route. We have reason to expect a large force in or near the harbor, as they are now drawing in their ships for the winter. The third battle group, indicated on the right of the main formation, comprises six warships and ten heavy transports, all of which are now loading here. The total force of soldiers in these ships will be twelve hundred, consisting of Admiralty Marines, Scots Guards, and Welsh Pikemen. This group will be under my command."

He paused as pole-wielding ensigns separated the battle groups and moved them into the vicinity of Santander itself.

"As we approach Santander, Captain Fotharta's group will bear off to the east and approach the coastline about twelve miles from the city. The soundings show that at high tide she will be able to take the ships within a half-mile of shore and rapidly land the Bretan force. As soon as they are ashore, her ships will sail towards the harbor itself. I will break off my group to the west and land troops about the same distance from the city, thirteen miles. Captain Endean's force of warships will head directly into the harbor to capture or destroy the enemy's battle fleet. The land forces will advance from both sides and converge on the city, which does not have any kind of physical barrier surrounding it. If all goes as planned, we will then demand surrender of the city, its dockyard, and all of their ships. We are prepared to allow them one hour to decide. At the end of that time, if a surrender is not received, the land forces will move into the town with the primary objective of seizing the dockyards and warehouses before the enemy can fire them."

Mairin admired the beauty of the plan's careful design and at the same time worried over the multitudinous ways it could fail. The first and most obvious problem was the rapidly-changing weather of early fall. A northerly gale could blow them aground or force them to beat into the offing for days on end until supplies ran out and they had to return empty-handed. How did they know a force of two thousand fighters would be enough to overwhelm the city's defenses? What if the whole Santander fleet escaped the harbor and forced a major engagement in open water, possibly under conditions where the Celtic warships could not adequately defend the transports?

As if hearing her thoughts, Richard was speaking to these very contingencies and providing plans to cope with them. He went on for nearly an hour, and by the time he finished, Mairin admitted that no possibility she could think of had not been planned for. That explained the fact that each order packet was at least an inch thick. The sheer complexity and size of the operation was astonishing. Once again she wished it was a month earlier, when the chance of a violent, unrelenting storm had been far less.

Another hour was consumed with questions, suggestions, agreement on details, and one or two genuine arguments. Occasionally

Collen weighed in but mostly Richard handled it, never losing his dis-
arming smile yet never conceding an important point. At last Collen
took the platform again while Richard edged his way around to where
Mairin stood.

"Comrades in arms," said Collen, "I think no one will resent my
request for a brief moment of silence, in which each of us in our own
way prays for fortune to be with us."

Conversations ceased. From the harbor, the sound of voices
drifted on the morning breeze, otherwise no sound echoed from the
ancient stones. Collen said, "Godspeed to us all," put on his hat, and
stepped down. Slowly and in surprising quiet, the captains and generals
and fighter chiefs filed out in ones and twos, a few smiling, the majority
somber and thoughtful.

Richard's hand caught her arm. He handed her a packet of orders
and said, "Walk out with me, Captain?"

Mairin turned to her fellow officers. "Go on ahead to the launch.
I'll join you shortly."

Kennat scowled and pushed her way ahead of Tierney and Jilleen.

"No one has slept here since we came back from Brest," Richard
told her as they passed under the archway. "We had the plans pretty
much laid before that and we intended a spring attack. A week ago my
father decided we could not wait, and he's right. We have to strike now.
They'll build all winter and by spring we could be too far behind to
ever catch up."

"I trust your father's judgment," Mairin said, "and yours. Aideen
must agree too."

"She does."

Halfway to the quay, Richard stopped and looked back at the castle.
"You remember the dance?"

"Of course I do."

"I was so happy that night. I couldn't believe my good fortune to
be with you."

"I was happy too."

"Will I ever dance with you again?"

His voice was light, his expression expectant. She gave no reply.

"I'd better get back," he said, and then he was gone.

Mairin turned and walked slowly towards the waiting launch, her heart filled with sadness for him, and for herself. As she walked, a memory surfaced. She was thirteen again, braiding her long auburn hair for the boy who would be there soon to take a stroll with her. Etain glared at her from the doorway, her face a mask of envy and spite. "You'll never be happy," she said. "Why bother with your hair?"

Brigid had seen that expression on her captain's face before, and was not surprised when Mairin strode past her without a word. Jilleen's excited utterance died on her lips when she saw Mairin's cold, closed look. The ten-minute pull back to the *Caillech* was accomplished in silence save for Brigid's muttered orders to the sailors.

"Captain Conmaicne, Captain Ulaid, wait for my signals," Mairin said curtly as the launch was secured to the davits. "Captain Gailenga, please come aboard."

She bolted up the rope ladder with a muttering Kennat Gailenga close at her heels. Seconds later they stood face to face in Mairin's cabin.

"Close the door," Mairin ordered.

Kennat complied. "I really should get back to my ship. What's this about?"

"It won't take long," said Mairin, tossing her hat onto the chart table. "I have a couple of things to get straight with you." Her voice rose in anger. "First, if you *ever* muscle your way in front of me again while serving under my command, I will rebuke you publicly and note in your record an inexcusable breach of naval etiquette. Second, there will be no disparaging remarks about Admiral Tredinnick in my presence. Great gods above, who do you think you are compared to him? Third, I want no reports of brutality coming from your ship. This is a war command, and my powers as senior captain are much greater than they would otherwise be. I will not *tolerate* the kind of behavior you have been warned of twice, especially not on this mission. If I should find out otherwise, I will see to it you are stripped of rank, pay, and privileges, and charged with violation of your officer's oath. You are dismissed."

"You can't—"

"I said you are dismissed. Return to your ship."

Heavy muscles bunched in Kennat's arms, but she said nothing. The cabin door nearly tore from its hinges as she went through and slammed it with a violent report. A full minute later, a soft tap sounded on the door.

"Enter," Mairin snapped.

Rowenna peered around the edge of the door. She wore a wary expression as if expecting a verbal salvo.

"Captain, Pendennis Castle is flying *proceed to sea*," she reported cautiously.

"Lieutenant, you can come all the way in," Mairin said. "You're always welcome in my cabin." She took a deep breath and eased herself into a chair at the chart table. "I was shouting, wasn't I?"

Rowenna glanced up at the open ceiling vent. "Not shouting so much as speaking forcefully, Captain."

"I was heard all over the ship."

"Yes, sir."

Mairin felt some of the anger drain away in the face of Rowenna's barely-suppressed grin.

"Well, the hell with it." She fingered the red-ribboned packet on the table. "Let's get underway, then we can both have at that pile of paper."

They went on deck together. The fresh northerly blew steadily. Under Sithmaith's sure command, the anchor was hauled, sails flashed out, the bow swung round, and once again, the *Caillech* put to sea.

"Signal our consorts," said Mairin. "Sailing order *Morrigan, Rosc Catha, Wexford.* Rendezvous as ordered, ten miles offshore."

Alone, she strolled forward into the bow. The wind filled and strained *Caillech's* vanilla-white sails and raised whitecaps sliced asunder by the ship's sharp prow. On either side, ahead and astern, dozens of other ships paralleled *Caillech's* course to the rendezvous point. A part of her thrilled at the sight of so many great vessels joined in a common mission. Another part turned over and over the risks that such a great undertaking entailed. And yet another part, deeper and less analytic, churned with feelings of love and hate and sweet remembrance and bitter regret. Deep in her thoughts, Mairin did not hear Rowenna's approach.

"Captain," Rowenna said lightly, "your hands are about to damage our bow rail."

Startled from her reverie, Mairin let go the rail and flexed stiff fingers.

"So they are!" she said with a laugh, which Rowenna shared.

"Tonight," Mairin said, "let's get up some music, dancing too if the sea permits. Serve out ale to the offwatch."

"Aye, aye, sir. I've heard it said you do a fine reel."

"With enough ale in me, yes."

They leaned together on the bow rail and talked of pleasant things ashore, while all around them, the greatest battle fleet in living memory gathered its strength for war.

In my long life I have often struggled with the sense that the universe is perverse, that there may be some truth in claims that Man is born only to suffer. The worst blow of all was the loss of my son, whose valiant spirit seemed to be the very lifeblood of our people, who embodied so many of the qualities we all long to have. Yet as the seasons turned and peace followed war, as the markets teemed with goods and babies cried and families gathered for meals for which they were duly thankful, my faith in the balance of life returned. I have multitudinous blessings: my wife, my daughter-by-marriage Liadan, my grandchildren Aideen, Conor, and Feth, my health, my writing, my home. What could possibly tip the scales against all that? As the end of my life draws near, only one deep pessimism threatens me: that we will not survive as a people, that forty-five centuries of the Celts on Earth will draw to a close, that our stories and poetry and love of nature will pass forever from the world. I battle this sense of foreboding every day.
Inner Thoughts, Uinseann Laigain

Chapter 23

The three-mile walk from his cottage outside Duncormick to the shores of the brackish tidal inlet was no longer as easy as it once was. *Not age alone,* Uinseann scolded himself, *but too much damned sitting. I write and read all day, and at age seventy joints and muscles stiffen when you do that.* Beside him, his gray-coated wolfhound Raffer ambled along, pausing now and then to sniff an interesting bit of earth or sprout of grass.

"You're not so young either," Uinseann advised the pony-sized dog. "Seven if I'm not mistaken. That makes us about even, boy."

A slight puff of sweet-scented morning breeze stirred the leaves and mussed Uinseann's flowing white hair.

"And I pulled off the hat trick again!"

He hated wearing a hat. In the past year Rionach had taken to insisting on his wearing one in all but the warmest weather. For the sake of marital harmony, he left the house sporting a fine wool hat which he deposited on a handy tree limb once out of sight.

"Don't let me forget it on the way back," he cautioned Raffer, who stared up with loving slate-gray eyes and possibly offered a faint nod of understanding.

He stopped to catch his breath after the steepest climb of the hike. From a low-hanging branch he plucked an unusually colorful maple leaf and tucked it gently in his vest pocket. It was a modest morning gift for Rionach, who collected autumn leaves and mounted them as gifts.

So early for trees to be trading in summer green for autumn gold! What was the date today, October 21? In his childhood, tress did not give up their verdant green till mid or late November. *How much life can change in two generations.* To Raffer, he cried, "get away from that!" The curious dog had buried his formidable nose in a hole that might well house an irritated skunk.

Now that he felt warm and relaxed, he walked down the slope with a long, limber stride trailing a reluctant Raffer who would have liked a slower pace. At the last bend in the trail he paused as he always did to take in the delightful view. *More splendid than usual today*, he told himself as he sniffed deeply of air scented by brackish water, mud, wet grass, damp leaves, and morning mist. The sun edged up over the forested horizon, sending mist-dimmed rays cascading over smooth water and setting ablaze with color the multicolored trees clustered along the shore. As if responding to a theatrical cue, crows launched into raucous cackling in an attempt to drown out chittering sparrows and cooing doves.

A score of flat-bottomed boats drifted along with the current, their silent occupants gripping fishing rods in hopes of catching a tasty dinner. He recognized the fishermen in the two nearest boats, and waved. The anglers waved back and one dared to shout hello, drawing a furious glare from the other thirty yards away.

Uinseann's own boat lay tied up to a tree above the tide line and he longed to take it out. A cool, misty morning was excellent for fishing, after all. Raffer posted himself expectantly next to the boat.

"Not today, boy," Uinseann said. The tall, scruffy ears sagged. "Go on, get wet!"

Raffer plunged joyously into the water and cavorted in the shallows, hoping to catch a fish in his huge jaws. Meanwhile, the shouting boater rowed himself ashore and slogged through the muck of low tide. Short as Uinseann was tall, Eimhin Finguine's tattered wool hat sprouted lures and hooks, his gray wool trousers featured more patches than cloth, and his plaid wool sweater stretched tight over a barrel-like torso. An ill-trimmed, grizzled beard reached to his chest. *Thirty-five years I have known this man*, Uinseann reflected. *How often his simple approach to life has embarrassed my finely-honed philosophy!*

Eimhin's hard-calloused hand felt like rough stone in his grasp.

"I hoped I'd see you this fine morning," Eimhin said in raspy voice. "You've been away?"

"Teach Munna first, then entertaining guests. They're still with us, but I took my walk anyway. Needed time to think."

The two old friends sat down on a weathered wooden bench.

"Aye, my friend the thinker!" Eimhin laughed. "Why not get in my boat and help me catch a fine dinner? You have the lucky hand, that much I know."

"Not today, though I'd love nothing better," Uinseann said, looking wistfully out at the gently-flowing water.

Eimhin studied him a moment. "Politics, I take it?"

"Politics. You must have heard about the western clans' envoys coming to Teach Munna?"

"Aye, and the Council's *swift* action," Eimhin said with pointed sarcasm.

Uinseann nodded. "Swift action indeed. We invited the envoys to stay with us a few days, get to know each other better."

"What sort of folks be they?" Eimhin asked. His stubby fingers struggled with a tangled fishing line.

"Very fine folks indeed. They've taught Rionach and I much about life in those regions. Very hard, especially where Rainait lives in Dromina."

"Hard for us too," Eimhin pointed out. "You know, those clans have reason for grievance with us. Did I tell you my father voted on the Council to include Cork and Kerry behind our Rampart? Aye, that he did, when I was a young lad. They'd always been friendly with us, me father said, it was not right that we left them out there. I think he was right."

"Time we put the past away and live for the future," Uinseann said. "Else we'll have no future. Enough on that! How's fishing this fine day?"

"Bah." Eimhin gave up on the snarled line. "One small one in the boat." His rheumy green eyes peered at the second boat, drifting a few hundred yards from shore.

"Curse him," he said, spitting. "Finnen got the fat one I wanted."

"You shouted at me to get his goat."

Eimhin raised his bushy eyebrows in mock surprise. "Did I?"

Raffer tired of cavorting in the shallows, bounded onto the shore, and shook his dense wooly coat, sending a spray into the air that sprinkled their clothes.

"Pretty spry," Eimhin said of Raffer, "for an old-timer."

Eimhin found a long stick lying by the bench and idly drew open spiral shapes in the damp sand.

"You know, I was thinking out there while I weren't catching anything, I have twelve grandchildren now. Six boys and six girls, isn't that an even bundle? Youngest, little Nevan, is but eleven, the oldest, fair Islene, is twenty-seven. And now two great-grandchildren, by the stars! I remember every birth and every hard moment when they were sick. Often enough Nuala and I took care of the babies ourselves. Not that we minded! They grow up fast ... too fast."

"Aye, I know it," said Uinseann softly. His mind filled with images of Aideen and Conor and Feth as yelling tots banging around his house.

"What troubles me now is this," Eimhin went on. "I am two years past seventy, imagine that! When you and I were young the Twenty Clans lived all over the midlands, and here in the south, and in the west too, we did. There were many more of us in those days, and no Rampart neither. The spring and summer and fall were fair and the winters not so bad, most times. We had to fight, the fair Earth knows, you and I both, but we always believed next month or next year would be better. I hoped my children would grow up in peaceful days, and their children too. Now," he paused and studied the spiral he had drawn, "now the wild clans are closing in and we have barely the strength to hold onto what we have. So I worry about my grandchildren and their little ones. They will have a hard time of it, harder than we did, in those days."

Finnen, whose boat had drifted off to the west with the tide, shouted for joy and hauled in another fish.

"Double curse him," Eimhin muttered without genuine rancor. "What does he use for bait? He won't tell me. If I get nothing more this morning, I'll go to his house and ask for my share. Now where was I? Yes, my grandchildren. Seven of the twelve are in the uniform and t'other five are not far behind. Uinseann, my friend, what is there for them? Just fighting and fighting until we're all gone?"

Raffer, his coat no longer dripping, padded up to the bench and settled with a heavy sigh next to Uinseann, who stroked his damp head.

"Old men must think the same old thoughts," said Uinseann. "That's the question I was pondering as I walked this morning. Where are *my* grandchildren? Are they here with me, bringing their own babies that I've lived long enough to see? Nay, they are not. Aideen is at sea, if fighting doesn't get her the sea itself might. Conor wants a family, dreams of it he does. The poor man can't put down a sword long enough to make it happen. And now my darling Fethnaid ..."

His voice trailed off. The letter from Feth had struck hard. Eighteen and riding off into the western lands, of which she knew nothing! Gilvarry and Rainait tried to reassure him yet their eyes betrayed their words.

"You mean the blond one with pigtails?"

"The same. No pigtails anymore. She's posted to the Line of Bows in the west. Almost killed in her first battle, not two weeks ago. Now she's riding off into Cork and Kerry trying to find more fighters for us."

Eimhin shook his head. "Ah, that is indeed a matter for worry. Nuala and I will keep her in our thoughts."

They sat silently for a few minutes, old friends content to watch the ascending sun burn away the mist and then sparkle off rippling water.

"You remember I told you once," said Eimhin, "about an old library I found?"

"You told me ... a long time ago."

Eimhin gazed up at the clear blue sky, remembering a time more than three score years ago.

"I was sixteen, maybe, a tough young buck and fast with my blade. Dublin wasn't safe even then, you know. We lived ten miles west and I was always curious about the old city, or what's left of it. Made my way to the edge of ruins and found a forgotten, dusty library in a deserted area. The fairies know how old it was. More dust than books! I went back there day after day for weeks, reading anything that didn't fall apart in my hands. History mostly. I read about the Egyptians and the Greeks and the Romans, they all had their day. Europe later, French and Germans and the English of course. Then the Americans and the Russians and the Chinese, all came to grief sooner or later. After the nations came the companies that made the machines, and then came the machines that ran the companies, and then the whole sorry mess fell apart, a thousand years ago more or less. We Celts survived it all, we go back to the Romans and even before them! At least four thousand years, can you think about so much time?"

Uinseann shook his head. Eimhin finished an elaborate spiral in the soft earth. "Celts were drawing these when mankind was young."

"A long time it is," Uinseann admitted. "Yet not so long, when we look out at the heavens and remember that all this was here long before us, and t'will be here long after."

Uinseann leaned back on the bench, his eyes settling on radiant cluster of maples and dogwoods and aspens straight across the inlet from them. Raffer had curled up and now snoozed to the mellow sound of their voices. Eimhin swept a soggy boot over his spirals and began to draw an intricate Tree of Life.

"Aye, that is true, that is true. I read the science books too, didn't understand them all. Forty-odd centuries is just a wink in time. The world is a great cycle and it turned afore us and 'twill turn after us. For all that, old friend, I come round to the idea that we add value to this green Earth. Not our bodies! Many a thing's larger or stronger or faster or more beautiful. But we *think* and that's the difference. We make art and write poems and sing songs and we love and cherish this fair land. We fish too, and sometimes catch dinner, at least Finnen does. Who knows about men over the horizon? All we know is this little corner of the planet from Bretan to Kernow to Wales to Scotlan to Eirelan where we speak the Gael—though some folks have a nasty accent—and do our best to live in peace each with each other. This is the corner where my grandchildren live, and I am fearing that it may not be around for *their* grandchildren." He stared out at the water and scowled. "Finnen's already headed home, the scoundrel."

"Perhaps," said Uinseann after a moment's thought, "we *are* the last generations to sit beside this arm of the sea and speak these thoughts in the Gael. I don't know, Eimhin. You know my belief, that we're not so important, that we're part of the endless succession of peoples and animals that have been granted the privilege of living in this glorious world. A world with enough fish for you and me and Finnen too."

"A good faith," Eimhin observed, "but for all that, I'd take the sword again in these creaky old hands and fight for my people. I'd go down fighting sooner than I'd go down spouting philosophy and so would you. Maybe there's a spirit in us older than your philosophy and deeper than my muddy thinking, a bit of our souls that won't let us lie down and fade away like the leaves falling around us or the snow melting away in the spring."

Which of us is the philosopher? Uinseann asked himself silently. *Which indeed?*

"As usual," he said aloud, "I have to walk back thinking on something new."

"Bah. I'm just an old man who wants things for the folk I leave behind."

They fell silent again, Eimhin drawing his tree and Uinseann gazing out over the water.

"Best I get started," Uinseann said at last. He got to his feet. "When our guests leave, we expect Etain Fotharta. How I do wish I could stay here and fish."

Eimhin lifted himself to his feet with a grunt. "Hard on your Rionach, fighting with her daughter year in and year out."

"Aye, it is. Worse all the time. I worry for my dear wife's health."

"She's a strong one, your Rionach. Outlive us all, she will. We'll see you at the house soon?"

"A few days. Our love to Nuala."

Eimhin climbed into his boat, pushed it from the soft sand and rowed off with vigor, his still-strong arms driving the boat against the tidal current. Uinseann watched him for a time, pondering all that they had said. Then he turned and headed back with Raffer along the winding, hilly path strewn with autumn leaves. An hour later, the burnt-wood smell of the oven fire from his own house reminded him how hungry he was. He found Gilvarry Muiredarg loading a cart with logs he split in the two hours Uinseann was away.

"Fine dry wood," Gilvarry observed, hefting a split log in his hands. "What else could a man want but a stone cottage, enough wood and peat for the winter, water and fishing nearby, and a wife to make it all a home?"

"I have no complaint," Uinseann said. He pitched in to load the last dozen logs into the cart. "Only that I have so much more to write, and maybe not so much time left to write in."

Together they pushed the heavy cart towards the cottage. The closer they got, the more overpowering grew the fragrance of baking bread. They parked the cart at the foot of the porch steps and began stacking logs next to the kitchen door.

"Your cousin says little of her home," said Uinseann in a low voice. "She speaks of her family, yes, but not of how they live."

Gilvarry did not immediately answer. When the logs were all stacked by the door, he wandered back into the yard with Uinseann following. They sat down in two rough-hewn chairs beneath a huge willow, its trunk carved by Uinseann himself with the Twelve Signs of Mystery.

"She says little," Gilvarry answered at last, "because life is hard for her, and dangerous. My home in Enniskean is far enough south that we don't see raids that often. Rainait's farm outside Dromina is too close to cursed Limerick. She lost a child in a raid last year and her home has been burned twice. These are things she can't speak of. I've begged her to bring her family to live in Enniskean but her husband won't hear of it and she agrees with him. Their clans—Phelans and Muiades and

Sogains and others—have lived and farmed in Cork and Limerick for centuries and they won't be driven off. Admirable, sure it is, but I'm afraid the next big raid might destroy Rainait and her whole family."

"I am sad for her," said Uinseann. "Well I know what it is to lose a child. It remains in your thoughts forever. As for her safety ... I think the tide is turning among the Twenty Clans. People are seeing things differently than they did fifty years ago when we built the Rampart."

"Because you're desperate yourselves," Gilvarry said, sounding bitter.

"Fear and desperation are an effective cure for prejudice and foolish malice. I hope it's not too late."

"Can Rionach do it?"

"I have faith in my wife. I've seen her overcome many things in her lifetime."

"But her daughter—"

"Is tied to the old divisions between the clans," Uinseann said, shaking his head with dismay. "And seems to enjoy sparring for its own sake."

Gilvarry considered a moment. "Perhaps if Rainait and I stayed, appealed to Etain directly?"

Uinseann managed a bleak smile. "If I thought that would help, I would beg you to stay! It would not work. She sees you and all the clans of Cork and Kerry much as you've always been seen among the Twenty Clans."

"Arrogant, ignorant, uncivilized clods."

"Exactly. Better you be on your way and enjoy the rest of this fine day riding among the trees. Where will you stay tonight?"

"With friends in Clonmel. Tomorrow I'll escort Rainait to Dromina and then head home."

Uinseann clamped a hand on Gilvarry's rock-hard shoulder. "We'll miss you."

Gilvarry smiled and grasped Uinseann's forearm. "And we will miss you. We'll see each other again, I'm sure of it."

"Hot bread," Rionach called to them from the kitchen door. "For you *hard-working* men."

"We *were* working!" Uinseann protested. "And hard, too!"

"Husband, where is your hat?" Rionach demanded.

She went back inside. Uinseann glared at Raffer, curled up at his feet. "You were supposed to remind me."

Raffer woofed once and resumed his guiltless doze.

Uinseann and Rionach sat side by side in wicker chairs on the porch, enjoying late-afternoon sun filtering through thinning trees. The cool, damp smell of early autumn saturated the air. Gilvarry and Rainait had ridden off towards home, saddlebags bulging with food and gifts.

Though they had been guests but three nights and two days, Uinseann felt a keen sense of loss when their horses disappeared down the road. Gilvarry was a warm and friendly man, full of stories and wise sayings, and about the same age as Domnall would have been, had he lived. At times Rainait joined in the light-hearted banter, at other times she seemed content to sit back with a smile and listen to the others. Uinseann read the pain in her eyes and knew exactly how it felt to be enjoying the company of friends and at the same time grieving for a lost child. Late each evening Rainait played her zither and sang songs in ancient Gaelic dialects.

"I hope we see them again," he said, taking hold of his wife's hand.

"As do I," Rionach said, squeezing his arthritic fingers gently. "I fear for Rainait."

"If we extend the Rampart, Dromina would fall south of it."

Rionach nodded and thought a moment before answering. "Ninety-five miles, husband, from Dungarvan to Tralee, if we are to protect all of Cork and most of Kerry. If you say a hundred with twists and turns, that's ... five hundred thousand feet. A million posts, ten forts, the road, the ditch, the watchtowers." She shook her head. "I wonder if we can do it again."

"We'd do the engineering but the people there would have to work as we did, fifty years ago."

"There is another way."

"Ah, yes, Padraic's plan. Keep armies in the field, go on the offensive against Dublin and Limerick, even Belfast if we have to with naval power. Dangerous."

"All our options are dangerous," Rionach said with a wan smile. "The rock and the hard place."

Etain was long overdue and Uinseann began to hope they would be spared her company. It was not to be. Hooves echoed through the woods and a moment later, three horses cantered into the cleared meadow in front of the cottage. In the lead on a sweat-shiny dappled mare rode Etain Fotharta, her gray-flecked roan hair spilling over a copper-colored cloak. *Still the most beautiful woman in the Province,* Uinseann reflected, *and never afraid to use that beauty.*

A few strides behind Etain, her brother-in-law Zephan rode a big black stallion. His dark-complexioned face was impassive as always, except for a slight narrowing of the eyes as he looked towards them. *Zephan is no Gorman. They look like brothers and there the resemblance ends. This man is tough, hard, and touches no drink. A formidable merchant with plenty of friends and allies. Married ... does he enjoy his sister-in-law's company as well? Says little and conceals much. He wants power as much as Etain does.*

Bram Fotharta, in full armor, rode opposite his uncle. *Dangerous-looking at any distance. He wears Gorman's scowl like a badge. Such a father! That is, the father who raised him, not necessarily the one who sired him.*

Rumors had always abounded; in Uinseann's mind the issue had never been in doubt. Short, blocky, dark-eyed Gorman was not this man's father. Bram's height and blue eyes came from a different father, a man who had been Etain's sometime-consort months before she married. For a fleeting moment, Uinseann felt a pang of sorrow for Gorman, whom he had not seen in at least a decade. *He must have always known the truth and could never escape sight of it.* What the man had done to his children, especially Mairin and Kellen ... there could be no excusing that. For that, the balance of the world demanded suffering and punishment.

The three riders dismounted in the yard and tethered their horses to the porch rail. Uinseann rose to his feet.

"Welcome to our home, Etain, Zephan, and Bram," he called out in formal greeting.

Etain merely nodded, omitting the polite reply ritual demanded. She said something quietly to Bram, who made no move to follow her into the house. Rionach followed them inside. Uinseann pondered his options and decided to stay outside with Bram for the time being.

The big soldier pulled a cloth from his saddle bag and wiped sweat from his face. Uinseann descended the porch steps with Bram watching him warily.

"Cold water," Uinseann said, waving a hand towards the covered well in the yard. "Can I get you some?"

Bram's heavy eyebrows lifted in surprise. "Yes. Hot. In this armor," he said haltingly.

Three long strides brought Uinseann to the stone-enclosed well, where he lowered the bucket, raised it again, and dipped a quart-size metal cup into the fresh water. Bram approached and took the proffered cup. *We're the same height,* Uinseann noted, *but he must weigh at close to twenty stone. No wonder Padraic has tolerated his bad behavior ... he would be worth four ordinary men in battle.*

Bram downed the water and handed back the cup.

"More?"

"No. Thank you."

Uinseann dipped the cup for himself and drank. Bram seemed uncertain whether to return to the horses or wait at the well.

"You have duty tonight?" Uinseann asked as he replaced the cup on its hook. "You're a long ride from the Rampart."

"Reserve at New Ross," Bram said. He looked back and forth nervously.

Uinseann leaned back against the well. Raffer sauntered across the yard towards his own water bucket on the porch and slurped in it noisily.

"Nice dog," Bram commented. "Must be old by the way he walks."

"Seven. Old for a wolfhound. You have a dog?"

"Once," Bram said, staring at his boots. "Long time ago." He looked up suddenly. "I'd like to know why you're giving me the time of day. Our families are enemies."

Uinseann laughed lightly. "Families aren't enemies, people are. I hardly know you at all. What I've heard about you from others, I don't like. But then you probably have no use for an old philosopher. That doesn't make us enemies."

"Conor hates me, you must know that."

"I know for a fact he does not," Uinseann replied sharply, meeting Bram's challenging gaze. "So far as I know, my grandson hates no one. You were cruel to him when you had the chance to be, and he remembers that I'm sure. But hate? No. He doesn't hate you. It's not in his nature."

Bram muttered something Uinseann could not make out. Audibly, Bram said, "You must have known my father, once."

Strange, the double-meanings in that question.

"Sure I knew him, when I was forty and still serving in the Line, and he was twenty and a fine figure of a man. Your father had a foul temper and a fouler tongue."

"He could fight with the best of them."

"Aye, that he could."

"So can I."

Uinseann eyed the long, powerful arms and rugged hands. "No doubt of that. The problem was your father could never stay away from strong drink and it ruined him. It will ruin you too, if what I hear is true."

Bram straightened to his full height and took a step away.

"None of your damned business," he said, clenching his hands into massive fists. "I live my life my own way."

Uinseann returned a smile, which seemed to confuse Bram yet further.

"I grant you that, Bram. We all have the right, within the limits of law and honor. What I said is true nonetheless. I didn't say it to offend you. Consider it unwanted advice from a man who has passed seventy years."

Raised voices drifted from the open front door.

"Best I go in," Uinseann said. "Take more water if you like."

Bram nodded, once again looking confused. He remained behind when Uinseann climbed the porch steps. Inside, Uinseann found his wife at one end of the dining table, her daughter at the opposite end with Zephan on her left. Speaking stopped while he made his way to a chair next to Rionach. He nodded to Zephan, who remained impassive, then to Etain, who returned an impatient glance.

"As I was saying," Etain said, turning back to Rionach, "you tried and failed to obtain the Council's approval of a formal and binding contract of alliance with the western clans. My information is that their representatives left this house hours ago. I would be interested to know what they were doing here."

She has us watched, Uinseann mused. *I am not surprised.*

Rionach waved a hand casually. "A social visit, no more. We spent much time trading stories and singing songs."

"Is that so?" Zephan said with sarcasm. "And the approval of Province soldiers going recruiting in their lands, was that a social matter as well?"

"An unofficial mission," Rionach replied, "and well within my authority as Speaker to approve when the Council is not in session. I would ordinarily have consulted with General Conmaicne. As you well know he is out of touch at the moment. I sounded out Gilvarry and Rainait on the wisdom of the plan and they agreed it was worth trying, if dangerous to the Province soldiers themselves."

"One of whom is your own granddaughter Fethnaid," said Etain. "A bit young and unseasoned for such a daunting and delicate task, is she not?"

"She risks her life working for our survival," Uinseann broke in, "while others debate and do nothing."

Etain sent him a furious glare. "I'll chalk that silly remark up to your advanced age," she snapped, "and get to the point of this meeting. Rionach, you and those whose votes you control want a formal alliance both with the western clans and the other Celtic states. Those I represent believe such alliances will cost us more than we receive, so we oppose any alliances beyond those already agreed to."

"Meaning the naval connection with Kernow and limited military cooperation with the others, nothing more?"

"Yes. It's a simple matter of votes."

"In theory, yes."

Etain leaned back in her chair. "I'm curious. In the case of a tie, the Speaker's vote can be weighed twice. You chose not to use that privilege last week. Why?"

Rionach took a leisurely sip of tea and stared at her daughter over the cup. Setting it down, she said, "Because the matter is too great to be decided in that way. Spending money on roads, yes, that I would break a tie vote on. Not binding alliances. I wonder if you would have shown the same restraint, in my position."

"No."

"I thought not. I appreciate your candor."

Etain laughed humorlessly and tossed her great mane to one side. *She uses that technique even here,* Uinseann marveled, *where it can do her no good. Force of habit, no doubt.*

"After the first of the year," Etain said, "I will sit in the Speaker's chair and add my extra vote against the alliances, if you propose them again. That kills the matter for at least another year. So why not settle this here and now and save the Council a repeat of all that wrangling?"

Rionach gazed out the window, making Etain wait impatiently for an answer.

"For the purpose of argument," Rionach began with a glance at Zephan and then at her daughter, "let us say you're right. The Council of Twenty is divided and as Speaker you can cast a deciding vote opposed to new alliances. I say that the army and navy will not follow you. They're already committed to the alliances I propose. Even as we speak, four warships from our Squadron, led by your own daughter, are en route to Falmouth and thence to Brest where they will take part in a unified attack on Santander in Spain. This attack will involve fighters from all the Celtic nations everywhere."

Etain actually gasped with surprise.

"General Conmaicne," Rionach pressed on, "will attack the army of the Ghaoth Aduaidh whether they choose to make us their target or sweep west into Cork and Kerry."

Zephan's fist struck the table. "Who approved those actions?"

"There are no formal treaties," Rionach answered him in a matter-of-fact voice. "Commodore Laigain acted in an emergency as she is empowered to do. General Conmaicne believes that destruction of the western lands will weaken us too and so we defend them for our own benefit."

"We are off the subject," Etain said. "When I take the Chair, I can reverse any and all of these unauthorized operations. The compromise

I came to offer is a guarantee of votes to ratify your proposed alliances, in exchange for your agreement that the Council's powers will be ceded to a single leader who will make all decisions needed for our defense and our survival in the coming year. This leader will decide how the new alliances are to be observed by the Province. What could be fairer?"

"The Chief of Clans will direct army and navy operations?" Rionach inquired.

"That's the whole point," Zephan reentered the fray. "It's been done before in a crisis and it's time to do it again. The Council is too divided and slow, even you must agree with that."

"Possibly I do," Rionach said. "And your candidate for this position?"

"By any measure," said Etain evenly, "Zephan is the obvious choice. He has the skills, the experience, and the support of the people."

Rionach stood and circled behind her chair. "Zephan, you're a man of considerable energy and ability," she began smoothly, her eyes on Zephan, "and no doubt could make a contribution, given the chance. Certainly many of the larger merchants support you. However, I plan to offer an alternate proposal to the Council."

Etain leaned forward with narrowed eyes. "Which would be?"

"I will propose Province-wide votes on two issues. First, to grant the clans of Cork and Kerry two voting seats on the Council, and second, to allow the leaders of our army and navy wider latitude in making decisions for our security. In the event of a deadlock on this proposal, I *will* use my tie-breaking vote, because it would be a vote used in the interests of democracy, which we all profess to believe in."

Zephan rocked back in his chair, stunned. Etain seemed to have trouble finding her voice.

"You are insane," she said finally. "You risk splitting the Province into warring factions that will never come together again."

"The people will decide. I'm comfortable with that."

"Why tell me this now?" Etain asked. "You could have made it a surprise at the next meeting."

"That would be your style, not mine, daughter. I have nothing to hide and this is not a clever behind-the-scenes maneuver. It's a life and death matter for the Province."

Etain rose from her chair, followed immediately by Zephan.

"Don't think you have won, *mother*. You have not. I'm glad you gave me time to plan my next move."

She stormed out with Zephan on her heels.

Uinseann led Rionach onto the porch and together they watched the three riders thunder into the woods.

"Never was *mother* spoken with such venom," Rionach said, her eyes filled with sadness. "To think that I could have raised such a child."

Uinseann put his arm around her frail shoulders.

"The most carefully planted tree may yet grow crooked," he said. "The world gives and receives in equal measure if we are paying attention. It could be that Etain is the price we pay for our many blessings."

Rionach sighed, her face sagging with fatigue. "There are times, husband, when I don't like your idea of balance, and this is one of them." She looked up and kissed him on the check. "I mean no offense."

He was about to offer an argument, then reconsidered. He drew Rionach's head onto his chest.

"You may be right," he agreed. "Possibly I take the concept too far in this case."

He led her into the cottage, and over a quiet dinner, they spoke of happier times, when they were young and knew nothing of politics or philosophy.

So far as my research discloses, Dublin's history stretches back at least three thousand years from today. Its founding somehow involved a Nordic people called Vikings, though my sources do not say exactly how this came about. As is apparent from the size of the ruins (which I was able to see once from a ship in the harbor), it was an impressive city during the Age of Machines. No doubt much history could be learned if it could be explored safely. Much of it is now unoccupied and in ruins, though substantial sections are still in use according to Oran. The city, or what is left of it, is dominated by a remnant of an old religious faith whose leaders consider the Twenty Clans to be godless and therefore dangerous. Like everywhere else in the midlands and the north, food supplies in the lands near Dublin are dwindling rapidly with the decline of agriculture in those regions. One might speculate that food has become a source of conflict inside Dublin, as elsewhere.

Seanlaoch Osraige, "Essay on Dublin"

Chapter 24

Had it not rained all night, he would not have heard them in time. Running feet make a racket in puddles and so Aodhan Saithne was able to turn an instant before his two assailants smashed him to the cobblestones and quite likely beat him to death. He knew them by their clothes: Redshirts from the Abbey Street Buidheann. Though the Redshirts didn't often prowl south of the river in broad daylight, that was no excuse for his daydreaming. They would not have waited to find out he carried no liquor or money and had only a half-eaten sour apple in his pocket.

By the time he faced the sound of the feet, they were two fast strides away, knives out, screaming to frighten and freeze him into inaction. Unfortunately for these two charging boys, Aodhan's father had taught him well. They were bigger than he was, and surely stronger too—yet his blade gutted one and slashed the throat of the other in the time of a lightning flash. Anguished cries gurgled briefly, blood gushed into muddy puddles, then silence. Aodhan wiped his knife clean on one boy's black wool trousers and slid it back into his belt pouch. He searched them briefly, finding a couple of churchcoins and a chunk of moldy cheese.

"Too bad," he said to their staring, lifeless faces. "I'm hungrier than you are, you bastards."

A quick glance around showed he was alone; it was yet early for anyone to be in the streets. He dragged the two bodies into a rubble-filled alley and buried them with refuse. Eventually they would be missed ... but they would not be found for long after that.

Now he quickened his pace along Dame Street, turned down an alley and emerged in the courtyard of Dublin Castle, an immense ruin grand even in its desolation. Many of its eons-old structures had crumbled, yet a few had been preserved, among them The Tower and The Chapel Royal which now housed the city's impotent government. Aodhan spit in the direction of the Tower, then guided his steps left towards the entrance to the castle's starling and tangled subterranean levels, home to his own Black Hats Buidheann and to half a dozen other gangs in truce with them.

Rain-washed stone steps led downwards to a massive oak door, entrance to the Black Hats' quarters. He rapped twice, a tiny porthole opened in the door, and a scornful female voice said "oh, it's you." The bar slid across and the door swung open, setting Aodhan face to face with the main object of his fifteen-year-old desires. Yvone Fergusa, also fifteen with flashing dark eyes and alabaster skin, offered him her best *keep-away-from-me* frown, which ignited him instantly.

"Have a minute?" he asked as she closed and barred the door. "For me, love?"

Her left hand came up and lightly slapped his face. "Shame," she said, then grabbed him and forced him into a small side-chamber. Fear of being caught heightened the feelings and when Aodhan tucked his shirt into his trousers ten minutes later, his whole body trembled with pleasure. Yvone winked at him and resumed her post at the door.

A single guttering lantern lit the long, damp, cold corridor leading to their rooms. The passageway reeked of something Aodhan could never quite put his finger on, akin to urine but fouler and perhaps older. He wondered whether in this labyrinth there might not be decaying dead bodies.

When he entered the room they called the Pit, his friend Flann, a year younger and a head shorter, tossed a shred of blue-green bread at him. The Oldsters of the gang let them occupy this strange, circular place. At some ancient time the room had featured four tiers of finely-upholstered seats arranged in a semicircle around a stage. Rats had long since eaten the upholstery and the wood frames rotted away in the damp, so all that remained of the chairs were skeletons of rusty springs and metal channels. Scattered among these remains were moth-chewed cushions and battered chairs scavenged or stolen from the homes of rival gangs.

On the stage rested the pride and joy of the Youngsters: an decrepit old piano that could still be played if errant pitch and missing notes were accepted. A skylight high above the stage, which leaked when it rained, was daily cleaned on the outside by the Youngsters, as it was the main source of light for their lair—they could not afford lanterns or big candles. The sky on this morning was shrouded in a thick gray overcast, so the skylight lit the center of the room and left the corners in deep shadow.

Aodhan batted the rotten bread aside. "Any food at all?" he asked Flann, who sprawled a lanky frame onto the least offensive of the cushions. "I'm serious. My mom and sister are hungry and so am I."

The red-haired boy sighed. "We're hungry too, Aodhan lad. Nay, no food. I asked the Oldsters yesterday and I asked today. They said all the food went south with the army. So we here get to starve."

"Goddam them." Aodhan kicked at a rat that scurried after the bread. He missed and the rat bolted down a hole with its find. "T'will come to nothing."

"I hear the Redshirts might have a stash of flour and dried meat," Flann said with a conspiratorial look. "I know we're supposed to be in a truce ... Christ, where'd the blood come from?"

Aodhan looked down in dismay. Blood covered the lower half of his pant-legs, the result of dragging bodies still oozing blood.

"Truce be damned," he said, flinging himself into a chair. "Two of them jumped me on my way here, might have had me too, 'cept for the rain puddles."

"Killed 'em then?"

"Sliced one and gutted t'other," he said proudly. "Hid the bodies, that's how I got the blood. Mother will slap me for it, too, the blood on the pants, I mean."

"Yer shirt's out in back too," Flann observed. "You had Yvone."

"That I did."

Flann cranked himself to his feet and slapped Aodhan's shoulder.

"You get all the goddam luck. Day's hardly started and you killed two Redshirt pigs and had a fling too." He strolled away, looking puzzled. "Don't care about the killings ... but I sure wish Yvone would let me in too. Why won't she?"

"Strict rule she has," Aodhan said, grinning. "Size is everything."

Flann whirled. "Bastard! I ought to—"

"Calm down! I was just teasin'. Take more baths or something, I don't know. There's other girls, Flann. Now about the food."

"Yeah, what about it?" Flann said, still simmering. "All right, the word is the Redshirts stole half a shipload of flour and dried meat from the docks, food supposed to go to the Bishop. They got it locked up and guarded in the old Post Office."

"Christ, that would be hard to get at," Aodhan said. "Their blessed headquarters is never unguarded. It'd be a bloody mess and we'd only get half of it. Father Faolin takes the other half to feed his fat face."

Flann's eyes flicked nervously towards the entrance. "That kind of talk could get you killed, Aodhan."

"I don't care. Curse the bastard, he doesn't shed tears when we get cut and die. Says God watches over us, doesn't say why God is starvin' us to death." Aodhan spit on the floor. "Piss on him and his religion."

"Calm down, brother," said Flann, eyes wide with alarm. "I don't like the priests neither, but the Oldsters say—"

"I don't care what they say anymore, times is different from when they were kids." He tried to push the anger in his belly down, but it flooded up anyway and he could not stop it. "Last week in church Faolin fires everybody up against the pagans in the south, calls them tree worshipers, says we should take the food from them because God hates them. I tell you this, Flann, they are tough mothers. My Dad's lost an eye already tryin' to break inside their wall. God better have his mighty hand ready or else none of our dads'll be seen in Dublin's streets again."

"I hate it when you talk like that," said Flann, his eyes turned on the dirty floor. "Makes me feel hopeless. Hungry's bad enough. Now I feel like just dyin'. Yer such a good friend."

Aodhan regretted his big mouth. Flann was a nice boy, one of his best friends, and Flann's mother was sick. His father beat him too, something Aodhan's father often threatened but never did. Flann had enough to worry about as it was.

He took hold of his friend's shoulder. "Look, Flann, we'll find a way to get food. I guess them guys jumping me has me in a bad place. Sorry, really."

"S'alright," his friend said with a bleak look. "Maybe our dads'll win the fight and then we'll all have plenty to eat. I don't know about God myself. If he was on our side he wouldn't make us live like this. Even my grandad says things are bad, much worse than when he was my age." He fingered a fading bruise on the side of his face. "Makes me Dad angry."

Three more Youngsters filed in from the door at the back of the room's highest tier. Yvone sauntered in first, hips swinging, followed by tall, burly Gordain Tuascirt and pale little Kieran Aradh. Aodhan cringed to see the twelve-year-old boy limping and breathing hard, yet smiling and laughing at the same time. Of all of them, Kieran needed more than stale bread and old cheese to eat, or he would not live to see the spring.

The newcomers gathered around Aodhan and Flynn, exchanging insults and taunts. Yvone winked at him. Maybe later there would be a chance ...

Gordain bent down and fingered Aodhan's pantleg. "Blood," he said, his baritone-shifted voice pitched well below the others. "What happened?"

"I had to kill two Redshirts this morning," Aodhan said with an offhand shrug. "That's their blood, not mine."

"Hid them well?"

"Very well."

"All right," the big sixteen-year-old said with a satisfied nod. "You all know about the Redshirts stealing the food. We're going after our share tonight. We'll be pretty much on our own. I talked to other gangs, not much interest in a fight with the Redshirts. A few said they'd help in exchange for a share."

"Cowards," Flann said loudly. "Goddamn cowards."

"We share only with those who fight," said Yvone. "No fight, no food."

"How many can we get?" asked Kieran. "Very tough to break the guard at the Post Office."

"I think fifty will do it," said Gordain. "More would be better."

"I want to fight," Kieran said. "This time I want to fight."

"Please don't start that again," Gordain said, always protective of the frail boy. "You'll be with us, help anyone that gets hurt, like always."

Kieran's green eyes shone with tears and he looked away.

"Next, we have to tell Father Faolin," Gordain said with a frown.

"Why?" Aodhan challenged. "I say screw him."

Gordain sighed. "I don't like him any more than you do, lad. The thing is, he has power with the Oldsters and with the other priests. And with the bishop for that matter. We piss him off and he talks about it from the pulpit, with names. You want to answer to yer Dad if that happens?"

Aodhan kicked at an empty crate, sending it flying past a scowling Yvone.

"Sweet Jesus, Gordain, he as much sent me Dad out to get himself killed! I haven't seen any of the priests or the bishops strapping on swords, have you? They preach war on the heathens and then sit on their asses. I've had enough of it!"

"Let's not get into all that," said Yvone, absently sharpening her long, shiny knife. "Right now we need food, the Redshirts might have some—I say might—and that's it."

"Fine," Aodhan said. "We tell Father Faolin. Leave me out of that part."

"No," said Flann. "You may hate his guts, but yer Dad knows Faolin pretty well. You have to go. All you have to do is smile and nod."

"Christ. All right, I'll go, just don't make me say anything."

Yvone slid her knife into its sheath. "I'll head out and start collecting people."

"Get everyone you can," Gordain said. "This won't be easy, sure it won't."

Aodhan watched with a tinge of regret as Yvone left first, perfectly-rounded hips swaying suggestively inside tightly-fit trousers. No chance for a repeat performance now ... but there was always tomorrow. He followed Gordain and Flann and Kieran up the steps and into the dank, shadowy hall, wondering all the while why she was such an obsession with him. He liked whiskey, when he could get it, but Yvone was much better than whiskey.

Father Faolin occupied second-story quarters on the north side of The Chapel Royal. Being one of Dublin's senior clerics, his brightly-lit apartment was clean, warm, and well-furnished. When a black-robed deacon responded to their knock and let them in, Aodhan's knees nearly buckled at the heady aroma of fried meat and fresh bread. He stole a glance at Kieran, limping behind him, saw the boy's stricken face, and wished they had left him in the Pit.

The portly priest was indeed about his breakfast: sausages and biscuits and fruit served on polished wooden platters. Not much was left, though even a few scraps would have given struggling Kieran a boost. The offer was not made. The priest bade them to sit on well-stuffed chairs until he finished. Aodhan clamped his hands on the chair's smooth arms and called up the image of knocking the fat man to the floor and stuffing the plates down his throat as dessert to his gorging. At last the priest gulped a rose-colored drink, wiped his jowls with a pure-white linen cloth, and turned his chair toward his three visitors.

"Now," he said cheerily after a belch, "what can I do for you fine boys this morning?"

"Father," said Gordain, "we have word there might be food across the river. Stole from the docks."

"Belonging to the Redshirts, like?" said the priest, narrowing his eyes. "Stolen from whom?"

"Don't know," Flann answered. The priest waited with narrowed eyes. "Probably from the bishop, Father."

"I'll get my share?"

"Of course, Father," Gordain assured him. "A quarter of everything we get, no one will know."

Faolin pondered a moment, then nodded. "All right, you can go. Got enough help?"

"Maybe fifty, Father," said Flann. "Should be enough."

"Maybe," said Faolin, looking dubious. "Won't look good if too many get killed."

Aodhan's temper slipped out of control. "Maybe you'd take that greasy knife from the table and come along, help us like."

Gordain sent him a furious glare. Too late: the words hung in the air, and Father Faolin was heaving his oleaginous bulk from the chair.

"Ye have a nasty tongue, lad," he said, taking a step towards Aodhan. "I'll speak with yer father when he returns."

Aodhan jumped out of his chair, breaking Flann's desperate grip on his forearm.

"You do that, ye fat pig, if my father comes back a'tall," he cried. The black-robed priest advanced on him until Aodhan's crimson-stained knife flashed out. "You try anything and I'll gut you like the two Redshirts I did this morning. You sit here and fill yer fat face when this poor boy is half-dead of hunger, and worry about the goddamn heathens in the Province while yer own people starve. I say good riddance to all of you."

As he fled out the door Aodhan heard Gordain's muttered "Christ Almighty." He ran down the long, shadowy halls until he reached the open air again. Rain had returned, a cold rain born on a cold wind, but Aodhan paid it no mind. He stopped in the middle of the Castle Green and sucked in clean, rain-washed air and tried to forget the stink of the food and ease the intense desire in his gut to go back and carry out his threat. He wished desperately for Yvone; the feel of her would empty his mind of rage and sadness.

"Aodhan," called out a breathless voice. "Wait."

Kieran had followed him and now stood bent over with pain, his slender body shaking. Aodhan took hold of him, shocked at the boniness beneath the heavy sweater, and led him back to the Pit. By the time he reached it the boy could no longer stand, so Aodhan lowered him gently onto a cushion.

"Kieran, why did you run after me? You should have stayed with the rest where it was warm, maybe that fat bastard would have given you something to eat after all."

"I followed you," said Kieran, coughing hard, "because you were right and because you stood up for me." Kieran looked up, tears streaking his sallow cheeks. "I won't live the winter, I know that. Sure I'd like to see my mother and sisters have decent food and wood to heat the place." His head sank again in a coughing fit.

Aodhan ran his hand through the boy's wispy hair. "I'll have no talk of dying, lad. We'll all be here in the spring if I have to kill every damn Redshirt in Dublin to get that food for you. I'll be right back."

He walked through the back of the stage to a filthy bathroom where on occasion the tap gave up a pitiful stream of water. Today he was in luck; he found a not-too-grimy cup and filled it for Kieran. When he returned, Gordain and Flann were climbing down the tiers, followed by Yvone, her straight black hair plastered down by the rain. He gave Kieran the water and helped him into a chair.

"I'm sorry, Gordain," Aodhan said before the older boy could tear into him. "I couldn't stand the sight and smell of that bastard stuffing his face when all our families go without and Kieran is ... well, he's sick is all." He dropped his hands to his sides. "Beat me up if ye want, I won't draw my knife."

Gordain stared at him a moment, then tumbled into a chair and hung his head.

"There'll be no beatings," he said. "I could strangle the cockroach myself. The fact is he's got power over who gets what and who does what. He could snap his fingers and the Black Hats would be no more. He has sway with the Oldsters and probably with the country clans and the shippers and God knows who else? The other priests don't cross him. Christ, he gets away with cheating the bishop!"

"So what happened?" Aodhan asked. "We go tonight?"

"We go," said Flann. "Faolin's on the outs with Father Loughlin, who's supposed to make sure the Redshirts stay in line. So he doesn't mind dealing out a little punishment to the dear father's flock."

"Did he say anything about me?"

"No, but you can be sure he'll do more than talk with yer Dad. I'd watch where I go alone for awhile."

Aodhan caught Yvone's worried look. It warmed him to think she cared about him for more than backing her up against a table in a dark room.

"How many so far?" Gordain asked Yvone.

"Close to fifty, anyway," she said. "Most of our usuals and a band from St. Stephens Buidheann."

"You trust them?" Kieran asked. His breathing steadied and a small amount of color returned to his ashen face. "They've done us wrong before."

"I know that," said Yvone, "and I don't like going to them. Truth is we need help and they offered four tough fighters for an eighth share. Worth the risk."

"Maybe," said Kieran. "I hope they don't betray us, is all."

"The plan," Gordain said, getting to his feet, "is to meet at St. Andrews at eleven. Dark cloaks with hoods, knives sharp, iron bars if you're strong enough. Clear?"

They all nodded and the group broke up. Gordain took Kieran under his wing, Flann cast a wishful glance at Yvone and followed the other two out. Aodhan waited until the big room was empty, then felt his face flush hot and his body tremble with anticipation. Yvone moved over to him, loosened the top buttons on her sweater, and kissed him in a way that drove him beyond all control.

"We're leaving at dawn to visit your father," Aodhan's mother said. She stood over the stove stirring a dented pot filled with sweetened oatmeal. "The boats leave Parliament Quay at first light. You'll be coming?"

Duana Saithne turned her head to look at her son. Aodhan scooped up his two-year-old sister Cara and lifted her high overhead, drawing squeals of delight.

"I'll try, mother," he said, setting the curly-haired toddler down gently. "We're going over the bridge tonight for food, we think the Redshirts have a stockpile."

Duana halted her stirring. "I wish you wouldn't go. Bad enough yer Dad is risking his neck and his one good eye. I don't want you coming home cut to pieces ... or worse."

Aodhan went to his mother and wrapped an arm around her slender waist. He was taller than her now, a position of strength he used sparingly.

"I understand, mother, I do. I wouldn't go if we didn't need the food so much. We don't have much left ourselves, and who knows how long Uncle Varnait can keep sending to us from his farm? My friend Kieran is so sick." He stopped, his throat closing at the memory of Kieran gasping for breath. "Well, we need the food, is all. Father Faolin is no goddamned help at all."

Duana tapped him lightly on the cheek. "Don't curse."

Aodhan let go of her, crossed the worn and cracked wooden floor of the second-story flat, and sank onto the single decent piece of furniture they owned, a sofa his father had made. From the next room, six-year-old twins Beacan and Bronach wrestled and screeched.

"Quiet in there!" Aodhan yelled. "Mum and I are talking." To Duana he said, "A couple of other things you should know."

She lifted the kettle off of the hot stove and set it in the oven to keep warm. "I don't suppose I'm going to like this."

"No, I suppose not. First, I killed two Redshirts this morning on my way to the Pit."

"Jesus, Mary and Joseph," she said, crossing herself. "Did you have to?"

"They ran at me from behind, so 'twas either them or me. I don't like killing, mother, believe me I don't."

Duana crossed the room and sat down next to him.

"I'm glad to hear it," she said, resting her hand on his. "And what else?"

"I cursed out Father Faolin to his face and he came at me and I said I'd gut him if took another step."

Duana sucked in a sharp breath. "Your father will not want to hear that," she said. "Why, son?"

"Because he was stuffing his face while my friend Kieran is half-dead 'cause he's sick and doesn't have enough to eat. Because the priest's a goddamn coward, tells other people to go fight while he sits there in the castle safe and warm. I hate him and I hate all the priests. Let 'em all go to hell."

Duana clasped her hands in her lap, then dabbed at her eyes with a threadbare apron.

"I'm sorry, mother, I truly am," Aodhan said, appalled that he had made her cry. "It's how I feel. And I'm not the only one. There's less food this year than last and less last year than the year before. Cara won't live to see my age the way we're going. All the priests think of is keeping the peace in Dublin and cursing the pagans of the Province. If God loves us and not them, why do the pagans have enough to eat and we don't? Tell me that, mum."

"I don't know, son," she said. She fixed her round, luminous brown eyes on him. "I understand why you feel this way, and truth be told, I am beginning to feel the same. God has abandoned us. Why, I don't know. The priests say we sin! Your father fixes roofs and floors and walls and pipes twelve hours a day every day except Sunday, and can't earn enough churchcoin or trades to keep us going." She reached out and brushed wavy brown hair from his forehead. "If you have to go tonight, go. Please be careful. If your father doesn't come back, I'll need you, son. I can't do it alone."

Aodhan kissed her on the cheek. "I'll be fine, mum. You take the little ones to visit Dad, don't wait for me if I'm not here. I'll see you when you get back."

She rose and started back towards the stove.

"It's only for the day," she said, "because the army plans to leave the lake the next day and attack the Province day after that. All I ask God to do is to send my husband back alive. I know you don't think much of prayer, Aodhan, but maybe say one for your Dad?"

"Sure, mum, I'll do that."

He knew he wouldn't, but saying he would was rewarded by her smile. On second thought ... he decided to pray anyway. It couldn't hurt, could it? That evening, when the last rays of an angry red sunset faded into darkness, he remembered his promise as he walked alone to the Pit.

God, I don't believe you are watching out for me and my kin one bit. On the chance that I am wrong, please keep me Dad safe. I don't care much about myself. Mum and the little ones need taking care of. That's all.

Probably not a very good prayer, but his anger kept welling up in his belly and made it hard to feel like a supplicant. Still, he had kept his promise.

Two bright lanterns illuminated the sinister Gothic front of the Church of St. Andrews, where Father Faolin weekly preached the dangers of sin and the evils of paganism. Kieran leaned his shoulder against one side of the entrance.

"You feel OK?" Aodhan asked him.

"Better," the boy said. "I shouldn't have run this afternoon, it brings on the cough."

"Everyone inside?"

"Most."

A scattering of candles threw long, creepy shadows onto the floor and walls of the church's cavernous nave. The room reeked of smoke and wet stone and ill-washed bodies. Amazingly, someone was playing on the pipe organ a hymn they sometimes sang on Sundays. The organ was in poor repair and many of the pipes sounded not at all or blared off-pitch. Despite that, Aodhan liked the sound and tonight it helped to ease his agonizing tension.

Gordain and Flann stood off to one side talking quietly. He had to search out Yvone: she was in a dark corner having an animated whispering session with two tall boys from St. Stephens Buidheann. He clenched his fists, jealousy infecting his already-troubled mind. They had made love twice today and now she flirted with two boys from another gang?

She turned slightly and caught sight of his angry glare. She said something inaudible to her companions, then came to him, grabbed hold of his hands and squeezed hard.

"Aodhan, stop it. I was just being nice to them, for God's sake. We need their help, in case you hadn't noticed."

He took a deep breath and swallowed hard.

"Sure. Sorry, Yvone, I'm wound up bad tonight. Worried about me Dad, about Kieran, about everything."

She leaned over and whispered in his ear, "I love you."

"I love you too," he whispered back.

Gordain gathered them into a circle and set out the plan.

"Most of you have been with us before," he began, his eyes scanning the group. "So you know we have to be totally silent. No talking once we get onto the bridge. Not a whisper. Weapons under cloaks, hoods up. The stores are supposed to be in the Post Office basement. If we find what we're looking for, remember, the point is to get out with it, not fight every goddam Redshirt that comes along. Got it?"

Nodding heads were his answer.

"All right, let's go. Rain and fog would have been nice, at least it's cloudy. Remember, when we get to the bridge, no talking or you answer to me."

Fifty or so hooded, silent figures slipped furtively along deserted streets, skirting the brooding ruins of Trinity College. The night was pitch dark, sans moon or stars, so Gordain allowed a couple of shaded lanterns to be carried. When they reached the south end of Tir Connell Bridge, Gordain stopped them for a moment, making sure they were all together.

Aodhan strained his ears to catch any stray sound coming across the black, swirling Liffey. He heard nothing save the contented gurgle of the water. He would not have admitted it to anyone, even Yvone, but he was far more nervous about this raid than any others he remembered. He had killed two Redshirts that morning, then cursed out a priest, acts that could have consequences if the God he did not believe was angry with him.

He felt his left arm shake. Yvone pressed her lips to his ear.

"Crushing me," she whispered.

"Sorry."

He took her hand again, gently. Gordain raised his arm and led them onto the bridge. He kept them away from the sides of the bridge whose stone railings had long since fallen into the Liffey. When they reached the opposite side, Aodhan felt inside his cloak and drew his knife, sharpened that day with his mother's kitchen whetstone. Yvone let go of his hand.

The hulking stone Post Office, headquarters of the Redshirt Buidheann, was less than two blocks ahead. A painful scene flashed into Aodhan's mind: a year ago at this very spot, he and two friends surprised a cart-driver and stole a two bags of fruit. They paid a dear price for their modest gain. His friend Harkin, always ready with a joke, crashed to the street with a thrown knife buried in his back. Later that day, Aodhan vomited up the first stolen apple he tried to eat, and never touched the rest. He told his mother the fruit fell off a cart.

He must've been squeezing Yvone's hand too hard again, for she shook loose and took a step away from him. Gordain lowered his hood and donned his Black Hat, and everyone else followed suit. In a fight, they had to be able to tell friend from foe.

The rubble-strewn front of the building was lit by two lanterns on either side of a wide entrance whose doors had long since vanished. No one was posted outside to challenge them. Aodhan hoped Gordain knew where he was going when they got inside. Surely a building this size would be a labyrinth no less confusing than Dublin Castle. He trusted Gordain to know; his tall friend had never led them wrong in the past. They started toward the entrance and had nearly reached it when a shrill whistle pierced the night, followed by the slapping of shoes on stones.

Aodhan heard Flann shout an alarm. Then bodies collided with bodies, screams of pain and shouts of anger echoed through the ruins, boys and girls stabbed and struck and wrestled in the darkness. In seconds Aodhan lost track of Yvone. For a horrified second he saw Kieran fighting with someone, then a rock-hard first sunk into his ribs and he fell, searing pain robbing him of breath. Someone stabbed down at him, cutting his arm. His father's training took over and his male assailant instantly lost his manhood. Aodhan winced at the cry of agony. He struggled up and no sooner found another opponent than a club hit his face from the side and he was down again, his face blazing with pain. Flann guarded him, taking and giving cuts, until he was able to stand again. Where was Yvone? Where was Kieran? He couldn't see them, all he knew to do was to cut anyone without a Black Hat. His knife made contact a dozen times, and he knew some of those he got would never get up again. Then he tripped over a body and fell hard on the stones. Before he could get up again a knife sliced his right side and a fist thundered into his left temple. The horrible sounds of the fight faded to a distant roar, and then to nothing.

Aodhan awoke to the cool touch of a wet cloth on his face. Ever so slowly his mind put itself back together. He was lying on his back on something soft. He opened his eyes and saw Yvone sitting next to him, her face ash-pale and streaked with blood. He was not in his own flat: he did not recognize this room at all. Morning light poured through a single large window. It was dead quiet. His mouth was dry, his vision cloudy, and pain throbbed from his head and everywhere else.

"Hello," she said softly. She dabbed at his face again. "Lay still, love." She retrieved a mug of water from a table. "I'll help you sit up, then drink all of this if you can."

She reached behind him and pulled on his back. Pain surged from his ribs and a mighty hammer battered his temples.

"Oh, Jesus," he gasped. He managed to sit up partway and down all the water in the mug. Then he sank back, eyes squeezed shut, sucking air and fighting not to groan.

Yvone took the mug from his shaking hand.

"Am I dying?" he asked her. "It's OK to tell me."

Her soft hand caressed his cheek. "No, no, sweet Aodhan, you're not dying. Your head is one big bruise, you left side is sliced open, and someone kicked your ribs while you were down. I don't think they're broken. The man upstairs from us is sort of a doctor, he washed the cut and stitched it up pretty neat."

He forced his eyes open again and waited until Yvone's worried face settled into focus.

"Where am I?"

"My place. It was closer than yours and we had to carry you. My Dad's gone to fight, like yours, and my mum is making tea in the other room. My little brother is asleep."

He took hold of her hand. "How did we do?"

"Pretty good," she said, turning her eyes away. "We got the food, well most of it, and we got the better of the fight, too."

"How many'd we lose?"

"I don't know exactly, three or four dead I think. Gordain is hurt but he'll live."

"You?"

She looked back at him and managed a wan smile. "Not too bad. Cuts on my head, and my left leg was stepped on, and one tooth is gone."

"Kieran?"

"He made it out OK too. Beat up a little. We made sure his family got plenty of the food and he's resting at home. He'll be all right."

"Tried to protect him, but ... "

"I know you did, love. I said, he's all right."

"Help me sit up again, put the pillows behind me."

She did as he asked. Tears of pain slid down his cheeks. After a few moments the worst of it passed and he was able to drink another mug of water.

"Who helped you get me here? Flann?"

"No. One of the boys from St. Stephens. They fought hard for us, Aodhan."

She seemed about to go on, then fell silent.

He stared at her. "Something you're not telling me."

"Let's have tea," she said, getting up. His right hand held onto hers tightly.

"What is it?" he demanded.

She sat down again and started to sob.

"Flann. He didn't make it."

He closed his eyes and gathered Yvone's shaking body against his own. And he prayed again.

Thank you God for taking away from me one of my best friends and a sweet boy whose father beat him. I think this will be my last prayer, whatever mum asks. If you're there at all, which I doubt, you have no love for me and mine.

I am now in the fifty-third year of my life and the thirty-fifth year of my service under arms. How often have I dreamed that the next battle would be the last, that we would win for ourselves a peace that would allow me to retire, to be the cabinet maker I always wanted to be, perhaps even to marry again? Yet there is ever another battle ahead, if not here in Eirelan, somewhere else among the Celtic peoples where our help is needed. It seems to me I am on a child's merry-go-round at a fair. The mules turn the gears, the table spins, the carved horses bob up and down in a circle, returning to the same place. Once again, I find myself at the head of an army, outnumbered, taking a desperate chance to buy another window of safety for my people. I detest the idea of killing, it sickens me. I have tried to make deals, offer concessions, do anything to keep from the spilling of blood, our own or others'. Tomorrow we will fight and I will kill as I must. If blood must flow, let it be the blood of those who would take from us what little we have left.

Camp Journal, Padraic Conmaicne

Chapter 25

Conor held up his hand, halting the column on the edge of a grove of trees. In front of them stretched an open meadow that Oran said extended all the way to the shore nearly a mile away.

"Silence down the line," he whispered to the Blade Captain leading the first century.

Moments later, Melvina approached with a squad of ten sharpshooters, each one carrying a sight-equipped crossbow. Oran stood absolutely still, listening.

"Voices," Oran said, though Conor could not hear anything over the rustling of the trees. "Coming up the other side of the rise. Probably a foraging party."

"Everyone down," Conor ordered. "On your bellies, except the crossbows."

Conor waved a hand to Melvina, who brought the sharpshooters forward. At her hand signal they formed a line parallel to the ridge ahead, cocked their weapons, went to one knee and loaded bolts tipped with fast-acting nerve poison.

"Wait for my signal," he whispered to Melvina. "If they don't see us, we'll let them go back."

"Women's voices," Oran said in his ear.

"You said no women!" Conor whispered back urgently. "What if it's a family, for all love?"

"Possible, not likely. I didn't see every soul in the camp. They have some women fighters. These will not be innocent bystanders."

"I hope you're right."

The voices were now distinct, three or four males, at least two female, bantering loudly and laughing. *Oh, how I hate to kill in cold blood,* Conor agonized. *Please go back.* The sharpshooters raised their crossbows to shoulder height and peered through telescopic sights.

Conor felt Oran's hand clamp on his bracer. "I doubt they'll stop, Conor. They probably collect berries in these woods."

Melvina's raised her right arm and fixed her eyes on Conor. Five figures topped the ridge and came sauntering towards them: three men in ill-matched leather armor with swords hanging from their belts, two women in dark tunics armed with long knives in belt-sheaths. They laughed loudly at a joke and paid no attention to their surroundings. And they were tramping directly for the woods where Conor's troops lay hidden.

"No choice," Oran whispered.

"I know that."

But it is five lives I order snuffed out, my friend.

One of the men drew in front of the others and stared straight into the woods—and saw them. He stopped and opened his mouth to shout. Conor nodded to Melvina whose hand slashed down. With a sudden *snap* that made Conor jump, ten bolts sizzled true and deadly to the mark. By training the squad divided the targets down the line: two bolts struck each forager in the throat and chest. A faint gurgling could be heard as they fell, then silence. *Not battle*, Conor cursed silently, *mere slaughter. Someone will grieve for each of them.*

Oran took a few steps forward, listening intently. He nodded to Conor.

"Column forward," Conor ordered the Blade Captain. "Melvina, keep your squad at the front. From here to the ridge they'll have to shoot without a command."

She issued the order in a low voice. Her sharpshooters moved into the meadow with crossbows cocked. Oran and Conor followed, and behind them the Blade and Bow centuries emerged in silence and spread side to side. Conor paused over the dead bodies until Oran tugged him forward.

Fifteen tense minutes passed while the two lines of battle formed in silence below the ridge: Bows above and Blades three strides back. Clattering of pots, chopping of wood and a thousand conversations from the campground masked what little noise the army made. By the time the last fighter was in place, a sliver of the morning sun crept above the trees to the east. By now, Padraic's force would be in line of battle, concealed in woods to the north.

Through the eye-slit in his helmet, Conor scanned his lines. The captains had done their jobs well. The Bows' line of nine hundred and the Blades' of eight hundred ran north and south two thousand feet to each side. Every archer's first arrow was knocked; every Blade gripped a javelin in his right hand, rectangular, heavy-bossed shield in his left.

The faint westerly breeze wafted smoke from hundreds of cooking fires. A flock of cawing crows circled overhead, alert for the chance to steal scraps. Now and then, a dog barked and someone laughed.

Oran hand-signaled Conor that he was going to the top of the ridge. He walked partway up past the Line of Bows, then sank to his belly, pulled his cape hood over his head, and slithered up through tall, wet grass to the top. Sweat poured down Conor's back as he watched his friend scan the enemy camp. Seconds later Oran slid down the slope and returned to Conor's side.

"Trouble," he whispered. "Boats unloading."

"More fighters?"

"No. Woman and children come to visit."

The sweat on Conor's back turned to ice. "Children?"

"And their mommies, scattering through the camp."

As if to reinforce his statement, high-treble shouts and squeals peeled out from the invisible camp. Conor imagined what now ran through the minds of his fighters: arrows and javelins felling innocent, the blood of dying children draining into the sand.

Decision time. We can't stay here and we can't retreat. And we can't kill the children. Too much to ask.

He motioned to a boy clad in light armor posted with Trev Fiachrach and his fellow pipers. The red-haired youngster, no more than ten, looked stunned for a second and then bolted to Conor's side.

"Run north," he spoke into the boy's ear, "fast as you can. Stay below this ridge. When you hit woods again you will find General Conmaicne. Tell him, 'children in the camp, silent advance, do not attack.' Got it?"

The barefoot boy repeated the words under his breath, nodded, and sprinted off at astonishing speed. He disappeared in seconds. Oran leaned close until their helmets touched.

"We have to attack now. There'll come looking for the foragers any second."

"I agree," whispered Melvina, who had joined them. "Bad, but we have to."

"No," Conor said. "At my signal, we'll advance to the top of the ridge, arrows and javelins at the ready. I'm hoping Padraic will follow my lead. I think he will. No pipes. Silence. Make sure all the pennons are raised high."

"We could all be killed," said Melvina.

"Yes. But we do not murder children."

Conor turned to Oran, who shook his head sadly. "Heaven protect us."

Conor gave the orders to the flag captain and the hand-signals flashed down the lines. He counted off two agonizing minutes. By now, all Bow and Blade captains had the order and his runner would be reaching reached Padraic.

Signals came back: *lines dressed and ready.* He motioned to Trev Fiachrach, who came to his side.

"Trev," Conor said, dropping to one knee, "I need to put your life in danger, son."

The broad smile Trev gave in answer struck Conor like a blow. "Already in danger, sir."

"I need you to advance to the top with us and then stand in front of the lines with me, in plain sight, ready to play. Do you know why?"

"I do, sir."

"All right ... let's go."

One last glance down the lines: banners at the ready, twenty-one hundred disciplined fighters ready to give all for their people. Conor drew his sword and raised it, and with Oran on his left, Trev on his right and Melvina a step beside Trev, he faced the sword to the front and started up the rise. The lines advanced with him in a long ripple. Five more steps. Four. Three. He could see the lake, and boats gliding towards shore. Two steps. Then he was on the top. Archers pulled bowstrings to half-draw, infantry behind them raised javelins overhead into throwing position. Conor took two more steps ahead with Trev at his side. The tartan-capped musician drew the blowstick of the warpipes to his lips and filled the bag with air.

Conor expected instant chaos, weapons grabbed for, spears and hammers thrown, screams of fear and anger, a sudden desperate charge against the line to break it. Instead, a strange silence descended over the camp. Everyone froze in position. Spoons of oatmeal stopped halfway to mouths. Hatchets chopping firewood halted in mid-air. Bathers in the lake's shallows stopped splashing.

Yet not a total silence. The children, now numbering a hundred or more, went on cavorting and shrieking and laughing. Mothers in arriving boats tried to collar and silence their charges, to no avail. They had already spotted their fathers and brothers and shouted their names or "papa."

Seconds ticked by. Conor swallowed acid and waited. A quick glance right gave him slight comfort: Padraic's banners fluttered in the breeze. The escape path to the north was blocked.

A tall, wild-haired man not far from Conor raised his battle hammer and started climbing the slope. Melvina's arrow slammed into the earth between the man's boots. The man stopped, lowered his hammer, and edged backward.

Leaving his line behind, Conor sheathed his sword and started down the slope towards the lake. He took five casual steps down the slope and stopped, pulled off his helmet and swiped sweat from his forehead with a gauntleted hand. The nearest enemy fighters stood not ten paces from him. Every eye in the camp that could see him was fixed on his unprotected, sweat-covered face.

Melvina's eyes widened in amazement. She drew another arrow, knowing full well that Conor would die before she could shoot it.

"People of Dublin," Conor shouted, "we came to destroy your army. If you kill me where I stand, the pipes this young boy holds will sound, and death will come to all of you. Yet we see children among you, and we of the Twenty Clans do not slaughter the innocent. My name is Conor Laigain. Who will speak for you?"

For what seemed an eternity, no one in the camp moved or spoke. Only the children ran about and pointed innocently at the deadly line of fighters on the ridge. One especially clear voice rang out, "who are they, mommy?" At last a dark-haired man clad in black leather armor stepped forward. In his right hand he grasped a gleaming sword, but he did not raise it.

"I will speak," he said, looking at Conor with hate in his black eyes. "My name is Iarlaith. Let us put the women and children in the boats. And then we will fight you."

Conor waved an arm at his massed fighters. "Iarlaith, by the time the last child is out of harm's way, a thousand of you will lie dead, and the rest will also surely die. You can see that the way north is blocked. If you go south, we will drive you against our armies guarding the Rampart. I am offering you and your wives and children life, or death. You have only those two choices."

Iarlaith moved backward slowly and gathered with three other men who had cautiously moved near him. A minute passed. Two. Conor's tunic soaked with cold sweat, rivulets poured into his eyes. Oran's eyes darted back and forth, alert for any sign of an attack. Melvina held her arrow at half-draw, watching everyone near Conor. The Blades held the javelins high, waiting for a signal or an attack on Conor. Trev Fiachrach did not move a muscle.

Iarlaith came forward. "What are your terms?" he said bitterly.

"Fighters must lay down their arms where they stand," Conor replied, no longer shouting. "Mothers and children may leave by boat the way they came. We'll open a gap in our line for the road north. You will pass through that opening and take the road back to Dublin, or wherever else you choose to go. Take with you your food and clothes and the memory of this morning, and remember that we spared your children and yourselves. It will *never* happen again. If you choose to gather against us once more, we will show no mercy."

Padraic, I hope you will not despise me for this. I had to act as my heart told me.

"It will be done," said Iarlaith. He spat on the ground and muttered a curse. "As you say."

Iarlaith called out in a loud voice, "we will surrender to protect the children!"

His answer was a low muttering, though no one seemed ready to dispute his decision.

Conor turned towards his battle line. "Lower arms."

The Blades rested the points of their javelins on the ground. Archers lowered bows but kept arrows nocked to the strings. Conor summoned another runner, a girl with short blond hair and a face that reminded him of Feth as a ten-year-old.

"Run to General Conmaicne, fast as you can, tell him we have a surrender, the enemy will march through this lines."

"Surrender ... march through his lines," she repeated, staring down. Then she was off, her feet fairly skimming the top of the grass.

In the silent camp, singly and in small groups, fighters laid down their arms and with lowered heads walked north towards Padraic's line, which opened to let them past. Women gathered the children together and climbed into empty boats waiting on the shore.

A full hour passed before the last of three thousand fighters disappeared into the woods behind Padraic's battle line. When Conor was certain they would not return, he sent his troops into the camp. The soldiers piled what could be used into wagons the Dubliners left behind, then burned the rest. Meanwhile, the wind that covered their

advance slackened and a cool mist fell, hissing in the flames of burning
tents and sending pungent smoke into the air. When the mist turned
to a cold rain, Padraic decided against an immediate march back to the
Province. A day's rest by the lake could be indulged in without risk.

Oran and Melvina wandered off together while Conor lingered
on the shore of the enemy's former camp. In the distance he heard a
welcome sound: the laughter and shouts of his soldiers as they built
the defensive palisade and dug the latrines. He sank onto on a rotten
stump, took out a cloth and mopped the moisture from his face, then
sipped water from a canteen to ease the fierce burning in his stomach. He wanted to be alone so no one, even Oran, would see tears
of relief running down his cheeks. Tomorrow morning, hundreds
upon hundreds of young men and women would go home to families
and friends in one piece. No missing limbs or blinded eyes, no empty
places at dinner tables.

"And yet," he said aloud, "I left their whole army alive to fight
another day."

What will Padraic say to that?

By nightfall the rain faded back to mist; wolves howled in the distance; a flock of noisy geese circled overhead and landed on the lake's
placid waters. The bolder of the geese strutted through open camp
gates and demanded a share of the evening meal. The dulcet tones of
flutes and guitars and pipes and concertinas rose over the crackle of
campfires.

Conor sat cross-legged in front of a hot fire that sizzled in the mist,
holding in his hands a book of poetry that he read from now and then.
Next to him, young Trev softly played his complex melodies on uillean
pipes. Oran and Melvina leaned against each other, paying little attention
to their companions. Conor was startled by Trev's knowing wink.

Good for Oran, Conor told himself. His friend had spent much of the
last five years alone, traveling Eirelan from the spring thaw to the first
storms of winter. Last winter, Conor recalled, Oran had been involved

with a woman whose name he could not recall. When Conor inquired about her in the spring, he was met with a stony silence that spoke volumes. Melvina was, so far as Conor could see, a warm and interesting woman, strong-minded and occasionally sharp-tongued but also, well, sensuous was the word. Oran needed someone to come home to.

As do I, he sighed inwardly. *As do I*.

"Sir?"

Conor had the impression his attention had been summoned more than once. Looking up, he regarded the flame-lit face of one of Padraic's runners, a tow-headed boy with an impish smile.

"Your pleasure, sir," the boy said with a formal salute, "the commanding general would appreciate a word with you."

Conor returned the salute. "Tell the general I will be with him in a moment."

The boy saluted again and skipped off into the darkness.

"You still seem worried," said Melvina. "You don't honestly think Padraic is unhappy with what you did?"

"You'll have to get used to our friend," Oran put in. "He has a tendency to look dejected most of the time, even when we win a battle without bloodshed. The price of being a deep-thinking poet."

Conor managed a wan smile at that. "The fact is that I took control of the situation in a way I had no authority to do. My Uncle Padraic appreciates initiative but he doesn't allow his commanders to do whatever pops into their heads. I let three thousand fighters live who may be back on us in the spring."

Melvina got to her feet, slapped twigs from her camp trousers. "We could have attacked, we had them dead. Sure as I'm standing here, our arrows and javelins would have killed some of their children, and then they would turned on us with vengeance in their hearts. How much blood would have been spilled?" She kicked at the damp earth with her boot. "Whatever Padraic says, I say you did right and I'll back you up."

Conor fished a comb from his pocket and brought order to his damp hair.

"My decision, but thank you for saying that. I'll be back soon. How about cooking something? My stomach says we haven't eaten yet."

"One of my specialities?" Oran asked, keeping his eyes on the fire.

"I meant for Melvina to cook. Or Trev. Not you."

"I am wounded, brother. I make a fine pan of fried dough."

"Like I said."

Conor retrieved his uniform jacket from his tent and headed off through the camp, winding among the tents and the blazing fires. It seemed to him that conversations died out as he passed and then resumed when he moved on. *Do they think I failed them? Did they want to attack?*

Padraic's staff had combined three tents to make one large one, open to the air in the center and closed off on the wings. Conor found his uncle in the open section, seated at a folding table with two of his staff officers. The aging fighter seemed no less immense in a sweater and baggy trousers than in his battle armor. Conor caught his eye and Padraic said something quietly to the two men, who adjourned to one of the side tents.

"Sit, Conor," he said, heaving himself to his feet. From a small campfire Padraic retrieved a pot and poured steaming tea into two mugs. Then he slumped back into his chair with a heavy sigh. Conor read fatigue on his face, though the bright blue eyes were lively and alert.

"I need to discuss with you, son, what happened this morning," he began after a loud slurp of tea. "Gods, that's hot!"

"Uncle," Conor began, " I realize that—"

A massive, scarred hand detached itself from the mug and waved him to silence.

"Sorry, I am the general, I get to talk first."

"Sir."

Conor shifted uneasily in his chair as his uncle's eyes stayed fixed on him.

"First, we agree that what you confronted was totally unexpected? We did not plan for a hundred tiny tots and unarmed mothers running through the camp."

"No, sir, we did not expect that. Oran can't be blamed, those children arrived just before we did."

"I'm not blaming anyone," Padraic said. "In war, the unexpected happens."

"Usually at the worst possible time."

"Yes." To Conor's relief, Padraic turned his gaze out into the camp. "I'm curious, though, how you decided to do what you did. I mean, what ran through your mind?"

"The one image I could not shake," Conor replied, "was of a Blade throwing his spear or a Bow shooting an arrow, and watching it strike and kill a child. I felt that if that were to happen—and I was sure it would—our soldiers would be demoralized and our enemies would fight like demons. Even if we won, the dead children and mothers would lie at our feet, and we would never, ever forget that."

"Nothing strategic or tactical, like trying a straight Blade attack without missiles?"

"No, sir," he admitted, his stomach beginning to clench and churn.

"Interesting," Padraic mused, "because that's what would have occurred to me. I would have attacked anyway."

Conor could find nothing to say to that.

"What would you do now, if our positions were reversed?"

Conor set down his mug and found a nearby campfire to stare at. "Relieve me of command, perhaps."

"Oh, no," Padraic said with a smile, as if laughing at a private joke. "I have a worse punishment in mind."

"Sir?"

Padraic took a long sip of his tea before going on. "Nephew, what you did today was possibly the most astonishing act of personal bravery I've ever seen. Any one of twenty Dubliners could have taken your head off before anyone could stop them. More than that ... it was bravery with a real purpose. What you decided, in the seconds you had, saved hundreds of our own men and women. To put it bluntly, you made a command decision that won a great victory and cost us *nothing*. Tonight thousands of Dubliners, including the mothers and fathers of those innocent children, wonder if we're quite the evil heathens they imagine us to be. And in this camp tonight, twenty-one centuries of dedicated fighters would follow you to the gates of hell if it came to that."

Conor started to answer but Padraic waved him silent.

"In short, son, you're as much a hero as your father ever was, and I bless my own wisdom in choosing you for this command. If Domnall is up there in the vast heavens, he's weeping tears of joy."

"Or shaking his head in disbelief."

That drew a laugh from Padraic. "Maybe so, maybe so. Now on to your punishment. The time has come," he said, his voice turning more formal, "for the torch to pass. From this day forward, you will command our armies in the field."

Conor felt the blood draining from his face. "Uncle, you're not old—"

"Not old enough to retire? How many others are serving out here with fifty-four years breathing down their necks? Still ... I'm not retiring. I'll run the army, make sure everyone is trained and equipped and fed and ready. I'll manage the forts too. And I'll fight as long as I can wield that heavy sword. The fact is, field command needs a younger man, who thinks fast and moves fast. That will be you."

Conor gulped his tea to ease the pasty dryness in his mouth.

"We'll talk more about it back in Rosslare," Padraic said. He turned his head at the sound of a sweet, high tenor singing an old Scottish melody.

"A fine voice," he commented with a sigh. "'Tis a lovely spot here, too, beside this lake. Do you suppose, Conor, our people will ever be able to live here again?"

"It is a beautiful lake, with those gentle hills surrounding," Conor agreed. "Especially this time of year when there's so much color."

He paused, his mind reeling with what Padraic had said. "Uncle, in the west Feth will be in my army."

The older man nodded slowly. "I know that, son. As I've had to send you into battle, so you'll have to send her. She's more of a born fighter than either one of us. Young as she is, she'll be of great help to you some day. I'll give you Melvina for the Bows, and Oran will go with you, of course. What about a Blade Commander?"

"Kellen Fotharta."

"Yes, I agree. Steady as they come. Two fine children of three in that family. A dirty shame that Bram didn't turn out better."

Conor was surprised at the bitter note in his uncle's voice as he spoke of Bram.

Padraic downed the last of his tea.

"Off with you now, join your friends, have a meal and enjoy the evening. I plan to eat, read and sleep in that order."

Conor stood and looked back down at his uncle.

"I'll do my best for you," he said.

"That was never in question," said Padraic lightly. "Goodnight, nephew."

"Goodnight, Uncle."

Conor made his way to the lakeshore. The smoke of campfires blended pleasantly with the pungent, wet smell of the lake. A fish jumped near shore and the manic call of unseen loons echoed over the dark water. *What a lovely place this would be to live,* he pondered. *A house atop one of these low hills, overlooking the lake. A dock and a boat for fishing. Even the name, Poulaphouca, has a melodious sound. A challenge to rhyme a word with that! What did it mean in ancient times?*

He heard Oran and Melvina laughing long before he saw them. They'd built up the fire, and as he approached, the savory scent of stew struck his nostrils. His tight stomach had relaxed and he found he was famished to the point of weakness. Trev Fiachrach was slicing off thick chunks of bread for dipping in the stew.

"So, were you cashiered?" asked Melvina as he approached.

"Padraic punished me in his own way," Conor replied. "Very creative."

"How" Oran asked with a suspicious look.

"By making me his field army general."

Trev stopped his cutting. "Punishment indeed, but fitting, if you'll allow me to say so, sir."

Conor grinned at the eleven-year-old. "Be careful, I'll make you my adjutant. Melvina, you'll command the Bows in the west when we take the field. I can have Kellen Fotharta for the Blades, if he's well enough. And you—"

"Will be sentenced to wandering the dangerous countryside," Oran finished for him. "What else?"

"Nothing for now," Conor said, sinking onto the soft grass near the fire. "Who made the stew?"

"Guilty," Melvina said, giving it a last stir. "Oran never touched it."

Oran held up an open hand. "I swear."

Melvina served out the stew in deep wooden bowls. Conor's first spoonful told him he would not have to bear with Oran's "creative" use of herbs and spices. Though they all sat together, Conor found himself talking mostly with Trev, since Oran and Melvina had much to say to each other. Trev proved to be a fine talker equipped with stories too colorful for one so young. In the course of an hour Trev played his uillean pipes and then a flute and then a shiny brass tinwhistle.

"Is there anything you *don't* play?" Oran asked after a lively reel on the tinwhistle.

"Guitar is not my best, sir," the boy admitted, "because I can't get hold of a good one. Dad says maybe on my twelfth birthday, if the farm has a decent year."

"We'll see about that," said Conor with a secret wink at his friends. "Now, all to bed. We break camp at dawn."

Melvina said goodnight and moved off to join her captains. Despite drooping eyelids, Trev kept playing until Conor ordered him into his tent. At last Conor and Oran were left to sit in front of the dying fire, while around them, the human sounds of the camp gave way to chirping crickets and croaking frogs, punctuated by the eerie hoot of an owl perched high in the trees.

Oran poked idly at the glowing embers. "You noticed I'm interested in our Bow Commander?" he ventured.

"You astonish me."

Oran glanced up and saw his friend's broad grin.

"It's okay with you?"

"Of course it's okay with me, not that it's any of my business."

"I want to say one more thing," Oran said, "before we both doze off sitting up. I've been scared plenty of times in my life, faced my own death more often than I like to think about. I have to tell you, I was never more terrified than when you marched down that hill alone and took off your helmet. I was certain you'd breathed your last."

Conor rested his chin on his knees and gazed at his friend over the dying fire.

"I don't know why," he said, staring straight into Oran's eyes, "but I feel we still have some time to go. Even in my darkest moments, a thought comes to me that we've not come to the end of our road. Call it a poet's idle imagining, if you like. I believe we'll go on if we stay true to each other and to our people."

Oran waved a hand over the hushed camp. "They'll be looking to you now, you know."

"Yes, I know. I'll need your help."

Oran smiled at him in the dim light. "Did you need to ask?"

Dearest Mother, I write to you from Dungarvan. This letter will go out by the coastal packet to Tralee and should eventually reach you. I was lonely when I wrote my last letter, the fort near Clonea was a dark, isolated place and I could not seem to make any friends. That all changed last week when I came here, where I met Fethnaid Laigain and Derdre Dal Reti. They have become my first real and close friends in the Province. Feth is related to important people in the Province, among them her uncle Padraic Conmaicne, the general of the army, and her older sister Aideen who commands their naval fleet. Feth got the idea to recruit fighters in Cork and Kerry and so tomorrow, she and Derdre and I along with two husky Blades will ride west towards Cork. I am hoping we will get all the way to Fahamore, but I can't promise. We plan to reach Tralee in a few weeks, where I can see Uncle Ruinaidh, Aunt Norah and my cousins. I know you worry and wish I had not volunteered last year, but I am now more certain than ever that I am where I need to be. My love to father and everyone.

Your loving daughter, Gwen.

Chapter 26

The riding distance from Dungarvan to their first stop, the town of Youghal at the mouth the Blackwater River, was no more than twenty miles. Any expectation the troupe had of following a well-maintained road vanished as they entered the rolling, forested Drum Hills. The "road" soon deteriorated into a rocky, twisting path overgrown with weeds and partially blocked with fallen tree limbs. Ruins of ancient houses near the road provided stark and eerie reminders that once, many centuries ago, people lived here in great numbers. Even more depressing was the fact that they had to ride single file, making conversation difficult. Ionhar, who had traveled this way before, stayed in the lead, followed by Feth, Gwen, and Derdre. An uneasy Keegan rode at the back, his eyes roving the path behind them and on both sides.

The three Welsh horses seemed contented enough with their lot. So far as Feth knew, Wales was mountainous and they had been bred for thousands of years to manage rocky paths far worse than this one, at a steady, moderate pace. Not so the big horses carrying the Blades. Keegan's Comhghall capered with excess energy, while Ionhar's heavy draft horse Breasal grunted and snorted and occasionally stopped entirely for a breather. On each such occasion the other four riders stifled laughter, not very successfully, while Ionhar attempted to make use of Arvel's doubtful advice.

Except for Ionhar's comical travails, Feth did not see much to smile about. The further they drew away from the safety of the Rampart and the friendly, pub-lined roads of the Province, the more she began to wonder whether she had made a wise decision. It was not only her own life at stake now, it was four others who had thrown their lot in with her. That they came willingly, even eagerly, offered small consolation.

Now I begin to see, she mused darkly, *why Conor seems so oppressed at times, and maybe why Aideen rarely smiles or laughs. It's is a hard thing to be responsible for the lives of others, especially when they're your friends.*

About halfway to Youghal, they left the Drum Hills behind and found themselves on more level ground where the trees did not so oppress the path. In late morning they entered a broad meadow divided in the middle by a narrow, swift-flowing stream, where they decided to stop for lunch. They unburdened the horses and set them free to munch juicy grass and drink from the stream. Overhead, the gloomy overcast cleared in favor of white, pillowy clouds gliding lazily from the north, set against a brilliant blue sky.

"Why are we talking so quietly?" Gwen wondered aloud. "Doesn't seem to be anyone around to hear us."

Keegan tore off a chunk of bread and scanned the edges of the meadow.

"That's just it, it's so quiet. There must be people living around here. Where are they? We're not that far from the town and we haven't seen a soul yet."

"We've just past the hills," said Ionhar. "No farming up there, my friends. So why follow this twisty road towards the Province unless you have business there? I think only merchants travel through here for big market days in Dungarvan."

Feth nodded agreement. She strolled over to the stream and dipped her cup in. The water was ice-cold and clean-tasting.

"You're quiet today," Derdre said from behind her. "Not like you."

Feth pushed damp strands of hair from her forehead.

"I'm worried. Wondering if this is a good thing to do. Missing Sean. Something like that."

Derdre sat down on the edge of the stream bank and gently tugged on Feth's sleeve to join her.

"Feth, it *is* the right thing to do," she said. "We all feel it. We need the help of these people, and they need us. It's time to forget all the history and the bad feelings of the past. My mother felt that way, so does my father. You're the one who had the courage to stand up and say so and actually do something! Maybe the high-level bargaining will work out, I don't know. I do know that people from here to the great ocean do not like us or trust us, and political talk in Teach Munna won't do much to change that. They need to see us for who we really are."

Feth fished a small, colorful pebble out of the stream bed, turned it over in her fingers. "That's what I think too but it's more than an idea now. Four of you are out here with me and that makes it my responsibility."

Derdre squeezed her friend's shoulder. "Have faith in us! We came because we wanted to. We believe in what we're doing. And speaking for myself, I believe in *you*."

"I do have faith in my friends. The trouble is, all my life my mouth has tended to get ahead of my thoughts. Acting in front of thinking, my sister Aideen says. Gotten me into trouble plenty of times. I didn't really have time to think about doing this. By the time I got done thinking, it would be too late."

Derdre took the pebble from Feth's hands and studied it a moment.

"My father taught me an old song once, it talked about how everything turns around, war to peace, love to hate. One of the lines was 'a time for every purpose under heaven.' There's a time to think and a time to act."

Feth got to her feet. "Sing that song for us?"

"Sure, if I can remember it."

They rejoined the others and conversation lightened as Feth joined in the banter. Derdre sang the old song, as many verses as she could recall. The meal finished, Ionhar and Keegan collected the horses and they pressed on for Youghal. The road broadened enough for two to ride abreast, so Keegan joined Feth at the front; the two banners now flew side by side. Gwen and Derdre rode together next in line. Ionhar and his sullen mount fell back to the rear position.

Soon enough they found themselves with plenty of company: dark-clad people on foot, some pulling small carts; larger carts drawn by oxen or horses and bearing whole families on the benches; and occasional solo riders. The road was not wide enough to get around carts so they stayed in the queue, drawing stares that ranged from curious to hostile. No one spoke directly to them, though it was not hard to overhear mutters like "what are they doing here" and "this means trouble, sure it does."

Keegan leaned over towards Feth. "I don't sense that we're welcome."

"I didn't expect we would be," she replied. "These people think we look down on them and that we live in luxury. Why would they welcome us?"

The bridge over the Blackwater River was a rickety wooden affair resting on time-worn stone pilings. The planks creaked ominously under the weight of Ionhar's great steed and its ponderous rider. Reaching the opposite bank, Feth drew them aside onto the grass to take in the arresting view. The river itself, despite its name, seemed suffused a deep blue color as if its water absorbed the sky itself. An unusual mixture of hardwoods set the banks afire with colors from deepest crimson to brightest yellow. As they watched, a small boat floated past, its sole occupant holding a fishing pole in one hand and a big flask in the other. He looked up, saw them, and to Feth's astonishment, smiled and waved with his flask hand.

"The only friendly face we've seen," Keegan said. "Now what's his story?"

"Drunk," said Gwen with a skeptical frown.

Feth shrugged but inwardly did not agree: the man's eyes seemed clear enough.

She led them back onto the road leading south into the town. The outskirts came on gradually, scattered cottages close to the road, one roadside market, a stable. They passed through one last grove of trees and then found themselves in the town proper, which was much larger and more crowded that Feth had envisioned. In her mind she had conjured up towns of the west as dreary, dark places, peopled by angry, sullen folk who cast anxious stares this way and that. Instead, she found herself in a town alive with busy people shopping and laughing and herding cranky children. Still, there were details that marked a struggle for necessities: well-worn clothes and shoes, dilapidated roofs and collapsed dwellings, litter in the alleys, cracked glass in shop windows.

People in the bustling streets gave way to their passage slowly and reluctantly. Many townfolk glared at them in silent anger, others cursed loud enough to be heard, in an accent that rang oddly in Feth's ears. Out of the corner of her eye, she saw Keegan detach his helmet from the saddle-strap.

"No," she said to him. "Not unless we have to fight."

"Your call," he said with a shrug.

A partially-ruined stone fountain occupied the center of the town square. The fountain's central spire, which must have reached thirty feet into the air at one time, now crumbled to half that height. The broad basin resting on the monumental base was largely intact, though bone dry; no water spewed from the mouths of weathered gargoyles. Feth rode Ioan straight up to the fountain and dismounted. Her comrades followed suit; they tethered the horses loosely to a wooden rail near the fountain's base.

The fleeting thought occurred to Feth, *they could take our horses if we let go of them. Yet we can't appear afraid and I need to show them we trust them.*

"Onto the basin," she told the others sotto voce. "Keegan, bring the banners."

Ionhar leaned down and whispered in her ear, "We'll be easy targets up there."

"Yes, I know. Come on, give me a boost."

Ionhar hesitated a moment, then cupped his hands and fairly tossed Feth onto the ten-foot-wide basin. The other four joined her, Keegan last up with the two banners. Around them, a crowd gathered until the square was packed solid to the nearby buildings. A constant low muttering charged the air with animosity.

Feth moved to the edge of the platform. "Citizens of Youghal!" she shouted, startling her companions. "A few minutes of your time?"

The crowd fell into a momentary shocked silence.

"My name is Fethnaid Laigain. My friends and I come from the Province to ask for your help."

Now the crowd recovered its voice and it was not a pleasant sound. "Help for what, so you can get fatter than you already are?" "Sure, now that you're going under you want our help, when you would never help us before." "Too bad, you came to the wrong place."

"Feth, this is ugly," Gwen whispered in her ear. "Maybe we need to move on."

Feth shook her head, raised a hand in the air and plunged ahead.

"I understand how you must feel. I'm asking that old grievances—"

"You have a lot of nerve!" a gray-haired man standing right below her bellowed. "You spit on us for generations and now you come *here* for help?"

Feth stared down at her accuser. "Sir, I am eighteen years old and I have never spit on *anyone*. Feel free to spit on me if it makes you feel better."

The scowled and dismissed her with the wave of a grimy hand.

"We are here today," she started again with a raised voice, "because a powerful army is gathering near Limerick. Within weeks this army will attack the Province and—"

Something big sailed through the air from the right; none of them saw it coming. It struck Feth in the ribs and knocked her off her feet. She fell hard onto the stone surface, managing to get her hands out and avoid smashing her mouth into the stone. As it was her mouth struck her left hand and her teeth cut deeply into her cheek.

Instantly her friends surrounded her, facing outward. Feth sat up with blood dripping onto her cuirass. An oversized melon lay at her feet.

"Feth, it's too dangerous," said Keegan. He lifted her to her feet. "Let's get out of here."

"No," she said. She pulled out a cloth to sop blood from her mouth. "I won't be shut up by a melon."

"Cowardly!" A booming shout burst from the crowd nearby. A powerfully-built man with a grizzled beard hoisted himself up onto the basin with difficulty. He was dressed in blacksmith's leathers and in his right hand he held a smith's hammer. Keegan and Ionhar edged between him and the three women, but the man's attention was focused on the crowd. He lifted his hammer high in the air.

"Cowardly!" he shouted again. "We are barbarians here? We throw *melons* at people who wish to speak? You all know me and I know you. Throw something again and you meet my hammer!"

He turned to Feth.

"Speak as you will, Fethnaid of the Province. There will be nothing thrown."

She spit out blood, took a deep breath, and started again.

"As I was saying ... the army near Limerick is six thousand fighters, maybe more. They may defeat us, and I know that would not bother most of you. I ask you to think on this: when they are finished with us, they will turn on you. Without the Province to draw the fire of the Ghaoth Aduaidh, they will be free to rape all of Cork and Kerry. And they will, mistake it not."

"Are you trying to say you care about us?" a man called out from halfway back in the crowd. "History says otherwise."

"I can't answer to history," Feth called back. "I can't make up for so many years of mistrust and bad feelings. I am alive now and I want to make our land safe for my children *and* for yours."

She stepped back and grabbed Gwen by the arm. "Say something."

"What? Feth, I'm not—"

"Tell them who you are and why you're here. Now!"

A wide-eyed Gwen stepped to the platform edge. After a moment's hesitation, she raised her hands to quiet the crowd, and began.

"My name is Gwen Cennedi! I was not born in the Province and my name is not of the Twenty Clans. I come from Fahamore Town on the coast near Tralee. I fight with for the Province because they keep the port of Tralee open and safe, so that we can live in peace and trade with other peoples over the sea. If the Province falls, Tralee will fall too. My brothers and sisters will have no future. I beg you, fight with me!"

She stepped back. Feth turned to Ionhar. "Now you."

The big man's ruddy face blanched. "Well ... "

"Go."

"All right, I'm going."

Ionhar stepped forward. "I am Ionhar Raithlinn." His bass rang with astonishing power through the square, silencing the muttering. "My kin live in Creagh, near Skibbereen. We have been storytellers for thousands of years. Our stories tell of a people who value poetry and music and laughter and who believe in living in peace and sharing the fruits of the Earth with our brothers. If the Province falls, all of Eirelan will sink into shadow and the stories will soon disappear. *We* will disappear. Help me to keep us in the light!"

The crowd stirred uneasily. No voices called out in derision.

"Derdre," Feth said. Derdre nodded and willingly stepped forward.

"I am Derdre Dal Reti, daughter of Mor and Dunlaith. My mother has rested under the Earth but two weeks, killed defending our people. She and my father taught me to respect all peoples, to value all life, to take it only when I had no alternative. I will fight for you. I ask you to fight with me."

Keegan did not wait to be prompted.

"My name is Keegan Cholmain! My father fell in battle six years ago. I fight to avenge him, yes, but also to protect my mother and brothers and sisters. I swear on my father's grave that I will fight to protect you also. I need your help, and I humbly ask for it now."

Feth seized the two standards, one in each hand, and held them high. "Will anyone fight with us?"

At first she was met with stony silence.

Then a woman of about thirty, with dark, flowing hair and broad shoulders, forced her way to the front. "I will."

"And me," came a male voice from the left.

It was the man who had waved from the boat. He had his fishing pole in one hand and a string of fish in the other.

"I'll fight!"

"Let me through."

"Get out of my way."

Forward they came, young and middle-aged, big and small, man and woman, until at least thirty waited below the banners. Feth jumped down, followed by her comrades. Some faces confronting her were eager, others determined or grim or cheerful. Feth sent only two away, a boy no more than twelve and a woman with a damaged leg who could barely walk. The rest were given written passes through the gates at Dungarvan and directions to the fort where they would be taken in.

"Anyone else who wishes to join our cause," Feth called out as the crowd began to disperse, "we will camp north of town tonight."

It's a start, Feth pondered as they rode north through the emptying streets of late afternoon. *All I had to endure was a well-thrown melon and a mouthful of blood.* She glanced back at her saddle bag. *And I have the melon!*

On the north edge of town they managed to buy fresh bread and fruit for themselves and feed for the horses. As they rode north into the country to find a campsite, a cold rain descended that by nightfall became a downpour. The horses, their heads bowed, slogged through the mud, while riders did their best to stay dry beneath oilskins. None of them relished the idea of pitching a tent in the mud and darkness, and all felt for the horses that needed dry shelter too.

A mile past the last houses of Youghal, they spied a light ahead and found that it belonged to a small, shabby farmstead. Smoke leaked from the cracked chimney of a large, square cottage. A lantern burned beneath an eave of the house, lighting the path to a barn that appeared to be intact and well-roofed.

They dismounted. Feth's boots sank into the muck and made a sucking sound as she walked up to the door. She heard voices inside, male and female, child and adult. The pungent scent of a hot meal and baking bread filtered past the doorframe.

She tapped lightly on the heavy door. The adult voices fell silent; a child called out cheerfully, "papa, somebody at the door!"

The door opened a crack. A back-lit face peered out at her. Then the door opened wider and Feth found herself face to face with a roughly-dressed, bearded man of middle age.

"Sir, I am Feth Laigain of the Province. I am traveling with four others—"

"I was in the square," he cut her off. Though the man wore a wary expression, she heard no anger in his voice. "They shouldn't have knocked you down like that. Doesn't mean I have soft feelings for the Twenty Clans."

"I don't ask you to, sir," Feth said, brushing water from her eyes. "We ask if we might shelter in your barn for the night? We'll pay you and we have our own feed."

A woman appeared at the man's shoulder. About the same age, Feth guessed, and very tired.

"Let them stay, Larkin," she said to him. "'Tis a foul night. They've done us no harm."

Larkin pondered a moment. "All right, you can use the barn. Take what hay you need."

"Thank you," Feth said, inclining her head. "A good night to you and your family."

Larkin nodded and closed the door. Feth trekked back though the mud to her friends.

"He took pity on me," she said. "Let's go."

The barn was neither large nor especially clean, but it was dry, well-stocked with hay, and occupied by only three cows and a passel of working cats. An hour later, the horses had gathered around a stack of dry hay and a trough of clean water, while their riders made a circle on the dirt floor about a small, flickering oil lamp. Keegan took on the role of server, carving bread and cheese and meat and passing around fresh fruit from the Youghal market. Feth insisted on slicing her hard-won melon.

"Is your mouth okay?" Gwen asked her.

"Stings a little," she admitted, "but at least my teeth are all there." She took a bite of the melon. "Very tasty."

"It wasn't funny at the time," said Derdre. "We should have been much more alert ... all of us."

"Sure we should have been," Ionhar said with a worried frown. "Next time Keegan and I stand close to you. Derdre and Gwen watch all sides."

Keegan did not comment. He held a piece of bread in his hand and smiled in Feth's direction.

"What?" Feth asked him. "My hair look funny?"

"Not at all," he replied. "I am remembering a moment not so long ago on a ship when I took a look at you and thought, what, this young woman is a fighter? When I watched you out there today, blood dripping out of your mouth, making them listen ... well, that's courage in my book."

"Keegan is right," said Ionhar, a massive hand wrapped around an apple. "It is one thing to wield a sword or loose an arrow. We are trained for these things and we do them. It is another to speak to people you do not know, people who are suspicious and angry, and get them to hear you. When Keegan asked me to come along, I said yes because I'm his friend and because I want to help these people. In truth, dear Feth, I thought it would not work. Now I believe we may yet be able to do this. Why? Because you know how to speak from your heart, and people who hear you will believe you."

Feth gazed at the flickering lantern. A flood of emotions swirled in her heart: love for her friends, security in their protection, terror that they placed so much trust in her.

"I am no saint," she said at last, "and no worker of miracles. All I can promise is that I'll do my best for you. We have a long way to go."

Splashing footsteps approached the barn. Keegan and Ionhar dropped their food and reached for swords. Yet there was no threat: a child's figure was outlined in the open doorway. The youngster moved ahead with halting steps; the lantern's pale radiance revealed a barefoot boy no more than eight, thin, dressed in a plain wool tunic. His black curly hair was plastered down over his eyes. He brushed the hair aside and stared with wide eyes at each one of them in turn. Then he found his treble voice, steady and self-assured.

"My father Larkin says that you are welcome in the house to share our meal."

"Please tell your father," said Feth, "that we are honored to accept."

The boy ran out and splashed his way back to the thatch-roofed house.

Feth nodded towards the remains of their meal. "All we can spare, save just enough for tomorrow."

Arms loaded, they dashed across the rain-soaked yard and entered the cottage through a back door held open by the boy. By Province standards, the interior of the house was dimly lit. Most of the light in the large, undivided room came from a blazing turf-fire in the hearth at the far end. The room was warm, smoky, and oppressive; its stone floor was clean-swept but heavily worn and cracked. Rough beds lined the walls on all sides. In the crude kitchen next to the hearth, two middle-aged women ladled what looked like stew into wooden bowls, while a third woman, much older, sliced a loaf of soda bread.

The center of the room was taken up by a single long table, far more rough-hewn than the table at Feth's home, with benches set on either side. An elderly man occupied the place of honor at the head of the table; Larkin sat on his right and another man about the same age at his left. Six more adults and children crowded the benches, including one young woman breast-feeding a baby. The children's faces and hands were scrubbed clean, but their clothes appeared handed down and much-repaired. Space for the travelers had been cleared at the end of the table.

Feth had no idea what proper behavior might be in this household, so far removed from her experience.

"We offer what food we have," she assayed, "for all to share."

The man in the place of honor rose to his feet slowly and with obvious pain. He bowed slightly towards Feth and her comrades.

"I am Nolin McParga, head of this household. You are the leader of this band?"

Feth wondered, *was that a note of skepticism?* Before she could answer, a teen-aged boy halfway down the table spoke up.

"I was in the square today, Grandfather," he said, drawing scowls from his elders. "She is the leader, make no mistake."

"Thank you, Genty," said Nolin, giving the boy a stern look.

"I am Feth Laigain, of Rosslare," Feth said with a friendly glance at Genty. "My friends are Keegan Cholmain, Derdre Dal Reti, Gwen Cennedi and Ionhar Raithlinn. We are grateful for your hospitality."

Nolin did not reply right away, leaving Feth wondering if she had already transgressed in some way. Meanwhile, the women transferred their food from the table to wooden platters so that it could be shared.

"You are welcome here," he said at last. "Take places at our humble table."

Nolin eased himself back into his chair. When Feth and her friends had seated themselves, he bowed his head and laid his hands flat on the table.

"We offer thanks," he said, "for the food we eat and the friends and family we share it with. Though we be poor in material things, yet we are rich in spirit. I invite the strangers at our table to eat and drink and above all to speak freely. At the table of Nolin McParga, all who come in peace and friendship are welcome."

"All are welcome," intoned the men and women and children.

With that formality over, the food trays were passed, and to her surprise Feth found the conversation turning friendly, lively, and full of humor. The travelers were besieged with questions about their homes and families; the subjects of war and fighting and the danger of the moment were assiduously avoided. The meal finished, stout was served out to the adults and cider to the children, who eagerly followed giant Ionhar to places by the fire, where he spun fantastic yarns of magic and great heroes of the past.

After a second mug of stout, Feth found herself desperately tired and imagined all her friends felt the same. She breathed silent relief when Nolin announced it was time for everyone to sleep. The children groaned their disappointment, as Ionhar had just begun a new story.

"We're grateful for the hospitality you have shown us," Feth said to Nolin. "I ask only that you remember why we came. We need help and we humbly ask for it from all who are able to give it."

Nolin reached out a gnarled hand to her.

"Fethnaid, you and your companions have been welcome guests," he said. "My sons and I will talk over what you have told us. Generations have passed since the Twenty Clans have shown us friendship. Perhaps a change is in the wind."

"That is why we are here," she replied, "to bring change. Goodnight to you all."

They moved towards the back door. Larkin called after them.

"Stay alert," he warned. "Though the army you spoke of is not yet near, raiding bands roam the night."

"No harm will come to this household tonight," said Keegan, his hand resting on the head of a tow-headed girl. "Any who come here to do harm will be cut down."

They filed out into the cold, windy night. Thankfully the rain had stopped and stars glittered among racing white clouds and a slivered moon. Gwen offered to take the first watch and moved off to sit near the barn door. Feth lay on a bed of hay near Keegan and fleetingly thought of asking him to hold her for the warmth of his body. No doubt he would have done so in the fashion of a brother, yet she refrained. It would have reminded her too much of Sean's embrace. Long after Ionhar and Gwen had dozed off, she lay awake.

"Keegan?" she whispered. "You awake?"

"Yes," he whispered back.

"They are so poor."

"In some ways, yes. They have a home full of love too."

"Love will not keep them warm or fed if the winter comes on like last year."

"We've all thought of that tonight. Especially those scrawny little children. They can't survive much."

"It makes me so sad."

She felt his calloused hand take a gentle hold on hers.

"Me too, Feth. But what can we do?"

Soon Keegan's hand relaxed and he snored lightly. Tired as she was, Feth stared into the darkness for a long time after, wondering why those children did not have shoes. Even the poorest children in the Province had shoes.

Dear Orlaith, I gave this letter to an Admiralty sailor in Falmouth, I hope he is true to his word and posts it for me. Guess what? Your big sister has been promoted! I was named second lieutenant of my current ship, the Caillech. I don't know that Mother will be proud of that, she never has been before, but it does mean more money I can send home for you and the other children so you can keep warm this winter in that falling-down old house. I am learning to curb my tongue, the same tongue that got me a scarred back a couple of years ago. I have high respect for Captain Fotharta. She cares for her ships and her crews and I trust her completely. I also have to tell you, my dearest sister, that we are in serious danger and I might not come home again. I don't say this to upset you, but if this is the last note you get from me, remember that I love all of you, even Mother who has always found me wanting.

Love always, Sithmaith

Chapter 27

The great fleet made for Brest under a lowering slate-gray sky and a sharp northerly wind that by mid-day hurled line after line of squalls at ships and crews. To keep his armada together under such conditions, Admiral Tredinnick ordered all ships to shorten sail and maintain as close a formation as possible. Even so, by sunset eight of the merchant ships had strayed out of sight and a further slowdown was ordered until errant vessels could be located. Finally all ships were accounted for, but rather than attempt to enter Brest Harbor at night, Tredinnick ordered the fleet to stand to in the lee of Ouessant Island. Though the conditions had never been dangerous, Mairin offered silent thanks that she was not carrying passengers. Anyone but the Admiralty's own marines would have been violently sick, and in a crowded ship that would have made everyone miserable.

At dawn the next day, the fleet would divide as planned and she could lead her battle group safely into the protected anchorage off Crozon to take on the Bretan Fighters. What would they be like? While she had put in at Brest many times, she had never strayed outside the city nor encountered any of their soldiers. They were said to be terrifying in battle, a true throwback to the wild Celts of old.

She enjoyed a friendly dinner with all her officers, and now was able to relax in her cabin as the ship stood to under slackening winds. Rowenna was officer of the deck; Sithmaith had retreated to her cabin to rest before taking the midnight watch.

With a tired sigh, she pulled off her boots and slipped into a loose, fresh tunic. She needed sleep, and more than an hour or two. At dawn she would need all her skills and experience to hold twelve ships together and bring them to a safe anchorage, in a place she had never seen. *The ship is in good hands,* she told herself, *there is no danger tonight except for sleep itself.* With a sigh, she dimmed the lamp and eased into her hammock. She closed her eyes, took slow, deep breaths, and luxuriated in the ship's easy rocking motion.

What a strange place this is. My house, yet not my house. Too small on the inside. What happened to all the big rooms? And why are all the shutters closed? It's so dark I can't see where I am walking. Someone is here with me. I can hear breathing besides my own.

I wish I could make it light. Who's there? Please answer me! I need to walk faster, get outside where the air is fresh and the sea so vast. My steps are so slow, and now there are hands on me. Please let go, whoever you are. No, don't turn me around, I want to get out of here. Who are you? No, don't do that. Let go of me, I've got to get out of this tiny, dark room with no windows! Let go of me. Please please please stop. Take your hands off me. Stop. Stop!

"Captain. Captain!"

Who is shouting that? My name is Mairin, not Captain!

"Captain, open your eyes. It's me, Mor."

Who?

She opened her eyes and the tiny, dark room gave way to the familiar sights of her cabin. An acid taste stung her mouth. The fresh tunic was drenched with sweat. Mor Dal Reti hovered over her, his strong surgeon's hands clamped like vises on her upper arms. Past his left shoulder the lantern gleamed brightly. Sithmaith's ashen, troubled face peered through the ajar cabin door.

"It's all right, Captain," Mor said quietly. He relaxed his fierce grip. "A little worse than usual this time. Can you sit up?"

He helped her onto the cushions in front of the stern windows. *Oh, yes,* she said inwardly, *a little worse I am sure. Sithmaith is scared out of her mind and she called Mor because she didn't know what else to do.*

"Thank you, Lieutenant," Mor said to Sithmaith. "You can go back to sleep."

Sithmaith nodded and closed the door. Mor dampened a cloth and handed it to Mairin. She pressed it against her face.

"The dark room again?" he asked.

"Yes." *Please, don't let me sob.* "Yes."

He put his arm around her shoulders and she sobbed with one hand clamped over her mouth.

"Mor," she said finally when she recovered her voice, "I hate myself like this."

"Do not ever say that," he said. "It's nothing you have control over. You wouldn't hate yourself for having the grippe, would you?"

She wiped tears from her face with the wet cloth.

"I don't understand why it stays with me. Why can't I be free of these memories? I don't even know if they *are* memories. Maybe just creations of an unbalanced mind."

Mor stood over her, thinking a moment.

"We've talked this over before," he said finally. "Most likely memories are at the root of these nightmares. That doesn't mean what you see in them is a recording of what happened. Our minds don't work that way, at least from what I was taught in school. You may have lost the ability to recall many things that happened to you as a child, yet the memories are still buried in your mind, lingering like dust in the corner of a room. You may have more dust than some others. It does not mean your mind in unbalanced."

She twisted the towel in her hands and shook her head. "I'm not so sure about that. I am the child of Gorman and Etain, and part of me never escaped Fotharta House." She held the towel to her mouth to stifle a sob. "I can't get out of it. I'll never get out of it."

Mor leaned down and rested his hands on her shoulders.

"Mairin, take a minute to calm down," he said with a soft, soothing voice. "That's the dream residue talking now."

"I really should quit, Mor," she said went on bitterly, her eyes fixed on the deck between her feet. "Quit and live alone somewhere, or may be sail off into the sunset."

Mor stooped to his haunches and looked up at her. "You are one of the best friends I have in life and the finest officer I have ever served with. The Province needs you and you know it. We all bear crosses, Mairin, we all have weaknesses. Every last human being on the planet. I say there is not a crewman on this ship who would want another captain, and that includes me."

She knew what he was doing. He had done it before. *Talking to me until the dream residue fades. And of course he knows I know what he's doing.* That circular thought brought a bleak smile to her lips. He smiled in response.

She got to her feet and at the wash basin rinsed the bad taste from her mouth. She took a fresh towel and mopped her face dry.

"Get some rest, Mor. Tomorrow will be a very long day."

He put a hand on the door latch. "You'll be all right?"

"Sure. Never happens twice in the same night."

He looked unconvinced, but nodded and went out.

"That was a lie," she whispered to herself after he closed the door. "Sorry, Mor."

She passed the long hours of night thinking about many things, mostly of Conor and a future with him that at this moment seemed very far away indeed.

The anchorage off Cruzon was a secure one and completely sheltered Mairin's twelve-ship battle group. Though the wind whistled and howled through the rigging, the surface of the sea near the ships only rippled. With any luck, Mairin thought as she relaxed in her cabin with a mug of tea, the storm would clear by morning and the reassembled fleet could weigh anchor for Santander.

Boarding the Bretan Fighters had gone smoothly. These men were on average older than the Admiralty Marines they had carried two weeks before, and less inclined to socialize. For the most part, they were a silent group, talking among each other in deep, rumbling tones and asking for very little beyond the bare necessities. Mairin sensed, though, an abiding desire for revenge against raiders who had plagued their coastal towns relentlessly.

With eighty of the Fighters aboard they had to be given the main cabin; off-watch sailors took over the forward hold. She cracked her cabin door open and listened for noise from the main cabin. Only the odd sound of heavy male snores drifted down the short corridor between the officers' cabins.

She glanced out the stern windows at the swaying mast lanterns of the other ships. Tierney's *Rosc Catha* bobbed at anchor a half mile away. The lanterns of Jilleen's *Wexford* and Kennat's *Morrigan* glowed in the darkness about a mile off. She carefully counted the eight lanterns of the transports and assured herself that none dragged an anchor. Her group would be ready to sail at first light.

A quiet tap at the door startled her. "Yes?"

Rowenna Briuin's face appeared around the partly-opened door. Her carrot-red hair was askew and bare feet stuck out beneath wool trousers.

"May I come in, Captain?"

"Of course, Rowenna."

"Sorry to bother you, Captain, but I could see your light was on. I can't sleep. Too much on my mind."

She slumped into a chair and gratefully accepted a steaming mug of tea.

"I can't sleep either, but that's normal for me," said Mairin, taking a chair opposite her first officer. "I can use the company, to be honest."

They sat quietly for a moment. Rowenna, her round, naturally cheerful face radiating melancholy, stared past Mairin out the stern windows.

"Truth is, Captain, I miss my family. Don't get me wrong, I love the service and being at sea. I miss them all the same."

"Tell me about them," Mairin prompted. "Oh, I know the basics from your record. I'd like to hear what they're like. If you'd like to."

"I would, Captain," she replied, smiling now. "I truly would. My father is a carpenter, a fine one too. He builds cabinets, chairs, tables, anything you like. He has a shop in our town, Stradbally, I a tiny place no one has even heard of."

"You'd be surprised," Mairin said. "Conor and I rode through Stradbally this past spring. We stopped and bought flowers at a market."

"You've really been there? I can hardly believe it. Anyway, my mother runs a little pub next to my father's shop. We all worked in the shop and the pub when we were young."

"How many of you are there?"

Rowenna laughed. "Three sisters and three brothers, I'm right in the middle. We have a big old house on the edge of town, not fancy and it's drafty in the winter, but lots of room."

She gulped at her tea, green eyes shining, freckled face flushed with the joy of memories and the love of her family. Mairin found own her hands squeezing the mug. With effort she relaxed her fingers and nodded to Rowenna to go on.

"I miss all of them, Captain," Rowenna said. "Three of us have gone away, two of my brothers serve in the Line of Blades and one sister has just gone to sea. My other two sisters, the youngest, are helping with the shops ... I suppose their time is coming too, to serve somehow. Captain, would it be out of line to ask about your family? I know you come from Bhaile Mhurain and your mother Etain sits on the Council of Twenty. And you have a brother?"

"Yes, I have a brother," Mairin said, trying to sound matter-of-fact. "Two brothers, actually."

Rowenna was waiting for her to go on, and she couldn't. Her throat closed and her mouth felt dry as dust. Envy, pain, sadness, longing welled up inside her. What to say? How could this young woman whose whole life had been spent in a loving family begin to understand the gulf between them? She could not even find words to deflect the conversation.

Rowenna sensed what was happening. Her smile faded to a look of panic.

"Captain, I'm sorry, I should not have asked. It was not my place—"

Mairin silenced her with a wave of her hand. "Rowenna, there was nothing wrong with your asking. My family, well, it's not something I can talk about easily. My younger brother Kellen and I are close. The rest of the story is not pleasant. Not pleasant at all. I ran away when I was fifteen and never went home again."

She gazed up at Rowenna's troubled, concerned face, and knew what the younger woman was thinking.

"You've heard me cry out at night?"

Rowenna shifted uneasily in her chair.

"Yes, sir. The partitions are thin. You dream about when you were young?"

"Yes, in a way. Didn't you ask Sinea about it?"

"She simply told me what to expect, but no more."

"Sinea and I served together for close to a year. First time it happened, it frightened her to death, just like Sithmaith last night. Imagine that, Sinea Danaan, frightened! She thought someone was killing me in my cabin."

"They must be terrible dreams, sir. Do you want me to wake you up?"

"I wake up on my own usually. Or you can call Mor, like Sithmaith did last night."

"There must be something Mor can do for you."

"He can ... but what he gives me makes it hard to wake up and focus in a hurry. Ashore, yes, sometimes I take his potion. Never at sea. I just don't sleep much, and sometimes I don't dream at all. The nightmares seem to come with pressure. You could say I'm under pressure now."

"I know that, Captain." Rowenna gazed out the stern windows a moment, as if struggling to understand what it was like to grow up without love. "Captain, do come to Stradbally again? Stay with us?"

Mairin managed a smile. "I'll do that, you can be sure. First time we have some leave. I'll bring Conor if you have room enough."

"We have plenty of room, sir. Conor would be welcome. I have a special man of my own in town, I hope to marry him someday when this war is over."

Ah, yes, Mairin thought bitterly, *when this war is over. When Conor and I can marry and have our children and maybe settle down in tiny Stradbally by the sea. When will that be?*

A sharp bump against the ship's hull made them both jump. Rowenna's tea mug clattered to the floor.

"What was that?" said Mairin. She spun in her chair to look out the stern.

Rowenna was already on her feet. "I'll find out, sir."

She opened the door and found Sithmaith outside it, with someone behind her.

"Captain," Sithmaith said, "Jilleen Conmaicne to see you."

She stepped aside and the young captain, her face bleach-white and her breath coming in gasps, strode into the cabin.

Mairin jumped out of her seat, her stomach suddenly knotted.

"I have to report, sir," Jilleen said as steadily as she could manage, "that Captain Gailenga may have lost control of her ship."

"You mean a mutiny?"

"I don't think so, sir. I'm not sure, but I think the Bretan Fighters may have seized the ship."

"Explain."

Jilleen leaned her hands on the table and took a deep breath. "I sent over a boat to ask for supplies we are short of. The boat crew came back, said that when they called for a ladder, the voice that answered cursed them. Male voice, in Bretan Gaelic, sir."

"Get dressed," Mairin said unnecessarily to Rowenna, who was halfway to her cabin. To Jilleen she said, "You didn't signal any of this?"

"That's why I came by boat, sir. Rowed myself here. No signals. *Morrigan*'s lanterns are out."

"Very smart, Jilleen. Get to *Rosc Catha* and privately inform Tierney. Then go back to *Wexford* and keep a sharp watch. I don't want a single word of this leaking out, it could wreck the whole operation."

"Sir," she said, saluting as she turned.

Moments later, Rowenna reappeared in uniform while Mairin was pulling on her boots.

"Inform Lieutenant Laigain of the situation—quietly. Then get my gig in the water. Wake up Brigid if you have to, two sailors. That's all."

"You're going alone, sir?"

"I'll take Sithmaith. I need you here to command the ship. I don't know what's happened, but whatever it is, it has to be handled fast and without violence. By the time word gets out I hope we're underway to Santander."

Rowenna turned to leave, then halted and turned back, her hands clamped hard on the cabin door.

"Please be careful, sir. This sounds very dangerous."

Mairin managed a wan smile. "No doubt. If I don't come back at all, you have command of *Caillech*, but overall command goes to Tierney Ulaid."

"Understood, sir," Rowenna said, her voice tight. "Good luck, Captain."

Mairin pondered what to take. No weapons, that was certain. A boat cloak . ... windy night to be out on the open water. She grabbed it and nearly ran into Brigid Auteini racing through the doorway.

"Gig's in the water, sir. Watch crew is curious."

"Let them be," Mairin snapped. "Let's go."

They slipped up the stairs through the hatch and onto the quarter-deck, where Sithmaith waited next to Rowenna by the wheel.

"You're with me," Mairin said to Sithmaith. To Rowenna, she said, "Command is yours, Lieutenant. Watch for signals."

"Aye, aye, sir," Rowenna acknowledged.

Mairin was glad she took the cloak: spray flew from the oars as Brigid drove the two brawny sailors to a fast stroke. Sithmaith rummaged in the gig's lazarette and found a rain jacket that she donned. In the light of the gig's stern lantern, Mairin caught a glimpse of her lieutenant's face. *Pretty calm considering the situation. She may have had a loose tongue but she has steely nerves. I'll need that quality in her tonight.*

Sithmaith leaned over to her. "May we speak, sir?" she said softly.

Mairin nodded. "Yes, it's all right. Lots of noise out here with this wind."

"What's your plan, Captain?"

"A fair question, Lieutenant, but I'm afraid I have no plan, only an objective. I've never been in this situation before, have you?"

Sithmaith smiled and shook her head. "No, sir, I have not."

"If the ship has been taken by the Bretan Fighters," Mairin went on, "it was not because they got drunk. So far as I can tell, they're a disciplined force. I suspect the problem has to do with Kennat Gailenga's harsh methods. You know her reputation?"

"I do, sir. I'm glad I haven't served under her. Probably she'd have strung me up from the main yard."

"More than likely, if you crossed her. I could be wrong, I guess it's possible the Bretans got out of hand on their own. However it happened, we have to find a way to fix it without letting any blood. We need the *Morrigan* and the soldiers on it. If we're allowed aboard I want you with me. Brigid will stay in the boat. Whatever happens, remember, we are trying to defuse the situation, not make it worse. You follow my lead. Is that clear, Lieutenant?"

"Very clear, sir."

Seconds later the dark hulk of the *Morrigan* loomed up, faintly outlined by the glow of *Wexford*'s bright lanterns a half mile over the water. Brigid guided them around to the ship's leeward side and brought the gig to rest against the hull beneath the quarterdeck's starboard rail. No voices called from above. Brigid and the two sailors lashed the gig to *Morrigan*'s hull cleats.

"Call," Mairin ordered Brigid.

"Ahoy, *Morrigan*," Brigid's strong bosun's voice rang out. "*Caillech*'s gig, two officers wish to come aboard."

No direct answer, only a confused welter of male and female voices.

"Should I call again, sir?"

"No. Wait."

A minute passed and more excited voices argued. At last the blood-streaked face of a Squadron officer appeared over the rail.

"Ladder coming down, sir," the officer said in a ragged voice. "Bring no weapons."

The rope ladder thudded into the gig.

"All right, Brigid, stay here and wait," Mairin ordered, her hands on the ladder. "Give us fifteen minutes. If you don't hear from me by then, cast off and report to Lieutenant Briuin."

"Aye, sir," Brigid said reluctantly. "Fifteen minutes."

Mairin climbed the ladder with Sithmaith behind her. They found the quarterdeck lit only by the dim glow of the binnacle light. The deck was crowded with dark shapes, some standing, some lying on the deck. One of the largest of the shapes approached.

"Who are you?" asked an impossibly deep voice.

"Mairin Fotharta, Captain of the flagship *Caillech*," she answered in as friendly a tone as she could muster. "With me is Lieutenant Sithmaith Laigain. We are unarmed. I would appreciate some light."

Silence. After a pause the towering man said to someone behind him, "do it."

What turned out to be an injured sailor lit the big lantern bolted to the mizzen. The sight that met Mairin's eyes could hardly have been worse. Three sailors lay motionless on the deck. Two ship's officers stood near the lantern, one holding her left arm in her right, the other bleeding from the forehead. Bretan Fighters with long slashing swords drawn packed the deck from the poop rail to the mainmast. The deck watch had crowded into the tops; the off-watch must have been caught below and was now being held there. The ship was eerily quiet. The faint slapping of wavelets against the hull seemed to ring in Mairin's ears.

The man who had spoken to her appeared big enough to topple the mainmast on his own. His left hand gripped his sword; his right was coated with dried blood. He stared down at her, his face indistinct because the lantern was at his back.

"Get us off this ship," he ordered, his voice laced with anger. "Or there will be many more lying on your deck."

"May I ask your name?" Mairin asked mildly.

"Reunan. I command here."

"You do not."

The sword rose gradually until it was about parallel with Mairin's throat.

"You may kill me, Reunan, but you do not command here. I do, by authority of the Bretan High Council and your own Chief of Fighters. Lower the sword. Now."

The big man's breath came heavily. A full minute of silence passed. A river of cold sweat poured into the small of Mairin's back.

"As you say," the big man rumbled, and lowered his sword tip descended to the deck.

"Where is Captain Gailenga?"

"In her cabin," he answered, less threateningly.

"Alive?"

"Yes. That could change."

"There will be no killing, Reunan. Will you allow me to receive a report from one of these officers?"

He took a step back and waved the sword toward the officers. The one holding her arm limped forward. Mairin recognized her at once: Ailis Eogain, who had served under as an ensign.

"Sorry, Captain, I can't salute," she said, in obvious pain. "There was an ... incident. Fighters were playing dice in the main cabin. Captain Gailenga ordered them to stop and used some rough language. A fight started, she drew her knife and after that, everything was chaos, sir, we couldn't stop it. I'm very sorry, Captain."

Eogain sagged forward and was caught by a quick-reacting Sithmaith.

"Is the surgeon here?" Mairin asked. *Step by step, now, the tension is easing.*

A young man stepped cautiously forward. "I am the surgeon, Captain," he said with a nervous glance at Reunan.

"Reunan, I ask that the surgeon be allowed to help the injured, ours and yours if there are any." Reunan did not answer immediately. "Surely that's a reasonable request."

The massive warrior took another step backward and waved his blood-coated hand at the surgeon. "Go ahead."

Mairin allowed herself a deep breath of relief. *There is always a tipping point, and we're past it now. There will be no more violence tonight on the Morrigan.*

"Will you allow me to see Captain Gailenga?"

"Say what you like to that bitch, so long as you get us into boats and off this ship."

He waved the sword again and a path cleared to the quarterdeck hatch. Sithmaith gently lowered the unconscious Ailis to the deck and followed Mairin down the ladder. As Mairin expected, at least twenty

Bretan Fighters held the main cabin. The remainder of *Morrigan*'s crew huddled together at the cabin's forward end, armed but having the good sense not to make a bad situation worse. No one appeared to be injured here.

Two fighters barred the entrance to the captain's cabin; Reunan ordered them to stand aside. Mairin opened the cabin door and found a battered, seething Kennat Gailenga staring at her wildly.

"Good, you re-took the ship," she shouted, leaping to her feet. "My crew was worthless."

"Sit down," Mairin barked, "and shut up."

Kennat was at first stunned, then enraged. She took a step back, glaring at Mairin with pure hatred. Mairin stepped into the cabin, followed by Sithmaith, Reunan, and three of his fighters. Kennat stood defiantly in front of the stern window bench, thick-muscled arms crossed over her chest.

"Listen to me carefully, Captain," said Mairin evenly. "In the presence of another officer, I relieve you of command of this ship and place you under arrest. You will be taken—"

Screaming an obscenity, Kennat sprang forward. Caught completely by surprise, Mairin reacted fast enough to get an arm in front of her face and deflect Kennat's vicious blow. The sheer force of it launched her into the air and backward into a heavy oak cabinet. Her skull struck the edge, her vision faded to gray, and the shouts around her seemed muffled under heavy blankets. When her vision cleared, she found herself sitting in a chair, held upright by Sithmaith. The young surgeon was anxiously fingering the back of her skull. Kennat lay sprawled on the deck in front of the stern windows. Pain flared in waves from the back of her head and threatened to make her vomit. The surgeon pressed a cool, wet towel against her head and the nausea receded.

Foolish, she reproved herself, *not to see that coming*.

"Did you kill her?" she asked Reunan.

"No," he answered, "much as I would like to. I leave that to you."

"Captain," the surgeon said, "you need a few stitches and you may have a concussion. Please let me take you to the surgery."

Not yet. She concentrated through the pain. *Not yet*.

"Reunan, will you and your fighters stay on the ship if I promise you good officers?"

Reunan cursed under his breath at Kennat, then turned to face Mairin. He seemed to regain his some of his composure.

"Yes. We came to fight the damn Santanders. We counted on you to get us there."

"All right. Lieutenant," she said to Sithmaith, "tell Brigid not to shove off. Reunan, allow the crew of this ship to light the lanterns on deck and give signals for me. Please ask your men to put away their swords and return to the main cabin. I'll have a new captain aboard within an hour. Her name is Tierney Ulaid, my friend for years and a fine officer."

"Your word?"

"My word."

He nodded and slid the deadly sword into a steel scabbard. "It will be done."

"One other thing," she said, losing the battle with grey haze over her vision. "Tie Captain Gailenga and load her into my gig. Signal Captain Ulaid, use my private code. She'll know what to do."

The gray darkened to black, and Sithmaith's reply, whatever it was, faded to an inaudible whisper.

One of the great frustrations of my work as an historian at this time in history is the gap of some ten centuries since we in Eirelan had contact with the great world far beyond the British Isles (as they were once termed). True, we have a connection to the Bretans who live on the continent of Europe—yet even they lead an insular and defensive existence on their fertile peninsula. We trade on Africa's coast and yet know little of the cultures we trade with. We know that the world is an immense place, once populated by billions of souls and dotted with cities that counted residents in millions. It is certain, of course, that machine civilization cannot have arisen again on any grand scale, for we would have been visited long since by such peoples. Now we live in an ever-colder era, and ancient history suggests that when climate changes drastically, great upheavals occur in cultures and civilizations. People begin to move, and in times of scarcity, look to take what they need to survive, by any means available. That is to say: they make war on their fellow man.

Seanlaoch Osraige, "What Lies Beyond the Sea?"

Chapter 28

The light of day gave way to a blazing orange sunset. On this evening, two days after Feth's departure, Sean sat on one of the bollards used to moor Squadron warships and heavy cargo vessels. His eyes followed the lamplighter going about his business in the town square while his mind drifted over the hours and days he had spent with Feth. Where was she tonight? Under the same stars as now began to twinkle overhead, with a great difference: she was far from the protection of the Province.

The lighter ignited the wick of the last lantern—the big, multi-lensed one mounted atop the square's central clock—then called out "six o'clock and all is well." Sean wondered briefly at that ritual: how old was it? Rituals fascinated him because they were relics of the past, survivors of bygone centuries when the ritual might have had more meaning than it did now. Everyone knew all was well, after all, and the clock reliably told the time! Still, there was something oddly reassuring about the lamplighter's call as it echoed among the shops and houses and inns.

He turned and gazed out to sea, hoping a ship might be approaching from far out. The lanterns atop the masts would slowly rise above the waters in the age-old proof of the earth's roundness. To see better he wiped clean his smudged spectacles and squinted for a full minute. No masts and no ships, only the blue and red buoys marking the ship channel at the harbor's entrance.

He made his way back to his room, pausing at Seamus the Bookseller's shop to chat about the latest arrivals on his shelves. Seamus, who lived above his shop and often stayed open late, knew of Sean's insatiable appetite for old texts and watched out for volumes not appearing on Sean's ten-page alphabetical list. On this occasion he had nothing new to offer, and he was worried about what would happen to his books if a raid broke through the Rampart. Sean did his best to reassure the seventy-year-old scholar, but when he left the old man's eyes were shadowed by doubt and worry.

Back in his room, he forced his mind onto the contents of the packet Oran had sent him. He had come up with a rough idea of what the loose papers said, because numbers remained numbers and occasional words resembled old versions of Gaelic, English, and German words. One sheet was a set of directions through midland counties; another was a list of military units and weapons; yet a third seemed to be a shipping manifest for a vessel unloading at Belfast. The book, on the other hand, was a puzzle he had made little progress with. Bound in high-quality leather, it appeared to be of recent vintage and printed with an excellent press. Its numbered pages were packed with text using a syntax and vocabulary far removed from any language he had studied. Most likely, he surmised, the language was an amalgam of several disparate tongues dating from the Age of Machines, languages for which he possessed no references at all. He was confident that over the long months of winter, and with the help of scholar-friends in Kernow, Wales, and Bretan, he would grind out a passable translation.

When the light from the window failed he lit a single oil lamp, put the translation task aside, and took up work on a chapter in his history of the Province. An hour passed. When his lamp sputtered in need of oil, he filled it, lit the stove to make tea, and leaned back in his creaky chair. He took off his spectacles and closed his eyes to rest them until the water boiled.

The tap on his door startled him from his wandering thoughts. Had he once again forgotten to pay the rent on time? Fortunately this turned out to be a welcome visitor: Vaughn Maeluidir, who had found lodgings for himself and Murel less than a mile from the town square.

"Vaughn! Come in! Was I expecting you? I'm somewhat absent-minded, as Feth will attest."

Vaughn smiled as he walked in. "I come unannounced. It's not a bad time?"

Sean cleared papers off a chair. "Not at all. Sit. I have fresh tea brewing."

"Fresh tea is welcome. And knowing your larder is usually empty ... "

Vaughn emptied out the contents of a canvas bag.

"Fresh fruit, two kinds of cheese, bread, and olives. Before she left, Feth ordered me to make sure you ate decently and I'm following orders!"

Sean poured hot water into a teapot which he set on the table amidst the welcome feast. "Feth ordered you, did she?"

"She did. Out of your hearing, of course."

Sean sat down opposite Vaughn and suddenly realized he was starved.

"Haven't eaten since breakfast," he admitted through a mouthful of apple. "Thank you for thinking of me."

Vaughn selected an apple for himself and waved it in the air.

"This is small payment for what Murel and I owe you."

"She's doing well?"

"Her leg is healing cleanly and so far as we can tell, our child is healthy and strong inside her. Two more weeks and the doctors say the cast will be off and she can walk again."

"Wonderful. Any luck finding work?"

Vaughn nodded. "Yes. You know a shop called Dunsmore's?"

"Furniture?"

"The very one. Not a block from our lodgings. Mr. Dunsmore is near eighty and could not find a skilled apprentice. I saw the sign in his window and walked in. He let me work for a few hours and then hired me!"

"He knows who you are and where you're from?"

"I told him before I even touched a tool. He said he had friends among the Maeluidir clan in the days before the Rampart. Can you believe it? Sean, I thought I was dreaming. So we can support ourselves and our child."

"Feth will be thrilled to hear it," Sean said. He gazed out the window into the darkness. "I do wish I knew where she was tonight."

"We're worried too." Vaughn reached out and covered Sean's hand with his own. "She'll be back, I'm certain of it."

"Strangely enough, I'm certain of it too. Not sure why, exactly, except that it seems to me she has a destiny to fulfill. I just miss her, more than I imagined I'd miss anyone."

"I felt that way when I worked in Wicklow and didn't see Murel and our child for weeks at a time. It was cruel punishment, yet our reunions were occasions for joy."

Sean saw Vaughn's expression change at his mention of their lost child. "Excellent cheese," he said to change the subject. "And the olives must be from Bretan?"

Vaughn brightened again. "So the shopkeeper said. At the price, I hope so!"

Sean broke out a dusty bottle of wine and poured two glasses. "My father sends me these bottles," he said. "They're supposed to be fine vintages. The problem is they all taste about the same to me."

Vaughn sipped his. "It tastes fine to me, that's all I can say."

"Your clan names," Sean said after sampling the wine himself, "are ancient if my memory serves. Long known in the midlands."

"My clan's home was Nenagh," said Vaughn with a wistful look, "and Clan Felmeda's ancestral place was Roscrea. Now those places are wastelands."

Sean looked over the top of his glass. "Your clans were both invited to move behind the Rampart with us. Our records show we were on friendly terms, yet I find no record of why they refused and remained in the midlands."

"I'm no historian, so I can only tell you what we were taught as children. The basic answer is, we loved our homeland! There is so much beauty there, Sean. We believed that the Dark Times, as we called them, would eventually pass. And I guess we hoped that the Province, hiding behind its new wall, would draw the full attention of the violent clans and they would leave us alone. We were wrong. The Rampart held and in time we lost everything."

"And once the Rampart gates were locked, no one else was let in."

"I think a trickle made it inside in the first few years. After that, the Province could no longer sort out who was attacking, and closed the gates to everyone. Probably I would have done the same thing. Now, the great clan houses have been burned and looted. Our clans will never have a home again."

Sean drummed his fingers on the table. "We came to assume that everyone outside of our wall was an enemy unless we were sure of the contrary. We could have let people in, from the midlands, the west too. Our population has fallen year by year, I don't know by how much exactly. If you wander the countryside you see that a lot of farms aren't being worked any more. And we can barely field big enough armies to defend ourselves, against a threat that's growing instead of shrinking."

"Feth has the right idea, then?"

"Of course she does! The trouble is that she's up against two or three generations of mutual suspicion and resentment. And some grievances go back further than that. In time, we could build new alliances—it seems like the western clans want that now. What Feth decided was that we may not have five or ten years to smooth over all our differences. We could fall to the northern armies next month."

Vaughn finished his wine and considered a moment.

"Sean, would it be too personal to ask if you hope to marry Feth?"

Sean laughed. "Too personal? Not at all. The answer is yes, I certainly do hope to marry her, if she'll have me. It does feel odd, though, knowing her all her life as something like a younger cousin and then suddenly ... well, you know what I mean."

"I do," said Vaughn. "I've known Murel since we were children too. Though we're about the same age."

Sean got up and blew dust off a second bottle. "Feth and I are very different people," he said with a worried frown. "Feth's outgoing, I'm quiet. She's a doer and I'm a thinker. She's—"

"What nonsense!" Vaughn cried. "Do you love her?"

"Yes. Of course I do."

"Do you find her beautiful? Does she excite you?"

Sean blushed slightly and nodded. "To no end."

"And she feels the same way?"

"She says she does."

"Then," Vaughn said, raising his re-filled glass in the air, "to your marriage!"

They clinked glasses together.

"You and Murel will always be welcome in our home. When we have a home, that is."

"And you in ours."

They finished the second bottle of wine, cleared off what remained of Vaughn's portable feast, poured mugs of tea, and sat cross-legged on the bunks facing each other.

I need better chairs, Sean scolded himself in a slightly hazy frame of mind. *And a sofa. For that matter, I need a bigger room!*

Vaughn waved a hand towards the shelves groaning with books. "I've only seen more books than this once in my life."

Sean lowered his mug and stared across at Vaughn. The haze in his mind cleared instantly.

"Where? A library? A bookshop?"

"When I was a youngster," Vaughn replied. His gaze drifted toward the patched, shadowy ceiling and he thought a moment before going on. "I was no more than ten at the time. We had books then, it was before we lost our home. My father loved to read. I got the idea in my head to find books for him as gifts for his birthday. I took to wandering into abandoned houses, ruins of old estates and castles, any place I thought I might find books. Most times I found nothing, and if I did they were usually waterlogged and useless. One time," he paused for effect while Sean held his breath, "I found a treasure trove, and by accident too. Want to hear about it?"

"Curse you, you know I do!" Sean cried. "Go on!"

Vaughn delayed by taking time to set his tea aside and recline on the bed with a tired sigh.

"On the western edge of the Slieve Bloom Mountains, there's an abandoned ruin called Leap Castle. Do you know of it?"

Sean forced himself to think through his excitement.

"Leap Castle ... twenty-five centuries old. Restored by Clan Cuallan a thousand years ago after the Age of Machines and used as their clan home. Supposed to be haunted."

Vaughn gave Sean a look of raised eyebrows. "Do you remember everything you read?"

Sean shrugged. "Mostly. Go on!"

Vaughn settled back on the bed. "Well, your memory is right on the mark, at least as far as our own clan stories tell the tale—including the haunted part. Doesn't every boy of ten want to poke around in placed supposed to be haunted? My friend Cedric and I set out from Nenagh to find the old castle. It's not that far, at most twenty-five miles, though my father would have killed me if he knew where I was headed that spring morning. Cedric and I covered the distance in one day and had no trouble finding the place. We actually slept inside its walls that night, hoping for ghosts!"

"And did you meet any?"

"We heard lots of strange sounds and imagined that we saw evil spirits floating in the night. No doubt nearly all in the imagination of ten-year-olds. In truth, Clan Cuallan had completely abandoned it, there was no one there. We explored the ruins for two whole days. And we found a secret room, high in a tower, where Clan Cuallan stored its library. They must have carted off books and manuscripts from libraries in Dublin and Belfast and who knows where else. There were thousands of books, so many we couldn't count them. And it was pitch dark, because there were no windows, so all we could see was what our candles showed us. I took a few books for my Dad, the best I could find."

Sean threw his legs on the floor and leaned forward. "You're not making this up? Just to torture me?"

"I am not. We saw what I said we did."

"And you think this great collection may yet be there?"

"Who knows?" said Vaughn, sitting up to face Sean. "I never went back after that one time. The tower wasn't damp and since it had no windows, water hadn't gotten in. The roof was intact, at least then. That was almost twenty years ago."

Sean walked over to the window and threw open the casements. A soft, cool evening breeze fluttered his drab curtains.

"I'd like to go there, see if the books survived. I know this looks like big collection," he waved a hand at his shelves, "but there are great gaps of knowledge that I can't fill."

Vaughn got to his feet and joined Sean at the window.

"My friend, it would be a hundred miles on foot from here."

"It could be done."

"*Could*, yes. But perilous. Raiding bands move through the area all the time. And even if you got there, you can't stay. There's no food."

Sean lowered his head. "Yes, of course. A passing thought."

"I shouldn't have mentioned it," Vaughn said with regret. "I didn't mean to make you feel sad about it."

"No, I'm glad you told me. Who knows, some day the midlands may be safe again."

"Of course," Vaughn quickly agreed. "There's always hope."

"If I live long enough."

The town crier made his last call, "nine o'clock and all is well." Vaughn pulled his coat from a wall peg.

"Best I be going," he said. "You'll come to see us soon? I moved us from the boarding house to a cozy room above Dunsmore's shop. It will do until I earn enough to get something bigger."

"I will, and soon. Meantime, my best to Murel."

"Feth is in our thoughts."

They shook hands and Vaughn took his leave. Sean sat down at his table, seized a pen and tapped it idly on the table as a vision, sharp and clear, formed in his mind.

A vast tower keep, forty feet across, twenty feet high, books all around and floor to roof. I enter carrying a lantern, the light drives back the darkness and I see the books, intact, dry, readable. Thousands I have never seen. All those books waiting for me.

Aloud he said with a smile, "and guarded by ghosts till I get there!"

On a warm, sunny day, he strolled along a tree-lined country lane with Feth at his side. They held hands and laughed and had not a care in the world. It did not seem strange to him that every tree they passed had books for leaves. He felt no urge to stop and pick any at the moment, after all, more were growing and he had plenty of time to gather them in. Once, Feth shot an arrow into a book for target practice, and he scolded her for it. When he pulled the arrow out of the ruptured volume, blood began to drip on the ground and Feth started to cry at what she had done.

Then night fell with terrifying suddenness and he lost sight of Feth. He called out and heard no answer, not even the sound of her crying. He ran and called and ran and called again. Once he slipped in the darkness and when his hands hit the ground, it was wet and sticky as if he were running in a bloody field. At last, out of breath, he stopped running and looked up: the moon was bright overhead now, red and angry-looking. Then he heard Feth's voice call out his name, and he saw her atop a far hill, alone. While he watched, hands seized her and she disappeared into the earth itself. He screamed for her, but no sound came out of his mouth. An insistent bell rang in the distance, tolling her death.

He awoke at the seventh strike of the town's bell as it called out the hour of seven. His stomach muscles ached with tension, his mouth was ash-dry, and tears streaked down his temples. Despite the chill in the room, his forehead was beaded with sweat.

"It's a good thing I don't believe in dreams," he muttered, sitting up. He stared at his trembling hands. "Must've been the wine."

He swung his legs to the floor and pushed damp hair out of his eyes. Deep breaths of cool morning air cleared his head, and presently he downed a glass of water and looked out the window. Two big ships had docked during the night, and now they disgorged Welsh battle horses by the score. In pairs they trotted down gangways, snorting and neighing at the world in general. Sailors exchanged shouts and curses with dockhands and merchant sailors. The morning Squadron packet was gliding to a slip in front of Squadron headquarters. A scattering of citizens sauntered about the square, and the bakery a few doors down the street sent forth the cloying scent of fresh sweet-rolls.

The barely-warmed water of the bath down the hall sufficed to cleanse the night-sweat from his body. Dressed and shaved, he felt the power of the dream fade, leaving him with a wine-induced headache. Not having to report to the hospital, he opted to splurge at the first-floor inn for a big pot of hot tea and a basket of rolls hot from the bakery. He carried with him the book that described Leap Castle. He was so absorbed in his reading that he did not notice the chair across from him scrape away from the table and be taken up by a visitor, who cleared his throat noisily.

"May I join you?" a thickly-accented voice said.

"Yes, of course," said Sean. He read two more sentences before looking up to see who owned the weird accent. "Oran!"

His brother leaned back in the chair, tired and unshaven, wearing the impish smile that drove away all dark feelings. The brothers stood and embraced hard and long, drawing stares from other guests. Finally they resumed their seats and both brushed aside tears of joy.

"It's been so long," said Sean. He poured Oran a steaming mug of tea and signaled to the Naomham the innkeeper to refill the bread basket. "Six months?"

"Yes," said Oran after a gulp of tea. "Far too long, brother."

"How long can you stay?"

"Only till tomorrow," Oran said with regret. "I have to go back out and scout the Ghaoth Aduaidh army. I'll be outside the gate before noon."

"You're thinner than ever," Sean observed. He pushed the pastry basket directly in front of his brother. "Finish them all."

"You should have seen me when I rode in from the north! I won't be out that long this time. Then we fight and after that I can add pounds at leisure or I'll lose them very fast indeed."

"That's not funny, Oran."

"True, though." He frowned at Sean's unhappy look. "All right, not funny. It helps me not to get too serious about death. Anyway ... you've heard Conor will command the army?"

"It's been reported, yes. That will weigh very heavily on him."

Oran nodded and lost his smile entirely. "It already has."

"I haven't seen Conor since last winter. How is he?"

"Inside, I'd say he's frustrated, sad much of the time, worried to death. Outside, not many people would see it."

"I would."

Oran nodded. "True. You and Conor have much in common, you both live mostly on the inside of your head. This winter, make an effort to see him. I think he'd like that."

"So would I."

Oran refilled their mugs with fresh tea. "Now, how is Feth? When can I see her?"

"Well west of here, Youghal or further by now."

"What?" Oran sat bolt upright. "Outside the Rampart?"

"Yes. Not alone, of course, she has four comrades with her, two Bows and two Blades."

"Whatever for?"

"She got it into her head that we're desperately short of troops, so she wangled permission from Rionach Laigain to go out recruiting."

Oran twisted his rough hands nervously. "I wish someone had asked me about that idea."

"There wasn't time and you were at Poulaphouca anyway."

"A dangerous plan, I don't need to tell you that. There are many folk outside the Province who would not mind seeing us go under at all. If they're careful what they say I guess they'll come back in one piece. Without any troops, though."

"Feth may surprise you."

"I hope she does. By all that's sacred we need more fighters."

"I'm worried sick about her."

Oran stared into his brother's eyes. "You love her, don't you?"

"Yes. Very much."

Oran was about to answer when Naomham parked himself over the table, awaiting payment. Before Sean could reach for money, Oran opened his belt pouch and extracted a single gleaming gold coin that he laid carefully in the astonished innkeeper's outstretched palm.

"That should cover this meal, plus dinner," he said.

The man stared at the coin briefly, grunted his assent, and moved off. Oran patted the pouch which jangled with coins.

"Is that filled with gold?"

"It is," replied Oran with a grin. "The sailors on the packet invited me to join their usual overnight card game. I hated to do it, but ... "

"Oh, I bet you did!"

"I'm honest. Merely clever."

"No comment." Sean got to his feet. "Let's go out and walk, Oran. There's more I want to say about Feth and other things, but not here."

Bathed in the warmth of an autumn sun, the town square had come alive. Shop doors banged open, a caravan of Welsh horses paraded north towards the fort, sailors flooded from the ships in search of decent food and entertainment, sellers in open air booths began to hawk their wares. Sean led his brother along the quay and over the causeway to the south part of the harbor, past Squadron headquarters, and thence among the stone ruins of the village of An Rinn. From here they had a view of the harbor and the sea, and could drink in the gentle, salt-scented zephyr. Later in the day, if the balmy weather held, the ruins would be dotted with blankets and picnic baskets, but for now they were alone.

Oran sat on a crumbling stone wall. Sean sank down onto soft grass in front of him and wrapped his arms over drawn-up knees.

"You and Feth?" Oran asked.

"Yes. From the moment I first saw her a few weeks ago, something in me changed. It was like I'd never met this woman before. Isn't that strange?"

"Not so strange," Oran replied. He lifted a pebble from the wall and tossed it into the surf. "I guess it would be to you ... you haven't seen Feth for nigh on two years, true? I didn't run into her often either, maybe once every six months or so in Rosslare or at a training camp where I was teaching. That was enough to see her shed the guise of the cute little girl with pigtails and emerge a striking young woman with rock-hard hands and as fast a bow as I've ever seen. Feth radiates something, I can't exactly describe it, but you know it's there."

Sean let his eyes drift over the open ocean. "You understand very well, dear brother. She has an inner voice, I think, that pushes her in certain directions. A mystic might say it's Domnall's spirit."

"I don't think you're a mystic."

Sean laughed lightly. "Far from it. The problem is that this inner voice is leading her to take frightening risks."

"And you're afraid you might lose her?"

"Yes. Terrified. I never nightmared until now, at least that I can remember. I awoke this morning feeling like I was lost in some horrible fairy tale. Blood everywhere."

They fell silent for a time. Over the water came the busy hum of the town and the port, mixed with the high-pitched cries of hunting terns and the soft lap of waves against the sandy shore.

"On these long journeys alone I have time to ponder our lives and the world around us," Oran said presently. "I'm no deep thinker like you, or Conor, that's sure." He held up a hand at Sean's protest. "No, it's the truth. I'm a competent scout and a sharp card-player and I can tell an off-color joke in a pub, but I lack your sense of history and I can barely skim the surface of Uinseann's subtle philosophy. I know only what I see and what I feel in my heart. One thing I know for certain ... nothing we look at today is fixed in time."

Oran waved an arm at the harbor, where a cargo ship made its way alongside a pier.

"We sit here and look out at ships built by our own craftsmen in the last ten years. We behold a town that has rested on this shore for forty centuries." He ran a hand over the rough top of the crumbled wall. "I'm sitting on a wall that someone built with his own hands before there was any town here at all. And surely men lived here thousands of years before the man that built this wall! What do you call it, the Stone Age? A thousand years from now, all of this may be gone. We live among the ruins of the Age of Machines, when men built great towers and buildings higher than the mountains, yet all of that has crumbled too unless we preserved it. Time passes over everything, and still the stars shine at night and the sun rises by day."

"Somber thoughts."

"Oh, not at all! Because the beauty of the world remains with us! How many times have I camped alone on top of a hill, and when I wake up I see a sunrise so exquisite my eyes fill with tears? The only thought that depresses me, brother, is that men and women still kill each other after so many thousands of years of killing. That human blood runs into the earth for no good reason at all. That's the mystery I can't fathom and wish I could. All of your histories and Uinseann's philosophies and Conor's poems can't explain it to me. It's the one solitary thought that makes me bitter and angry. It would consume me if I didn't have the glory of the world to see every day and people around me to love and cherish."

"And this is not philosophy? If it isn't, I don't know what is."

"Poor man's philosophy," said Oran with a laugh. "Not worth writing down."

How wrong you are, brother! Aloud, he said, "Feth wonders about the same question. On the field of battle she can kill without a thought, yet she can't sleep trying to understand why she had to do it."

"Best we never come up with a satisfactory answer to that question," Oran said. "I think we're better off wondering than knowing, on the whole. Anyway, I'm glad for you, brother. You've always spent too much time alone with your books and your inkwell. As for worrying about her, think of it this way. It's painful ... yet it's a pain that means you have a powerful connection to another human being. Worrying is a small price to pay for having a woman like Feth to love."

"That's an unusually romantic viewpoint for you. Any special reason for it?"

Oran laughed. "Guilty as charged. I have met someone new. We haven't had much time together yet."

"Enough time to worry about each other?"

"I would say yes."

"Then I can say I'm happy for you too." Sean got up from the grass and joined Oran on the wall. "I want to show you something."

"Sure. What is that book, anyway?"

"A history of Eirelan's castles. The book must have been written in the Age of Machines. This copy dates back about a century, when they still had publishers in Dublin." He opened the book to the drawing of Leap Castle. "Have you ever seen this place?"

Oran shaded the page with his hand. "Leap Castle? The old haunted ruin in the midlands? I've camped on the grounds two or three times."

"You're not serious!"

Oran gave him a puzzled look. "What's so special about it?"

Sean's hands trembled with excitement. "When were you last there? Was this tower intact?"

Oran looked off over the harbor, searching his memory.

"Hmm ... maybe two years ago. So far as I can remember, the tower was sound. I prowled around some but I never tried the wooden stairs, they looked rotten. Why?"

Sean put his finger on the tower. "In a room at the top of this tower there may be thousands of books, taken from libraries all over Eirelan. Books that may date back ten centuries or more— if they've have held together this long. Copies like this one too. Manuscripts. Records. Who knows what else? The dream of an historian's lifetime."

"How do you know this?"

"The man Feth and I rescued outside the Rampart, Vaughn Maeluidir, came by my room last night. When he was ten years old, that's twenty years ago now, he and a friend climbed into that tower and found the abandoned library of Clan Cuallan. They were too young to fully appreciate what they found, but Vaughn remembers it clearly. The room was dry and nothing had been touched. Anyway, I think those books are still there."

"And you want to find out?"

"More than that, I want to bring them back to the Province. They may be our only chance to recover so much knowledge. Will you help me?"

Oran stood and strolled to the shoreline, with Sean following.

He's trying to think of a way to say no, Sean thought. *To tell me it can never happen.*

"Sean, it would be risky, that much is obvious. I move through those regions mostly at night. During the day I stay hidden or at least inconspicuous. It's possible I could get you there, the question is whether we could get back alive, let alone with a train of wagons full of books."

"Vaughn as much said the same thing."

"He was right."

"So it's all right for you to risk your life for military reasons, but not for me to rescue a part of human history, part of our own history, of who we are?"

Oran laid as hand on his brother's shoulder. "Sean, I don't place a high value on my own life. I've come close to losing it a hundred times. I'd take the risk for you. But think about how Mom and Dad would feel if we died out there? What about Feth? And what if you were killed and I had to come back alone? How could I live with that? Trading your life for books and papers?"

Sean walked back to the crumbled wall with Oran following. He gently set the book down on the stones and pulled his sweater up to his neck.

"Look at this. Not a mark. And no ribs showing."

Oran stared at him. "So?"

"Now look at this."

Before Oran could stop him, Sean pulled up his brother's sweater, revealing a torso of prominent ribs, the flesh laced with old scars and colored by recent bruises.

Oran forced his brother's hands away. "That means nothing, Sean. We do different things, that's all."

"No, it does mean something! It means you've put your life on the line a hundred times, as you said, for your own reasons. My life is my own to sacrifice, just like yours. If you don't help me I'll do it alone."

"Sean, calm down." Oran sat on the wall again and waited for his brother to join him. "You'd be lost before you went ten miles." He sighed before going on. "By heavens, you are still a stubborn kid!"

"You're only four years older, dear brother. And I'd be careful about making me out the stubborn son. Mom and Dad might not support your opinion."

"Fair enough," said Oran with a wry grin. He stared into his brother's eyes. "All right, I'll give it some thought. Maybe in the winter, we can do it. Depends on the weather and on what happens in the next month. Promise me you won't trek off on your own, alone or with Feth in tow. She's daring enough to go with you."

"I promise," Sean said. "And I'm sorry for shouting like that. I'm so glad to have you here, alive and well, and then I start a fight. Not what a good brother does."

Oran smiled and laid his arm across Sean's shoulders.

"No one could ask for a better brother than you," he said gently. "And I do understand about the books. If I could, I'd go up there right now with a train of wagons and dump the whole library on your doorstep."

"I know you would."

Oran leaned forward and put his face into his hands.

"You're exhausted."

"Yes."

"Let's walk back. You go to bed and sleep all day. With what you paid Naomham we can have his best cuts of lamb for dinner, and talk all evening over his finest stout."

Oran got to his feet with effort. "I'd like that above all things, Sean."

An hour later, Sean sat at his table working while Oran snored softly, buried and warm under fresh linens and clean blankets. It brought back to him memories of their shared room in Kilmore Quay, a room that like this one overlooked the ocean.

Oran always fell asleep when his head hit the pillow. I read by the flickering light of a candle until Dad or Mom appeared in the doorway and mouthed a silent "time to sleep."

He entered into his journal:

Oran is here on a rare one-day visit. Who knows the man I was with today? Conor, surely. Possibly no one else. Disguised by the naughty smile and bawdy jokes and sharp hand at cards, there is a soul unlike any other on this Earth. How fortunate I am that he is my brother.

Then he drew out a fresh sheet of paper and returned to work on his translation of the mysterious book from the north.

Padraic my brother, I write to you from Kilmore Quay. I came here to be with our dear friends Niamh and Hagan while I awaited news of the battle with the Dubliners. We now have word that your battle plan was a success and my son's quick thinking averted bloodshed. We don't have all the details yet, I hope you approve of what Conor did to save lives. Now that I feel this great relief, I can pass on other news. Seanlaoch has become attached to my wild child Fethnaid. Did you know that? A strange combination there, to be sure—let us hope that cerebral Sean will slightly temper Feth's impulsive nature. As for my least favorite subject, politics, the time is not far off when momentous decisions will have to be made concerning the Province. You know this, of course. Etain is maneuvering hard to see Zephan moved into power. For the moment, Rionach has blocked her and has alternate proposals ready to hand. I will see you in Clonmel, along with Rionach and Uinseann, where we need to talk when you can spare the time. I will sleep well tonight knowing you and Conor and Oran are safe.

Your loving sister, Liadan.

Chapter 29

It felt strange to be riding home on a borrowed military horse. Though the gelding was a worthy steed, to be sure, strong, well-fed, easy to manage, Conor longed for his massive stallion, for Treasach's wild impulsiveness never far from the surface, for his snorting and rearing as he neared his home stable.

His belly was empty and his body exhausted. The march back to Wicklow from Lough Poulaphouca had taken up much of the previous day. He slept only a couple of hours at the Wicklow fort before riding south to army headquarters in Rosslare, where he huddled with Padraic and his staff all day to work out the transfer of forces to the west. By the time he was able to break free, it was late afternoon, he'd had nothing to eat, and the azure sky of morning was turning a threatening gray. Now, less than a mile from home, a cold northerly wind spit raindrops at his back; the night promised to be stormy. He longed to rest in front of a hot fire in the great room and gather in a full night's sleep in his own bed. It might be his last for some time.

Would that Mairin was there waiting for him! He yearned for her now, both in spirit and in body. Of course she was not there, in fact he had no idea where she was in the vastness of the ocean. Tomorrow, if Aideen could be found in Rosslare, he would demand to know where she had been sent, and why.

Rounding the last familiar curve in the road, he spied the friendly porch lanterns of home, already lit as early twilight descended. He led the placid horse into the stable, unsaddled him, and gave him the stall next to Treasach, who banged his paddock impatiently.

"Too late now, boy," he said, running his hand down the long, dignified snout. "Maybe tomorrow we'll take a ride."

Treasach understood and turned contentedly to his hay. Conor pulled the heavy barn doors shut, crossed the yard and found Kellen waiting for him on the porch. They shook hands and Conor was elated to feel returning strength in Kellen's grip.

"It's a great moment for the Province, Conor," he said, holding Conor's hand in both of his.

"I'm sure the stories are far more glorious than the reality," said Conor with a rueful smile. "I'm made out a hero because I didn't have the heart to order the death of children. The fact is I took a big chance and the odds fell my way."

Triona appeared in the doorway, wrapped her arms around Conor's neck and whispered in his ear, "welcome back." Her trembling body pressed up against his.

The three friends retreated into the warmth of the great room, where Conor hoped to see his mother waiting.

"My mother's not here?" he asked.

"She left for Kilmore Quay two days ago to visit the Osraiges," said Triona. "She was worrying herself sick and I think she needed close friends to be with while she waited for news of the battle. She sent a note saying she'd be back tomorrow."

Conor nodded and eased into a well-stuffed chair near the fire. "I'm glad she did. The wrangling at Teach Munna wears out her spirits."

Triona took a chair opposite him and Kellen folded himself gingerly onto a sofa.

"Still hurts," he admitted, pressing a hand to his damaged side, "but my personal physician says the bones are knitting well."

"He's been a good patient on the whole," said Triona, "though at times he's also been a naughty boy."

Kellen fixed his eyes on Conor. "Conor, even if I can't fight, I have *got* to go to the west with you."

Conor turned to Triona with a questioning look.

"I can vouch for his being able to travel, if he needs to," she said. "No fighting."

Conor leaned back in his chair and said, "Well, I'm not sure."

"Please, Conor," Kellen pleaded. "I cannot miss this fight."

Conor laughed and winked at Triona.

"What's so funny?"

"Padraic signed the orders today," said Conor, still smiling. "All I needed was Triona's approval. You'll command the Blades in the western army. That is, if you're willing to serve under me."

"Oh, that was cruel!" Kellen cried. "You've been around Oran too much!"

"When do we leave?"

"Tomorrow, by land and by sea if the weather permits. Oran has gone on ahead to Dungarvan and will be scouting the enemy in the next week. We'll start assembling the army in Clonmel, have it ready to fight by the end of the month."

Conor spotted Triona looking at him expectantly. He knew what she wanted.

"You want to go?" he asked her.

"I'll serve where I'm ordered, Conor, but yes, I'd like to go."

There are reasons to say no, Conor told himself, *all personal and therefore unfair.*

"I'll make sure you're assigned to the field army," Conor said aloud, trying not to sound conflicted about it. "The better to keep an eye on my Blade Commander."

"Thank you," she said with a look that seemed to say, *I know you could have refused.* "I'll report to medical headquarters tomorrow."

"Have you eaten?" Kellen asked him. "As you can see from the apron, my cousin was hard at work when you arrived."

"The last meal I had was a stale bun at dawn."

"Leave it to me," said Triona.

She disappeared into the kitchen. Kellen added wood to the fire and poked at it idly.

"Two of my friends stopped by earlier today, off-duty Blades," Kellen said. "Bram has been heard in pubs speaking against you and your family. Mairin's name has also come up."

Conor's tired body turned rigid with anger.

"I wanted you to hear it from me."

"Not a thing I can do about it," Conor said, slamming a fist into a palm. "Padraic would flay me alive if there were an incident now."

"There can *never* be an incident," Kellen said. "Not with you being made a general."

"No, I guess not." He leaned back in the chair and closed his eyes. "I don't suppose there's any word of Mairin?"

"I went down to Squadron HQ yesterday to find out," Kellen replied. "Couldn't get in to see your sister—she was on her way out to her ship, I was told—but I talked up a doe-eyed ensign at the main desk. *Caillech* is not expected in port any time soon. You have no idea at all where she is or what she's doing?"

"I asked when I was on Aideen's ship, she gave me a vague answer and no details. I'll see her tomorrow, if I have to draw my sword to get into her office."

Triona returned from the kitchen carrying a food-stacked tray that she set down on the table in front of the sofa. Another trip produced a second platter bearing three tall steins and a froth-topped pitcher of cold ale. They all dug in and conversation turned for a time to the pungency of the cheese and the spiciness of the sausage. As the storm outside pounded the solid, drafty old house, pitchers of ale vanished and the three friends found their way to laughter and song and a poem recited by Conor. Fears for the future gave way to joyful memories and hopeful plans for the winter and spring. As midnight neared, Conor felt himself sinking under fatigue and the effects of a half-dozen tankards of ale.

"Can't keep my eyes open," he said with a modest slurring of words.

Kellen got to his feet and swayed slightly. "I am retiring," he announced.

"Goodnight, Kellen," Triona said. She was sprawled the length of the sofa with her head propped on a pillow.

Kellen ambled slowly towards the staircase, clamped his hand on the banister, and ascended one careful step at a time. Moments later, his bedroom door banged shut.

Conor got to his feet, surprised that his own balance seemed so far off. "See you in the morning," he said to Triona.

She reached up from the sofa, seized his hands, pulled him down and kissed him deeply. Her arms circled behind him and held on with fierce strength. Somewhere in the cloudy corners of his mind, resistance and judgment tried to gather their forces. It was futile. Ale and raw desire and the faint perfume of her neck overwhelmed him, and then there was no turning back.

He awoke to the sound of rain beating hard on his bedroom window. It was past sunrise, surely, though not much light filtered through dense storm clouds. Was she still here? No—his searching hand found no warmth beside him. Of course she would have moved back to her own room in the night. It would not be well to have Kellen see the two of them emerging together.

His head was foggy from the effects of the ale, yet his mind was clear enough for a torrent of conflicting feelings to surface. Guilt over being unfaithful to Mairin. Temporary relief from the surging tension in his body. Affection for Triona, who was a fine, sensitive woman and a lover of startling intensity. Worry that he had drawn her too close and raised an expectation in her mind. And beneath it all, a nagging uneasiness that questioned whether his love for Mairin was all he imagined it to be.

He allowed himself a few more minutes of comfort and private thought while rain lashed the window and wind buffeted tree branches against the siding. Would Kellen suspect? He had been quite drunk and might not remember much. He guessed that Triona would be nonchalant, at least he hoped she would, for he knew his own acting skills were minimal. Would it happen again? Did he want it to happen again?

With a puzzled sigh, he threw off blankets and shivered until garbed in a warm sweater and woolen trousers. He added heavy socks and padded softly down the hall towards the staircase. Kellen's door was closed.

He found Triona in the kitchen tossing chunks of firewood into the big black-iron cookstove. She wore bulky clothes as he did, but the memory of her lithe, strong body flashed into his mind and a fresh surge of desire followed it. He stood awkwardly in the doorway. She smiled, walked up to him and kissed him lightly on the cheek.

"Good morning," she said. "Sleep well?"

"Yes," he said. "Triona—"

She pressed her index finger to his lips. "Shhh. Don't apologize and don't worry about me. I wanted you and I acted on impulse. To be honest, I wanted you since I first saw you. I loved every second I was in your bed and I feel great this morning. Even if it never happens again, I will remember it with joy."

He gently grasped her restraining hand.

"I was worried," he admitted. "T'was a time when I slept with any woman I desired and did not think a thing about consequences ... but that time is long past. I made love to you last night and I treasured the feelings too."

Triona moved back to the stove and lifted the whistling teakettle from the stove. "You love Mairin and want to marry her and have children?"

"Yes."

"Then that's what I wish for you," she said while pouring the steaming water into a pot. "I mean it, Conor. I don't deny that having you would please me no end. I also care about you, more deeply than I probably should."

As she turned to face him, he leaned forward and kissed her forehead.

"And I care about you," he said. "Whatever happens, we'll always be friends."

She smiled, but did her eyes glisten with tears? The moment passed as Kellen's weight creaked on the staircase in the great room. By the time he came through the door, Conor was seated at the kitchen's square table sipping his tea and Triona was sliding a tray of biscuits from the oven. Kellen looked surprisingly fresh for someone who should have been hung over worse than Conor.

"Pleasant day!" he commented. "Triona is spoiling us, Conor. Ever since I came here, she has tea and pastries ready before I get up!"

He sat next to Conor, and a moment later Triona joined them.

Conor glanced out the kitchen window, streaming with rain. "No troops going out by water today. I'm going down to the harbor to see Aideen, if she's still here. Kellen, if you feel up to it, can you head up to army headquarters and report to Padraic? He'll need help getting the wagon trains ready to move west. Tell him I'll be there by mid-morning latest."

"On my way as soon as I get my gear together," Kellen said. "Triona showed me how to bandage and pad my ribs, and I've already ridden a horse without any problem."

They chatted amiably for a time, then Kellen carried off a half-eaten biscuit to his room. Conor got up and swallowed the last of his tea. Triona seized him and kissed him hard. When their lips parted, tears streamed down her face.

"You said—"

"It's not what you think," she said in a broken voice. "I'm crying because I wonder if we'll all see each other again, like this."

He brushed her tears aside and stroked her hair.

"We'll all be together again, I'm sure of it."

He held her against him, fighting to maintain his own control. Finally she broke away and headed for the stairs.

The rain abated slightly by the time he saddled and mounted a rearing Treasach, who had "gallop" in his eyes. Reluctantly Conor was forced to rein him in: the road was pocked with deep ruts and holes concealed by puddles. When he reached Squadron Headquarters at Rosslare Harbor, he left his stallion in an open-sided stable and splashed his way into the long two-story building. He stepped up to the receiving desk, currently occupied by a young ensign with pulled-back black hair and a distinctly cool expression.

"Yes?" she asked without a greeting.

I'm not in uniform, he realized, *let alone in a field army general's uniform.*

"Is the Commodore in?" he asked politely.

"And you are, sir?"

"Conor Laigain. Her brother."

The ensign's eyes widened and she applied a pleasant if somewhat artificial smile.

"Did you have an appointment?"

"Appointment!"

"I'm sorry, the Commodore left orders—"

"That's enough, Ensign," came the familiar cutting voice.

Aideen, her uniform wet and hair dripping, stepped out from behind a partition.

"Come in, Conor," she said without warmth.

Following her, he realized that he'd never seen her inner sanctum. It was far smaller and less grand than he imagined. A plainly-furnished square room no more than five paces side-to-side, it was brightly-lit by an all-glass back wall facing the harbor. Her framed Commodore's certificate hung on one wall and the Great Seal of the Province dominated the opposite wall. An immense desk was buried in papers, folders, and charts. Two plain chairs pushed up against the wall offered sparse seating for visitors. He took one of the chairs and moved it in front of her desk.

"Tea?" she asked him.

"No thanks."

She walked behind the desk and slumped into a high-backed chair. From a drawer she extracted a towel and mopped at her dripping hair.

"Just got in, I'm a bit wet."

"You were sailing in this?" he asked in astonishment as a fresh squall rattled the windows.

"No choice," she said. "I sailed out yesterday to meet with the Channel Squadron captains until late last night, then beat my way back in at first light. I have to see Padraic this afternoon about transporting army units. Damn gale was right in our face."

"So this is *really* a gale?" he asked cautiously, recalling their last conversation aboard her flagship.

"Of course, who told you it wasn't?"

He was about to make an irritated reply when he saw that this was a rare time Aideen was innocently needling him.

"Just checking," he said with a wink. "I was wrong the last time."

"So what brings you to my office?"

That sounded a bit like, what dragged you in? Bite your tongue, let's not get off on the wrong foot.

"I wondered if you had any word on Mairin?"

"No," she said, her gaze directed at the desk. "Not so far."

"I'd like to know where she is and what she is doing."

Aideen sighed as if to say, *I knew you would ask that.*

"Close the door, Conor."

He did as she asked. Aideen swiveled her chair and stared out at the whitecapped harbor for a long moment before answering.

"Remember I told you she was on a mission not authorized by the Council? My stated powers as Commodore extend pretty far, but not as far as sending four of our warships in support of a major attack led by the Kernow Admiralty. The objective is to capture Santander City, on the coast of old Spain. It's a huge operation, the fleet alone will number over one hundred ships. Mairin at this moment should be transporting Bretan Fighters to make the assault. I don't expect to get any word for at least a week. Satisfied?"

Conor felt the blood drain from his face.

"The Council still doesn't know about this?"

"They do now. I told Rionach, of course. Eventually she told Etain Fotharta when it was too late to make any difference."

"This is not at all like you," he said. "You of all people believe in strict compliance with policy."

She met his gaze, something she did not often do.

"It's not a decision I took lightly," she replied in a tense voice. "Our whole future at sea is at stake. I had to do it."

Conor stood and walked over to the window. The storm was getting worse, if anything. Every ship in the harbor was triple-lashed to its pier and even so they were rocked by towering waves that crashed over the breakwater.

"How dangerous is her mission, exactly?"

Aideen fiddled with a set of chart dividers. "I don't truly know. Collen Tredinnick is a superb fleet commander and he has all his best people with him. The attack is as well-planned as any could be. With all that, we can't control the weather or the strange fortunes of war."

"No. On land or at sea."

"Mairin Fotharta is the best captain in the Squadron, maybe one of the best anywhere. If anyone can bring our ships home in one piece, she can."

"You genuinely admire her, don't you?"

Aideen glared at him. "Yes, does that surprise you? Why do you think I want her, no, *need* her, to stay at sea? Because she *is* the best, that's why. That she and I don't especially like each other makes no difference at all."

"You don't like her because she's attached to me."

"Maybe that's true," Aideen admitted with a shrug. "My point stands, she's the best I have." She looked up at him. "Anything else?"

He circled around desk to stand in front of her. "I head for the west later today ... by land."

A particularly powerful blast of wind rattled the windows.

"Sure I couldn't offer you a ride on my corvette?"

"Land will do fine."

"You now command the field army, I hear. Feth will be there too?"

"Yes."

"What's the current assessment?"

"We'll be facing an army two or more likely three times our size, one that is no rag-tag bunch of raiders. The Ghaoth Aduaidh get more disciplined every year. Oran will let us know details soon. I don't need to tell you that if we can't break this army, there's no guarantee the Rampart will hold."

"No, you don't need to tell me that," she said in a weary voice.

"You still have the envelope I gave you?"

She looked uncertain for a moment, then nodded towards wall-mounted safe.

"Yes," she said heavily, "it's in there."

Conor leaned over her desk. "Aideen, why not come up to the house and rest a few hours? Mother will be home soon and I know for a fact there are fresh biscuits in the kitchen."

His suggestion drew a wan smile that faded with a tap on the door. An ensign's head poked in.

"Senior staff in five minutes, sir," the young woman said.

"Yes, Ensign, I'll be there."

Aideen stood and smiled at him, about as warm a smile as his memory of her stretching back to childhood could recall. "I would come ... but you see I can't."

She extended her hand. "Good luck, Conor. I am ... "

She faltered, and as he took her hand she stepped forward and embraced him.

"I am very proud of you," she said in his ear. "Really I am."

When she released him, she turned away to the window. He stood dumfounded and speechless. Finding his voice after a few seconds, he said, "And I am proud to be your brother."

Riding Treasach back home in driving rain, his insides churned with what had just happened.

Aideen had never hugged him, at least not since they were children. She had deliberately exceeded her authority in sending Mairin to lead a war mission without so much as informing the Council. And she said she was proud of him! Had it not been raining so hard, he would have looked up to see if the sky was falling.

By the time he reached Laigain House's barn, the churning gave way to a feeling of peace. *At least we had kind words between us. If I lay dying two weeks hence, I can call to mind the last words I spoke to her and pass from this world knowing they were not said in anger.*

"It's been a surprising night and day, big boy," he said as he toweled water from Treasach's mane. "Don't you think?"

His own words brought to mind a saying of Uinseann's. How did it go exactly? *Never be surprised by life, it is the plan of Nature to surprise us.*

Treasach, with a less philosophical outlook, snorted, reared his head, and whinnied.

"I'll take that as a yes," said Conor.

Hours later, Liadan returned to an empty house and found Conor's note tacked to the front door. She pulled it down and read:

Mother, I am sorry we missed each other. I waited as long as I could. I go directly from army headquarters west to Clonmel where I will command the field army against the Ghaoth Aduaidh. Visit me there if you can. Love, Conor.

She sank into a porch chair and stared at the note for a long time. *I knew the time would come. Domnall, my love, if you watch over us from a place beyond this world, help your son. He will need it.*

How would I tell my own life, as a story? "Once upon a time there was a man named Ionhar who worked on his father's farm and told stories to children. Then one day he decided that he had to become a fighter and he left the well-kept farm and the friendly town and went to another place where he put on armor and a sword and fought to keep people safe from harm." Simple enough and true as far as it goes. I could not explain to children that the people I fight against, at least some of them, are desperate for food and good land and will do anything to get them. Others who stand across the battle line are there for adventure and yet others simply want what someone else has. I do believe in my heart that we must hang onto a way of life where each man has hope his children will live in peace and tell stories of love and kindness and Celtic honor. So I fight on. I miss the morning splendor of purple mists over Roaringwater Bay, the haunted silence of the Skibbereen countryside, the hum of my village, the laughter of our cottage. Oh, father, would that I could come back to Creagh to stay! So say I, Ionhar Raithlinn, Storyteller of Creagh, this twentieth day of October, the year 999 as the Province reckons.

Chapter 30

At dawn they departed the home of Nolin McParga. A brisk, cold wind dried the roads, such as they were. Five miles down the winding, overgrown path leading west from Youghal, they came upon a wide clearing in the woods where Feth called a halt. Much as she wanted to push on, she knew they had to hone their skills further to prepare for the coming fight. Derdre fashioned a target from a rotted hay bales lying by the side of the road and practice began. Keegan and Ionhar looked on while the three archers galloped, circled, and loosed arrows for a full hour. Later, as the horses rested and grazed, the travelers ate a cold breakfast of bread and cheese, and savored cakes given to them as a parting gift from the McPargas.

"A huge amount to learn," Gwen commented. In one hand she held a piece of bread, in the other Arvel's tactics manual. "They've been at this for centuries and we're just starting."

"We can't do anything complicated this fall," Feth said, her own copy of the manual open on the grass in front of her. "I'm sure Arvel will train for the simplest maneuvers."

Derdre returned from filling her cup with cold water at the nearby brook. "I've got the hang of the horse, and the recurve feels okay. Compensating for moving crossways to the target is really hard."

"You all looked pretty sharp," Keegan put in. "I would suggest one thing."

The three archers looked up from their manuals.

"Be ready to use the sword too. If the battle lines are too tangled for arrow fire, you'll have to charge in with the horses."

Feth turned around to watch Ioan grazing contentedly near the brook.

"I'd hate to attack that way," she said. "The horses would be hard to replace, and we grow to love them too."

"They'll be armored?" asked Ionhar.

"Yes," Feth replied, "Arvel says they're used to the extra weight of chainmail. They'll be covered in it and they're trained for charging too. The saddle has a special strap to use when you fight with a sword. All the same, it would be a last resort."

Keegan reached over and borrowed Gwen's copy of the tactics manual. He leafed through the first few pages. "You have a name?" he asked.

"A name for what?" Gwen inquired.

"For the new force. Line of Bows, Line of Blades, Line of what?"

Feth stared at him. "I hadn't thought of that! Arvel gave us the banner, black with the red dragon and crosses. Maybe he's come up with a name ... he didn't mention anything."

"We won't fight in line ordinarily," said Derdre, "and the insignia is the red dragon holding arrows in its talons. Why not the Red Dragons? It would acknowledge our debt to the Welsh."

"Yes, that would be perfect," Feth agreed. "Gwen?"

"Yes."

"If Arvel or Conor haven't come up with a name when we get back, we'll suggest Red Dragons."

Gathering up their picnic remains and errant arrows, they mounted and rode west toward the sprawling ruins of Cork. The map Sean provided guided them surprisingly well. When they passed the crumbled tower of Barryscourt Castle—noted by Sean in the map's margin to be some three thousand years old—she knew they were not far from the old city and the River Lee.

The road straddled the northernmost part of Cork Harbor. More than ten centuries after the fall of the Age of Machines, and at a distance of two miles, the sight of the wrecked city was chilling. Great skeletal towers rose high above the rubble, rusted steel twisted into all sorts of unsettling forms. Here and there, a tall stone building had better withstood the ravages of centuries, yet appeared all the stranger for it: big glassless windows gaped like hundreds of empty eye sockets. From the mass of decaying wreckage drifted an unfamiliar musty odor. The horses lifted muzzles into the air, shook their heads and whinnied at the strange, unnatural scent.

From her school days Feth remembered pictures and drawings in old, fragile books of what the city might have looked like in the Age of Machines. It seemed unbelievable that such cities could be built. Where did all the stone and metal and mortar come from? How did they build structures so tall and slender? And why?

"How much Sean would want to be here," she said to Derdre, who was riding next to her. "He'd wander around for weeks, taking notes, making sketches, digging for interesting things."

"So would I, given the chance," said Derdre. "I love history. When we get back to Dungarvan you have to get me copies of Sean's work."

"Of course," said Feth. "We'll all get together and let him talk for hours."

Derdre drew her horse closer to Feth's until their flanks almost touched.

"You love him, don't you, Feth?"

"Yes, I do. I miss him so much."

Derdre fell silent for a long moment. Then she said, "When the winter comes on it will snow and snow. My father and I will host a dinner at our house, with a roaring fire in the hearth. You'll be there, and Sean, and Gwen, and maybe Keegan and Ionhar too." She turned towards Feth. "I am, ah, rather fond of Keegan."

"I hadn't noticed!"

Derdre laughed. "Okay, I guess it's obvious. I could be wrong, but I think Gwen likes our giant storyteller."

Feth twisted around in the saddle. Gwen and Ionhar rode close together ten strides back. Keegan waved amiably from the rear of their column.

"You're not wrong, I'm sure. When we sleep tonight, make sure you're closer to Keegan than I am!"

Derdre gazed up at the azure sky. "Anyway ... we'll all eat plenty and then we'll have hot cider and spiced wine and Sean will tell us of history and Ionhar will get us laughing and crying with his stories. It will snow all night but we'll be warm with our friends and we won't care at all." She turned towards Feth, her bright blue eyes glistening. "Feth, is my imagination getting the better of me?"

"My grandfather Uinseann taught me that under the sky all things we hope for are possible." Feth turned her gaze towards the north. "The only fly in your ointment is an army of fighters massing near Limerick. They have it in mind to take your home and mine away."

"Well, they're wrong about that," said Derdre, her voice turning steely. "They'll never set foot inside the Rampart, not this fall, not ever."

They fell silent for a time, then Derdre drifted back to ride with Keegan, leaving Feth alone at the lead. The disturbing ruins crowded in upon them, rising on either side of the dusty road, a towering forest of broken stone, shattered bricks and rust-orange metal.

"Terrible reminders," said Ionhar, his rugged face sad. "I do not tell stories of the Age of Machines, especially its dark and troubled ending, because the stories depress everyone who hears. How could such things be built and then abandoned? Who once lived here and what truly befell them a thousand and more years ago? What night-marish times did they live through?"

"I've heard camp stories," said Keegan, "that in places like these, the agonized souls of that age walk through the city at night, howling and crying."

"And you believe such stories?" Feth scoffed.

"Would you camp here alone, tonight?" Keegan retorted. He swept his arm at the great piles of rubble and tumbling monuments. "I wouldn't."

Feth picked up the pace. She did not believe in ghost stories but time was wasting and the immensity of this wreckage, crowding them so hard on either side, made her tense and morose. Not any too soon for the riders, great mounds of rubble yielded to collapsed houses and shops and then to scattered stones and hollow foundations. Sean's map suggested the next decent town they would enter was Ballincollig on the River Lee, two miles past the west end of the old city.

Road traffic picked up and once again they drew stares from fellow travelers, some curious, some suspicious, some hostile. They rode in a tight group, Feth and Keegan ahead and Ionhar, Gwen and Derdre three abreast a pace back.

Topping a rise in the road, they beheld a sight as different from the depressing remains of Cork as could be imagined. The River Lee meandered through a shallow valley south of the road, and a mile ahead, surrounded by tilled fields and small, neat cottages, was Ballincollig. They edged their horses off to the side of the road to gather in the welcome and familiar sight.

"The Province has no monopoly on beauty," Derdre said. "What a peaceful place!"

"Maybe," said Keegan, his eyes focused north of the town. "What's happening there?"

Smoke billowed from behind a small hill north of town.

"A lot of smoke for chimneys," Ionhar observed.

"Screams," said Gwen. "I'm sure of it."

"To arms," said Feth, yanking on her helmet. "Let's find out what's up."

Together they thundered down the winding, hard-packed dirt road, dodging carts and people on foot along the way. At the outskirts of town they swerved north off the road and galloped over harvested fields. Men, women and children running towards town fled past them, terror etched on their faces.

Feth halted Ioan and shouted at one man running for his life.

"What's happening? Why are you running?"

The man stopped, stared at them and then pointed north. "Raiders!" he screamed, and then kept running.

"How many?" Feth called after him, but he did not turn round.

"I hope it's not a hundred," said Keegan, his big horse circling nervously.

Ionhar's sword scraped out of its sheath. "Let's find out."

Feth tapped Ioan's flanks. The five of them raced up the hill and at its crest found the source of the smoke: the thatched roofs of four stone-walled cottages threw flames high into the air. The cottages clustered around a common yard; a red-roofed barn lay fifty yards beyond, its broad doors flung wide open. In front of one cottage, a woman held four children close to her; in front of another, an elderly couple clung to each other, their faces resigned. Seven saddled horses strained at tethers tied to a well in the center of the yard. The riders of those horses, sword-armed raiders clad in black leather trousers and fur pelts, emerged from the barn lugging leather bags.

Down the hill they plunged, dismounting on the fly. Feth, Derdre and Gwen lined up between the well and the barn and drew arrows. Keegan and Ionhar sliced the enemy horses' tethers and a single bellow from Ionhar sent them fleeing in all directions.

The seven raiders dropped their booty, drew swords and charged. Three arrows fired at close range slammed with killing effect through leather and flesh. The remaining four men leaped at Keegan and Ionhar at a dead run. Feth had a hard time sorting out what happened in the next moment. Steel clanged on steel, heavy boots ground into dusty earth, Ionhar bellowed a foul curse, Keegan's blade disappeared in a blur. Then it was over. The four attackers lay still in the dust, blood pouring from fatal wounds. Two of the heads were nearly severed from their bodies. Feth had never seen Bladesmen go about their work at this range: it astonished her that men so large and powerful could move so fast, that a blade could slice and stab faster than the eye could follow.

Yet it was *not* over ... ten more riders crested the hill to the north of the hamlet, expecting no doubt to meet up with the other party. Seeing the carnage in the yard, they pulled their horses up hard thirty yards away. A tall, red-haired man riding the biggest horse waved a curved sword in the air as if in threat.

Keegan scooped up one of the booty bags. "Want this?" he roared at the man. "Come and get it." He tossed the bag in their direction.

"Come on," Feth muttered, her eye sighting down her arrow. "Come on."

The red-haired man peered at them, then wheeled his horse, and leading his comrades he galloped north in a spray of dust and stones. Ionhar pulled off his helmet and began wiping his sword on a cloth.

"Curse the cowards," he said. "Not even decent exercise."

He walked slowly towards the terrified mother and her children and spoke softly to calm them.

The danger ended, people from the town streamed over the rise into the hamlet. A bucket brigade drew water from the well and fought to extinguish the burning thatch. Then more screams erupted from the barn. Feth pulled off her helmet and ran there, her friends at her heels. She drew a quick breath at what she found. Four men and two boys all lay dead, their blood staining fresh-cut hay. Feth found herself surrounded by wails of anguish and angry curses. She backed out fast, her stomach roiling and her face flushed scarlet with rage.

"How I wish they had attacked," she said bitterly to Gwen.

Keegan's massive hands balled into fists. "We could have cut them all down ... now they may go after someone else. We could trail them, Feth."

"I'd like nothing better, but no," she said with regret. "We've got to go on."

Feth led them across the yard to their horses. Before they mounted, a middle-aged man wearing a shiny silver chain around his neck approached cautiously, with many townfolk following him.

"My name is Ravelin," he said with a slight bow, "mayor of Ballincollig. You are all from the Province?"

"We are," said Feth, "and I'm sorry we didn't arrive earlier. We grieve for your losses, Ravelin."

"We're grateful for your help today," Ravelin said, "though we don't expect help from the Province and its soldiers. May I ask how you came to be here at all?"

"My friends and I are traveling among the peoples of Cork and Kerry seeking fighters for our army. These raiders," she nodded towards the corpses, "were probably foraging for an army of the Ghaoth Aduaidh now gathering near Limerick. When it reaches its peak strength that army will attack the Province's western border. We need more fighters and we're asking for your help."

A woman stepped when forward when Feth finished. She was easily fifty, with wispy gray hair, a heavily-lined face, and rough hands.

"My name is Kennocha, midwife of the town," she said with an angry edge. "Do you think this is the first time our kinsmen have been murdered? Except for today, the Twenty Clans have peered out from behind their Rampart and done nothing! Why should we fight for you?"

"We fought for you today," said Ionhar gently. "And I am not born of the Twenty Clans, nor is she," he said, laying his hand on Gwen's shoulder.

"We need to make common cause again," Feth said. "There was a time when our peoples were friends and we are here to show we want that time to return. If we can't defeat this army, all of our lands are forfeit, yours and ours."

"We've been told of the proposed new alliance," said Ravelin smoothly, "and we also heard your Council voted it down once again. We have no reason to—"

"Enough, Ravelin!"

A tall, strongly-built young man pushed his way to the front. Tears streaked down his cheeks and his hands were coated with blood.

"My brothers died in that barn!" he cried. To Feth he said, "I'll fight. Tell me where to go."

"And I!" shouted the woman holding the bow. "They were my kinsmen."

"Here!" a male voice called from the back. "Let me through."

The crowd closed in on Feth and the others. Friends and kin of the murdered townfolk and many others volunteered, thirty-seven in all.

As before in Youghal, each recruit was given a map and a hand-written pass to Dungarvan fort. When the last pass had been given out, Feth and her comrades helped the townfolk move the bodies of their loved ones onto carts. The corpses of the raiders had already disappeared. Chickens and a stray dog returned to their yard, the dog sniffing hard at blood-soaked earth.

Before mounting the five travelers gathered around the well and drank their fill.

"Your thoughts?" Derdre asked a silent and frowning Feth.

"What I saw in the barn made me sick," Feth answered her. "I am trying so hard not to hate, but I can't understand why men would do this to such peaceful folk as these. Ionhar, do you know why?"

The big soldier turned his ruddy face upward to the graying sky. "In my heart I can't understand it, no. In my stories there are many kinds of people, Feth, some good and some evil. There was a time when men believed evil spirits caused evil, but I don't think that's right. To me evil is just a thing, like the rain and the stars and the bounty of the earth. It is."

The next town of their planned route was Macroom, some fifteen miles west of Ballincollig. The townfolk of Ballincollig warned them not to go to that town; it was said to be walled off and unfriendly to any stranger. Feth decided that they would backtrack two miles and take a road south toward Bandon, a town beside the river of the same name. Thence they would travel along coast to Clonailty (a port where coaster vessels called) and after that in quick succession Skibbereen, Bantry, Kenmare, Killarney and finally Tralee where they would take ship for Dungarvan.

The road southeast from Cork to Bandon was little-traveled and overgrown; at times it was hard to see exactly where the road was at all. Feth gratefully conceded the lead position to Gwen, who seemed to have the best eye for following the right path. The overcast deepened all afternoon, cold rain spit from the sky, and the road wound about as if determined not to follow a straight line. Feth began to worry that they would not reach Bandon or any kind of habitation before nightfall.

Ionhar took the rear position in line and began a long and hilarious tale that kept them laughing in the face of the deepening gloom of the landscape and the realization that they were utterly alone on this dreary road. Nor were they made more comfortable by the howl of wolves somewhere off in the rolling hills. Feth recalled her father's fireside stories of wolves that roamed Eirelan in the Age of the Ancient Kings. The cry of wolves was rarely heard inside the Rampart, where they were hunted to protect livestock, but here in the open country, the clever predators lived in abundance and by timeless instinct hunted in packs. Possibly, Feth worried, one of those packs was now shadowing them, slavering over a meal of horseflesh and maybe human flesh as well.

Ionhar reached the end of his story and at the same time, down a long, steep, grassy slope, the River Bandon appeared in front of them. Spanning the river below were the remains of a long-destroyed bridge, its massive stone pilings disturbing the river's easy flow. Enough daylight remained that they could make out the road leading away from the opposite side of the fallen bridge. There was no obvious way to get across.

"Maybe it's not too deep," said Keegan. "I can try it with Comhghall."

"Too dangerous," Derdre said. "The water is swirling everywhere near that bridge so currents would be strong. Even if it's not too deep, the bottom is probably full of rocks. If your horse slipped you would both be swept into the current."

Keegan stared at the bridge for a long moment. "You're probably right."

"Look for a ford?" Gwen suggested.

"It's getting too dark," Feth said. She slapped a fist into her palm. "Sean warned me that there was no way to tell from his old maps which bridges might still be usable. I don't think I was listening. I'm sorry for this."

Keegan bent down to look into her face.

"Feth, we're in country we don't know. The folk in Ballincollig didn't know about this bridge, or they would have warned us about it. Besides, there *must* be a way across, the road on the other side looks like it's used."

Feth pulled out Sean's map and cursed the evening gloom. Derdre lit a candle lantern and held it out over the map.

"I see the bridge. There's something else shown here but I don't know what that symbol means. And here's a ford about two miles upstream."

"The trouble is, by the time we can get that far, it will be pitch dark," said Gwen. "We can't risk trying a ford in total darkness, even if we could find it."

Wolves bayed again, louder and closer.

"And the wolves are not going to wait," Gwen finished. "We'll have to fight them."

"Maybe not," said Ionhar. He pointed down towards the river. "Look there."

He pointed down towards the river. A light shone on the opposite bank a few yards downstream of the wrecked bridge. As they watched, the light began to move out over the river. Moments later the light blinked on and off three times at even intervals. Derdre covered and uncovered her lantern twice. The moving lantern signaled twice in return.

"Some kind of ferry?" Feth wondered. "Or someone trying to lure us down?"

The wolves barked and yipped, now very close.

"We have to take the chance," said Keegan. "Or we face the wolves up here."

Feth took another second to think. They had run out of options.

"All right, let's get down there," Feth decided. "Helmets on. Ionhar and Keegan, go down first leading the horses, if we lose them we're finished. Gwen and Derdre and I will cover you. Derdre, put out the lantern and let our eyes adjust, there should be just enough light to shoot by at close range."

"Which it will be," Gwen muttered. "Point-blank I think."

Keegan and Ionhar started down the slope leading the skittish horses. Even the Welsh-trained battle steeds capered at the anxious yipping and rank scent of hunting wolves. Feth, Derdre and Gwen drew arrows and formed a defensive line backing down the slope. They descended as fast as they dared in the poor light. Gwen tripped once and fell backward heavily, leaped to her feet cursing and caught up. Keegan and Ionhar reached the riverbank safely and needed all their combined strength to restrain the panicked horses. Seconds later the archers joined them. They gathered the horses behind them near the water's edge and formed a semi-circle to defend them. They found it darker by the river as the last of twilight ebbed.

"Not enough light to be accurate," Feth decided. She slid her bow into its holster and drew her sword. Derdre and Gwen followed suit.

Feth glanced over her shoulder: the boat's lantern had reached mid-river.

"It's quiet," Feth whispered. "Gwen, does that mean they gave up on us?"

"I'm afraid not," Gwen whispered back. "They get quiet when they're ready to attack."

And attack they did. Seven wolves bounded out of the forest from all sides and leaped at the armored fighters. Derdre stabbed repeatedly at a wolf whose jaws were clamped onto her forearm. Gwen dueled with two wolves and managed to kill one before the other toppled her and pinned her down in the mud. Feth retreated a step from a leaping wolf and caught it in mid-air with her blade. It backed off, bleeding and snarling and biting for her legs. Keegan and Ionhar, whose size kept them from being bowled over, killed three almost immediately with sword-thrusts. They continued to slash and stab until six of the seven attackers lay dead. The last alive was a powerful male still atop a struggling Gwen. Ionhar grasped a handful of the wolf's thick fur, pulled it off Gwen, and flung its writhing body far out into the river.

Feth dropped her sword and knelt down beside Gwen. In the dim light she saw blood streaming down her friend's pallid face. Derdre knelt down on the other side while Keegan and Ionhar tried to gather the panicked horses.

"Help me sit up," Gwen gasped, spitting out mud.

"I can't see much," said Derdre. "Did he bite through anywhere?"

"I don't think so," Gwen said, her breathing steadier. "Not for lack of trying."

They helped Gwen to her feet. Keegan and Ionhar brought the capering horses back from shallows. Ionhar managed to locate and light a lantern which he gave to Derdre. She looked each of them over including herself.

"We're lucky," she said. "I see no deep punctures, which are very dangerous. A lot of washing and antiseptic should be enough. Sort of like a battle."

"I'll take human fighters any day," Feth said with some relief. "What a stink they make!"

"We have company," said Keegan.

The boat's light had reached shore. It was indeed a ferry, long and flat, with a small central cabin and a big oil lantern mounted in the bow. The bow glided into the mud and a short, thick-set figure leaped out. The man held a smaller lantern in his hand, revealing a scowling, florid face creased with lines, long white hair pulled together in the back, powerful arms and shoulders, and oversized hands. The man's scowl softened when he saw how bloodied they were.

"Lucky for ye I saw yer light and came across," he said. "My name be Feargal, Feargal the Boatman these forty years and more. Ye want to get across?"

"We do," Feth replied. "We'll pay."

The man's rheumy blue eyes lit up. "Pay me? With what?"

"Coin of the Province. Sure you can see who we are even through the mud."

"Oh, I see who ye are well enough," Feargal said through a gap-toothed grin. "Soldiers all, or ye'd be dead in the muck by now. For Province gold, you get my best service. Come aboard."

They coached the skittish horses onto Feargal's heavy raft and when they were all aboard, the grizzled boatman drove a long pole into the muck and with surprising ease, muscled the raft out into the Bandon's current. Derdre, whose father had given her extensive first aid training, retrieved their medical kit and by the light of the boat's lantern treated their many wounds. She dipped a clean towel repeatedly in the river, washed every cut, dampened another cloth with sting-ing antiseptic and swabbed the wounds to stop infection. Meanwhile Ionhar moved among the horses, whispering and mumbling in his deep bass, until their sides no longer heaved with stress.

"Might I ask what soldiers of the Twenty Clans be doing here?" Feargal asked he poled the raft steadily towards the far shore. "Yer pretty far from home."

It seemed to Feth a simple question; she heard no rancor in his voice.

"Recruiting," Feth answered him. "Soldiers for our army."

Feargal frowned at spat on the deck. "Much luck will ye have with that in Bandon Town."

"Why is that?"

"Not just that the people there don't like ye. They hate ye. Lost twenty, thirty folk last year alone in the raids. Then they were swindled by a sharp fur trader from Wexford."

"We'll try anyway."

"Have it your way. Remember I warned ye."

Feth rejoined her friends at the raft's port rail.

"Very promising," she said, her spirits sagging. "Should we turn back?"

"Nay," said Ionhar. "We have time yet."

"A few scratches," Keegan said with a smile. "They threw a melon at you in Youghal and we got thirty-four. I say we go on."

"Yes," said Derdre. "All the way to Tralee."

Gwen, the worst-injured, held a cloth to her lacerated forehead.

"Can't stop now," she said. "Thirty-seven this morning and they didn't like us either."

Feth, tears in her eyes, took each of their hands in turn.

"We go on," she said. "All the way to Tralee."

"Imagine what life was like here when that bridge was new," Keegan said. The boat's powerful bow lantern outlined in deep shadow the ragged foundations of the massive stone bridge. "How many people lived in these parts, do you suppose? What did they wish for? What did they fear?"

"I bet they didn't fear packs of wolves," Feth said.

"There are worse things in this world to fear than wolves," said Ionhar. "Maybe when the end came what they feared most was each other."

The Santander navy is now estimated to number some 100 ships of all types with at least 50 of these two and three-masted vessels capable of shipping more than 100 fighters each. Their designs—often copying ours—are steadily improving, and their newest vessels are nearly as weatherly and fast as our own. Seamanship also has advanced greatly from a decade ago. They are in a position to build ships faster than we can and also have access to a larger population for crews and embarked fighters. It is the judgment of this committee that within a year the Santander navy will be the equal of our own in numbers even when combined with the Province Squadron. Unless prompt action is taken, we may lose our ability to defend Celtic ports and ships from Santander attack, with dire consequences that need not be further explained.

Report of the Admiralty Strategy and Planning Council
Respectfully Submitted to Collen Tredinnick, Fleet Admiral

Chapter 31

"The Caudillo and his High Council would like the answers to a few questions, this afternoon," said High Council Secretary Agurne Ganborena. He blew a cloud a blue cigar smoke at the ceiling, drawing an irritated look from the man seated behind the desk. "For example, why can't we keep squadrons at sea in winter, when there is still cargo to be seized and coastline to be raided?"

Almirante Joseba Bastegieta's sea-weathered hands gripped the edge of his polished oak desk until the knuckles blanched. He struggled to hold his temper in the face of such ignorance.

"I shall be happy," he said in a pleasant if strained tone, "to tell the Caudillo and his counselors yet again why operations at sea in the winter months are dangerous and gain us very little for possibly great loss. There are very few ships worth seizing. Winter storms bring ice and snow. Seamans' hands and feet freeze. Spars and masts shatter and fall to the deck. Ships are lost in blizzards. Daylight hours are short and skies are usually cloudy, making navigation difficult at best."

Ganborena narrowed his small, close-set eyes; his voice took on a harder edge.

"You should be prepared, Almirante, to offer better excuses. The Caudillo has been patient for almost ten years, has spent much money on building up your navy. It is now strong enough to destroy our Celtic enemies once and for all and seize the ocean lanes for ourselves."

"You forget, if I may say, the fact that the Celts are no longer the only ones on the seas."

The Secretary dismissed this remark with a wave of his hand through his own smoke.

"Oh, yes, yes, the ships from the north again. I advise you not to bring that up."

Bastegieta let go of the desk and poured himself a tall beaker of wine.

"For you?" he offered.

"Yes. Thank you," said Ganborena. "You always have the finest wines in your office."

Bastegieta handed over the beaker and downed two gulps from his own. In truth, he never broke out the really good wine for this arrogant *cabron*.

"It is easy," he said to Ganborena, "to simply count ships and fighters and decide we now have the edge. It is quite another, Secretary, to win battles at sea. The Cornish Admiralty is a formidable force, and with the Province Squadron added—"

"Ships sailed by women!" Ganborena shouted, spilling his wine on the carpet.

Bastegieta set his own glass down on the desk and glared at his guest but kept his voice level and quiet. "I was not aware the Council Secretary had engaged their ships in battle."

"You know I have not," Ganborena snapped. "My delicate stomach cannot stand the rigors of the sea."

Bastegieta got up and walked to broad windows overlooking the shipyards. With his back to Ganborena, he said, "Then you have not seen their heavy ballistae firing razorhead bolts that maim ten men at a time. Or heard the strange ripping sound of a hundred arrows cutting down your crew and fighters by the dozens. Or observed their superb ship-handling and utter fearlessness in battle, even when it is hand-to-hand and we have the advantage in strength and numbers. No doubt you have seen none of this, in the interest of your delicate stomach. I do assure you, warfare at sea has little to do with the organs between the legs."

"Careful, Almirante," said Ganborena. "Insulting me would be a mistake."

Bastegieta turned and bowed slightly. "I am merely trying to provide you with accurate information, so far as it is in my power after some thirty years at sea in the service of the Caudillo—and his father before him."

Ganborena sipped his wine and blew another acrid cloud of smoke.

"I merely inform *you*, Almirante, of what the Caudillo wishes to hear from you."

He stood, drained the beaker, and left his burning cigar in a glass tray.

"I shall leave you," he said, donning his cloak. "You are expected at three."

Bastegieta watched him leave, then threw open the casement windows to clear the room of the vile smoke. A fresh breeze off the harbor poured in, and he drank of it, wishing yet again that he was at sea and not confined here amidst politics and corruption. In the spring, he told himself, he would take out a squadron himself, whatever the Caudillo might say.

The pendulum clock in the corner of his office read almost noon. He decided he would lunch at home today, calm his spirit and prepare his mind for another trial with the Caudillo and his insistent, prating Councillors. Leaving word with his aide, he left Armada Headquarters and took the long route home through the open markets. It was a fine autumn day, at least to a sailor: stiff, steady north wind, perhaps scented with a yet-distant storm. The open markets near the harbor did a brisk business today. Hundreds of bright-colored banners snapped in the wind, vendors called out in loud, happy voices the great bargains to be had ... only today! Bastegieta loved the markets and envied the simple life of the men and women who worried only over buying low and selling high. He stopped at a booth run by a woman he knew from childhood, Katalin Lurrieta. Once a tall, willowy woman with a slender waist and fetching eyes, she was now the fleshy, somewhat ill-kempt mother of four. Still, she was a happy woman and she greeted her old friend by his first name.

"Jose, welcome!" she cried. "I have not seen you since summer! The market is not good enough for an Almirante, eh?"

"Foolish woman!" he said, smiling. "No, my navy pay is not up to your prices!"

"Hah!" she laughed. "Today a special discount for navy officers. A gift for your beautiful wife?"

"Yes, a gift for Terese." His eyes scanned delicately-crafted rings and brooches and necklaces. Terese had so many of these!

"You wish an unusual gift today? I have just the thing."

She retreated into her tent and returned with an open wooden box.

"All Celtic," she said proudly. "Taken from Eirelan, Scotlan, Bretan, Wales, by your own ships. What could be better, Almirante?"

True enough, the box held many exquisite earrings, bracelets, hair clasps, and perfume bottles. Some of the glasswork was truly extraordinary. Yet it was an unfamiliar item that caught his eye: an intricate three-pointed knot fashioned of leather and decorated in silver, mounted to a delicate silver chain. He lifted it carefully from the case and examined it more closely.

"What is this called?"

She set down the box and took the piece from him. "If I'm not mistaken, Jose, a Celtic Knot. We get them now and then. Supposed to be used in a marriage proposal, I've heard said. I can't be sure, you understand. And I think you're already married, old friend."

"True," he said, taking the trinket back from her. "Still, it's romantic, wouldn't you say? I'll take it, Katalin, how much?"

She waved a thick, calloused hand. "Not a pesata, Jose. Promise you will stop by more often."

He smiled at her and tucked the gift into his pocket.

"I will do that, and thank you," he said, touching his broad, gold-trimmed hat. "My best to your family."

"And to yours," she said.

His modest home rested atop a knoll, giving it a view out over the town. He had designed it himself, and his heart swelled with pride as he strolled up the steep, dusty path. No one would mark him for wealth: the house was but one story, fashioned of plain brick and tile, and offered no grand turrets or sweeping terraces. Yet from its broad front porch all of Santander Bay could be seen, and beyond that the great blue ocean itself. The rear veranda faced west—the light of the dying sun often accompanied their late suppers.

Terese did not see him approach. Her back was turned; she was watering potted and hanging plants that converted the front porch into something of a garden.

His boot struck the first wooden step.

"Jose!" she cried, her lovely face instantly alight with a smile that melted his heart. She set down her water jug and kissed his cheek.

"Is there not a meeting today, with the Caudillo?"

"Yes," he said, pulling off his hat. He sank into a wicker chair with a sigh. "This afternoon. I spent much of the morning with Señor Gonborena and his filthy cigars. I needed an hour at home with my wife before facing that gaggle of armchair warriors."

Terese sat next to him. With her apron she mopped sweat from her brow.

"It is a pleasure, my husband, but I have nothing prepared. You will have to make do with the cold lamb from yesterday and fruit pie. And olives I bought this morning."

"My dear," he said, taking her hand, "that is so much better than the fare at the officer's mess. I don't hear the girls, are they here?"

Terese shook her head. "Just as well, if you want a quiet lunch. They quarreled all morning! You would think twins of ten years age could get along better. I sent Usua to your mother and Sendoa to mine. I needed a few hours of peace! They'll be back soon. So we will lunch alone, Jose."

He eyed her suggestively. "Half an hour for lunch, and half an hour ... ?"

"It would not cloud your mind, Almirante?"

"It would not," he said. He rose, lifted her to him, and kissed her deeply. "Indeed it would clear my mind wonderfully. Let's have our lunch second, shall we?"

Slightly more than a half hour later, Bastegieta reluctantly donned his gold-trimmed black uniform and made his way out onto the front porch, where Terese was setting out lunch on a table between their chairs. He was enjoying himself so much that he nearly forgot the gift in his pocket.

"Ah, I have something for you, courtesy of Katalin Lurrieta." He pulled out the Celtic Knot and handed it to Terese. "She tells me this is a Celtic Knot, and so far as she knows it's used for a marriage proposal. I suppose it's a little unusual but I thought you would like it."

Terese studied the leather charm with fascination. "It is indeed unusual. What do you suppose the three points represent?"

"I don't know," he admitted, "and Katalin doesn't either. Maybe I can find out. I imagine it somehow symbolizes the family. Would you marry me again, dearest?"

Terese draped the chain around her neck and seized his hands. "I would marry you ten times again, husband. No one could be happier than I am."

She kissed him and then pressed a hand to his chest.

"Now eat your lunch! Any chance Mikel might return today?"

"A chance," he said between bites. "Our son has his own way of doing things, even at seventeen. He shows much initiative in his scouting work."

Terese smiled and said, "He has always made you proud of him."

"I suppose all fathers are proud of their sons," he said, snaring an olive from the bowl. "I will say as Almirante too that Mikel is a fine seaman."

A high-pitched shriek warned them that the twins approached. They pelted up the dusty hill, racing to see who reached the porch first. Twins they were, but identical they were not, and longer-legged Usua made it first, setting off an argument about whether the race was fair.

"Naughty girls!" said Bastegieta with mock severity. "Come here this minute."

Black-haired Sendoa and her brown-haired sister climbed the steps, their shoes and clothes coated with dust.

"Stand before me," he ordered, drawing giggles. They drew up at attention.

"Your mother reports bad behavior," he said, struggling desperately to keep a straight face. "Is this true?"

"Yes, father," said Usua.

"Yes, father," Sendoa repeated.

"Punishment is five lashes." He pulled the long feather from his hat and swiped each of them five times. "Now behave."

"Yes, father," they both said, giggling again.

He stood and kissed Terese. "Time to go, love. I shouldn't be late tonight."

He strolled at an easy pace towards the Caudillo's palace, his thoughts on his son. Selfishly, perhaps, he had kept seventeen-year-old Mikel away from the fighting, giving him instead command of a fast two-master and assigning him to constant patrol duty. Any day he should be returning from a final voyage north as far as Wales, and when he returned, he would be safe for the long months of winter.

The Caudillo's immense palace, intended to show off the city's great wealth acquired from a century of piracy and trade, sprawled some three hundred yards from one end to the other. An architectural masterpiece it was not, or so Bastegieta thought each time he approached it along a manicured stone walk lined with trees and sculptured shrubs. Too many towers, spires and domes, too many colors of blue and green and pink and lavender, too many gilded doors, too many statutes and gargoyles. In fact, he hated the building ... yet he never failed to praise its magnificence when the opportunity arose. It did not pay a man even in his high position to irritate Caudillo Erramun D'Etcheverry, the third of that name and supreme ruler of Santander these past nineteen years. Bastegieta's wife and three children lived well because he kept the Caudillo happy.

Or as happy as the dour-faced, snappish, wiry man ever managed to become. He greeted Bastegieta in his private dining room, where a sumptuous lunch served to his High Councillors was being cleared away.

"Joseba," he called out from the far end of the long table, "please be seated."

D'Etcheverry wiped grease from his chin and sipped coffee while Bastegieta took the proffered chair and removed his hat. Twenty-six well-fed faces, many flushed deep pink from never-empty wineglasses, turned and stared at him. Gonborena sat on D'Etcheverry's right. His face was coldly composed and he smoked another giant cigar whose smoke he was careful to direct away from the Caudillo.

"Your Excellency," Bastegieta said, "and honored ministers. I am pleased to be here. I report that of seventy-eight fighting ships available for sea service, sixty-four have returned safely to the harbor. Four were lost in recent engagements with the enemy, ten others recently dispatched to assault Tralee in Eirelan have not yet reported in. Twelve new ships, the finest we have ever built, will be completed in the yards this winter. In two more years we will be in position to overwhelm the Celtic navies and seize control of the seas."

"Always two years more," complained Frantzisko Arostegi, D'Etcheverry's political advisor and no friend to Bastegieta. He glared down the long table from his place at the Caudillo's left hand. "We build and they build, and always it is two years, Almirante. It is long past time that we seize the day. The attack on Tralee, for example—"

"Was premature," Bastegieta interrupted. His temper rising, he gripped the arms of the chair. "However, because the Council demanded it, I authorized it. I sent ten ships under Capitano Zornoza, but I advised you of the risk. More than that, I have often pointed out that we are moving too fast."

Arostegi fumed at the interruption. "Almirante, I have heard enough of this. I—"

The Caudillo's hand clamped down on his forearm.

"I will not hear this argument again!" D'Etcheverry barked. "My order, Almirante, is that we prepare for full attacks in the spring, and launch winter attacks as weather permits."

Bastegieta inclined his head towards D'Etcheverry. "As you wish, Your Excellency. I merely point out that as my grandfather once told me, do not poke a lion with a stick unless you are prepared to fight him."

Bastegieta did not sleep well and left his wife's side before dawn. Fixing himself a cup of hot coffee, he crept out onto the front porch, wrapped himself in a heavy blanket against the night's chill, and turned over in his mind the orders he'd received from the Caudillo. He hated the idea of sending out his ships in the dead of winter, subjecting crews to frostbite and the ships to vicious storms. He would obey, of course, but in a way that would protect his ships as much as possible. Perhaps some raids to the south, strike at the African ports which stayed warm? It was worth considering.

When the glow from the eastern sky threw enough light over the sea, he arose and turned his powerful tripod-mounted telescope towards the harbor. A two-master was making its way in, flying a full suit of sails in the light airs. He studied the ship's pennants and breathed a sigh of relief; it was Mikel, returned from the north at last. His son was safe and would be home by the time Terese cooked breakfast.

Still, it seemed odd that he was in such an apparent hurry. Bastegieta held the telescope on the ship as it drove through the harbor, never slackening sail until it reached the pier. Odd indeed! Perhaps something was up. He went inside, stole into the bedroom where Terese still slumbered, and traded his robe for trousers, a warm shirt and soft-soled boots. When he returned to the porch, he saw Mikel in full uniform running up the path to the house. Bastegieta descended the steps and met his son in the yard.

Mikel tore off his hat and saluted. "Almirante," he said between great gulps of air, "I have an urgent report."

Bastegieta grasped his son's arms. "What is it, Mikel? Quickly."

"Yes, sir. I looked in at Falmouth and found it empty. Plymouth too. Then Brest, nothing. Not a single warship. I made for home and located their fleet, followed them at a long distance. Twelve miles outside the harbor when I last saw them."

"How many?"

The boy's eyes widened. "Before the fleet broke up, at least a hundred, father. Warships and heavy transports. Some forty on their way in now, all warships."

"Mother of God."

Bastegieta raised the heavy barrel of his telescope and trained it out to sea. First, nothing. Then he saw it: the great battle fleet, black and white flags streaming from topmasts, in flawless attack formation. Alarms rang out in the town and the klaxons sounded from his own Armada Headquarters. The entire Cornish navy was about to burst into the harbor, where most of his ships lay helplessly at anchor. And what about the transports, where did they go? He swiveled the telescope east and found a chilling sight: battle pennants of the feared Bretan Fighters, approaching the outskirts of the city.

Bastegieta straightened up and turned to Mikel.

"Father, I must get my ship ready to fight," the boy said, ready to run again.

Bastegieta took hold of his hands. "My son, your little ship will mean nothing now. Here is what I ask you to do. Go inside, change out of your uniform, gather up your mother and sisters and take them in our carriage. Drive south to your grandfather Imanol's farm. Waste not a second, my son, their lives may depend on it. I will follow when I can."

"But father—"

"Teniente Bastegieta, do as you are ordered. Now go!"

Mikel fled inside. Bastegieta raised the telescope again, focused its powerful lens on the Celtic fleet's command ship leading the rest. He made out a brightly-uniformed, grey-haired figure poised in the bow, more than likely his own counterpart. A fighting seaman, who knew his business well.

"I did warn them," he said to himself. "And now the lion has come for his lunch."

My daughter Derdre, I post this note from Falmouth, it should reach you soon. I know how deeply you grieve the loss of your mother. Each time I awake aboard ship I hope that her death has been a terrible dream. I take comfort that we have each other to love and cherish, and her sweet memory. Her death has made me think hard about my own life. You know how we were talking about retiring from service and moving to the country? I am thinking now that I will do it anyway, come spring. I am not far from forty-two and I'd like to enjoy the next phase of my life bringing medical care to the folks in the countryside. I'd even consider practicing outside the Province where I'm told trained physicians are a rarity. I will keep our home in Dungarvan where we have so many friends, if that is something you would like. You will give me a few grandchildren to spoil terribly? My daughter, know that I love you and miss you each day and hour.
Your loving father, Mor.

Chapter 32

"Mor, you don't have to watch me every second," Mairin grumped. Mor, who had been lost in his own thoughts, turned to her.

"Captain, I do understand," he replied with a knowing smile, "that you're a responsible officer and would never think of going against your medical officer's direct orders. On the other hand," he nodded towards the mizzentop, where two lookouts scanned the horizon, "if one of them were to call out 'sails to starboard,' I'm concerned you might scurry into the crosstrees for a better look. And that, we cannot have."

"Ach," was her comment.

"Yes, sir," he replied, and turned back to stare into the *Caillech*'s wake.

Off to starboard and a ship length astern, *Morrigan* under Tierney Ulaid's command sailed a parallel course. The eight heavy transports in loose formation followed the two warships, shepherded from the rear by Jilleen Conmaicne's *Wexford* and *Rosc Catha*, now commanded by brevet-Captain Vevina Monaig. Insistent signals during their first hours out of Brest had been needed to inform the merchant captains of what Mairin expected; since then, they had done a fair job of keeping station.

Fortune smiled on them so far: they were within a half-hour of Tredinnick's timetable. Since departing Brest, the combined Celtic war fleet had plunged south through rolling seas with a steady following wind. Thirty miles north of Santander Bay, the sprawling fleet split into three sections, with Captain Endean's battle squadron continuing straight south, Richard's squadron and its army of Marines, Scots Guards, and Welsh Pikemen sheering off to the west, and Mairin's group carrying Bretan Fighters tacking to the east. *Caillech's* barometer rose and fell a few points during the day, but so far gave no sign of an impending storm.

Soon after the lower edge of a swollen sun touched the western horizon, *Caillech's* lookouts reported that the sails of the other squadrons could no longer be seen. They were on their own.

Rowenna stood near the helm, feet spread wide, her eyes roving fore and aft. Sithmaith had posted herself in the maintop with Mairin's best glass, adding her eyes to those of the lookouts for any sign of trouble. So far, Mairin reflected, she had worked out well; whatever insubordinate streak she may have had was not apparent. She had to admit Mor had a point about the crosstrees. Her head throbbed and a faint dizziness came and went. *Damn Kennat Gailenga! I will see that she is not only broken but made to work in the dockyards for the next ten years.*

Mor asked, "what did you say, sir?"

She gave him a startled look. "Sorry, Mor, mumbling to myself."

He nodded, rubbed his hands absently on the smooth, varnished rail.

"Much to worry about," he said in a distracted way.

With all that has happened, she chided herself, *I have forgotten than this man, as dear a friend as I have, lost his beloved wife not a week ago.*

"You're thinking of Dunlaith?"

"Yes ... and Derdre too."

"You must be very proud of her. Strong, bright, attractive, and I would guess a tough fighter."

"Like her mother in many ways, yes."

"How old is she now?"

"Twenty, plus a couple months."

"You'll see her again soon."

"I do hope so, Captain."

"Twenty," Mairin repeated with a sigh. "I'll be twenty-nine next month, but I feel about fifty today."

He glanced up at her with concern. "Anything besides your head?"

"Wrenched my back, too. It always hurts anyway. The old injury mostly."

"Remind me."

"Fell from the foretop when I was an ensign, someone broke my fall and saved my life. My back was never the same."

"Ah, yes, I remember. I'll give you some herbal relaxer."

Rowenna turned and caught Mairin's eye. "Captain, we'll sight land from the tops in about a half hour. Wind is falling off and veering east."

"I'd just as soon have light airs for the landings," Mairin remarked. "Tough making Santander if we have no wind, though."

"Yes, sir."

"As soon as land is sighted, shorten sail to reefed topsails and start soundings. I want one ensign on each side, we can't afford a mistake in these waters. Lieutenant!" she called up to Sithmaith, who lowered her glass and leaned over the mizzentop rail.

"Sir?"

"Take charge below, get them ready."

"Aye, aye, sir," replied Sithmaith, already sliding down a backstay.

"Lieutenant," Mairin said to Rowenna, "handle the loading operation. I'll take this station."

Rowenna hesitated. "Captain, may I ask how you are?"

"Tolerable," she answered. "I've been better, no doubt."

"No doubt, sir," said Rowenna with a concerned look. Then she hurried forward and snapped out orders for the boats to be set on the davit hooks.

As night fell over the rolling sea, the twelve-ship flotilla glided ahead towards the Spanish coast, aiming for a point east of an abandoned town marked on the charts as Santoña. Mairin took the wheel herself, assuring a watchful Mor that with a light following wind the effort was near to zero. Despite the light airs and calm seas, this part of the voyage presented the greatest sailing hazard. The charts indicated shoals in these waters; the ships had to thread among them using the compass and continuous soundings. As had been planned, each ship mounted a single shaded blue lantern at the top of the mainmast and the formation shifted to line ahead, with *Caillech* at the front and Jilleen's *Wexford* at the rear. Though the shoreline five miles distant showed no lights, Mairin demanded minimal noise on all the ships. The ensigns calling depth from the chains were ordered to face the quarterdeck and report in a low voice.

As Mairin expected, the Admiralty chart was accurate in every detail. Within a half-mile of the anchor point, Mairin ordered the lantern flashed three times, to which *Morrigan* and then all the other ships responded. When Jilleen's signal was received, Rowenna gave the order to strike topsails. *Caillech* glided to a halt, the anchor was carefully lowered from the cathead without a splash, and *Caillech* swung round the short cable until its bow facing windward. Mairin's stomach clenched tight as she watched the merchant haulers; a slip here could cause a collision. At last *Wexford's* lantern could be seen swinging in a slow arc. All twelve ships lay at anchor on a gentle swell no more than a mile from the coast of old Spain, a land as unknown to the sailors of the Squadron as the far side of the world.

Mairin released her hands from the wheel and flexed her fingers, not realizing she had gripped it long after *Caillech* dropped anchor. Sithmaith appeared in the hatchway halfway up the steps, her face outlined by light from below.

"Captain," she said quietly, "the Bretan chief would like to come on deck."

"Of course," she replied. To Rowenna she said, "Lower the boats. Ensign Velnowarth in the longboat, Ensign Auteini in the launch. Hold the gig, I may need it."

Sithmaith ascended the ladder once again, this time followed by Fighter Chief Herenal Iocilin. To Mairin's relief, the towering warrior had maintained strict discipline among his rugged fighters, eighty powerful men armed with a frightening array of weapons. Master Sechnaill, by far the strongest sailor aboard, had struggled mightily to heft the spiked mace Herenal himself carried into battle. Yet he whirled it about one-handed like a child's ball on a string. Mairin came close to pitying the Santanders who would find themselves facing these fearsome and vengeful men in battle.

In spite of his size, Herenal glided across the quarterdeck without making a sound. Mairin's eyes barely reached to his chest. He bowed slightly as was their custom.

"Captain," he said in an subdued rumble, "we are ready. I wish to say that we are in your debt for bringing us to the lair of our enemies. Long have they raided our coast and taken from us, killed and seized hostages. Repayment is finally at hand."

Mairin dipped her head in reply. "The Province of the Twenty Clans makes common cause with you, Herenal. Santanders have preyed on our ships and our coastline also, and they must be stopped for the good of all. May fortune go into battle with you."

He smiled down at her. "Fortune is good to have, Captain. The honed blade and the whirling mace will fell our enemies. Now, we can come up on deck?"

"Yes. Quietly as you can. No speaking, we want to alert no one. Sound carries well over calm water and it's a quiet night."

In surprising silence, eighty gear-laden fighters climbed the fore and aft steps and clustered near the boats. Crews silently lowered the launch and longboat from the davits; the heavy boats touched the sea without a ripple. The rowers descended first followed by the two commanding ensigns, then ten fighters packed themselves into the launch, eight into the longboat. Once all was made secure, the ensigns took tillers in hand, whispered commands to the rowers, and they were off. A quarter-hour later, the boats returned empty. Meanwhile, boats from the other eleven ships passed *Caillech*, making no more sound than the light splash of oars. An hour after the final trip of *Caillech*'s longboat, the last of *Wexford*'s boats passed close by. When they disappeared into the darkness, Mairin ordered their lantern extinguished. Soon all of the ships had gone dark.

The wind died almost entirely; only a puff now and then trembled furled sails. *Caillech* rocked gently on a light swell. When the boats were stowed and lashed down and the ship secured for the night, not a sound was heard from any direction, nor could any light be seen from shore or sea.

Mairin's head throbbed, her back ached fiercely, and she was very tired. Mor, who never once left the deck during the operation, noticed her leaning on the starboard rail.

"Captain," he whispered, "please go below and rest till first light."

She turned and read the deep concern in his face, visible in the faint light of the binnacle.

"I will, Mor, I will. Fifteen minutes with my officers first, including you. Lieutenant," she said to Rowenna who was posted at her right elbow, "officers and crew chiefs to gather below. All hands below may take a meal, deck watch rotated down in three hours for a meal and sleep."

"Aye, sir," Rowenna acknowledged.

To Sithmaith, who was posted at the starboard rail, she said, "Lieutenant, please come below for the conference, ensigns too."

"Aye, sir."

Mairin straightened up with difficulty and with Mor close at her side, took the stairs one at a time, silently cursing Kennat Gailenga at every step.

The wardroom table was large enough for eight and could be partitioned off from the main cabin at the captain's choice. Though some captains preferred the wardroom to be closed off at all times, Mairin did not share this preference. On this occasion, however, she wanted a private word with her officers and crew chiefs and so the partitions were in place. Rowenna and Sithmaith took seats at the table, leaving the aft-most chair open for the captain. Mairin normally stayed on her feet in such meetings, rare as they were, but this time she took Mor's whispered advice and sat down.

"First," she began, "reports from all departments. Sailing Master?"

Nya Gailenga took a step forward. "Ship is becalmed in seven fathoms, sir, anchor in heavy muck and gravel. Glass is drifting down, I expect wind by morning, probably from the northeast, light airs building during the day. If I'm right we can reach the offing on schedule for our rendezvous."

Thorough, complete, and clear, Mairin observed. *I miss Cholmain's weathered face ... yet this is a fine sailing master too.*

"The western squadron would have a harder time with a northeast wind."

"Yes, sir, they would."

"Weapons Master?"

Eavan Sechnaill's powerful form was braced against the port bulkhead behind Sithmaith.

"As ready as we can be, sir. We ran five drills while you were out, er, recovering from your injury. Every bow is restrung, every sword is sharp, every ballista lubed and the sight calibrated. We have incendiaries at the ready as well."

Mairin nodded and turned next to Brigid Auteini.

"Launch and longboat secured, sir," the bosun reported. Your gig is on the davits for quick use, as you requested."

Next the watch chiefs, Ciar Loigde and Lavena Ulaid, reported status of their crews: both watches at full complement.

"Surgeon?" she asked Mor, who to her mild irritation hovered behind her chair.

"Sick bay is empty. Medical supplies are in order and ready for use."

Mairin's back protested as she twisted enough to make eye contact with him.

"Be ready to sand the deck, make sure it's assigned."

"Yes, sir," he answered with a grave look.

She took brief reports from ensigns and lieutenants, then allowed a moment of silence to intervene while she gathered her thoughts.

"All right," she said finally, "the ship is ready. Let me remind everyone what will happen tomorrow. Weather gods permitting, *Wexford* will weigh about thirty minutes after first light and lead us back through the shoals into open water. At that point the transports will detach and sail for their home ports of call. Warships will form in line ahead with *Caillech* at the front and make for a point fifteen miles north of Santander Bay, where we'll rendezvous with Captain Tredinnick's force.

If we see no enemy ships in the area, we'll sail into the bay in support of Captain Endean's attack. Questions?"

There were none.

"It's no secret," she went on, "that I was injured last night on the *Morrigan*. I lost some blood and my head feels like I had a terrific night in a pub." That drew relieved smiles. "I am blessed on this ship with an extraordinary wardroom and a superb crew that knows its duty, so I don't need to run around barking orders. Tomorrow will be a hard day. The ship itself will be conned by Lieutenant Briuin. Lieutenant Laigain will lead our deck force if we get into a fight, which I regard as likely. I'll focus my full attention on command of the squadron as a whole. I rely on my ensigns for signaling."

She nodded towards them, and each murmured a quiet "aye, sir."

"Everyone not on duty is to eat and then rest, myself included. We'll lie at anchor six hours and we need to use that time well. Neptune's blessing to all tomorrow. Lieutenants to my cabin, the rest of you are dismissed."

The ensigns folded back the partition and lashed its sections to the bulkhead. With the Bretan Fighters gone, the main cabin had been restored to perfect order. Some sailors sat at the long tables eating and talking, others lounged in their hammocks strung along the bulkheads, reading or writing. Mairin got up carefully and turned into the passage leading to her own cabin.

Once inside, Mairin sank into the cushions in front of the stern windows, pulled off her hat, and tried to relax knotted back muscles. A memory flitted through her mind: Conor's strong hands massaging her back, months ago, in very different place from this.

"Close the door," she said to Sithmaith, who reached behind her to comply.

"Rowenna, could I trouble you to wet a cloth?"

Rowenna grabbed a clean towel from a locker, soaked it in fresh, cool water from the tap, and handed it to Mairin, who pressed it to her eyes. It eased the headache, if only temporarily. After a half minute, she laid the cloth aside. She waved her officers to sit at the chart table.

"I know I look like hell," she began with a wan smile. "Despite appearances, my mind is clear. We've had very good luck so far, how long it will hold we don't know. I hope Nya is right about the glass and the wind, I'd hate to be stuck here. With any decent wind, we'll be able to make it out and help with the main attack. I have two things I need to say. First, Sithmaith, I'm pleased so far with your work as second officer. You've minded your tongue and gained the respect of the chiefs, masters and the crew."

Sithmaith reddened. "Thank you, sir."

"Second ... Rowenna, if we're in a fight and I'm unconscious or dead, you have to take instant command of the ship and notify Tierney to take over the squadron. You are clear on that?"

"I am, sir. Though I hope it will not come to that."

"No more than me," Mairin said. "Now, we all rest. Make sure I'm called before first light."

The lieutenants headed for their own cabins. Mairin pulled off her boots, climbed into the hammock, draped the cool cloth over her eyes, and drifted off. She did not hear the cabin door open minutes later. Mor padded in on stockinged feet, doused the lantern, draped a blanket over her, and left her to sleep.

The eastern sky glowed a dull rose-violet when Mor entered Mairin's cabin six hours later. She lay as he left her, and he regretted having to wake her. A concussion of that violence demanded more rest. He hovered over the rocking hammock for a second, then touched her shoulder.

"Captain," he said. "Captain." Her eyes fluttered open. "Lie still a few more minutes. I'm having tea brought in."

She beheld a blurry version of Mor's face. "Yes ... all right ... I hear you," she said through a dry mouth.

A sailor entered the cabin holding a steaming pot of tea and a basket of rolls, which she placed on the table. Mor thanked her and she slipped back out.

"Take it easy a minute or two more while I pour the tea. Then get up slowly, Captain."

Seeing out of the corner of her eye that it was still quite dark, she obeyed his request. In truth, the horrible throbbing in her head had faded to a faint, dull ache. She watched as he poured two mugs of tea and dumped tan-colored powder into one cup.

"No doubt that's mine," she said, easing herself to a sitting position. Her back protested, but her head did not flare with pain.

"Yes," he said, handing the mug to her. "A potion of muscle relaxer and headache powder, nothing to dull the senses. You feel better?"

"Some." She took a long draft of the tea.

"I need to take a quick look, Captain."

She set her feet on the floor and inclined her head. His fingers parted her hair.

"Swelling is down," he said. "I got you up a half hour early. You have time to get cleaned up and eat something."

"Did you sleep?"

"A few hours," he said, offering her a bread roll. "I've had a hard time sleeping since Dunlaith died, and I'm worried about Derdre. Troubling dreams, not as bad as yours but I wake up in a sweat. Did you dream?"

She sipped at the spiced tea and relished its soothing effect. "Not that I remember. Maybe a knock on the head isn't so bad for me."

"Not my prescription for bad dreams."

Mor set his cup down and gazed out the stern windows. Pink sky glimmered in reflection on a rising sea.

"I hate breaking out the sand barrels."

"We'll be lucky if no blood is shed this day."

"I know, Captain." He chewed absently on the roll. "If we gain the victory, we may have some relief on the seas for a time. And we can go home for the winter, which I want above all things."

"I think we'll beat them."

He nodded. "I think so too."

"I'll have to carry the full load today."

"You'll be fine. Take it slow for the first half hour. By the time you go on deck the herb powder will take effect."

She smiled and obligingly took a big bite out of the warm roll. He gulped the rest of his tea, saluted, and closed the cabin door behind him. Her mood lifted from the night before; the hot tea and nourishment spread energy into her aching body.

Her quarter galley's primitive shower offered a thin stream of surprisingly warm water. *Mor ordered it from the cooking stoves. I wonder if he actually slept at all.* Five minutes was enough to wash away dried sweat and blood. The fresh uniform tunic sagged appallingly until she cinched the belt in and pulled the fabric tight against her body. Her cabin was cool, so topside must be colder: she added a sweater and donned her uniform jacket over that. The mirror then displayed a figure that appeared strong and fleshed out, a triumph of clothes over weight loss. Her face looked drawn, nothing to be done about that. *Now I see why captains who serve till they're forty look sixty.* She added her hat, and as Mor advised, climbed to the quarterdeck a bit more slowly than usual.

It was a lovely morning. The cold breeze from the northeast was a blessing in itself: it meant they would not have to claw off tack after tack. Yet it would be the devil for Richard, on the opposite side of Santander, for he would have this freshening breeze straight on his bow. Though the sky overhead was clear and brighter stars lingered, angry crimson clouds on the eastern horizon promised a coming storm. From her memories of Admiralty training she summoned up the words in old English, *red sky at morning, sailors take warning, red sky at night, sailors' delight.*

Her four commissioned officers preceded her on the quarterdeck. Rowenna leaned on the starboard rail with Sithmaith next to her while the ensigns chatted quietly at the port rail. All of them straightened up and saluted as she made her way to the wheel.

"Good morning, Captain," said Rowenna. "All ships secure at anchor, dawn in twenty minutes."

"Very well. Let's hoist a mast light, white this time."

Sithmaith moved off to get this done.

"How are you this morning, sir?" Rowenna inquired.

"Much better, Lieutenant. We have a fair wind. What's the glass say?"

"I think the Sailing Master has it right, sir. Glass is falling slowly. The wind will strengthen yet it could shift on us too. Best we not linger."

"My thought exactly. Signal *Wexford* to get underway as soon as Captain Conmaicne believes advisable."

Rowenna passed the order, and seconds later the bright lantern above *Caillech*'s maintop began to flash. Matching lights came on along the whole line of ships. Jilleen's signal returned, *underway in ten minutes, all ships prepare to weigh.* *Caillech*'s crew leaped into smooth action. The capstan groaned, drawing the ship over the anchor. The deck watch swarmed up the masts and out onto the yards, readying topsails. Then a lookout reported *Wexford* was underway, followed immediately by *Rosc Catha.* One after another, the merchantman weighed and the line of ships drew out of the anchorage. Second to last was *Morrigan*, then *Caillech.* As soon as the anchor cleared the water, Nya Gailenga shouted commands to the tops, topsails dropped from yards and the ship gathered speed.

Mairin had no reason to interfere: her officers and crew knew their work. Twenty minutes of careful threading among shoals brought all the ships into clear water, just as the first rays of a blazing red sun poured over a rolling violet sea. The sight was startlingly beautiful and every sailor on every ship who could steal a glance did so. At their discretion the merchanters bore up until they were close-hauled heading north. Each of them signaled the Squadron ships farewell and godspeed and then flashed out a full suit of sails. Their task finished, they knew a storm was brewing and they wanted to reach a friendly anchorage.

As planned, *Caillech* and *Morrigan* drew up to the other two ships, then *Caillech* moved to the front followed by *Morrigan*, *Rosc Catha*, and *Wexford.* Jilleen Conmaicne doffed her hat as *Caillech* passed her ship.

Their point of sail was an easy one ... Richard's would not be. Mairin looked out over the sea in his direction and pondered his options. With the wind out of the northeast, he could gamble and sail almost straight east, hugging the coast close-hauled on the port tack. This would abandon the plan to rendezvous with her in open water though it might get him to the mouth of Santander Bay in good time. The risk would be negotiating shoals close to shore with an onshore wind that could shift further into the north. If Richard held to their planned rendezvous, he would have to beat upwind, yet the overall distance was not great and his warships were certainly weatherly and well-handled. Which would he choose? She stared at the chart for two long minutes, finally deciding that Richard would make for the rendezvous.

Back on deck, she told Rowenna of her call. "You agree, Lieutenant?"

Rowenna's pale green eyes played over the rising sea ahead of them. "I do, sir. Too much hazard hugging the shore in these conditions. I trust the charts well enough but these are unfamiliar waters to us. I believe Captain Tredinnick will make for open water."

"Get someone in the crosstrees with my best glass, I want him spotted as soon as possible."

Mairin strolled forward to the bow, now beginning to plunge and bite through rising rollers that would soon be whitecapped. The Spanish coast faded to a thin dark line on the horizon. Somewhere on that horizon almost directly to port lay the city of Santander. The landing forces would have moved into position during the night and would launch their coordinated assault exactly one hour after sunrise. Miles Endean's battle fleet should already be fighting its way into the deeper reaches of the harbor to threaten the city from the sea.

Overhead, high wispy clouds marched ahead of the coming storm, still many hours off ... or so she hoped. They could not end the day outside the harbor and near the coastline, that much was certain.

"Captain," said Sithmaith, suddenly at her elbow. "Lookout in the crosstrees reports sails, sir."

Forgetting Mor's caution, she bolted forward at Sithmaith's heels. The lookout, a wiry young woman with tousled black hair, landed with a thud from a long backstay-slide.

"Captain," she said nervously, waving a quick salute, "I count at least seven sail, maybe more, two points to starboard. Just the masttops visible, I see no flags."

"Thank you, good work." To Sithmaith she said, "go." The lieutenant seized the glass and assailed the mainmast.

Mairin joined Rowenna on the quarterdeck. "What do you think?"

"Either Captain Tredinnick sailed during the night," Rowenna replied, "or that isn't his squadron."

"I don't think it's him."

"Signals from other ships, sir," called out Ensign Velnowarth from the mizzentop. "They've all spotted the sails, sir."

"Acknowledge we have too, Ensign. Signal line abreast, *Wexford* and *Morrigan* to port, *Rosc Catha* to starboard."

"Yes, sir."

Ensign Auteini ran up the flags. *Caillech* and *Morrigan* luffed their courses for a short time allowing the other two ships to catch up and take positions along the line. Then courses were reset and the four warships gathered speed in a strengthening wind. Mairin stayed near the wheel, now in Nya Gailenga's own hands, with Weapons Master Sechnaill at her right elbow. Sechnaill knew the call to arms could not be long in coming.

Sithmaith made her way back down to the maintop and called to the quarterdeck.

"Ten sail, Captain, not Admiralty. I make them a Santander raiding squadron heading for home. Not hull up yet, pushing hard. I'm sure they see us too. I also have Captain Tredinnick's ships on the horizon directly off the bow."

"Can they be seen from where you are now?"

Sithmaith trained the glass forward. "The Santanders, yes, sir."

"I'm coming up."

Mairin climbed the mainmast and entered the top through the lubber's hole, something she could not recall doing in seventeen years at sea. Taking the glass from Sithmaith, she found the Santander fleet. Ten big ships under full sail, holds most likely bulging with spoils from raids along coastlines and attacks on merchant ships. If they were not stopped they would crash into the rear of Miles Endean's battle fleet.

She lowered the glass. "Your assessment, Lieutenant?" she asked Sithmaith.

"My guess is we can cut them off."

Mairin pondered the options a moment. "We can't guess. Follow me."

She climbed down carefully, her back now aching from the effort.

"To my cabin," she said as they passed Rowenna near the wheel.

The three of them gathered around Mairin's chart table which displayed the Admiralty's large-scale chart of the area.

"I have Captain Tredinnick here," Rowenna said, marking the spot with a pencil. "We are here, and the Santander group is here. Their speed will be at least nine knots, ours is seven, Captain Tredinnick's effective speed towards this point," she marked a point of convergence about five miles ahead of their current position, "is four knots, at best."

They all stared at the dots Rowenna had made and considered speeds and the wind.

"They might offer battle," Sithmaith said, "take us on ten to four and break off before Captain Tredinnick can help out."

"Possible," agreed Rowenna, "yet I think they'll try to pass on into the harbor. They must guess something strange is going on to see us here."

Mairin weighed the options. No way Richard would be able to intercept, the best he could do would be chase. In her mind's eye, she saw him pacing his quarterdeck, cursing the wind, knowing what was about to happen and powerless to do anything about it.

Ten against four, for a time. Yet they can't be allowed to pass.

"Bring the ship to arms," she ordered. "Heavy armor issued to all hands except sail handlers. Hoist the battle pennant and signal to all ships: we will attack."

My first entry in over two weeks. This morning I passed through the Rampart gate at Clonmel and began my journey towards Limerick. The weather could not please me more: overcast, fog, mist and light rain. As it is now growing cold, I have provided my faithful Seara with a wool blanket. I can tell she was bored with the stable and longed to be on the road again. I had only one day to spend with Sean, yet I am grateful even for this. How little time we have had together in the past decade! And how much I gain from listening to the product of that deep and penetrating mind. He misses Feth. And I miss Melvina Eogain, the steely hardness of her body and the softness of her eyes and lips! If the universe has any mercy to spare for me, it will grant me more nights with her. My last thought for now will be of Conor, who this day bears the burden I knew would someday be his to bear. He speaks often and longingly of Mairin, yet I wonder if she can be what he imagines her to be. Written ten miles out from Clonmel this 25th day of October, 999.

Journal of Oran Osraige

Chapter 33

It was a strange day, threatening in some way Oran could not quite define. Not that this was unknown terrain to him, far from it. He had traveled the road from Clonmel to Tipperary many times. The road itself was still a decent one, built to last by the Province and maintained until the withdrawal to the Rampart. In the youth of his grandparents, this road would have been well-traveled. The chimneys of cottages along the way would have spewed aromatic smoke of turffires. Light would have poured from windows to cheer up this dark day. Now these cottages were abandoned and roofless.

This was lovely country: the splendor of the Comeragh Mountains, already capped with snow, the shining and peaceful River Suir, the looming ruins of Cahir Castle. Wild horses still ran here too, left behind from the great breeding farms of old. Sometimes in open pastures he saw magnificent steeds, wild and wary, roving in bands of ten and twenty. Never would they let him get close, though. Each time he passed through the old county of Tipperary, his heart sank at how much of Eirelan and her history had been lost to the Twenty Clans in their desperate retreat.

So it was odd that he felt out of place in this familiar landscape. Out of place ... or watched? Yes, that was it: the feeling of being watched. He was wary of that feeling, for it was too easy to indulge the imagination when alone in such country and on such a day. He did not believe in a supernatural sense, yet often enough in his travels the feeling of being watched turned out to be the fact of being watched. He halted Seara in a place where the woods closed in on the road and let her snack on high grass while he sipped the last of his warm tea. Mainly, he was listening. His eyes were no better than the next man's but his ears were unusually sharp, whether from birth or long experience he neither knew nor cared. He could isolate sounds one by one. Seara chewing and muttering to herself. Water dripping from trees. The soft gurgling of a brook a few yards from the road. His own heartbeat. And one other sound, or rather chain of sounds. A snapping twig. Crushing of damp leaves in mud. Another twig.

In fluid motions that revealed nothing, he spoke softly to Seara and replaced his flask in the saddle bag. In the same motion he lifted out a compact crossbow, already loaded with a bolt and cocked with a safety latch on the trigger.

"Good grass, Seara?" he cooed. "Have all you like."

The safety latch off, he concealed the weapon between his body and the saddle. Another snap of a twig. Close. In his peripheral vision to the left, movement. Fifteen yards, maybe. He turned his body slowly as if to stroll in that direction ... and brought up the crossbow to rest on his left arm, his right eye staring down the sight. Partly obscured by a glistening green holly bush, a hooded figure halted ten paces away. The stalker's nervous panting created puffs of fog from warm breath striking cold, damp air. The face he could not see, nor did he spy any weapon raised in his direction.

"Halt where you are," he warned, "or you are dead."

The hooded figure did not move. The breathing grew faster, louder.

"Who are you?"

This time he heard a muffled, indistinct reply.

"I didn't get that. Push your hood back."

A hand came up to comply and then the figure disappeared into the brush. A sudden crunching of wet leaves and twigs told Oran his stalker had fallen.

Ye gods, the oldest trick in the book. I walk ahead to check this out and get a knife in my gut or a bolt in my forehead. He took a few cautious steps forward and stopped.

"That trick won't work, friend, not with me. Get up."

No answer. *Curse my luck. I can just get on Seara and ride away.* As if to urge him in that direction, Seara whinnied loudly behind him.

"Yes, I get your opinion, little lady," he said under his breath.

He sighed and started forward, crossbow aimed where the hooded figure fell. The holly bush obscured his vision. He expected at any moment to see something deadly hurtling at him. Two steps away, he leaped forward, crossbow aimed ... and saw the hooded figure sprawled face down in the tall, wet grass. The outstretched hands were those of a woman.

He laid his crossbow down and knelt beside her. Gently he turned her onto her back. She was young, that was certain, not much into her teens. Her face was bruised and mud-streaked, her long, chestnut hair soaked and tangled. Her eyes were closed.

With a dry cloth from his pocket he mopped her face and then examined her hands. Rough, with blood under the nails. Her sweater left a gap above her trousers, exposing a strip of belly that was yellow and purple with bruises. This woman had been beaten and could even now be dying.

Deciding it was best not to carry her, he raced back to Seara and pulled out his medical kit, food, water, and a blanket. He covered her to the neck, dampened a towel and touched it to her eyes and forehead. After some fumbling, he found the capsule of smelling salts and waved it twice under her nose. Her eyelids fluttered and then opened. Light brown eyes stared up at him in sheer terror. She tried to rise and he pushed her back gently.

"Please don't hurt me," she sobbed. "Please don't hurt me."

"It's all right, I'm a friend." He took hold of her hand. "I almost killed you with my crossbow, you shouldn't have come up on me like that. Now lie still until I can decide how badly you're hurt."

The terror in her eyes lessened and the hand that he held squeezed his. He smiled and laughed lightly.

"Ah, that's better, young lady. Now look at this face. Do I look like someone who's going to hurt you? Of course not. Can you drink some water?"

"I think so."

He let go of her hand, raised her head slightly and brought the canteen to her lips. She drank greedily, then sank back, breathing hard.

"Thank you," she said. "I was so thirsty. Who are you?"

"We'll get to that in a minute. Let's start with your name and how you came to be out here, alone."

"My name is Bethia MacLaren."

"And?"

He studied her while she briefly pondered her answer. How old was she? Not a child, certainly, maybe fifteen? Probably quite pretty under better circumstances: a wide mouth, friendly eyes when the fear faded from them, a delicate, straight nose and rounded chin. Her clothes were torn and soiled yet well-made of fine wool.

"And I was lost."

"Uh-huh. Well, I'll accept that for the moment."

From his food bag he pulled out a fresh roll already packed with butter ... planned for his dinner. He handed it to her. "Hungry?"

She nodded and dove into the roll.

"I'll talk while you eat. My name is Oran Osraige, from Kilmore Quay in the Province. I know you were not lost, at least that's not the main reason you're out here alone. I also know you're from Belfast or thereabouts, from your accent." He looked down at her belly. "You've been beaten, recently."

Though she kept eating, tears filled her eyes.

"Right, let's not get into that. Before I get you up I need to know if you're hurt in some way I can't see."

"I hurt everywhere," she said. "I threw up some blood yesterday."

"Well, that's not good. Would you be willing to lie flat and let me touch your ribs? I promise that's all I intend to do, Bethia."

She studied him a moment, then nodded and laid back. He reached under the sweater and felt the ribs on both sides, as high as decency allowed.

"I don't feel anything broken," he said. "And your color is better. Can you stand if I help you?"

"I think so."

He set the blanket aside, crouched and threaded his right arm under her armpit.

"Very easy, let's try it."

She gave out a muffled moan of pain as he lifted her. She was not as small as she looked lying down, just a couple of inches shorter than he was.

"Bethia, look at me."

Her pupils seemed normal size and her color did not fade. He led her to Seara.

"Lean against my horse."

He retrieved his crossbow, blanket and saddle bags. "Feel a little better?"

"Yes, I think I can manage now. Thank you, for helping me."

She turned and took an unsteady step away from him.

"Wait a minute," he said, laying a hand lightly on her shoulder. Her whole body froze as if he were about to assault her. "I'm not leaving you here alone. You wouldn't go a hundred yards."

"You've done enough. You don't owe me anything."

She turned to face him, head down.

"I'll tell you the situation straight," he said. "I'm on my way to Limerick to scout the position of an army gathering there. I can't abandon you here and I can't give you my horse. Taking you back to Clonmel now will waste more time than I can afford. That leaves taking you with me. But it's up to you, I don't force anyone to do anything."

She shifted nervously from one foot to the other. "I came from the army you're going to spy on."

"Really?" *Now that could be very useful.* "When did you leave them?"

"Three days ago."

"You were beaten by someone in the army?"

She nodded. "My father hit me. Then I tried to leave and got caught by sentries."

"And you got away somehow."

"Yes."

"I'll tell you what," he said, "how about coming with me? It won't be for very long, then I'll get you back to the Province. That is where you were trying to go, isn't it?"

"I was just wandering, really. I didn't think the Province would let me in."

"I have to keep moving. You'll have to decide now whether to trust me or no."

She walked a few unsteady steps along the road, and for a moment he thought she would keep on going. Then she turned and came back to stand in front of him. From somewhere inside her cloak she produced a small, shiny knife.

"I know how to use this, when I'm stronger. And I can shoot a bow too."

"Did you have one?"

"Yes," she said, her voice trembling. "A fine one. They took it."

He tilted her chin up so her eyes met his. "You should know that I won't harm you."

"I know." She put the knife back in its hiding place.

"One other thing, Bethia," he said in a deadly serious tone. "I tell funny stories when there is someone to tell them to. If you don't laugh, I'll have to cast you loose."

Fear danced across her face. Then she realized he was putting her on. She managed a weary smile.

"I haven't laughed in a long time, Oran," she said. "I'll do my best."

He helped her up onto Seara, who seemed pleased enough with the new, lighter rider.

For the last hour of their travel, Oran led them off the main road leading towards Tipperary, a large town he avoided after his first visit there almost ten years before. For reasons he could never uncover, a city that was once a gem of Eirelan (or so Sean told him) was now a haven for all sorts of unpleasant folk, including road bandits who prowled the countryside robbing and more often than not leaving their victims for dead. So he skirted the village of Cahir and led them into the foothills of the Galtee Mountains. He liked to imagine that the rolling verdure of these ancient smooth-topped peaks concealed tombs of long-dead giants who roamed Eirelan in a mythic past. More than any place he had seen, these mountains spoke to him of time reaching beyond man and beast alike.

Bethia said little in the three hours since he found her lying in the grass, and it was just as well. Oran had much to ponder on his own. Of all the times for him to be saddled with someone needing help! Many times in his travels he had chanced upon persons injured or starving or just plain lost, and he always made sure they were given aid or could find their way again. Never had he been forced into taking someone with him.

He led them into a deep valley that followed a rushing stream. In a small open space on the bank, concealed by dense woods, he halted Seara and helped Bethia down. An hour later, they sat together beside a warm, crackling fire. Oran cooked hot cereal, poured hot water into mugs, and emptied a few spoons of powder into each mug, telling Bethia to stir it up.

"What is it?" she asked.

"What does it smell like?"

She sniffed the fumes. "Apples?"

Oran nodded and sipped from his own mug. "A little taste of home. My mother makes that, apple cider powder with spices added. Don't ask me how she does it. Reminds me of home when I'm traveling."

Bethia sampled hers and nodded approvingly. "Good." After another sip she said, "Tell me about your home, Oran?"

"Sure," he replied. He set aside his cereal bowl and cradled the cider mug in his hands. "All you want to know. I have a question first. When I found you today, why did you keep coming towards me and not answer when I called out? You must have seen my weapon."

"I saw it."

"And?"

She sighed and brushed tears from her eyes. "I didn't care if you killed me."

He stared into the flames and nodded. "I thought it was something like that. Do you trust me enough to tell me what happened?"

She started to sob.

"Would it be all right," he asked, "if I came around to your side of the fire?"

"Okay."

Oran slid around and wrapped his arm around thin, shaking shoulders. From his pocket he took a clean cloth and dabbed the tears from her face.

"How old are you?"

She took a deep breath to steady herself. "Fifteen."

"You traveled with the Ghaoth Aduaidh?"

"From Belfast. With my mother and father and two brothers."

"Your father is a fighter?"

"And one brother, Sloane. Tormaigh is only ten."

"Isn't it unusual for whole families to travel with the army?"

She shook her head. "Not this time. They plan for us to settle on Province lands."

"That might be a bad plan."

Bethia jumped as a nearby owl suddenly announced its presence.

"Just a friendly owl," Oran said. "Go on."

"One night, my mother told my father she was going back north to her father's house in Donegal and taking me and Tormaigh with her. My father struck her hard and told her never to say that again. I tried to protect her and he hit me too."

"Why did your mother want to leave?"

"I don't understand it all, Oran. My mother said the soldiers will die for nothing. She worried we would not be safe if something happened to my father and Sloane."

"But you left on your own?"

"I did. After my father hit me I wanted to get away from him. Three nights ago when everyone was asleep, I took my bow and a pack and left camp. And I almost made it past the sentries. They were drunk. They ... they ..."

Sobs surged up in her again and he drew her more tightly inside his arm.

"It's all right, Bethia, I know what they did," he said. "You don't have to say."

With his free hand he stroked her hair. She fell silent, crying and shaking. For a long while he held her next to him. Now and then he tossed a small dry branch on the fire, while the owl hooted contentedly and the stream gurgled, paying no attention to them.

"Anyway," she said when she could find voice again, "I killed one of them with my knife. The other two laughed and pinned me down and tore at my clothes. They meant to kill me when they were done with me. Then I heard voices and the sentries ran off. I got away and just kept going, I had no idea which way was which. Hitched a ride on a wagon for ten miles. Then I really did get lost." She paused and swallowed hard. "What they did to me ... that's why I didn't care about dying."

"We won't talk any more of that," Oran said firmly. "You're with me now and no one dies in my care." He dried her tears again. "Now, I took you along on your promise to listen to my stories and to laugh at the right times. So far you have not laughed once, so you are not keeping your bargain with me."

He watched her struggle between a pain that would plague her for years and a longing to feel some relief, however fleeting. Finally a faint smile won out. She wiped her eyes with his cloth and turned to him.

"I'll do better," she said. She took a swallow of her cider. "I'm not a child. You wouldn't recognize who I was a week ago."

"The thing is, Bethia, you are *exactly* the person you were a week ago. I'd like to get to know that person, and when we get back to the Province there are others who will want to know you. Or you can find your way back to Donegal, if that's what you want."

"No. I never want to go back there. I want a different life for myself."

Oran made them some more cider, then stood and walked a few steps towards the stream to stretch his legs. Its swirling waters sparkled red in the light of their campfire.

"Bethia," he said, "you must *never* let yourself believe that evil done to you makes you less human. You are still Bethia MacLaren, a person of value, and you have much to offer the world."

"Why did they hurt me, Oran?"

"I don't know the answer to that," he said, battling the rage that welled up inside him. "I see much cruelty in the world, and much love and kindness too. Some people think one can't exist without the other. Maybe that's right. Or maybe there's an evil god somewhere that meddles in human affairs." He rejoined her at the fire, where she sat watching him with eyes that now seemed a little less filled with anguish. "Finish your cider, then get some sleep. When I'm traveling I rest and doze but I have to keep watch."

She laid down, rested her head on a saddle bag, and pulled a blanket over herself. Her eyes were already closed when she said, "thank you, Oran."

Her breathing soon settled into the deep, slow pattern of sleep. Oran slid back a few feet and braced his back against a big tree as he always did at night. His knife and loaded crossbow lay within inches of his fingertips He pulled a blanket over himself against the chill of night and watched the fire die out to embers.

The night grew steadily colder and a steady wind rustled the branches of the trees. The clouds dissipated and a few brighter stars twinkled through branches. Once he heard the eerie shrieking of a fox, and often the hooting of the owl hunting somewhere nearby. Otherwise, this was a silent place as he knew it would be. Three times before he had camped on this very spot. Once when he was eighteen, once when ... when ...

His hand clutched the knife and his body tensed for combat. *What is that noise? Ah, yes, I have company!* Bethia had shifted her body and moaned in her sleep. Now she breathed easily again. His thudding heart slowed and his body relaxed. Overhead the clear sky began to glow. *Time to get ready to move.* He sat awhile longer under the warm blanket, pondering courses of action and making choices among alternatives he did not like.

Finally he roused himself with a cold shudder and fed the fire's glowing embers with twigs and branches. The fire rekindled slowly and then blazed up hot and noisy. *Something far back in our history*, he pondered, *that makes us feel safer when a fire lights up the woods around us, warms our cold bodies and crackles in our ears.*

He fetched a pail of water from the stream and found Bethia awake when he set it on a grate over the fire. She sat up and rubbed her eyes.

"Good morning," he said. "How do you feel?"

She rubbed her bruised stomach and ribs. "Not so bad. Rested anyway. I didn't sleep at all for two days. Can I make the tea and oatmeal?"

"For yourself," he replied. "I'm riding into Cahir to get you a horse. I have a friend there who will do almost anything if the price is right. I shouldn't be that long, it's only three miles to the town."

A look of panic crept into her face.

"Bethia, you'll be fine," he said. He crouched and took hold of her shoulders. "No one will find you here, and I'll be back soon."

He saddled Seara and rode off through the woods, letting the little mare gallop when the trees gave way to meadows that once had been tilled for crops. By the time he reached the edge of the town, the violet eastern sky was tinged with pink. His aged friend Aodhagan complained bitterly about being awakened at this early hour, then quieted at the clinking sound of Province coins in Oran's pouch. In short order he rounded up a horse, saddle, blankets, and saddlebags, and sent his wife to the house of a friend who made and sold clothes. She returned with an armload of women's garments and looked more pleased than her husband at the sight of five shiny gold coins offered in payment. A brilliant sliver of sun edged over the horizon as Oran rode Seara and led a frisky gelding back into the woods.

He could smell his campsite long before he could see it. He found Bethia bent over something cooking on the campfire.

"Is that fish?" he cried, dismounting.

"Yes," she replied nonchalantly. "I hope you like trout."

He tethered the two horses to a tree and handed her the bundle of clothes.

"Not sure these are your style," he said. "The good part is they're new and clean."

She set down the flat stick she was using to cook with and took the bundle from his hands.

"You bought me clothes?"

"I did. Go off and change and we'll bury what you have on. How did you get the fish?"

She looked at him with friendly derision.

"You're a scout, you must know how to sharpen a stick with a knife and stab them as they go by. I cleaned them with my knife."

"Yes, well sure. I just didn't expect, er—"

"That I would know how," she finished for him.

"You change," he said lightly, "and I'll get this served up for us."

When she returned in clean and surprisingly well-made clothes, he barely recognized the battered, suicidal girl of yesterday. The close-knit wool sweater fit decently as did the wool trousers, and the cloak draped over her arm would keep her warm in the colder weather he knew was coming. They sat and ate hot fish and drank tea, and he found her breaking into a smile more often.

"I feel so much better," she said, rubbing her arms to savor the feeling of the fresh clothes. "You'll see, I won't be a drag on you. I know how to cook, I can sew, hunt with a bow—if I had one—I can read and write, and throw a knife. And I make up poems."

"Do you now?" he replied with raised eyebrows. "My friend Conor and his mother Liadan are both poets, too. You'll have to recite one for me tonight."

"My poems are probably not much compared to theirs," she said, poking at the dying fire with a stick. "They help me to keep going when I feel bad. I wrote one this morning in my head."

Oran reached into his tunic and took out a sheathed knife that he handed to Bethia. She slid out a gleaming ten-inch blade.

"Something else I bought from Aodhagan," Oran told her. "I want you to carry it on your belt."

She turned it over and over in her hands while a tear dripped down one cheek.

"Thank you, Oran. I'm not used to getting gifts."

"Not exactly a gift," he said. He leaned back against a tree, relishing a last bite of the fish. "It's for our protection. *If* you actually know how to use it."

Detecting the challenge in his voice, she got up and walked about twenty paces into the woods. There she used the knife to carve a crude "X" into the trunk of a white-barked poplar. She walked back to the campsite, turned, and hefted the new knife a few times in her hands. Then, squeezing the blade in the fingertips of her left hand, she raised it to shoulder height, paused a second, and threw with a quick, snapping motion. The blade flew faster than Oran could follow with his eyes. The tip buried itself deeply into the cross of the "X."

"Better than I could have done," he admitted. "Remind me to stay on your good side."

She retrieved the knife, slid it back into its case, and fixed the strap to her belt.

"Shouldn't we be moving out?"

"Right. We have a long, hard ride today." He got to his feet and started packing up their gear. "The gelding is a little spunky, you might say. Would you rather ride Seara?"

She gave him a scalding look.

"Sorry. The gelding is yours. He needs a name."

She paused while washing the frying pan in the stream. "I'd like to call him Vengeance."

"Hmm, a harsh name for a horse. Still, it's your choice. Vengeance it is."

They rode out to the northeast, avoiding the roads, and soon found themselves surrounded by the spectacular scenery of the Glen of Aherlow, framed by the Galtee Mountains on the south and the Slievenamuck Ridge on the north. In the middle of the Glen, Oran called a brief halt to rest and water the horses. Bethia gazed all around her and breathed in the cold air deeply.

"It's so fair and peaceful here," she said. "I would like to just stay here and live, wouldn't you, Oran?"

"Aye, one of my favorite places in all of Eirelan. There are a few folk still living in these lands, though not many since the Twenty Clans left. Who can say of the future? Maybe a time will come again when you can live here in peace. I hope it does."

With gentle pressure on her shoulder, he turned her to face him.

"Bethia, you do understand that my mission is to scout the size, position and plans of the army your father and brother will fight in?

The Province means to destroy this army, all of it. You can still turn
around and ride off, wherever you want to go. You don't have to come
with me."

She looked up at him and seized his hands in her own.

"*You* don't understand," she said. "I left because I wanted to. My
mother will escape with Tormaigh, one way or the other. I hope Sloane
makes it out alive, he's been a good brother to me. And I want death
for two certain men in that army. I'll do anything to see that happens."

"Then you ride with me."

They mounted again, rode past the tiny village of Lisvarrinane
where smoke rose from the chimneys of a few small cottages. When
the lovely glen passed behind them, Oran led them northwest over
open country where they saw occasional crumbled remains of farm-
houses and towns and no inhabitants at all. Bethia reminded him of
his promise to talk about his home, so he told her of his childhood
in Kilmore Quay, of his friendship with Conor, of his hopes for the
future. At times he saw her smile in his direction, at other times she
looked straight ahead, her face rigid with anger and sadness.

*What a strange fate has come upon me! I have always traveled alone, and now
I have a companion. If a companion had been offered to me, would I have chosen
a slight fifteen-year-old girl? Hardly. A thirty-year-old Blade twice my size, more
likely. Still, she rides well, cooks, and throws a knife a damn sight better than I
can. Maybe she's a decent poet. Sean has a saying he quotes from one of his dusty
old books, "accept the unexpected, it may be good fortune in a clever disguise."*

*What was it I said to Sean? Something like, "the only thought that depresses
me is that men and women still kill each other." That wasn't quite right. How
depressing it is to think of what happened to this poor girl. I cannot even fathom
her suffering. Always there is a balance, writes Uinseann Laigain. In the name
of balance in the world, may those men who tortured Bethia MacLaren be struck
down, may they die slowly and in agony for what they did to her.*

I arrived here in Clonmel three days ago, this is my first chance to write a short note. We have been blessed with decent weather to prepare the army. The camp stretches along the south bank of the Suir for nearly a mile. Kellen and Melvina are drilling and training the soldiers without letup, as they must, while Arvel works the horse-archers in open fields to the south of our camp. Without these three to help me I would not sleep at all, little as I can sleep anyway. Recruits from the West are trickling in, more each day. Some of them never even saw Feth and her band, they are coming along with friends and relatives who did. Triona is here too, I have seen her once in the medical tents. I am not happy with myself for what happened at Rosslare, and thankfully it cannot happen again now that we are in camp. I tell myself that no harm has been done. A poor excuse for what I did.

Private Journal, Conor Laigain

Chapter 34

"General. General Laigain. Wake up, sir."

Bradaigh Cumain shook Conor's shoulder.

"What? Yes. I'm awake," Conor mumbled.

He forced his eyelids open and beheld the concerned face of his young companion. Bradaigh straightened up and took a step backward. Conor swung his legs over the edge of the cot and let out an "ah" of pain. The old hip injury, he reminded himself, from his first year in the Line of Bows. It always stiffened up sleeping outdoors on a cot.

"Are you all right, General?" asked Bradaigh with a frown.

"Oh, yes, sure, Bradaigh," he replied, getting to his feet. "What time is it?"

"Five, sir. As you requested."

"Five, yes, that's what I said."

"I have hot water on the fire outside, sir."

Conor smiled warmly at his dedicated aide, one week on the job. Bradaigh had come into camp the same day he had, talked his way past sentries, and offered his services as an aide. Conor remembered him well from the fight at Wicklow, a strong-looking boy of fourteen, saddened by his brother's death, who kept his head in the tower during the Dubliner attack. Bradaigh had trimmed his straw-colored hair and now proudly wore the red tunic and black belt of the Blades, with a single silver pin on his chest signifying his service on the general staff of the army.

Conor took a step towards Bradaigh and studied his face. "And how much sleep did you get?"

A faint smile towards his own cot. "Enough, sir."

"I'm sure."

Conor pulled open the tent flap. The welcome balmy respite from autumn's cold winds and chill rains held so far. Overhead, stars blinked their friendly light and a crescent moon hung lazily near the horizon. The camp was quiet at this early hour. Across from his tent, light glowed in the tents of Kellen and Melvina. The sprawling mess tent near the riverbank never went completely dark. At this early hour, cooks would be filling giant pots with honey-sweetened oatmeal for breakfast and pounding out biscuit dough. Conor sniffed the air. Yes, the first batch of morning biscuits was baking. The scent made his mouth water.

Bradaigh stepped past him to the fire he had built. Using a rag pulled from his pocket, he lifted the hot brass pot from its hook and carried it inside.

"I'll make the tea, Bradaigh," Conor told him. "Can you ask my commanders if they'd like to join me?"

"Of course, sir."

Bradaigh proudly donned his black tam and strode with a purpose towards their tents. *He has an easy stride,* Conor noted, *and a fine build. Three years and he'll be ready for the Line of Blades. I hope he will not have to serve, will not have his unmarked young body decorated with scars like mine.*

His aide returned minutes later followed by Kellen and Melvina, both wearing plain sweaters and trousers. Kellen had already collected biscuits and Melvina set on the table a family-sent jar of blueberry preserves.

"You both look as tired as I feel," Conor observed as they took chairs around the table. "Up early or up late?"

"Oh, early," said Kellen "Though it does seem like I just laid down."

"Same for me," Melvina said, leaning forward and rubbing her eyes. "I bedded down early enough and then stared at the tent roof for two hours."

Bradaigh served out tea and biscuits with jam, then backed away towards his cot.

"Oh, no you don't," said Conor, his mouth already full. "Sit down and eat. I need you at full strength."

Bradaigh obeyed with a show of reluctance though Conor knew his aide was pleased to sit with them. He moved his desk chair over and served himself. Conor could not resist having a bit of fun. He waited till Bradaigh took a huge bite out of a biscuit and then asked, "what's our numbers situation, Bradaigh?"

Bradaigh looked up in panic. Conor and his comrades laughed and Conor held up his hand. "Swallow first!"

Bradaigh grinned, swallowed, gulped tea, and then replied, "Blades, twenty-two hundred fifty-three as of late yesterday, Bows sixteen hundred twelve, and a hundred twenty Welsh horses, sir."

"New recruits from the west?"

"Over seventy so far."

"Message for General Laigain, marked Private."

The quiet, treble voice came from a messenger silhouetted in the tent's open flap.

Bradaigh got up and accepted the envelope from the shy boy, who beat a quick retreat. Conor set down his mug and held the envelope next to the lantern.

"From my mother," he said, tearing it open. It read:

Conor, sorry we missed each other at Rosslare. I closed up the house and asked Aonghas and Shelagh to feed our horses and make sure the cats have water. Then I rode to Clonmel and took a room at the Inn of the Autumn Leaf. Can you spare time for an evening meal? Send a note to the Inn. The food is very good, perhaps better than your camp kitchens. Love, Mother.

"Everything OK?" asked Melvina.

"Fine," he replied. "She's at the Autumn Leaf in town and wants me to come for dinner."

"Go, by all means," said Kellen, pausing in his attack on another biscuit. "Melvina and I can handle things here. You need a few hours out of the camp."

"And you don't?" Conor said. "No, we all go, tonight. The army won't self-destruct if we're away for two hours. Bradaigh will know where we are, it's barely five minutes' walk from here."

"Would it be all right to ask Triona?" Kellen asked.

Oh, just what I need. But how can I say no? It would look very odd.

Conor pasted on a smile. "Triona? Of course, of course."

"I'll issue a pass," said Kellen affably.

A trumpet sounded the camp's wakeup call.

"It's settled, then," Conor agreed, "the Inn tonight. Bradaigh, send a message to my mother, tell her four of us will come for dinner at seven o-clock."

"Sir," said Bradaigh. He served out the rest of the biscuits, then retreated to his writing desk in a far corner, lit his lantern and started writing.

Kellen stood and stretched side to side, then bent over from the waist and straightened up.

"Doesn't feel too bad," he said, a hand on his damaged side. "Conor, when can we expect to hear from Oran?"

"He'll stay out until he sees signs the army is ready to move, then he'll fly down here as fast as the little mare can carry him. I'd guess no more than a week."

"So we'll have, what, two days after we hear from him to get the army in the field and into position?" asked Melvina.

"It should be enough," Kellen said. "The roads are dry and hard."

Bradaigh showed him the message he had written. Conor nodded and the young aide ran out to find a messenger.

"I'll take my leave, Conor," Melvina said. "First drills at five-thirty."

She set off at a fast pace for her tent. Kellen lingered behind.

"Conor, Bram is here," he said quietly.

"He must not be happy under your command," Conor said, trying to sound nonchalant.

"That concerns me nothing," replied Kellen coldly. "I can't turn him away, he reported with orders. I just wanted you to know."

"Maybe it would be best if we had it out, once and for all."

Kellen's warm features took on a hard cast. "No, it wouldn't. I don't think you appreciate how important you are to the rank and file fighters here. Morale is high, but it won't stay that way if you're hurt or worse yet, killed. I mean it, Conor. Stay away from him."

Conor smiled bleakly at his friend. "Chances are I won't even see him. Keep him away from Triona."

"I'll slice his balls off personally if he goes anywhere near her."

Now the camp was coming alive: tent flaps flew open, bells clanged, and nearby, gangs of cooks muscled massive iron cauldrons of oatmeal over roaring fires.

"I'll be off too," said Kellen, touching Conor's shoulder. "Tonight, then."

"Train them hard, my friend," said Conor, his eyes sweeping the camp. "Train them very hard."

"No need to worry on that score," Kellen said with a smile. "The Blades will be ready. Make sure you tell me if there's any word of Mairin?"

"Instantly."

"I'm very worried about her, Conor."

Conor ran a hand through his too-long and tangled hair. "So am I."

Kellen made off for his own tent. Conor stood alone briefly, hands in his trouser pockets, trying to settle the feelings coursing through him and clear his mind for the long day ahead. Bradaigh returned on a run, his boots fairly flying over the soft grass.

"You didn't have to run," said Conor, wrapping an arm across the boy's wide shoulders. "My mother won't even be up yet!"

"Duties to perform, sir," Bradaigh said, only slightly winded. "Remember, you have a meeting with the Quartermaster and his staff at six."

"The Quartermaster?" Conor groaned. "You don't say."

"Yes, sir, the Quartermaster. Time for you to clean up and dress."

"Is he in a good mood, by any chance?"

"I doubt it, General. I'll try to schedule him later in the day, next time."

The Inn of the Autumn Leaf offered surprising elegance for this modest border town. The innkeeper, Brenna Sechnaill, proudly informed all guests that the inn had been operated by her family for three centuries with ne're a single complaint from a guest. The structure did not impress from the outside: a narrow brick front, a steep brick staircase leading to an ornate oak door, a post-hung sign bearing in burned-in letters the name of the establishment and two painted autumn leaves, one red and the other yellow. The door led into a nondescript anteroom for the hanging of wet cloaks and depositing of muddy boots. Just beyond that, a guest found himself in a cozy parlor dominated by a massive hearth, furnished with overstuffed chairs, varnished tables, and four large paintings, autumn scenes done in oil, each wild with color and fine in detail. The back of the parlor opened through an archway to an equally-elegant dining room seating ten. A staircase at the rear of the dining room led upstairs to six comfortable and spotlessly clean guestrooms. It was a commonplace in Clonmel that the bath serving these rooms was the best for many miles around, offering blistering hot water and soft towels of the best linen.

Though Conor and his three companions were famished and anxious to taste the products of the Inn's kitchen, they graciously accepted Brenna's tour of the Inn. Liadan trailed behind, wearing a smile and rolling her eyes—out of Brenna's sight—at the wildest exaggerations of the Inn's illustrious past. The tour ended with a detailed explanation of the bath's complex hot water system. Then portly Brenna returned them to the dining room and disappeared into the kitchen.

"I'm glad we came dressed," said Conor softly to his mother. "Sweaters and trousers would have been frowned upon!"

"Oh, not really," Liadan replied. "Domnall and I used to come here now and then, when we were first married. Brenna and Gildray make quite a show of things, but they welcome anyone who takes off their shoes in the foyer. I can tell she's bursting with pride to have the army's leaders here in full dress!"

Conor had to admit with a tinge of guilty vanity that they did make an impressive threesome. His own general's uniform was a variation on Padraic's choices. A solid black wool tunic with long sleeves was drawn at the waist by a gold belt matching a gold cape. His own hard-earned decorations were pinned on the left side of his chest, the gleaming gold eagle of his rank on the right. Kellen wore the crimson tunic of the Blades, with silver belt and cape, his rank shown by a silver medallion of crossed blades inside a gold crest. Melvina's tunic and cape were deep blue and her belt sky-blue; her emblem of rank was a silver longbow with arrow drawn inside a silver crest. Her decorations, Conor noted, included five for personal valor and three for serious wounds in battle. He idly passed a hand along the heavy scar on his face. *We all bear the marks. Luckily her face does not show hers.*

And then, Triona. The physician's garb did nothing whatever to conceal her tall, striking beauty. Long waves of medium brown hair cascaded onto a pure white tunic. A maroon belt drew attention to a slender waist beneath a not-so-slender chest. Her service medallion, a simple cross of white gold, was pinned to the front of a maroon, open-fronted jacket. *It is more than a man should be asked to bear,* he cursed silently. He managed not to walk close to her at any time on the way from the camp to the Inn.

The dinner fare did not disappoint. Brenna served the courses herself, though her chef-husband occasionally popped his head in the room to accept compliments. They were joined mid-meal by four other guests, two well-dressed merchants and their wives, who tactfully avoided questioning their military dinner companions about the army and its plans. Conversation over after-dinner wines in the parlor turned to literature; both Liadan and Conor were pressed into reciting a sonnet of their own. When the big pendulum clock struck nine, the two couples sensed that the other four wished to speak alone and retired to their guest rooms. Brenna added wood to the hearth, filled their glasses one last time, and left them alone.

"Camp food will taste pretty awful after this," said Melvina, holding up her wine glass. "Thank you, Liadan, for this wonderful meal."

Liadan waved a hand. "It's the least I can do. I feel so helpless sitting around with stacks of paperwork near a warm fire while you're working twenty hours a day in the camp."

"It wouldn't be so bad," said Kellen, slumped deep into the padded chair, "if we didn't have such a relentless general. Liadan, you raised a hard man in Conor."

"Oh, hard as stone," Conor retorted with a grin. "It was a lovely dinner, Mother. Thank you. We all needed a short break."

"Brenna will talk about this dinner for years," said Liadan. "Your should know that she and Gildray have three children, all of them are with your army now."

"Oh," said Conor, his stomach tightening a little. "She didn't say anything about that."

"She told me before you arrived. She would have talked about them all night in other company. Not in front of you."

Kellen leaned forward and set his empty glass on a table.

"Conor, I'm heading back. I'm getting sleepy and I still have hours of work to do."

"Me too, I'm afraid," Melvina said, getting up. "And you two should have some time alone together."

"Likewise," said Triona. "I have the early shift tomorrow."

For a brief moment, Triona caught Conor's eyes and he saw hurt there. Then everyone said goodnight, leaving Conor alone with his mother by the hearth. Brenna reappeared, collected empty glasses, refilled theirs and left the bottle on a table.

"I can't stay long, Mother," Conor said, fingering the narrow stem of his glass. "I have to get back too."

"I understand," she replied, eyeing him with a look of curiosity.

"What?" he asked. "Did I spill on my uniform?"

She sighed and put down her glass. "Conor, my son, we share many traits. We both write poetry, we both tend to melancholy ... and we both have a keen sense of intuition about people. True?"

He shifted in his chair and did not look up.

"I guess that's true, mother," he said warily.

"It did not escape my notice that you avoided Triona all night. You sat furthest from her, never met her eyes, and rarely replied to anything she said."

Trapped. What's the point of denying it?

"So should I assume you two had an argument at Rosslare?" Liadan pressed. "What was the argument about?"

Then he did look up. "You know perfectly well there was no argument."

"Yes, I suppose I do," Liadan said with a sigh. She took a sip of her wine. "Rather the opposite, I would guess."

"Yes."

She swirled her wine in the glass and gazed into the fire through rose-colored liquid.

"Say something, Mother. You're not as disappointed as I am, that much I can tell you."

"I'm not disappointed in you, son," she said, turning back to face him. "How could I be disappointed in a son who sits here in the uniform of a general, loved by his friends and respected by everyone who knows him?"

Conor stared sullenly into his drink. Liadan put her glass down and reached out to hold his forearm.

"Conor, you are a young man of twenty-eight years. You love a woman who's almost never home and even when she is, you don't have much time alone. And you're not yet married to her." He started to interrupt and she waved him quiet. "Oh, I imagine you've already asked her! And no doubt she said yes. If there's any justice in the world, you'll be happy together some day. Meantime, don't tear at yourself for whatever happened. Triona is young and beautiful. So beautiful she reminds me of Etain when we were young. To my eyes she is about as desirable as a woman can be."

He nodded sadly. "It was just more than I could handle. After a half dozen ales, alone with her in that house. I was tired and lonely. Kellen went to bed drunk, and ... well, it happened."

Liadan smiled and her hand closed tighter on his arm.

"I know you feel that you somehow hurt Mairin, but after all, we're made to carry on our race! Without that powerful desire, where would we be? So long as it's between the two of you, there's no real harm. Your father and I were engaged for more than a year, and I had a bit of fun then."

"You didn't!"

"Of course I did. I was young and sweet-looking once, you know. I never asked, but I'm sure Domnall sowed some final wild oats, too. That never meant a thing to either of us. After we married, we were faithful to each other. As you will be. Making love to a fine woman you care about is nothing to be ashamed of, son. Will it happen again?"

He hung his head in his hands. "I want her, that's true enough. Now we're in a different place and the chance will not come up. Kellen would not see it the way you do."

"No, I don't suppose he would."

"I don't expect to see her again, after this campaign."

"Then it was only one night, and you should remember it for what it was, exciting and satisfying. Then leave it be."

Conor reached over and placed his hand over Liadan's.

"Thank you, mother. For understanding. I wanted to tell you."

"I know, dear son. You have other burdens to bear than this one."

He rose to his feet and embraced her. Then they separated, her hands on his arms.

"I'll be here as long as you are," she said. "I know you can't come often. Any word of Mairin?"

"None," he said, moving towards the foyer. "Aideen told me about her mission, the one that wasn't authorized by the Council."

"Your sister knows what she's doing."

"I know she does."

He donned cloak and hat and opened the Inn's door to a blast of cold wintry air.

"Aideen said the strangest thing to me before I left her office," he said. "She said she was proud of me."

Liadan froze, a smile tugging at the corners of her mouth.

"And what did you say?"

"I said I was proud to be her brother."

"She's always has been proud of you, Conor." Liadan's eyes brimmed with tears. "She has a hard time telling you. I'm glad she did. Good night, son."

She kissed him on the cheek.

"Good night, mother," he said, kissing her in return.

The pleasantly cool autumn night had indeed vanished, and Conor was glad of the cape which he drew tightly around him. A sharp wind from the north whistled down the street, stirring fallen leaves and bits of paper. The big clock in the town square showed it was past ten: pubs were closed and the street, though well-lit, was deserted. He made his way at a slow pace towards the camp, pondering his mother's reaction to his revelation.

He found Bradaigh slumped over at his writing table, a stack of reports and messages under his arms. The boy awakened as cold air swept through the tent.

"Oh, sorry, sir, I should not have been sleeping," he said, straightening up and rubbing his eyes. "I was trying to get all these sorted before you got back."

Conor began stripping off his dress uniform. "Bradaigh, go to bed, now. We'll get an early start again at five. I'm tired too."

Bradaigh headed towards his own cot.

"Two people came to see you," he said while he tugged off his boots. "A big man in the Blades, said he knew you."

"Name?"

"He didn't say. Not very polite about it, either."

"That's all right, I know who it was. Who else?"

"Surgeon Bairrche stopped here after your dinner. She left a private note there, on your cot."

Conor sat down on the cot and opened the folded note from Triona. *Conor, you didn't have to treat me like I had a disease all night. I wasn't going to blurt anything out. It must have seemed strange to your mother that you would not even look at me. Aren't we still friends? T.*

He closed the note and folded it over again. His sigh must have been audible throughout the camp.

"Everything all right, sir?" asked Bradaigh from beneath his blanket.

Conor pulled off his own boots and donned wool sox against the night's chill.

"You're almost sixteen, Bradaigh?"

"Yes, sir."

"You notice girls, then?"

"Indeed I do, sir. For some time now."

Conor got up and went to Bradaigh's writing table, where he put out the lantern.

"Dealing with girls can get quite complicated, Bradaigh."

"So I've heard, sir."

Conor heard the boy's lighthearted mock. *No doubt he knows plenty.*

"Sleep well, Bradaigh. I'm stepping outside for a breath of fresh air."

With the camp lights extinguished and the night clear and cold, the full glory of the Milky Way stretched over his head. Stars by the million, he remembered from his boyhood lessons. "How tiny we are," said his teacher, "compared to the immensity about us." Another memory surfaced, Grandfather Uinseann speaking to him one night when he visited Duncormick: "Whenever you feel yourself important, Conor, go outside at night and look up at the sky. It is best that we feel small." *Grandfather, I feel small enough tonight.*

He gazed out over the vast camp, at the tents stretching off into the darkness, the vague figures of sentries moving deliberately along the fence. Over the rustle of the wind came the occasional cough from a tent, and further off, the barking of a dog in the town. The wind whipped at him and tomorrow his soldiers would battle stiff fingers and cold feet.

They would fight soon, before the heavy snows came, of that he had no doubt at all. They had to be ready, as ready as he could make them. All his responsibility now, all those souls looking to him to keep them alive and bring them victory. This time, he knew, victory would be paid for dearly. He could not keep them all alive. Possible he could not even keep himself alive.

Two people came to see me, Bradaigh said. One, a man who hates me for reasons that don't even make sense, who would like nothing better than to see me dead at his feet. The other, a warm and tender woman who made love to me and whom I have hurt and now owe an apology. What a strange people we are, Grandfather.

*Feargal let us bed down with our horses in a smelly old stable. It
seems we always end up in barns! And for extra coins he found
hay and oats for our horses. Bandon Town was like Feargal said,
dreary and hostile. No one would listen at all. Feargal also told
us that the roads south and west from Bandon are terrible, so we
are turning northwest towards Crookstown and Macroom as I
originally planned. We'll deal with Macroom when we get there.
Then it's on to Killarney and Tralee. We have to be reach Tralee
in ten more days to get transport on a Squadron ship back to
Dungarvan. Gwen and Ionhar are getting closer all the time, so
are Derdre and Keegan. That's fine for them but it also makes
me miss Sean more. I hope he misses me too.*
Journal of Fethnaid Laigain

Chapter 35

Feth and her companions recrossed the Bandon River on Feagal's
ferryboat and rode northwest through rolling hills and thin forests
towards Crookstown. At times it was difficult to follow the remains
of the ancient road, which snaked about in ways that defied any sort
of logic. Gwen hazarded a guess that the road followed long-forgotten
property boundaries. Ten miles of easy riding brought them to a region
of well-kept small farms and thence to the town itself. Feth called a
halt as the broad country path changed into a rough cobblestone street
with thatched-roof cottages on either side. Further ahead, they could
see more substantial buildings of stone and brick.

The street seemed strangely deserted for mid-morning on a cool,
clear autumn day. They dismounted and let the horses graze on high
grass.

"Now this is odd," said Keegan, voicing all their thoughts. "No
signs of destruction, decent farms nearby, a clear day ... and no one in
the streets. I don't hear a sound."

Indeed, as he fell silent, all they could hear was a faint rustle of the morning breeze and the occasional snort of their own horses. No smoke rose from chimneys despite the chilly air.

"Should we go around and make for Macroom?" asked Derdre. "One way or another, it doesn't look like we'll find many recruits here."

Ionhar pulled at his thick red beard. "I'd like to find out what's going on."

"Your call, Feth," said Gwen.

Feth hesitated, weighing the potential danger against her own curiosity.

"If we go through, I suggest we button up our armor," Keegan warned.

"I may regret this," she said finally, "but let's try it, buttoned up like Keegan said."

Mounted again and fully armored with weapons at the ready, they set the horses at a slow walk down the deserted street towards the center of town. Every door and shutter was closed and some were nailed shut. Here and there, a small cart or wagon rested by the side of the road; one cart held a few apples that they fed to the horses. The neat central square of the town was fronted by boarded-up with signs swinging in the wind: "Liam's Leather Goods" and "Dealla's Bakery" and "Lugaid's Fresh Meat."

"I don't think we're in danger here," said Feth, pulling off her helmet. "Those apples weren't rotten. There were people here, and recently. Now where are they?"

Ionhar sniffed the air. "I smell smoke, yes?"

"Yes," said Gwen, "turf fire. From upwind," she pointed towards a street leading north from the square.

"Let's go," said Feth.

They headed down the empty street at an easy trot. The smoke-smell grew stronger block after block. At the edge of town they found its source: the chimney of a small thatched-roof cottage with flower-boxes hung beneath its two front windows. The shutters hung open and the front door rested slightly ajar. They dismounted in the street and tethered their horses to a wooden lamppost.

"Feth, let Ionhar and me go up there," Keegan said.

Her first impulse was to say "no, I'll go." *Don't be silly*, she scolded herself. *Send the big guys.*

"All right," she agreed. "We'll be ready here."

Covered by the three archers with arrows at half-draw, Keegan and Ionhar advanced together to the cottage's front door.

"Hello?" Keegan called out from the threshold. "Anyone inside?"

"Of course there's someone inside," returned the instant, irritated answer. "I'm inside. Who do you think is tending this fire?"

The female voice was high-pitched and crackly. Feth, Derdre and Gwen relaxed their bowstrings and joined Keegan and Ionhar at the door. Feth took an extra step forward and pushed the door fully open. An old woman sat on a rickety chair in front of the hearth, a poker in her bony hand. Her gray hair was wispy yet not unkempt; her sweater and long wool skirt were clean and mended. Many, many years showed on her lined face, though alert blue eyes fixed on Feth.

"If you mean to kill me," the woman said harshly, "do it quickly. My time is near anyway."

"We don't mean to kill you," Feth said. She laid down her bow on a window ledge. "My name is Fethnaid. May we come in to speak with you?"

"Fethnaid of the Twenty Clans, eh?" said the woman, eyeing Feth's armor and uniform. "Come in, I suppose. What you'll be wanting with old Glynis Cruachain I surely can't guess."

Derdre and Gwen followed Feth into the cottage's single room, brightly-lit by the two windows at front and two more at back. Keegan and Ionhar had to duck to make it under the low-hanging lintel. They found the cottage clean and well-stocked. Tall stacks of dry peat took up much of the back wall. The wall to the left was one long larder, its floor-to-ceiling shelves neatly stacked with crates of flour, wheels of cheese, boxes of dried meats, and jars of preserves. A small cot occupied the space beneath the front window to the left. A table and benches took up the room's center.

Glynis motioned them towards the table. "Sit there," she said, giving the fire a last poke.

They took to the benches as she asked, with Feth sitting nearest her. The benches creaked ominously under Keegan and Ionhar.

Glynis turned her chair in their direction.

"As I said, my name be Glynis Cruachain," she said, "and I am in my eighty-first year. Old enough to remember the Twenty Clans and how they left us to the wolves. So you will pardon an old woman if she wonders what brings you to her home now."

"We've come from the Province of the Twenty Clans," Feth admitted, "though we were not all born there. Ionhar Raithlinn and Gwen Cennedi," she nodded towards each of them, "are from towns far from the Province. My other friends are Derdre Dal Reti and Keegan Cholmain. My full name is Fethnaid Conmaicne Laigain and I am in my eighteenth year. We're honored to be under your roof, Glynis Cruachain."

"Young you are to be so armed and armored," Glynis observed. She reached out and ran her long, gnarled fingers along Feth's bracer, then stared with rheumy eyes at Keegan's scarred face. "You have fought long and hard, though you too be young."

"Yes," Keegan said. "Seven years in the line."

"Hard times," she sighed, staring at the hand-hewed surface of the table. "For all, it seems. Colder too, so much colder than when I was young as you."

"Why is the town empty?" asked Gwen. "So far we found no one but you."

"Afore I answer," said Glynis, her suspicion returning, "I should hear what brings ye here to Crookstown."

"We expect to fight a great battle soon," said Feth, meeting the woman's watery gaze, "and we need fighters to help us."

"So what I have heard is true," Glynis mused. "Even the mighty Province be hard-pressed these days. Imagine that."

"My mother was killed two weeks ago!" Derdre cried. "Don't make light—"

Glynis held up a blue-veined hand. "Take no offense, young woman, I meant none. And I grieve for you, truly I do. Forgive me if I feel little sympathy for the Province, hiding these many years aback your great wall while the rest of us suffered. I have lost my husband, three of my five children, four more yet of my grandchildren."

"I know there is bitterness here in Cork," Feth said after a moment of silence, "for things that happened before I was born. I can't answer for that. If I live long enough, I'll do what I can to make amends."

Glynis smiled with raised eyebrows. "Will you, now? Strange to hear those words from a Province soldier."

"There will be no chance for any of us," Gwen said, "if we can't destroy the army of the Ghaoth Aduaidh. There will be chaos, everywhere. You may not live to see it, Glynis, but your children and grandchildren will."

Glynis nodded slowly, turned and poked her fire absently, then faced them again.

"So I have lived to see the day the Twenty Clans come asking for help," she said without rancor. "What a queer place the world is, how things turn about. 'Tis easy to forget what matters in this life. Easy to be angry, not so easy to forgive."

She fell silent, drifting into memories. Feth waited a moment before intruding.

"Glynis, can you tell us why you're the only one here?"

She looked up, startled. "Oh! Yes. I almost forgot you were here. Well, they're all gone to Macroom. I don't like the Macroomers or their town, so this year, I stayed put. Too old to move about now. My children and grandchildren will be safe, or so they think."

"Why would they be safe there?" asked Ionhar, leaning forward on his forearms. "Macroom is not far away from here?"

"Nay, but eight miles or so down the road," she replied. "Macroom is a place of old castles and much water. With help from the towns and farms nearby, they rebuilt the castle walls and connected them, and in some places the water itself protects them. Strong as your Rampart it may not be. Safe enough from raids until the snows come."

"So," said Keegan, "they have armed men and women there?"

"Many," Glynis replied. "They swagger and shout and believe themselves invincible. I can't say about that. A noisy, dark place, and I love my cottage. So here I stay. If all goes well, the townfolk will return in a month. Perhaps I'll be here to greet them, perhaps not."

"What would happen to us," asked Feth, "if we went there?"

The woman's face darkened. "T'would not be a healthy thing for you to go there. They might not let you past the gate. If they do, they might not let you out again. Five more fighters like you they could use."

"You said *many* fighters," Keegan observed. "How many?"

"Over a thousand, when all have come in from the countryside and the towns."

Feth's hands clamped onto the table top. *A thousand fighters!*

"They'll not fight for you," Glynis warned, "unless you possess a magic spell to work on them."

"I have no magic in me," Feth admitted. "None at all."

Glynis studied her a moment. "I am not so sure. There is more than one kind of magic in this world. If you had time, I would tell you about the different kinds of magic."

"Time is what we have least of right now," said Feth. She stood and reached out to help Glynis to her feet. "If I live into the spring, would you let me come back and learn about magic?"

"Of course," said Glynis with a surprised smile. "Remember I am eighty-one, Fethnaid. And the wild ones may have me yet."

"We can take you with us," Ionhar said. "You could ride on my horse."

"Nay, nay," she said, reaching for a fresh brick of peat. "Here I stay. Good fortune to you." She turned and smiled at them. "If you go to Macroom, ask for my oldest son Liam."

"The leather shop," said Keegan.

"The same. He is important in Macroom too, does much business there."

"Thank you for speaking with us," Feth said.

"You were taught well, Fethnaid," said Glynis. "Come back, if you can."

Outside they found that the fair day was gradually giving way to overcast carried on a damp, chilling breeze. Glynis's Cruachain's shutters banged shut as they walked their horses down the empty street. After two short blocks the buildings thinned out and a dense forest closed about the road. Feth called a halt at the edge of the forest and they ate a standing lunch.

"What are you thinking?" Keegan asked her. "Try it, or go around to Killarney?"

Feth unfolded a map and pressed it against the side of her horse. Gwen and Derdre held the corners against the breeze.

"Not easy to swing around it," said Ionhar, his thick finger tracing the road ahead. "The road goes right between this water and that, and who knows where a bridge might be except this one leading into town?"

"They might let us pass," Derdre said, without much conviction. "From what Glynis said, though, we might come out the other side minus our weapons and our armor. And maybe our horses too."

Feth listened and nodded, then folded up the map and tucked it inside her saddle bag. She took two steps away from her friends, her eyes searching the deeply-shadowed road ahead. *I am uncertain once again. Was my father ever uncertain? Is Aideen? Hard to imagine my sister standing here like I am, wondering what to do. Four other lives besides my own are at risk here.*

She felt Keegan's heavy hand on her shoulder. "Feth, we can't pass this by. If Glynis is right about their numbers, we have to try."

She turned and read agreement in the eyes of the others.

"Then we go," she said, "with standards flying."

Into the forest they rode, with Feth and Gwen at the lead, Derdre and Keegan next, and Ionhar guarding the rear. The contrast with the morning ride from Bandon could not have been more extreme. In place of a pleasant road wandering through open meadows and thin woods, they were oppressed by a narrow path snaking between tree trunks. Oaks and maples and cedars and poplars, their leaves turned and ready to fall, obscured the gray sky and left them riding in a mossy-smelling gloom. They saw and heard no one and encountered no signs of human habitation, save for one broken wagon wheel, long rotted and rusted.

"What a gloomy place!" cried Gwen in an especially dark grotto. "Reminds me of a haunted path near Fahamore Town."

Feth looked over to see if Gwen was spinning a yarn. "Trying to make me more edgy than I am already?"

"Not at all," Gwen said, shaking her head. "That place scared us to death. Though I think the grownups might have told us fireside tales to stoke our imaginations."

"It isn't really haunted though?" Derdre asked.

"I think it is, in some way."

"How do you know?"

"When I turned twelve, I accepted a dare to walk that whole path in the dead of night, maybe two miles, by myself."

Ionhar edged his horse up behind Gwen's. "I need to listen carefully," he explained with a wry smile. "This might be a story I can use!"

"Don't laugh," Gwen scolded him, "or I won't tell it."

"We want to hear it," Derdre said. "Or at least I do."

"Me too," Keegan put in, "if Derdre promises to hold my hand tonight in the dark."

Gwen glared at him but went ahead with her tale.

"It was late spring," she began. "My friend Lanty, the boy who dared me, walked with me to the edge of the woods. At the last minute he changed his mind and took back the dare. He liked me and didn't want me to get hurt. I said nothing doing, Lanty, you opened your big mouth in front of the other kids and now I'm going. I thought he might offer to go with me, but he was too scared himself. So I took my candle lantern and plunged in. It was a night with no moon and it was summer so all the trees had leaves. A hundred paces in and without that lantern I could not have seen my own hand in front of my face."

Gwen paused as the horses negotiated a washed-out section of the road. Knowing now she had a captive audience, she took her time about going on.

"I think I walked about half the distance and nothing happened. I felt pretty cocksure then so I stopped for a minute to tie my shoe. And then I heard it."

She delayed again, enjoying the uneasy silence of her friends.

"What I heard was music, very faint first. Instruments alone and then voices too. I froze in my tracks and tried to figure out where it was coming from. The trouble is, no one lived in those woods and there were no towns within miles of where I stood. Even though I stayed put, the music and singing got louder on its own, as if the performers were coming towards me!"

"After a minute or so I could make out the words they were singing. The words were old Gaelic, I could barely make them out. The song was about a girl who had a baby but no husband. She went to her father's house for shelter and he turned her away into the cold night, so she and her child died in the snow. When the song ended the instruments played on awhile and then faded out too. I stood still a long time, waiting for the music to come back. When it didn't, I started walking again."

"I reached the other side, circled back on the roads, and got home very late. My father was furious until I told my story. Then he was quiet. So was everyone else. The next day, I wrote down all the words I remembered and played the melody on my flute. That night I played and sang the song for all the oldsters in the town. No one had ever heard it. Even the minstrel who was at least eighty and seemed to know every song ever written said it was unknown to him."

Feth felt a cold chill creep up her spine. "Did you ever walk the path again?"

Gwen smiled. "Every summer till I left home for the Province. I never heard that song again, or any music at all."

"What do you think it was?" Keegan asked, without a trace of skepticism.

"I don't know, Keegan," Gwen replied. "Maybe my imagination made it all up for me ... though how it made up the old Gaelic words and a strange melody, I will never know. There is much mystery about the world, you know. You in the Province are so busy worrying about tomorrow—with good reason, I admit—you don't have much time to wander the woods at night and listen for echoes of past ages. My father said to me that we Celts have lived here nigh on five thousand years, and certain it is that something of us has soaked into the earth beneath our feet. I think what I heard was an echo from the past, a song sung in Eirelan ages ago. Maybe the scene it described actually happened near those woods. Maybe I walked over the bones of that young mother and her infant."

"Do you think that was some of the magic Glynis Cruachain had in mind?" Feth asked.

"Maybe it is," Gwen replied. "If we come back here again, we can ask her."

"A good tale indeed," Ionhar said. "I'd like to retell it, especially when I go home again."

"Feel free," Gwen said. "Just don't change the truth of it."

"I will not," Ionhar promised. "I never change true stories."

They moved on through the oppressive, dark forest, talking little, each of them pondering the meaning of Gwen's story. The road twisted and turned through deep glens for a time, and then, quite suddenly, the woods gave way to an open meadow covered by rolling mist and fog. Feth held up her hand and they drew together in a line.

"We must be near the water, I can smell it," said Derdre. She drew her cloak tighter around her throat. "The town can't be a half-mile ahead, somewhere in that fog bank."

Ionhar pulled a kerchief from his belt pouch and wiped drops of mist from his face.

"Not to be overcautious," he rumbled, "but I suggest we put on our helmets and have weapons to hand."

"Helmets, yes," Feth replied, "and the standards. No weapons. It's obvious enough as it is that we're armed. We're not seeking a fight."

Keegan moved up parallel with Feth, carrying the Celtic Cross next to her Red Dragons banner. Though the mist-soaked pennants drooped so that emblems could not be seen, they held them high nonetheless. Into the fog bank they rode. Once inside it, they could not see ten paces in any direction.

Suddenly Feth heard a sound that did not come from their horses. She reined in Ioan so fast that Gwen and Derdre almost bumped her from behind.

"Voices," Keegan whispered. "Up ahead. Lots of them, mixed up. We're hearing the town, can't be more than a quarter mile ahead."

They started their horses forward again at a slow walk. So far as they could tell, the decently-graveled road here ran straight ... right up to massive doors ten feet high. A palisade of six-foot sharpened stakes stretched away from the doors into the fog. Their cautious approach was watched with interest by two crossbow-armed sentries posted on a platform level with the top of the palisade.

Felt halted them ten yards away and they all dismounted. Before Feth could speak, one of the sentries shouted, "wait there."

"Not exactly welcoming," Keegan muttered.

"They don't know why we're here," said Gwen sotto voce. "At least they didn't take aim at us."

Ten minutes passed. Then they heard the sound of a heavy bar being slid aside from inside the gate. The sturdy doors creaked open and one woman clad in leather armor strode out toward them. A bow and quiver were slung on her back. Gray-brown hair pulled back over her ears glistened with moisture. Her stride was quick and agile.

"Gods above, she's an archer!" Gwen said.

"Not a happy-looking one either," added Ionhar.

The woman stopped two strides in front of them and scanned them briefly. Dark eyes peered out beneath heavy brows; a pale scar creased her chin from one side to the other.

"My name is Aife Luachra, I command the Fighters of Macroom. You are?"

Confident, formal ... but not threatening.

Feth offered a shallow bow and gave their names.

"You are the leader?" she said to Feth with raised eyebrows and a glance toward Keegan.

"We're companions," Feth replied, "but I speak for all of us, yes."

"Three Bows and two Blades," Aife commented. "You're a long way from home, soldiers. You must know that Macroom is a guarded town and the gates are now closed until the danger of raids passes with the coming of winter. We will let you pass through unhindered, if that is your wish."

"We're grateful for your offer," said Feth, "but we did wish to speak with you before moving on."

"About?"

"About the army of the Ghaoth Aduaidh."

Aife nodded with a guarded look. "The North Wind, yes, we know about them. As you can see," she swept her arm towards the palisade, "we're prepared. And we expect that the attack will be directed at you and not at us, as it was three years ago. You'll forgive us for not being sorry about that."

Hold your temper, Fethnaid. She doesn't have all the facts.

"We'd like your help in fighting them."

"And why would we want to do that?"

"To protect yourselves."

"That doesn't seem to follow."

"I think I can show that it does," Feth said, keeping her tone breezy. "Would you let me speak to the town's leaders?"

"You're speaking to one of them."

"Of course. I'd like to speak to all at once."

Aife seemed to argue with herself for a moment. "I could consider that, but I need some reason."

Now it was Feth's turn to pause.

"Tread lightly," Derdre whispered. "Try the numbers."

"When we last fought the Ghaoth Aduiadh," Feth said, "how great was their number?"

Aife's eyes narrowed. "We heard two thousand, perhaps a few more. You mauled them badly a mile outside your fort at Dungarvan."

"Did any of the defeated trouble you?" Feth asked.

"They did, in bands of a hundred or so. Our defenses held."

"We know they are coming with three times two thousand."

Aife's whole body stiffened, though she struggled to keep her face impassive.

"Six thousand? That cannot be."

"My friend speaks the truth, Aife Luachra," said Ionhar. "Six thousand, or more yet than that."

"This time," Gwen added, "they travel with siege ladders, battering rams and catapults. And with their families too. They mean to have our lands, once and for all."

"And if they can't get them," Feth continued, "they will turn west and take yours."

A long silence intervened. Aife turned away for a moment, staring towards the town shrouded in fog. Then she faced them again.

"Come in and shelter for the night. We'll hear you out." She stepped forward and ran her fingers along Feth's bow in its saddle holster. "A fine bow," she observed. "You have skilled bowyers in the Province."

"Not the longbow I'm used to," Feth said. She pulled out the recurve and handed it to Aife. "We shoot these from the horses."

Aife hefted the bow and drew lightly on the string.

"No doubt you are skilled in using it," she said, handing it back Feth.

"No doubt."

Aife nodded, then turned and led them through the gates into the fort-town of Macroom.

Their quarters for the night turned out to be a vacant corner of Macroom's food warehouse, stockpiled with enough to supply three thousand people for thirty days. A dark, windowless place to be sure, yet it was dry and clean. They were given a large flask of water, a smaller one of ale, a bag filled with cheese, bread, and dried fruit, and a single oil lantern. It cast a pale reddish glow over the mounds of sacks and boxes and gave their faces a pink tinge.

"I don't like being separated from the horses," grumbled Ionhar. "I've grown quite found of cranky old Breasal."

"I take Aife's word they'll be given back," Feth said. "I think we have her respect."

"I was getting tired of barns," Gwen said. She sprawled out comfortably on a pile of soft flour sacks. "I'll take dry and quiet for tonight."

"It may not be that quiet," Derdre commented. "Warehouses and rodents go together, my friend. Expect to hear some scurrying about when we put out the light."

As if on cue, they all heard a faint meow, then another, lower in pitch.

"The ancient guardians of warehouses!" Keegan laughed. "Not many rats around with that crew at work."

Feth stared into the dark corners, searching for the hidden hunters. "I miss our cats at Rosslare. Mother won't let them in the house, it makes her sneeze, so I always go out to the barn to play with them."

"Considering what these people think of us," said Keegan, sitting cross-legged near Feth, "this is better than we could expect."

Derdre made a makeshift chair from three crates. "We'll have to be very careful what we say because they're proud of their defenses. If all you're worried about is a roving band of fighters, they would hold up. Aife told us they've fought off two or three hundred at a time. With the advantage of the palisade and the lakes, a thousand fighters could hold this place against a determined attack."

"Not against the army of the Ghaoth Aduaidh," Keegan said, "even if we bloody their nose first."

"No," Derdre agreed, "not against that."

Feth took out a brush and made an attempt to yank tangles from her matted hair.

"I've been thinking about the numbers," she said. "We were told there are over three thousand people inside this fort, and Aife nodded when I mentioned a thousand fighters. A full third of everyone here? That means virtually everyone not a child or too old is called a 'fighter.' The question is, how many of them can be as strong and skilled as Aife?"

"Half, perhaps," said Ionhar. "Yet even five hundred strong fighters might hold this place against a large band of raiders. They have to be convinced it may be different this time."

"Even if they believe what we say about the size of the Ghaoth Aduaidh force," Gwen said, "they might still decide to wait and see what happens in the battle. It's possible, isn't it, that we kill each other off to the last man and woman?"

Keegan paused in his re-stitching of a torn saddle bag. "Sure it's possible. All they need here is for enough enemy fighters to die, and they're safe. They know we'll kill many of them even if we lose or draw in the end."

Feth turned the hairbrush over and over in her hands.

"We *need* these fighters," she said. "I have *got* to find a way to convince them."

Ionhar was about to comment when double doors on the far side of the building creaked open on rusty hinges. From the shadows emerged a short, silver-haired man dressed in a black sweater and gray wool trousers, with a blue-dyed leather cloak thrown back over hunched shoulders.

"I am Liam Cruachain," he said, coming into their midst. He shook each of their hands in turn. "I understand you spoke with my mother this morning."

"We did," replied Feth, "and we found her well. We offered to bring her here with us, but she said no."

"It was kind of you to offer," Liam said ruefully. "She has her own mind about staying in her cottage." He stared briefly at the stack of weapons and armor. "I've traveled often inside the Province, selling my leather goods at open markets. So I have no special animosity towards you or your people. Not an opinion widely shared, I can tell you."

"You know why we're here?" Feth asked him.

"Yes, Aife told me. You will get your chance to speak to the assembled leaders of Macroom and its allied towns."

"What kind of reception can we expect?" Derdre asked.

Liam shook his head. "Not terribly friendly, I have to say. It's already known that the offer of the western clans to make a formal alliance has again been turned down, and this fanned old flames of resentment."

"It was a tie vote," Feth said in a small voice, "and there's still a chance it will succeed."

"Be that as it may," Liam replied, "it hardened hearts that our envoys Gilvarry and Rainait tried for months to soften."

"Will you support me?" Feth asked with an outstretched hand.

"I can't promise that. I'll listen with an open mind, which is more than you'll get from most of the others. Aife seems worried by what you told her and her opinion carries much weight."

"The danger is real," said Ionhar. "We're not here for ourselves alone."

Liam moved in front of the huge fighter. "I know that, Ionhar. Truly I do. The alliance among all peoples of the south and west, I believe in. Stripping our defenses now, that I'm not sure about."

He stepped back and turned to face them all. "They'll come for you soon. I warn you that tempers will be tried. Be prepared."

He turned and departed into the shadows.

A full hour passed before a young woman with a sword hanging from her belt came to retrieve them. Outside, a cold heavy rain pelted down and Feth was grateful they had to walk only a hundred yards through slick mud to their destination, a long, low building with a broad, lantern-lit porch. They hung dripping oilskins on the porch and followed the woman fighter inside. It was warm, at least: a big hearth at the back of a large, square room blazed with a hot fire. Four amber-glassed oil lanterns hung from rough-hewn ceiling beams. A single square table made of thick, ten-foot planks took up the room's center. Three sides of the table were occupied; five chairs nearest the door had been left vacant. Feth took the center chair, Keegan to her right with Derdre next to him, Gwen to her left with Ionhar by her side.

Liam Cruachain, now dressed more formally in a splendid leather jerkin, sat at the far side of the table opposite Feth, with Aife Luachra at his left hand. On his right, a red-faced man well past middle age, with powerful forearms and a dense gray beard, scowled in their direction. Feth scanned the rest quickly: ten in all, five men and five women, the majority middle-aged and a few white-haired. None looked like they had come for a pleasant fireside chat.

"I will lead this meeting, though you should know," Liam said to them, "that we are not a government. Those seated here come from Macroom, Crookstown, and other towns and villages and farms in this region. You have met Aife Luachra," he nodded in her direction, "who commands all our fighters. On my right is Sleven Orbraige of Taiscumar, chief of our fort defenses. The rest may say their names if they wish to speak."

"My name is Fethnaid Laigain," Feth began, fighting to keep her voice steady with every eye in the tense room upon her. "My friends are Keegan Cholmain and Derdre Dal Reti, of the Province, Gwen Cennedi of Fahamore Town in Kerry, and Ionhar Raithlinn of Creagh, in Cork."

"Welcome," Liam responded. "Speak what you came to say."

Before Feth could start, a white-haired man with a patch over one eye said, "Fighters not of the Twenty Clans?" He pointed a bony finger at Ionhar. "Why do you fight for them?"

"Your name, sir?" Ionhar asked politely.

"Uscias Glendamnacht, of Toames."

Ionhar leaned back and spread his great hands wide.

"My answer, Uscias, is that I am a man of stories. Stories written down in Gaelic and passed on these many centuries in Eirelan. They tell of our culture and our beliefs down through the ages. I believe that if the Province falls, all of Eirelan will turn wild and violent, and soon my little town in the south and its farmers will be no more. The books will disappear and men will live only from hand to mouth. I wish more for my children, when I have them."

The man seemed taken aback by Ionhar's heartfelt answer. He turned his gaze on Gwen and said, "and you?"

"My town," said Gwen, "is not far from Tralee. My father and mother and I are musicians, and I think music as I know it would disappear when violence and want is everywhere. So in a way, I am fighting for my own family."

"Very admirable, if foolish," Sleven commented derisively from across the table.

Feth cast a worried glance at mighty Ionhar—but the big man's ruddy face showed no reaction beyond a nod. He would not rise to the bait. Nor would Gwen. The room fell silent.

"We are not official emissaries," Feth said, turning her gaze from left to right. "As you can plainly see, we're soldiers. But we're here as ourselves, a singer, a musician, a story-teller, a potter, and me, just a plain girl from Rosslare. We want families and children and a future that isn't full of fear and killing. The same as you."

"It's a waste of my time, listening to this child," scoffed Sleven, his black eyes on Feth.

"There will be none of that!" Aife snapped. "Friend or no, she stands in the Line of Bows and that is honorable. Mind your tongue, Sleven."

The big man's red face flushed to purple ... but he offered no challenge to Aife. Feth waited a moment to see if anyone else spoke. No one did. A couple more faces seemed receptive to listening.

Now, all hangs in the balance. The room is hot, my tunic is soaked with sweat that chills me, and some part of me wishes I were back in Rosslare. Yet I must do this. It may be the difference between death and life for my people.

She felt Keegan's reassuring hand rest lightly on her back.

"I did not intend to appeal to you as friends," she began. Left to right, she met each pair of eyes focused on her. "I know you have grievances against the Twenty Clans that go back generations. I am only eighteen and I have no way to change what has gone before. In a short time, our army will leave the Province and meet the army of the Ghaoth Aduaidh in the field, where we will fight to the death. All of us here will be in that fight. We came to Cork and Kerry asking for help so we can destroy this army completely, not just fight it to a bloody draw."

"You have a strong force here and a sturdy, well-planned fortification. You have defended yourselves well from what Aife has told me. What I must tell you now is that if the Ghaoth Aduaidh fail to break us and then turn west for spoils, you will fall to them. They are bringing at least six thousand fighters this time, trained and equipped better than in the past, with siege weapons and artillery. Even if we kill half of them, can you stand against three thousand at once, so armed and armored? No. They will sweep over your defenses, take everything you have, and perhaps settle on your lands as they hope to settle on ours. Their families travel with them; they do not plan to go back north."

She paused and sipped water from a mug in front of her to salve a mouth and throat gone dry with tension. Some of the faces had turned uncertain. A few showed genuine fear. Was it her imagination ... or did Aife offer an faint nod?

"You heard my friends Gwen and Ionhar. They're fighting for towns far from the Province's border. I will be fighting for my own people, but I ask you to believe I am fighting for you too. All of us are. We fight for our civilization, not just for the Twenty Clans. I seek your help in one battle, a battle that could bring peace to all of us for years to come. After that, we may become friends as we once were. Or we may not. I ask you to remember what is at stake. If we fall, you will fall with us, and sooner rather than later. I believe this in my heart. I know my father believed it too, while he lived." She fought back tears, but one slid down her cheek and fell onto the table.

Chairs creaked and the fire snapped. No one spoke for a long moment. Then Aife leaned forward and met Feth's eyes.

"You know that what you ask would leave us nearly defenseless here?"

"I do know that. In truth, Aife, you are not safe now."

Liam waved a hand around the table. "Does anyone wish to speak further with these soldiers?"

"Whatever we may decide," said Uscias, "you have shown courage in coming here and speaking to us as friends. That in itself sways my judgment."

"We will discuss the matter now," said Liam, "and let you know our decision before the midnight bell."

A short time later the five travelers found themselves back inside the warehouse. They doffed dripping cloaks and gathered around their lantern.

"Never been so nervous," Feth said. "It was blazing hot in there, and the angry faces! I can't even remember what I said."

Keegan wrapped his arm around her shoulders. "You said what needed to be said, Feth."

"Aye, that you did," said Ionhar. "No one could have done better."

Gwen located her flute and began to play softly, a warm and sweet melody in a major key. It was a song Derdre knew and she sang the words in old Gaelic. Ionhar managed to heat a pot of water over the lantern and served out lukewarm tea. Keegan resumed his stitching ... and they waited. Feth fished a dry sweater out of her saddlebags and leaned her back against a stack of flour sacks. She closed her eyes and basked in Derdre's soothing voice.

I did the best I could, she told herself. *I don't think I convinced many people there. It was nice what Keegan and Ionhar said but Conor would have done it better.* It was done now. It was ...

She drifted off, warmed by the tea and relaxed by the music. Hours passed. She awoke with start; Keegan was shaking her and saying something. When her vision cleared, she saw Aife standing at the edge of the lantern's glow. Keegan pulled her to her feet.

"Five hundred fighters," Aife said, "the youngest and strongest, led by me. The rest will stay here for defense. In the morning we will work out the details."

Feth extended her hand. Aife took it in a hard grip.

"Did you argue in our favor?"

Aife smiled. "I did. We archers must stick together. In the morning, then."

She turned and left them alone.

"Five hundred fighters," said Feth, mostly to herself.

"Five hundred," repeated Derdre. "It could mean everything, Feth."

They sat and talked together for awhile, then Gwen put out the lantern and they laid down to sleep. Feth lay awake listening to the cats prowling among the crates. One brushed its soft coat along her fingertips. She stroked its back until a loud purr rattled in the darkness. When it went back to its hunting labors, Feth slept.

*October 23, 999. Weighed anchor 5:45 am Kernow time, lead-
ing squadron from anchorage. Wind NE seven knots, weather
high overcast, barometer falling, starboard tack. At 6:38 am,
merchanters split off for home, Capt. Fotharta signaled line
ahead, Caillech now at the front. Proceeding to rendezvous point
off Santander Bay. Ship is ready for battle.*

Jilleen Conmaicne, Capt., Wexford

*Private log: Last night while we lay at anchor off the coast of
Spain, I was thinking about a will. I don't have one and never
gave it a moment's thought. Who does at my age? I don't have
anything to give to anyone, really. Most of the clothes I own are
my uniforms and my seagoing scrubs. Everything of any value to
me is in this little cabin, and if I am killed chances are good this
ship may be gone too. Mostly I treasure the gifts I have received
from Innis. I hope he misses me as much as I do him.*

Chapter 36

Mairin's head still ached vaguely. Her thoughts were crystal clear.
Five minutes to make a plan, all the time it took to don full fighting
armor: cuirass, bracers, cuisses, pauldron, gauntlets, greaves and finally
the helmet. While lacing and tying she kept glancing down at the chart
of the three converging squadrons. It was a straightforward problem
in naval warfare ... with tremendous consequences hanging on the outcome. Question: how can four ships delay ten ships long enough for
six more ships to arrive and even the odds? One obvious option was
to launch firebombs with the ballistae and try to set them afire. She
dismissed this idea: they would be expecting this tactic and have fire
brigades ready. Her opponents would simply sail on past and put the
fires out on their way into Santander Bay. It would not work.

"Delay," she muttered to herself. "Engage less than all ten, pref-
erably four or five, make the others come about." She bent herself

awkwardly over the table and scribbled with a pencil held in her fingertips, all that the awkward gauntlets left exposed. Overhead, the ship quietly went to arms.

The fifth minute was nearly gone when she had it. Plenty of risk, of course, but risk attended anything she attempted now. Could she count on absolute precision from the other ships? Would the wind hold? How could the plan go wrong? The last question was easy to answer: *more ways than I have time to think about.* She drew a quick sketch. With a sigh and a final moment's thought, she picked up the scrap of paper and carried it to the quarterdeck. The last few archers had just crammed their way into the fighting tops. Rowenna and Sailing Master Gailenga stood side by side aft of the wheel; Brigid Auteini had taken the helm as she always did in combat. Sithmaith roved back and forth along the rails, checking every part of the deck and the tops. Mairin motioned her to come onto the quarterdeck, where she spread out the paper sketch on the top of the binnacle box.

"Any changes?" she asked Rowenna.

"No, sir. Wind steady, edging from northeast to north. Santanders flying for the bay, Captain Tredinnick has tacked twice."

"I'll bet. He'd be paddling with oars if he could. That won't help us in the next thirty minutes. Here's the plan," she said, tracing with her finger. "We'll shift to line ahead, *Caillech* followed by *Morrigan*, *Rosc Catha* and *Wexford*. Gauge our speed to pass close in front of their line as if we intend to launch a broadside of bolts. What we *will* do when we cross them is come hard about to starboard, shoot up into the wind, sail into the slots between the center ships of their line. As we pass between them, ballistae will fire grappler bolts with lines secured to cleats, try to snag their wheels."

Sithmaith nodded with admiration. "Break the wheels free from the deck, maybe snap the rudder cables in the process. With a following wind and sea they'll slew broadside. They'll need time to transfer rudder control to lines belowdecks, while the other ships shoot by us."

"And Captain Tredinnick's squadron intercepts those ships," Rowenna said. "Elegant, Captain."

"Lots of variables," Mairin admitted, "but we have excellent ballista crews and we'll get multiple shots at each wheel. With any luck one bolt will snag through the spokes and shatter the wheel itself or yank it up from the deckplates. Then we'll have a fight on our hands, at even odds. Master, how long till we intersect the Santanders?"

Nya Gailenga scanned the sea with bare eyes; no scope was needed now.

"Twelve minutes, give or take, sir."

"Lieutenant," Mairin said to Sithmaith, "this is tricky signaling. Please work it out with the ensigns. Send, ask for reply and then repeat. There can be no uncertainty."

"Aye, aye, sir." Sithmaith called for the ensigns and huddled with them at the port rail.

Eavan Sechnaill had been listening to the conference. "I'll get the bolts rigged, sir," she said, already on her way to the arms lockers amidships.

A minute later, one ensign at each rail flashed the hand flags. A full minute was needed for the first send, then a minute's delay, then another minute while the signals returned.

"Signals received and acknowledged, sir," Sithmaith reported.

Mor Dal Reti emerged from the hatchway in full fighting armor. He directed four sailors to distribute sand barrels along the deck from poop to forecastle.

"Can you work in that?" Mairin asked him with a glance at his armor.

"If need be," he said with a tense smile. "I think everyone fights today, Captain."

She nodded, then turned her glass on the rapidly-closing Santander ships. It seemed to her that they had already been in a fight, and recently. Where? And with whom? Lines were roughly knotted, black scorches along the decks and hull spoke of fires, and many of the crew appeared to be injured. She distinctly made out one man on a topsail yard with a bloody bandage on his head. Had they won? Were their holds now stuffed with spoils from Province cargo ships? And did they carry prisoners? This last question was especially worrisome, because in the battle to come she would destroy these ships in any way she could, including setting them afire. She had to hope that whatever spoils the Santanders might carry, no human prisoners had been taken.

She searched for the Santander flagship; its bow would be emblazoned with an elaborate and colorful coat of arms. There ... in the center where she expected it. On that ship her adversary was watching them, trying to guess what she planned. Who was he, she wondered? What training? For what did he fight besides plunder? As battle neared he would raise a speaking trumpet, used by some Province captains too. *I don't need one,* Mairin mused, *because we train to sail and fight in virtual silence. The Santander ships with all those fighters jostling with the crew on deck are noisy as a county fair at noon. No wonder their captains need trumpets.*

One thing her glass told her certain sure: the deck of every oncoming ship was crammed from rail to rail with boarding fighters, lean and muscular men who traded the protection of armor for speed and sheer strength. Some of them showed signs of injuries too, yet that would hardly signify in a battle. They would still be dangerous, tough fighters.

"Mostly heavy hammers and pikes," she observed to Mor. "They've learned that swords and knives are not effective against our armor. And they've learned too fast about building better ships and sailing them well. Collen is right, if we don't defeat them now, we never will."

"Aye," he agreed. "I've watched them these five years I've been at sea, and they're no longer like other raiders. They've built a real navy. Somewhere in Santander is a man who knows the naval business as well as we do."

"Five minutes, sir," Rowenna reported. "Wind north-northeast, about ten knots."

Sithmaith returned from the bow. "Ballistae loaded and lines attached, sir. Crews know what they're shooting for."

Mairin trained her glass on the rest of her squadron. Line ahead now, about two hundred yards apart. A bit too much.

"Lieutenant," she called to Briuin, "signal to close up by fifty yards, also be ready for a final maneuver in the event they spread out." Seconds later the two ensigns flashed their flags and waited for return signals.

Caillech eased her way a trifle and the others closed up. Mairin turned the glass again on the enemy flagship ... and there he was. A big-chested man with long, flowing white hair, posted in his ship's bow, speaking trumpet at the ready. His vessels had not slackened sail a bit, in fact they had set spankers to increase speed. The flagship's helmsman fought to hold his ship on a steady course with so much sideways pressure on his ship's stern. The fighters on deck, the raised boarding ramps and the sailors waiting to cast boarding hooks were a precaution only. Her adversary planned to blast right through them and keep going into the safety of his home port. And into the rear of Miles Endean's attack force.

"Three minutes, sir," Rowenna called. "I set reefed royals to account for their higher speed."

Mairin watched to see that her other ships kept exact station. This was the crucial moment. If they were not in the right position in two minutes, they could not execute the sudden turn she hoped her silver-haired opponent had not thought of. More than likely, he assumed the Province ships would do what they generally did: use the advantage of long-range ballistae and longbows to hammer at him from a distance, wounding or killing some of his crew and doing minor damage to his rigging. He was prepared to accept a short period of bombardment to get home and see what was happening in the harbor.

"Two minutes," Rowenna reported. Then louder, she called out, "Battle silence on deck."

"Ballistae, ready fire," Sithmaith ordered in a steady voice.

Ratchets on the heavy bolt-throwers clicked as the crews cranked thick, twisted skeins to the full-draw position. Eavan Sechnaill strolled both sides of the ship, occasionally whispering advice to a crew. The ballistae chiefs had to account for the drag of the trailing line and cast the bolts over the heads of the fighters crowding the rails. Mairin's stomach churned with unvoiced doubts. *A tricky shot under any conditions. Yet Eavan trains them well. How much I have counted on her these past two years!*

"Ready about," Rowenna said to Brigid. "One minute."

Mairin held her glass on the Santander captain. He was staring straight at her as if he knew she was his direct nemesis. Dark skin, tanned and weathered, handsome in a rugged way. A curly beard darker than his hair. An expression of calm and power and confidence. Was that a smile of disdain? *The worst sin of combat at sea: overconfidence. He thinks he has me. If he can't get past me, he expects to crush our four female-crewed ships before Richard gets here.*

Just as she lowered the glass, *Caillech* crossed the course of the first Santander ship in their line. Then the second ... the third ...

"Starboard helm!" Rowenna bellowed. "Loose sails as she bears up!"

Brigid's powerful arms swung the wheel's spokes into a blur. *Caillech*'s bow leaped to starboard and headed straight into the eye of the wind. The Santanders plunged through rollers no more than two hundred yards away. Mairin turned her glass on their commander: he was screaming orders that she could now hear, though the words meant nothing. *Board them*, no doubt. *Take those womanish ships!*

The four Squadron ships, bows into the wind and slowing rapidly, threaded between the oncoming five ships at the center of the Santander line, at fifty yards' separation. Too far for boarding planks yet well within range of the ballistae.

Caillech slid between the Santander flagship and the next ship west of it. The *whump* of the portside ballistae broke the silence on deck. Bolts tipped with grapples sailed over the gray-green sea towards the enemy flagship. The first shot flew a trifle low and toppled a fighter standing at the railing. The second bolt arced too high and slammed into two crewmen on the ship's far side. The third ballistae crew found their mark: the bolt flew over the top of the wheel and its grapple caught fast in the wheel's spokes. Before the stunned helmsman could move his hands, the trailing line snapped taut and the wheel erupted from the deck in an explosion of planks and splinters. Wheel, bolt and entangled helmsman slid across the deck and struck the port bulwark with an audible crunch. The ship flew on past *Caillech* and within a hundred yards was rolling broadside to the wind and waves.

Mairin looked to her other ships. All had snared one ship, and with excellent shooting, Jilleen's *Wexford* had crippled two. Five Santander vessels including the flagship now slewed about, in danger of ramming each other, while five others shot downwind. Meanwhile *Caillech* had lost all of her way and Rowenna screamed out sailing orders. She backed a topsail, whipped the bow through a full turn, and sent *Caillech* plunging south towards the crippled ships. Very little time to attack, Mairin judged: that veteran commander and his captains would get the damaged vessels under control soon enough. Yet every second brought Richard's six line-of-battle ships closer. At this moment his squadron plunged through the waves no more than a mile away. One more tack and he would hurtle headlong into the battle.

"Take the flagship," Mairin ordered Rowenna, and to Sithmaith, "Ballistae load razor-heads, shoot for fighters. Archers concentrate on sailors and the man with the trumpet."

Caillech bore down on the drifting Santander flagship. *Morrigan*, *Rosc Catha* and *Wexford* came about as fast as *Caillech* and now raced downwind to the attack.

Richard was coming about. Mairin studied his new heading: he meant to attack the undamaged Santanders, who had worn and were beating hard upwind to help their comrades. *You read my mind, Richard. Cut them off.*

Mairin stepped up next to Rowenna. "Close as you dare."

"Aye, sir," she said.

Seconds later, *Caillech* slid alongside the Santander flagship and spilled wind to match the other ship's drift. Furious activity and much shouting on the other ship's quarterdeck showed they were fighting to get rudder control back. Where was their commander? Mairin spotted him near the quarterdeck hatch ... sans his speaking trumpet. She did not need her glass now to tell he had discarded his smug expression. He bellowed orders in a huge voice, trying to clear deck space for his crew to control the ship with sails. Fighters scrambled to get out of the way, but short of going below, they had nowhere to go.

"Two minutes of chaos," Mairin said to Eavan Sechnaill at her elbow. "Open fire."

At Sechnaill's command, *Caillech*'s full armament opened its man-killing barrage. Ballistae executed rapid–fire drill, sending across volleys of high-speed bolts to tear at human flesh. Bolts that missed enemy fighters punctured sails and severed lines. Longbow archers in *Caillech*'s fighting tops picked off Santander sailors in the rigging and concentrated heavy fire on the quarterdeck. So long as the ships stayed too far apart for the boarding ramps to fall, the advantage was all *Caillech*'s.

No one could control the wind, and after a minute of this withering fire, a sudden powerful gust whipped the enemy ship's stern in

Caillech's direction. Before Rowenna could maneuver *Caillech* further off, the two sterns collided with a resounding crunch, doing no special damage but allowing the Santanders to drop the rear boarding ramp. It descended on *Caillech*'s poop deck with a deafening crash, smashing flat the taffrail and ramming its steel anchor-pike into the deck planks. In an instant, Santander fighters leapt up from sheltered places behind the bulwark and poured onto the ramp.

In the seconds it took Mairin to drop her visor and draw her sword, she saw Sithmaith pounding down the starboard rail at the head of her deck force. Then, it was melee and she could no longer see what was happening anywhere except the few feet around her own body. The fury of the fighting told her that many Santander fighters had gotten across, some no doubt wounded with arrows, others untouched. Battle hammers crashed into steel helmets and breastplates, pikes clanged off of pauldrons and greaves, armor and skill fought power and fierce determination.

Mairin slashed and stabbed, her long training taking over from conscious thought. The smell of blood penetrated her nostrils, and each time she fell to the deck, her eyes beheld the crimson of fresh blood. Pain flared from wounds in her thighs where pikes found openings in the armor's joints. The salt taste of blood flooded her mouth, one eye lost vision from blood oozing down her forehead. Shouts of rage and shrieks of pain deafened her. In one spare second as she struggled to her feet yet again, she glimpsed archers in the mizzentop, firing salvo after salvo at the ramp to cut off the flow of fighters.

Suddenly *Caillech* shuddered under her feet and with a wrenching screech the boarding plank slid off the deck and plunged into the cold, swirling waters between the ships. They were free and clear, for the moment. A man directly in front of her, bleeding from a dozen wounds yet still fighting, stabbed at her chest with his pike and connected. Steel plating saved her life but she slipped in blood and tumbled backwards. His battle hammer came up for the killing blow. Before it descended an arrow split his skull open and he fell heavily on top of her. In a second she was back up and the fighting went on. Bodies collided with her on all sides, she slashed at anything not wearing armor and Squadron-green, took a stunning hammer blow to the shoulder and again tumbled hard to the deck. Her vision grayed for a moment, then cleared, and she leapt to her feet, bloody sword ready.

At last, there was no one left to fight. All of the boarders lay dead or dying and the two ships rolled on the waves a hundred yards apart. Ballistae and longbows maintained steady fire until the range became too great. Mairin staggered backward and nearly toppled down the two steps onto the quarterdeck, where bodies lay everywhere, enemy and their own. Rowenna, her helmet torn off and blood pouring down the both sides of her head, leaned heavily against the wheel. Brigid Auteini and Eavan Sechnaill were nowhere to be seen. Nya Gailenga crawled out from beneath a Santamder corpse and struggled to her feet. A gasping Sithmaith clutched the starboard rail. The two blood-spattered ensigns supported each other at the port rail.

Mairin yanked off her helmet and took stock of their situation. The ship was under control: Rowenna called out sail commands in a voice trembling with pain. High in the rigging, sailors worked furiously at yards and sails. She had them underway with full topsails, and Mairin saw why. The enemy flagship had regained its rudder and was steering to ram them in the bow. *Caillech* eased ahead enough to avoid a collision but not fast enough to dodge the enemy's forward boarding ramp. It slammed onto the forecastle and more fighters poured over.

Mairin jammed her helmet back on and ran forward at Sithmaith's heels. Once again it was a deadly struggle, nothing to do but let instinct and experience guide her hands and feet. Five times she was struck hard and fell heavily to the deck. Once as she lay there she slashed at unprotected ankles and a screaming Santander fell across her legs. The Santander fighter directly in front of her was struck through the chest by an arrow and fell. Another fighter leaped into his place and swung his pointed hammer, grazing her helmet with a blow that would have killed her had it struck squarely. She slashed his arm, nearly severing it at the elbow, then stabbed his belly. He fell dead at her feet.

Dimly she was aware they were fighting as they trained to fight: a battle line holding port and starboard sides just aft of the forecastle, giving the fore and main tops a clear line of fire. Another minute of slashing and stabbing passed before the boarding ramp tumbled into the sea. Mairin took a heavy blow on her back from behind, turned to see a fighter's pike heading straight for her face. She ducked and plunged her blade into his throat. He fell backward, wrenching her sword loose from her hand. She pulled it loose and fought on. A minute more of blistering longbow fire from the tops ended this second battle.

Mairin climbed over and around bodies to reach the quarterdeck, where she found Rowenna held on her feet by a bloody-faced Kensa Velnowarth. Sithmaith, blood-coated sword clenched in her hand, sagged against the mainmast. Nya Gailenga worked the wheel and calmly called out sail commands. *Caillech* was now well clear of the enemy flagship, which had set its own topsails and was trying to escape the fight.

"Stay with her, Nya," Mairin ordered, and in a loud voice cried, "Ballistae, load firebombs."

Wounded sailors clambered over bodies and re-manned the eight heavy weapons. Bloodied fingers struck matches, lit touch holes in the round incendiary spheres, and laid them gently into firing trays. Sithmaith personally took command of one ballista whose chief lay dead in a pool of blood near her weapon.

Caillech overtook the flagship and drew up parallel a hundred yards away.

"Fire!" Mairin shouted. "Tops shoot fire crews and pumpers."

The flaming bombs flew over and shattered on the enemy ship's deck, spewing deadly liquid everywhere. Men caught fire and plunged overboard. Burning sails spread the conflagration to lines and yards and masts. Deck planks soaked with incendiary flared up, forcing bucket and hose crews away. Crews manning pumps and fire hoses were shot down by *Caillech*'s archers faster than they could be replaced. Nya maneuvered to keep them just within range so the rain of incendiary continued nonstop.

Where was he, Mairin wondered? *There.* The white-haired captain bellowed orders to his crew until two arrows at once plunged into his neck. He fell into the flames licking at his feet. Mairin searched her heart for pity, and found none. *He was so sure of himself,* she remembered. *And now he has paid the price.* For ten full minutes, *Caillech* dogged the doomed ship. By then, the enemy ship was fully ablaze and boats carrying panicked survivors were splashing into the water. *Caillech* steered away and upwind of her.

Mairin could at last pull off her helmet and let cool fresh air clear her throbbing head. Someone handed her a wet towel and she mopped blood from her face.

The deck from taffrail to bowsprit was a nightmarish landscape of dead and wounded, of moans and rattles, of cries for help and curses in a foreign tongue. With a sailor's help Mairin clambered atop an arms locker amidships.

"Caillechs," she cried out, "we have our ship, but this fight is not over yet. If officers or watch chiefs are dead or wounded, next in command step up. The deck must be cleared. Santanders go overboard, dead or alive. The surgeon will direct getting our wounded below, then retrieve our dead and lay them in the main cabin. We'll honor them when we have time. Get to work."

She climbed down and approached Rowenna, held up by Ensign Velnowarth. Rowenna's normally ruddy face was the color of chalk yet her eyes burned bright and clear.

"How bad are you hurt?" Mairin asked her.

"Took a hammer strike square on my back. My legs are numb and the pain is astonishing. You, sir?"

"Bashed and cut half to pieces. Brigid?"

Rowenna waved a hand towards the poop deck stairs. "There, sir. Dead."

"Ah." Five years of friendship, vanished. "Eavan?"

"Also dead, sir."

She could only swallow and nod in reply.

Edwina Auteini, a blood-soaked cloth pressed hard to her left forearm, approached from the portside.

"Can you signal, Ensign?" Mairin asked her.

"Yes, sir, if you could tie this cloth on my arm?"

Mairin knotted the soaked cloth over an ugly slash.

Mairin made her way to the starboard rail. The Santander flagship was a tower of flame and would presently sink. Next down the line from *Caillech*, *Morrigan* poured firebombs and arrows into its own crippled opponent. There had been a deckfight there too, and she saw no sign of Tierney Ulaid on the quarterdeck. Vevina Monaig's *Rosc Catha* had drifted further downwind and was now struggling to come about; her opposing number blazed from stem to stern. She raised her glass and found Richard's squadron, a mile to the west, locked yardarm-to-yardarm with his own opponents in a tumultuous fight.

Where was *Wexford*? There: partly obscured by *Rosc Catha*. Jilleen had beaten off her opponent and left the Santander ship adrift and afire. *Wexford*'s decks were clotted with dead and wounded and worse yet, *Wexford* was in terrible danger. Jilleen's ballistae had managed to tear wheels from *two* ships, and the second one, as yet unengaged, was beating upwind to take revenge on *Wexford*. Jilleen showed no signs of running, indeed *Wexford* had backed topsails and awaited the attack.

Valiant, Mairin told herself with a sinking heart, *but unless we get there to help, she'll lose her ship, and her life.*

"We have another fight on our hands," she called out to her assembled officers. "Nya, flash out everything we can, head for *Wexford*." She pointed to their sister ship and the Santander vessel cleaving the waves to attack her. "Mor, clear and sand the decks, fast as you can. Ensign," she said to Velnowarth, "get Lieutenant Briuin below and then help ready the ballistae for another engagement. Make up new crews if you have to. Lieutenant Laigain, re-form your deck force, check arms and armor, make sure the tops have ammunition."

Sithmaith, her face plastered with drying blood, nodded and offered a wan smile.

"Got my breath back, Captain," she said. "We'll be ready."

Mairin gazed into her eyes, searching for concealed fear, and found none. *You saw it, Captain Endean. A born fighter, this one.*

"Ensign," Mairin said to Edwina, "signal *Morrigan* and *Rosc Catha*, *make for Wexford as soon as possible*. Signal *Wexford*, *avoid engagement*, send it twice."

Nya Gailenga drove the ship hard towards *Wexford* as Mor and his team hurriedly cleared the decks and scattered sand that turned pink on hitting the planks.

"Signal from *Wexford*," Edwina reported. "*Captain Conmaicne not in command ... insufficient crew and time to get underway ... will fight here ... help appreciated. Kylee Dunlainge, First Officer.*"

"Neptune save us," Mairin said hoarsely. "Nya, will we make it?"

The Sailing Master shook her head. "No sir, we will not. The enemy ship will pull alongside *Wexford* before we can. Unless ... unless we ram them."

"Yes, Captain. Time enough for that."

Mairin had seconds to consider that option. An enemy ship loaded with unbloodied fighters, her own ship's crew much reduced and Jilleen's worse off yet. Once the Santander grappled with *Wexford*, *Caillech* could not use its ballistae, let alone firebombs. A furious boarding fight that they might well lose, with two ships at risk. *Caillech*'s virgin-oak bow timbers were heavily braced for just this occasion.

"Master," she said to Nya, "stove them in."

"Aye, aye, Captain, stove them it is."

"All hands, brace for collision!" Mairin shouted. "Archers in the tops, hold on and prepare to fire. Ballistae aim forward. Clear the forecastle."

Two hundred yards. The Santander captain, a tall black-haired man, saw what they intended and screamed orders to his crew. Though his ship came about sharply, it could not avoid *Caillech*'s onrushing bow, which struck the Santander ship dead amidships with a shuddering crash. *Caillech*'s bowsprit plunged over the Santander's deck and snapped off. Mairin's hands slipped on the wet rail and she slid forward in wet sand. Fighters from the enemy ship made a desperate attempt to board *Caillech*'s forecastle, then found themselves barraged by archer fire from the tops. They gave up quickly.

To Mairin's relief, the two ships broke loose from each other and began to drift apart. Nya backed topsails and swung *Caillech* away, revealing to all on her quarterdeck the horrible damage to the Santander ship's hull. Seawater poured into splintered ten-foot gash extending from the rail to below the waterline. Sailors instantly manned her pumps and streams of water poured from her scuppers. Her captain put his ship before the wind to get the damaged side away from oncoming waves. *Wexford* was safe from attack.

A sailor burst through the quarterdeck hatch.

"Captain, we're taking water in the bow. Carpenter is working with a crew in the hold."

"Start the pumps, find anyone you can. Nya, bring us alongside *Wexford*. Ensign Velnowarth, take over signals, send to *Morrigan* and *Rosc Catha*, *hold station and await orders*. Ensign Auteini, come below with me to get that bleeding stopped. Lieutenant Laigain, you have the deck, I'll return shortly."

Mairin followed Edwina down the hatchway, fighting rubber knees and blurring vision at every step. The scene in the main cabin was shocking. Mor had stripped off his armor and was working furiously, assisted by his trained medics. She counted fifteen dead lying on the floor covered by Sacred Cloths. As he worked Mor gave his triage report: twenty-two with serious wounds though likely to live, five in dire condition, the rest either uninjured or with minor wounds. With a total complement of seventy-five, that left her less than half a crew, barely enough to sail the ship, keep a work crew in the forward hold and man the deck pumps. Rowenna Briuin was strapped into a bunk. Mor whispered in Mairin's ear that paralysis was a possibility from her injury.

And what about me? My head is exploding, my back is in agony, every muscle and joint is bruised or strained, and I've lost a bucket of blood, not to mention the fractured skull I already had. In short, I'd replace myself if I could. I can't.

A medic helped her out of her armor and bandaged the worst of her oozing wounds. After a brief word with Mor, Mairin made her way to her cabin, where she rinsed blood off her face and hands, donned a fresh working tunic and clean boots, added a sweater and uniform jacket. She took a long pull on a bottle of wine, spared two seconds to comb sweat-drenched hair, and dared a glance in the mirror. Not bad: her quick makeover disguised pretty effectively how torn and battered she felt. The crew needed to see her in one piece.

She took one more minute to lean with eyes closed against the cabin door. *The horror of this is not lost on me. Tomorrow and for a long time to come I will be heartsick over the friends and shipmates I have lost today. Now I have to bring my squadron together, form it into line ahead, rendezvous with Richard, and make all possible sail for Santander Bay. If our bow will take the pounding and if the pumps can keep up with the water in the well. And if we make the harbor and if it's safe to go in. We may yet have to fight again.*

On deck after a painful, slow climb up the stairs, she found Sithmaith pale and weak from blood loss. She sent her below with Velnowarth; Edwina Auteini had returned to duty and took over signaling again. Acting crew chiefs had assumed their duties the deck had been swept clean of bloody sand two bilge pumps amidships spewed a steady stream of water through the scuppers lookouts manned the tops and a skeleton sailing crew stood ready at each mast.

Rolling on the swell fifty yards to port, *Wexford* had also managed to clear her decks and send up a short-handed sail crew. Kylee Dunlainge, her head bandaged and one arm in a sling, saluted Mairin from the quarterdeck.

"How is Jilleen doing?" Mairin called across to her.

"Poorly, Captain," Kylee shouted back. "Our surgeon is doing what he can."

Further away, *Morrigan* and *Rosc Catha* signaled ready to sail. *Morrigan* added regrets that Tierney Ulaid had died of her wounds.

Directly downwind of *Caillech* and *Wexford*, the ship they rammed rolled on beam ends, and with a bubbling hiss, sank below the waves. A couple of her boats rowed hard for the Spanish coast. Left behind in the sea, at least a hundred drowning men cried out their anger and fear.

"You would have killed us all," Mairin said under her breath. "Let the sea have you."

Ten minutes later, *Wexford* signaled she was ready to make sail.

"Signal to all ships," Mairin ordered Kensa Velnowarth, who had returned to the deck. "Make sail for Santander Bay, line ahead, *Caillech*, *Wexford*, *Morrigan*, *Rosc Catha*. Ensign Auteini, get us underway."

Caillech's sails flashed out, a bit more slowly than usual, and the damaged bow began to plow through the rollers. Tired and battered sailors stored ballistae, allowing the main courses to be set. Archers deserted the tops and went below. Body armor was stripped off, cleaned and made ready for reuse. A regular watch of the least-injured assembled itself on deck. The remains of the bowsprit were cleared away; a replacement would have to wait for the harbor. A sailor brought up a mug of cold tea for Mairin, which she sipped gratefully at the remains of the starboard rail. Sithmaith Laigain returned to duty with more color in her face and took her station near Nya Gailenga at the helm.

A mile to the west, Richard's squadron had finished its own repairs and formed line ahead parallel to them. *Ajax* signaled they were ready.

It was purely a personal matter ... but she had to know.

"Ensign, signal *Ajax*," Mairin ordered Kensa. "Send *a hard day* question mark."

"Sir?"

"Just send it."

"Aye, aye, sir."

A minute later *Ajax* answered.

"*Ajax* replies ... replies ..." Kensa hesitated, her eye glued to the glass.

"Yes?"

"I think it reads *may I have this dance,* question mark."

Mairin brushed away tears of relief. She couldn't see him clearly—but she knew he was there.

Int én bec, ro léic feit, do rind guip glanbuidi;
fo-cheird faid os Loch Laig, lon do chraib charnbuidi.
The little bird has whistled from the tip
of his bright yellow beak;
The blackbird from a bough laden with yellow blossom
Has tossed a cry over Belfast Lough.
(Anon. circa 800 A.D.)

Chapter 37

RyAnn MacLaren ladled out stew from the steaming pot. Her younger son Tormaigh held two bowls tightly in hands large and well-formed for his nine years of age.

"Give the larger one to your father and the other to Sloane," she told him quietly. "Then come back for yours."

The tow-headed boy nodded and took slow, careful steps from the fire to the felled log where his father Lucharba and older brother Sloane waited. Lucharba set aside the flintstone he was using to hone his sword and took the bowl without a word or change of hard expression. Sloane, now seventeen, broad and strong, accepted his and smiled at Tormaigh. RyAnn dished out Tormaigh's portion, then one for herself, and sat on a broad stump across from Lucharba. Tormaigh crowded up against her.

It was the second night since Bethia disappeared and RyAnn was almost certain she would never see her lovely daughter again. That she escaped the domination and violence of her father was a cause for joy. How had she escaped the sentries? Rumors spread in the camp that a sentry was killed two nights ago. Could that possibly have involved Bethia who left that very same night? Maybe she had gotten away clean, or maybe the sentries caught her, used her, killed her and dumped her body deep in the woods. She would never know. The first swallow of stew churned in her stomach and she set the bowl aside.

Sloane was watching her. When Lucharba finished slurping his bowl, he tossed it into the grass and stumped off in the direction of the privies. Tormaigh got to his feet and retrieved his father's bowl. Sloane set his own bowl on the log and crowded onto the stump beside his mother.

"I should kill him for it," Sloane said, his hands twisting with anger. "I really should."

RyAnn put her arm around his shoulders. "It would not bring her back, my son. And you should not hate him. Your father was a good man once, you're old enough to remember. Now he's so bitter and sad that he can't act any other way."

"He hit Bethia and that's why she left," Sloane said, still angry. "He will never hit you again, mither, that much I can tell you."

Tormaigh, blond and freckled and too thin for his wide frame, came over and put his arm around RyAnn. "We'll see her again, mither, I know we will," he said in his boy soprano. "Bethia is smart, smarter than any of us. You'll see."

RyAnn wiped tears from her cheeks. "You're right there, my little one, she is a bright girl and pretty too."

Sloane got to his feet, retrieved his sword, and slid it with an angry scrape into its scabbard.

"Did not have to happen," he said, in a baritone now deeper than his father's. "Still, what's done is done. Mither, in the morning I think we'll break camp, all the captains are saying so. Take Tormaigh and get out of here, back to Limerick, soon as you can. Maybe you'll find Bethia there."

With a heavy sigh, RyAnn started cleaning the bowls and the pot with water and a tattered brush. She sent Tormaigh to fetch more water. To Sloane she said, "You know this will all come to nothing."

"Maybe, maybe not," he replied with a shrug. "We have a chance."

"The leaders promised that three years ago. Your uncle Kelvan died for that promise."

Sloane stared at the ground. "What do you want me to do? Run away?"

Before Ryann could answer, Tormaigh returned with the water.

"Your father will come back drunk," RyAnn said to her sons. "Sloane, please don't bait him. Tormaigh, you—"

"Can I go to the big fire with the other boys?" he broke in. "I promise not to drink any ale."

"Just as well," she said, mussing his hair. "Be quiet when you come back, if your father's here."

Tormaigh pulled on an extra sweater, kissed his mother's cheek, and dashed off among the tents to the nightly bonfire, where the younger boys and girls sang and danced and no doubt explored new ways of looking at each other. Sloane assembled all his armor and weapons and started cleaning and sharpening them again. Though it was not late, RyAnn lay down on her bedroll in the tent to rest. She was utterly spent, not having slept an hour since Bethia disappeared.

She lay with her eyes closed, listening to the camp. Nearest by, Sloane fussed nervously with his gear and hummed a battle hymn. Further away, songs and laughter, clanging of pots, shouts of anger, the cackling of crows hunting for easy meals. She let her mind drift back five short years, to a time when she had four children, not three or even two, when Lucharba did not drink to forget and did not strike out in rage, when they lived in a decent cottage on the west edge of Belfast in the shadow of monumental ruins.

The boat Lucharba had bartered two days of bricklaying for was barely big enough to hold the six of them together with lunches and fishing poles and buckets. Yet hold them it did, and bore them over the placid surface of Lough Neagh safely enough. It was a warm, sunny afternoon at the height of summer, breezy enough to blow the bugs away, canopied by a sparkling blue sky that promised a storm-free day. Lucharba rowed hard for a time, then turned the oars over to Sloane, at twelve already a large boy with broad shoulders and strong arms. An hour's rowing brought them into a cove sheltered from the main body of the huge lake. Here fishing was usually good and a quiet sandy beach offered a place for a picnic. Sloane hauled in the oars, Lucharba baited hooks, and little Eithne squealed with two-year-old delight when RyAnn splashed cool water in her face.

"Mither, I'll take her," said Bethia from the bow. "You fish."

"Thank you, I will," said RyAnn. She passed the tot forward to Tormaigh, her serious-faced boy of four, who then passed her to Bethia, at eleven a decent cook and willing babysitter. RyAnn eased past Sloane to the stern, where Lucharba handed her a pole with a line and hook already baited. Briefly she admired the pole's fine reel, Lucharba's craftsmanship learned from his grandfather.

"Now, my dear wife," he said, "let's see which of us really knows how to catch Dollaghan Trout!" He leaned over and kissed her, then resumed watching the tip of his own pole.

Less than a minute later, RyAnn's pole was nearly torn from her hands. "I've got one!" she cried. "A big one! Sloane, get ready with the net!"

Twenty yards from the boat, the trout soared from the water and landed with a mighty splash.

"Hah, you don't have him yet!" cried Lucharba. "Shall I help you?"

Her withering look silenced him. She did have a struggle on her hands, one that lasted a full ten minutes. Sloane and Tormaigh shouted encouragement, Lucharba offered friendly but unwanted advice, and Eithne watched with wide-eyed wonder from the tight grip of her sister. Finally, and not long before RyAnn's hands tired out, the powerful trout gave up the battle and Sloane scooped him from the water into a net.

"Ye gods, he is a big one!" Lucharba said. "Five pounds if he's an ounce!"

Sloane managed to get the still-thrashing fish unhooked and secured in their basket. Lucharba re-baited RyAnn's hook and then barely had time to grab his own pole from between his knees before he too had a strike. He brought his fish in easily, another trout barely half the size of RyAnn's lucky catch. By the end of a full hour, they each caught at least two trout, to the delight of Eithne who shrieked with delight at the sight of the splashing, struggling fish.

Lucharba rowed them ashore and Bethia built a fire with wood collected by the boys. RyAnn tended Eithne's diaper while Lucharba cleaned the fish and shucked the precious corn, once a cheap buy at the market, now a dear one. Soon the delicious odor of fresh filets frying in grease watered every mouth. The two boys and Bethia held corn cobs on sticks near the flames, and when the cobs were hot and soft, they smeared them with salty butter. Everyone ate fresh trout and corn until they could eat no more. Eithne sat down at the edge of the water and amused herself splashing under Lucharba's watchful eye, giving both Bethia and RyAnn a break from their duties.

"I've heard," said RyAnn with a raised eyebrow, "that you have your eye on a boy."

Bethia blushed scarlet. "Oh, mither, it's nothing. He's just a boy, is all."

"Does he have a name?"

"Of course he has a name. It's Neill."

"Do we know his family?"

"I don't think so. They live north of town. I see him at the market, his family has a booth selling woolens."

RyAnn thought back twenty-five years and the face of a young boy swam into her mind. His name was Sethne and she was very fond of him for a time.

"You may ask him to dinner, if you like."

Bethia blushed again, this time smiling. "I'd like that, mither, thank you. Next week, maybe."

RyAnn kissed her daughter's smooth forehead. "You're a lovely girl, Bethia, you can afford to be choosy. Just like I was when I married your father."

"I'm a long way from that!"

"Not so long as it will seem," RyAnn said with a gentle laugh. "Retrieve Eithne, will you? She's getting so muddy."

Bethia scooped up her giggling sister. RyAnn broke out a basket of sweet apples for their dessert, and then they all sang songs until Lucharba was forced by the waning light to gather them all aboard again. Sloane insisted on rowing and Bethia took Eithne again, so RyAnn was free to sit back in her husband's arms the whole way.

It was that very day, when they returned to their thatch-roofed cottage, that a neighbor told them of the raid on the grain warehouse by warriors pouring out of ocean-sailing ships. That winter in Belfast, flour was scarce and then gone entirely. The hunger began and Lucharba scavenged and stole and grew pale and sad and angry. Eithne fell ill and died. And that winter was only the first of harder ones to come.

She dozed off, and when she awoke the camp was far quieter than before. Her heart ached with the lingering image of Eithne, sweet blue-eyed Eithne, taken by the coughing sickness at four but in truth destroyed by hunger. She died in Lucharba's arms, arms that could not find enough food to keep her strong in the long and terrible winter of that year. From that moment on, their lives had been so very different.

Tormaigh, true to his word, returned and now crowded against his brother on the log. Sloane was talking to him in a whisper. Lucharba was nowhere to be seen. Campfires blazed to ward off the approaching cold of night. RyAnn draped her heaviest cloak over her shoulders and set water over the fire for tea.

"No sign of your father?" she asked the boys.

"I saw him," offered Tormaigh. "He was with a bunch of his friends."

"Drunk?"

"Yes."

RyAnn brewed a big pot of tea and served mugs out to her sons and herself. She did her best to speak of happier times, an effort largely in vain. Sloane had gone silent and Tormaigh worried that he might lose the brother he adored after losing a sister he loved. After a time they simply sat together on the log and drank the dregs of the tea, saying little.

At last Lucharba staggered into their camp, pushed Tormaigh aside and sat next to Sloane, who got up immediately and edged away into the shadows. RyAnn backed up a few steps, knowing how quickly Lucharba might strike out at her when he was like this.

"I'm hungry," he said, staring at her with unfocused eyes. "Give me more stew."

"Husband, the stew was gone hours ago. I have bread—"

"Bread!" he cried, leaping up. "I want no cold bread."

He advanced on her and she knew what would come next. Then Sloane was between them, eye to eye with his father.

"Get out of my way, boy," Lucharba rasped.

"I told you yesterday," said Sloane, "that your days of violence in our family are done, old man. And I meant it."

With a bellow of rage Lucharba swung wildly with his fist. Sloane dodged easily, then slammed his own big fist into his father's chin. The older man toppled without a sound into the soggy grass. Sloane drew his sword and raised it to strike a death blow.

"Sloane, please don't."

It was RyAnn's voice. She came forward and laid a hand on his sword arm. "I don't want his blood on your hands."

Rage and disgust overwhelmed him. He spun away from his mother and gagged out his dinner into the grass. Tormaigh emerged from the shadows and laid a hand on his brother's back.

"'Tis all right, Sloane," he said. "He deserved it, he did."

"Carry your father into the tent," Ryann told them. "Right away boys, please."

When they returned, she said, "Tormaigh, you and I will leave before dawn while your father's still asleep. Sloane, go and spend the night with Hegan and his family. We'll say farewell now."

"But mither—"

She threw her arms around him. "Go, my son, go."

Sloane wrapped his powerful arms around her, and she felt the sobs shaking him.

"I am sorry, dearest boy," she said, stroking his head. "If you can, save yourself and come to us in Limerick. Do not give up your life for nothing. You know where we'll be."

He released her, embraced his brother, whispered something in his ear, and ran off into the gloom. RyAnn held Tormaigh under one arm, her heart sinking under the weight of so much loss.

"Pack up everything we need and then go to sleep," she said, finding her voice. "I'm going to walk along the lake for awhile and then I'll be back."

She kissed Tormaigh on the forehead, drew the cloak around her shoulders, and headed towards the lakeshore a hundred paces from their tent. In daylight the shoreline of Lough Gur was crowded with bathers and children and women washing clothes. Now it was deserted. To her the lake seemed no more than a pond, being a mile north to south and less than a half mile across. Until their coming, it had been surrounded by dense forest. In the past weeks the army had cut down the whole west side of the lakeshore for camp space and firewood.

One night in Limerick, before they came here, she had heard a toothless old man seated at their outdoor dinner table declare that the lake was among Eirelan's most ancient sites, that the spirits of Celts from eons past dwelt amid the crumbled stones and rested beneath the clear, still water. And now, at night, when dying fires lit the glassy surface, she felt a tingle in her bones remembering the old man's words. Perhaps it was so! Celts like herself walked this very shore in the dim reaches of time before writing and steel and hatred and want had ever visited Eirelan or Scotlan, the land of her birth and ancestors. If she listened hard enough, she wondered, could she hear them? As she watched the lake and listened for its ancient voices, some measure of peace crept into her heart.

Then another feeling came over her. Neither sorrow nor wonder nor fear, more a sense that eyes were watching her from the forest-dense shore on the other side. Yet it was more than that. A feeling of attachment, of connection with something or someone on the other side. A terrible thought crossed her mind: did Bethia lie dead in those woods? Was her cherished daughter's tortured young spirit calling out to her?

She started around the shoreline and did not stop until she was blocked by a solid mass of blackness, trees clustered so close together that even the bright moon overhead cast no light beneath them. A primitive fear overwhelmed her, froze her in place. She could go no further.

She retraced her steps and gazed across the lake again. The heart-freezing feeling faded. Perhaps it had nothing to do with her. It might be just as the old man had said: ancient Celtic spirits roamed here and called out to the living. Yet, she considered, if Bethia walked among those spirits now, at least she was in the company of friends who would lead her to the light.

She smiled at that thought, and turned away.

This morn I heard a dove's lamenting cry.
I asked, 'what can your sadness signify?'
It said, 'I mourn for you and not for me,
For in your heart much weeping do I see.
I asked, 'when will this weeping pass away?'
It said, 'when that will be, I cannot say,
But this I know: the cleavéd heart will heal,
As surely as the heavens are a wheel,
Which turns above the world, in wondrous night.'
So said the dove, at early morning's light. ·
Bethia MacLaren

Chapter 38

"That's a touching poem, Bethia," said Oran when she finished. "You should write it down."

"No need," she replied. "I keep all my poems in my head."

She walked to the water's edge and rinsed out the pan she used to heat leftover fish for breakfast. They were camped on the south bank of the Morning Star River, not far from the village of Bruff. The river was a quiet one, flowing smoothly and silently through a gentle countryside Oran felt much attached to. He visited this place on his first journey outside the Province, when he was a young wanderer and not a scout for the army. Every year since, some fourteen years now, he stopped at this very place.

He paused in his packing and smiled at her. "I had in mind a copy for myself."

"Tonight, I'll write it down," she said with a tolerant sigh.

Oran finished gathering up and stowing their blankets, ground cloths, and other gear. *How wonderful it would be to stay right here for a week, fishing, exploring, sleeping near the river. So peaceful. It's hard to grasp that less than six miles from this idyllic place, thousands of fighters are gathering, fighters who mean to take my homeland from me and destroy my people.*

With a sigh that Bethia overheard, he tightened the girth straps on their horses and took a last glance at the placid, fish-filled river.

She swung herself easily into the saddle. "You would like to stay here."

"Indeed I would, Bethia," he said, mounting Seara. "Indeed I would. Maybe another time."

They rode along a trail that followed the easy curves of the river for a five miles. When the river's course turned more sharply to the west, Oran led them across a ford into woods on the opposite bank. Once in the woods he turned north, passing by the town of Bruff on the east. There was no path through these woods, so Oran set a slow pace that allowed them to talk quietly.

"Gur is a beautiful lake," said Bethia. "Not big like Lough Neagh near home in Belfast. Even a strong wind barely ripples it. At night it's so smooth it makes a mirror for the stars and the moon."

"My brother Sean tells me that Lough Gur is an ancient gathering place. Celts and the people who came before them have lived on its shores for at least seven thousand years. Seventy centuries! Or so one of his dusty old books tells him."

She pondered that. "It's hard to think of that much time," she said finally. "Tell me about Sean and his books."

"Well, to start, he's an historian."

"And what is a ... historian?"

"Someone who studies and writes about history."

"History of what?"

"Well, Sean studies just about everything he can get his hands on. He's already written a short history of the Province, and now he's working on a longer history of Eirelan going back to the Age of Machines. He writes other things, too, just things he thinks about."

Bethia looked over at him, her eyes wide. "He must be smart, then."

"Very," said Oran with a grin. "I guess he's the smartest person I know. He's also a wonderful brother. Makes me very lucky."

"You'd be a good brother to have too. Where does Sean live?"

"In Dungarvan, a port town. I saw him the day before I left." He frowned. "We had kind of an argument."

Conversation halted as they came upon a narrow, bubbling creek at the bottom of a deep ravine. Oran spent several minutes looking for the easiest place to traverse it.

"Where was I? Oh yes, the argument. Sean loves books above all things and he found out where there might be a big stash of them. The place is way up near Birr, in a pretty dangerous area. He wants to go up there and see the books, bring them back if he can."

"Will you help him?"

"I'd like to. I had to warn him it might be impossible. I don't want to lose a brother over a few books."

"But he doesn't see it that way."

"No, he doesn't."

Bethia paused to think and then said, "My father didn't believe reading and writing were important."

"Yet you know words very well, enough to make up poems. How did you learn, then? A school?"

"No, the last school we had in Belfast closed when I was six. My great-aunt Aigneis grew up when schools were common. She never stopped reading. She taught me almost every day until she died last year. I'm teaching my brother Tormaigh." Her voice caught in her throat. "Or I was. Now he won't learn at all."

Oran reached over and touched her shoulder. "Tell you what. In the winter we'll visit Sean, and then you'll see more books than you can read in a lifetime."

Her face brightened. "You're sure he won't mind?"

"Mind?" Oran laughed. "Sean takes to anyone who loves words like he does. I'm a bit of a disappointment to him in that respect ..." he trailed off.

Snowflakes drifted down among the trees. Oran halted and peered up at a dark gray sky.

"You don't like snow?" asked Bethia, swishing her hand through the flakes. "I love it."

"So do I, when I'm not worried about someone tracking me."

"Oh. Right. I didn't think of that."

"I don't think we have to worry yet," he said, sniffing deeply. "The air doesn't smell right for real snow, cold enough but too dry. Three weeks off yet."

"I do like snow," she repeated, mostly to herself. "We liked to play in it."

Oran heard pain in her voice and saw her wiping tears from her face.

"I know," he said gently. "You miss your family. I'll make sure you get a new family. I promise."

She sniffled and pulled a kerchief from her belt pouch. "I trust you," she said, wiping her eyes. "You know, you're not as funny as you said you were."

He laughed out loud and then had to cover his own mouth. They were getting too close to the lake make much sound now.

"Fair enough," he said with a much softer chuckle. "Tonight when we camp I'll tell you funny stories."

I'll have to select them carefully, he considered. *The funniest ones, I can't tell to a fifteen-year-old girl.*

They rode on in silence for a time. Snowflakes continued to swirl about, though never enough to cover grass or make a trail. Up and down the road, through swales and over rises but always in woods that seemed to go on forever. After another hour passed they crossed a broad, burbling creek where they paused to let the horses drink their fill and top off their canteens and jugs. After the creek the woods gradually changed from oaks, alders, and elms to pines and firs. Holly and myrtle crowded the forest floor so they had to weave their way more carefully than before.

"It's so beautiful," breathed Bethia. "The smell alone is so sweet."

A half-hour's slow ride brought them into a small clearing where Oran halted Seara. He dismounted and Bethia followed suit.

"How far away are we?" she asked with an uneasy glance at their closet-like surroundings.

"Just over a mile from the south shore, I think. I've never stopped here in the woods, no reason to with the lake so close by. We'll find out for sure after dark."

Bethia paused in her unsaddling of Vengeance. "At night? How do we find our way there and back?"

"Compass and our own footsteps. Ever seen a compass?"

"No, I don't know what it is, even."

He reached into a pocket and took out his compass, a birthday gift from Conor years ago. Kernow-made, it was shiny brass with a spring cover engraved with his family crest. He popped open the lid and rotated case until the gold-plated needle settled on "N." Bethia watched with fascination.

"That 'N' means north," he explained. "The 'S' is south and so on."

Her eyes widened. "It works everywhere?"

"It does," Oran said. He snapped it shut and tucked it back in his pocket. "Without it I'd have been lost a thousand times."

He finished unsaddling Seara and let the two horses wander and nibble on whatever they could find. "What's this?" Bethia asked. She held up a small, metal-sided lantern.

"My own invention," he said with a note of pride. He took it from her and held it over his head. "The whole army uses it now for night marches. Only the bottom is glass, colored red, so dim light goes towards your feet and nowhere else. When we walk to the lake, our boots will leave a visible trail that we can see with the lantern on our way back. I usually scuff a little to make it easier to see. The compass helps to make sure you're headed in the right direction if you lose your tracks."

He set the lantern down and took a light hold on her upper arms. "It might be better if you stayed here with the horses."

"No!"

"You know what they'll do to you if you're caught. You killed a sentry."

"I know. I don't care. I don't want to stay here alone."

He let go of her and shrugged. "All right, you go. Make sure you have that new knife handy."

She drew the gleaming blade from its belt sheath and ran her thumb over the honed edge.

He turned back to the campsite and pulled all the blankets from his saddle bags. "It's going to be a cold night. We can have a small cooking fire but that's all."

She started gathering dead branches and twigs.

"There's more than one kind of cold," she said. "I'll take this kind any day."

Two hours passed while they made a fire and enjoyed a dinner of hot tea and sausage and dried fruit. By Oran's watch, it was now past eight and the cold was settling in. Heavy overcast yielded to wind-blown clouds sliding from north to south. The risen moon, more than half full, set the drifting clouds aglow. Normally, Oran preferred moonless, starless nights for scouting and traveling, but tonight the luminous moon was just what he wanted. From the shore of the lake, they would have a clear view of the enemy camp bathed in moonlight.

Bethia had been quiet and pensive the whole time. The cleaned-up versions of his best stories barely brought a smile to her lips. And he knew why. Her family, all the family she ever knew, was camped not more than two miles from their campsite. In that same camp, two men who attacked and forced themselves on her now lifted pints of stout and told the tale to rapt comrades.

"Bethia," he said in the silence that followed his last story, "I know this is hard for you. You must be feeling a lot of things that don't fit together."

She looked up, tears glistening in the fading light of the fire.

"Yes," she said, her voice shaking. "I'm angry and sad and lonely all at the same time. My father should never have brought us here, and those men ... those men should die for what they did to me." She wiped her eyes on her sweater and struggled to smile. "I'm sorry I didn't laugh at your stories, they really were funny and I liked them. Especially the one about your father catching you and Sean drinking his whiskey in the barn."

Oran poked at the embers with a stick. "You'll like my father, when you meet him. He was Domnall Laigain's best friend when they were kids, that's why Conor and I grew up like brothers. Domnall died twelve years ago and to this day my father walks down to the end of the pier at Kilmore Quay and weeps to think of it. My mother and Conor's mother Liadan are close too. I love my family and I hate being away from them so much."

To his surprise, Bethia reached across and took hold of his hand. "You're lucky to have such a family, Oran."

The woman emerges from the girl, he thought. *The woman takes my hand and offers sympathy.*

He squeezed her hand gently. "And now we have to be off."

He poured a bit of water over the embers, which died out with a faint hiss. Then he gathered up his lantern, compass, sword-belt, and pocket-sized naval telescope and donned his black, hooded cloak.

"You can carry the lantern," he said. "We won't use it till later. Make sure your knife is handy. No talking once we start, just tap me if you need to say something, then whisper directly in my ear. Got it?"

"Got it," she said, taking the lantern. "I'll be one step behind you."

He opened the compass and read it one last time in the moonlight. Then they plunged into the trees. Thereafter every sound they made, every snap of a twig or crunch of pine needles, rang in Oran's ears. He was used to that nerve-induced sensation; in truth the spongy carpet of needles made their footfalls almost inaudible. Bethia seemed instinctively quiet behind him. After a half hour of steady walking he slowed their pace and stared straight ahead, trying to catch the first glimmer of the lake. He could smell water. It had to be nearby.

He felt a light touch on his shoulder. Bethia was pointing off to the left. *Good eyes!* he thought. *Probably better than mine.* For there, through a slight thinning of the trees, moonlight gleamed from placid water. He leaned over until his lips brushed her ear and whispered, "well done." He pocketed the compass and headed towards the shore. He halted them in the first line of trees and shrubs.

Bethia stood next to him, her body touching his. Through all the heavy clothing, he felt her trembling.

The glasslike surface of the lake shimmered with moonlight. Along the far shore, a thousand campfires blazed up and cast a yellow-orange glow on the water. Oran was stunned to see how far the camp extended—it covered more than a mile of shoreline from northwest to northeast. The woods had been cut back for hundreds of feet from shore, the stumps plainly visible in the glow of the campfires. In the stillness of the night, voices, shouts, laughter, and singing carried perfectly across the lake.

Oran drew out his telescope and swept it from far left to far right, then back, pausing now and then to note specific details. He could hear Bethia's rapid breathing next to him and knew intense feelings must be welling up inside her. He passed the glass to her briefly, and when she was satisfied, took it back and stowed it away. Then, standing absolutely still, he listened intently for a time. Now and then the general clamor died down and he was able to pick up snatches of conversation that he would write down in the morning. Over the course of several days, such bits and pieces could be fitted together in a coherent picture.

When the campfires died out and voices dropped low, he touched Bethia's arm and led her back into the depths of the pine-scented forest. Twenty yards in, he lit the special lantern and in its faint red glow was easily able to retrace their exact path to the clearing. They found Seara and Vengeance standing with sides touching for warmth and companionship.

"Are you all right?" he asked her.

She leaned against him and cried. He wrapped his arms around her trembling body and whispered in her ear that he understood how she felt. After a minute she found her voice.

"My mother must be sick with worry. I wish I could get word to her."

"And I wish I could help you," he said. "Right now there's no way. After the battle is over ... well, I can't promise anything but maybe we can find a way. Now, into our beds."

A short time later they lay buried under layers of blankets on beds of soft pine needles.

"What could you tell?" she whispered.

"More folk than I expected," he said. "I would say there are close to ten thousand in that camp. Bethia, when you were there, how many women and children were there? I mean, if I said there were ten thousand altogether, how many would you say are fighters?"

"I'm not good at big numbers, Oran," she said after a pause. "Most of the families stayed back in Limerick. I'd say one out of three were not fighters."

"That means at least six thousand fighters, then. Two days ago, were more still arriving?"

"Oh yes," she said immediately. "Many more, maybe hundreds every day. There were always new tents going up and more trees cut down."

"Where is all the food coming from? And what kind of food is it?"

She thought for a moment. "I heard it came from Limerick. Just enough to live on, not that we got much more at home anyway. Sometimes the new people brought fresh things and shared them."

Her words were beginning to slur with oncoming sleep.

"One more thing," he said. "Your hand is on your knife?"

"Yes."

"Be careful about using it. I might get up during the night."

"Don't be silly."

"Right. Sorry."

"Good night, Oran."

"Sleep well, Bethia."

He lay fully awake long after he heard her breathing slow and deepen in sleep. His mind churned with details of what he had seen and heard. One conclusion was already inescapable: this would be the largest army the Province had faced in a long time. Assembling and supplying such a large force took time and planning and logistics, and all that effort did not go into a single scavenging raid. These people, whatever mix they might be of rogue clans and hard-nosed Belfasters and foreigners, had it in mind to break through the Rampart and settle their families on the Province's land.

He drifted in and out of light sleep. Twice he came fully awake with his hand gripping the sword, once because the horses made a fuss over something, and again because Bethia had left the tent for a few minutes. Otherwise it was quiet, and by the first light of day he felt rested. From the icy feel of the air on his exposed face, he knew the temperature had fallen below freezing.

Crawling out from beneath the blankets, he built a small cooking fire and heated water for tea and porridge. Bethia emerged soon after him and took over the cooking while he fed the horses. After a satisfying hot breakfast it was off to the lake, where he studied the camp in daylight. Bethia was certainly right about the pace of new arrivals: the camp was growing by the hour along the northeast shoreline of the lake. In crystal clear air his fine sliding telescope revealed details of armament, armor, siege weapons, assault ladders, and perhaps most ominous of all, harsh drills to instill battle discipline. *Our one great edge,* he pondered in dismay, *disappearing in front of my eyes. They have watched us, and learned.*

For two more days, while the weather held clear and cold, they watched by day, listened in late evening, and huddled under blankets at night. The third dawn was no dawn at all. Heavy overcast and a wet smell to the air promised an end to the fair weather. And their food was nearly gone. When they reached the shoreline, Oran saw that they need remain no longer: the tents were going down. By afternoon, the huge army would be on the move.

"Where will the women and children go?" he asked Bethia on the way back to their camp. "They can't possibly follow the army."

"No," she said, "the plan was that we would move back to Limerick town and camp there, wait to hear when we could claim our new farms and houses."

"Is that what they told you?"

"That's what my mother said, yes. New farms and houses."

Fifty yards from their camp, Oran stopped dead. Bethia bumped into him and opened her mouth to speak. His right hand shot up for silence. Male voices could be heard through the trees, speaking rapidly in a Belfast brogue. Oran crept forward until he could see the clearing through pine branches. Three men, scattering their gear and intending to steal their precious horses. He turned and saw Bethia already had her knife out. He drew his sword and led them forward, trying to stay concealed till the last possible instant.

A snapping twig gave them away. One of the men shouted a warning. Oran charged into the clearing with Bethia at his heels. One fighter held the reins of their horses, a second man's arms bulged with pickings from their camp. The man who shouted drew a sword and charged Oran, but long training in the Line of Blades could not be overcome. Oran's sword flicked the man's blade aside and plunged into his belly. The man groaned once and fell face forward. Bethia's knife flew into the neck of the man holding the gear: he dropped without a sound. The third man had time to drop the reins and fling his own knife at Oran. He dodged enough that the knife missed his heart and instead sunk into his chest beneath his left shoulder, sending a torrent of pain into his neck and down his arm. Ignoring the pain, he charged the man, who hesitated a split second and then bolted into the woods.

Oran sank to his knees, his sword tumbling to the earth. Through graying vision he saw Bethia retrieve her knife and sprint after the fleeing man. She was not gone long. When she returned, panting hard, she knelt next to him, her eyes fixed with horror on the knife blade sticking deep in his chest.

"Did you kill him?"

"I did."

"Good, very good. That'll buy us time." Slowly he lowered himself onto his back. "Bethia, you're going to ... have to ... pull the knife out. Slow and straight. Can ... you do that?"

She nodded, set her own bloody knife aside, and with slightly-trembling fingers grasped the handle tightly.

He bit down on the sleeve of his sweater. "Now."

Pain forced muffled curses and groans from his mouth. When the tip cleared his flesh, the pain slackened enough for him to speak.

"Good girl," he said, panting hard. "Now, the medical kit from our bags."

His thoughts raced while she scrambled for the saddle bag. *Did not hit my heart or a big vessel, or I'd be dead. Let it bleed some, try to get cloth out of the wound, apply the liquid, bandage, wrap. Not much time, we have to get out of here. Pain will die back slowly. Can I ride? We'll find that out very soon.*

Bethia worked fast now with steady hands. Oran liked the look on her face, determined and hurried, no sign of panic.

"All right," he said, his breath coming easier. "Find the scissors ... good ... and a square bandage ... yes, that one, and a roll of white cloth. Right. Now dig for a stoppered vial of green liquid. Keep looking ... that's it. Unclasp my cloak and spread it away from the wound. Cut a big slit in my sweater and my shirt so you can see the wound itself."

"Yes," she said softly, "I can do that. My mother taught us some things. I was scared for a minute, Oran, but I'm okay now."

She took the scissors and quickly exposed the wound.

"How does it look?"

She leaned over and looked close. "I don't think any fabric went in with the knife. That's good, isn't it?"

"Yes, lucky for me. How much blood?"

"Some, it's kind of oozing."

"Bright or dark red?"

"Dark."

"Okay, now you have to do three things. It's going to hurt me, I may even pass out, so listen carefully. First, take a clean cloth in the bag, put a little water on it from your canteen, and wipe the blood away. Then right away pour the green liquid on the wound, try to get it inside if you can. Then press the square bandage on it, wrap the rolled cloth under my arm and over my shoulder, tight enough to squeeze the bandage on the wound. Got it?"

"Yes. I know that part. Which part will hurt you the most?"

"The liquid, curse it. Without it the wound will infect, so it has to be."

She arranged what she needed carefully.

"You're doing really well, Bethia."

She nodded. Her young face was a study in concentration. "Okay, I'm ready."

She swabbed the wound clean, opened the vial, and after a moment's hesitation, poured the antiseptic mixture. Oran knew what was coming from long experience. An iron poker straight from the fire lanced into his chest. He sunk his teeth deep into his sleeve and the gray winter sky overhead blackened. When he came to, he saw that Bethia had taken full advantage of his senseless interval. She had the wrapping finished and was tying the ends in a neat knot. His jaw ached and his right hand was clenched so tight it was hard to open it. The wound blazed like fire which was good. That burning might save his life.

She pulled the shirt and sweater edges back together and re-fastened his cloak.

"Now for the hard part," he said while she re-stowed the kit. "I need to get up and onto Seara. We have to get moving, those men will be missed."

He elbowed himself up to a sitting position and saw stars briefly. *I haven't lost much blood yet. That will change while I ride, without stitching of the wound. No choice. I have to get us away from here or we'll both die.*

Bethia got onto his right side and tucked her head under his arm. She pulled and he drove with legs that seemed made of rubber. Pain flared from the wound again ... then he was standing and leaning against Seara. Bethia needed only seconds to load the horses and free their reins. He stepped into the stirrup and swung onto Seara, who stood frozen in place. The horses smelled blood and it made them uneasy. Bethia mounted Vengeance, and they were off.

When the terrain permitted, he set Seara to her fast trot, a pace she liked and one that made for a smooth ride. If they could make twenty miles by sunset they would reach the pass through the Galtee Mountains, and there be safe from attack. He planned to go directly though the pass and stop in a town called Kilbeheny where he knew a blacksmith. From there it was no more than twenty-five miles along a decent and safe road to the fort at Clonmel, where Conor gathered the army.

By noon they covered much of the distance, under a dark wintry sky that sometimes spit ice pellets and sometimes flakes of dry snow. He called a brief halt in a sheltered glen, where they fed the horses the last of the oats, ate a quick meal of dried beef and fruit, and rode on. By mid-afternoon, Oran felt his strength ebbing. It was nothing new to him, in fact he expected it. The bandage on his chest was soaked with blood. His hands and feet grew numb with cold despite heavy gloves and sox, his thighs ached from the effort of riding, and his vision blurred slightly every now and then. Still he pressed on, a silent Bethia riding close behind him on Vengeance. Seara knew much was amiss: he saw it in the odd tosses of her head, the frequent nervous snorts. Still she held her pace, and at times he imagined she made a special effort to smooth out her stride.

His admiration for the young woman from Belfast climbed very high indeed. She had killed two men, saved him from bleeding to death, and now rode with a determined look that showed not a hint of fear. The unwanted burden had become a steadfast companion to whom he owed his life. Again, Sean's words came back to him, "*accept the unexpected, it may be good fortune in a clever disguise.*"

They reached Kilbeheny by nightfall and at the very end of his strength. On the outskirts of town stood the cottage and workshop of

Jarlath Ethra. Oran knew the blacksmith well and stopped to see him often on his travels beyond the Rampart. Jarlath's wife cooked astonishingly tasty meals, served out at a vast table at which Jarlath's brood of nine children shouted and laughed and begged Oran for stories of his travels. Oran always brought treats and gifts for the children, and even on this urgent mission his saddle bags held nine spinning tops he had purchased in Dungarvan.

Oran knew something was wrong even before they dismounted. No children cavorted in the yard; the shutters of the big thatched cottage were closed and latched; no light shone from the barn's windows. And not a sound could be heard from the town a half mile down the road.

"Where is everyone?" Bethia asked.

"My guess is Jarlath and everyone in the village fled into the Galtees, took their horses and carts and enough food to last two or three weeks."

"Why would they do that?"

"They know of the army at Lough Gur and they also know that army may come straight through here. Would you want to be here then?"

"No," Bethia said with a troubled look. "I wouldn't."

"So they took everything they could and vanished. Anyway, Jarlath won't mind my staying a night or two. The cottage door has one of his big iron padlocks on it, but the barn should be open."

Bethia dismounted and had no trouble sliding the heavy barn door aside.

"Now help me down."

Oran was barely able to swing his leg over the saddle. His knees buckled and as Bethia tried to bear his weight, her shoulder pressed into the wound. A gasp of agony escaped his lips.

"I'm sorry!" she cried, struggling to hold him up.

"It's all right," he said, sucking in deep breaths against the pain. "Into the barn, let me down, bring the horses, then close the door."

She eased him onto a mound of hay well away from the door. On their own the two horses found a feeding crib that still held some oats. Bethia tugged the heavy door shut and instantly they were plunged into near-darkness.

"Lantern," he said. "Take the shade off the side, keep it away from the hay."

She got the lantern out and lit it. Without its night shade, it cast a warm glow that revealed a an anvil and forge, plunging tub, chunks of pig iron and slag piled in a corner, horseshoes hanging on nails everywhere.

Bethia sat down next to him on the dirt floor.

"So there's no one here to help us," she said with a dejected look. "We're alone."

Oran leaned back against the hay. Slowly the pain in his chest eased.

"It's all right," he said, taking one of her hands. "We have a little food left, the horses have feed and water, and we're dry and snug for now."

Her hand tightened on his. "I'm really scared, Oran. What are we going to do?"

"Scared," he said with a laugh. "After what you did today? Nonsense! First I need you to change this bandage, and then we're going to eat and rest. You can recite poems for me. After that we'll figure out what to do."

"Aren't you ever scared?" she challenged him. "Ever?"

"Look at me." She turned her head upward. "Of course I'm scared, lots of times. It's a good thing, too, being scared keeps you alert and you don't take stupid chances. Now dig out the medical kit and we'll get started."

The fear in her eyes faded as she took care of the bandaging and then spread out their remaining food. They ate and drank in silence for a time. Oran felt some strength returning afterwards, though not enough, he knew well, to ride hard all the next day. Bethia told him when she changed the bandage that wound was not bleeding now. That was because he was sitting still on a pile of hay. Mounting and riding a horse would break it open. He pondered the options while Bethia recited some of her poems.

"You have a real talent for it," Oran told her. "You'll enjoy meeting my friend Conor. An interesting combination, poet and knife-thrower."

"You're making fun of me."

"Not at all, Bethia. What I mean to say is that I'm glad you're here with me."

"Really?"

"Really. You're quite a young woman and a fine partner."

She brushed away a lone tear that ran down her cheek.

"Thanks for saying that. Being with you has, has made a big difference for me. I want to make a new life for myself. So ... what about tomorrow?"

"Ah, yes, tomorrow," he said casually. "Well, I have a plan worked out. You're going to go on alone to Clonmel."

She looked up in alarm. "Alone?"

"The fact is, I'll never be able to ride twenty-five miles. If I lose any more blood I'll fall off the horse and then we'll both be stranded. I'll be safe here for a time. The enemy army may not come through here, and even if they do, it won't be for two more days. So here's the plan. I'll write you two notes, one for the gate commander at Clonmel, the other for Conor Laigain. The first one will get you inside the Rampart, the second will tell Conor where I am and why. You'll also take him all my notes. Those are the most important thing, not me. You've got to get those notes to Conor. He'll send out fast riders right away, and with any luck they can carry me out of here in time."

She twisted her fingers together. "And if they don't?"

"I'll hide out in the loft, they'll never find me."

I don't like lying to her, he told himself, *but she has got to be made to go.*

"Sure," she said. "Whatever you say."

"Now find my notebook and the pencil. And when you've done that, take some of that wood stacked in the corner and build a fire in Jarlath's forge. We'll be warm tonight."

While she stoked the forge and got a fire going, he wrote steadily. The note to the gate commander was short, just enough to get her through in a hurry with an escort to Conor. The second note would lie on top of his notes on numbers, weapons, armor, route of attack, and probable timetable. To Conor he wrote:

Conor: this young woman's name is Bethia MacLaren, from Belfast. She can tell you her own story. All I can say for now is that she saved my life today. I had a tiny accident and had to camp out in a barn in Kilbeheny. The sketch below will tell you exactly where I am. I need a surgeon to make some repairs before I can ride out of here. Not much time, the great beast is lumbering down the road. This above all: keep a smile on your face, General. - Oran

He folded the notes and tucked them into a waterproof pouch of oiled leather. The barn warmed quickly as Bethia stoked the forge. She came and sat by his right side and he tucked her under his arm.

"How do you feel?" she asked.

"Not too bad," he said honestly. "You did everything right this morning. If I stay quiet until help comes I'll be fine."

"I won't get lost tomorrow?"

"No, I'll draw you a map. You'll go south from here a couple of miles and take the older, less-traveled road that runs east through Clogheen. You'll cross the River Suir and then you'll be almost there. If you start at first light, you can cover the distance by noon. Be careful with Vengeance, don't push him too hard. He'll be well-fed and watered by morning. Watch out for ruts and washouts in the road."

She snuggled down deeper against him. One of her hands sought out his and held on.

"I'll make it," she said firmly, sounding sleepy now. "I won't let you get killed, Oran."

"I know you won't," he said. He stroked her hair. "I still have thousand stories to tell you."

In the morning, he felt strong enough to get to his feet. Moving around cautiously did not tear open the wound. He leaned on barn door frame, watching Bethia ride hard down the road and disappear around a bend.

Good fortune, dear Bethia. Whatever happens to me here, I hope the world has a kindly plan for you.

I have seen General Laigain write in his journal, and it seems like a good idea so I am going to start one. Mother and Father make sure we all learn to read and write well, they say it is part of our heritage. I am almost sixteen now and have major responsibilities here. 'Tis my great fortune to be aide to General Laigain. At times I find it hard to imagine him in battle, he is such a warm and quiet soul, yet I saw him command and fight at Wicklow as fiercely as any man alive. He reminds me of Uncle Ultan, never seems to shout or get angry with people, though he has plenty of reason to at times. The soldiers love and respect him as they did his famous father Domnall. He is said to be a poet though I have not seen any of his poems. Would it be wrong to ask? He does not smile much. Who would with the weight he is carrying? I do my best to keep things straight and fend off minor problems that take up too much time. We are days from battle now. Morale is high. Everyone is nervous, me included. Time to go to work.

Journal of Bradaigh Cumain

Chapter 39

"Twenty-two more volunteers from the west arrived from Dungarvan today, sir," Bradaigh reported.

"My sister is still busy."

"Aye, it seems so, General. The heavens know we need every one."

Conor bent over the basin in the tent's corner and splashed water on his face. The water was pleasantly warm.

"And thank you for the warm water, Bradaigh," he said, mopping his face with a towel.

He eased his aching body into a chair and made an attempt at combing unruly hair.

"With respect, sir," said Bradaigh, approaching with a steaming mug of tea, "you could use a haircut."

"True enough," Conor agreed. "No doubt there's gray starting to show."

Bradaigh handed him the cup and peered at Conor's hair.

"Not that I can see, sir," he said.

"Good."

"In this poor light, that is."

"Uh-huh."

Conor enjoyed the banter with his broad-shouldered young friend, who seemed to sense when it would lift his mood. Bradaigh was already much changed from the angry and sad boy he met in Wicklow Tower.

It had been a strenuous sixteen-hour day, never a moment's rest from an hour before dawn until now, when the invisible sun had long since set. The run of three clear, cold days came to an abrupt halt: now a chill, damp wind ruffled the canvas and made it seem colder than it was. Kellen, Melvina, and Arvel allowed no letup in the endless training. Arvel managed to acquire a hundred more horses from his homeland; now three hundred of the small, fast horses regularly thundered over the broad, flat meadow Arvel used for practice. Two hundred riders were well enough trained to ride and shoot confidently, and a hundred more would be ready in two or three more days of grueling work.

Kellen and Melvina had each formed an auxiliary unit composed of Feth's new recruits from the western regions. There was simply not enough time to train these willing fighters in the complex maneuvers of the Lines of Blades and Bows, so they were armed and armored as separate fighting forces. Kellen's all-male infantry unit wore chainmail and carried javelins, short swords and round shields. They would be used to harry the enemy's flanks and reinforce weak points in the main battle line. Melvina had armed her mixed male and female auxiliaries with fast-loading crossbows, easier to master than the longbow. In a close-range fight they could pour out salvos of bolts that would kill just as efficiently as longbow arrows.

"No word of my sister's whereabouts?" he asked Bradaigh, who was laying out food on the table for a cold supper.

"Nothing recent, sir. I asked several of the newest recruits, they saw Feth over a week ago. Dinner is ready, if you're hungry."

"Yes, I'm hungry," he replied. "It's just the energy it takes to eat that I'm lacking."

Nevertheless, he dragged his chair to the table, and as he did so the tent flap opened. Melvina's face poked through.

"Conor, a brief word?"

"Absolutely not," he replied. "Come in, sit down, and eat."

She came in, a study in exhaustion. Mud coated bare, hard-muscled calves, long russet hair tumbled loose from a metal band, and most striking of all, a blood-soaked bandage adorned her forehead from one side to the other. As she sagged into a chair, Conor stared at the bandage in alarm.

"What was *that* from?"

Her eyes turned upwards. "Ah, yes, that. Loaded crossbows are tricky to handle in fast maneuvers. One of the recruits fell and the bolt went, er, somewhat astray." She took a mug of tea from Bradaigh with a grateful nod.

"It could have killed you," he said with an irritated look. "Stay further away."

Instantly he regretted both the words and the tone.

"Sorry, General," she said. "My mistake, it won't happen again."

"Melvina, I—" he began.

She sighed and held up her free hand. "Conor, don't apologize. We're both so tired we can't see straight."

Conor smiled and handed her a chunk of bread. "Sorry anyway. I'm getting short with everyone, including myself. Bradaigh, come eat with us."

The aide had posted himself a few steps away as he usually did. Now he pulled up another chair and with relish cut himself a thick slice of cheese.

"Now, business first," said Conor. "Aside from your brush with death, everything okay?"

"The Line of Bows is ready, strength is seventeen hundred twenty, all well-trained. The best we have from here to Wicklow. The auxiliaries are coming along fast, we'll have to be careful how we use them. They're proud of what they're doing."

"Uinseann will be here tomorrow with members of the Council. We'll hold the Service of Citizenship night after next. You did need something, right?"

"Not business, really."

"Ah. You're worried about Oran."

"Yes."

"I've been worried about him for most of the last decade," Conor said lightly. He raised an eyebrow and said, "You must have gotten pretty close."

"We had a full day together, the day after we reached the Rampart and released the field army. We strolled into Wicklow, had dinner in a pub, and then, well, they had a room available and we stayed. General Conmaicne probably missed me, but he let it go. Oran must have told you."

"He told me the general idea. Padraic knew where you were."

Copper eyes looked up in surprise. "How?"

"A staff officer saw you two together in town and opened his big mouth."

"Oh, boy, that's not good."

"Relax," Conor laughed. "I know my uncle wasn't angry. You reported by six the next morning."

"I was so tired I couldn't see straight, but I was there! Anyway, we had a couple of hours the next day and then he was gone. Yes, we got very close in that time. He's a wonderful man, your friend Oran."

"He is indeed," said Conor. His mind drifted back to childhood days. "Strange that we're not at all alike and yet so attached to each other. We like some of the same things, like good stout and strong, beautiful women." Melvina grinned at him; Bradaigh stifled a laugh. "He's wandered this whole country for fifteen years. The first time he took off past the Rampart, I thought his father Hagan would use him for a scarecrow. He does what he likes to do. Without him, we'd be just about blind. The problem is it gets more dangerous year by year."

Melvina nodded and thought a moment. "He has a brother ... Seanlaoch?"

"Yes, younger by four years."

"Oran seemed surprised I hadn't heard of him or his writings."

"His books and monographs are used in all the schools now, but not when you and I were studying."

"How can he have done so much by, what, twenty-four?"

"Sean got started early," Conor said, smiling as he recalled the scholarly boy. "By the time he was ten he'd read every book in the town library and most of the private collections around. He wrote his first pamphlets on history when he was fourteen, and in the last ten years he's written a great deal more."

"Why?"

"Why does he write? He's worried sick we'll forget who we are and what we're fighting to preserve. We lost so many books and records when we retreated behind the Rampart, there wasn't time to collect all the libraries and bring them here safely. So Sean is collecting and reading and digesting everything we have left on the history of our people and writing it down for later generations."

"A worthy task," Melvina murmured. "I bet he wears spectacles?"

"He does, usually sliding down his nose. Otherwise he looks quite a bit like Oran, in a softer, gentler way. The strange thing is, my wild little sister Feth always had a crush on him, and now I hear that Feth and Sean are, well, an item." Conor paused in thought. "Feth is a hard one to read, though. Impulsive, mouthy, daring too, yet there is another side of her that sends a chill up my spine. Hard to define, something ancient in the blood, maybe? No doubt Sean sees it too."

Bradaigh cleared off the table and went outside the tent to fetch more hot water from the cooking fire. When he returned moments later, he wore a wide-eyed expression.

"A problem?" Conor asked him.

"Not exactly, sir," he said. "You have another visitor."

"Well, who? Commander Fotharta?"

"No, sir. General Conmaicne."

The tent flap parted and the opening was suddenly filled with a cloaked figure. The hood of the cloak nearly touched the frame of the tent. Conor and Melvina, tired as they were, got up in a hurry. The hood slid back, revealing the smiling, craggy face of Padraic Conmaicne.

"A fine aide," he said, smiling down at Bradaigh. "He insisted I give my name."

Padraic maneuvered his vast form into the tent. Bradaigh edged behind him to close the flap against the wind.

"I am here incognito!" Padraic said brightly. He tossed his cloak to Bradaigh. "Not official at all, Conor. I came to see if I can help in any way." He caught sight of Melvina's damaged forehead. "I don't approve of wounds in advance of battle."

Melvina put a hand to her bandage. "I've already been chastised. Would you believe I tripped, sir?"

"I would not."

"How about a loose crossbow bolt?"

"That I believe," Padraic said. He laid a broad hand on her shoulder. "Just be careful. You are of great value to this army and we can't afford to lose you."

To Conor's astonishment, Melvina blushed deep red.

"Thank you, General," she said in a small voice. To Conor, she said, "I'm going to my tent, Conor. Thanks for dinner. Good to see you, General," she said with a slight bow.

Bradaigh caught Melvina's *come with me* look and followed her outside.

Padraic peered uneasily at the folding camp chairs. "Perhaps I'll take the bed," he said, and settled his bulk onto the wood-frame bunk, which nevertheless creaked ominously.

"Tea, Uncle? The pot has plenty."

"Yes, that would go well, Conor. Damnably cold ride along the military road." He took the steaming mug from Conor. "I repeat, I am not here to check up on you. If I didn't believe in you, you wouldn't wear the gold cape. I just wanted to see how things were going. You'll be moving out soon, I think."

Conor turned his chair to face Padraic. "I expect word from Oran any day. I could use another week, sure, but we'll be ready."

"Numbers?"

"Blades twenty-three hundred eighty, Bows seventeen hundred twenty. Arvel is nearing a full complement of three hundred horse archers. Feth's sent back over two hundred volunteers so far, they've been formed into auxiliaries. Kellen made up a century of light-armored auxiliaries with javelins, Melvina equipped hers with fast-firing crossbows."

"Hence the wound."

"Yes."

Padraic tapped the bed frame absently. "Two inches over and she would have been killed. Make sure she wears her helmet at all times on the field, you and Kellen too."

Conor nodded assent.

"Citizenship ceremony?" Padraic asked.

"We'll induct the auxiliaries as citizens before we move out. Uinseann is already in town. You'll be present?"

"Of course. Two hundred volunteers!" He shook his head. "My little Feth. Any word on her whereabouts?"

"She's supposed to be in Tralee by tomorrow, take a coaster to Dungarvan and get up here by nightfall. God forbid the weather is bad for sailing, they'll never get back overland fast enough."

"I believe Bram is here, yes?"

Conor was caught off guard by the question. "He was here last night looking for me. He's spoiling to have it out with me and I'd love to oblige."

"Nephew, that's a brawl that must *never* take place. It's not just that he's likely to kill you. No, don't protest! You might well kill him at the same time. What exactly would that prove? No, there will be no fighting, no matter what he may say about you or me or Mairin. Give me your word on that."

Conor met his uncle's challenging look. "All right, my word. But tell me this. Where does all this hatred come from? I never tormented Bram, yet he seems to despise me. Gorman loathes you and Etain seems to have it in for our whole family. I asked Uinseann once, years ago, if this feud goes back over generations. He said no and that's all he would say. I know my father broke Gorman out of the army for drunkenness. That doesn't seem enough." Padraic said nothing so he pressed the issue. "I didn't help matters any by what happened at Kellen's cabin. Yet I didn't see that I had any choice."

"You didn't," Padraic agreed. He set the mug aside, lifted Conor's sword from the foot of the bunk, pulled it from the sheath, and idly studied its gleaming blade. "There's much more to the story."

"I'd like to hear it."

"Not here," Padraic said. He replaced the sword and heaved himself to his feet. "I know it's a foulish night, but the wind will be cut off down at the river near the bridge. Walk with me?"

"Of course, Uncle. I'll leave a note for Bradaigh. He gets worried when he doesn't know where to find me."

A minute later, two cloaked figures emerged from the tent and made their way out the east gate of the camp. A winding path leading off from the road took them down to the water's edge. Here, the Suir's black currents swirled and gurgled around timeless stone pilings. Conor took a deep breath: no smoke of campfires down here, no reek of sweat, no blended odors of stewpots and bread and hot grease. Instead, he relished the musty scent of old stone and mortar, the clean fragrance of cold running water, the calming odor of damp earth. Above them, friendly lights of the town cast a dim yellow glow on the rippling waters.

Padraic leaned his shoulder against a stone arch and ran a hand over its jagged surface.

"Built by hands of men twenty-five centuries ago," he murmured, his deep voice seeming to blend with the sound of the river itself. "Did they have to fight for survival too? I wonder."

"Probably they did, Uncle. Sean Osraige says that's the story of our land and our people."

Padraic sighed heavily. "I'm sure he's right. Well, onto other things. It's hard to see it now, Conor, but once I was a tall young man with a smooth face, bright blue eyes, and a decent head for stories. Oh, I was never so handsome as you! Still, women liked me anyway and I had my share of fun. Most of it innocent."

"Mother says you were pretty wild."

Padraic's bushy eyebrows climbed. "Oh, she does, does she? If that isn't the pot calling ... well, that's off the point. I suppose I was a bit of a stallion."

"Until you met Pegeen."

"Yes, my dear, dear Pegeen. Oh, what my life might have been had she lived! Well, that was later anyway. Before I knew Pegeen, I knew Etain Fotharta. So did a troupe of other young bucks in those days. She was the most beautiful woman any man could lay eyes on. A man's mouth watered just to see her, and other parts of his anatomy had something to say too. Well, she and I enjoyed a couple of nights together and then to my surprise she became rather attached to me. For the next few months we spent a lot of time together, maybe courted is the word. I felt like I loved her, for all I knew about love then. With Etain it was hard to sort out real feeling from the passion she drew out of men."

"Anyway, I began to dream that I'd marry this beauty. Then word got back to me that she was, well, enjoying the company of someone else. I didn't want to believe it except that the source was unimpeachable— your father. When he told me, I flew into a rage and told Etain what I thought of her, though it broke my own heart to do it. Strange thing was, she denied nothing and to me seemed unbearably cold about it. A month after that disaster I met Pegeen and fell in love with her. I didn't see Etain at all for three months. Then one night she came to see me and claimed she was pregnant with my child! I threw that back in her face. I said 'how can you tell it's mine?' She admitted she couldn't be sure yet still had the audacity to ask me to marry her! Needless to say, I said no and she cursed me in ways I didn't think a woman like her knew about. Then she threw herself on a besotted Gorman whom she'd already slept with. She convinced poor gullible Gorman the child she was carrying was his and they married, even before I married Pegeen."

He paused his tale as laughter burst from the bridge above. Young male voices, *probably soldiers*, Conor thought. *A good sign ... so long as they stay out of the pubs.*

"She can't have hated you all these years over that, Uncle."

"When you hear the rest, her reaction may seem less irrational. The trouble really started when she gave birth to Bram six months after she married Gorman."

Conor was getting an uneasy feeling in the pit of his stomach.

"Six months is an early birth but not unheard of," he commented warily.

"The 'premature' boy-child weighed ten pounds at birth. Etain's lover after me was five-feet seven and thin. And while blue-eyed children sometimes spring from two dark-eyed parents, it's as rare as flowers in January, Conor. Gorman's eyes are nearly black and Etain's medium brown."

All at once the river's soft murmur seemed inordinately loud in Conor's ears. He could find nothing to say.

Padraic heaved a great sigh. "So, it's almost sure Bram is my son, as Etain claimed. I never saw the child but your mother did and she knew immediately what the truth had to be. I was desperate to make sure no rumors reached Pegeen's ears. And in the three short years she lived with me, I don't think they did. Then she died after losing our first child, oh what a tragedy that was."

Padraic's voice broke. Conor could hear him breathing heavily in the darkness.

"Gorman was a weak man to begin with," he struggled on, "and he had to know Bram was not his and most likely mine. After that I think he despised Etain ... though he managed to have two more children by her. And I suppose Etain blamed me for all her woes, though in truth the whole debacle was her own fault."

"So, I am being told that Bram is my cousin? After all these years, that is what I am being told?" Conor said with anger rising in his gut. "And who else would know about this, Uncle?"

Padraic walked to the river's edge and gazed up at the town. "Your father before he died. Uinseann and Rionach, of course. And your mother."

"My mother! I can't believe she never told me."

"A promise to me, Conor, that she would never break."

"What about Mairin? And Kellen?"

"Possibly they suspect. I have no way of knowing what they think."

Conor struggled to control his anger. "Uncle, I am twenty-eight years old. Isn't it a little late to be telling me this? You know I've been seeing Mairin for two years."

"And what good would telling you have done?" said Padraic, on the defensive.

"Then why tell me now? You didn't have to."

Padraic ran a hand through long gray hair.

"No, I didn't. I've agonized over this ever since the incident with Bram. You see, Bram is almost certain he's my son. He told me so to my face five or six years ago. He was drunk and stumbled into my office at Army HQ. I dragged him out into the woods and he spewed at me for most of an hour. Maybe he guessed when he was young, maybe he overheard a fight between Etain and Gorman. He didn't say. Bram envies you, envies the family you have, what you've done with yourself, how people look at you. He's convinced you are where you are now because I favor you. He has no idea I've had to push you from behind with all my strength."

"In truth I think he hates me more than you, but after many years hate grows like a cancer until a man can't remember exactly what it was for or who it was directed against. That's why you have to be careful of him, son. He has my strength, almost, and that makes him very, very dangerous."

Conor took a few steps away and turned his face into the wind that seeped into the sheltered spot. Down the river, campfires flickered for as far as he could see. Above the town to the north, brilliant lanterns blazed atop the high tower of the vast stone fort. His flare of anger subsided. *What is the point now? And what would I have done differently, had I known all along? Nothing.*

"Uncle, wouldn't it be better if we sent Bram back to one of the forts, away from here?"

Padraic shook his head. "I can't deny him the right to fight, Conor. Whatever else he may have done, and however undisciplined he may be at times, he's fought honorably in the Line of Blades as long as you. Unless he does something bad enough to break him out of the army, he goes with his unit, and his unit is here. We need every sword, and on the battlefield, sober, Bram is a terrific fighter, worth three ordinary men."

Neither spoke for a full minute.

"Uncle," Conor said finally, "there is a question I need to ask you. Not about Bram directly. About something he said to me two weeks ago in Rosslare. The day after the incident at Kellen's cabin."

His mouth went dry and his heart thumped against his chest. Padraic waited silently.

"Bram implied Gorman harmed Mairin. I don't mean striking her, I know about that part, I mean ... "

"You need say no more, son," said Padraic with a deep sigh. "I get the idea."

"And?"

Padraic cursed under his breath. "Etain was away from their home much of the time, left the children alone with Gorman and a housekeeper who is now dead. So I suppose it's possible. But to be honest, Conor, I don't see it. Not from what I know of Gorman. It doesn't fit. More likely Bram made it up. Only Mairin can tell you the truth of it."

"How could I ask Mairin that? I can't, Uncle. It will have to be left as it is. I tell you this: if Bram ever says it again, I will run him through. You can't ask me to let it pass."

"No, not this," Padraic admitted. "When our business here is finished, I'll deal with the matter. In my own way." He seemed about to go on, but instead cursed again and slammed one massive fist into the other. "Enough of this, Conor, we have to talk about the army now. What needs to be done?"

Conor struggled to refocus his mind. "We're still short of weapons and armor. If anything breaks we have nothing to replace it with."

"I'll crack heads tomorrow," Padraic said with feeling. They started up the bank together. "I'll have supper with your mother and Uinseann and take a room at the inn. Call on me if you need me. Just remember, you are in command here. That's absolute."

"Yes, sir," he said, saluting as they parted at the road. "Thank you, Uncle, for telling me what you did. I'm not angry about it."

He added silently, *we all do things we're sorry for later, like making love to someone on the spur of the moment when you're engaged to someone else.*

"Good night, nephew," Padraic said. He stepped onto the bridge and headed into town.

Conor turned towards the camp and then stopped. Too many feelings welled up inside him to go back to his lonely tent just yet. He strolled back down to the river's edge and perched on a boulder. Bram ... Padraic's bastard son! Why had he never seen it, or even suspected it? Now that he knew the truth, it all fit. Take away Padraic's scars and lines and weather-beaten skin and the resemblance was surely there.

He lowered his head as thoughts of a young Mairin in that vile household overtook the matter of Bram. How much had she suffered? What if Gorman had forced her, abused her, as Bram wanted him to think? Like him she was twenty-eight now, but could wounds so deep ever completely heal? He scooped up a handful of pebbles and tossed them into the black waters, one at a time, thinking bleak thoughts. Perhaps Mairin would never return. Perhaps he himself would lie in the dust, a week hence. Perhaps—

"General."

He started at the voice directly behind him.

"Yes. Yes, Bradaigh, what is it?"

"Message from the fort, sir, the captain on duty requests that you come."

"Any word why?"

"No, sir. He says it's urgent."

"Right." Conor hopped off the boulder and led his aide up the bank. "Go back to the camp, alert Kellen and Melvina. Get the signalers together, sound no alarm unless the fort sounds it first."

"I have it, sir," said Bradaigh over his shoulder. The boy sprinted off into the darkness.

Conor crossed the bridge into town and strode at a fast clip towards the fort. *Don't run*, he warned himself. *The sight of the army commander pelting down the street will send rumors flying.* Who was on fort duty tonight? The name came to him: Muirios Dunlainge, a twenty-year veteran and long stationed here at Clonmel.

Conor covered the four blocks through the town quickly yet inconspicuously, waving and calling out greetings to citizens he knew. The fort itself was unlike any other in the long chain of forts, nearly all of which had been new-constructed along with the Rampart itself. This gigantic edifice of granite and mortar, in its earliest incarnation a church of one of the old rites, dated back like the Suir Bridge at least twenty-five centuries. Impregnable walls three feet thick and an eight-story tower that gave it a commanding view ten miles to the north and west made it the Province's key defense point in the west.

Conor ascended the long stone staircase leading to the fort's ornate double doors, now closed tight to shut out the cold wind. He entered the cavernous Common Room through a small side door and was met inside by a young tower-watcher, a boy of ten at most, who led him to the staircase at the base of the tower. Ascending its eight flights behind the sprightly boy, Conor felt an occasional twinge in the leg he fractured five years before in defense of this very fort.

The open roof level of the tower was a tense place; that much Conor sensed as soon as he made the top step. All of the watchers leaned over the rail of the west parapet, the four alarm trumpeters held instruments at the ready, and Muirios Dunlainge himself manned the telescope which was also aimed west. He saluted and then accepted Conor's extended hand; they knew each other well.

"Muirios, good to see you. What do we have?"

"Take a look, General," the white-haired, slight man said with a nod towards the telescope. "Force approaching, but I'll be damned if I can figure out who they are."

Conor stepped forward and trained the telescope onto the road leading west towards Clogheen. He saw torches first ... and then a column of soldiers walking four abreast, led by a standard-bearer. In the pale light of the tower's great lanterns, Conor made out some uniformity of weapons and body armor. And there were archers! None of their usual foes used the bow and arrow in combat.

"We've had them spotted for at least a half-hour, sir, saw them five miles off where the road goes over the rise. You know the place, General."

"Yes," said Conor, straightening up. "Very strange. Discipline in the ranks, archers, leather armor, and coming on slow as if not to raise the alarm."

"That's how I read it, sir," agreed Muirios. "I have the fort itself on quiet alert, Blades massed at the west gate, Bows and ballistae crews on the shooting platforms. I didn't want to send the town into a panic."

Conor moved to the west parapet, where two of the watchers quietly stepped aside. One he recognized, a honey-haired girl with shiny hazel eyes.

"Liadan Cumain, yes?" he asked her.

"Yes, General," she answered, beaming that he recognized her. "My brother is your new aide. I asked to be sent here. We have a cousin in town that I stay with, off-duty."

"Your brother is a fine aide, Liadan. You must be proud of him."

"Thank you, sir. I am."

Conor looked west over Liadan's head. The unknown fighters advanced at the same unhurried pace. One by one they extinguished torches as they came under the full blaze of the fort's lanterns.

"I'd say about five hundred," Conor said. "Give or take."

"Yes, sir, that's my count too," said Muirios. "A quiet lot."

"Very."

Five hundred disciplined, well-armed fighters ... from where? And what did they want?

"I'm going to the gate," Conor told Muirios. "Send a runner to the Inn of the Autumn Leaf, General Conmaicne is there now."

"Is he, sir?" said Muirios with raised eyebrows. "Liadan," he said, "did you hear?"

"Yes, sir," she said, pleased to be chosen. "What shall I tell him, General?"

"Tell him what we've seen and ask him to come to the fort. Then run to the camp, find your brother at my tent and ask him to come here too, fast as he can."

Liadan Cumain bowed slightly and bolted down the stairs. Conor and Muirios followed at a more modest pace; who could keep up with a twelve-year-old at full tilt?

Two sentry platforms rose fifteen feet high on either side of the west gate. Conor and Muirios threaded their way through the assembled Blades and climbed one of the platforms. At the top they found the Blade captain on duty.

"General Laigain," he said, saluting. "Piaras Briuin."

"Captain," said Conor, "If you would, rejoin your men below, listen for my orders."

"Sir," he said with a parting salute.

"Someone coming," Muirios said. "Woman archer, from the looks of it, and a tough one at that."

The bow-armed woman now approaching them was of modest height and graceful stride. A chainmail gambeson covered her torso from neck to thigh, heavy wool trousers were tucked into black boots, and a long sheathed dirk swung from a metal-studded black belt.

As she neared, Conor made out a hard-featured face of dark complexion. She looked up straight at Conor and spoke with a strong, commanding voice.

"My name is Aife Luachra. I command the Fighters of Macroom."

"I am General Conor Laigain, commanding the Province field army."

She took two steps closer and pulled a folded note from a belt pouch.

"A note addressed to you," she said, holding it up. "May I deliver it?"

Conor turned toward Piaras, who waited at the bottom of the steps. "Captain, move your Blades back and open the gate." Turning back to Aife, he said, "I'll meet you below."

He climbed down the steps as the sentries pulled aside massive iron bars and swung the gate inward. Conor walked through and directly up to Aife. She handed him the note. He knew the loopy, clear script immediately: *Conor: these fighters have come to help us. Please treat them well. I will be back soon. Feth.*

He folded the note in half again and held it in a faintly-trembling hand. *Shades of our fathers, Feth, what have you done? Five centuries of armed, trained fighters? It can hardly be believed.*

He held out his hand. "Welcome, Aife Luachra and the Fighters of Macroom. Please bring your force ahead."

She took his hand, then waved a signal at her troops, who resumed their advance towards the gate.

"General Laigain," said Aife, "my soldiers are tired and hungry and cold. We've been marching for three days with very little rest."

"You'll be taken care of immediately," he told her. "Do you have a title you want me to use? I'd prefer you call me Conor."

The hard features eased towards a smile and she shook her head. "No title, Aife will do. Fethnaid is your sister?"

"She is."

"Impressive. And persistent. You would know that."

"Yes. Possibly headstrong too."

Aife now smiled broadly. "A quality I admire, Conor. I suppose that word has often been applied to me."

He led her inside the gate, where Piaras Briuin waited expectantly.

"Captain, order your lines to parade salute."

"Sir."

Piaras shouted out three quick commands. The two lines of a hundred each turned to face each other ten feet apart, came to rigid attention, then lifted their swords to a forty-five degree angle overhead.

"Clear the Common Room, fast," Conor ordered Muirios. "Have all the stoves fired, get the room warm, bring in all the water and food we have on hand. I'll send more from the camp. Quarter the fort watch in the army camp tonight, anywhere we can find space in tents. Go."

The veteran captain saluted and ran for the fort, just as the Macroom Fighters began to enter the gate. The first few inside paused and stared warily at canopy of swords and the heavily-armored men who held them aloft. Conor led Aife down the aisle and her fighters followed.

"You do us an honor," she said in a low voice to Conor.

"You do us a great service," he replied.

An hour later, the vast nave of the old church hummed with the cheerful voices of five hundred warmed and fed fighters. The Common Room's eight big woodstoves drove out the chill, long dining tables groaned with steaming pitchers of tea, wicker baskets of warm bread, cauldrons of lamb stew and platters crowded with applecakes. Hundreds of blankets had been handed out and soldiers with blisters attended by army surgeons. At the front of the room, on the raised platform that once served as an altar, Conor sat at a table with Aife, Melvina, and Kellen. Padraic, who had eaten with them, now strolled around the room, talking with individual soldiers, listening to their needs, telling his own stories or laughing at a joke. Slowly the room quieted as tired soldiers ate their fill and then felt the full weight of their exhaustion.

Padraic, appearing even bigger than usual in his full dress uniform and cape, ascended the high pulpit and waited for silence. Then his rolling bass echoed from the stone walls.

"Fighters of Macroom! I know you arrived here exhausted by your march and wondering what kind of reception you would get. I hope we have managed to make you feel warm and comfortable. Tonight you will sleep well and safe within these ancient walls."

He paused to let the echo die and then went on.

"Decades of suspicion and distrust have passed since the Twenty Clans and the clans of Cork and Kerry drank at the same table together. You are here today because one soldier in my army, a young archer named Fethnaid, had the courage and audacity and humility to reach out to you and ask for your help. It is help we desperately need. This battle is not one where we seek only to hold our Rampart, to defend ourselves as best we can. We need a victory that will bring peace to our lands and to yours."

He nodded towards Conor, Aife, Melvina and Kellen.

"Tomorrow we will make our plans. Anything you need, ask and we will try to provide it. We are all one army now, brothers and sisters of the sword and the bow." He bowed his head slightly. "May the powers that guide all our destinies smile on us. Good night to you all."

Conor, his heart filled admiration, watched his uncle slowly descend the steps in the silence that followed.

"He is much more than a mere soldier," said Aife. She looked at each of them in turn. "As are you all. I am glad we decided to come."

"Most of us are just ordinary people, trying to hold on," Conor said.

Aife nodded and raised her tankard of ale. "Death to our common enemies, then."

To that, they all drank deep.

An hour later, Conor found Bradaigh still hard at work at his desk. Blond hair tumbled down around his exhausted young face. Conor laid a hand on the boy's shoulder.

"To bed, Bradaigh. We start early again tomorrow."

"Yes, sir," he replied. "At five."

Conor pulled off his boots and sweater and collapsed on his cot. Bradaigh straightened up the papers on his desk, put out his lantern, and with a tired sigh climbed into his own cot.

A minute of silence passed. Then Bradaigh said in a low voice, "General? Could I ask about Driscol tonight?"

Conor told him the story of his brother's death at Ballynamult. Bradaigh sobbed once at the end.

"Thank you, General," Bradaigh whispered. "I'm glad you were with him."

"I'm glad I was too, Bradaigh. Sleep now."

And Bradaigh did sleep, but Conor did not. In the still darkness of the tent Conor beheld once again the terror in Driscol's eyes, heard the last breath rattle in his lungs.

Why does that one death affect me so? he asked himself. The answer came after a time. *Because I saw the spark of life expiring in Driscol's eyes and I was utterly powerless to help him. How I do hate and despise the violence of this world.*

Dear Father, we are camped on the shores of Lough Leane, as beautiful a place as I have ever seen. I don't know if the letter will reach you before I see you again. I write to feel close to you. After our success at Macroom, Killarney was a disappointment. The prosperous fisherman here have their own survival plan. They have built shelters on islands in the lakes, and take refuge there whenever raiders are in the area. They are not at all worried about the future and take no heed of our warnings. Feth tried her best but no argument she could make (and she leaves none out) made any difference. Today which is dark and rainy we must make our way to Tralee and then home to Dungarvan. I have become fond of Keegan Cholmain, a fine, tall man from Tramore. You will meet him, I hope, when we are together again. My thoughts as always are of you and of my mother whose face I see each night when I close my eyes.

Your loving daughter, Derdre.

Chapter 40

From first light they had ridden hard. Derdre, Gwen and Feth's horses pounded the soft green turf of the meadow until it was more mud than grass. The archers fired a steady stream of blunted arrows at moving targets provided by Keegan and Ionhar in full armor. When the overcast began sending down a light, cold mist that made footing too treacherous, they gathered on the grass for a late breakfast and set the horses free to graze and rest before the twenty-mile ride to Tralee.

Feth was seething. Her friends saw it in the fierce power of her shooting, in the harsh sound of her voice while they practiced, in her silence and bleak expression as they gathered around a hissing fire. Ionhar served up dried salt fish and bread provided by the thoughtful though uncooperative fishermen of Killarney. Seeing that her friend was still in a black mood, Derdre tried to make pleasant conversation.

"Delicious," she said, nibbling on the fish. "I wonder if they export this through Tralee?"

Gwen answered her. "I think that they do, because—"

"If our ships are gone," Feth cut in bitterly, "they won't have a damned port to export through."

"Feth— " Keegan began.

"I don't want to hear it, Keegan!" she cried. "Not one person volunteered. Not one! They sit out there on their stupid islands and watch while the rest of us bleed. They don't see what's about to happen, if we lose." Her voice fell. "It's not right. Not right at all."

They ate in silence for a time.

"Fethnaid," said Ionhar, his broad face thoughtful, "in the end we can only tell the truth as we know it. What others do with that truth is beyond our power. You may as well rage against the birds for singing or the wolves for hunting."

"Failure is failure," she answered him. "Philosophy can't change that."

"Did we do our best?" Gwen asked. "Did we try?"

"We did," Keegan answered her. "Feth, that's all we can do. Please don't feel like it was you who failed somehow. You've done so much already. You don't even know what effect your words may have, as time passes. Let's leave it at that."

Derdre put her arm over Feth's shoulders. "Now eat some fish. We need our strength, and it *is* tasty."

Feth looked up at each expectant face, the faces of her dearest friends.

They need me to lead, not drip with self-pity, she scolded herself. *Pull yourself together, Feth.*

"Right," she said, forcing her best available smile. She took a big bite of salt fish. "Practice went well anyway, don't you think?"

She saw each of her companions visibly relax, and conversation flowed more easily while Ionhar served out hot tea. An hour later, their gear stowed in saddlebags, they set out on the wide, well-traveled road to Tralee. They would arrive in the port city one day ahead of the date a Squadron ship had been promised to take them back to Dungarvan, so Feth saw no reason to hurry.

She joined in the usual banter, yet inside she still raged at the indifference of the Killarnees. For five long, rainy, windy days they rode among the scenic lakes, as far out as the end of the peninsula, stopping in towns large and small, talking to farmers and merchants and fishermen, and to no result. The people of this region were on the whole prosperous and content and did not worry much about the occasional raid that rarely penetrated beyond the big town of Killarney itself. They'd been received affably enough in most places, and just as affably told they could fight their own battles. Now she turned her thoughts to going home, to seeing Sean—however briefly—feeling his arms around her, breathing in his scent, making love to him.

But first ... there was Tralee, where they might have a full day to recruit among folk friendly to the Province. Even better, Gwen knew the town and its people. Tralee thrived on ocean fishing and commerce, and in both cases benefitted heavily from the Province's warships and merchant fleet. The people of Tralee held the Province in high regard, and had more than once been offered full citizenship in the Twenty Clans. Each time, they respectfully declined, preferring to maintain their long history of independence and self-government. Still, Gwen was unsure whether they would offer to send fighters. Tralee maintained its own militia to defend the port and the surrounding towns from sea-raiders. Stripping those fighters away from the town, even for a short time, could spell disaster in the event of a seaborne attack breaching the protection of the Squadron.

Gwen, riding as usual beside Ionhar, now moved up next to Feth at the front.

"If we have enough time," Gwen said, "I'd like to see my cousins. They'd put us up for the night. Their house is not much to look at but it has a wonderful view of the harbor."

"Sure," Feth replied, "I'd like that. If we have time." She turned her gaze at the lowering gray sky. "The wind is northwest now, that would be good to sail out with. It will be up to the Squadron captain to say, if our ship is already there."

Gwen frowned. "Any chance we could be stranded?"

"If I heard Aideen say it once, I heard it a thousand times, 'wind and tide, wind and tide. You can fight one but not both'."

"Did she take you out on ships sometimes?"

"Oh, yes," said Feth, smiling at the memories. "Lots of times, until she made captain."

"Then why didn't you go into the Squadron?"

"Because I knew I'd always be looked at strangely. Aideen is fourteen years older than me, she made captain when I was eight and commodore when I was fourteen. If I got promoted, it would look like favoritism, and knowing Aideen, she would *never* let tongues wag. I knew it was best I choose another service. I think she was relieved when I started archer training."

"But General Conmaicne is your uncle. Conor's too. And he promoted Conor."

Feth nodded. "Sure he did, and he'll promote me if I deserve it. It's just a different situation. The army is much larger and promotions to officer rank come as a matter of course if you do a good job. The Squadron's officer corps is much smaller than the army's and promotions are done very formally. Aideen names every captain, and she may be commodore a lot longer than Uncle Padraic will lead the army. So ... here I am."

They passed a small lake teeming with mallards, gadwalls, pintails, and wigeons.

"I envy them, don't you, Feth?" said Gwen. "Swim around all day, eat your fill of fish, enjoy the scenery."

"Yes," Feth sighed, "I suppose I do. I guess I'd be a noisy duck."

Gwen laughed. "A sweet, noisy duck, Feth. What kind of duck would Sean be?"

Feth felt a thrill in her thighs at the mention of his name. *Oh, we have to have a little time, Sean, we just have to.*

"He'd be much quieter," she said. "His feathers would be in soft colors. And he would sometimes dive down just to look around, see what he could see. Sean would be a curious duck."

"You miss him."

"Oh, yes, I miss him so much. I want to ... well, you get the idea."

"Sure."

Laughter burst out behind them. Derdre and Keegan rode side-by-side at the back of their group. His big hand held hers.

Gwen twisted around in the saddle and looked past an amused Ionhar. "What's so funny?"

"Naughty joke!" cried Derdre. "Keegan should wash his mouth out with soap!"

"I heard it," said Ionhar, as gravely as possible. "Naughty indeed."

Gwen dropped back next to Ionhar, and they rode on at a gentle pace with Feth again alone at the front. Before long they passed through Farranfore, an abandoned town that Sean's handwritten notes said was supposed to be haunted. The town's cemetery lay at the side of the road, next to a ruined stone church and a quiet stream. Feth decided it was as good a place as any to rest and water the horses. They all dismounted and wandered among overgrown, weathered gravestones. Keegan forced back weeds covering one of the tallest markers.

"John ... O'Malley," he read with difficulty. "The birth date is gone, but the death date is 2877."

Ionhar bent down to read a marker at his feet. "This one says 2798."

"And this one 2924," Gwen put in, on her knees to read a flat stone. "All these are from the last days of the Age of Machines. These people must have lived in a hard time."

Feth wandered towards the back of the graveyard, where a tall, eroded Celtic cross of green stone watched over the graves. "Let's say a prayer," she said. "This is a sacred place."

"Yes," agreed Keegan, "we should."

They gathered themselves around the cross.

"Ionhar," Feth said softly, "would you?"

The red-haired giant nodded. "My words may not be the same as yours, being from Creagh. Perhaps it doesn't matter."

He took a step forward and laid his hands on the scarred surface of the cross.

"We gather here, Fethnaid and Derdre and Gwen and Keegan and Ionhar, to remember and honor those whose remains lie at rest beneath our feet. We do not know these gentle folk, nor do we know their lives, their hopes and dreams, nor how they died. From earth did they arise, and to earth they have returned, in the unending cycle of birth and death. May this ground be forever undisturbed and may this cross, the symbol of the Celts from the furthest of past ages, watch over them and bring them peace. So say we all."

"So say we all," they repeated.

One by one, they laid hands on the cross and returned to their horses. They rode on in silence, each pondering the meaning of the place they had been and the words Ionhar had spoken.

Another hour passed till the air took on the salty tang of the ocean, and the distant sounds of a busy town touched their ears. Soon they were passing neat cottages and inns and pubs. They drew polite nods and greetings from fellow travelers on the road.

Gwen led them through the center of town to the pier, where they stopped at a pub overlooking Tralee Bay. A hanging sign announced in neat, burned-in letters that this was the "Seaside Tavern" whose proprietor was "Drystan of Wales." Inside, a smoky-timbered room was brightly lit by a wall of windows facing the harbor. They took a table near the windows and ordered stout and sandwiches from a friendly barkeep, who gave their soiled uniforms a brief glance but made no comment.

Three merchant ships were moored at the docks, one unloading and two loading, with cargo bound for ports throughout the Celtic world. In the bay itself, single-sailed skiffs plied the gentle waves.

"Cold day for sailing," Keegan observed with a shiver. "A warm pub for me."

Gwen laughed. "Keegan, you're what folks call a land-lubber! This is a fine sailing day, steady wind from the northwest, no storms in sight. People here love to be on the water. My family has a boat like those and in fair weather we sail it all the way to Tralee and back. Fahamore Town has its own harbor," she said proudly. "I wish we had time to go there so you could see it."

"Someday we will," said Ionhar, resting his hand on her arm. "And you'll see Creagh too."

The innkeeper delivered sandwiches piled high with ham and a huge pot of steaming-hot boiled potatoes slathered with butter. After a week of cold rations eaten outdoors, the five travelers demolished every bite and called for seconds. Meanwhile, tables filled and emptied and no one approached them. The main meal cleared to bare plates, they accepted the barkeep's offer of spiced cider and apple cobbler. For the first time in many days, Feth felt some of the tension melt away.

"It almost feels strange," she commented, "to sit in a warm pub again and be ignored. This seems like a wonderful town, Gwen, but the question is, will they give us any help?"

"It's hard to say. I would guess—"

Gwen's eyes widened to saucers as a slender, black-haired young man strode straight up to their table. Gwen jumped out of her chair and hugged him.

"Brennan!" she cried with her head over his shoulder. "Oh, Brennan, it's wonderful to see you!"

"Hi, Gwen," the young man said tenderly. "I heard you were here."

They parted to arms length and Gwen brushed tears from her cheeks.

"Friends, this is my cousin Brennan Cennedi. Keegan ... Ionhar ... Derdre ... and Feth."

He took each of their hands in a strong grip. "Welcome to Tralee, all," he said, sliding into an extra chair. "I overheard someone in our shop talking about Province soldiers in this tavern. We knew from Gwen's letter you were coming this way, so I figured it had to be you. Mom and Dad will be thrilled to see you, Gwen. We worry about you like crazy, you know that."

"I know," she said, her voice trembling with emotion. "But look who I have to watch out for me!"

"A formidable group," Brennan acknowledged with a smile. "Can you come up to the house? We'll feed you more than sandwiches ... and we have hot water for baths and washing clothes."

"I hate to think what we must smell like," admitted Feth. "We're used to it by now."

Brennan sniffed the air. "You notice no one is sitting nearby."

They all laughed. Feth imagined her aching body enveloped in hot water and savored the idea of a fresh-smelling tunic, clean leggings and dry socks. Yet the Squadron ship could arrive at any time and they had a mission to accomplish.

Gwen caught Feth's uncertain look. "Brennan, we'd like nothing better, but we did come here for a reason as I explained in my letter. What do you think? Will Tralee help us?"

Brennan accepted a glass of stout from the barkeep and took a long pull on it before answering.

"Gwen, it's a close thing. When we got your letter a couple of weeks ago, Father brought the issue to the Council of Elders, and a minority supported sending the militia. We have to consider that this town can be attacked from the sea at any time. The Province Squadron patrols the coastline as best it can, yet often enough raider ships slip through. Then we have to defend ourselves."

Feth opened her mouth to speak but Brennan held up his hand.

"Feth, I know what you're going to say. If the land battle Gwen warned us about is lost, the Province may fall and there'll be no more ships defending us at all. We know that. It's just not that easy to send away your best fighters to fight a battle none of them may come back from."

Feth frowned and stared at the table. "Macroom sent us five hundred fighters. Their best too. And they are none too friendly with the Twenty Clans."

"Word of that has reached here," Brennan replied, "and to say it surprised everyone is an understatement. The truth is, they have a fortified town and we don't. And our main hazard is from the sea. If you could guarantee that a Province fleet would guard the harbor and the coastline while the militia is away, it might make the difference."

"You must know I can't promise that."

"But Gwen said your sister is—"

"Brennan!"

Gwen glared at her cousin, who saw his mistake immediately.

"If there were time, Brennan," Feth said, cutting off his apology, "I'd make the proposal to my sister, as you say. The problem is, there won't *be* time. When our transport arrives we have to leave, with or without fighters from Tralee. You'd have to take on faith that the Squadron would protect you as best they could while the militia is away. As to soldiers not coming back, what can I say? None of us here at this table may come back either. We will all be there on that day, when it comes. And it will come, sure as day follows the night."

"We know that too," Brennan said with a look of deep concern. "And I dread to think of losing Gwen." He paused, swallowed hard, and went on. "Keep in mind that you all volunteered, even you, Gwen. You've already made your decisions. The young men and women of the town have made no decision, and the town does not feel it should force them to go with you."

There is the opening. Feth glanced at her friends. *Sure, they all heard it. Now they're waiting to see if I dare use it. What's to lose? If I don't try, we may leave here with nothing.*

She looked straight at Brennan. "Would the town let us ask for volunteers?"

"You mean, assemble the whole force and let them make their own choices, one by one?"

"Yes. That's exactly what I mean."

Brennan stared out the windows for a long moment before answering.

"It could be seen by some," he said, choosing his words carefully, "as interfering with the town's right to provide for its own defense. We're not part of the Province, after all."

"Neither Gwen nor I are Province-born," said Ionhar, his big hand holding hers, "yet we volunteered. In a time such as this, should not every man and woman choose for themselves where their duty lies?"

Brennan nodded slowly. "That's an argument you could make. How many of the townfolk it would convince, I don't know. It seems to me you should at least have the chance to make your case. Gwen, take your friends up to the house for the rest of the day. I'll send word or come myself when I know what the decision is. I wouldn't count on anything, Feth." He stood and pushed his chair to the table. "Welcome again to Tralee. I wish the circumstances were different and you could enjoy what our town has to offer."

He kissed Gwen on the cheek and went out.

"I had to try that," said Feth without much hope. "I don't feel very good about it, though. It looks like I'm trying to steal their militia from under their noses. And he's right, I can't promise protection for the town."

"We're all tired and Brennan is right," Gwen said, "we're probably driving away the tavern's business. We can see the harbor from the house, in case a Squadron ship comes in. How about it, Feth?"

"I guess. I do need that bath."

Keegan laid a sizable stack of Province coins on the table and they headed out to their horses. After two hours of the tavern's warmth and comfort, the cold, misty wind had them all shivering as they followed Gwen up a winding road to a bluff overlooking the town. Rounding the last turn, they beheld a ramshackle house that seemed to have been built in pieces over a long period of time—as indeed it had. The center section of the house, two stories high and hardly bigger than a large cottage, was constructed of weathered stone. A large single-story addition with walls of rough-hewn logs attached to one side of the stone center, while on the opposite side, an even larger two-story addition fronted in whitewashed brick sprawled nearly to the edge of the bluff. A heavy-timbered barn with a sagging roof provided shelter for their horses, who seemed at home enough in the company of goats, pigs, cows, sheep, and chickens.

With Gwen's younger cousins at school and her Uncle Ruinaidh at his furniture shop, they found themselves alone in the care of Aunt Norah, a slender woman with graying brown hair and soft voice who made them feel instantly at home. By late afternoon the travelers had luxuriated in a warm bath, washed their uniforms and dried them in a special room overheated by a pot-bellied stove, and groomed their hard-worked horses. Then the children returned: ten year-old Ina, a tow-headed girl with an infectious giggle, fifteen-year-old Niocol, a slender, tall boy with a serious expression and a strong interest in Ionhar's stories, and his sixteen-year-old sister Paili, a dark-haired beauty who found Keegan something of an eyeful. At dusk Brennan and Ruinaidh returned with news that Feth did not find heartening: she would be allowed to ask for volunteers, but no more than one hundred of the militia's four hundred would be released. Disappointed as she was, she reminded herself that one hundred was far better than nothing. She made sure her disappointment did not show as everyone gathered at table for supper. Partway through the meal, talk turned to the coming battle and Feth's request for help from the town.

"We appreciate any help you can give," she said to Ruinaidh, a careworn man in his middle forties with the hard-calloused hands of a carpenter. "Your militia is well-trained and armed, so they can be used immediately. There'll be almost no time left for training when we reach Clonmel."

Ruinaidh set his pipe aside as Norah served out heavenly-smelling lamb and potato stew.

"We'd like to do more," he said honestly, "but the people of the town have cause to fear for their safety. The Spaniards, from where is it, Santander? They're a vicious enemy and we've spotted their ships off-shore in the last few weeks, waiting for a chance to attack. Your ships have chased them off so far, yet we have to be able to defend ourselves too."

"We know that, Uncle," said Gwen, seated between Ina and Paili, "and as Feth says, we appreciate what the town is offering."

"But you would like the whole force," put in Niocol, seated on his father's left.

Ruinaidh glared at his son. "Your opinion wasn't asked. Pass the bread to your sister."

"It's all right," Feth said. "Everyone has to make their own decisions, Niocol. Sure I'd like the whole force, because we believe our enemy will be twice our number or even more. Still, numbers aren't everything, or we would have lost long ago."

"Are you going to fight, Gwen?" asked Ina, who sat next to her tall cousin.

"Yes, I'll be there, Ina. I'll be all right. Look at those two big men stuffing their faces! They'll protect me, don't you think?"

"Maybe yes, maybe no," said Paili with a frown. "Maybe you should stay here, Gwen."

Norah finished serving the stew and took a seat next to her husband.

"Gwen has to go, Paili," she said. "These are her friends and they're counting on her."

"We all protect each other," said Keegan. "Ionhar and I usually fight next to each other."

"Would you show me your weapons and armor after dinner?" Niocol asked.

This drew another sharp look from his father.

"We will," Ionhar said, "if it's all right with your father."

"*After* he finishes his school lessons," said Ruinaidh with a sidelong glance at Niocol.

"Can I go too, father?" asked Paili, her eye on Keegan.

"No," he said with a shake of the head, "you girls help your mother tonight, she's had a long, hard day."

The conversation turned to the children's studies in school and the furniture shop and the price of flour and eggs. The main meal finished, Norah served up a delectable cream-topped pudding that drew muffled compliments from everyone. The festive meal was crowned by hot, strong coffee that came in through the port; rare though it was, Ruinaidh had a 'secret source' that he dared not disclose.

Though the steaming, rich brew was a great pleasure, Feth felt the ache of homesickness creeping over her. How long had it been since she sat with her family over a meal like this, bantering and trading stories and laughing at jokes? Her thoughts drifted back years, not so far as when her father was alive, but to the time in her life when Conor and Aideen and Padraic came home often and Uinseann and Rionach still lived nearby and Oran and his quiet, bespectacled brother Sean visited with their parents Hagan and Niamh. How the great room in Rosslare had sounded then! The smells around her now made the feeling worse. The scent of burning wood blended with the smoke from Ruinaidh's pipe. Grandfather Uinseann smoked one too, and she remembered sitting on his lap and watching him go through the ritual of emptying it, filling it, and lighting it, over and over.

During one of Ionhar's stories, Derdre leaned and whispered in her ear, "are you okay?"

"No," she whispered back. "I'm not."

She muttered an excuse about the call of nature and quickly excused herself, grabbed her cloak off the peg and ran out onto the covered porch with its view of Tralee and the harbor. She heard the door open and close at her heels.

"I saw you getting quiet," said Derdre, "and your mind was miles away."

Feth wiped at the tears streaming down her face. "All those people, a loving family together ... I miss that, Derdre. We had it for awhile in

Rosslare, even after my father died. Mom and Padraic and sometimes Uinseann and Rionach, Conor and Aideen and me. Now it's lucky when two of us are there at the same time! I am so homesick for a home that isn't even like this anymore."

They clasped hands tightly and stood shoulder to shoulder at the porch rail. The air had cleared of mist and the wind freshened out of the northwest, bringing on a clear, moonlit night. Below, the soft lights of the town spread along the shore of the bay whose waters gleamed with reflected moonlight. The laughter of children and the clop of horses' hooves over cobblestone streets echoed up the hill.

"I know how you feel, Feth. I see Norah and I think about my mother. There were usually just the three of us, after my brother died, but sometimes we had big dinners with all our friends and everyone talked and laughed. Like tonight. I dread how it will be with my mother gone, forever."

Her voice broke into sobs and Feth held onto her tightly with both hands, while she cried too. All the tension and anguish of the past weeks spilled out into each other's arms. After a time, Feth swallowed hard and found a clean cloth in her pocket.

"We'd look just fine going in like this," she said, mopping her face. She handed the cloth to Derdre. "Norah will think she poisoned us!"

Derdre laughed and dried her own tears.

"I needed to let that out, Feth," she said. "I guess you did too."

"I did. Thanks for coming after me."

At that moment the sweet sound of Gwen's flute wafted onto the porch.

"Let's go in," Feth said. "I want you to sing."

"Only if you do."

"Don't be funny."

They went inside together. The family had adjourned from the table and drawn the chairs into a wide semicircle around the blazing hearth. Gwen was playing a lively jig that had the children cavorting in the open space between the chairs. Five jigs and reels later, the children fell exhausted into chairs and Gwen switched to songs that Derdre knew. For an hour more, Gwen played and Derdre sang, often in the old Gaelic that sounded strange to their ears, and sometimes in English too.

In the midst of one especially touching song, Paili leaned over and whispered in Feth's ear, "I wish I could sing like that. Mother says I have a raspy voice."

Feth whispered back, "Don't feel bad, no one likes my singing either."

Paili smiled broadly, and they went back to listening.

As the hour of nine approached, Norah packed the children off to their rooms to work on school lessons. Long before he finished his lessons, Niocol crawled out of his bedroom window and crept silently to the barn, where he spent the next hour watching all five travelers clean and polish weapons and armor. He managed his clandestine return through the window in time for the night prayer.

Ruinaidh gathered everyone in the great room. With one arm around Niocol and another around Ina, he bowed his head.

"Please join hands, all. Another day and night we have passed in good health, with enough to eat, warmed against the cold. For this we are truly thankful. We welcome our cousin Gwen and her comrades into our hearts where they will always remain. May their path be safe and their dreams fulfilled. We will greet the new day with a quiet mind and a calm spirit."

The children kissed their parents and went off to their rooms. Feth and her comrades were given a large upstairs room to themselves, complete with soft straw mattresses and wool blankets. For once, Feth was able to find sleep quickly and slumber untroubled until first light.

Feth waited until the others headed out to the barn to ready the horses, so she could steal a few seconds alone in front of the bedroom's full-length mirror. For once she was not completely disappointed. Her straight blond hair, still damp from the bath, was clean and combed. The skin of her face was shiny red after a scrubbing with soap and hot water. Her uniform's tunic and leggings showed not a speck of mud or dust. She stood straight and square to the mirror and found something to admire in hard-muscled shoulders, a tiny waist, and a modest chest measurement. *Taller would be nice*, she admitted, *but clean and lean will have to do*. She added her cloak, drew its waist-cord tight, donned her cap, and strode out the front door.

The fierce northwest wind billowed her cloak wildly and nearly tore off her cap. Derdre waved from the barn, where she and the others were saddling and loading the horses. Brennan, now wearing his brown and tan militia uniform and decorated hauberk, was poised at the edge of the bluff with his eye glued to a long, gleaming brass telescope.

"A fine scope," Feth commented as she came to his side. "See anything?"

He lowered and collapsed the glass. "An empty harbor and beyond that, a wicked-looking sea." He ran his fingers along the shiny instrument. "Kernow-made, cost my grandfather a fortune forty years ago. He gave it to me two days before he died."

He handed it to Feth, who accepted it with great care. "Can I take a look?"

"Sure. I need to leave anyway. You're welcome to come into town, or stay here, whichever you like."

She slid open the instrument and trained it on the shining waters of Tralee Bay. No small sailboats out today: the wind was too strong and gusty even in the sheltered waters. Along the north shore of the bay, houses and shops dotted the shoreline for at least a mile from the town. Smoke rose from chimneys and fled instantly downwind. Beyond Rough Point lay the Magharee Islands, a hazard to returning ships for millennia.

She was about to lower the glass when a moving speck caught her eye. A fleck of green? A pennant?

She handed the glass back to Brennan. "Look," she said. "I think I see something."

He trained the glass. "Yes ... yes ... it's a ship. Three master, just clearing the point, plunging like the devil. Province warship, Feth, I'm sure of it. But ... "

"What is it?"

"More than one ship."

"How many?"

A full minute passed before Brennan answered. "Ten, all flying the Squadron ensign." He turned to Feth with wide eyes. "Did you order a battle fleet to pick you up?"

"Hardly! I begged for one ship and was lucky to get that."

"See for yourself."

She trained the full power of the scope on the lead ship. What was it that was out of place? Then her stomach tensed: it flew a solid red pennant from the foremast.

"Injuries aboard," she said, handing Brennan the glass. "They've been in a fight."

As if on cue, bells pealed out from the town below.

"Emergency signal," said Brennan. "We need to move. Can I get a ride?"

"With Keegan," Feth called over her shoulder as she ran for the barn.

Feth leaped onto Ioan, Brennan crowded behind Keegan on Comhghall, and in seconds they were pounding down the twisty road into town. Feth led them to the wharf which was rapidly filling with militia, ambulances, and citizens. The riders dismounted in the square near the pier. Brennan entrusted Feth with his telescope and ran to report to his chief. Feth trained the glass once again on the flagship which now parted the waves well within the bay. As she watched, sailors struck courses, reefed topsails and readied the anchor at the cathead. The gold lettering on the flagship's bow at last steadied long enough to read: *Nore*. Aideen's flagship. Her commodore's pennant streamed from the mizzen.

"My sister has come to call," she said.

"Aideen Laigain," Gwen said with a note of awe. "I've heard a lot about her. Is she much like you?"

"No," Feth said, with a sideways grin at Derdre, "I wouldn't say we're that much alike."

Shortly the *Nore* came to and dropped anchor a mile out in the bay, leaving room to swing southeast around its cable. One by one the other five ships did the same, each one pushed rapidly by the stiff wind until all six ships' bows pointed northwest. Moments later a small boat splashed down from the *Nore*'s side and a dark-green-uniformed officer with black hair descended into it. Four sailors pulled hard, driving the gig through wind-whipped water toward the pier. Brennan returned with a white-haired woman carrying a staff of office, whom he introduced as Toiréasa Cearrnaigh, Mayor of Tralee, and a uniformed, red-haired man of middle age named Midir Cormaic, Chief of the Tralee Militia.

The gig slid along the pier and made fast to a ladder. The officer that climbed the ladder and headed towards them was not the crisply-uniformed, perfectly-coifed sister Feth was accustomed to being awed by. Aideen wore no hat; her coal-black hair was plastered down with salt spray; a worn boat cloak billowed out in the wind; beneath it her tunic was torn and bloodied; and both forearms were bandaged. To Feth her sister looked drained of all color.

Aideen caught Feth's eye and nodded slightly, then advanced with her hand out to the mayor, who spoke first.

"Commodore, welcome to Tralee," the Mayor said. "May I ask what has happened?"

"What has happened," said Aideen in a hoarse tone, "is that I finally caught up with the Santander fleet lurking in these waters. Twelve ships. Sighted them yesterday morning near Blasket Sound, spent all day chasing them, and engaged off Brandon Bay early this morning. Burned two and gave the rest plenty to remember us by. Last we saw them, they were making sail for Spain, where a surprise awaits them. Mayor, I have critical cases that must come ashore."

"Of course, of course! We have everything ready, your injured will get the best care we can offer. You know Militia Chief Cormaic?"

Aideen shook his hand. "I do."

"My troops will help with your wounded," Cormaic said. "How long will you be here?"

"Only long enough to make minor repairs and treat the injured. I must be at sea again by sunset. We could use help from carpenters."

"I'll send out a call," said Cearrnaigh. "Anything we can do to help, Commodore, please ask. If you'll excuse us, we'll get to work."

They hurried off, shouting orders as they went. Aideen sighed, pushed wet hair off her forehead and turned to face Feth.

"Well, sister," said Aideen, "I am your transport. I don't suppose this is what you expected."

"No, sir, it isn't," said Feth. "May I ask if you're okay?"

"Feth, you don't need to be that formal," Aideen said with a tired wave of her hand. She glanced away momentarily as the first longboats loaded with stretchers tied up at the docks. "I'm better off than those sailors. Now who are your friends?"

"Brennan Cennedi, of Tralee," Feth said. "His cousin Gwen and Derdre Dal Reti, Line of Bows, Keegan Cholmain and Ionhar Raithlinn, Line of Blades."

Aideen paused when shaking Derdre's hand. "Your father is surgeon on the *Caillech*?"

"Yes, sir," Derdre replied.

"I am so sorry about your mother," Aideen said.

Derdre swallowed hard. "Thank you, Commodore."

Aideen turned to a surprised Feth. "You can go aboard now or later, Feth. As I said, we'll be sailing by sunset at the latest. Now, I need to be getting back—"

"Aideen, wait," said Feth.

She was instantly sorry she used her sister's first name, but Aideen did not seem to notice.

"Yes?" she inquired.

"I'm going to ask for volunteers from the Tralee militia, and if we get any, they'll need transport too."

Aideen glanced at Brennan and then at the uniformed men and women crowding the pier.

"How many?" she asked Brennan.

"I don't know, Commodore," he replied. "The town authorized up to a hundred. Under the circumstances," he waved a hand towards the stretchers being loaded into waiting ambulances, "it could be more. I'll check with the Mayor and Chief Cormaic."

Brennan left them and disappeared into the crowd.

"How have you done so far?" Aideen asked Feth. "To be honest, I didn't think you'd get anyone."

"I think about seven hundred, not counting Tralee."

Aideen's eyes widened in amazement. "You're not joking."

Ah, that set her back, Feth exulted. *For once, I caught her off guard!*

"I am not."

"How?"

"I'll tell you later," she said, seeing Brennan returning.

"They released everyone," he said to Feth. "It's your show, Feth."

"I need to go," she said to Aideen. "See you aboard?"

"I'll wait," Aideen replied. "I'd like to hear what you have to say. You can tell them we'll take anyone who volunteers."

Feth studied the crowd, which fell silent as boat after boat unloaded wounded sailors, some moaning in agony. Citizens walked alongside the ambulances, offering comfort to the wounded. The militia, four hundred strong, all waited to be addressed.

"Keegan," Feth said quietly, "get your horse and Ionhar's."

He looked at her quizzically but did as she asked. He returned seconds later with Comhghall and Breasal. "Lift me on Comhghall," she said. "Gwen, take Breasal. Stay back for a minute."

Keegan's powerful hands clamped around her waist; she glided upward until she could swing into the oversized saddle. From its holster she withdrew the Province banner and held it in her left hand, the reins in her right. Then she maneuvered the big horse down the pier to the boardwalk where the militia were assembled. She raised the Celtic Cross banner so that it waved in the stiff wind.

"Good people of Tralee," she shouted, her voice echoing off the nearby buildings. "My name is Fethnaid Laigain. I serve in the Line of Bows in the army of the Province. You know my uniform and insignia. With me are Keegan Cholmain and Ionhar Raithlinn in the Line of Blades, Derdre Dal Reti and Gwen Cennedi in the Line of Bows. By now you have heard that our warships attacked and drove off an enemy force that was trying to attack your city. Thanks to these brave sailors, your city is safe ... for a time. The Province is not. The army of the Ghaoth Aduaidh massing near Limerick numbers more than six thousand fighters. In days that army will attack the Province and try to destroy it completely. Our own army will meet it in the field.

Already we've enlisted many volunteers from Cork and Kerry, even from Macroom, to help us. We need more."

She wheeled Comhghall about and motioned to Gwen, who rode forward on Breasal.

"This is my friend Gwen Cennedi," Feth called out. "Most of you know Gwen's family. Her Uncle Ruinaidh has a furniture shop in your town. Her cousin Brennan serves in your militia."

Feth backed her horse away. Two more boats pulled up to the pier and began unloading stretchers. One stretcher carried a young, fair-haired girl whose trailing hand dripped blood on the flagstones.

"My friends of Tralee," Gwen called out in a clear, ringing voice, "when I was a little girl, I sat on the seashore near my town of Fahamore and watched the ships go by. Some of those ships carried goods and people and others flew the pennant of the Province Squadron. My father told me that those warships protected us, but I didn't understand from what. Later on I learned that there were people in the world who wanted what we had, little as it is, and that we had to fight to keep it. Now I wear the uniform of the Province and I fight with them. Why? Because I know that if the Province falls, there will be no more ships to defend us, and within a year, the Spanish raiders will strip Tralee and all the towns on this coast of everything. This beautiful, ancient city will fall into ruin like so many others in Eirelan! So I ask every one of you to fight at my side in this coming battle. These sailors now coming ashore fought for you and for all of us, so let us repay them, our blood for theirs."

Feth rode forward again and set her horse beside Gwen's.

"By sunset today," she said, "these warships must set sail for the Province. If you want to fight with us, come to the pier with your kit and weapons and armor. The Commodore told me no one would be turned away."

Feth and Gwen dismounted from the huge steeds. Gradually the townfolk dispersed and the militia followed, talking among themselves in small groups. Meanwhile the last of the boats discharged its wounded and pulled away from the pier, leaving only Aideen's gig and her four sailors.

"What do you think?" Feth asked Brennan.

"I think you'll get more than a hundred," he said, "but how many, I don't know. I need to go up to the house, I left my kit there in the rush. I'll be back soon."

He kissed Gwen on the cheek and trotted away.

Aideen had listened from the top of the ladder near her gig. She motioned to Feth to join her.

"You realize it will be a rough ride back to Dungarvan," she said. "This gale is only going to get stronger tonight."

"I know that, Aideen, but sick fighters will get well ashore soon enough. You know we need every one."

"I do," Aideen said. She gazed out at her ships for a long moment. When she looked back at Feth, a smile creased her lips. "Something tells me I should order the ships to be ready for quite a few passengers."

She climbed onto the top rung of the ladder and paused.

"You grew up when I wasn't watching," she said with a cocked eyebrow. "I am ... astonished is the word."

She dropped into the gig and the sailors pushed off for the *Nore*.

"Trouble?" asked Derdre as Feth rejoined her friends.

"No," Feth replied, "Just sister-talk." She scanned the now-deserted wharf. "Nothing left to do here. Let's enjoy the town while we can."

With Gwen leading them, the five travelers strolled into Tralee's business district. On the street they passed Ruinaidh hurrying towards the wharf with a sack of carpenter's tools slung over his shoulder. They ate lunch in a quiet tavern. The owner, an elderly, bearded man wearing a cheerful plaid apron, lingered at the table after he refilled their glasses of stout for the third time.

"No payment," he said in the Tralee brogue. Then he said something in a dialect they did not understand.

"An old saying from my home in Connemara," he said, seeing their puzzlement. "It means, *may your enemies never meet a friend.* Good luck to ye."

The squadron cleared the protection of the harbor and faced the full brunt of the northwesterly gale. The *Nore*'s bow plunged into a heavy swell and then as their heading swung due south the heavily-loaded ship began to corkscrew. Quickly the lee rail filled with seasick militia. Feth left Keegan and Ionhar below, where they joined a card game of off-watch sailors. Gwen and Brennan chatted quietly at the taffrail, catching up their lives and trading stories of childhood. Derdre lingered on the quarterdeck talking with the officers.

Feth clamped her hands tighter on the bow rail as the ship plunged and recovered. She loved the sense of wild motion, the smell of the spray, the fierce power of the oak-timbered vessel as it sliced through whitecapped waves. She glanced up and watched a young crewman, her own age perhaps, make a minor repair to a mainmast forestay. *That could be me up there*, she reflected. *It is a great life, Aideen. If I had two lives to live, I'd be a sailor like you in the next one.*

Dear Mother, I have been wounded and the surgeon is not sure I will live. One of my shipmates is writing this down for me. Don't worry, I am not in too much pain, they gave me something for it. It was a terrible battle and many of my friends were hurt, or already lie beneath the sacred cloths. I wanted to tell you and father and Luiseach and Piran how much I love you and all of my kin and friends in Killurin. This may be farewell, and if it is, know that your daughter fell defending her people.
Cairenn Dunlainge, Sailor First Class
Squadron Ship Rosc Catha, at sea off Santander Bay

Chapter 41

"Ensign Auteini," said Mairin, "take the ship to arms. Course south by southwest. Ensign Velnowarth, signal Captain Tredinnick, we will pursue to the east. Make to our ships, *follow Caillech*."

Having seen enough, she lowered the glass. Eight Santander two-masters fled the harbor for the open sea, beating hard into a relentless north wind. They had escaped Miles Endean's attack fleet, seemingly without much damage. Of course, their flight meant almost certainly that the city was taken and the remainder of their fleet bottled up or destroyed. Indeed, the smoke now plainly rising from the city might be burning ships. Seeing the oncoming warships, the Santanders split into two groups, with four each headed west and east.

"Captain Tredinnick acknowledges, sir," said Velnowarth. "He'll take the other group."

Mor Dal Reti chose that moment to emerge from below. He had stripped off his armor and blood covered his clothes. A stethoscope hung from his neck.

"Captain," he said with an insistent look, "I will ask you to come below if you can spare fifteen minutes. You have wounds that need attention."

"Not a good time, Mor," she replied curtly.

Around them, the ship silently returned to arms, the least injured climbing into the tops and the rigging, the limping assigned to ballistae and the deck.

Mor stared out over the sea. "I speak under correction, Captain, but it seems like we won't engage for some time." When she made no reply, he persisted. "Please, Captain. You've lost a good pint of blood already."

"It will hurt like sin, no doubt."

"Yes, sir. No time for a sedative. The antiseptic will deaden the area some."

She sighed heavily. "All right, let's go. Fifteen minutes, doc."

She followed him below. The main cabin had been restored to some semblance of order. The dead had been moved into a forward hold and the seriously injured lay in their hammocks. Mor led her into the surgery where a vacant table awaited.

"Clothes off, " he said, shutting the door behind him. "I'll make this is fast as I can."

"My apology, Mor," she mumbled as she pulled off her boots and then her tunic. "Hard day."

"Captain," he said with a hand on her shoulder, "we've been friends for too long to worry about such things. Now lie back and let's see what we have under these bandages. Hmm, not too bad ... not too bad here either ... oh-oh."

She swore a blue oath. "I never like your oh-ohs."

Mor leaned in closer and dabbed gently at a pike wound on her upper left thigh. "Deeper than I thought."

The attending surgeon's mate, a very young sailor with a friendly, round face, handed her a rolled up towel.

"Captain, best to bite on this."

Mairin set it between her teeth. Mor finished cleaning the wound, then lifted a bottle of green liquid that Mairin knew all too well. "This is the worst part, Captain."

She pulled out the towel. "Sure, you always say that."

He smiled and nodded patiently. She bit down on the towel and gripped the sides of the table. He poured the antiseptic.

Pain exploded from her thigh and radiated like fire against flesh through her torso. Her teeth cut into the towel and her hands clamped with rigor mortis strength onto the wood of the table. Dimly she was aware of the surgeon's mate pressing a cold towel over her face and urging her to take deep breaths. *Not easy*, she thought somewhere beneath the pain, *with a rag in your mouth*. Slowly, the first burst of pain faded as the antiseptic's deadening power took hold. The mate pulled off the cloth and took the towel from her mouth.

"Shades of Cuchulain," she said, gasping.

"I know," he said, already stitching on the wound. "I knew it would be bad, Captain. I'll get the stitching done before much sensation returns."

The mate mopped her face with another cold cloth.

"Thank you ... Tara, isn't it?"

The young woman blushed. "Yes, sir, Tara Briuin, the first officer's cousin."

She was beginning to feel the needle and had to speak through clenched teeth.

"How's your cousin doing, Tara?"

"In good spirits, sir," Tara answered. She dipped the towel in cold water and pressed it to Mairin's forehead. "She's sleeping quietly now."

"Mor?" Mairin asked.

He did not look up from his work. "Captain, it's hard to say. Nothing was broken. I'm hoping the spinal cord was only shocked. In that case the weakness in her legs will be temporary."

"You are hoping."

"Yes, sir."

He finished stitching. With Tara's help he applied a fresh, antiseptic-soaked bandage to the wound and wrapped it tightly in place.

"Agh, more stinging," Mairin commented.

She sat up and watched the surgery spin for several seconds. Tara handed her a steaming mug of beef broth, which she sipped until the room steadied. Mor washed his hands and came back to her.

"You'll be all right for awhile, Captain, but as soon as we're free and clear you need food and rest. Sithmaith too. She's back on deck against my advice."

"How many others out of action?"

"Ten cases that need more attention when we reach a hospital ship. None critical."

"Do you expect any more deaths?"

Mor leaned against the table, head down. "No, sir. We lost seventeen. May they be forever blessed." He looked up, reached for her head. "Some gashes there too, Captain."

"Later." She eased herself to her feet.

"Better than before," she said in a husky voice. "More or less. Tara, would you help me get my armor on? You can spare her a few minutes?"

Mor nodded. "Another fight is likely?"

"Yes. You'd better dress."

Tara followed her into her cabin, where her bloody armor lay in a pile. With Tara's help, she cleaned it off and donned it again. When Tara set her helmet on, it scraped the wounds on her forehead and she barked out a curse.

"Oh, I'm sorry sir," Tara cried. It was then that Mairin first noticed the livid bruises on the girl's face and the dried blood on her left temple.

"No, no, it's not your fault," said Mairin, adjusting the helmet. "You were a great help. Now into your armor ... and thank you."

The relieved young woman fled the cabin. Mairin turned to the chart of Santander Bay. The exit due north from the harbor was clear of shallows, while the eastern and western approaches shoaled at low tide to two fathoms. The ships she had seen in her glass were smaller by half than the ones they fought earlier. What would they draw? Surely near two fathoms, it depended on the keel design, ballast, and how much cargo they carried. With the wind out of the north, their leeway would be forcing them towards the shoals.

"So," she murmured, "make them take the biggest chance."

On deck, Sithmaith leaned heavily on the binnacle, her fair skin the color of bleached sailcloth.

"Captain," she said with a wan smile, "you look pale, sir."

Mairin laughed. "If I only had a mirror, Lieutenant." She glanced along the deck and up at the tops. "We're a bit thin up there, aren't we?"

"Best we can do," Sithmaith said, her eyes following Mairin's. "We're down by twenty-six. I have all the ballistae manned, each crew one short. Four sailors are on the forward pump as you can see, we have one foot in the well so far. Bowsprit is fished, won't take a lot of strain. Tops are short eight. I didn't think we could afford taking any more from the sail crew. Bosun Auteini and Master Sechnaill have been replaced by their mates until you say otherwise, sir."

"No changes now, Lieutenant. Well done."

"Thank you, sir."

Mairin glanced at the wheel and struggled for a name. Sithmaith leaned over to whisper in her ear.

"Keriann McClura, sir, Scots girl. Tough and reliable, sir, by Brigid's notes in her record."

Mairin nodded. In the bow she spotted Sechnaill's mate, a woman she knew well: Maeve Skyburiow, native of Kernow, experienced and well-liked by the crew. Smaller and leaner than Sechnaill, known to be the finest swordwielder in the Squadron. Soon both ensigns came up from below, patched by Mor's quick fingers. Mairin breathed even easier when Sailing Master Nya Gailenga emerged up through the forward hatch and made her way aft with a slight limp and a bandage wrapped over her forehead.

"Nya, two points to port and set everything she'll bear without the overloading the bowsprit. Keep the pump going, we need all the speed we can get. With the storm coming and the injuries aboard, we don't have time for a long chase. I aim to cut them off just as they cross the shoal, if they make it at all. It will be close, even for ships of that size. Ensign Auteini, signal to all ships, *line ahead on Caillech, prepare to attack.*"

While these orders were being carried out, Mairin turned her glass on the ships they pursued. In line ahead formation, they sailed straight for the shoal, with every sail they had set and drawing. As she expected, they were struggling with leeway: every few seconds the helmsmen would luff up into the wind and then fall off again. *I was right*, she thought. *They're gambling that they'll get across at high tide and then hope we'll give up the chase. No taste for a fight.*

She swung the glass west, where Richard's ships bore down on the other four Santander vessels. His tactic was the same as hers: pour on speed to intercept.

Sithmaith appeared at her elbow. "Captain, may I look? My glass, well, I used it as a weapon."

Mairin had to laugh. "Yes, Lieutenant, be my guest."

Mairin scanned her ship again while Sithmaith used the glass. The forward pump spewed a steady stream of seawater, to be expected given their speed through the water and the plunging of the damaged bow through the rollers. Astern, *Morrigan*, *Rosc Catha*, and *Wexford* held station, their tops no better manned than *Caillech*'s. She glanced at the barometer: falling faster now. Three more hours of daylight left, and soon after that, a storm would churn these seas into a fearsome cauldron. If the battle for the harbor had been won, as she believed, she had to get her ships and her injured crew inside its protection before the storm delivered its blow.

Sithmaith handed back the glass. "Thank you, sir. May I ask about Lieutenant Briuin?"

"Sleeping," said Mairin, her stomach clenching with worry. "Mor is optimistic."

Mairin trained her glass again and was not surprised to see the Santanders lightening ship.

"There goes their water," she said to Sithmaith. "Probably food and everything else too."

The sea behind the Santander ships was quickly littered with hundreds of barrels and crates, spare sails and yards and repair timbers. At the last, the four massive boarding ramps were unhinged and tossed into the sea.

"They're gambling everything," Mairin said. "Lieutenant, let's get the lead going. We'll be cutting it close."

Sithmaith quickly assigned an experienced sailor to cast the lead weight from the forechains.

"And a half four," the sailor called out. A moment later, "by the mark four."

"Strike topgallants," Mairin ordered.

The two lines of ships were now sailing parallel to each other a thousand yards apart, *Caillech* and her companions skirting the edge of the shoals, the Santanders now directly over them.

"By the mark three."

"Reef the courses," Mairin ordered. "Fall off the shoals a point."

"Not much under our keel," Sithmaith said quietly. She leaned over the starboard rail as if trying to see the bottom three fathoms below.

"And a half three," came the reassuring call, and then "by the mark four."

"We're clear," said Sithmaith.

"Ship aground!" cried Ensign Velnowarth.

They did not need a telescope to see that the Santander ship second in line had slewed sideways and lost all forward motion. In quick succession the next two ships followed suit. The lead ship sailed on past the shoals into open water.

"Ensign, signal to our consorts, *attack grounded ships with long-range fire. Caillech will pursue.* Nya, let's get moving."

"Aye, aye, sir."

The Master bawled out commands for *Caillech* to set every sail to the royals. Their prey, a thousand yards off to starboard and a full mile ahead, did the same. Nya Gailenga knew how to make chase, and she let pass no chance to gain more power from the sails. Within an hour, *Caillech* closed the gap to three hundred yards back and a hundred yards abeam of the other ship, whose stern letters read *Navarre*. Mairin could now study her adversary, a tall, lanky man clad in a red tunic, fairly young she judged, calling out orders calmly on his quarterdeck. Now and then he stared in her direction.

"He must know he can't get away," said Master Skyburiow, using her own glass to study their opponent. "He tossed his ramps and they carry no firepower. Why keep this up?" She turned her glass astern. "The other ships struck, Captain, after a taste of firebombs. Boats launched, they're hightailing it for shore."

"Three new ships for our fleet," Mairin commented, "if we have time to retrieve them. Master, load firebombs."

Skyburiow's portside ballistae crews set naphtha-filled shells into firing trays and lit torches. *Caillech* gradually drew parallel to her opponent at a hundred yards' separation.

"What's going on there?" Sithmaith said from the rail.

From the Santander ship's quarterdeck hatch emerged a dozen long-haired men, bare-chested, hands bound behind them, dirty gags stuffed in their mouths. They were guarded by four sword-wielding fighters who poked their stumbling charges along until all stood swaying weakly at the port rail.

"Hostages," breathed Ensign Velnowarth. "We can't fire them."

Mairin raised her glass and focused it on the gagged men. She studied each hostage, one at a time, at the maximum power of her scope. After a full minute, she lowered the telescope.

"Master," she said to Skyburiow, "light bombs and open fire. Archers, shoot!"

A hail of arrows whizzed over the open water, followed in seconds by the flaming canisters.

"Captain!" Velnowarth cried. "Why?"

"Not a mark on any of them," Mairin said calmly. "And tattoos in Spanish."

Four ballistae volleys later, his ship aflame and decks littered with dead, the enemy captain struck his pennant. Mairin halted their fire, allowing *Navarre*'s crew and fighters to extinguish the fires and crowd into boats. *Navarre*'s captain climbed into the last boat, and as it rowed away, he stared back at Mairin with an expression that seemed poised between rage and admiration.

For just a brief moment, Mairin felt pity for him—until her eyes drifted down to the fresh bloodstains on her own deck. Then all pity vanished.

All of remaining daylight hours were consumed by the task of bringing four abandoned ships into Santander Harbor ahead of the threatening storm. The ship taken by *Caillech* was the easiest, once temporary repairs to fire damage had been carried out and the dead sent to a watery tomb. The three ships hard aground on the shoal were rapidly crewed but could not be floated off until the approach of high tide, an hour before sunset and barely that much ahead of the storm piling up in the north.

So it was at twilight that *Caillech* sailed into the harbor under topsails, trailed by her three Squadron consorts and four Santander two-masters. Spread before them was a scene of wreckage, burnt ships, flotsam and jetsam, bodies drifting on the sea, and fires glowing and smoking in many parts of the city, all illuminated by a blood-red sunset in the west and the pallid flares of lightning to the north. The largest fire by far ate away at an immense, garish structure at the harbor's southern end. The precious shipyard had been saved.

Mairin had given Ensign Velnowarth command of the *Navarre*. At the moment, Sithmaith conned *Caillech* from the quarterdeck while Ensign Auteini took a long-delayed meal below with the port watch. With Nya Gailenga at the wheel, Mairin felt at ease climbing into the foretop with Mor to watch the extraordinary scene unfold before them.

"Innocent people are suffering tonight," Mor said, his hands clasped and elbows resting on the foretop's railing. "All through this city, people are dying or fleeing for their lives. How sad that it had to come to this."

Mairin pulled off her hat and fiddled with its insignia pins. "That it came to this was their own fault. Decades of preying on ships at sea and coastal towns. I admit, they've never been especially vicious and didn't kill unless they had to. But they harmed and frightened so many innocent people, there's justice in this." She waved a hand at the terrible devastation.

"Justice?" Mor said with a bitter edge. "I find it hard to see much justice in the world, Mairin. Was Dunlaith's death just? Or Brigid's, or Eavan's? What I see is the killing, on and on and on, no end in sight. Kill or be killed, it seems like that's the only principle the world offers us."

Distant thunder rumbled over the ocean. An Admiralty pilot boat arrived and signaled them to follow to an assigned anchorage. Mairin watched her flotilla for a time, especially the skeleton-crewed Santanders. There were no problems; each ship was efficiently brought to and anchors lowered into the placid waters.

Mairin turned to face north. "Time we battened down, Mor. It'll be a wild night from the looks of it, even here in the harbor."

"Amazing lightning," he commented as a brilliant bolt erupted from a distant, towering thunderhead. "Mairin, I'm sorry I sounded so bleak. You did a brilliant job today. Every dear comrade we lost died in gaining a victory we had to have. I can't tell you how much I admire you."

She laughed self-consciously. "Mor—"

"I mean it."

"Do you know," she said, turning to face him, "what a warship's captain absolutely needs to have?"

"A hard skull?"

She fingered the shrinking lump on the back of her head. "That helps, yes. What I had in mind was the ability to suffer and not show it to your crew. That's a skill I learned long before I signed up."

"You do it well," he conceded. "Yet all the same, they know what you feel. Every officer and sailor down there knows."

"Maybe they do," she said, sighing. She looked out again at the smouldering city and the harbor filled with the detritus of war. "So many gone, Mor."

"Tomorrow we'll say goodbye," he said, his hand on her arm. A sudden cool breeze rippled the sea around *Caillech* and the thunder ascended another notch in volume. "Best we go below."

"Some sleeping potion tonight, Mor. It keeps me from dreaming. I don't want to dream, tonight."

Dear Kenwyn, I enclose copies of documents that came into my possession recently. One set of papers was taken from a ship that was attacked off the coast of Wales, another set was brought in by one of our scouts operating in the north of Eirelan. The language in both cases appears to be the same, but I am struggling with its origins and translation. Some words seem to be old German for which I have decent references. Other words are neither German nor English and certainly not Gaelic. I believe it is important that we understand this language because its speakers may be a threat to both the Province and to Kernow. With your access to so many more books, can you help? Please answer when you can. My best regards to your lovely wife Tryfena. I hope the children are well.

Your friend, Sean

Chapter 42

Sean could not remember how long he had been wandering in this desolate countryside, nor did he know where he was. The grass was dry and dusty brown, the trees gnarled and leafless, the sky overcast, the air sultry and still. Lightning flickered on the horizon and the faint echoes of continuous thunder broke the eerie, oppressive silence. It seemed as if he had been walking through this strange land for a long time and yet the distant, snow-capped mountains drew no closer.

One thing he was certain of: those mountains were the site of a great library, pristinely preserved from vast ages past. For that reason alone, he had to fight his weariness and go on. What was that lying on the ground not far ahead? Not one thing, rather many indistinct shapes. He started to run over grass that had turned a deep shade of red. Oh, the shapes were bodies, lying in pools of dried blood! Hundreds, thousands of them, with Province uniforms torn and bloodied. They had lost, then. On this field lay Feth, and Oran, and Conor, and he should be lying there with them.

Coward that he was, he had to find his books. Nothing to do except keep walking through the bodies towards the mountains. He stumbled over a body and did not dare look down to see who it was. Thunder pounded in his ears, loud and sharp, and a voice called out his name. A familiar voice.

Not thunder! An insistent knocking at the door, and a visitor calling to him. He opened his eyes to a cold room lit by slanting rays of morning sunlight. His mouth tasted sour and his back ached.

"Nightmare again," he muttered, and louder, "Coming, just wait, I'm coming!"

He stumbled the few steps to the door and unlatched it. Outside stood a slender woman in her mid-fifties, of medium height, light brown hair flecked with gray, and sparkling brown eyes.

"I thought you'd be awake at this hour!" cried Niamh Osraige.

"Mother, it's all right," he said, embracing her. "Was I expecting you today? You know my memory."

"No, no," she said, walking past him. "This is a surprise visit!"

She laid her leather valise on his paper-littered table and hung her cloak on a peg.

"I must look terrible," he said, with a glance down at his disheveled clothes.

She smiled and nodded. "Yes, your hair is a mess, you haven't shaved, and you slept in your clothes." She walked over to him, mussed his tangled hair, and kissed him on the cheek. "I wouldn't have you any other way, son."

Sean pulled out a chair for her and he slumped into one opposite her.

"I don't like the look in your eyes," she said. "Something besides too little sleep, I think."

"Bad dream," he told her. "A nightly occurrence these days." He pulled off his smudged spectacles and absently cleaned them on his shirttail. "Mixed up, like most dreams. The common thread is guilt that I'm sitting here and I should be out there fighting in the line, not huddled back with the medicos."

"Nonsense. You can't see worth beans without your spectacles and you know it. And you've never trained for it. Treating our wounded is just as important as fighting."

He sighed and set the spectacles down on the table. "Yes, Mother, that all makes perfect logical sense. My dreams don't seem to agree with the logic."

Niamh regarded him with a tender look and took hold of his hand.

"Our dreams tell us many things," she said, "but they are not the guides of our lives. Be proud of who you are and what you are doing for your people. That's what your father and I have taught you, yes?"

"Yes." He managed a smile and kissed her hand. "Now what brings you here?"

"First of all, to see you, and second," she glanced at her valise, "I have customers in spite of the dire circumstances. We have to go on with our lives as best we can."

"Father often comes along."

"Yes," she sighed, "I wanted Hagan with me. The day I planned to leave, your Uncle Wynn came down from Wicklow unannounced."

"So let me guess, they've been out fishing every day together?"

"Right. Who am I to stand in the way of those two liars?"

Sean grinned and felt his dark spirits lift. His uncle Wynn was a cheerful, funny man, a strong contrast to his sober, thoughtful father. The brothers did indeed indulge in marvelous fish stories whenever they went out together.

"They've been pretty quiet the last few days, though," said Niamh, her smile fading. "Even Wynn looks worried most of the time. All three of your cousins are now serving, somewhere."

"Even little Selia?"

"Sean," Niamh laughed, "little Selia is sixteen. She's gone to sea with the Squadron."

"I'm a bit behind," he said, frowning. "I get lost in my work, I guess."

"Word of your brother?"

"Not yet. Conor promised a message whenever Oran shows up."

"And Fethnaid?"

"I think she's okay. We got word a big force from Macroom arrived at Clonmel last night, and that's on top of hundreds of other volunteers. She's amazed everyone ... including me."

Niamh raised an eyebrow. "You love her?"

"Yes. Very much."

"You have to admit you're an odd combination."

"In some ways. Feth believes in my work, she wants a family and a home. And she and I, well ... we, well ..."

"Well what?" Niamh's eyes twinkled with mischief.

"You know what I mean."

"I hope I never get so old I don't!"

They both laughed until tears ran down their faces.

"So, you plan to marry her, if she'll have you?"

"I do."

"Then I have something for you."

Niamh reached into her valise and withdrew a hinged box made of dark, polished wood. She set the box on the table and opened the lid, exposing to a sunbeam an array of necklaces, broaches, pins, rings, and bracelets pinned to a velvet cushion.

"My latest collection," she said proudly.

Sean leaned over and looked closely. "Exquisite as always, Mother. No one can come close to you, as far as my amateur eye can tell."

"Thank you," she said, blushing. She reached into the box and carefully removed a woman's necklace, a delicate chain of alternating gold and silver links coupled to a gold heart set with a pink tourmaline. "What do you think of this one?"

She passed it gently into his hands.

He studied the stone closely. "Remarkable color. Truly one of your finest. Which shop does it go to?"

Niamh closed the box lid.

"Would you like to give that to Feth?"

"Mother, this is a valuable ... "

Niamh waved him silent. "I made it for you to give, son, if you want to."

He lifted the pendant to catch more sunlight.

"It would look beautiful on her," he said softly. "Thank you, Mother." He stood and kissed her cheek.

Niamh took a small metal box from her valise. "Here's a case for it," she said, "with soft padding inside. Now, I have to be going, son. I have a five or six calls to make and then I'll take the late packet back home if the weather holds fair. You expect Feth today?"

"I can't be sure," he replied. He placed the pendant in its case and set the case atop a bookshelf. "I hope so."

Niamh stood and held him close.

"Be careful, son," she said, her voice catching in her throat, "and give our love to your brother, when you see him."

"Of course, Mother. Tell Father I'll visit as soon as things quiet down here. I promise."

Niamh brushed tears from her face.

"Now, clean yourself up before Fethnaid arrives!"

"Yes, Mother," he said as if a small child again. "Your son will be sparkling clean and well dressed within the hour."

And so he was. The unreliable bath cooperated with a more or less steady stream of tepid water. One set of clean clothes remained from the last wash day: blue sweater, black wool trousers, and boots that showed only minor wear. Putting the room to rights took longer than he expected because he often stopped to read something he was trying to put away. Finally, he set clean linens on the bed, fluffed the pillow, and opened the window to freshen stale air.

By the time he reached the pub on the first floor, lunch was being served. He had not planned to stop, then suddenly noticed his knees trembled from hunger. When had he eaten last, exactly? Not being able to remember, he took a seat in the corner and downed a large bowl of soup. He drew a glare from the innkeeper when he asked for a third slice of bread. It had just arrived along with a gruff "here you are" when his ears caught a sound over the din of conversations. The Squadron horn!

He threw coins on the table, pulled on his jacket and fled the room with bread in hand. He was not alone in his race to the pier: doors flew open throughout the town and the wharf filled up rapidly with civilians and naval personnel. Working his way around to the far right, he found stacks of crates awaiting shipment. He climbed to the highest crate to get a clear view of the harbor.

Ten Squadron warships in an orderly line had rounded the point. He wasn't sure whether to exult or lament. Feth was supposed to meet a single warship in Tralee. That ship might be part of this group ... or it might not. As the ships neared, he made out red flags and battle damage that signaled injuries aboard. And who were the brown-uniformed soldiers standing at the rails?

Naught to do but wait as the ships struck sails and glided towards the pier. He was certain the Commodore's pennant flew from the mizzen of the lead ship. Aideen Laigain led this fleet, then. *Not an unattractive woman*, he recalled. *Cool, efficient and imperious*. When they were younger, Aideen had little time or patience with Conor and often needled him openly. Yet Feth seemed fond of her big sister and often spoke of Aideen's good advice.

And there she was, on the flagship's quarterdeck, two steps behind the wheel, hands clasped behind her back. Her ship struck all its sails save a single topsail and swung its bow toward the slip on the far side of the pier. As it came about, he got a clear view of the forecastle and his heart leapt for joy. Feth and her four comrades leaned casually against the port rail. He waved frantically but Feth was not looking in his direction. Shouting would surely embarrass her.

He leaped down from the crates and with a multitude of apologies forced his way to the boardwalk. Another chain of "sorry" and "excuse me" got him to the front of the crowd. The flagship's two gangplanks thudded down onto the dock. First off came the brown-uniformed troops, most of them looking pale and walking with an unsteady stride. Ship's officers shouted for an aisle to be cleared through the crowd, and shortly these soldiers were led off by an officer from the port HQ. Then followed Keegan, Ionhar, Derdre, Gwen, and Feth last of all. Her hair drooped over her forehead and her tunic and cloak were soaking wet. When she spied him at last, she cried out his name, sprinted past her grinning friends and catapulted into his arms.

He locked his arms around her and said into her ear, "I missed you so much."

"Not as much as I missed you."

They kissed long and hard, drawing amused stares from sailors and civilians alike. When their lips parted, Sean guided her through the crowd, holding her as close as he could. His joy at seeing her alive and well was diminished only by the thought of how soon they must part again.

His heart sank when his eyes focused on the clock next to the bed. Two and a half hours gone! Feth lay in his arms beneath the blankets, her breathing deep and relaxed. The strong, lithe body pressing on his was noticeably thinner than it had been, the lovely young face drawn and pale. He wanted to keep her there for weeks, sheltered and warm and fed, take walks in the country by day and sit together at night holding hands and talking. Now ... thirty minutes left, and he had to wake her.

He kissed her forehead and called out her name. Again. She stirred, her eyes fluttered open, and her mouth spread into a welcoming smile. He kissed her and then said, "it's time to get up, love."

"Oh, no."

He drew her against him, a last time, and felt his body surge with desire. So little time; it could not be. With infinite reluctance he struggled out of bed. The room, usually cold, was warmed by the fire he had kept going in the stove. Feth's clothes hanging above it had fully dried. Sean dressed himself and took her clothes down for her.

"Dry and warm," she said thankfully. "Except my sox."

"Take a pair of mine," he said, rummaging in the battered old bureau. "A shade too big is better than wet."

By the time she pulled on her boots he had spread the table with dark bread and strawberry preserves and smoked salmon. Feth attacked the simple meal hungrily.

"Now tell me about the Tralee Militia," he prompted.

"Four hundred in all, pretty well trained and armed, too. We have over three-hundred and fifty with us. That brings the whole force of reinforcements to at least a thousand."

"And I worried you'd get killed or come back with nothing."

"Either one was a possibility," she said, waving a chunk of bread. "I'll tell you about the whole journey another time."

"Does Conor know about this latest contingent?"

"No," she said with satisfaction. "I could have sent a messenger ahead but I thought I'd surprise him instead."

"Oh, he'll be surprised all right."

"I only hope we're not too late."

"I don't think so. Conor promised me word when Oran returned, and I've heard nothing yet. That means the army hasn't left camp."

Feth looked down at herself. "I've lost a few pounds, I guess."

"You have," he agreed. "We'll have all winter to put it back on you."

"Yes. Yes, sure we will."

She stopped eating and stared at the table. He reached out and took her hand.

"We have to believe in that, Feth. We'll make it through."

She nodded slowly and set the rest of the food aside.

"You're coming with us?" she asked.

"Yes," he said, clearing the table. "The medical wagons will follow at the end of your troop train. Thank the stars the roads are in good condition. That won't last much longer."

"I don't know if we'll be able to see each other in Clonmel," she said. She wrapped her arms around his waist from behind. "Maybe we should say goodbye right here. I don't want to do it in public."

He turned, kissed her lightly, and said, "sit down for a minute."

She gave him a curious look but did as he asked. He took the opposite chair and extended his left hand, the fingers wrapped around something small. After a few seconds' pause for dramatic effect, he spread his fingers and set the shiny box on the table.

"Open it," he invited.

She raised the lid and lifted the pendant out, her eyes turning into green saucers.

"Sean, it's beautiful!" she gasped. "Where did you get it?"

He stood and moved behind her. "My mother was here this morning and left that for me to give you." He took the pendant from her hands and set it around her neck. She got up and stood in front of his cracked, foggy mirror. Tears streamed down her face.

"I've never had anything so perfect," she said, her voice breaking.

He drew her tight against him.

"It means that I love you, Feth Laigain. I love you with every part of me."

She held him fiercely. "I love you, Sean Osraige. With every part of me."

They embraced for a full minute and then parted to arms length. Sean brushed the tears from her cheeks.

"I guess we've run out of time," he said.

She lifted the pendant off her neck. "Put it back in the case and keep it here. Anything could happen in the next week and I would die if I lost it."

"Let's not talk about dying," he replied in a ragged voice. "Let's think about living and being together."

He replaced the pendant in its case and stored it behind books on a top shelf.

"By next week at this time I'll take that down," he said, "and put it on you again in the town square, on a moonlit night."

"Promise?"

"Promise."

Sean dowsed the fire in his stove and retrieved his rarely-used key from a hook in his cabinet. Donning their cloaks and taking hold of travel bags, they headed out into the square, where late afternoon gloom was fading into night. The lamplighter was already making his appointed rounds. All of the great lanterns at the wharf burned bright, illuminating damaged warships and work crews busily repairing them.

"Do you want to find your sister?" Sean asked.

"No time," said Feth, quickening her step. "We'd better get moving. The column is being marshaled at the transport depot across from the hospital."

They walked quickly among the closed shops and lantern-lit houses of Dungarvan. Fog crept in off the sea, mixing with misty air, giving the town a silent, somber feel. Feth stopped once to admire a white-washed cottage with a "For Sale" sign posted in its tiny front yard.

Soft light shone from its windows and smoke curled from the chimney. Wilting flowers sagged tiredly from window boxes.

"I don't suppose we could ever have something like that," she said wistfully.

"Probably not," he replied, taking her hand. "Still, no harm in checking it out when we get back."

"Yes," she whispered, mostly to herself, "when we get back."

Two blocks short of the transport depot they came upon the first wagons loaded with Tralee Militia. Every canvas-roofed wagon was jammed with fighters talking quietly among themselves. Heavy draft horses stamped impatiently, their flaring nostrils spouting clouds of steam into the cold, damp air. Driving lanterns were lit, illuminating soldiers' faces in a soft yellow glow. Feth stopped at the third wagon where a young man had called out to her.

"Sean," she said, "this is Brennan, Gwen's cousin."

They clasped hands. "Feth spoke very highly of you," Sean said. "She wants to take me to Tralee to meet your family."

"You'd be welcome any time," said Brennan. "I'd love to talk to you about history, and so would my father. Tralee is an old city with a rich past."

"It is indeed," Sean agreed. "And there's so much I don't know about it."

"Maybe this winter?" said Feth hopefully. "See you in Clonmel."

In the next wagon, several of the soldiers seemed very young even by Province standards. Feth pushed back the hood of her cloak and rested her hands on the side of the wagon.

"I know it was a hard trip to get here," she said, looking at each soldier in turn. "Is everyone all right?"

A woman with a quiver on her back answered. "Just about all of us were sick," she admitted, "but I think we have our stomachs back. It wasn't like sailing around Tralee Bay! You spoke at the pier, yes?"

"Yes. I'm Feth Laigain. I'm the one who got you into this!"

That drew smiles from nervous faces.

"I'll be at the head of the column, if anyone needs anything. Welcome to the Province, and fortune be with us all."

"You feel responsible for them," Sean said, walking beside her again.

"I *am* responsible, for everyone I recruited, Sean. A thousand lives in my hands."

"They volunteered, Feth. You told everyone what they were getting into."

"Sure they volunteered," she said as they passed the last of the troop carriers. "I still laid awake every night, seeing their faces in the air above me."

Sean drew her aside before they reached the front of the column.

"You feel alone right now," he said quietly. "When you get to Clonmel you'll be with Conor and lots of others who command the army. Everyone shares the burden, Feth. Everyone."

She looked up at him, her eyes catching the light of the roadside lanterns.

"I'm so glad I have you," she said, burying her face in his sweater. "I was never really lonely with you to think about."

"Feth!" a deep male voice called out.

Ionhar stumped up to them wearing his usual warm smile.

"This must be Seanlaoch," he said, offering a massive hand. "Feth did mention your name once or twice while we were traveling."

"No doubt she exaggerated my merits and omitted my faults."

"I did not!" Feth protested. "I'm sure I said you were forgetful."

The three of them walked together past the lead wagon. Keegan, Gwen, and Derdre held the five horses, who seemed fit and ready despite the rough voyage. Sean greeted each of them and they conversed lightly for a few minutes to ease the tension in the air. Then an officer wearing the insignia of the Transport Service on his chest came up leading his own horse. He walked with a pronounced limp.

"Captain Eochaid Loigde," he said, shaking her hand. "Feth, I served with your brother many times. I hope I see him tonight. We're ready to move out. I'll ride at the front of the wagons, and I'll post another officer at the rear of the column behind the medical wagons. You and your friends can ride between me and the first transport. I'll set as fast a pace as I think safe, probably take five hours in this fog.

We'll stop at the halfway point to rest the horses and let the passengers stretch."

Feth nodded. "I'm curious ... how did you know me?"

"Conor spoke of you often enough!" Eochaid laughed. "There is some resemblance, you know."

Eochaid mounted his horse and took his lead position.

Feth whispered to Sean, "see you soon," mounted Ioan, and called out in a loud voice, "Tralee Militia, we are moving out."

How she changes! As soon as she mounted, her face hardened, her head tilted back, her voice turned sharp and commanding. An amazing transformation, in the blink of an eye.

He strolled back along the column, found himself a spot in the last wagon, greeted his comrades, and settled into a corner. A minute later, the wagon in front of them started forward, the driver spoke a word to the draft horses and the wagon lurched ahead, gravel crunching loudly under the wheels. Five minutes more and the lights of the town completely vanished in the fog.

Sean leaned back against the side panels of the wagon, closed his eyes, and began to write words on his mental slate:

I now begin an account of the battle that took place on November blank, 999, in which the army of the Province of the Twenty Clans and its allies from Cork and Kerry fought a powerful force gathered by the Ghaoth Aduaidh, the "North Wind." This coalition of violent clans of the midlands and the north was formed by the Belfaster clans in the year 978 ...

I knew at the moment I put my arms around him and kissed him, that night, it was going to be my hurt in the end. I wanted him so much and when the chance came I took it. What a mistake that was! Yet how can it be a mistake when I don't regret it at all? Maybe it was all my fault, but Conor should have treated me with respect at the Inn.

Journal of Triona Bairrche

Chapter 43

The panoramic view from the lofty tower of Clonmel's fort on a bright, cold morning was worth the long climb and aching leg. Frost glistened on low-cut turf for miles around, all the way out to the edge of the woods. To the south, Conor's eyes drifted over the town's rooftops to the army's camp, where hard training and maneuvers were already in progress. Sunlight glimmered on the silvery River Suir as it wound its peaceful way through the town and the prosperous farms east and west.

Many miles beyond his sight to the northwest, the army of the Ghaoth Aduaidh massed in great numbers, and in that same direction Oran Osraige watched the enemy by day and by night. Conor had long since learned not to consider Oran overdue, because his friend always returned when his work was finished and not a moment earlier. Yet it could not possibly be long until the enemy army would reach full strength and move on them. The first heavy snows of winter would descend by the first week of December, and he was sure his adversaries planned to be resting comfortably inside the Province's homes and hostels by then.

His army was ready, or as ready as it was going to be. The Macroom Guards had been supplied with all the additional arms and armor they needed and under Aife's command would be used as a swift attacking force or a ready reserve. Arvel Rhydderch's three hundred horse archers drilled as much as horses and riders could stand and would be a potent harrying force in battle. The army's fighting core, its Line of Blades and Line of Bows, had been brought to perfect discipline by Kellen and Melvina. Padraic reviewed Conor's strategic and tactical plans, offered suggestions, and in the end approved entirely. Now what Conor needed most was for Oran to return with information on the enemy's size, composition, route of advance, and most importantly, when they would approach.

He took one last glance over the gleaming meadows, then told himself with a sigh that fifteen minutes was all the indulgence he could afford. He had an apology to deliver, much as he wanted to avoid it. He dared not face Liadan again until he made things right with Triona. With a polite nod to the fort captain, he started back down the long staircase.

Four tents each ninety feet square had been joined at the center to form the army camp's field hospital. One section, a surgery and recovery area, featured a canvas-covered wood floor and a large heating stove to keep patients warm and comfortable. Minor injuries and illnesses were treated in the infirmary area; the third zone housed medical files, references, and lockers for the staff. The fourth area served as a storage depot for medical supplies and equipment.

Conor entered the administrative section and asked the desk attendant where he might find Triona Bairrche. The nurse told him Triona had gone to the mess tent for breakfast and was expected back any moment. Outside, Conor found Triona walking towards him, head down in thought. She wore a deep red cloak over her hospital whites and a wool cap pulled down over her ears.

She stopped abruptly two paces from him. "General Laigain, good morning," she said, offering a salute.

Conor moved closer to her and said quietly, "Walk with me."

"Sir, I am due inside."

"Triona, please."

She glared at him but allowed herself to be led past the hospital complex into a dense grove of trees along the river bank. She turned her back to Conor, who knew better than to touch her. How to start?

"The other night at the inn. Inexcusable. I'm very sorry," he said, stumbling over his words.

"Very eloquent," she replied, still facing away. "I don't suppose it was your idea to invite me in the first place?"

"No, it wasn't. I—"

"I lived in your house for the better part of a month." she said, turning to face him. Though she kept her voice low, her ivory face flushed with anger. "It was at *your* invitation, to take care of your friend and my cousin. I make the mistake of wanting you for one night and then I am treated like someone you don't even know. In front of your mother, for pity's sake! I can't imagine what she thought was going on. Or Kellen for that matter."

She brushed tears from her face.

"I know, Triona. I don't have any defense. I tried to make it look like we weren't as close as—"

"As close as we are? And how close is that? I was just a night of fun for you."

"Please don't say that," he said, daring to reach out a hand.

She backed up out of reach, pulled off her cap and worked it in her hands.

"All right, I admit it was my fault to start with. I grabbed you, not the other way around. I didn't expect you to show any affection for me in public, but to treat me like I didn't exist ... it hurt and I didn't understand it."

He stepped forward and reached for her hand again. This time she accepted his hand.

"The truth is," he said, moving close and looking into her eyes, "that I like you very much and if I were free I'd get down on my hands and knees and beg to be with you again. The fact is I'm not free, I'm committed to someone else. I let my feelings for you get out of hand and it made a mess. Is it possible for us to be friends?"

After a moment's hesitation, the hand he held squeezed his.

"Of course it is, Conor." She pulled his hand up to her lips and kissed it. "Of course it is. Friends, then."

He kissed her hand in return. "I'll walk you back. I expect we both have work to do."

They left the trees and ascended the bank. Conor realized that touching her again was a serious mistake. She was unbearably beautiful and the touch of her hand on his lips brought flooding back the memory of her next to him and around him. *Never again*, he warned himself. *Disaster lies that way.*

Triona was about to enter the hospital when they heard a shout. Bradaigh pelted up at a dead run. In his hand he clutched a well-worn leather pouch that Conor recognized as Oran's. He dared not think why Oran was not standing there instead of Bradaigh.

"Sir," his aide said between gulps of air, "rider came through the Rampart gate with this."

With trembling fingers Conor opened the pouch and withdrew a packet of papers. Blood drained from his face as he read the covering note from Oran.

"Where's the rider, Bradaigh?"

"I left her at your tent, sir. Young woman named Bethia, about my age."

He turned to Triona. "Oran is wounded and holed up in a barn in Kilbeheny. Twenty-five miles away."

"I'll go," she said. "He'll need attention right away."

She disappeared into the hospital.

Conor sent Bradaigh in search of Kellen and then sprinted the three hundred yards back to his command tent, where a frightened and exhausted Bethia MacLaren clutched the reins of her horse.

"Bethia," said Conor, keeping the urgency out of his voice, "welcome to Clonmel. My name is Conor Laigain."

"Yes," she said, offering a slight bow. "Oran told me about you."

"I know you've had a hard ride. When did you leave Kilbeheny?"

"At first light. I think I rode about four hours. I never stopped once. You'll help Oran?"

An accent I don't remember hearing, Conor noted. "Of course, we'll have him back here by sundown, don't worry."

Triona came running up, a canvas bag slung over her shoulder.

"Bethia, this is Doctor Bairrche, she's going out to help Oran. Can you tell her what kind of wound he has?"

"Knife went in ... here," she pointed to her chest a couple of inches below the collarbone. "I got the knife out and poured some green stuff into the wound. He bled a lot while we were riding yesterday."

Kellen pounded up in full armor, helmet in hand, with Bradaigh by his side.

"Bradaigh filled me in," he panted. "Should I go?"

"I'd go myself," said Conor, "but you know we can't leave now. Pick four strong Blades who can ride and get them here fast." Kellen fled towards the drill field. "Triona, take the map, ride Treasach. He could carry you both if Oran can't ride alone. Bradaigh, draw four fast horses from the stables, saddled and ready to go."

The young aide bolted towards the stables.

"Sir, I'd like to go," said Bethia. "Oran saved my life. I just need another horse."

Conor nearly assented. But the slender young woman was plainly worn out from the grueling ride and might slow down the rest.

"Bethia, I have to say no. They'll bring him back, don't worry. Bradaigh will make sure you get hot food and have the doctors take a quick look at you. You won't be far away and I'll let you know as soon as Oran comes in. Is that all right with you?"

She looked disappointed. "I understand."

Conor himself took the reins of her spent horse and with Bethia led him to the stables. On the way, Triona and her four armored companions thundered past in a spray of mud and twigs. He turned Bethia over to Bradaigh and returned to his tent, where an anxious Melvina awaited him. She seized his arms in her steely hands.

"Conor—"

"Come inside," Conor said with an arm over her broad shoulders. "Sit."

She took a chair at his paper-littered table. "So?"

"Triona's on her way to Kilbeheny with four Blades on fast horses. Oran should be safe until they get there."

"Should be?"

"Will be, unless the Ghaoth Aduiadh's advance guard reaches the town first. I have no idea what kind of scouting they do if any."

"How badly is he hurt?"

"The girl Bethia said he had a knife wound in his chest."

"Oh, that's not good." Melvina held her head in her hands. "I am so tired, Conor. And now this."

Conor took another chair and rested his hand on her back.

"Go to your tent and rest. Two hours at least. Your captains can handle the morning training."

She looked up, pushed strands of hair from her face. "I really shouldn't."

The tent flap parted and Bradaigh stepped through.

"General, one of the younger nurses was going off duty, so I let her take charge of Bethia. She seemed a little afraid of me. And here are the latest dispatches, sir." He handed Conor a fistful of envelopes. "I put the most urgent one on top, it's from Squadron Headquarters at Dungarvan."

Conor tore open the message from the fleet and read: *General: Commodore Laigain's battle fleet sighted off the coast of Cork en route from Tralee. Beating against adverse winds to make port in Dungarvan. Will keep you apprised of their progress. Rylee Monaig, Port Captain.*

"What's up?" Melvina asked.

"Aideen's fleet has been sighted returning from Tralee, having a hard time making Dungarvan with this damned north wind."

"You think Feth and her group are aboard?"

"Likely though I can't be sure. If Feth is with Aideen, I owe it to her and her comrades to wait as long as I can. Thanks to them we have seven hundred extra fighters. On top of that, Arvel thinks she should command the horse archers."

"Conor, I know she's well-trained and an excellent fighter," said Melvina uneasily, "but she's awfully young for that kind of responsibility."

"I said as much to Arvel," Conor replied, "and he didn't change his mind. Arvel has fought as long as Padraic, even longer, I'll have to go with his judgment. Now back to the subject of rest. As a favor to me, not an order."

She stood up and took a deep breath. "One hour, then, in my tent."

"We'll all eat dinner together tonight, Melvina."

Melvina forced a smile. "Yes, I'm sure we will."

When she was gone, Conor set about to read the rest of the dispatches. Bradaigh worked quietly at his own desk. After some minutes passed in silence, Bradaigh set his pen down and turned toward Conor.

"General, could I ask you a question?"

Conor set the dispatches on the table. "Of course."

"Do you think it would be wrong to offer Bethia my friendship?"

"I don't think it's ever wrong to offer friendship to someone. Keep in mind we don't know much about her yet."

Bradaigh toyed with his pen. "Sure, I know. I was thinking that she's all alone here and she must be scared."

"I'm sure she is," Conor said, getting to his feet. "Go see her later on. Take your time and let her talk, you listen and answer her questions. She's probably been through quite an ordeal. Remember that things you take for granted may be very different for her."

"Thank you, sir," said Bradaigh, smiling. "I'll do that, when there's time. Right now, you have to go to the command tent, then the training field, and then the fort. Here's your list."

He handed Conor a neatly printed tabulation of times, places, and people.

"Sorry, sir, I know you're tired too."

Conor mussed Bradaigh's hair. "Not your fault, Bradaigh. You know where I'll be."

Outside the tent, Conor found the clear start to the day giving way to a lowering deck of dreary gray clouds. A damp night ahead and probably fog as well.

As he made his way to the command tent, his thoughts turned to Mairin. No word from her or about her in weeks, only Aideen's telling him of the clandestine mission to Spain. His longing for her mixed uncomfortably with his memory of holding Triona's hand and his undeniable desire to have her again.

"So your soldiers have been well cared for?" Conor asked.

"Better than I could have expected," Aife replied. "We'll be ready to fight."

She stood next to Conor at the center of the bridge over the Suir. Below, the river spoke as it always did, in soft, mellow tones that seemed unusually loud in the depths of a dense fog. Only the nearest and brightest lights of Clonmel could be seen. The lanterns mounted on the bridge's main pillars cast an eerie white glow on the water below.

When Conor fell silent, Aife said, "I've heard that your friend, the scout, was injured."

"His name is Oran Osraige. The party that went to retrieve him should be back by now."

"The fog would slow them down."

"Yes, I guess it would."

"You and Oran are close?"

"Like brothers."

"I can send a company of my troops out to search, if you like."

"I appreciate the offer, Aife, but it shouldn't be necessary. If they got out of Kilbeheny in one piece they'll take it slow on the road back. Oran had a knife wound, he might not be able to ride on his own."

"You'll send word when the party returns?"

"I will."

Aife gazed down at the murmuring waters.

"Tomorrow morning is the ceremony of citizenship?"

"It is. I made it clear that no one is required to come? We offer citizenship to anyone who fights for us, but it's a gift of thanks, not an obligation."

She nodded. "I understand. Will your uncle be there?"

"Padraic? Oh, yes."

"He's an impressive man. I'd like to know him better, if the chance comes."

"I hope you get that chance. He's a man of many parts, Aife."

Aife laughed quietly to herself.

"What are you thinking?" Conor asked.

"Of your sister, Fethnaid," she replied, still smiling. "A bold young woman, she is. I suspect she has quite a temper, I saw it in her eyes when the town's councillors sniped at her. She's learned to mind her tongue when needs be. Young to have learned that already."

Images of his sister in furious contestation with him, Liadan, Padraic, Aideen, and anyone else in range flashed before his eyes. It was his turn to laugh.

"It seems she's learned fast," he said, "because she was born with a sharp tongue and a willingness to turn it loose."

"My fighters," Aife said, her eyes boring into his, "will expect her to lead us."

"Not in your place, surely?"

"No, not in my place, but at the head of our column, wherever that may be when the time comes. Fethnaid came to ask our help, and among my soldiers, that means a great deal. It means a great deal to me."

"Then she will lead the column. I give you my word."

Aife turned and leaned backward on the wall. "I'm told you're a poet."

"I write poetry," he admitted, "but as to whether I'm a poet, that's for others to judge. What about you? When you're not dressed for combat?"

"I have a small farm outside of Macroom," she said with pride. "My children help me work it. My oldest son is twenty, I have a daughter seventeen, another son fifteen."

"Your husband?"

"Beneath the soil."

"I'm so sorry, Aife. How did it happen?"

"Four years ago, the year before we built our town wall. It was the year you last fought and defeated the Ghaoth Aduiadh. They turned west and split into wild bands. Barram died defending our town. It was as Fethnaid warned us would happen again. I knew she was right."

Aife pulled a loose stone from the wall and tossed it down into the river.

"A lovely place, Clonmel," she said with a sigh. "Perhaps you'll see my town someday, Conor. We have our poets, too."

"I'd like that. Our peoples have been apart too long."

"Fethnaid has already done much to pave the way for understanding." She drew her cloak more tightly around her shoulders. "I should get back to my soldiers, Conor. You'll wait here for your friend?"

"I will," he replied. "Thank you for the company, Aife."

"It was my pleasure," she said with a shallow bow. Then she disappeared into the swirling fog.

Another anxious half hour passed while Conor paced the bridge. The fog grew still denser still until Conor could see no lights in the town at all. A cold mist wafted on the east wind, chilling him through layers of cloak and sweater and shirt. It was an altogether forbidding night, one that cried out to be described in verse. Lines danced in his head, a couplet and then a quartet:

> *Enclose me, fog and mist, my friends,*
> *Wrap formless arms around me.*
> *No sun, no moon, no stars above,*
> *No earthly lights shine through thee.*

The next line was half-formed when the faint clatter of hooves on cobblestone echoed from the town. How many? Not moving fast, that much was sure. Then one of the horses whinnied and snorted: Treasach!

He stationed himself beneath the lanterns on the town side of the bridge. The clattering drew nearer and was joined by muffled voices. Treasach snorted again; he hated walking. First to emerge from the darkness were two mounted Blades, then Triona on Treasach, then two more Blades. Triona halted Treasach next to him and dismounted.

"Where is he?" Conor cried. "Didn't you find him?"

Triona turned away from him. Her shoulders trembled as if she were crying.

"Triona, answer me!"

Laughter issued from the darkness. "Never fear, old fellow. I'm just a bit slow today."

"Curse him!" Conor shouted. "He set this up!"

"Yes," said Triona, turning. She had been trembling with laughter. "He insisted."

A moment later, little Seara trotted out of the fog into the lanterns' light, bearing her chuckling owner.

"Help me down," he said, "and don't touch the left shoulder if you please."

Conor clamped his hands around Oran's waist as he dismounted. He embraced his friend gently and whispered into his ear, "I should kill you for that!"

"You almost didn't have to."

"Doctor?" he asked Triona.

"Weak from blood loss," said Triona. "Otherwise sound. Bethia did the right things."

"Should he be walking?"

"Just let Conor help me," Oran said. "I'll take it slow, doc."

Triona nodded. "I need you in the hospital for a half hour or so. Food and rest tonight or I'll have you strapped down."

Triona turned to lead Treasach away.

"Triona ... wait," Conor called to her. When she turned about, he said, "thank you. And thank the others for me, too."

She looked into his eyes for a long moment. Then she turned away with Treasach's reins in her hand.

"You know," said Oran as they set off at a slow pace, "I could almost swear there's something between the two of you."

"Just friends," Conor said lightly. "When we pass my tent I need to send Bradaigh after Melvina. She's been sick with worry all day."

Oran frowned at the quick change of subject, but let it pass.

"How much has Bethia told you about herself?" he asked Conor.

"Not very much. She was pretty frightened and exhausted. Bradaigh seems rather taken with her."

"Bethia was raped trying to escape from the army we're about to fight."

Conor stopped in his tracks. "*Raped?*"

"Beaten too. She was lucky to get out alive. Bradaigh needs to tread lightly."

"He will," Conor said as they resumed walking. "He's a good lad with a sense of humor. She needs a friend close to her own age, someone she can confide in if she wants to."

They reached Conor's tent where Bradaigh stood outside the entrance, beaming at the good news.

"Welcome back!" he cried to Oran. "The whole camp ... well, let me go find Commander Eogain."

He sprinted off into the fog and they continued towards the hospital tent. Triona waited outside with a nurse.

"We need to talk, tonight," Oran said before going in.

Conor gave Triona a questioning look.

"Let him rest a few hours," she said. "Warmth, food, water, and dry clothes will give him some strength back."

"Right. I'll set up a late meeting for all the commanders, you can join us then."

Oran nodded and let the nurse lead him inside. Triona hung back.

"He'll be all right," she said, touching Conor's arm. "I'll see to it personally."

"I owe you," Conor said, his hand covering hers.

Not too quickly, she slipped her hand away and went inside. By the time Conor reached his tent, Bradaigh had returned and was pouring hot tea.

"You found Melvina?"

"Yes, sir. She'll visit the hospital when the last mock battle ends. Very relieved, sir." He handed Conor a steaming mug. "I'm glad he made it back OK, General."

Conor looked up at the young man's sincere face.

"Thank you, Bradaigh. So am I." He took a long sip of the tea and felt the knot in his stomach relax. "Senior officers' meeting at nine o'clock tonight. Is the mess tent still serving?"

"Yes, I think so, it's not seven yet. They'll bring it here, sir, you don't have to—"

"No," said Conor, rising. "I'll eat with the soldiers tonight. You too."

"Yes, sir. The mess tent it is."

Kellen joined them for a time, and together they circulated among the tables of Blades and Bows and auxiliaries. He found morale high and even more to his liking, the fighters from Macroom and the other recruits were mixed in with the regulars. Back in his tent, Conor worked steadily with Bradaigh to read and answer dispatches, draft final orders for the line of march, and send a short note to his mother at the Inn. At twenty minutes to nine he declared a break, sent Bradaigh to check on Bethia, and withdrew from his travel bag a leather-bound book of old English poetry. It seemed like he had barely started when Bradaigh returned and said, "five minutes, sir. Sorry to break in on your reading."

With a sigh Conor closed the book and set it on a shelf. "Do you like poetry, Bradaigh?"

"Yes, sir, what I've read. Maybe I could read some of yours?"

Conor got up, smiling. "Oran says my poetry is maudlin."

"Maudlin?"

"Never mind, you can judge for yourself. My hat is straight?"

"Yes, sir. You should add the cape, sir, for this meeting."

Bradaigh handed him the gold cape, which he donned and then added a cloak to ward off the cold, soggy air. In the command tent he found Kellen and Melvina and their senior captains, Aife Luachra and a big man with her he had not met. A wan-faced, smiling Oran was talking with Melvina. Conor had told Bradaigh to arrange the chairs in a circle for this last conference. Conor took a seat next to Aife, who whispered an introduction to her deputy commander, Eibhear Uaithne. Bradaigh drifted into a corner to listen.

"I won't keep you long," Conor began. "We all need rest tonight. I'm happy to say we have our spy back in camp," he nodded towards Oran, "somewhat damaged though able to tell a tall tale, I'm sure."

"When have I ever told a tall tale?" Oran said in a hurt tone. "You wound me, General!"

The guffaws that followed were music to Conor's ears. *I'm glad we can all still laugh,* he told himself. *There won't be much laughter after tonight.*

"Lead on," he said to Oran. "Save your jokes to the end, Captain Osraige."

Oran saluted briskly. "Yes, sir, jokes at the end."

Oran turned serious and in the next thirty minutes relayed from memory detailed observations of the enemy army's approximate strength, weapons, armor, discipline, and training. Then the questions began and went on for another forty minutes, until Conor sensed Oran was tiring. He was about to call a halt to the meeting when a messenger stepped inside the tent and whispered in Bradaigh's ear. Bradaigh looked puzzled as he slipped behind Conor's chair and whispered, "Transport Chief Eochaid Loigde at the main gate, sir. Asks that you come, important."

Conor remembered the name, and the face too. They'd fought together in the Line of Blades many times until Eochaid's leg was savaged by an enemy mace. What was Eochaid doing at the camp gate at this hour?

He waited a moment for a gap in the conversation.

"I think we need to break up and let Oran get some rest," he said. "You can all go and do likewise. Kellen and Melvina with me, please. Oran too if you're up to it."

Conor waited as the others filed out.

"What's up?" Kellen asked.

"Not sure," said Conor. "Eochaid Loigde, Transport Chief at Dungarvan, is asking for me at the main gate. Bradaigh, we didn't expect a supply train tonight?"

"No, sir, not to my knowledge."

"I know Eochaid well, and if he says it's important, it surely is. Oran, don't fall over on me."

"I'm much better, chief," Oran said with a half-salute. "And Melvina will catch me, should I totter."

"No doubt. Well, let's go."

Eochaid was chatting with the sentries as they approached the fog-shrouded gate. Seeing Conor, he came to attention and saluted. Conor returned the salute and then extended his hand.

"Eochaid, good to see you," he said warmly.

"And you," he replied. "It's been awhile, Conor."

"It has, my friend. Two years? Now what brings you to the gate at this hour and in this miserable fog?"

"Train coming up, sir. I rode ahead to let you know."

The rumbling of wagon wheels now penetrated the fog.

"We weren't expecting supplies tonight."

"Not supplies, Conor. Troops it is. Well, you'll see."

Five horses striding abreast emerged from the fog and into the light of the gate's lanterns. On the far left and right, his Blade comrades Keegan Cholmain and Ionhar Raithlinn rode massive mounts. Between them, two archers rode the smaller Welsh horses. One was a tall woman with black hair and the other of average height with flaming red hair. Keegan held the Province banner the dark-haired woman the red dragon banner of Arvel's horse archers.

In the center, a step ahead of the others, his sister Feth sat ramrod straight on her own Welsh horse, in full uniform and crested helmet, her cloak thrown back over her shoulders. She advanced her horse an extra step and saluted Conor crisply.

"General," she called out in a surprisingly hard and authoritative tone, "Fethnaid Laigain, Line of Bows. My comrades are Keegan Cholmain, Ionhar Raithlinn, Derdre Dal Reti and Gwen Cennedi. I am authorized to offer you the services of the Tralee Militia commanded by Midir Cormaic. Total number three hundred fifty-four, fully armed and ready for battle."

Conor heard Oran mutter behind him, "I wish Padraic could see this."

"The Tralee Militia is welcome," Conor said after an astonished pause. "We'll shelter them in the fort tonight."

"Yes, sir," said Feth. She saluted again, then started the column forward again.

Eochaid whispered in Conor's ear, "I couldn't believe it myself."

Conor turned to a wide-eyed Bradaigh. "Hustle up to the fort. All the beds and blankets for the Macroomers should still be there. Get everything set up. I'll roust out the quartermaster for food. Move."

It was near the hour of midnight when Conor was at last able to return to his tent. Bradaigh lay face down on his cot. Conor draped a blanket over his sleeping form. Exhausted as he was, Conor was determined to read again before retiring. His weary mind struggled with the old English:

> Red Rose, proud Rose, sad Rose of all my days!
> Come near me, while I sing the ancient ways:
> Cuchulain battling with the bitter tide;
> The Druid, grey, wood-nurtured, quiet eyed,
> Who cast round Fergus dreams, and ruin untold;
> And thine own sadness, whereof stars, grown old
> In dancing silver-sandalled on the sea,
> Sing in their high and lonely melody.
> Come near, that no more blinded by man's fate,
> I find under the boughs of love and hate,
> In all poor foolish things that live a day,
> Eternal beauty wandering on her way.

"Would that I could write like that," he said with a tired sigh. "Let's try another."

His eyelids were drooping when he heard the tent flap rustle. He glanced up and saw Feth's head poke through the flap.

"Can I come in, Conor?"

He leaped up and wrapped his arms around her.

"Welcome back, dear sister," he said into her ear. "And well done. Well done indeed."

Paragraph 27.4. Burial at Sea. When it is necessary to commit the bodies of the dead to a final resting place while at sea, the traditions of the Kernow Admiralty shall be observed as set forth herein. Each body shall be sewn into clean, unused sail-cloth, knotted at the foot end for attachment of a stone weight of at least twenty pounds. The body shall be placed on a handled plank and covered by a Sacred Cloth bearing the Celtic Cross of Unity and Sacrifice. The plank shall be set on a raised platform level with the starboard or port rail of the ship. At the head end of the plank, a sailor or officer shall be stationed. Conditions permitting, all hands shall appear on deck in full dress uniforms for the service, which shall consist of the playing of the Air of Farewell followed by the Captain's reading of the Prayer and the List of Names. As each name and service record is read out, the plank shall be raised and the body and weight slid over the rail, the Sacred Cloth to be retained aboard ship. Although not required, the Captain is urged to say a few words to the assembled crew at the conclusion of the ceremony.

Province Squadron Regulations
Section 27: Deaths in the Line of Duty

Chapter 44

Tara Briuin brought the *Air of Farewell* to a mournful close and lowered her tinwhistle.

"Off hats," Sithmaith ordered.

Mairin opened the black-covered book and with some difficulty focused her eyes on the *Prayer of Burial at Sea*, filling in the underlined blanks as she read.

"We the company of the Province warship *Caillech* stand at attention before the bodies of our eighteen comrades who have fallen in battle. Their names will be inscribed on the mainmast, joining all others who have served this ship and perished in her service. So long as *Caillech* sails the high seas, they sail with us. Let us resolve to remember them, tell their stories, honor their service, revere their ultimate sacrifice. They died so that we may live, so that our people may survive. We now commit their bodies to the ocean, from whence all life arose. It is our belief that from Nature we spring and unto Nature we do return, in the unending cycle of life and death. Goodbye to each of them, they will be missed."

She closed the book and took from Sithmaith's trembling hand the list of names.

"Bosun Brigid Auteini, age forty-five, twenty-four years' service."

Brigid's body plunged into the sea.

"Weapons Master Eavan Sechnaill, age forty, twenty-two years. Watch Chief Ciar Loigde, age thirty, fifteen years."

Fifteen more names, and then the last, the youngest to die.

"Midshipman Kacy Finguine, age fifteen." Mairin's voice broke. "One year."

She knew the youngster: a cheerful, eager girl from Wicklow, anxious to please, always ready to do the dirty work. *Her life extinguished at fifteen. Of all the letters I must write, this is the one I dread the most.*

She handed the list and the book to Sithmaith whose face was streaked with tears. Composing herself with a deep breath, she brought her voice up to command volume.

"Caillechs, it is sad day for all of us. Those who now lie at peace beneath the still waters were our friends and comrades. We have a treasure of memories to cherish, and we will tell their families and friends at home of the honor their actions brought upon them as individuals and upon our vital service. Now it is our duty to care for our injured and make the ship ready for sea. Anyone not on duty wishing to visit one of the other ships in our task force is free to do so."

She nodded to Sithmaith, who called out "ship's company, dismissed."

In total silence, both watches filed down the fore and aft hatches, the more severely injured leaning on sounder comrades. When the last had gone, Mor followed with Sithmaith and Ensign Velnowarth and finally Mairin herself, leaving Ensign Auteini with the deck watch.

Mairin retreated to her cabin, closed the door, and slumped onto the bench in front of the sunlit stern windows. She tried in vain to calm the welter of emotions flooding through her mind.

It was late morning of the day after the battle. The furious storm they barely outran had at last blown itself out. Boats moved freely to and from the hospital ship *Morning Star,* where surgeons worked to repair so many hundreds of battered bodies. Now the town itself was quiet, yet it had not been so during the stormy night. Enraged Bretan Fighters overran the control of their officers and took revenge for decades of Santander attacks on their ships and coastal villages. Blood ran in the streets and screams carried to the anchored ships over the roar of the wind.

Moving her stitched leg carefully, Mairin changed into a working tunic, sweater, leggings, and boots. At each movement, her wrenched back threatened to spasm and bruised muscles flared with pain. She dared a glance in the mirror to see how much hair Mor had cut away to clean her scalp wound. Not too much: the shaved spot could be combed over. Nothing could be done at all about the dark circles under bloodshot eyes.

A tap on the cabin door. "Enter."

A slightly-built young woman entered and saluted. "You sent for me, sir."

"Yes, Ensign, sit down. Tea?"

Kensa Velnowarth nodded politely. "Yes, thank you, sir."

Mairin watched the twenty-year-old officer out of the corner of her eye while she fetched the tea from a sideboard. Dark hair cut shorter than was typical, deep-set blue eyes, a sharp nose, and broad forehead combined to give Kensa a determined, almost cold look. *Intense* was the word that came to mind. Mairin set out two mugs of tea and took a chair opposite Kensa.

"Thank you, sir." Kensa's hand trembled ever so slightly. "It's been a tough day for me, Captain."

"For all of us. I served with Brigid Auteini off and on since I was an ensign like yourself. Eavan Sechnaill saved my life in a fight off the Welsh coast. Yes ... a very tough day."

Kensa set down the tea and withdrew a sheaf of papers from her tunic. She swallowed hard and arranged neatly-drafted papers on the table.

"Ready to report, Captain," she said in a steadier voice. "Summary of dispatches from Admiral Tredinnick, status of our own ships and crews, and *Caillech*'s condition and supplies. Also, Captain Tredinnick has signaled, requesting that you pay a visit to his ship when convenient."

"Thank you, Ensign, we'll get to your reports in a moment. When you return to the deck, signal Captain Tredinnick I'll honor his request in about two hours, if that's acceptable to him."

"Aye aye, sir."

Mairin took a sip of her own tea and met Kensa's eyes briefly. *Shaken by the deaths, to be sure, but still thinking and working.*

"Ensign, you will serve as acting second lieutenant."

A smile, instantly suppressed. "Thank you, sir. I'll do my best for you and for the ship."

"I know you will. Your seamanship is outstanding, there's no question about that. I ask you to bear in mind that an advance in rank, even a temporary one, is an acknowledgment of your work and your quality. You can be proud of where you now stand. Remember that you depend at every moment on everyone who serves under you. You need their loyalty, and that is earned more by attitude and competence than bare authority in our service. Do we understand each other?"

"Perfectly, sir."

"You do understand that your rank is temporary? If and when Rowenna Briuin returns to service you will be an ensign again, at least for a time."

The warning did not erase Kensa's barely-suppressed elation.

"Now your reports."

The first, her summary of the Admiralty's dispatches, told the tale of a vicious fight on land and sea. On land, the Santanders' militia forces refused to surrender the town and battled the attackers for three long hours. In the end they could not hold out against the Bretans attacking on one front and the Marines, Scots Guards, and Welsh Pikemen on the other. At sea, thirty-seven Santander warships awaited Miles Endean's battle fleet. Eighteen had recently returned from voyages and thus were manned and ready to put up a fight; the other nineteen were moored for the winter and devoid of crew. Twelve of the manned ships were taken in bloody boarding actions; the other six were threatened with incendiaries and when they refused to strike colors, were set afire in a furious barrage led by the heavily-armed flagship *St. Vincent*. A last-ditch Santander attempt to fire the dockyards failed: four Admiralty line of battle ships drove their way to the piers and landed ten companies of Marines, who brushed aside resistance and doused the flames before much damage was done.

"On to our ships, sir," said Kensa, shuffling the papers. "All vessels will be ready for sea no later than tomorrow. We have a total of seventy-four officers and crew in hospital. Ninety-two burials today."

Kensa stared at her own notes as if having trouble believing them. A moment of anguished silence intervened.

"Captain Conmaicne?" Mairin asked.

"Doing better, sir. Lieutenant Briuin is also improving and is expected to recover completely, in time."

Mairin felt some of the endless dread drain out of her at this news. Perhaps their losses had come to an end and her list of letters would not lengthen.

"As to the *Caillech*, sir," Kensa went on to her third sheet of notes, "we're sound and ready for sea. The bow has been shored up and sealed, the carpenter says we can expect only minor leakage even in a storm. New jibboom is set and rigged, railings and other deck and gunwale damage repaired as needed. Armor has been cleaned and repaired, weapons supply adequate for another engagement."

"Well," said Mairin, leaning back in her chair, "let's hope we won't need the weapons, Lieutenant."

First time she was called that, Mairin noted with amusement. *It sounded good to her, as well it might.*

"Agreed, Captain. Will there be anything else?"

"Not at the moment. Efficient reports, prepared under trying conditions. Please take the deck and signal Captain Tredinnick, if you would."

"Aye, aye, sir."

Mairin sighed when the cabin door was closed. Twenty years old and an acting lieutenant. How old had she been? Only a year older, promoted after the battle off Strumble Head on the Welsh coast. *Then why does this woman look so terribly young to me?* She answered her own question: *because it has been a long, hard eight years since I made lieutenant, my body is no longer young and flexible like hers, and I have seen too much death. Especially in the last day.*

She spent the next two hours at the dismal task of writing letters to the families of the deceased. The letter to Brigid Auteini's husband, whom she knew well, had her in tears. Worse than that was the letter for the parents of fifteen-year-old Kacy Finguine. She did not know them at all; the address she had in Kacy's file was a tiny town north of Gorey called Hollyfort. How to tell them that their fresh-faced, enthusiastic daughter, at sea only a year, would never come back to them? She started the letter three times and crumpled up each attempt. As she started the fourth, a tap on her door was followed by Sithmaith's "Captain, may I see you?"

"Yes ... come in, Lieutenant."

She brushed tears from her face but there was no concealing what she was about. Sithmaith came in, closed the door, and then, with an appalled look, said "I'm sorry, sir. I can come back."

"No, sit down, Lieutenant," Mairin said. "This will be your job someday, though I don't wish it on anyone. I'm having a hard time with the letter for Kacy Finguine."

Sithmaith ran a hand through unwashed hair. "She fought right next to me, sir. I saw her go down, get back up and keep fighting. She—"

She broke off, buried her face in her hands, and fought down sobs that shook her body.

"I'm sorry, Captain," she said through her fingers. "I can see her face when I took her helmet off."

Mairin retrieved two glasses of water. Sithmaith gulped down hers and wiped her face on her sleeve.

"I came to report that we have a message from the Admiral. He's asking for all captains to repair aboard *St. Vincent* at four o'clock today. I acknowledged for you."

"Yes, thank you. I'll be leaving the ship shortly. *Morning Star* first, then *Ajax*, then *St. Vincent*."

"I'll have the gig ready, sir." She paused, her eyes drifting to the crumpled drafts. "Would you like me to try the letter for Kacy, sir? I knew her pretty well."

Mairin pondered the offer and decided it might help Sithmaith to write something.

"Yes, please write a note and sign it. I'll add my own and we'll send both."

Sithmaith stood and saluted. "Give my best to Lieutenant Briuin, sir?"

"I will."

When the lieutenant had gone, Mairin struggled through a note for Kacy's parents, folded it and placed it with the others, a stack far higher than she had ever had to write. Then she paced the narrow confines of the cabin, pondering the wisdom of going to see Richard. She knew she looked a mess and there was no time for a shower. That was a mere excuse: the genuine reason was her emotional state, steady enough to run the ship and hold its anguished crew together, yet vulnerable to a man she had a great deal of affection for, who would understand and probably share her grief. Didn't the mere fact of being on his ship prevent anything from going too far? This last thought in itself was disturbing. *Why should I have to rely on circumstances? I am engaged to a man who loves me and is waiting for me to return.*

Not going seemed unthinkable, however. Who could tell when their paths would cross again? And so she did her best to clean up, turned command over to Sithmaith, and climbed into the waiting gig. The pull across to the *Morning Star* gave her time to gaze out over the bay, as fine a safe anchorage as could be wished for. The entrance was a bit narrow and shoaled on both sides, but once in, the harbor was completely protected from the violence of the Atlantic. Of the town, which spread along the shore of the harbor to the south, she could see only what lay near the shore. The buildings and houses she could make out were painted in bold colors and had a pleasing architecture utterly different from anything in the Celtic world of her own experience. What the town's connection was with the vast inland areas of old Spain, she could not imagine. No doubt this was a place Seanlaoch Osraige would love to visit and study.

What she could see clearly was the dockyard, and an impressive one it was. Sixteen spacious and well-designed dry-dock slips, every one holding a partially-built warship. Scores of open-sided sheds protected huge piles of fine timber, some rough-cut and some already hewn into smooth masts and spars and planking. On the east side of the dock-yard stood five large buildings that appeared to be residences, probably quarters for the thousands of sailors and fighters the Santanders had been putting to sea for decades. Taken all in all, it was an immense resource. Collen Tredinnick had been dead right: the Santanders meant to overwhelm them at sea and had been very close to accomplishing it. Whatever the terrible cost had been, it was a cost that had to be paid.

Though the hospital ship *Morning Star* was not much longer or wider than a line of battle ship, it was a true three-decker from stem to stern, with long rows of portholes on each side providing light for each of the two inside decks. Mairin climbed the wood-stepped ladder to the quarterdeck, where she was piped aboard and greeted by a salut-ing officer garbed in a standard Admiralty blue-with-red-trim uniform, adorned with caduceus insignia on both shoulders.

"Captain Fotharta," he said with a touch of formality, "welcome to the *Morning Star*. I am Ensign Kenver Hurdon. May I provide you with an escort to see your wounded?"

Mairin returned his salute. "Yes, thank you, Ensign."

Kenver turned and snapped out an order to a midshipman rest-ing his elbows over the port rail. The young man, obviously caught woolgathering, spun about and quickly assumed a horrified and then respectful expression.

"Captain," he said, approaching a few steps. "Medical Midshipman Deveril, at your service. Please come with me."

Under the baleful glare of Ensign Hurdon, Deveril led her down the quarterdeck hatch to the ship's Surgery Deck. The Constant Care Ward stretched from the stern windows a hundred feet forward to a bulkhead amidships; forward of the bulkhead four fully-equipped sur-geries extended forward to the bow. Dozens of hinged glass ports lit the ward cheerfully. Special gimbal-mounted bunks were bolted to the deck every seven feet along the sides, one bunk next to each porthole; a medical chart swung on a cord attached to the end of each bunk. Ventilators connecting to the open deck above ensured movement of fresh air. At the head of each bunk, a small, ship-style shelf held a stoppered flask of water, books, writing paper, clean cloths, and personal effects.

"This is the ward for the most seriously injured," Deveril said. "As I recall, two of *Caillech*'s company are here."

He led her down the center of the cabin to two bunks head to head on the portside. Mairin recognized both faces above the reach of the blankets. On her left lay Danu Eogain, ship's cook and the only other male serving on *Caillech* besides Mor Dal Reti. Though Danu's face was not marked in any way, he was not conscious. Deveril glanced at the chart.

"Severe internal trauma," he said in a low voice, "with internal bleeding. We're hopeful he'll recover."

"How hopeful?"

Deveril forced a smile. "The doctor's notes seem cautiously optimistic, Captain."

On the right was Lavena Ulaid, chief of the starboard watch. Lavena was awake and watching them. Bandages covered much of her face including her jaw and mouth.

"Broken leg and fractured jaw," Deveril whispered in Mairin's ear. "Leg amputation is a possibility."

Mairin stepped closer and found Lavena's hard-calloused hand beneath the blankets.

"Chief, you look about as bad as I feel."

Lavena's eyes sparkled with laughter.

"You'll have to stay behind so they can take care of you. We'll have you back home soon."

Mairin saw the anguished question in her eyes: *will I lose my leg?*

"You'll be climbing the ratlines before you know it. We need you back, all the youngsters on your watch are skylarking."

Lavena's eyes smiled gratefully and her hand squeezed Mairin's.

"I'm off to see Rowenna," Mairin told her. "Be well, my friend."

Mairin visited seven other Province sailors from other ships in her battle group, then Deveril led her down a narrow spiral staircase to the Recovery Ward. This deck extended the entire two-hundred foot length of the *Morning Star*. In addition to the special bunks, each patient was provided with a chair bolted to the deck. The patients here, nearly all male and numbering a hundred or more, were awake, alert and reading or talking to comrades. Mairin's ears detected a mixture of accents: the strong burr of the Scots Guards, the softer gutturals of the Welsh Pikemen, the rugged rhotic speech of the Bretans, the light, airy Gaelic of Kernow.

Deveril consulted a clipboard hanging on a peg next to the staircase. "Four *Caillechs* here, twelve others from your ships."

"Lieutenant Briuin and Captain Conmaicne?"

"Let's see, those two are bunked next to each other, they should be ..."

He looked down the long cabin, but it wasn't necessary to search. Rowenna Briuin had seen them and was waving from her bunk near the bow end of the ward.

"I can find the rest," Mairin said to Deveril. "You've been most helpful."

"My pleasure," Deveril replied. "Captain."

He touched his hat and headed back up the stairs.

Mairin found Rowenna dressed in a sweater and trousers, seated in her chair with a book in her lap. Jilleen, occupying the next bunk aft, wore a plain, loose-fitting tunic that left space for thick bandages on both legs and her right arm near the shoulder. Another bandage covered the left side of her face from nose to temple. Her lap held a portable writing table on which rested a half-written letter. Her bunk was littered with crumpled sheets and addressed envelopes.

Rowenna set her book aside and made to rise.

"No one gets up," Mairin said, easing herself onto Rowenna's bed. "I'm getting down."

"Your back?" asked Jilleen.

"You could say that," Mairin said. She fixed her gaze on Jilleen's lap table. "That could have waited, Jilleen."

The young woman's naturally beautiful face, partly obscured and pale, flashed a wan smile.

"I needed to do it, sir. For myself. Rowenna's been a great help in finding the right words."

"How many?"

"Sixteen." Jilleen waved the unfinished letter. "Including Ensign Kinneard, a Scots girl promoted three weeks ago at the fall exams. She begged to ship out with me. Now I wish I'd turned her down."

Mairin shook her head. "You can't take the blame for that, Jilleen. She might have shipped with me, or Kennat or Tierney. All I can say is that when you see the dockyards here and the ships they planned to build and send against us, you'll know no one died in vain. They'd have beaten us next year, or the year after that."

"You've done the service already?" Rowenna asked.

"Yes, this morning. It couldn't wait."

"No, of course not."

Jilleen twisted in her chair to look out the nearest port. "My ship is in good order?"

"I'm assured it is," said Mairin. "You know Kylee's quality."

"Of course I do." Jilleen's left hand absently fingered the bandage on her face. "I wonder what I'll look like when this comes off?"

"The surgeons on this ship are the best you could have," Rowenna put in with an encouraging smile. "You may have a scar, but with a face like yours, who would notice?"

"Rowenna is—" Mairin began.

"What am I thinking?" Jilleen cried. "Gods above, sixteen shipmates gone and I worry about my face!" She hurled the lapboard to the deck; the sudden *crack* momentarily silenced conversations in the ward.

Mairin retrieved the board and laid it on the bed. A doctor drifted towards them but Mairin motioned him away.

"Jilleen," she said quietly, "you did everything a ship's captain could do for your ship and your crew. I've read the battle reports, you were bleeding to death and still had hold of the wheel and command of the ship. You held your sailors and officers together through a terrible fight, kept your ship and sent the Santander to the bottom. And you were ready to fight again. Don't ask more of yourself than that." She ran a finger along the scars on her own face. "None of us comes away unscathed, in the end. These are the insignia of honor. If you have a scar, wear it proudly."

Jilleen took a deep breath. "I'm all right, Captain, really. It's not the wounds, it's the shock of losing so ... so many at once. I wasn't prepared for it."

"And you think I was?" Mairin laid a hand on the younger officer's shoulder. "No one is prepared for this. Get as much rest as you can, do what the medics tell you. I don't want to leave you here. The same goes for you, Lieutenant," Mairin said to Rowenna. "Rest and recover. I'd like to sail in two days if at all possible."

"I'll be aboard," Rowenna said firmly. "Sithmaith is holding up?"

Mairin nodded. "She's done well. We made a good choice in her. She sends you her best."

Half an hour later, Mairin's gig glided among the anchored ships, heading for the *Ajax*. The bosun's pipe sounded as Mairin stepped on the quarterdeck. She was met by the officer of the watch, a tall, slender lieutenant with his arm in a sling and a bandage on his neck.

"Captain Fotharta, welcome aboard," he said with a friendly smile. "Lieutenant Hellyns, acting first officer, at your service."

She returned his salute. "Lieutenant."

A moment later Richard emerged from the quarterdeck hatch and stepped up to her with his right hand extended.

"Captain, good to see you," he said in a breezy tone. "We're still fixing things, as you can see. Let's go below. Lieutenant, carry on."

"Aye, aye, sir."

Richard led her down the stairs. Once inside his cabin, the door closed, she leaned heavily on his chart table.

"Mairin, sit down," he said gently, his hand on her arm.

She eased herself into a chair. Richard went to a sideboard and poured out two glasses of port.

"This may help a little."

"Thanks."

The port was as smooth as she expected. Richard sat down across from her.

"So, how are you?" he asked.

"Lost quite a bit of blood, bruised everywhere and my back is killing me. Added to that, we had a slight incident coming down here so

I wasn't in the best of shape to start with. You look like you escaped without a scratch."

"I heard about your *incident*," Richard said, swirling the ruby-colored port in his glass. "You really went aboard that ship with the Bretan Fighters holding the deck?"

"What else could I have done?"

He waved a hand at her. "I wasn't criticizing, just admiring."

"Oh. Well, it was worth a concussion to get rid of that bitch once and for all. I can't believe Aideen let her hold her commission this long."

"As to the battle," he said, "I was lucky indeed. We boarded two Santander ships. The first time, I got knocked flat in the first couple of seconds. Just stunned, but by the time I could see straight it was over. The second time, I ended up behind one of our biggest Marines. He cut a path through like a scythe, left nothing for me to fight."

"What were your losses?"

"Eleven Marines. You?"

"Eighteen dead on the *Caillech*, seventy-two overall."

"Oh, Mairin." He reached out and took her free hand. "I am so sorry."

"I've lost people before," she said, easing her hand away, "but never anything like this. The deck was awash with blood. Old friends, youngsters ... "

He refilled their glasses and searched out her eyes.

"Are you OK?"

She took a long sip of the port and waited for its warming burn to settle into her stomach.

"I'm doing what I need to do but my soul is at the bottom of the bay with my sailors and officers. Richard, I knew the life would mean accepting death at sea, sometimes in battle. It comes with the job. And I knew this was a dangerous mission. The thing is, I've never seen my deck covered bow to stern in dead and dying. I've never lost two old friends I loved and respected. And I've certainly never lost a fifteen-year-old midshipman. Call me weak if you like, my heart is in pieces."

To her surprise, his eyes shone with tears. "Call you weak?"

She'd never seen him even close to losing his composure.

"One of the Marines, a fine strapping lad from Lanreath, died in my arms. The last thing he asked me was if we'd won, and he lived just long enough to hear the answer."

A sob surged through his body. "I'd really like to hold you."

She stood and he took her into his arms, her head resting on his shoulder. She held him too, feeling in her hands the steely strength and also the trembling of his powerful body.

After a moment, she said, "I must reek. Sorry."

"Blood, sweat, antiseptic, and sea water," he said into her ear. "Perfume to a seaman."

She had to smile at that. "Richard, you are something."

"So are you." He eased her out to arms' length. "We're due on the flagship soon. Would you consider having dinner with me, here, afterward? All I can offer is ship's fare, but it would be private and my cook wasn't hurt much in the fight."

"I shouldn't."

"Because you're needed on your ship, or because you don't want to spend time alone with me, even in this cabin where ensigns and bosuns and God knows who else knock every ten minutes?"

She lowered her head and made no answer.

"Mairin," he pursued, "if past is prologue I won't hear from you again after this. Indulge me."

She stared at him and said nothing.

"What a stupid thing to say," he said, slamming a fist into his palm. "Forget I asked. I'm tired and sad and really not fit company anyway."

She teetered on the fence a moment longer, then decided.

"I'll be here. Let me go back to *Caillech* after the meeting on the *St. Vincent* so I can clean up. I can't stand myself this way."

"Fair enough. You sail tomorrow?"

"Most likely the day after," she said, getting to her feet. "I'll delay as long as I can to get my injured back to their ships. What about you?"

He stood and poured an extra ounce of port in her glass.

"We'll be here for about a week. Most of the Marines will stay behind to guard the shipyard until we can station a permanent force here. My father wants the yard working at full tilt by the end of the year. Half of the ships in the slips now will go to the Province Squadron."

She downed the port and handed him the glass. "I hope we can crew them."

"You might need to use men."

"The heavens forfend."

She climbed the stairs to the quarterdeck with Richard following.

"Men make decent sailors and officers," he quipped, loudly enough for nearby officers to overhear. "Give it a try."

"So do women," she retorted. "*You* give it a try."

"She has a point, Captain," put in a grinning Lieutenant Hellyns. Under Richard's mock-angry glare, he added, "in a manner of speaking, sir."

She paused at the quarterdeck rail and touched her hat. "Until later, Captain."

She climbed down to the waiting gig. Her sailors had been provided with sizable chunks of iced cake that they now tried to gulp down.

"Sorry, Captain," the bosun's mate said, sweeping crumbs from her tunic.

"Is it good?" Mairin asked.

"Very tasty, sir," the other sailor answered.

"Then you should have saved a piece for me."

"Yes, sir," said the bosun's mate with a grin. "Where to, sir?"

"Admiral's flagship ... the *St. Vincent*. There."

She pointed to a warship easily half again the size of *Caillech*. The *St. Vincent* was anchored somewhat apart from the other ships in the fleet and was already surrounded by ship's boats of all sizes.

As the gig glided over a glassy-smooth bay among the busy warships, the sounds of command and work and laughter lifted Mairin's sagging spirits. It was the life she had chosen, a life on the water, and yes, a life of fighting for her threatened people. All the ships around her now, and all the men and women aboard them, shared that life and that purpose. She sniffed the air: scented with wood and resin and sewage too as they passed near each ship. Woodsmoke poured from galley stacks; below decks the cooks prepared hot evening meals for exhausted sailors and officers. The autumn sun descended behind the taller buildings of the dockyard, outlining them in a contrast of orange glare and deep shadow. She wanted to go home ... yet she felt at home here too, among the ships, even after so costly a battle.

Did I flee to this life to escape something? she asked herself. *And is it now so much a part of me that I can't give it up ... for anything or anyone?*

The gig bumped against the towering *St. Vincent*, startling her from her thoughts. It was an even longer climb onto the double-decked warship, an ascent that had her seeing stars of pain by the time she set foot on the hallowed quarterdeck of Collen Tredinnick. The piping stopped and there he was, coming towards her, hand out, resplendent in his uniform of blue and gold.

"Mairin," he said, taking her hand in both of his, "welcome to the *St. Vincent.* Walk with me?"

Mairin nodded to Flag Captain Berdinnar and five or six more officers standing nearby. Collen led her out of earshot a short distance down the starboard rail.

"I am forever grateful," he began with a hand on her shoulder, "to you and your comrades for what you did yesterday. You knew the sacrifice it would mean and your losses were heavy. Everyone in your task force will receive Admiralty Crosses and I will propose you for the Medallion of St. George. We're building a stone memorial in the shipyard to record the names of those buried here in the bay."

"Thank you, sir."

He turned his gaze over the lovely bay, now shimmering with slanting orange sunlight. His eyes found the *Ajax*, anchored about a mile away. "I may be out of place in saying this ... you know my son is extremely fond of you."

"The feeling is mutual, Admiral."

"If you and Richard should ever decide to become closer than friends, I personally would welcome it. Of course, that's a father talking now. My son is a very lonely man. So am I, for that matter, since Ebrel died. But he is young and I am not, and I had twenty-eight wonderful years with the woman of my dreams." He sighed, tapped the ornate siderail with his palm. "It's none of my business, I realize that. I hope I'm not making you uncomfortable."

"Not at all," she replied. "I just don't know what will happen now. The world seems to be coming apart, our part of it anyway."

"So it is," he replied distantly. "So it is."

"And Richard must have told you I'm involved with someone else."

"He did, and I understand." He straightened up and smiled at her. "Whatever happens, remember you're always welcome in my home. Now, come below. Your old taskmaster is waiting to see you."

"Captain Endean?"

"The same. He's hiding out in my cabin."

"Nothing would please me more. Lead on, Admiral."

Candles. Not something she expected to see on a ship, given sailors' abject fear of open flames. She noted with hidden amusement that while each of the four candles rested in an ornate brass holder, each holder sat on a large dinner plate. Still, it was a nice thought, and she commented on it when he opened the cabin door for her.

"Where, pray tell, did you find candles?" she asked, taking the chair he slid out for her.

"To be honest," he said, sitting opposite her. "I sent a boat in to scour the dockyards. They found these candles. As a bonus my crew discovered an amazing cache of vintage wine in the closet of the Santander admiral's office. Try some?"

"Yes, thank you."

While he poured, she gazed out the stern windows. With the tide flowing into the bay from the ocean, *Ajax*'s stern faced the town. Lights twinkled there, and from this distance they could easily have been the lights of Wexford or Wicklow. Only the burnt-out hulk of the ugly palace marred the sight.

She felt entirely better. She was eternally grateful to her crew for providing warm water. Six soapy minutes in her quarter-galley's shower erased the stench of battle, rinsed blood from her hair, and made her feel fit for company again. Deciding against the formality of a dress uniform, she donned a dark green uniform shirt, jacket and lightweight trousers. With her hair combed over the shaved gap, the image in the mirror no longer appalled her. She dashed on a touch of perfume and then regretted it: the expensive fragrance was a gift from Conor.

As if reading her thoughts, Richard handed her a glass and said, "you look beautiful, Captain Fotharta."

She tried the wine. Well-seasoned, fruity though not sweet.

"You look dashing yourself, Captain Tredinnick."

As indeed he did. He too had opted for informality: a light blue shirt, open at the collar, wool vest in deep blue tucked into black trousers, with a black belt trimmed in red. His black wavy hair was combed back. The flickering candles lit up the sea-blue of his eyes.

"To us," he said, raising his glass, "and to victory."

She clinked her glass against his. "To us and to victory," she repeated.

The cook tapped on the cabin door and carried in the first remove, a vegetable soup spiced with local herbs lifted from the dockyard's stores. That and each dish to follow were hot and delicious and complimented by a steady flow of fine Spanish wines. Mairin found herself slowly unwinding. Her head no longer throbbed and her stomach unclenched for the first time in weeks. Richard kept up the flow of lively conversation, and before long she found herself laughing till tears flowed. She could not honestly remember how long it had been since she laughed for the sheer joy of it.

The dessert of boiled pudding went down easily, the cloth was cleared, and Richard poured out the dregs of their third bottle.

"Sit with me," he invited, nodding towards the padded bench below the stern windows.

She got up and joined him on the soft cushions.

"I don't have cushions like these," she commented, pressing her fingers into one. "Mine are hard and lumpy."

"I'll send these over tomorrow morning," he said, lifting one up. "Plenty more in Falmouth."

"Thank you, that would be nice."

"You can remember me whenever you're sitting on one."

She reached out and touched his face gently. "I'll remember you for more than cushions, Richard. I'm glad I came tonight, it will be a wonderful memory."

"I'm glad you came too. I hate to think two more years will pass before I see you again. At least answer if I write?"

"I will."

They fell silent for a time. Finally he turned to her, his handsome face solemn.

"Mairin, we only have a few more minutes and there is something I need to say."

He paused and swallowed hard. "It's just this. I love you, and I want us to be together. Maybe you already knew that, maybe not. I don't want us to part with you wondering what I'm about. I know you have a commitment to someone else, and I respect that." He stopped, seemed about to go on, then shrugged. "That's all," he finished, looking down at the deck.

"Richard," she started. *Yes, that's his name. But what to say? How do I tell him I'm frightened and sad and happy and torn apart all at once? That I have no answer he will want to hear?*

"I'd be lying if I said I didn't love you. It doesn't seem right to love two people, but I do, and I already told Conor I would marry him." She took his hand in hers. "We're very much alike, you and I, and because of that it seems obvious to you we'd be happy together. As much as you know about me, there are still things you don't know, and if you did, you might feel differently. On top of that, how could we ever spend any time together? Or did you want me to quit, like Conor does? It's not that simple, for me anyway."

"I understand that," he said, staring into her eyes. "I wasn't making a practical statement or laying out careful plans for the future. I love you and I want to spend my life with you. Let's leave it at that."

He stood up, drew her against him, and hugged her gently. When he kissed her, it was on the forehead.

"We'd better call it a night," he said, his voice unsteady. "I won't forget about the cushions."

She leaned forward in his arms and with tears in her eyes, kissed him long and deeply.

"Goodnight," she said, moving a step back. "A favorable wind, dear Richard."

"A favorable wind, love." he replied, his face anguished. "And a red sky at night."

Dear Caemgen and Feidlimid, it is with great sorrow that I must report the death of your daughter Echna in recent action off Tralee. Echna served the Province with great distinction for fifteen years at sea, most recently as a Sailing Master, a rank of high distinction and responsibility. I can tell you that she will be terribly missed by her fellow officers and shipmates. Please accept my sympathy and deep personal regret. Echna's name and service will be added to the Scroll of Honor at Squadron Headquarters in Rosslare, and she will be awarded the Province Medal of Valor posthumously. She will of course receive the fullest military honors at the service of burial, if that is your wish.

Aideen Conmaicne Laigain
Commodore, Province Squadron

Chapter 45

Unable to sleep, Liadan donned a cloak and crept down the stairs of the Inn. The first faint rays of dawn shone in the east, the time of day she most favored for walking in the countryside. She was surprised to find the Inn's parlor occupied: her father-in-law lounged in one of the big chairs near the stove, writing by the light of an oil lamp. He glanced up when the stairs creaked beneath her feet.

"Daughter, you're up early," Uinseann observed.

"So are you, father," she said, walking towards him. "Or shall we both admit we didn't sleep last night?"

He laid aside his writing pad with a sigh. "I suppose we must. I don't sleep well in strange places anyway."

She focused on his writing tablet. "The *Credo*?"

"What else? I'm four score and ten, how much longer do I have to finish it?"

"Plenty of time. I'm taking a walk, you're welcome to come."

"No," he said, rising stiffly. "I should get myself cleaned up and dressed. I have to think about what I'm going to say."

She smiled at the tall, elegant man whose gray eyes so resembled Conor's. "You're never at a loss." She rose on tiptoes and kissed him on the cheek. "I'll be back soon."

During the night a sharp northwest wind had blown away the fog. Liadan found herself strolling out of Clonmel on a late autumn morning of extraordinary beauty. The eastern sky glowed in soft shades of magenta and orange, fading into the purest blue overhead and pale violet in the west. The air was cold, dry and head-clearing.

She set out at her usual fast pace, heading east on the narrow road that meandered through town and then followed the banks of the River Suir. On her left, the Rampart followed the line of the river; on her right, rolling fields of well-kept farms stretched south for as far as the eye could see. Steep hillsides were kept trimmed by color-marked, bushy-coated sheep, whose bleating suggested they were contented on this chilly morning.

She had walked this way before, years ago, and remembered the farms, especially the one she now passed with its herd of Black Angus cattle, whitewashed house with red shutters, and curious round barn topped by an oversized rooster-weathervane. She almost turned aside into the farmyard; at this hour breakfast would be on the table in the house, hot frying bacon and eggs and thick slices of fresh bread. Perhaps another time, when she could linger and get to know those farmers, let them speak with pride of their farm and their herd and tell her the tale of the circular barn.

A mile down the road, the first watchtower east of Fort Clonmel interrupted the Rampart. Two figures moved around the open-sided top, ever-watchful of the lands to the north. They would be especially vigilant today, knowing that somewhere in the northwest, a great army was descending on the Province, bent on smashing through the Rampart and taking their lands. It was her children, she lamented, more than the Rampart, who now stood between that army and the farmstead. The blood of Conor and Fethnaid might soon be spilled into the earth so that this farmer she'd never met could hold onto his lands and his cattle.

Another time, words and verses would have flowed into her mind in a torrent, faster than she could write them down. Not this long-feared morning. Try as she might to enjoy the glory of the sun peaking over the hills, pouring its brilliance over frost-covered fields, she could not.

Suddenly from behind her, a mockingbird perched in a tall oak burst into raucous song, launching into call after call of imitations, one of which sounded suspiciously like the signal horns of the watch-tower. She turned and spotted the full-throated, long-tailed singer, who seemed to be staring straight down at her.

"Thank you," she said with a slight bow. "You're doing your best, and it's an impressive song. Maybe another day I'll come back to enjoy it more."

I speak to birds, she laughed to herself. *It is well I remember, Uinseann would say, that I am no more significant than my feathered friend up there. We both live on the earth, and today I worry and he does not. Who is to say which of us will have better fortune in the days ahead?*

She listened awhile longer, then reluctantly turned and headed back. She had much to do today, much to endure. All three of her children would be in the same place, if only for a short time. She feared most for Feth, her youngest, her little one, but her heart bled for Conor, who bore the weight of so many thousands of souls. Even Aideen, cool and self-contained, was beginning to show the endless strain of com-mand, her face fissured by the same lines of worry as Domnall's in the last years of his truncated life.

The town was awakening when she returned to its cobblestone streets. While many townfolk had fled, other citizens poured in during the night to witness the Ceremony of Citizenship. Never before had citizenship in the Twenty Clans been granted to so great a number at once and under such unusual circumstances. The Council of Twenty would be present; all of the Elders led by Uinseann; the high com-mand of the army and navy; and the field army itself drawn up for review. Despite the danger and worry in the air, it was pageantry and solemnity on a scale seldom seen in anyone's lifetime.

Liadan went upstairs to dress in her own official robes, adding at the last the medallion Domnall wore on the day of his death. She was brushing her hair when a tap sounded at the door.

"Come in, it's not locked," she said.

In the mirror she saw Rionach enter, already garbed in her Council robes.

"Sit, mother, I'm nearly ready."

Liadan fussed a few seconds more, then turned towards a smiling Rionach.

"You've always worried about your hair," the older woman said, "when anyone else would gladly trade for it! Uinseann tells me he wasn't the only night-owl, or should I say morning-owl?"

"Too many things on my mind," said Liadan, taking a chair next to Rionach. "The walk helped some, especially the mockingbird who imitated the watchtower trumpets! Did you sleep?"

Rionach shook her head. "Poorly. I'm restless when I don't sense my husband next to me. No matter. Will your stomach accept some tea and rolls? Padraic is already downstairs. As you might imagine, his appetite is unaffected."

"My brother's appetite survives anything," Liadan said lightly. "You know Fethnaid came in late last night? Conor sent a message."

"Not just came in! She had most of the Tralee Militia at her back!"

"I don't understand how she did it. Volunteers, yes, I expected she might get a few. The Macroom Guards and now this! It doesn't seem possible."

"Perhaps Feth sees only the need to try and not the likelihood of success," Rionach mused. "Like you I was quite certain she'd return a week after she left, empty-handed and disheartened. She's taught me a lesson, old as I am. How does the old expression go: nothing ventured ... "

"Nothing gained. Failure and heartache narrows our thinking, do you suppose?"

"Whatever the explanation," said Rionach, rising from the chair, "she's made a difference already."

They found the Inn's small dining room crowded to capacity. Liadan nodded to other Council members and breathed a sigh of relief when she did not see Etain. The day would be hard enough without having Padraic and Etain in the same room, not to mention Rionach who had outmaneuvered her in the Council. Uinseann and Padraic sat together and rose from their chairs when Liadan and Rionach approached. Padraic loomed larger than ever in his full dress uniform, massive chest adorned with every commendation the Province offered, alongside decorations of valor from Kernow and Wales and Bretan. Uinseann now wore the blue and tan robes of an Elder.

Uinseann and Rionach bade farewell and left together, Uinseann needing to gather his fellow Elders together and Rionach her Councillors. Liadan took a chair across from her brother.

"I understand you plan to fight in the line," she said with a tone of disapproval.

"And you think I'm too old?"

"A year older than me, last time I thought about it."

Padraic nibbled at a biscuit before replying.

"You may be right," he admitted. "On the other hand, there are times when a man must do something out of love or conviction, however foolish it may seem to others."

"My philosopher brother," she said. She took hold of his hand. "I know why you're fighting. And I know what it will mean to Conor to have you nearby."

"Sister mine, old I may be," he said, "but my sword is still fast and my armor thick."

Liadan laughed. "Maybe your head is thick too."

"Maybe it is!" he agreed, laughing with her. He gulped the last of his tea and got to his feet. "I must be off."

With that he left the room, boots clumping heavily on the wooden floor.

By the time Liadan climbed into the reviewing stand, the ceremony was about to commence. From a tall mast in the reviewing stand's center, a Province flag waved in the morning breeze. On each side of it, twenty banners flew from shorter masts, one for each of the ancient clans. The crimson-tuniced Line of Blades, armor plate and mail and steel weaponry gleaming in the brilliant morning sun, extended six hundred feet from end to end and three deep. On the flanks of this massed phalanx, the blue-tuniced Line of Bows extended the line another five hundred feet and two deep. Those who would be given citizenship, more than a thousand soldiers, were assembled closest to the reviewing stand: Macroom Guards on Liadan's left, Tralee Militia on the right, and between them, the auxiliary light infantry and crossbow units, the former uniformed in maroon and the latter in gray, each unit proudly bearing its own standard.

Directly in front of the reviewing stand, Conor rode Treasach, who for the occasion was draped in a brilliant gold blanket. Melvina and Kellen flanked him on horses adorned with blue and crimson blankets; on the far left and far right, Aife Luachra and Midir Cormaic, commander of the Tralee militia, were mounted on horses draped in silver blankets. At the top of the risers, Trev Fiachrach and ten other musicians stood ready to play a special anthem he had composed for the occasion.

The Council of Twenty occupied the second tier of the risers, though a head-count would have come up with twenty-two men and women. Gilvarry Muiredarg of Enniskean and Rainait Phelan of Coumduffmore had taken places on either side of Rionach as her guests. Liadan by chance found herself between McCrae Dal Reti, an old friend, and of all people Etain Fotharta, looking resplendent and haughty. On the first tier, Uinseann occupied the center position, flanked by Padraic and Aideen and Arvel on one side and by three Elders of the Clans on the other. The remainder of the seats were occupied by mayors, army and navy officers, and invited guests from Kernow and Wales.

To Etain's obvious displeasure, Liadan leaned over in her direction to get a direct view of Aideen, whom she had not met coming in. Tall, slender, elegant, a striking figure of authority in deep green and gold, features that from this distance looked so much like her father. The report of the battle off Tralee had reached Clonmel, and with it the losses Aideen's ships had sustained. Perhaps alone in this huge gathering, Liadan knew the depth of anguish that lay beneath that commanding presence.

Where was Feth? Liadan's eyes searched the assembly field from end to end and spotted no mounted archers. She was about to ask McCrae what he knew when a strange sound echoed over the meadow, a low keening that rose higher and higher in pitch until it imitated the howl of a wolf. Over the keening of the horn came the thundering of hooves: three hundred black-mailed horses ridden by black-uniformed, black-armored riders whose curaisses bore the insignia of the red dragon with arrows grasped in its long talons. The archers' hands were free; they directed their Welsh battle steeds by boots and stirrups alone. Beneath the black, silver-crested helmets no faces could be seen, yet Liadan had no trouble spotting Feth riding at the front, holding high the banner of the Red Dragons. Horses and riders pounded along in a perfect chain past the left flank of the Bows, behind the phalanx of Blades, and then past the right flank of Bows. All the while the strange horn of the ancient Celts blew, a sound that gave Liadan a chill up the spine.

Feth suddenly pulled up her horse, the horn fell silent, and with flawless discipline the riders formed into three long, straight lines of a hundred each. Archers drew recurves from saddle holsters and held them at the ready. The Welsh horses made no motion at all, so trained and bred were they to keep still and silent at a single voiced command.

"Magnificent," whispered McCrae. "Liadan, who leads them?"

"Someone who was once my little girl."

McCrae stared at her in surprise. "Fethnaid? It cannot be!"

"It is, old friend."

McCrae turned his eyes back towards the Red Dragons and said again in a hushed voice, "magnificent."

Liadan glanced sidelong at Etain, who must have overheard them. "You must be most proud of Kellen," she assayed.

Liadan saw Etain's luminous eyes widen in surprise. For a moment she seemed not to have a reply. Then with a wary look at Liadan, she said, "I am, yes. Thank you."

Liadan glanced up at the sky to see if it was falling. It was not.

The uillean pipes, fiddles, and trumpets led by Trev now intoned the *Hymn of the Twenty Clans*. Many present sang the old Gaelic words, with feeling if not always on key. From somewhere in the direction of the Red Dragons, Liadan heard a female voice of haunting beauty drift over the field. Who it was she could not tell. When the hymn ended, Uinseann stepped forward to a lectern and waited for silence.

"Please be seated," he said to those in the reviewing stand, who had risen from their seats for the hymn.

Then, in a ringing voice that belied his age, he began the service.

"Many of you here today," he said, sweeping his eyes over the field, "have never set foot in the lands of the Province, and possibly you expected you would not be welcome here. I hope we have shown you that this is not so. Everyone from the lands of Cork and Kerry who is ready to do battle for the sake of all is our friend and ally, and will forever be welcome among the Twenty Clans of Eirelan."

He paused and allowed silence to descend on the multitude.

"One thousand, two hundred and eight of you now stand before me, awaiting the grant of citizenship. Citizenship comes with no obligation except one, which is that neither you nor your successors will ever raise a hand against the Twenty Clans. Once allies, eternally allies. So it has ever been, since the founding of the Province a thousand years ago, and so it is today."

He paused again, sipped water from a mug handed to him, then took up in his right hand the staff of the High Elder. Hewn from an oak growing on the shores of Lough Ennell in the time of the Province's founding, the staff was straight and finely polished, its head carved in the shape of the Celtic Cross, whose ancient meaning as the "Circle of Unity, Cross of Trials and Suffering" was inscribed in old Gaelic around the center of the staff.

With his free hand, Uinseann pulled the hood of his cloak over his head and began the formal rite.

"And now I begin the ritual of citizenship. The words I use you will understand, though a thousand years ago the exact words in the older Gaelic tongue were different. Let us all now stand. Those in the field should remove their helmets."

Liadan and everyone in the reviewing stand rose to their feet. At last she saw her younger daughter's face ... and it surprised her. Even at this distance, something subtle had changed since she'd last seen Feth. *Thinner, yes, but that's not quite it.*

The child is gone, she lamented. *That's what I see.*

"We are the people of the Twenty Clans of Eirelan," Uinseann intoned, "founded on the shores of Lough Ennell. In us flows the ancient blood of the Celts from time out of mind. Our creed is to cherish all things about us, living and not living, return what we use, live gently on the land. In our hearts we value our fellow man, hate no one, take from no one, rule over no one. With our minds we see that all of life is mystery, and death a part of the unending cycle of the world. We fight as we must, to defend our right to live and partake of the wonders of the earth. All who fight with us, wherever born, become a part of us and rightfully share in the life of the clans."

Uinseann looked up to the clear blue sky, then raised the great oaken staff high over his head. His voice rose in pitch and power.

"All who pledge to fight with us in the great battle that is to come are now citizens. You and your husbands and wives and children and their children will be welcome in the Province unto the last age of man in Eirelan. You may come and go in our lands, own property, and enjoy all the protections of our laws and customs. Your names will be inscribed in the roll of the Twenty Clans as of this day and shall never thereafter be erased. So say I, Uinseann Danaan Laigain, High Elder of the Province in this year nine hundred and ninety-nine. May fortune smile upon all of us in the days to come. Amen."

He lowered his staff, pushed back his hood, and stepped back. Trev Fiachrach's uillean pipes sung out, alone at first and then joined by all the other musicians assembled, playing the closing hymn he'd written. To Liadan's ears it was a melancholy melody of extraordinary beauty, suffused with joy and sorrow, longing and fulfillment. It said to all those assembled and listening in silence, *we are not a grandiose people who celebrate our own merit and raise ourselves up high. We are the people who live in the world, not above it, and we treasure love above all things.*

A soft, cool breeze wafted through the lofty stone tower of Fort Clonmel, where Liadan and Aideen had for the last two hours watched the departure of the great army. The main body of fighters had long since disappeared down the road leading towards Clogheen. Feth's company of horses brought up the rear of the column, and they too vanished in the woods that closed in over the road to the west. The covered medical wagons now approached that point; behind them rumbled the artillery wagons loaded with ballistae; and last of all, just now emerging from the Rampart gates, the heavy-duty wagons of the supply train, piled with munitions, food, tents, camp gear, and every other item needed for a field army on the march.

"Do you remember Seanlaoch?" Liadan asked, breaking a long silence.

Aideen seemed at first not to hear, then awoke from her distant thoughts to answer.

"Seanlaoch? Oran's younger brother you mean? Not very well. Wasn't he the boy with spectacles who was always reading and asking pesky questions?"

Liadan frowned at her daughter. "Fifteen years ago, yes he was, if you want to put it that way. He's twenty-four now and a writer and historian. You haven't read *anything* he's written?"

Aideen shook her head in irritation. "Mother, when exactly would I have time for pleasure reading? In the last five years I've barely had time to brush my teeth."

"Of course. I shouldn't have asked."

After a pause, Aideen sighed and drew up straight.

"I'm sorry, mother, that was uncalled for. I'm exhausted, I hurt, and ... well, it's been a bad week. I'll try to read Sean's work, next chance I get. Maybe this winter. I'm sure it's worthwhile."

Liadan looked out onto the road again, where the supply wagons drawn by the teams of draft horses now lined the road west. Moments later, the Rampart gates swung shut and sentries slammed home the iron bars.

"I take no offense, Aideen, you know that," Liadan said. "I would like to know why your eyes carry so much sadness in them."

Aideen pulled off her dress hat and ran a hand through coal black hair flecked with gray.

"Three years ago, mother, we lost twenty-two sailors all year, half to accidents and the rest to fighting. Two years ago, the same number to accidents and forty-three to fighting. Last year, ninety-six to fighting alone. This week, I buried over eighty, and I have no idea what Mairin Fotharta's losses may be."

"No word yet?"

"None. For all I know, we could have lost those four ships and I had no authorization to even send them in the first place. The Council may have my job over that. To tell you the truth, mother, I don't think I'd care if they do."

"Rionach would never let that happen. Never. And you'll get your spirits back, this is exhaustion talking now."

Aideen shook her head sadly. "Not so. Just look at me! If people saw us together they'd think you're the younger. My body is tired, my mind is tired, and there's no end in sight. Even if we've taken Santander, we have other enemies out there, maybe stronger than the Spaniards. I've been at sea twenty years, since I turned twelve, and it's making me old and bitter. So yes, I wouldn't mind being sent off to a desk somewhere, or maybe retired altogether. Let someone else lie awake all night wondering how to hold things together for another day or another year. Or write the letters to the grieving families."

Liadan moved to her daughter's side and touched her shoulder.

"I had no idea you felt like this. You never say much when you're home."

"How often is that?" Aideen flared bitterly. "And what home? A place where I sleep a few times a year? I'm thirty-two, I have no home of my own, no husband, no close friends, nothing. Just work, and worry." She drew in a deep breath, then another, and managed a forced half-smile. "This is nothing but self-pity, pure and simple. I made my choice and I have to live with it."

Liadan was about to reply when one of the two sentries on duty suddenly appeared at Aideen's elbow. She was a short girl of about twelve with long curly hair and freckles. Her companion, an older and much taller girl, waved at her to come back, to no avail. Both girls had been under the watchful eye of the Fort Captain, a middle-aged man with a grizzled beard, who had told them to keep their distance from the visitors. Now he glared at the girl from his post near the telescope, but he did not try to intervene.

"Excuse me," the girl piped in a thin voice, "would it be all right if I asked you a question?"

Aideen looked down and despite her foul mood, smiled at the girl.

"Of course it is. What's your name, sentry?"

"Nainsi Ulaid, from Rathgormuck , ma'am. Not far from here."

"Well, my name is Aideen Laigain and this is my mother Liadan. What would you like to ask?"

"My sister," she glanced at the tall girl, "says you're an officer in the navy. We don't see navy people in my town so I wanted to know if she's right."

"Why, yes she is," said Aideen, showing the girl her hat and insignia. "I'm the Commodore, which means I get all the work and none of the fun. That's what this gold cross-and-anchor means on my hat."

She handed her dress hat to the youngster, who handled it with reverence. Liadan looked on with a smile, mentally thanking Domnall's spirit for sending this child over to them at this moment.

"I'd like to be in the navy," Nainsi said, handing the hat back, "but I don't know how. I'm twelve, that's supposed to be old enough."

"It's old enough, barely, but your mother and father would have to sign some papers."

Nainsi frowned and looked off towards the west. "My father is there, with the army."

Aideen put her hand on the girl's frail shoulder.

"I'm sure he'll come back soon and then you can take care of it."

Nainsi seemed unsure. "Would you write my name down and help me if I need it?"

Aideen turned to Liadan in a panic. Liadan reached into her belt pouch and handed Aideen a small writing pad and pencil.

"That is Nainsi Ulaid, Rathgormuck," she said, writing. She tore off the sheet, folded it, and slid it into a pocket. "There. You let me know if you need any help."

"Thank you," Niansi said. She walked back to where her sister watched with amusement.

The Fort Captain stepped over and said, "Sorry, Commodore, I told them not to bother you."

"No bother at all, Captain," Aideen said. "I always need new recruits."

He nodded and returned to the telescope, which he trained on the disappearing remnants of the army's supply train.

"I have to go, mother," Aideen said. "I'll walk you back to the Inn."

"You can't linger for tonight? You could bunk with me, my room has two beds. A decent night's rest, a hot bath and breakfast would do you good."

Aideen considered the tempting idea, then shook her head. "I'd love to, mother, really I would ... but I can't. I'm awaiting word from Spain, my ships are damaged, I have crew in the hospital, and orders to get out. I'll stay in Dungarvan until we have news of the battle, then I have to go back to Rosslare."

"If you must," said Liadan with regret.

Minutes later, they stood outside the Inn. Liadan embraced her daughter and took hold of her hands.

"Before you go, Aideen, I need to say one thing to you. You said up in the tower that you have no close friends to confide in. I know you and Conor have been at odds since you were children. That never surprised me, you have different ways of looking at the world. Even so, you might find that you have more in common now than you think. Try talking with him. He loves you, you know, and he'd do anything for you."

Aideen turned away. "I've treated him badly, mother. Many times. Mostly out of envy, I suppose. He has plenty of reason not to like me."

"Conor has a very forgiving heart. You might find him a valuable friend."

Aideen gazed into her mother's eyes for a long moment.

"We got started on a friendship these past weeks, at least I thought we did. When he comes back, we'll talk again." She paused and swallowed hard. "I do hope we get that chance."

She kissed Liadan's cheek and strode down the quiet street. Liadan watched her first-born until she turned a corner and disappeared.

"Oh, my children," she said to herself, "what a time we live in."

She sat down on the steps and wept.

We feel we are ancient, we speak of the past,
As if we have lived through the ages of time.
But the blazing of sunset was here long before us,
And long past our going will moon and stars climb.
What dell in this land is not salted with blood?
Oh Eirelan, the suff'ring and anguish you bear!
Yet many a poet has sprung from your gardens,
Many a songbird has music'd the air.
At last what we have, is the greatest of things,
The spring of all meaning, the font of delight:
'Tis our love for each other, the tend'rest of feelings,
That holds us together, 'gainst falling of night.
Conor Laigain, 995

Chapter 46

A golden eagle, buoyed by a gentle easterly breeze, glided high above the late autumn landscape west of Clonmel. Into the setting sun she soared, telescopic eyes scanning the meadows below for moving prey. She was not especially hungry but as night approached, a meal arose in her avian-hunter mind as a desire if not a genuine need. At times she followed the road below, because it offered a cleared path through dense woods where prey were hiding. As the sun plunged below the western mountains, she crossed the River Tar and on its bank spotted a ginger-colored stoat. Down she plummeted ... but it was not to be. The stoat vanished into the woods seconds before her grasping talons could do their deadly work.

West of the river she beheld a sight strange to her eyes: vast numbers of men and their horses and wagons, gathered in a broad meadow. She circled out of sheer curiosity and picked up that odd yet familiar scent rising from flaming stacks of wood. Some of the men below stared up at her, though they could not see her as well as she could see them. A second circle and then she moved on along the general line of the road, soaring high and low, until she came to a place where roads crossed each other. There she spotted a brown mink skittering across bare gravel, and this time she succeeded. Talons clamped down in an unbreakable grip, wings beat hard, and it was done. She flew north a few miles to a secluded meadow where she could enjoy her meal. She found the meadow occupied as well. Flames were everywhere, the scent of meat hung in the air, and strange, loud sounds offended her sensitive ears. It had to be the next meadow then, and there she was finally allowed to devour the fresh-killed mink in peace.

"About two miles north of the road crossing at Mhisteala, sir," the scout reported between gulps of air. He stood before Conor and Oran, holding the reins of his sweat-covered horse. "Camped for the night. Not more than ten miles from here."

"You saw no advance scouts?" Oran asked, still fuming that Conor had forbidden him to do the job himself. "And were you seen?"

"Let him catch his breath!" Conor intervened. "Eremon, isn't it?"

"Yes, sir, Eremon Loigde."

Bradaigh took the reins from Eremon's hand and led the horse away from the camp's westside sentry post. Eremon, a slight young man who seemed determined to grow a sparse reddish beard to age his cherubic face, emptied his belt flask of water.

"Thank you, General," he said, his breath restored. "My throat was dry." To Oran, he said, "No, sir, I saw no scouts. I don't believe I was seen. I heard the camp from a mile away, hid my horse, and crept through the woods on my belly. As you told me, sir. They're a damned noisy lot, I could have sneezed and played my harp and no one would've noticed."

Conor turned away to conceal a smile. Oran attempted to maintain his composure but finally failed too.

"Fine work," Oran said, slapping the anxious Eremon on the back. "I mean it, well done. Go get your dinner."

"Yes, sir," he said, saluting with relief.

Conor and Oran headed back for the big command tent where the army's officers and general staff were gathering to discuss the final plan for battle.

"It'll be tomorrow, then," said Oran. His hand touched the bandage on his chest.

"Are you all right?" Conor asked. "You've done more today than you were supposed to."

"Ah, it hurts a bit, not bad. Problem is I have no energy. I couldn't wield a child's sword."

"Nor will you be wielding any sword," said Conor firmly. "I mean it, Oran. Get into armor, yes, and stay with me, but no fighting. It's bad enough I have to worry about Padraic who's too damn old to be in the Line."

"I wouldn't let him hear you say that," said Oran quietly. "And to be honest, I wouldn't want to put your idea to the test. He may not be young but he's the strongest man I've ever seen. There may come a time tomorrow when you need him."

Conor stopped a yard short of the tent entrance.

"I know," he said, facing Oran. "I know I need everyone. I'll fight myself if it comes to that. I just can't shake the thought that someone I love dearly is going to die tomorrow."

As if on cue, Feth, Derdre and Gwen came up at a fast walk and, not seeing Conor and Oran in the gathering darkness, plunged into the tent. Oran put his hand on the nape of Conor's neck and leaned in close to his face.

"My friend," he said softly, "the only thing we can do now is to seek victory. Who lives and who dies is out of our hands."

They entered the tent, which was now nearly full. Bradaigh came in behind them, his alert eyes scanning the room to see if everyone was there. His lips moved silently: *Kellen, Melvina, Fethnaid, Gwen, Derdre, Arvel, Padraic, Aife, Midir, Oran, Conor. Me.* Plus assorted senior captains, deputy commanders, aides, and the chief of the medical unit. He was satisfied.

"All senior staff present, sir," he reported to Conor.

"Thank you, Bradaigh," said Conor. To Oran, he whispered urgently, "sit down!"

Conor walked to the front and stood before the ten-foot map displaying the region between the army's current location and the position of the Ghaoth Aduiadh force. Bradaigh took a seat in front of him and set his notepad on his knee.

"We've heard from our scout," Conor began, "who tells us our enemy is camped here." He pointed to the map north of the town of Mhisteala. "That's about ten miles from our camp. No doubt they've been watching us too since we left Clonmel. Given the huge size of their force, they can't use any of the smaller roads near here. They'd have to split up into three or four sections and even then they'd make slow progress. So I believe, and Oran Osraige agrees, that they'll march at dawn and come straight for us. General Conmaicne?"

"I agree," said Padraic from the last row of chairs. "We should keep the scouts watching all the roads but their path seems almost certain now. The only question is where we collide."

"And that place needs to be of our choosing," Conor went on. "In three hours, around midnight, we'll break camp. It's a moonless night and with the east wind we can expect it may rain at some point, so make sure every soldier has rain gear handy. The main body of the army will move straight for Mhisteala, reaching it in less than two hours' time. Feth, you will lead your full division of twelve hundred up this smaller road that branches off in Kilbeheny. Halt your column as soon as you can hear their camp, then wait. By dawn they'll move south. Send out a scout to make sure they've passed the crossroads, then take to the road in their rear. Stay far enough back not to be seen."

"Understood, General," Feth said. "We'll be in position."

Conor traced a position on the map with his finger.

"We're aiming to engage them in a broad meadow two miles west of Kilbeheny. The general terrain is flat with a moderate rise east of the battlefield that will screen our movements. The meadow itself is about a half mile wide, extending evenly on both sides of the road. Thin woods border it, the trees are not very dense, underbrush thick and tangled. Kellen, the Line of Blades will stretch across the road from one side to the other. We have almost twenty-four hundred, so we'll form three battle lines of eight hundred each, three feet to a man. Melvina, we'll need to set up the shooting platforms ten feet high to give you a clear line of fire. Leave the usual gaps for troop and wagon movements. You have enough archers to cover the whole line. The ballistae will mass on the flanks. General Conmaicne will lead a force of two hundred in reserve, to be used wherever they're needed. Questions so far?"

There were none.

"Melvina, as soon as the main body of their army is in range, your archers and ballistae will open up with long-range fire, as heavy a bombardment as you can. Make sure the supply wagons with arrows and bolts are right behind the platforms."

Melvina merely nodded. Conor smiled at her briefly to say, *sorry, I know you knew that.*

"This is our vise, comrades. We want their force caught between the main battle line, here, to the east and Feth's division attacking from the west, here. They know they heavily outnumber us and judging by their past tactics, they'll try to smash our line right at the beginning by sheer weight of numbers. Feth, you have to wait until they're fully committed. I'll sound four long blasts on the trumpets to let you know. When you commit your force, attack with everything you have. You'll have to decide on the exact spot to strike. I don't need to tell anyone here that the Ghaoth Aduaidh are tough and trained fighters, not street thugs like the Dubliners, so I don't count on any panic. Still, they won't expect a heavy assault from the rear and it may rattle their captains into decisions that give us an opening. If the plan works that far, the only thing left is the fighting. Be ready for signals at all times. Senior officers must hold themselves from combat or we risk losing our coordination. Surgeons, draw the wagons up a half mile behind the battle line. Quartermaster, the supply train remains here. Questions?"

There were a few: exact dispositions along the line, signals, location of reserve arms and armor. When he had answered the last question, Conor caught Padraic's eye from the back, the slight nod of his uncle's head. He knew what Padraic silently asked.

"As General Conmaicne has often told you, friends, battles are won by skill, courage, brains, and discipline, not by numbers. We're outnumbered two to one ... but we're fighting to keep our homes and our families safe from harm. There's nothing fancy about our plan, we know from long experience that clever designs collapse in the fury of battle. If we keep our heads, make quick adjustments, and use our firepower to maximum advantage, we will destroy the enemy. And that is our goal, not driving them off, but destroying them. Our friends from the west fighting with us need a total victory and I believe that when the sun sets tomorrow, they will have one. May fortune smile upon us all."

Two hours later, as a light rain began to fall, Conor threw on an oilskin, raised the hood, and told Bradaigh where he would be. Then he set out alone to walk along the Tar, a wide, shallow river lacking steep banks. Dark and misty though it was, he could see easily by the light of the camp's lanterns and cooking fires. He strolled at a leisurely pace, savoring the pungent smell of burning wood blended with the subtle flagrance of clean water and damp grass. Now and then he heard laughter in the camp, and as he passed near campfires his ear caught snatches of conversations.

"They have the best fried clams anywhere, I'm telling you."

"Beautiful? I'll say she's beautiful."

"Lend me your string wax, will you, I can't find mine."

A fish jumped in the river, then another, and another.

"Don't you wish we had poles?" asked a familiar voice behind him.

"You move quietly, Feth," he said as she came up beside him.

"I don't weigh much, brother," she said, springing on her toes. "Can I walk with you?"

He stopped and looked down at her earnest face. In spite of the sinister black uniform and the fierce red dragon on her chest, the pale light revealed the face of his little sister.

"Of course," he said, resuming his stroll along the bank. "How are you doing?"

"Nervous," she admitted. "Scared. A little sick." She paused as a burst of female laughter echoed over the camp. "I don't think I could laugh right now. I know what needs to be done, and I'll do it."

"I know you will."

She stopped and gazed out over the rippling river. "Conor, why did you give me the command?"

He found a smooth stone and skipped it out over the water. He counted the skips *sotto voce*, "one, two, three, four ... five."

Feth took an insistent hold on his arm. "I need to know."

"For the Red Dragons ... Arvel suggested it. Arvel has been fighting now for almost forty years, I wouldn't think of questioning his judgment."

"And the rest?"

Conor skipped another stone. "Aife asked for you. So did Midir. I spoke with some of the other recruits, from Youghal and Crookstown, and they all said the same thing."

"Why would they want me to lead them?"

"Because they know your courage, and because you dared to beg for their help for the good of all. Aife said it best. It's a question of respect, in the end. You earned the right to lead them."

Feth found herself a stone and skipped it.

"Four." Her hand found Conor's and held it in a tight grip. "All the time I was off in the west, I laid awake at night wondering if I was doing the right thing. I feel like the life of everyone I brought here is in my hands. Sean argued with me about it but he didn't change my mind. Or my heart. Do you feel that way?"

"Of course I do. It's why I always dreaded command, avoided it as long as I could."

"Do you get used to it?"

"Padraic never has."

"Really? He always seems so calm."

"He's a great actor, our uncle. Better than me for sure. Maybe you'll be more like him."

Feth fell silent, thinking. Two more fish jumped in the river, one close to them.

"I really do wish we had our poles," she said. "Maybe another time."

She let go of his hand. "Time for me to get back to my soldiers. I won't see you again for awhile."

Conor wrapped his arms around her and held her, and then she was gone. He took his watch from a pocket and held it so the nearest campfire's faint light struck its dial. It was time to move.

Derdre, riding on Feth's left, carried a red-shaded lantern so she could keep track of the time. Feth leaned toward her and whispered, "how are we doing?"

"A little past four."

Feth brought Ioan to a halt. Aife and Midir, her companions at the front of the column, did likewise. Behind them, the four-abreast line of nine hundred foot soldiers reached back along a half mile of narrow, winding road. Bringing up the rear of the column, Gwen and Derdre led the double- column of Red Dragons. A gentle rain fell, cool but not cold, softening the turf and gravel enough to quiet the horses' footsteps.

After decades of neglect, the road shown on the map was now a road in name only. It was heavily overgrown, with dense shrubs crowding in both sides and tree branches hanging low overhead. Feth had no way to tell exactly where they were, not a single landmark, so she was forced to guess at how fast they moved and how far they yet had to go. She estimated they were no more than a mile from the main road ahead, and the enemy army.

They dismounted and listened. As dawn was yet two hours away, the silence of the woods was undisturbed by so much as a single songbird. Nature was mute ... yet there was *something* faint in the air, coming from up ahead. Muffled voices, the clank and scrape of metal on metal.

"Pass the word," Feth whispered to Aife, whose fighters were at the head of the line. "We'll halt here. Drink, eat, and rest. Absolute silence."

Midir came forward and gave Feth a questioning look. She nodded in response. It had been agreed that this compactly-built Tralee man would be the one to go ahead on foot. His night vision was unusually acute and he was an experienced hunter who made no noise even when moving fast.

He disappeared quickly out of range of the red lantern. Feth considered: Midir would have to move carefully, weave his way through deadfall in the road that would surely slow him down. Say three miles an hour, one mile out and back. Forty minutes. Dawn's first light would brighten the overcast on his return. She told Derdre to mark the time. Then, they waited.

The army passed through the tiny town of Kilbeheny in silence and halted two miles east of the larger crossroads town of Mhisteala. The logistics staff swiftly posted lanterns along the whole line of battle and marked it with powdered chalk. As soon as this was done, Kellen sent his heavy-armored Line of Blades fanning out to either side. Melvina stayed on her horse, riding from flank to flank, supervising the positioning of portable shooting platforms and the forty heavy ballistae.

Conor drew out his watch and held it under Oran's lantern.

"Just past four," he said softly. "Feth should be in position by now." He scanned the eastern sky, still dark beneath the overcast. "First light at five and then they'll be on the move."

"Unless they sleep late and have a nice breakfast," Oran quipped.

"I don't think so with these people. The thing that worried me most about watching them at Lough Gur was the discipline. It's almost like someone is coaching them in our own methods."

Conor's eyes searched ahead to where the road crested the hill. "You have a rider out there?"

"Of course, brother, my best scout is at the crossroads."

"Sorry," said Conor with a sigh, "you know your business."

"It's a deadly business we're about today, and no mistake." Oran's gaze followed Melvina as she rode yet again from flank to flank, stationing her archers on the platforms. "I'm quite fond of that woman, Conor."

"I know you are," Conor said, "and she of you." He paused and swallowed hard. "My mouth feels like beach sand."

Oran pulled a flask from his belt. "Sip this."

Conor pulled out the cork and lifted the flask to his lips.

"Shades of Emer!" he gasped. "What is that?"

"Welsh whiskey," Oran said with a grin. He slid the flask back on his belt. "Courtesy of Arvel."

Conor gulped plain water from his own flask. "You might have warned me," he complained. "I still owe you for hiding out in the fog the other night."

Oran turned his face upward, closed his eyes and savored the cool mist coating his cheeks and forehead. "Not a breath of wind and this light rain. I love this kind of day."

"So do I," Conor agreed. "They called it 'a soft day' in the old tongue."

"A day to walk and think and then sit by a turf-fire."

Many a man and woman will see the beginning of this soft day, Conor said inwardly, *but not the end of it.*

Sean pounded a stake into the soft earth, ran the tent rope through a hole in the stake and pulled in the slack. The last corner of a surgery tent rose into place. He tied off the line and moved to the next tent awaiting assembly. A young woman in a doctor's white tunic was already pounding in one of the stakes. She was quite tall and lovely, that much was apparent even in the shadowy light of the lanterns.

"Seanlaoch Osraige," he said, extending his hand. "Orderly and general factotum."

"Triona Bairrche," she said. Her grip was firm. Huge dark eyes stared at him; ivory cheeks tinted with rose glistened with mist. "Physician."

She thought a moment as their hands parted. "You're Oran's brother ... the writer."

"Yes. Have we met?"

He added silently, *I think I would remember you.*

"I don't think so," she replied while moving on to another stake. "I know Oran's friend Conor. I stayed at their house in Rosslare for a couple of weeks when my cousin Kellen needed care."

They drew the ropes taut and tied them off.

"I've read some of your work," she said. "I liked it but it left me with a lot of questions. Maybe we can talk about it some time?"

"I'd like that."

I doubt Feth would, he cautioned himself. *This is a dangerously alluring woman.*

Triona laid her hammer on a table. "Help me get these tents ready for surgery?"

"That's what I'm here for."

They worked together alongside others in the dim lantern light for a time, setting up tables, lamps, instrument bins, bandage stations, and pharmacy cabinets. Twenty surgery tents were soon ready to receive wounded. Scores of horse-drawn ambulances loaded with stretchers were lined up on either side of the road.

"That's it, then," Triona said, sitting down on top of a crate. Sean sat next to her, feeling pangs of guilt because he seemed unable to ignore Triona's striking beauty.

"First light in a few minutes," she murmured with a glance at her pocket watch. "Then it will begin. How I do dread it."

"Imagine how Conor must feel, leading the army."

Triona nodded and said in a thready voice, "My heart is with him." She wiped tears from her cheeks.

Is it my imagination, or did that sound like they're more than acquaintances?

Sean twisted his hands together to stop the trembling. "My girlfriend is out there, Conor's sister Feth. And my brother Oran."

"My cousin Kellen, too," Triona said, "and so many friends. All of the Province is out there today, everything and everyone we love and value."

A soft note was sounded on a trumpet.

"The call to get ready," she said, standing. "I'm happy we met, Sean."

"We'll meet again," he replied. "Fortune to us all."

He located the surgery tent he was assigned to and absently put a few last items in the right places. A bottle slipped from his shaking hands but did not break when it struck the rain-softened grass. He put it back and drew in a deep breath.

Suddenly, from a half-mile down the road came the blast of trumpets. Then silence. And then, after what seemed like an endless time, the cry of massed warpipes.

A surgeon standing next to Sean said, "It's started." Under his breath the man added a prayer, "let us offer thanks for the time we've been given on this Earth."

Dear Oran, I leave this sealed note in my tent for you should I not survive the battle, and you do. If you read this, I am gone. You know I'm not well-schooled so I can't say anything clever or poetic. I have not felt much love in my life, and have not seen or heard or experienced many things to laugh about. Mainly I have worked hard and tried to do right by my comrades and friends, and I have fought for my people. My body bears the scars of that, you have seen them. I just wanted to tell you that in the short time we had together, I was made to feel more alive than I ever have before.

Remember me — Melvina

Chapter 47

The great army of the Ghaoth Aduiadh, led by Belfasters and gathered from throughout the north and midlands of Eirelan, passed through a deserted and silent Mhisteala, and like an enormous snake, bent itself left onto the road leading to Clonmel. Though a light mist fell on them, these seven thousand fighters, armored in leather and chainmail and carrying every sort of weapon for cutting, stabbing or crushing flesh, were hardened to the elements and paid no mind to it. To a man they were spoiling for the fight. No drunkards here or oldsters or children: tough, lean, muscular men who meant to drive the army of the Twenty Clans into the mud and seize the precious tilled lands and seaports of the Province for their own. Their scouts watched the route ahead ... and paid no attention to the road they had already traveled.

On that road, a mile north of the town and the crossroads, Feth led her force ahead. For the tenth time, she mentally recited her own numbers: Auxiliary Knights, one hundred sixty-five; Auxiliary Crossbows, one hundred eighty-seven; Tralee Militia, mostly swordsmen but some armed with pikes and battle hammers, three hundred

fifty-four; the Macroom Guards, five hundred two, forty-three archers
and the rest well-armored infantry; and last but not least three hundred
Red Dragon archers riding armored Welsh battle horses. Total, fifteen
hundred and eight.

"Attack to your right, Feth," Conor had ordered, late the night
before. "I'll hammer on both flanks, try to get them to thin the center
for an assault by Padraic. Hold back no reserve, use every man and
woman, press the attack. Keep your Dragons on the move, strike hard
and fast, everywhere along the line, infuriate them, make them lose
their cohesion. Watch for an opening, you'll know it when you see it.
Do not attack until you hear four blasts on the trumpets."

*"Hit them," he said. "Hit them as hard as you can and never let up." I
hardly recognized my own brother. The poet was gone, the kind and gentle man
vanished. He pounded the table with his fist, a strange fury glowed in his eyes. And
I intend to do exactly as he ordered. I will strike the Ghaoth Aduaidh like Ionhar's
hammer.*

They had reached the outskirts of Mhisteala. Here the road widened and turned to firm, level gravel. Though the enemy army was
more than a mile ahead of them, she could now hear individual voices,
shouted commands, the scraping of swords sliding from metal sheaths.

"Helmets," she whispered, and buckled her own on. All along the
line, soldiers donned battle helmets, drew bows from holsters, took
final sips of water, and stood ready. A few vomited as quietly as they
could along the side of the road.

Feth nodded to Midir, who walked forward on foot into the town.
When he reached the intersection of the roads, he peered around the
corner of a building towards the east. He waited two minutes, then
waved them on. The tail of the great snake had passed around the
bend of the road, out of sight.

Feth started Ioan forward with Gwen on her left and Derdre to
her right. As agreed, the main body of the Red Dragons trotted to the
front of the column and fell in behind the three leading riders. Feth
herself commanded one century, Derdre another and Gwen the third.
Each of them unfolded a Red Dragon pennant and slid it into a saddle
holster. The Tralee Militia, Macroom Guards, Knights and Crossbows
raised high their own battle ensigns.

When the three lead horses reached the crossroads, Feth held up a minute to allow the column to compress from the rear, and then started Ioan forward again at a slow walk. Between her knees she felt him sucking in deep breaths as if storing up a reserve of oxygen. *He knows the battle is upon us!*

Through the town they maintained a narrow front, twelve soldiers wide. On the eastern edge of town, the treeline receded from the road and they were able to mass fighters on a hundred-soldier front. There, Feth picked up the pace, urging Ioan to a faster walk. One more bend in the road, two hundred yards ahead, and they would be seen. The light easterly breeze carried with it the sour smell of sweat and the musty odor of damp leather emanating from seven thousand bodies.

Feth halted the column, drew her bow from its holster and raised it overhead, the silent signal for all fighters to draw arms. Arrows were knocked to bowstrings, crossbows cocked and bolts laid into firing channels, javelins seized in sweaty hands, swords drawn from scabbards and circular shields raised up by gauntleted left hands.

Then, a strange silence descended on the battlefield. The smell was still in the air but the clatter and shouts of a high-spirited army readying itself for battle ceased. Feth looked a question to Gwen and Derdre, who shook helmeted heads. The silence maintained for two full minutes. Sweat poured down Feth's back; Ioan tossed his head impatiently from side to side.

"What's happening?" she whispered to herself. "Is—"

She jumped at the sound: a single long cry of the battle trumpets. Once again, silence, for two agonizing minutes. Then the howl of great warpipes shattered the silence, and seconds after that came a deafening thunderstorm of battle bursting over the land. Feth patted Ioan's mail-covered flank, then raised her hand overhead signaling that no one was to move or make a sound. Not that sound mattered much now: she could hear nothing but the horrifying din of clanging metal and human cries. The urge to ride ahead and see what was happening was almost overwhelming.

Listen for the trumpets, she told herself. *Four blasts. You must hear the trumpets.*

The Line of Blades, twenty-two hundred trained, conditioned, battle-hardened fighters protected in steel and leather and mail and armed with the short sword and javelin, bisected the meadow from south to north, their flanks protected by ballistae and archers. Each man stood at parade rest, rectangular shield in his left hand, throwing spear—one of two he carried—in his right, point touching the soft, grassy turf. The visors of red-crested helmets had not yet been lowered; that would happen at the call to battle announced on this field by Conor's voice and the orders of twenty-two century captains.

Twenty paces behind the double-line of infantry, eighteen centuries of archers in the Line of Bows were massed atop ten-foot-high shooting platforms. In lighter, more flexible armor and wearing blue-crested helmets, each archer held her longbow in her left hand and rested her right on the top of the belt-quiver loaded with the first thirty arrows she would loose into the enemy's ranks. Three special platforms in the center and on the left and right supported the long-range field ballistae, each crewed by four powerful women who could on command take up longbows slung on their backs. At full elevation, the ballistae could reach enemy positions five hundred yards away, and a bolt descending at that range would punch through the heaviest armor. To the rear of the platforms, wagons loaded with arrows and bolts could supply the maximum rate of fire for hours of steady fighting.

Between the two lines, at the head of his hand-picked reserve double-century of veterans, Padraic Conmaicne casually leaned an arm on the nearest shooting platform. For this battle, he had traded his gold helmet crest and cape for Blade-red, telling a dismayed Conor, "I want no question when the fight begins. You command the army today." Standing nervously on the right of Padraic's force, four teen boys clutched long-snouted trumpets beneath their cloaks to protect them from the mist. And next to them, Trev Fiachrach chatted calmly with twelve other boys and four girls who would sound the warpipes when battle commenced, and beat the drums for the advance.

Conor sat astride Treasach and swept his eyes over the field a last time. He could find nothing to change or correct. A thousand years of fighting for their survival in Eirelan left very little to chance or luck. The army was ready. Kellen rode along the line in front, talking with soldiers and captains; Melvina did the same for her line.

Across the broad meadow, a mile distant in plain view, an army very much larger than their own massed its forces. There would be few surprises: they had fought the Ghaoth Aduaidh five times in the past two decades. What the enemy lacked in standardized, finely-made body armor and long-range weapons, they more than made up for in numbers, ferocity, and determination to fight on even when the battle turned against them.

Oran, who was gathering reports from his scouts, now rode up on Seara.

"Feth is ready," he said. "Final estimate from counters I posted along their route of march is seven thousand, give or take. Morale seems to be very high."

Conor scanned the enemy lines with a pocket telescope. "Five horsed officers out in front now, one with fancy armor and a shiny brass helmet. My counterpart no doubt."

He collapsed the scope and downed water from a flask to dilute the acid burning in his gut.

"How are you?" Oran asked.

"Sick. Soaked with sweat. Stomach burning. Mouth sour."

Oran laughed softly. "Nothing unusual there."

"No." He twisted in the saddle and caught Padraic's eye. The giant fighter, who in his full armor dwarfed even his biggest comrades, nodded his reassurance.

Bradaigh, in uniform and armor for the first time in his life, rode up on a frisky young mare.

He reached across and handed Conor a sealed note.

"From Squadron Headquarters in Dungarvan," he reported. "Messenger's horse nearly fell dead getting it here."

Conor tore open the seal and read silently:

Dearest brother, I am sorry for many things I have said to you in the past, especially in the recent past. My heart and soul and spirit are with you. If our father watches from another place, may he guide your hand today. My love to you. Aideen.

Oran saw the tears filling his eyes. "Bad news?"

Conor barely heard him. "What? Bad news ... no. From my sister. An apology, and her love."

Conor folded the note and tucked it into a saddle pouch. Oran shook his head in astonishment and stared up at the oppressively dark sky.

"It should really fall down on us. The sky, I mean."

Conor wiped his eyes with the back of his hand. Through clearing vision he spotted the enemy general riding along the road straight towards the center of their line. The black-horsed rider reached a midpoint between the two armies. There, he reined in his horse, pulled off the gleaming helmet, and waited.

"What's he about?" asked Kellen, who had ridden up with Melvina.

"Wants to talk, I would guess," Oran answered. "I don't like it, Conor. These folks don't share our code of honor."

"He's alone and five hundred yards from his own line," Conor said. He strapped on his helmet and left the visor up. "Oran, with me. Kellen, open the line."

Kellen barked a command that opened a small slot in the center of the Line of Blades. Conor and Oran rode out across the meadow at an easy trot. Conor studied his adversary as they approached him. A hard, bearded face, early middle age, powerful body, missing his left ear. Close enough now to see his expression: calm, almost quizzical.

Conor halted Treasach a few paces away.

"I am Conor Laigain," Conor said with a polite nod. "My companion is Oran Osraige."

The man dipped his head in return. "Miach Ciannachta, Chief of the Ghaoth Aduaidh. Where's the big man? Not ill, I hope?"

The man's Gaelic carried the strong, harsh burr of Belfast.

"Not at all," Conor answered in a breezy tone. "Today he has a sword in his hand and is anxious to use it."

Miach cast his gaze around the broad, mist-covered meadow. "A fair day for a battle, is it not?"

"Fair enough," said Conor with a glance at the gray sky. "You have an offer to make?"

"I do. Bloodshed can be avoided if we are granted lands inside the Province, where the fields are yet green and the snows not so heavy as in the north."

Oran brought Seara up a stride. "How many settlers did you have in mind, altogether?"

"Twenty-five thousand," Miach answered him. "Maybe a few thousand more as time passes."

"All our lands are owned and in use," Conor said. "Even if we were inclined to welcome you after fifty years of needless bloodshed."

Miach smiled broadly now. "Surely room can be found? Perhaps the lands bordering the Rampart on the north. Much of those regions lie empty."

"You must know," Conor replied, "that we would allow that only if you dispersed all along the border. No large settlements. And you would be subject to our laws and government."

"We would govern ourselves," Miach said, good humor fading.

"This is a charade," said Oran. "You knew we would never accept."

"Possibly I did," Miach admitted. "I wanted to see who led you today."

"Now you have," said Conor. He scanned the front ranks of the enemy force from far left to far right. "Oran reported to me that you were coming with an overwhelming army."

"And so I have."

"You should have brought more," Conor snapped. "This won't be enough."

Before Miach could hurl an angry reply, Conor wheeled Treasach and pounded back towards the line with Oran by his side. They galloped through the gap, which quickly closed. Conor spun Treasach about in time to see Miach reach the front of his own lines.

"They'll be coming now," he said to Kellen and Melvina. "Ready the lines."

To the anxious-faced trumpeters he said simply, "call to battle."

In perfect unison the boys swept their trumpets out from beneath their cloaks and blew one long blast. Blades jammed one javelin into the turf and drew the second for their first throw. Five hundred of the strongest archers raised hundred-forty-pound-draw longbows to high elevation for maximum range. Ballistae crews cranked windlasses to full draw, locked the pin and loaded the firing channel with lightweight, long range bolts. Trev and his fellow musicians readied their warpipes.

"Maybe not a bad guy in a pub," said Oran lightly. "Miach, I mean."

Conor had to smile. "We'll invite him to one, if he lives."

The Ghaoth Aduaidh began a slow advance, led by the five horsed officers, their line wavering only slightly as they came on. Conor admired the training that represented.

They were almost in range. It was time.

He drew his sword and shouted, "Army of the Twenty Clans, you are called to battle. Sound the pipes."

At the same instant, Trev and his comrades unleashed the warpipes and Melvina's raised arm chopped downward. Long-range archers loosed a volley and another and another, three in ten seconds. They knew the exact range and there was little wind; the arrows soared up and poured down on the Ghaoth Aduaidh fighters like a cloudburst. Ballistae, elevated for maximum range, cut loose all along the line; bolts whistled through the air and plunged into the massed fighters. The relative quiet of the field of battle now filled with screams of agony and the barked commands of officers trying to maintain order in the face of the barrage. The mounted officers including Miach rode up and down the line, steadying their front ranks.

The charge picked up pace. They came at a trot now. Two officers' horses were struck by arrow fire, tossed their riders and galloped off the field. Miach himself at last dismounted, slapped his fine steed, drew his sword and joined the charge. At a hundred yards separation, the entire Line of Bows opened fire, eighteen centuries of hard-muscled and endlessly-trained archers firing an arrow every six seconds. Sprinting warriors stumbled over writhing, howling comrades. At fifty yards, heavy bolts from forty ballistae whistled in flat trajectories over the Line of Blades and plunged into the charging ranks, severing heads and punching through torsos. At Kellen's command, twenty-two hundred Blades launched javelins at the charging lines, drew swords, and braced for the impact.

Conor winced at the horrific crash as body met body, weapon struck shield, sword cleaved flesh, and hammer crushed skull. His right hand instinctively went to his father's sword; he longed to dismount and plunge into the line.

"We've held," Oran said. "But by the stars they have a huge army."

Conor nodded grimly. Seven thousand was probably too low an estimate now that he could see the full enemy force arrayed against his own. The Line of Blades had indeed withstood the tremendous assault, giving ground here and there, breaking nowhere. While the Blades went about their grisly work of stabbing and gutting, the Bows continued a steady barrage of arrows, precisely aimed so as not to hit their own fighters. The rate of fire subsided in favor of accuracy, yet still Ghaoth Aduaidh warriors fell by the score with each passing second. The ballistae fell silent: the forces were too closely packed. Their crews drew longbows and added to the withering arrow fire.

Five minutes passed. The sheer mass of the Ghaoth Aduaidh army pushing forward was hard to resist and the Line of Blades bent backward at the flanks. Kellen split his third line in the middle and used it to reinforce the flanks, while Melvina's archers concentrated fire in the center. The rain of arrows had the desired effect: the Ghaoth Aduiadh center began to thin out in favor of pressing ever harder on the Province's endangered flanks.

Conor signaled Padraic, who trotted up quickly despite his bulk.

"Ready your attack on the center, General."

Padraic motioned to his two hundred veterans, powerful men all, seasoned by a hundred battles, many his comrades and friends for decades. Padraic gathered them into a double rank of one hundred, posted himself in front, and led them to the center of the Blades' line behind the third rank.

Conor turned to Oran. "Here goes, my friend."

He twisted in the saddle and pointed to the trumpeters. "Four blasts," he shouted. "Now."

The boys lifted their brass instruments and blared out four times in perfect unison. Seconds later, they were answered by the mournful cry of the Celtic horns. Feth was attacking.

When the sound of battle rang in the air, the waiting became unbearable. She longed to ride a hundred yards ahead and gain a view of the battlefield. Yet she dared not. Conor would know the right moment. Four blasts of the trumpets, and she would unleash every-thing at once.

She glanced left and right, where Derdre and Gwen on their steeds waited at the head of their companies. Her one thousand infantry were massed on her right side: Tralee Militia furthest away, then the Knights and Crossbows, and nearest Feth, Macroom Fighters led by Aife Luachra. Swords were drawn, crossbows loaded, arrows nocked, javelins at the ready.

How long, she wondered? Close on five minutes now. The sound was deafening. Then, over the roar and clatter of battle, came the four trumpet calls. She pointed to her own signalers, who answered with a long blast of the Celtic horns.

Raising her bow high overhead, she looked right and left again, then tapped Ioan's flanks signaling a trot. A hundred yards to the bend in the road and the rise that hid the battlefield from their eyes. Fifty yards. Her force held together, horses trotting and foot soldiers falling back a few yards. Sweat poured down her forehead under the helmet: she shook her head to clear her eyes.

She rounded the bend and through her visor slit beheld the rear of the Ghaoth Aduiadh's vast army. So many! In an instant she saw that so far, Conor's script was being followed. The enemy was bending back the Blades on the flanks. According to plan, Melvina's archers had unleashed a concentrated barrage on the center.

Feth halted her column while the infantry caught up and then angled their front to the right. A shout arose from the enemy's rear ranks. They'd been seen!

"Attack!" she screamed.

Her infantry force pounded over soft turf towards the enemy's right. Javelins, bolts and arrows slammed into the rear ranks of the enemy, felling many fighters who never saw death approaching them. Feth waited until the lines collided and then urged Ioan to a gallop. Down the line she flew with the Red Dragons to assault the enemy's left flank and take the pressure off the Blades there. They plunged ahead and wheeled at fifty yards, loosed a continuous volley, rode in a wide circle and attacked again. And again. And yet again.

Ghaoth Aduaidh commanders quickly responded to the assault by turning the rear ranks to face the new threat. Seeing the comparatively small size of her force, they did what Feth hoped they would do: defend their rear lines and continue to press the main attack against Conor's front. Yet the fury of the auxiliary force's attack was enough to drain strength away from the right side, allowing Kellen's Blades to straighten their battered line. Feth led the Red Dragons in nonstop bombardment of the left, forcing the rear ranks of the enemy to face her with shields held high, unable to answer with sword or javelin. On this flank also, she saw the standards of the Blades advance, take back lost ground.

The Ghaoth Aduaidh's center ranks thinned further under the relentless bombardment of the Line of Bows shooting from platforms. That was where Conor planned to send Padraic's force at the right moment, in an attempt to split the enemy line and compress its flanks into immobility.

Feth drew her Red Dragons up three hundred yards from the enemy's line and waited for Gwen and Derdre to join her.

"We can break them!" Derdre shouted over the din.

Gwen stood high up in her stirrups. "I can see General Conmaicne's banners, he's in position. Wait ... he's coming on!"

At that instant, the arrow barrage on the enemy center ceased, meaning that Padraic was striking the line now. Victory or defeat hung on whether the center could be broken.

We can't shoot either, Feth told herself. *Every miss will hit our own fighters.*

She jammed her bow into the holster, drew her sword, and cinched across her thighs the Welsh saddle's special belt, designed to hold the rider in place for close combat.

"Ready charge!" she bellowed out with her sword held high. "Dragons, ready charge!"

The moment I dreaded, she told herself. *The moment I send my friends into the cauldron of death.*

She twisted right and left and through her visor slit saw three hundred swords lifted into the air. Ioan, his flaring nostrils drenched in the smell of blood, snorted and scraped at the ground.

"Charge!" she screamed.

Ioan bolted ahead and galloped over the field. Big, bloody, desperate fighters loomed in the eye slit of her helmet. Ioan smashed into two fighters and trampled them beneath spiked iron hooves. And then Feth was fighting for her life. Swords and hammers struck at her from all sides. A pike bounced off of Ioan's heavy mail. Derdre flashed in front of her and disappeared into the enemy's ranks. She slashed at heads, stabbed at chests, wheeled Ioan left and right, took heavy blows that nearly unhorsed her a dozen times. Blood spurted and spattered everywhere. Ioan stumbled and then regained his footing. Some remote part of her brain told her Padraic's banners were near. So very near.

A thrown hammer glanced off her helmet, stunning her. When her vision cleared, her eyes focused on a crimson Celtic cross emblazoned on a rectangular shield, gripped by a towering man in heavy armor whose mighty sword cleaved a man in two with a single swipe.

The break in the center was complete. Padraic's veterans instantly exploited the opening, attacking with renewed fury to the right, while Feth's auxiliaries poured into the gap and pressured the left. The gap widened to fifty feet, then a hundred, despite frantic efforts by enemy officers to restore their line. Feth's Red Dragons, much reduced in number, disengaged from the center and pounded the turf to harry the enemy rear again, trying to compress the divided force even further and open a field of fire for the ballistae.

Conor heard Padraic's voice saying in his head, *the most dangerous time in a battle is when you think you've won.* He turned to Melvina, waiting on her horse next to him. "Extend the lines."

"In the trees it will have to be hand-to-hand."

"I know. No option now."

She rode off in a spray of mud. Seconds later her own signal trumpets blared three quick bursts. Three companies of archers at each end of the shooting platforms dropped their bows, snatched up light shields, drew their swords, and sprinted down the ramps into the woods on both flanks. They arrived none too soon: the Ghaoth Aduaidh captains screamed out orders to extend their own lines and outflank the Blades, who could stretch no further. Conor watched long enough to see the Bow companies engage in vicious combat on both flanks, then turned his eyes away. Many an archer would perish in the woods today. Yet they would exact a heavy penalty for their losses and seal the fate of the enemy.

Kellen rode up. "Time to roll, Conor."

"I agree. Drummers, sound the advance."

Instantly the warpipes ceased their cry. Trev and his comrades threw down their instruments and grabbed hold of huge kettle drums. In unison they thundered, *BOOM-boom-BOOM-boom, LEFT-right-LEFT-right.* The Line of Blades picked up the cadence and began grinding ahead with renewed fury. Over the echoes of the drums, two long blasts sounded on the Line of Bows' treble trumpets, signaling the ballistae to open fire again, aiming for the compacted enemy ranks. Bolts shot out in flat trajectories into still-dangerous masses of uncowed enemy fighters.

Conor's eyes searched the field for Oran, who had ridden straight up the center and into the enemy rear to give a message to Feth. He breathed a sigh of relief: there was little Seara blazing back through the gap at astonishing speed.

Oran flipped up his visor. "Reached her," he said between gasps. "Three charges, she's lost a lot of Dragons but they're still hammering away. Her auxiliaries haven't given an inch. Feth's fighting a great battle, Conor."

"She knows what I need now?"

Before Oran could answer, the Celtic horns howled a single long cry.

"She knows."

Oran vanished through the gap in the lines.

Feth circled Ioan around the medic from the Tralee Militia. He was on his knees, frantically trying to stop the bleeding from a gaping pike wound in Derdre's chest.

"She's dying, isn't she?" Feth asked him.

He did not look up from his labors. "Not if I can help it."

I must fight on. That's all I can know for now. She sheathed her sword and raised her bow high overhead. "Dragons, ready attack!" To her four signalers she called out, "one long blast."

They raised their Celtic horns and blew until their young faces turned purple.

Feth kneed Ioan and they were off, a hundred and fifty now, to assail the enemy rear ceaselessly, while on the right, the valiant fighters from Cork and Kerry redoubled their attack at the sound of the horns. As they passed the center of the line and opened fire, Feth caught sight of two Blades leading the advance left. One was a tall man wielding a sword with blinding speed, the other, shorter and broader, swung an enormous spiked battle hammer. Keegan and Ionhar, side by side, hacking and bludgeoning their way ahead to the ceaseless beat of the drums.

In the end it was a slaughter that sickened Conor. The Ghaoth Aduiadh fought on to the last man. Not a single fighter fled or let go of his weapons, and so the killing had to go on and on. One of the last to fall was Miach Ciannachta himself, his gleaming brass helmet crushed like so much paper by Ionhar Raithlinn's descending hammer. Finally, Conor was able to silence the drums. The incessant whiz of arrows ceased, ballistae crews fell exhausted next to their machines, Blades and auxiliaries sank to the ground where they stood. Ambulances and medical wagons thundered past the shooting platforms and fanned out over the field of human wreckage. Doctors and assistants struggled to save those who could be saved, of either army, and give final comfort to those whose lives were fast slipping away.

At that very moment, as if Nature herself was appalled at the scene of carnage, a gentle snow of thick, puffy flakes drifted down over the blood-drenched field, coating the dead and dying with a shroud of white. Where they fell on bare earth, flakes turned crimson and melted.

Conor dismounted from Treasach and waited for his commanders to assemble. Oran rode up, looking white-faced and exhausted but unharmed. Melvina and Kellen had taken wounds at the very end of the battle, Melvina slashed in the leg and Kellen concussed with a huge lump on his forehead. Both dismounted without help. Minutes later, Padraic arrived at the front of his remaining veterans. His armor was completely coated with blood as if dipped in a vat; the great helm dangling from one hand was dented and its crest stripped off. The double-sized battle sword in his other hand dripped blood from its tip.

Last to arrive was Feth, leading her limping horse whose coat of mail was half torn away. Her helmet was gone entirely and blood streaked down both sides of her face. One leg guard was missing and the exposed leg oozed blood into her boot. Only Gwen walked beside her, leading her own mount.

"Where's Derdre?" Conor asked her.

"Alive," Feth said in a distracted way, "but not by much."

"Will she live?" Feth asked, her hand holding Derdre's.

Triona brushed red hair back from Derdre's ashen face. She was unconscious, her breathing rapid and shallow.

"I don't know, Feth," Triona said softly. "The pike penetrated far enough to do serious internal damage. It barely missed her heart and the aorta. We did all we could for her."

Sean wrapped his arm around Feth's waist and pulled her closer to him.

"She's a fighter," he said to her, "and I'll stay with her, Feth. You need to get some rest. Please."

"He's right," Triona said with a gentle smile. "We'll watch out for Derdre."

Gwen, at the foot of the bed, stroked Derdre's foot under the covers. Her face was streaked with tears.

"She took that spear for me," she said in a shaken voice. "She saw it coming and took it for me."

Feth let go of Derdre's hand and took hold of Gwen's.

"You would have done the same for her. We all fought for each other."

Gwen nodded but did not move away from the bed.

Sean led Feth out into the snowy night. A blanket of white covered the lantern-lit fields, a strange and jarring contrast to the moans of suffering that drifted from the hospital tents. Little rejoicing was heard in the camp of the victorious army; too many friends and kinfolk had fallen for that. Every man or woman left alive was filled with grief for lost comrades, brothers and sisters and cousins and friends gone forever.

Feth said nothing as they walked, their boots making a trail in the snow. Sean could think of only one thing since he had first seen her coming towards him, torn and bleeding but alive: he had not lost her. At the moment, nothing else much mattered to him. The long day of dread was over.

"It was the sword charges," Feth said. "I wish there had been some other way. So many ... well, it was too bad, that's all. Really too bad."

"You had no choice, Feth. You heard what Conor said. Many lives were spared because of what you and your troopers did."

"Maybe, but it's hard to think of it that way. I suppose ... oh, Sean, I'm just too tired to think anymore."

They reached her tent, which she had planned to share with Gwen and Derdre. Gwen had not returned so for the moment it was empty. Sean led her in, lit the candle lantern hanging in the center, and eased her down onto her cot.

"I should really check on my troopers again," she said, looking up at him. "The other fighters too. They all fought so hard for us. For me."

He sat down next to her. "No, not now. You've got to rest. I'll check on every one of your fighters personally if it takes all night."

"And Derdre."

"And Derdre."

He swung her bandaged legs up onto the cot, pulled off her boots, and dragged blankets over her. He leaned down and kissed her, though her eyes were already shut.

"I love you," he whispered.

"I love you," she whispered back, and then she slept.

He walked slowly back to his own tent and lit a lantern. Opening his journal, he wrote with a shaking hand:

On November 8, 999, the Army of the Twenty Clans and its allies triumphed at the Battle of Mhisteala. Seven thousand fighters serving the cause of the Ghaoth Aduaidh have been returned to the earth from which they came. The cost in blood for this victory is almost too much to contemplate. Nearly two thousand brave men and women of the Province and our allies will never again see the sun rise over Eirelan. Many more are wounded grievously. Let us hope that their sacrifice brings peace for our people and for those who fought with us, on this dreadful day.

Then, adding a cloak against the cold, snowy night, he went back out to the tents where lay the wounded of Macroom and Tralee and the other towns of Cork and Kerry. At midnight he entered the tent where Derdre lay, her condition unchanged. He took hold of her hot, moist hand, and through the long hours of night, amidst the moans and cries of the wounded, he wrote the rest of the battle's story in his mind.

As a matter of logic and reason, I can justify the terrible losses we have taken, for this threat might well have overwhelmed us in years to come. Outside of logic and reason, the reality of what has happened is not so easy to accept. I have lost crewmen before and I have seen shipmates die. This past week has been different, has affected me differently. Brigid and Eavan gone and Kacy's life ended before it began. I feel as though a dark shadow is following me, depressing my spirit, forcing on me a feeling of emptiness and futility. I don't know what awaits me ashore. Is Conor alive? Is he missing me? He does have a way of lifting me out of the darkness.

Personal Log, Mairin Fotharta

Chapter 48

"Course due north, sir, speed four knots, barometer steady."

Acting Lieutenant Kensa Velnowarth saluted as Mairin climbed onto the quarterdeck. Ensign Auteini, posted at the port rail, wore a calm expression as she saluted in turn.

"Very well, Lieutenant, carry on."

A quick scan of the deck satisfied her that the acting lieutenant had worked out well so far. The ship drove toward Eirelan flying courses and topsails, well-trimmed for beating upwind. Astern of *Caillech*, the *Wexford*, *Morrigan*, and *Rosc Catha* held station. A cold, light breeze from the northwest blew steady for the three days since the squadron left the protection of Santander Bay. It made for slow beating upwind yet was easy on the ships and their injured crew members. A thick deck of gray cloud hung perpetually overhead, darkening the days and turning the nights ink-black: not a single star or sliver of moon gave them company. Now and then, snow flurries drifted over the deck. The crew and officers packed away summer tunics and donned wool trousers and sweaters, warm sox, stocking caps, and waterproof jackets.

Mairin was thankful for the slow, quiet passage. Her crews suffered both from physical injuries and the aching loss of comrades left behind in the waters of Santander Bay. Given the easy roll of the sea, Mairin permitted all ships to light stoves below decks for warmth, and galley fires for hot food. Mor was satisfied with the progress of his patients, especially Rowenna Briuin whom he allowed a stroll about the ship every three hours.

Her own body no longer protested every move. Mor's herbal remedy relieved the back spasms. Though the deep wound on her thigh throbbed, Mor confirmed it was not infecting and would heal cleanly, albeit with a pronounced scar. *What's one more? At least this time my face was spared.*

She caught Kensa looking at her out of the corner of her eye. She remembered well what it felt like to serve as officer of the deck under the watchful eye of the captain.

"I'll go below, Lieutenant. I'd like a position report at the end of your watch."

"Of course, sir," Kensa said, saluting.

The extra twenty degrees of warmth in the main cabin was welcome. The two long mess tables were in use for writing letters and playing games. At the forward end of the starboard table, a card game was in progress; Mor was dealing a hand to Rowenna and two sailors of the port watch. Mairin strolled down and stood behind Meig MacDunnough, whose broken, encased left leg was stretched out beneath the table. Across from her, Bosun's Mate Steren Retallik played one-handed with the other arm in a sling.

Mor finished dealing five cards face down on the table. "You can be dealt in, Captain—before we look at our cards!"

"What're the stakes?" she asked, noting green chips in the ante pot.

"Green is one ale, red five," Rowenna explained. "Ashore, of course, sir."

She took a seat next to Meig. "Deal me in."

"We each started with ten of each," said Rowenna, the banker. She pushed two stacks in front of Mairin. "So far Steren is doing well, as you can see, sir." Indeed, the dark-haired, quiet young woman appeared to have doubled her stake.

"At my expense," noted Meig.

"And the game?" Mairin asked.

"The old Admiralty stand-by," said Mor, dealing her a hand. "Five card stud, nothing wild."

A half-hour later, Mairin wondered at her luck: she'd drawn away all of Steren's winnings and added more besides. She found herself unwinding, laughing at jokes, telling a couple of her own, paying close attention to the cards and the poker faces around the table. She knew Mor saw it, in the way he smiled at her approvingly now and then. Meig and Steren were naturally uneasy at first, but soon loosened up. Rowenna concentrated hard and played skillfully, without much luck of the draw.

Mor was fine company as always, though an indifferent poker player.

An hour into the game, a yawning Sithmaith emerged from her cabin. Seeing the game, she collected a mug of hot tea and took a seat next to Mor.

"Captain," she said, "you seem to be cleaning up."

"More luck than skill. Why don't you take my place, Lieutenant? You're not on duty for at least an hour. I have work to get to in my cabin."

"In fact, you can deal," Mor said, handing Sithmaith the deck. "Captain, a moment of your time?"

He followed her through the main cabin and into her own, which was distinctly colder. Mairin eased onto the soft cushions sent by Richard. Mor joined her an arm's length away.

"Leave the door open," Mairin said. "Let some of that heat in here."

"It's great to see you laugh again," he said, his eyes turned towards the gray, rolling sea. "Therapy for me too. I don't think I've laughed once since I lost Dunlaith."

"I worry about being seen that way," she replied, following his gaze. Two hundred yards astern, *Wexford*'s bow smoothly cleaved the modest waves. "In the Admiralty they would never think of it, a captain playing cards with sailors."

"No, I suppose they wouldn't," said Mor, turning to face her. "I see it this way, Captain. We have much in common with the Celts of Kernow. Yet many differences too. For example, we look on the roles of men and women differently, and also how authority is acquired and used. We believe in discipline as much as they do, we try to achieve it in a different way. So I'd say there's nothing wrong at all with a captain playing cards with the crew ... in our service. It humanizes you, and those sailors are hardly going to forget you're the captain simply because you enjoy a game with them."

"A windy analysis," Mairin commented. "Almost as if there's something else you have to say and are not anxious to say it."

Mor stared down at his hands. "I suppose that's true."

"Don't keep me waiting for bad news, Mor. What is it?"

He met her eyes. "When we get back to the Province, I plan to take a leave of absence."

"Oh."

"I've been at sea almost constantly now for five years and I'll never see forty again. My wife is dead and I hardly ever see my wonderful daughter. I have brothers and sisters, too, and nieces and nephews I rarely get to spend time with."

He got to his feet and paced in the small space of the cabin.

"During the battle, I found myself face to face with a man half again my size who swung his mace at my head. Helmet or no, my head was coming off if that mace connected. Well, I got my sword up in time, deflected it, and then an arrow from the tops split his skull." He paused, reflecting. "I've been in battle before, you know that. When I was young, I fought three years in the Line of Blades. Fighting doesn't scare me. The thing is, if he'd killed me, so much of my life is left unlived, and my daughter is left alone."

The cabin was silent for a time. The ship rolled easily in a regular motion, creaking as its timbers worked slightly.

"So," Mor said at last, "to be honest, I don't know that I'll come back at all. I'm a doctor and my skills are useful on land as well as at sea. Bringing babies into the world would be a nice change from sewing up wounds."

He sat down again near her. "I'm sorry, Mairin."

She turned to him and managed a wan smile. "Well, maybe I'll have one of those babies for you to birth, Mor."

"Nothing would please me more. And there are plenty of fine surgeons I can recommend, I wouldn't leave you to hunt on your own."

"Of course. I know that. It's just, well, it's a lonely existence out here and you've been someone I could talk to. You probably know more about me than anyone, even Conor."

Or Richard, she almost added.

"We'll still be friends, see each other ashore, write letters."

"Yes."

"And besides, I thought you were planning to marry Conor and have children? That would mean retiring soon, or at least changing your duty."

"That was the plan." She got up and retrieved the Celtic Knot from a drawer, laid it in Mor's hands.

"Conor gave this to me before we sailed from Wicklow. After taking a tongue-lashing from Aideen about how much I'm needed at sea."

"Needed, yes. We're all needed," he said, handing the amulet back to her. "No one is indispensable, Mairin, even you. And we've beaten the Santanders for good. This may be the best time for you to make a life with Conor."

Mairin returned the amulet to the drawer and stared out over the sea, where fog was gathering as evening came on.

"Before we left Wicklow weeks ago," she said in a low voice, "Aideen told me she's planning to rename the Squadron the Province Battle Fleet. We'll be getting as many as ten more ships, if we can crew that many. The Fleet will be divided into two squadrons, each commanded by a commodore. She offered me the eastern squadron based at Dungarvan. All secret information, Mor."

"No doubt," he said, shaking his head. "And you didn't say no."

"I didn't say yes either. I asked for some time to think about it. She wants five years."

Shouts and laughter echoed down the corridor. Someone in the card game had won a big hand.

"Her way of making sure you stay," Mor said. "Give you a promotion and make it sound like no one else can do it as well."

"Something like that."

"What would Conor say if you accepted?"

"I think ... he would take back the proposal and look elsewhere. And I couldn't blame him."

Mor got up and stood next to her. "Mairin, she can't *force* you to serve. This is a still a volunteer service. The problem is, with you it's not just duty and obligation, is it? There's a part of you that doesn't *want* to give up this life. Am I right?"

"You know the answer to that."

Mor touched her shoulder and turned her to face him. "I can only say this, Mairin. The Squadron may be the only life that's ever meant anything to you. That's the penalty of your childhood. But don't think it's the only life you can ever have. You're more than the uniform you wear, more than a fine officer and fighting captain. You *can* have another kind of life, if you want it enough."

Mairin smiled and brushed away a tear. "I have a hard time convincing myself of that."

"Take my word on it," he said with a smile. He stepped towards the open door. "I should take a look at my patients. How are you doing?"

"Well enough," she said. She stretched her back. "Your herbs work wonders."

When he was gone, Mairin spent an hour at her desk, writing reports and log entries. At the watch change she donned a jacket and wool cap, intending to go on deck. Yet she found herself sitting at the stern windows again, lost in thought.

Of course Mor is right, there's a part of me that's terrified of leaving the service. I've only been two people in my life, a frightened girl running through the snow to escape a house of horror, and a sailor, midshipman, ensign, lieutenant, and captain of the Province Squadron. There's no third piece, Mairin by herself, intact, loving and loved, secure and confident, stripped of her uniform and title and abilities. Conor imagines he sees one, so does Richard. Men often see what they're looking for, what they want, whether it truly exists or not. Yet Mor doesn't want me in that way; is his opinion truly objective? Is he right that I could make the change?

A half hour passed. A tap on the cabin door made her jump.

"Yes, enter."

A tall, slender young sailor entered. Mairin could not quickly bring her name to mind.

"Lieutenant Velnowarth's watch, sir, she requests that you come on deck."

"Tell her I'm on my way."

Sithmaith was already walking the quarterdeck, ready to take over the watch from Kensa. Only a light air rippled the sails. Thickening fog reduced *Wexford*, two hundred yards astern, to the shadowy outline of a ship.

"Where do you have us, Lieutenant?" Mairin asked Kensa.

"No sightings at all today, sir," she said, pulling a sheaf of paper from her pocket. "My calculations based on course and speed have us thirty miles due east of Wexford. I checked my figures with Lieutenant Briuin and she agrees, Captain."

"All the northing we need, sir," Sithmaith commented, "but once the sun sets we'll be totally blind."

Mairin pondered the options. She planned to reach port tonight but there was no reason to take chances.

"Very well, we'll heave to for the night. Three lanterns on all ships, stay within sight of at least one other ship. Signal *Wexford*, have her pass it along. Also ask *Wexford* if she could host a captains' dinner."

As Kensa gave the orders, Mairin drew Sithmaith aside at the starboard rail.

"I plan to go aboard *Wexford*, Jilleen can't leave her ship. You have command but keep Lieutenant Briuin informed. Officers may have a private dinner with wine, serve out some to the crew, two glasses each. Minimal watch on deck, just make sure no one drifts into us or us into them."

"I have it, sir," Sithmaith said. "Please give my best to Kylee. We roomed together in Admiralty training."

"I'll do that."

"*Wexford* replies they will host dinner, sir," Kensa reported. "At your convenience."

"Gig in the water," Mairin ordered, then went below to don a decent uniform jacket and regulation hat.

By the time Mairin climbed down into the gig, the three brilliant lanterns of *Wexford* could barely be made out through the fog. The surface of the sea was quiet, nothing more than a gentle swell to distinguish it from an inland lake. The splash of the oars and the coursing of water along the gig's hull seemed unnaturally loud. With the falling of night, the four ships created a small island of diffuse light in the blackness.

Kylee Dunlainge welcomed her to the quarterdeck. Mairin had last seen the soft-spoken, flaxen-haired young woman on a blazing hot day in Rosslare, two years ago. Kylee was sitting for the lieutenant's examination. Aideen chaired the panel of three captains and for reasons Mairin could not fathom, seemed to have it in for the candidate. Kylee's fair skin turned beet red and sweat poured down her face and onto the lapels of her dress jacket as Aideen did her best to rattle the desperate ensign. The third member of the panel, Grania Eogain, tried to deflect the worst of the grilling and baiting, as did Mairin. The deliberation after the exam erupted into a furious argument between Aideen and Grania, a fight that threatened to turn physical. Mairin assumed the distasteful role of peacemaker for Grania's sake as well as Kylee's. In the end, they had passed the ensign. Mairin recalled the incident now as one more reason she disliked the Commodore so intensely.

"Lieutenant, great to see you again," she said to Kylee, taking her outstretched hand. "I bear greetings from Sithmaith Laigain."

"Captain Fotharta, welcome to the *Wexford*. Please say hello to Sithmaith for me."

"I'll do that. Shall we go below?"

Kylee hesitated and lowered her voice. "If I could have private word, Captain?"

"Of course."

Kylee led Mairin to the taffrail.

"I never properly thanked you for helping me get my promotion. I know Commodore Laigain opposed me. I saw Captain Eogain soon afterward and thanked her, but somehow I never had a chance to see you alone after that."

"As a matter of fact," Mairin said in a quiet voice, "Commodore Laigain did not vote against you. None of us did."

"I heard that—"

"That there was a shouting match? Yes, that's true, but it was not over your passing or failing. Grania Eogain was outraged at how you were treated, and so was I. I played peacemaker because I was afraid the Commodore would void the exam and make you take it over. You were clearly qualified, Kylee. Then and now. I could not understand why the Commodore took such a dislike to you."

"Oh, I knew why, Captain."

Mairin leaned back against the taffrail. The fog soaked up sound and no one was standing nearby.

"Suppose you tell me."

The young woman fell silent for a moment, her eyes staring out into lantern-lit vapor.

"It was the worst moment of my life, Captain. I worked so hard ... well, it doesn't matter now. Anyway, what happened was that I got married about a month before the exam. I did everything that was required, filed the papers with Squadron HQ, made sure they got signed. Two days before the exam, Commodore Laigain caught me coming off my ship and waved a piece of paper in my face. She wanted to know why I was sitting for lieutenant when I obviously had other plans for my life. She said it right in front of other officers and sailors! I wanted to melt through the dock planks but I defended myself as best I could. I said the regulations said nothing about marriage being a bar to promotion. She shouted something like "don't quote regulations to me, you know what you're doing" and stormed off. I was serving under Tierney Ulaid then, she heard the whole incident from the quarterdeck and told me she'd lodge a formal complaint with the Council of Twenty itself. I begged her not to, so she didn't. Two days later, well, you were there."

"Yes, I was there." *And I let it go on, far too long.* "I'm sorry that happened, Kylee. The important thing is you got the promotion. And you did get married?"

"Oh, yes, sir, I did! Steafan and I have a small farm north of Waterford. He served in the Line of Blades till last year, when he lost an eye in battle. Doesn't keep him from farming, though. I'll see him soon, I hope. In the winter we'll have time together."

"I'm sure you will. If this damned fog lifts I'll have you in port by noon tomorrow."

Kylee leaned closer to her. "I'm glad I finally got the chance to thank you ... and for more than I realized. Now let's get after the stew, shall we?"

Kylee led her below. The wardroom's table was laid with a white linen cloth and set with gleaming silver and sparkling glassware. The lantern over the table was shaded to cast a soft glow over the room. The other two acting captains, Vivina Monaig of the *Morrigan* and Caitin Cumain of the *Rosc Catha*, were on their feet with wine glasses in their hands. Jilleen Conmaicne, looking pasty-white and thin but sipping wine and smiling nonetheless, lounged in a comfortable padded chair. Mairin knew Vivina, surely the tallest officer in the service, only slightly through Tierney Ulaid. Caitin Cumain, an impeccably-dressed officer with striking pale blue eyes, she did not recall at all. After an exchange of greetings, Mairin was handed a glass of wine and asked to make a toast.

"I want this to be a happy occasion," she began, "and so all the toasts after this one should be funny. I think we must drink once to fallen shipmates. To our friends no longer with us."

Glasses clinked together in a moment of silent remembrance. Then they took seats and waited expectantly while the cook, a middle-aged woman with a gap-toothed grin and infectious laugh, ladled out steaming lamb stew followed by a great basket of blazing-hot biscuits.

"Fresh Spanish vegetables," Kylee said between heaping spoonfuls. "I took the liberty of sending a party ashore to see what they could come up with." She raised her glass. "Good wine, too, don't you think?"

Jilleen lifted her glass. "To the damned Spaniards, may they continue to tend grapes and stay off the high seas."

"Hear her!" came the chorus.

At the end of two hours, Mairin felt the creeping drowsiness induced by three bowls of stew, a half-dozen fresh biscuits, two slices of frosted almond cake, and numerous glasses of wine. She was happy to see a hint of rose creep back into Jilleen's face.

"Wonderful meal," she said to Kylee. "My thanks to your cook and the crew. As the old woman of this group, I have to call it a night. If you wouldn't mind, I'd like a few minutes with Captain Conmaicne."

The other three officers bade her goodnight and exited to the quarterdeck, leaving Mairin alone with Jilleen. Mairin poured the dregs of the last bottle of wine into Jilleen's glass.

"How are you?"

"Physically, getting stronger," Jilleen said after a sip of the wine. "Considering I was nearly dead when the battle was over. Spiritually, I feel like someone peeled off my skin and left the flesh exposed. I never imagined I would see so many marks on my roster, 'killed in the line of duty.' Never."

Mairin emptied her own glass and fleetingly wished she had yet another bottle for them to share.

"Our only consolation is that their sacrifice meant something. You saw that shipyard? They would have been back next year and crippled us from Eirelan to Bretan."

"I saw the shipyard," Jilleen said. Her mind seemed to drift away for a moment. "And you're right, it was necessary."

Jilleen absently touched her fingers to the bandage covering the left half of her face.

"How did it happen?" Mairin asked her.

"Unbelievably bad luck. With so many crew down, I took the wheel myself. Blood was running into my eyes so I pulled my helmet off to clear my vision. At that exact moment one of the Santanders threw a knife that bounced off the binnacle cover and sliced my face open. Can you believe that?"

"Your eye ...?"

"No, not my eye, thank the stars." Jilleen paused, struggling for composure. "I guess being vain about your looks isn't officer-like. Truth is, I'm only twenty-three and Innis likes the way I look. I don't want to end up hideous."

Mairin set her glass on the table and laid a hand on Jilleen's forearm.

"Innis will still want you, if anything more than before."

"I guess."

Mairin lifted her sweater, exposing a long scar on her belly, evidence of a pike that slid under her cuirass. "You could play chess on my body beneath these clothes. You've met Conor? Well, he makes a little game out of it. And I do the same with him."

Jilleen stared at her. "You're putting me on."

"I am not. You want details?"

Jilleen burst out laughing and Mairin joined her.

"You're a good friend, Mairin."

Mairin squeezed her hand and then got to her feet. "I have to run before I fall asleep. Kylee is doing well?"

"First-rate. She should be considered for as a posting soon."

"I agree." Mairin set her hat on and donned her jacket. "See you ashore."

"Ashore it is, and the drinks are on me."

Vivina and Caitin had already departed when Mairin reached the fog-bound quarterdeck. Kylee stood near the wheel; an ensign leaned against the taffrail with hands clasped behind her back, staring out into the fog. Mairin's gig crew waited at the port rail.

"We fed your crew well, Captain," Kylee said. "Did we not?"

"Yes, sir," replied one of the two young sailors.

"Thank you, sir," said the other.

"Thanks for a wonderful dinner," said Mairin, taking Kylee's hand. "I'll see you ashore. Pray that the fog lifts!"

"I will, sir."

The gig eased away from the *Wexford* towards the barely-visible lights of the *Caillech*. About halfway across, Mairin noticed one of the sailors cocking her head to one side.

"What is it, Matty?" Mairin asked.

"I thought I heard voices, sir. Not ours."

"Up oars."

The gig glided to a silent halt on the calm sea.

Matty was right, there were voices, and they could not be coming from the Squadron ships. *Too loud,* Mairin told herself, *and there is something else. Not Gaelic of any dialect.*

"Row," she whispered, "quietly as you can. Make sure we don't bump the side."

The two sailors eased their oars back into the water and gently pulled the gig the remaining distance to the *Caillech*, where they fended off the ship's hull.

"Leave the gig in the water for now," Mairin whispered.

She climbed the ladder and was met by Sithmaith.

"You hear what we did?" she said in Sithmaith's ear.

"Yes, sir. I've ordered total silence on the ship."

"Signal *Wexford*, all lanterns out, silence, unknown ship nearby, pass on the signal."

Ensign Auteini climbed to the mizzen lantern, shuttered it in the proper sequence, then put it out. Other sailors had extinguished lanterns on the main and foremasts. Only the dim binnacle lamp now glowed on the quarterdeck.

When Auteini returned, Mairin took hold of her arm.

"Ensign, go below, get a writing pad and pencil, come up and stand near the binnacle. Write down everything you hear, phonetic spelling. Go."

"Look," Sithmaith whispered.

With *Wexford*'s lanterns now out, a faint glow penetrated the fog astern to starboard.

"Towing, I think," Mairin whispered to Sithmaith. "That regular clank has to be oars. They have boats out, two, maybe three."

Sithmaith nodded but made no answer. Auteini held her pad in the binnacle's glow and scribbled phonetic renderings of commands and responses drifting over the water.

"Masts, sir. Three I think." Sithmaith pointed to the brightest glow in the fog.

Seconds later the tops of three masts could be clearly seen, lit by lanterns not unlike those carried by the *Caillech*. The remainder of the mystery ship was no more than an indistinct outline in the glow, sliding slowly past.

Mairin lifted the speaking trumpet off its hook near the wheel and aimed it at the ghostly lanterns.

"What ship are you?" she called out.

The voices and rowing sounds stopped. Then the lanterns went out, one by one.

"Unfriendly," Sithmaith said sotto voce.

Mairin raised the trumpet again.

"We are the Province Squadron ship *Caillech*. I repeat, what ship are you?"

No answer. The rapid clank of oarlocks resumed.

"Launch a boat, sir?" Sithmaith suggested.

Mairin had been weighing that option.

"I'd love to get a good look but it could turn into a fight. We have no idea how many boats they have or how they're armed."

She tapped her palm on the rail in frustration.

"No, we'll maintain a silent watch. At first light I want someone in the main crosstrees, we might be able to sight them when the fog clears."

She turned to Ensign Auteini.

"Ensign, go below and copy out your notes fair, leave them in my cabin."

"Lanterns, sir?" asked Sithmaith.

"No, let's stay dark for the night. There could be more than one ship out there. I'm going below, the deck is yours, Lieutenant."

"Aye, sir."

In her cabin, Mairin doffed her hat and jacket and waited for Edwina's notes before closing the door. The ensign delivered them ten minutes later, carefully copied onto a sheet of log paper.

"Best I could do sir, the words were totally strange to me," she said, handing Mairin the sheet.

Mairin glanced at it quickly.

"Good enough, Ensign. It was very hard to make anything out. Thank you."

"Sir," she said, saluted, and closed the door.

Mairin tried to concentrate on the words, but exhaustion and the effects of the meal and the wine weighed down her eyelids. She set the paper aside, undressed and laid in her bunk, her mind full of questions about what they had seen and heard. Even so, sleep came quickly.

The wedding chapel was filled with friends and relatives, naval officers and common sailors. A scowling Aideen Laigain sat with arms crossed over her chest in the front row. It was spring: a fair and fragrant breeze wafted through open windows. A piper played a sweet melody. At the front, facing the congregation, an Elder in tan robes waited to conduct the ceremony.

She entered the chapel from the rear. Not in a dress uniform, rather in a long, deep-blue gown with an embroidered veil covering her head and face. The piper should have kept playing, yet he stopped when she entered. She had to walk to the front of the chapel in total silence. The Elder smiled, then looked questioningly left and right. Conor approached from one side and Richard from the other. Each extended his right hand.

Horror and embarrassment washed over her. How could this happen? Which one was she marrying? She opened her mouth to scream and only a whisper came out. Conor turned his back and ran away, and then Richard did too. From somewhere high in the chapel's loft, she heard Etain laughing. She had to escape! She ran down the aisle. The gown tripped her and she fell hard, to the laughter of the assembled company ...

She awoke to the sound of a cabin door opening and closing in the hall, probably Rowenna's. The dream swirled in her mind. The bedclothes beneath her were soaked. *Oh, please, I hope I didn't cry out this time.*

She lifted herself on her elbows: the fog glowed a soft gray with pre-dawn light. Her chronometer read five-thirty-three.

A light tap sounded on the door.

"Enter," she croaked. Her throat was parched dry and her head ached. *Yes, the wine.*

Rowenna slipped in and closed the door behind her.

"Good morning, Captain," she said quietly. She eased herself gingerly into a chair, holding her back straight. "Gets stiff when I don't move around."

Mairin took a chair opposite her, found a brush and struggled to straighten out tangled, damp hair.

"How did you sleep?" Mairin asked her.

"Pretty well, considering," said Rowenna. "Mor says about two weeks for me to be fully mobile again, no problems after that."

Mairin set the brush down. "Rowenna, did I wake you?"

Rowenna seemed confused for a moment. "I beg pardon? Oh. No sir, not at all. Honestly, I heard nothing. You had a dream?"

"Yes." She cursed under her breath. "Different. Strange. Not exactly a nightmare. Not pleasant though."

"Sorry, Captain. I took the liberty of asking for hot tea and rolls."

"Bless you. The wine is not helping my head at all." She glanced out the stern windows. "Still fogged in, I see. Strange, last night, that ship passing us in the dark."

"May I see Edwina's notes, sir?"

"On the desk."

Rowenna reached over and took the sheet. She read the phonetics aloud.

"Hardly a word that even seems familiar."

Mairin nodded. "I agree. We'll turn that in at HQ as soon as we get in. On another subject, I have some bad news."

"Sir?"

"Mor is leaving the ship. He wants some time for himself, time to spend with Derdre and his kin."

Rowenna stared at her, shocked and then troubled. "Oh, that is hard news, Captain. I don't know him like you do, sure, but he's been really good to me. To everyone. He's like a father to the youngsters. Will he come back?"

"I don't honestly know," said Mairin, turning the brush over in her hands. "I would guess not."

The tea and rolls arrived and they spoke of more mundane matters, the needs of the ship, replacements for the crew, promotions, plans ashore. Slowly the residue of the dream faded from Mairin's mind and the wine-induced headache subsided. A pleasant hour passed while the watch changed and the fog glowed more brightly. Kensa Velnowarth reported from the deck that a breeze was coming up from the north, the fog was lifting, and lookouts saw no sign of the mystery ship. Mairin dressed and climbed to the quarterdeck.

A cold, dry northerly breeze scattered the fog into great puffs of white drifting south, and overhead, a pale blue sky promised fair weather. The other three ships of the squadron stood to in line, sails backed to hold position. Kensa saluted; the port watch waited at sailing stations.

"Signal to all ships," Mairin ordered, "Make sail for Wexford." She paused, then added, "Black ensign to the mast."

Yes, she added inwardly, *the black ensign. Ninety-two we have left behind.*

It is strange what strikes fear into a man's heart, and what does not. I fought in the line at Mhisteala, maybe the last time I will ever do so, knowing age has slowed my sword and my step—whatever I may have said to Liadan. Yet I knew no fear there. Tomorrow morning, I will to ride to the house of Etain and Gorman Fotharta, to bring an end to the strife now threatening my nephew's happiness with a woman who was so terribly wronged by these two. Bram may be there too, he survived Mhisteala and I am told he fought hard and bravely. Is it the uncertainty I fear most? I have no battle plan for this mission, only that it must be undertaken, and the result must be obtained.
Journal of Padraic Conmaicne

Chapter 49

Padraic paused his horse at a hand-lettered sign reading "K. Fotharta" nailed to a tree. A path led off into the woods, to Kellen's place. No doubt he was there now. The great battle was three weeks in the past and with the Rampart now well-manned and secure for the winter, he had released his senior commanders for a week's absence.

He was sorely tempted to turn his sixteen-hand stallion Alastar down that path and see for himself the artwork Conor described to him. Maybe later, he could do that. Now, he had to click his tongue and send Alastar cantering ahead to the place where the road divided. A sign at the fork reading "Bhaile Mhurain" pointed left; the other branch of the fork was not marked but he knew well where it led. The lands lying in that direction had been held by Fotharta Clan since the founding of the Province. He turned right and held Alastar to a trot as he passed down the overgrown lane. In his youth, all of the many houses and cottages and farms had been occupied and this road was a cheerful route. Over the decades the dark force of Etain and Gorman drove away most of their kin and left the ancestral lands barren.

He passed many vacant cottages, their lightless windows staring at him like the eyes of the dead.

In his mind's eye he saw the great meadow open up before him, a half mile before he reached that point. The gray, cold day suited his mood, yet now as if to spite him, the clouds parted and brilliant sunshine lanced downward. When he reached the meadow surrounding Fotharta House, the great, ill-maintained manor was bathed in brilliant autumn sunlight from one side to the other and assumed a sort of tired magnificence. He urged Alastar to a gallop over the flat, brown grass, and the stallion responded, stretching long, powerful legs and carrying his ponderous rider with contemptuous ease. As he neared the house, Padraic reined in Alastar to a walk, circled the house completely, then halted in front and dismounted.

No one emerged to greet him though he knew Etain expected him. He tapped Alastar's hind quarter, telling him he was free to graze close by. Then he ascended the stone stairs worn concave by more than a millennium of use. As he reached the top step, one of the two double-doors swung open and Zephan Fotharta stepped onto the veranda. Padraic kept his distance, knowing that short-statured Zephan would find his size threatening. So far as he could recall, he had never crossed the man; nonetheless Zephan's greeting was distinctly cold and formal.

"General Conmaicne," he said with a slight nod of his head. "Welcome to Fotharta House."

Padraic nodded in return. "Only Padraic today, Zephan. I left the uniform in Rosslare."

Now he did step forward, offering his hand. Zephan took it, but only for a second.

"Please come in. Etain is expecting you."

He led Padraic inside and closed the creaking door. The house was nearly as cold indoors as out. The prevailing odor was musty and stale. Zephan started off down a long center hallway that led to a massive, winding staircase.

"Forgive the temperature," said Zephan without turning. "The house is far too large to heat in winter. We only use rooms on the second floor."

Padraic made no reply; his eyes scanned the walls and empty rooms as they passed. He could recall being inside twice, before he met Etain.

In those days, Gorman was a fellow Blade and he invited Padraic and Domnall to holiday dinners given by his parents Keondric and Areinh. The house was still alive in those days, with light and warmth and people.

At the top of the staircase, Zephan turned right and started down another hall. Here it was distinctly warmer, cleaner and brighter, though the silence was oppressive. Zephan opened a door on the left and Padraic followed him into a sitting room whose two enormous windows faced out on the great meadow. Sunlight poured into the room, which was elegantly furnished and had none of the dank odor of the first floor. A fire crackled in a hearth.

Etain awaited him in a simple, straight-backed chair placed in front of the rightmost window; her gray-streaked auburn tresses hung over the chairback. She wore a long dress of fine, shimmering burgundy velvet, cinched at the waist and flowing below, a silver band in her hair, and no jewelry on her hands. Zephan backed out and closed the door, and only then did Etain turn her head towards the door. Though he had steeled himself for this moment, Padraic felt a shudder pass through his body.

Her beauty was still a force of nature, and in this warm light and in that stunning dress it was overwhelming. So different from the Etain he encountered every time he appeared before the Council of Twenty! Those encounters took place in a crowded room; she wore dark traveling clothes and tied back her hair; and often as not she was arguing vociferously with him or someone else. The woman he now beheld was more beautiful than the fiery politician yet also reduced in some way that almost disappointed him. Her face was serene, almost sleepy, and the years melted away. His eyes perceived the lines and creases yet they seemed if anything to outline rather than diminish her extraordinary dark eyes, slender, straight nose and wide, upturned mouth.

"Padraic," she said softly and with a smile, "please sit." She motioned to a bulky oak chair a few feet from her. "There's wine on the table, if you'd be so good as to pour."

He knew what she was doing, of course, and he knew she knew he knew. It was ever a game with her, the assertion of power over a man with her mere presence. He poured two glasses of wine, handed her one, and settled into the chair. Out of the corner of his eye, her could see Alastar wandering about the meadow, munching here and there. Etain sipped her wine and regarded him over the rim of the crystal glass.

"I saw you coming," she observed, "on that fine black stallion. You've had him a long time, have you not?"

"I have," he said, willing to play his role for the time being. "Alastar is over twenty now, I expect I'll set him out to pasture him soon. Probably set myself out to pasture too."

She nodded and smiled more broadly, showing perfect teeth that seemed too numerous for one mouth. "None of us is getting younger. Yet I'm told you fought at Mhisteala."

"I did. Possibly the last time, if I'm honest about it."

"You were always honest, Padraic," she said, eyes boring into him. "Your son Kellen deserves a great deal of credit for the victory."

"I don't see Kellen except by accident on the road. And Bram?"

"He acquitted himself well on the right flank. Is he here?"

Her eyes drifted back to the window. "He's here, though *where* he is at the moment I can't say for sure."

"Etain, I—"

"Yes, yes," she cut him off with a sharp wave of her hand. "I know you didn't come here to make idle chat with me. I was just trying to be polite, Padraic."

She turned those huge eyes on him, let the corners of her mouth sag and assumed a look somewhere between a pout and genuine hurt. *No woman should have this kind of power and cleverness*, he muttered inwardly. *I excuse my young self for every sin I committed with her.*

"It's a good wine," he countered genially while filling his own glass again. "More for you?"

"No, thank you. My doctor forbids even this much, he says it fights the medicine he's giving me."

"Are you ill?"

She smiled again. "Dying, actually."

He sat up straight in the chair. "That's going too far, Etain. I'm used to your little word games but that is not funny."

"Perhaps not funny, yet true nonetheless. Oh, I'm not going to drop dead at your feet. The doctor in Bhaile Mhurain gives me two or three months, at most. A growth that can't be stopped or taken out, he says."

Padraic set his glass on the table and leaned forward.

"I am sorry, Etain." He fought the impulse to reach out for her. "Are you in pain?"

In answer, she rose from the chair with a grimace. Her face turned sheet-white for a moment and she was forced to hold onto the back of the chair.

"As you can see," she said in a raspy voice of barely disguised agony, "even I am not so good an actress as that." She took a few steps towards the hearth and stood in front of it, facing Padraic. "I'll stand here a bit, I get cold easily."

"Does Gorman know?"

"He does. I didn't want him here as I was dying, he'd be drunk all the time anyway. So he took ship three days ago for Wales where he has old friends. I doubt he'll ever return to Eirelan. Zephan will care for me and then the house will be his to do with as he chooses, a small reward for his loyalty. I forced Gorman to sign over his rights to me before he left the country."

"And after Zephan?"

"Would come Bram, whom I will bar in my own will. I expect Zephan will hand the estate over to Kellen, which is for the best. There's no bad blood between them, so far as I know."

"You left out your daughter."

"Mairin would never come here."

"It's partly of because of her that I came to see you."

"I guessed that. Conor expects to marry her, does he not?"

Padraic felt uneasy sitting while she stood, so he got up himself and moved the chair she'd been using next to the hearth. As she slowly lowered herself onto it, he turned his own chair to face her. Now she was in shadow, and the gray tinge of her color more obvious. *She's telling me the truth, then. I should feel some kind of relief, yet all I feel is an aching sadness for her.*

"Conor would like to marry your daughter, yes. The problem I came to see you about is Bram, who taunted Conor about what may have happened to Mairin in this house. I'm not asking for the truth about that. What I'm asking is that Bram be silent about it, now and forever. With Gorman gone and you ... ill ... what happened here will never be spoken of again. If Mairin chooses to tell Conor, that's her own decision."

Etain was silent a long time when he finished. Her eyes seemed fixed on the curtains yet focused into another time and place entirely. At last she did look at him again.

"We're now talking of your son, Padraic, you know that."

"Yes, I know that. You should have told me the truth when I still had a chance to be a father to him." He held up a hand to silence her response. "No matter, that was over thirty years ago and can't be undone now. Bram resents my treating Conor like a son, and he seems determined to ruin any chance his innocent sister has to be happy. I can handle his hatred of me, but he needs to leave Conor and Mairin alone and be silent about whatever he knows, or thinks he knows."

"What did he say to Conor?"

"He implied that Gorman ... that Gorman might have done more than beat Mairin. That he, well, that he raped her."

Etain stared at him with shocked eyes. Her head fell into her hand and he saw tears drip past her fingers.

"Not true," she whispered. "Gorman never did that, I'm sure of it."

"Then why did Bram say it? Just to be cruel?"

"Mairin *was* taken against her will in this house. Not by Gorman."

"Who then?"

"Bram did it. Yes, Padraic, your blood son."

He was stunned into speechlessness. Etain wiped tears from her cheeks and stared at the floor.

"You'll ask me how I know, and I'll tell you. When Bram was sixteen and Mairin was twelve, I came home unexpectedly one night,. Gorman had passed out downstairs and I left him there. We had a housekeeper then, a Scottish woman named Beathag, who met me at the top of the stairs. She heard strange sounds coming from the third floor which we didn't use except for guests. When she went up to investigate, she caught Bram coming out of a guest room, his clothes half dragging behind him. In the room she found Mairin on the bed, bruised, unable to speak. I need give no more details about her condition."

Padraic heard a snapping of wood and realized his right hand had twisted off the stout oak arm of the chair.

"What did Bram say when you questioned him?"

"The bastard grinned and said nothing. I saw in his eyes that he'd done it."

"How many times?"

"He insisted that was the only time. Since I never saw Mairin act like that before or after, I have to believe he was telling the truth."

In desperation Padraic poured himself another glass of wine and slugged it down.

"And Gorman? What did he do about it?"

Etain turned her head away from him to gaze into the fire. More tears poured down her cheeks.

"I never told him," she said. "He would've killed Bram instantly. Whatever else you may think of Gorman, he had that much honor left in him."

"And *didn't* Bram deserve to die for it?"

"He did. But he was your son, Padraic, and I ruined him. He was what I made him, with Gorman's help. I couldn't watch him be killed in front of my eyes. I loved you the night Bram was conceived."

"As far as you're capable of love, that might be true."

Now she did look up and fix him with the full power of luminous dark eyes shining with tears.

"I *did* love you. The great mistake of my wretched life was letting you get away from me. I should have stayed with you, I know that. I was drunk on my own power over men and when you left me for someone else—"

"I never left you! You took another lover and I wanted no part of a share and share alike arrangement. I told you that the night you came to me, claiming you carried my child. Don't change the past to excuse yourself now."

"Yes, all right," she said, eyes flashing anger. "I was wrong. I made a mistake that cost me a decent life, and after that I kept making more mistakes. Some days I hated Bram and some days I loved him. I think he sensed the hate more and it led him to attach himself to Gorman. But he is your son still! If anyone is to kill him for what he did, it has to be you."

Padraic got to his feet and stood at the window. "And so you did *nothing?*"

"No, I did something. I went to Bram the next day. He was already tall and strong, he could have killed me with a swipe of his hand. I told him three things. First, I would spare his life by not telling Gorman. Second, he had to leave the house immediately for military training and return only on leave. And third, I would slit his throat while he slept if he ever touched Mairin again. He knew me well enough to know I'd do it."

"And Mairin? What did you say to her?"

"For a couple of days Mairin did not speak and did nothing beyond eating and sleeping. When she finally began to speak again, I tried to question her about it, and she seemed to have no idea what I was talking about. None. Mairin is no actress, like me. In a roundabout way I asked Kellen, who was eight at the time, if he knew anything. He said no, and I believed him."

"And Mairin never said another word about it?"

"No."

Padraic turned to face her. "Etain," was all he could think to say.

Etain buried her face in her hands.

"Nothing you can say would make me feel worse."

She began to sob, and despite his rage at the destruction she had caused, he could not bring himself to hate her. He poured her a glass of water from a flask on the table and brought it to her. The slender hand that accepted the glass shook as if she had palsy.

He touched her shoulder. "I didn't come here to make you feel sad. I came here for your help to deal with Bram. Something I can do that doesn't mean killing him."

"I hoped in dark moments that he'd die honorably in combat, but he's like you now, there are few men on this earth who can bring him down. Surely no greasy-haired barbarians from Belfast."

Padraic waited while she struggled to regain her composure. He felt completely unmanned by her obvious illness and by her brutal honesty with him. And despite himself, he felt compassion for her.

"It's not right that you die here in this lonely old house, with no one but Zephan and Bram for company."

She sighed. "And where would I go?"

"You have friends. Other relatives."

"Political allies. Cousins who despise me."

"Does Kellen know you're dying?"

"No, nor would he care."

Padraic hefted a log into the diminishing flames. "You mistake him. He may have no love for you, yet he's an honorable man and I think he'd care for you."

"Respect my wish in this," Etain said, meeting his eyes. "Please say nothing to him. Or to Mairin."

"And Rionach? I am to keep this from her also?"

"Yes, especially her."

"She would be here in an instant, you know that."

"Of course I know it," Etain snapped. "And I'd spend my last days on this Earth trying to apologize for a lifetime of disappointment and heartache I caused her."

"If you change your mind," Padraic persisted, "I'll take a message for you."

"If that satisfies you, fine."

Padraic sank back into the damaged chair.

"And now what am I to do? Tell Conor? He'd try kill Bram, then, and I can't let that happen. Conor is too precious to me, to all of us, and despite himself he'll have to lead the army after me. If Mairin truly doesn't remember, the past is best left buried. The one important thing is that Bram remains silent. Help me, Etain. Please. I don't want to kill him."

Etain sat quietly for a full minute, the rising flames reflected from her eyes.

"There may be one way," she said at last, "that does not mean his death."

"I'm listening."

"He has friends in Bretan." She paused long enough to wipe her face with a white handkerchief and sit up straighter, though the movement caused obvious pain. "I think if the right offer were made, he might accept being transferred to their Fighters. You and I both know he'd fit in with that bunch better than he does here."

Padraic pondered her words. The transfer itself could be easily arranged: Bretan's Chief of Fighters had been his friend for many years. With the force needed to hold Santander the Bretans were overstretched. Tephaine Seznec would be pleased to get his hands on a powerful, trained Blade.

"It could be done," he said to her, "if he gave me his word on the other subject. What would that word be worth?"

"I don't honestly know," she said, her eyes searching the flames for an answer that was not there. "It's the best chance you have. All the other options are more dangerous."

Quiet descended as Padraic tried to digest the stunning information she had given him. Etain lost herself in thoughts that revealed themselves only in a slight narrowing of her eyes, a trembling movement of her lips. The moving sun slanted into the room and a beam caught Etain's hair.

Oh that my heart could hate this woman, he lamented, *but sitting here brings back memories I wished never to think on again. What could have been, Etain, if you had been faithful to me.*

"I'll do as you suggest," he said at last. "Where will I find him?"

"Since he's not here," she said with a heavy sigh, "I expect he's in a pub in Bhaile Mhurain boasting over his part in the battle."

Padraic rose from the chair and stepped over to help her up. She waved him off.

"No, I can still get up on my own."

He cringed at the pain she must be experiencing already -and two months before the release of death? She straightened fully, pulled the long dress smooth and set her hair back over her shoulders. With a supreme effort she restored the full beauty of her face and serenity of her bearing.

"I will not see you again," she said. "I ... I ..."

Her control failed utterly and her body shook with sobs. He wrapped his heavy arms around her and felt the loss of flesh concealed by the folds of rich fabric. For a long time he held her as she cried. At last, he lowered her gently into the chair, kissed her fevered, damp forehead, and left the room. He was glad for not seeing Zephan again as he raced to escape the house; he did not want to be seen with tears streaming down his face.

Bhaile Mhurain at first glance appeared to be a copy of many other villages scattered over the Province of the Twenty Clans: a cluster of buildings and cottages set at a crossroads; a cemetery at the edge of the village with markers dating back fifteen centuries and more; a tiny village hall that also housed a library; shops that supplied townfolk and nearby farmers with necessities brought down from Wexford; a stable and blacksmith; and a single well-made stone house occupied by the owner of the town's small armory.

Next to that fine house stood the pub that made Bhaile Mhurain a desired destination of travelers. The sturdy oak-paneled structure had been built thirty-odd years ago by an industrious young man from Wexford named Maghnus Loigde. One year after the pub opened, Maghnus was killed in a wagon accident. Thereafter it was run by his wife Doireann, a short, stocky woman with a friendly smile and great skill at telling bawdy stories. She never remarried and her only child, a son named Quinlin, was deaf from birth and could speak only a few words. He served as cook and soon became famous for his fresh bread, home-cured ham and fiery, secret-recipe mustards. Doireann offered only the finest ale, beer and wine, while Quinlin produced sumptuous sandwiches accompanied by deep-flavored soups and followed by the best hard-frosted cakes for miles around. Anyone traveling in the region made it a point to pass through Bhaile Mhurain to spend an hour or two in Doireann's place.

Padraic tied Alastar to a hitching post outside and gazed up at the beautifully-painted sign:

"M & D" it still read after all these years, for Maghnus and Doireann. The first time he had come here, a twenty-year-old Blade with a taste for beer and women, his companions were Gorman Fotharta and Domnall Laigain. Maghnus was already dead and a young, feisty, black-haired woman ran the pub. When he and his two friends started to bellow their stories and spill stout on the floor, Doriann's acid tongue and flailing broom quickly reined them in. He smiled at the memory. Could she be here after all this time?

A married couple in their thirties came out through the ornately-carved door. They eyed him briefly, nodded a polite greeting and made their way down the street. Padraic entered before the door swung shut and found himself in a place that smelled familiar: the scent of lemon oil that Doireann used to daily polish the oak tables and chairs and bar. There was one change: the pub was now divided in half by a full-height wooden partition whose pass-through was covered by a green brocade curtain.

Pipe smoke swirled about, yet the pub was not stuffy; every one of the many windows was cracked open at the top. The cold air filtering in did not compete with the blistering heat of a vast black-iron stove taking up the center of the room. Three of the ten tables were occupied by local families. He heard one tiny girl with curly hair whisper loudly to her mother, "who is that man, mommy? Is he a giant?" Her mother shushed the little girl and smiled at Padraic in embarrassment.

And then Doireann bustled through the curtains bearing a tray of empty glass steins. So focused was she on her task that she went straight behind the bar on Padraic's right and took no notice of him. He sidled up to the bar and slid partway onto a stool.

"Doireann?"

The woman spun from the barrels where she was filling the steins and eyed him between wisps of gray hair tumbling over her sweaty forehead.

"Yes, can I—"

She stopped, closed the tap, and moved closer to him. Seated as he was, she still had to look up at him.

"I know you," she said, her eyes taking in his face and his vast, sweatered torso. "A long time ago, yes, I was young and you were too."

She stared down at the bar and bit her lip. When she looked up, bright blue eyes glittering with recognition. "Padraic. Padraic Conmaicne. General of the army."

"*Now*, Doireann," he said quietly. "Then, a rowdy young buck that spilled stout on your floor and lusted after your young lady patrons."

She leaned forward and set both work-hardened hands on the polished oak bar.

"Thirty years it's been," she said, her memory searching for details. "You traveled with Domnall Laigain then, may his soul rest in peace, and Gorman Fotharta too." Her eyes narrowed at Gorman's name. "I never thought to lay eyes on you again, me in this tiny backwater town and you leading the army."

"Your memory is good," he said, feeling his heart lift from despairing sadness. "I'm alone now and I promise not to spill stout on your floor." He glanced around the room. "It's still a wonderful place, even finer than I remember. You keep the drinkers behind the curtain these days?"

She nodded and went back to filling the steins. "I do, Padraic. Most of my business is families. Even back there I allow no nonsense. Quiet drinking and pipe-smoking, or you get the broom."

"Anyone I might know back there now?"

She loaded the filled steins, four of them, back onto the tray.

"Possibly. Gorman's son Bram and three town lads, Blades all."

"Do me a favor?"

She smiled broadly, revealing gaps where teeth had once been. "Sure."

"Take two stouts back, and I'll follow you."

She looked puzzled but unloaded two of the steins and headed though the curtain with Padraic following. The back room was darker, having only one window, and a bit cooler too since that window was cracked open more than the rest. Two long tables with benches, each seating eight or ten, took up nearly all of the floor space. One table was empty. At the other, four young men sat together, two on each side. The largest of the group sat with his back to Padraic.

Doireann set the tray down. The oversized patron said, "what took you so long? And where're the other two stouts?"

"Button yer smart mouth," Doireann snapped as she unloaded the steins. "Gentleman there said to serve two."

All four sets of eyes followed Doireann's nod to where Padraic waited inside the curtain. One of the men got to his feet quickly, then two others. Bram remained seated.

"I have business with Bram," Padraic said in a low, commanding voice. "Private business, soldiers. When I'm gone, there'll be a round on me."

Each of the three muttered "sir" and stepped around him into the front room. Doriann bustled past him with her empty tray.

Padraic lowered himself onto the bench opposite Bram and took a long draft on cold, finely-brewed dark stout. At this close distance, he saw both himself and Etain sitting across from him. The tall, broad frame, heavy jaw and blue eyes were pure Conmaicne ... but Bram had his mother's wide mouth, fine, straight nose and wavy, thick hair.

"General," Bram said, setting his stout down. "Or should I use father for this conversation?"

The sneer in his tone was obvious, yet it had a forced, tired quality.

"Padraic will do," he replied. After a pause, he said, "I've just come from your mother."

"You knew she was ill?"

"I did not. I came to speak of other matters and she told me."

"The news must've pleased you."

The rage that welled up from his belly was almost too much to contain. He downed half the stein and took a deep breath before replying.

"I loved your mother once. I loved her the night you were conceived. And her death will grieve me. That's the truth of it, son, believe what you will."

The sneer vanished from Bram's face. He opened his mouth to speak, then looked down quickly and wrapped powerful hands around the stein.

"You'll miss her?" Padraic asked him.

"Yes," Bram said. "I will."

Padraic caught Doireann's face peaking through the curtains: she held forth a pitcher of stout. Padraic nodded, she slipped in and topped off their steins, then vanished again through the curtains.

"What your mother and I spoke of was the future," Padraic said. "And the past too. The details I won't get into, but there's something I need to ask of you, and I'm prepared to offer something in return."

Bram gulped down half of the refilled stein and mopped his mouth on his sleeve. Beads of sweat broke out on his broad, unscarred forehead.

"I doubt I'm going to like this."

"For the moment, listen. Etain told me you have friends in Bretan, that you might like to transfer to their fighters."

"I tried already. They didn't like my record."

"I can make it happen, in fact I can see to it you're placed with any unit you like, anywhere in Bretan."

Bram looked up with eyes that were both suspicious and hopeful.

"Why would you do that for me?"

"I'd do it in exchange for a promise, your word of honor as a soldier and citizen."

"Promise of what?"

"That you'll never again speak to anyone of what happened in Fotharta House when you were children."

A look of panic came into his eyes. "What did Mother tell you?"

"I believe she told me the truth."

"Then you came here to kill me."

"No. I came here to obtain your silence. So I repeat: I'll do whatever it takes to get you into Bretan, into their Fighters, with a clean record. What you do after that is your own affair. My price is silence."

Bram got up and wandered over to the window. Outside, the afternoon sun had sunk behind the next building, throwing the room into a gloomy gray light.

"And if I say no?" he said with his back to Padraic.

"Then you will not leave this room alive."

Bram turned and smiled. "You look to be unarmed."

"I carry no weapons."

"I'm much younger than you."

Padraic sighed and stared at his stout. "Please consider what I'm offering. It costs you nothing."

Bram sat down at the far end of the table, thinking.

"A clean record?"

"Yes. Anywhere you want to be posted. Brest, a coastal town, the interior. Beautiful women there, great food and wine. Warmer than here, too. Just keep in mind that if you cross their line, it's not a stockade or a demotion for punishment. They'll hang you. Once you leave the Province, you're beyond my protection."

"I'd be able to come back?"

"You're a citizen, you can always come back."

Bram sipped at his stout and drummed fingers on the table.

"I asked for your word," Padraic pressed him, "and I would have to accept it. Some day I *will* be too old to kill you, and not too long after that I'll be food for the worms. I'm hoping there's enough of me in you that you'd keep a solemn oath."

Quinlin, wearing an apron and a jaunty wool cap, entered to light a lantern and then left quickly. The low rumble of conversations from the front room grew louder as patrons arrived for an evening drink and meal. At last, Bram lifted his stein and drained it. He banged it hard on the table.

"Make the arrangements," he muttered. "Draw up the papers and get word to me where and when to meet you."

Padraic got to his feet. "I'll do that," he said, "but today, I want your word."

He reached out his hand.

Bram stood and looked at him straight. He took Padraic's hand.

"It's a fair deal," he said. "I'll do as you ask."

Two hours later, Padraic unsaddled Alastar in Laigain House's barn. To his relief, he saw no sign of Treasach: Conor was still with Oran at Kilmore Quay.

The sun had long since set, and a overhead brilliant stars and a gleaming half-moon shone upon fresh-fallen snow. Padraic crossed the yard with a slow step, ascended the porch stairs, and entered the great room. Liadan sat near the hearth, a teacup in one hand and a book in the other. Seeing him, she set the book aside.

"How did it go, brother?" she asked. "Did you see Etain?"

Padraic sank onto an overstuffed sofa near her.

"I did."

"And?"

"Conor won't be back tonight?"

"No, it's just you and me. Why do you ask?"

He eyed her teacup. "Could you make a pot? There's a great deal I need to tell you."

My heart is heavy for so many grieving among our people, their eyes beholding empty places at the table. By whatever fortune watches over my family, my children have all come home alive— though they bear scars on their bodies and in their souls too. Conor who is so like me in spirit and thought clings to his dream of a quiet home and a loving family, with Mairin who has changed in a way I cannot quite fathom. Is my intuition over-zealous where my son is concerned? Despite the victory over the Santanders, Aideen seems more worried and tense than ever. Yet I have hope that she and her brother might learn to share each other's burdens. My heart bleeds for my dear Feth, who accomplished so much in so little time, and in whose eyes I see a new sadness that comes of leading others into death. She is betrothed to a fine and understanding man who will support her and love her, and for that I am grateful. As Uinseann often says, we must be content with life and love and the beauty of the earth. All the rest is dust in the wind.

Journal of Liadan Laigain

Chapter 50
December 14, Province Year 999

The Great Celebration of the Millennium was at hand. With the official date of December solstice only a week off, the proud townfolk of Dungarvan were putting the finishing touches on decorations for their town. Mourning wreaths were lifted from doors and replaced by wreaths of bright red and green holly. Colored lanterns on wooden posts illuminated every street corner. Clan banners flew proudly from cottage rooftops, and merchants' shop windows glowed with candles at dusk. Every gathering place was filled nightly by citizens eager to hear readings of histories and stories and poems and revel in sweet music and song.

Feth and Sean stepped out of his rooming house into a snowy night that was cold indeed, yet the crisp air was redolent of woodsmoke and turf fires. Feth pulled her hood over her head and playfully drew Sean's stocking cap down over his eyes. He retaliated with a handful of powdery snow thrown in her general direction. Then they wrapped arms around each other's waists and strolled through the snow towards Mor and Derdre's home.

"When we were riding somewhere near Cork," Feth said, "the ruins I mean, Derdre talked about a night like this. She said it would be snowing and we would all come to her house. And she was right!" She paused and sighed. "I just wish she hadn't been wounded so bad."

"She seems to be getting stronger," Sean said, "and she has Keegan who loves her as much as I love you. Suppose they'll marry soon?"

"Sure. Gwen and Ionhar too."

"How about us?"

Feth kissed him lightly. "Mother wrote back, she's making plans with Niamh. Maybe two months."

"That pair!" Sean laughed. "What fun they must be having! They've been friends since before we were born."

They turned a corner and left the square. Halfway down the next block, they approached the cottage Feth had admired before the battle. It was cheerfully decorated with lanterns and candles and colored banners. Snow lay thick on its many shrubs and evergreens. Feth stopped and rested her hands on the white-painted fence.

"Too bad," she said. "That's really too bad."

"Why? I thought you liked this house."

"Oh, I love it! But the sale sign is gone. Someone bought it."

Sean brushed snow off the top of the fence post.

"Well, it's too small anyway."

Feth slapped his snow-covered coat. "It is not! It's a perfect size. Any idea who got it?"

He leaned back nonchalantly against the fence.

"As a matter of fact, I did."

"What?" She spun to face him and nearly fell on the slippery walk. "You bought it? How? Don't put me on about this, Sean Osraige."

"I'm serious, love. I should say *we* bought it, because *we* will have to pay for it. I borrowed money from my father and from a scholar friend. *And* from a bank. *And* I spent every other farthing I had."

"Oh, Sean, I love you." She wrapped her arms around him and they kissed long enough for passersby to chuckle. "It will be our home forever. I'm so excited, you could never give me a better present. When can we move in?"

"As a matter of fact, the house is empty now and those are my decorations," he said, lifting her off her feet. "Unless you want to wait until we're married."

"I'd rather not," she said with a grin. "I want someplace where we don't have to be so quiet."

"Such a naughty girl!" He kissed her again and then pulled her along the sidewalk. "Come on, we're late already! And I'm starved."

They skipped along through the snow, tumbling down once and brushing themselves off and then throwing snow at each other. At the next corner they ran into Gwen and Ionhar, also heading for Mor's home. The big man carried a monstrous basket under one arm and Gwen lugged a bulging canvas sack. They fell in together to walk the final block.

"May we know what's in there?" asked Sean, his fingers on the cloth covering the basket.

"The biggest ham you'll ever see," said Ionhar, "and Gwen has four cakes she made fresh today. She's already making me fat!"

"Do you know what Sean did?" Feth asked, eyes sparkling.

"It wouldn't have anything to do with a cottage, would it?" said Gwen.

"You knew!" Feth cried.

Gwen laughed in reply. Feth poked Ionhar in the ribs. "I suppose you did too."

"We happened on Sean coming out of the house last week," Ionhar explained, "so the secret was out. He swore us to silence!"

"I remember," said Gwen, "how you talked about the house one night when we were in Killarney. Your spirits were so low ... until you talked about that cottage. You described it so well I could picture it."

They reached the fence gate of Mor's home and made their way up the snowy walk to the ajar front door. Light streamed from the windows and reflected off virgin white snow blanketing the yard. They walked in and found the house's front room filled with five of their friends. One settee was taken up by Vaughn and a very pregnant Murel. Derdre sat next to them, smiling and laughing but Feth caught the grimace on her friend's face when she shifted position in the chair. Mor and Keegan were laying food out on the dining table.

"Welcome, welcome!" Mor cried when he saw them enter. "Food goes here. Ah, Ionhar with his ham! And look at those cakes! We'll be eating all night, my friends."

Soon the table fairly groaned with food. Everyone took a platter and loaded it up while Mor filled mugs with steaming hot spiced cider from a kettle hanging in front of the hearth. Keegan filled a plate and brought it to Derdre, then took a chair next to her. Feth and Sean seized the other settee, a small one that pressed them comfortably close together. Gwen and Ionhar took the big sofa, and Mor settled into a chair near the hearth so he could pile the wood on. For the next two hours, they savaged the ham, devoured dozens of biscuits, reduced cheeses to rinds, burned tongues on fresh-roasted potatoes drenched in butter, and overstuffed themselves with Gwen's frosted cakes.

At last, when not another bite could be eaten, Gwen retrieved her flute and began to play, and soon Derdre joined in with song after song. Feth nestled close to Sean, her hands wrapped in his, and dreamed of what their own house would be like. They would have parties like this, invite all their friends, tell jokes and sing and dance, remember the past and plan for the future.

By midnight sleepiness afflicted everyone. Vaughn and Murel were the first to leave, then Gwen and Ionhar and Keegan, who was staying in their flat until Derdre was well enough to move into a place with him. An exhausted Mor said good night and retreated to his upstairs room. As the fire died down, Feth and Sean were left alone with Derdre.

"You should get to bed too," Feth said to her. "Need any help?"

"No, no," said Derdre with a tired wave, "I'm fine. In fact I feel pretty good, most of the time. Father says full healing will take another month or two." She got to her feet with effort. "See? Not quite up to shooting yet, but by spring I'll have the bow in my hands again."

Derdre spotted the anguished look on Feth's face. "That's why I waited up. Feth, you have got to stop blaming yourself for this." She touched her ribs just below the heart. "Any one of us could have taken a hit with a spear. Lots of our comrades did not come out alive. I've told Gwen and I'm telling you, I was there because I wanted to be, and you know it. We all were. The charge you ordered was the right decision, it may have won the battle."

"I know," said Feth. She got up and pulled Sean to his feet. "I've thought it all through a million times. It's just different when I see you."

"I'll be fine, I have the best doctor in the Province." She took Feth's hand and led her towards the door. "You'll have a great house and we'll be neighbors! What could be better than that?"

Feth hugged Derdre gently. "Nobody ever had a better friend. I mean it."

Sean hugged Derdre too and then retrieved their coats from the coat stand. Sean pulled the door open and snow tumbled in over the threshold.

"Look at that snow!" cried Derdre. "It's just what I said Feth, in Cork. Isn't it?"

"Sure it is," said Feth. "Exactly as you said."

"Good night to you both. See you soon."

They strolled back to the rooming house through snow a foot deep and still piling up. Sean's room was ice cold so they undressed quickly and dove under heavy blankets. Feth pressed her nose onto Sean's warm chest.

"Wow, that's a cold nose!" he exclaimed. "And your hands are cold too!"

"Well, do something to warm me up."

He did, and a full hour later Feth slept soundly in his arms. He was tired too, but sleep would not come. His mind glided over the snow-covered fields to the north, to a hidden room in an old castle's tower, a room overflowing with books and manuscripts that might be the last copies left in the world. Somehow, he had to get there.

"My mother and Niamh are planning Feth's wedding. Why not combine the two? Oran could do double-duty as best man!"

Conor slid his arm over Mairin's shoulders. They huddled under the protection of Laigain House's broad porch, sheltered from heavy snow swirling in the light of the lanterns. At their back, the great room of the old house was filled to capacity and then some: Uinseann and Rionach, Padraic and Liadan, Kellen, Aideen, Oran and Melvina and Bethia MacLaren, Hagan and Niamh Osraige filled every seat and chair save for the small divan Conor and Mairin vacated for a breath of cold night air.

"Yes, I suppose that makes sense," Mairin answered after a pause.

Conor eased her shoulders around so they faced each other, virtually eye to eye in height.

"Don't get too enthusiastic about it," he said, then regretted saying it when her tepid smile vanished. "Look, Mairin, since the moment you stepped off your ship, over a month ago, you've acted like I was a stranger. You don't want to be alone with me, you don't want to make love, and it sounds like you don't want to get married. Was it that long ago I proposed to you at the Fair? I just don't understand what's happening."

Laughter burst from the great room; Uinseann and Hagan were trading bawdy stories again.

Mairin turned away from him, took a steps down the porch, and leaned forward with her hands on the rail.

"You look like you're on a ship," Conor observed. "Maybe that's where you'd rather be than here, with me."

He walked to her side and to his surprise she turned and put her arms around him.

"I'm sorry," she said in a strained voice. "I know things aren't right with me, Conor. Please don't be angry."

"I'm not angry," he said, holding her. "I'm worried. About you and about us."

"I don't know what to do. I want to be fair to you. If I accept Aideen's offer—"

"I'll be lucky to see you a day a month, and that's if I live in Dungarvan."

She held him at arm's length and looked into his eyes. "Yes, that's right. And that's not counting when you have to be away with the army."

"I told Padraic I'd accept field army command again, if he needs me, but not regular service. He's not happy about it but he understands. If you were home I'd be there most of the time."

"You're sure about that?"

Conor's hands tightened on her arms. "You're evading the main issue, Mairin, and you know it! I'll make it work somehow, the question is whether you're going to stay with me or marry the navy."

She broke free of his hands and turned her back. He took hold of her again, harder this time, and said, "sleep here tonight. With me. I want you."

"You've had too many ales."

He released her and stepped away. "Strange thing to say to a man who proposed to you, stone sober."

She stood frozen for a moment, then marched back into the great room without looking at him. Conor was left alone, cursing his loose tongue and wishing he could take back the whole conversation. He stood alone on the porch until the door opened again and Liadan gave him a look that said, *I know things aren't right but you need to come in.*

The great room felt shockingly warm after the freezing outside air. Liadan and Niamh had spread the festive meal out on the long table and everyone had taken a place. Conor and Mairin took one end of a bench across from Oran and Melvina. Bethia perched next to Oran, her eyes popping out at the sight of so much food. Uinseann sat at the head, and when everyone was squeezed in, he asked for silence and the joining of hands.

"We kin and friends here gathered are thankful for this bounteous food, for warmth in the midst of cold, for the company of those we love and whose lives have been spared. The world gives and the world takes, in an unending cycle whose mystery we cannot fathom. Let us always remember to love one another, share what we have, and look out upon the wonder of Nature with awe and humility. Amen. Now," he said, raising his head, "let's do justice to this meal!"

The assembled company concentrated on passing bowls and platters and baskets, with the usual confusion of which way to pass. Finally Padraic thundered a command to pass left and after much laughter and mock protests, order was restored. Kellen took on the duty of filling the stout pitchers and Melvina kept young Bethia supplied with spiced tea. Soon a relative quiet descended amidst occasional cries of "wonderful stew!" and "who made this?" and "here, have some more of this." Conor overhead Bethia whisper to Oran, "I've never seen so much food at one time."

While Conor did his best to join in the fun and devour his share of the food, the depressing exchange on the porch had closed his stomach and dampened his spirit. Soon the main dishes were cleared away and from the kitchen issued a stream of frosted cakes and fruit pies and warm boiled puddings. Cries of glee accompanied Liadan's announcement that thanks to Aideen, coffee strong and hot would be served as a special treat.

"Say what you will about tea, even the finest," Padraic said between gulps, "coffee is the beverage of kings, don't you agree, Hagan?"

Oran's father nodded vigorous assent. "Without a doubt. I raise my cup to Commodore Laigain, and I will not ask how you came by so much of it!"

They all laughed and toasted Aideen, who blushed and smiled in a way Conor could not ever remember seeing. Now and then he found Mairin's hand under the table and held it, mostly for his own reassurance. On the few occasions their eyes met, Conor sensed uncertainty, even fear, and that troubled him deeply.

When everyone declared themselves full to overflowing, the table was cleared and moved aside, more coffee was served out, and sated diners settled back into chairs and sofas. Conor sat with Mairin for a time, his arm around her, while Oran and Hagan engaged in a battle of wits and Rionach was enticed to tell stories of life in her childhood more than seven decades ago. In the midst of one of Kellen's lengthy and complex card tricks, Conor whispered "I'll be back" in Mairin's ear, gathered up his heavy coat and hat, and went out to shovel a path to the stable. Oran followed him, helped with the shoveling, and leaned against a pillar in the barn as Conor filled feed-bags.

"Should I ask," Oran began, "or would you rather not talk about it?"

Conor finished stuffing Treasach's bag with oats and then stroked the stallion's massive neck.

"I don't care," he said with resignation. "I just can't understand what's gone wrong. In October at the fair, I gave her a Celtic Knot and she cried with joy and said yes, I'll marry you. Now she seems like a different person. Distant. Afraid, maybe. We haven't made love once since she came ashore, she doesn't even seem to want to be alone with me. Yet she says she still loves me."

"What do you think she's afraid of?"

"I think what she fears the most is that she'll regret giving up the Squadron. It's been her whole life since leaving home, the only life that means anything to her."

Oran followed Conor as he emptied and refilled water troughs in the stalls.

"That could be very hard, Conor. I sometimes wonder how I'd handle not wandering around the country when I like. In the last fifteen years I've been to every corner or Eirelan, most of Kernow and Scotland and Wales, even been to Bretan, that garden spot over the sea. Staying in one place all the time would be a trial for me, at least in the beginning. It's different for you. You *want* a place to call home, you even have the details all worked out in your head. You probably know what your writing desk will look like, where you write poetry after the children fall asleep."

"You know me too well."

Oran shrugged. "The point is, both you and Mairin have new obligations now and people are counting on you. Did you ever think that one reason Aideen has fought to hold onto Mairin is that she's *afraid* of losing her? How would you feel if you had to take the army into the field next spring and Kellen said 'sorry, Conor, I have some painting to do. Maybe next battle.'"

"If you're trying to cheer me up," Conor said with a dark stare, "it isn't working."

"I was just pointing out that what Mairin feels is not so hard to understand if you consider your own case fairly."

Conor finished the water troughs and found a brush. Treasach shook his big head with delight as coarse bristles dug into his dense coat.

"Did you say anything to her you'd like to take back?"

"Possibly I did. I said something about her being married to the navy."

"Oh, very sensitive."

"All right!" Conor threw the brush against the stall, making Treasach jump. "I wasn't at my best. Crucify me."

Oran picked up the brush and set it back in Conor's hand. "Tomorrow, brother, talk to her again. Remember the life she's had and the burden she carries from it. Don't try to blot it out or make her forget about it, she can't. Help her deal with it. Show her you're the best friend she has, not someone who demands something from her."

Conor sighed and patted Treasach's flank. "I think I forgot that tonight. I must have sounded like a whining schoolboy."

"Let it go for now." Oran flopped onto a hay bale while Conor resumed grooming his stallion.

"You hear anything from Triona Bairrche?"

Conor gave Oran a sharp look. "No, why do you ask?"

"Merely curious. Where does she live?"

"Waterford, I think."

"Beautiful woman," Oran observed, visualizing her hovering in the air above him. "She'll be a catch for someone."

Conor did not answer. He set the brush aside, patted Treasach and said "good night, boy."

When he moved towards the door, Oran caught his sleeve.

"Make sure you kiss her before she leaves."

Conor nodded and pushed open the barn doors. The snow fell unabated, so heavily that it obscured the porch lanterns not a hundred yards away. Together they slid the doors closed and made tracks through snow piled inches deep on their shoveled path. When they reached the porch, a roar of laughter poured from the house. Then a fiddle started up, joined seconds later by a banjo.

"Your mother and Padraic are getting started," Oran said.

Conor paused at the door to listen. "It's good to hear mother play again. She hasn't taken the fiddle off the wall since summer. They'll be wanting your concertina."

"Aye, that's so. It's in my bag," Oran replied. "Time to dance, my friend, and leave the troubles of the world behind."

Oran pushed the door open. Chairs and divans had been shoved against the wall. In the room's center lithe Bethia MacLaren danced on her toes in the ancient style, back stiff and hands on hips. The young woman's joy was unalloyed since the day Oran located her brother Sloane, grievously wounded at Mhisteala, now recovering in the army hospital at Clonmel.

Oran's concertina joined Liadan's fiddle and Padraic's banjo, and the dancing began in earnest, while the stout flowed into tankards and the silent snow blanketed the Earth.

Alone in her bedroom, Triona Bairrche dipped her quill into ink and wrote on the small sheet of parchment. After one sentence she paused and stared out the window. It was not a letter she wanted to write, in fact it frightened her half to death. Yet she'd had put it off as long as she could and now it had to be written and sent. It was not a long letter nor did it need to be, and soon added the final period and signed it.

> *Dear Conor, I hope all is well with you and your family in Rosslare. There is something I must tell you. I am carrying a child and it is yours. I had thought to keep this from you because you have plans for the future that do not include me or the child growing within me. In the end I decided that would be wrong. You have to know, and now you do. Please do not think badly of me. I am not sad because it will be a beautiful child and I will raise him or her as you would have wished.*
> *Love, Triona.*

She waited for the ink to dry, folded the note in half, and slipped it into an envelope addressed to Conor. Tomorrow morning she would post it.

With a heavy sigh she rose from the writing desk and stepped to the ice-frosted window. A lovely snow drifted down over the houses and shops of their corner of Waterford town. She sat down on the window seat and watched the children below laughing and shouting and cavorting in the white powder, and she remembered what it was like when she was down there among them, not so many years ago.

How simple things were then. How very simple.

An excerpt from the next book in this series, *In the Bleak Midwinter...*

In the bleak midwinter,
Frosty wind made moan,
Earth stood hard as iron,
Water like a stone.
Snow had fallen,
Snow on snow, snow on snow,
In the bleak midwinter,
Long, long ago.

- - Christina Rossetti
(Gaelic trans. from old English
by Myghal Keigwin)

Dear Oran — Feth and I moved into our new cottage today on St. Mary Street. We'd hoped to wait till we were married but the previous owner already moved out, so why not? Feth is thrilled, of course. She pressed Keegan, Ionhar and Gwen into service moving all my books and papers (a big load) and my other furnishings (a small load). You really had to see it, mighty Ionhar hitched to a wagon like a draft horse with Keegan and Gwen pushing from the rear, through streets covered with ice and snow. Derdre waited at the cottage and helped Feth and me unpack everything. The house does need some attention like cracks in the chinking that leak cold air and a well pump in the kitchen that takes about six pumps to yield a cup of water. As you know I am so handy with mechanical things. On top of that, I'm back to teaching so I'm gone until late afternoon. Please come to see us after the Millennium Celebration, bring Melvina if you like. We have a spare room (what luxury!) You and I have so much to talk about.

Your loving brother, Sean.

Chapter 1
December 20, Province Year 999

"Banning, please return to your seat!"

Sean pleaded with the fidgety seven-year-old for the third time that day, and his very considerable patience was wearing thin. His mood wasn't helped by the fact that the drafty classroom was cold—the day's allotment of firewood for the stove had run out—and his back ached fiercely because Feth had enticed him to ...

He pushed thoughts of a scantily-clad fiancée into the background. Banning, his long, sandy hair wildly askew, scowled impishly and crept back to his chair. Just keeping thirteen children aged six to ten in their seats all day, listening, reciting and writing was a daunting task and while Sean loved every one of them, after seven hours he was just plain tired. Thank the heavens he had help coming today.

"Now, children," he announced over the chatter, "children please listen! I promised you a special treat today at two o'clock and that's what the clock says." Out of the corner of his eye he saw his guest speaker stroll past the frost-coated windows. "And if you'll just sit quietly for a moment, he'll be coming right in."

At least that piqued their curiosity and quieted them down. A moment later, the door in the back creaked on its hinges and his guest took a step into the room. All the children twisted in their seats to view the newcomer. Youthful eyebrows rose and shining eyes widened to saucers. Ionhar Raithlinn, Feth's massive friend from the Line of Blades and Storyteller of the Town of Creagh, was an impressive sight even without his armor. His enormous cape-covered shoulders scraped the doorframe on both sides. Huge black boots caked with snow thudded heavily on the classroom's planked floor. When he doffed his tall, rumpled hat, chunks of snow fell on nearby students, who giggled and tried to brush it onto their comrades.

Ionhar smiled to all the children and came forward to Sean, who offered his hand in the fervent hope the fighter would have mercy on his writer's fingers. To his relief Ionhar grasped his hand gently, then pulled off his heavy cloak and hung it on a peg. The children watched him silently, expectantly.

"Children, this is our guest today. His name is Ionhar Raithlinn, from the town of Creagh which is near Skibbereen—for those of you who paid attention in our geography lesson this morning. Ionhar fights in the Line of Blades and he is also a storyteller. His ancestors have been storytellers for many centuries. Please say hello to Ionhar."

"Hello Ionhar," they dutifully chorused.

Sean nodded to Ionhar, who sat down on a sturdy stool Sean had arranged for him in front of his teacher's desk. Sean moved his desk chair to a corner to listen, thinking enviously, *it's easy to keep kids quiet when you're so big you can barely squeeze through the door!*

"Hello, my children," Ionhar said, his voice warm and deep. "Today I am going to tell you a wonderful story that my father taught me and his father taught him. But first I'd like to tell you a little about my town. Your teacher told you its name, Creagh, and where it is, which is near Skibbereen." He pointed to the map of Eirelan on the wall to his left. "My town lies along the River Ilen where it becomes quite wide, you see it there? It's a very beautiful place and the town is so old no one even knows when it was first lived in. It's not nearly so big as Dungarvan where you live, I think we have only three or four hundred families and everyone knows everyone else."

"Do you have schools?" a little black-haired girl up front asked timidly.

Ionhar gazed down at her with great affection. "Oh, yes, we have a school, a little cabin all by itself."

"Is it cold too?" asked Banning, drawing laughter from the other children.

"Aye, it's just as cold as we are today, sometimes," Ionhar said, joining in the laughter. "We have a saying, though, that goes like this: cold is bad, hunger is worse, but ignorance is worst of all."

Sean silently thanked him for saying that.

"Anyway, Creagh is a fine place to grow up and I hope you will all come to see it some day. We are as proud of our town as you are of yours. Now, on to the story. It's called the Journey Over the Sea and it's about a great ship that sails west over the ocean and finds very strange creatures and peoples none of us have ever seen!"

Now the perpetually-noisy room fell utterly silent. Even Sean, tired as he was, found himself drawn in by Ionhar's resonant and flexible voice, his ability to play multiple characters and paint pictures in words, his unique gift of creating a seamless fantasy that riveted the children to their chairs and had Sean sitting on the edge of his own chair waiting for each new scene to unfold. When Ionhar finished, Sean was astonished to see that the street outside was darkened by twilight and the ticking pendulum clock on the wall read three minutes past four.

Ionhar stood and stretched his vast frame. Sean approached him, took his hand again, and whispered in his ear, "many thanks, dear friend. We expect you and Gwen for dinner."

Ionhar nodded as he donned his cape and hat and the students resumed their chattering.

"Keegan and Derdre too?" he asked.

"Not this time. Keegan took her out to Ballynacourty Point. They're staying two nights in a cozy inn attached to the lighthouse, or so he told me. They'll be back for the Celebration."

Sean walked with Ionhar to the door.

"She didn't seem that strong last time I saw her," Ionhar observed.

"Keegan rented a pretty luxurious closed carriage. That man won't let anything happen to her!"

Ionhar laughed. "Sure that's true. Tonight, then."

"You'll come again to help me out?"

"Try to keep me away." Ionhar waved a hand to the children. "Goodbye, little ones. And *behave* for your teacher. When I come back in a few weeks, anyone who gets a bad report will not hear my next story."

Sean hoped Ionhar understood his look of undying gratitude.

"All right, children," Sean called out, "time to go home. Make sure you dress in all your clothes, it's snowing again."

When they had all bolted out the door, many with coats unbuttoned and hats in hand, Sean slumped back in his chair, clasped his fingers behind his head and grinned. He planned to stop at the wine shop on the way home and buy a bottle of whatever his purse could afford. Ionhar's parting comment was worth that much and a great deal more!

Feth waited on a hard wooden bench in the tiny anteroom while Mor Dal Reti finished with his last patient of the day, a woman who'd brought in a coughing, cranky four-year-old girl. Outside, twilight was descending and the lamplighter was at his business in Dungarvan's town square. As he lit each lantern, its soft glow illuminated snowflakes drifting lazily down to add to the thick layer already covering the stones. *So very peaceful and quiet,* she thought. *And so ... right: Mor the physician tending to the needs of a young family. So utterly at odds with the scenes of horror I witnessed at Mhisteala.*

The door to Mor's little surgery opened and the mother emerged with her pacified girl.

"Keep him warm," Mor was saying, "and give her that draught every four hours. if she's not better in two days, make sure you bring her back."

"Thank you so much, doctor." The woman donned her heavy coat and dressed her daughter. "We'll pay our account at the end of the week."

Mor waved a hand at her. "Whenever you can, Brid. My best to Artegal."

When the door swung shut, Mor looked down at her. "Next?"

Feth stood and gave him a quick hug.

"Doctor, what's your prescription for a happiness ache?"

Mor's eyes twinkled. "Well, that depends, Miss Laigain. Where exactly does it hurt?"

Feth solemnly laid a hand over her heart. "Here. Right here."

"Nothing to be done, I'm afraid," said Mor with mock solemnity. "Perhaps it will pass of its own accord."

"I hope not!"

More pulled off the white smock he wore when seeing patients and hung it on a peg.

"Any special reason you came by?" he said, donning his coat and hat.

"I'll tell you while we walk home," she said.

Outside, they linked arms and strolled through the lantern-lit square.

"First reason is to invite you to dinner. I know Derdre's away, and Sean and I are having Gwen and Ionhar over. Can you join us?"

Mor patted her gloved hand. "Feth, I'd love to, really. But to be honest, I'm just exhausted. I had a delivery this morning at four a.m., a difficult one at that. And I've been seeing patients since eight. Tonight I just want to sit in front of the fire and rest. Give me a rain check?"

"Sure. And we'll all be together for the Celebration anyway."

"And the second reason?"

"You're really tired," Feth said, linking her arm a little tighter in his. "It can wait."

Mor stopped and held her at arm's length. "I'm never too tired to hear out a friend with a problem. To be honest, Feth, I'm almost sure what's on your mind anyway."

"Derdre," Feth admitted. She drew him on and they resumed their stroll along a street that led to Feth and Sean's cottage.

"You don't really need to explain," Mor began. "You're wondering how far she's really recovered from the wound."

Feth felt a pang of anguish stab at her stomach. The frightful image of Derdre lying on the battlefield, bleeding from a pike wound in her chest, flashed into her mind, as it often did in dreams.

"Good evening, Mor," said a man passing them. The man tipped his snow-covered cap.

Mor tipped his in return. "Coinneach, good to see you."

"Derdre is in overall fine health," he said after the man had passed on. "And as far I can tell, she'll live a long life, have children, do almost anything she wants to do."

Feth held them up to look into a shop window, still illuminated by a shaded lantern. It was a clothing shop featuring some fine winter coats and sweaters in the display.

"But," was all she said.

"But I think it's doubtful she'll be able to fight in the line again."

"Are you sure?"

Mor started them along the street again.

"Not completely, no. Still, my best judgment is that it won't happen. The problem is that the lance cut so many muscles in her chest, right through to the back, on her right side. If the lance had gone in on the other side, she'd have died of course. As it is, the lance barb missed major blood vessels and organs. So she recovered and in another month will have her full energy returned. The muscles were repaired as best they could do in the field hospital, but they had to work very fast. The rest of the healing is natural. Derdre will be able to ride a horse, carry a water bucket, or lift a baby out of a crib. Maybe even shoot a light target bow. But draw a powerful longbow, ten or twelve times a minute? Or crank the windlass on a ballista? I don't think that will be possible."

"Does she know that?"

Mor laid a hand over hers. "I've tried to prepare her for the idea, suggesting she not hope for too much. That she's alive is a great gift to all of us."

They reached Feth's cottage and stopped at the gate in the picket fence.

"In a way I should feel happy," Feth said, idly brushing snow off the tops of the fenceposts. "She'll be one friend I can come home to, if we have to fight again. And of course, we *will* have to fight again."

Mor nodded. "I know how you feel, Feth. I lost my dear wife to war and I very nearly lost my only child. The thought that Derdre won't be facing death in battle is a comfort to me in some ways. But I also know how she feels, how much she wants to be at your side when you take the Dragons into battle again. Leaving the Line of Bows after just one year's service is going to be very hard for her take, especially when Keegan goes off to fight."

Feth gazed at her wonderful, beautiful little cottage and thought of the man she loved so dearly who would soon be home to share it with her.

"Maybe," she said, "maybe in the spring things will really be different and we won't have to fight again, at least for awhile."

Mor laid an arm over her shoulder. "No one hopes for that more than me, Feth. Can you imagine how wonderful it is for me to bring babies into the world, after five years at sea mending sailors who are hurt and sick and desperately missing their homes? To mend little ones like Brid's daughter, to attend and comfort someone who is dying at the end of a long life?" He let out a tired sigh. "This is what I want my life to be. I want Derdre and Keegan to give me grandchildren and then I can spend my hours making sure they grow up healthy and strong too."

Two children tumbled by, shouting and shrieking and throwing snowballs at each other.

Mor followed them down the street with his eyes.

"I want them to never know what a sword or a longbow are, except as exhibits in a museum."

They both fell silent as the children's joyful sounds drifted into the distance. At last, Feth unlatched the gate and turned back to face Mor.

"You're sure you won't come to dinner?"

"Sure," Mor said with a smile. "My best to Sean and the others. See you for the Celebration!"

Mor kissed her forehead lightly and headed down the street towards his own house three blocks away. Feth watched him until he turned a corner, her thoughts and feelings whirling about like the snowflakes falling around her. *So many sides to everything*, she pondered. *I can never get things clear in my mind until I can talk them out with Sean. Tonight we'll talk after Gwen and Ionhar leave, by the dying fire in our drafty great room.*

She went inside, started a blazing fire, and began work on dinner. As she sliced the cheese, she tossed little bits onto the table for Rascal, their young male cat rescued as a tiny kitten from their own back yard.

"You do love your cheese," she said, grinning at the fast-growing tabby. "I wish you'd kill the mouse that runs around the house every night."

Rascal's large green eyes offered no hint of apology.

"Pass that ale pitcher!" Ionhar demanded. "Feth, how can someone so young make such a fine stew?"

The four friends were gathered around the rugged square table, which they had pushed as close as possible to the hearth. Soft, flickering light came from two thick candles resting on the stone mantle. Feth was actually pleased with her effort—an immediate benefit of asking her mother Liadan to send her recipes and hints for the kitchen. Gwen, whose specialty was baking, had provided a huge loaf of crusty bread fresh out of her oven to dunk in the lamb stew.

She glanced at Sean and cast him a secretive wink. He'd been so skillful at keeping the conversation away from any talk of war and fighting and politics. Between Sean's charming history lessons, Gwen's recollections of her childhood—so different from Feth and Sean's—in a tiny town on the Atlantic coast near Tralee, and Ionhar's hilarious tales, Feth had needed to do nothing but laugh, stoke the fire and serve out helpings of stew from the black iron pot hanging above the flames.

"Natural talent," Sean said to Ionhar. He retrieved the ale pitcher from the window sill, where drafts kept it cold. "Feth has many natural talents. Cooking, shooting a bow, public peaking, and then there's ... "

"Sean Osraige!" she cried. "Behave yourself."

Sean's eyes twinkled in the firelight. "I would if I had a fiancée who behaved *herself* !"

All four roared with laughter. Feth thought, *I could never imagine loving anyone so much as I love this man.* Then she saw Gwen lean over and kiss Ionhar's ruddy cheek and knew the bond between them was probably just as strong as her bond with Sean.

The stew and bread demolished, Feth cleared away the dishes to make way for dessert, a cake provided by Gwen. She talked over her shoulder as she sliced through the thick, crunchy frosting.

"What did you decide about a wedding?"

Gwen took a strong hold of Ionhar's thick hand. "Feth, much as we'd like to have it here, we really must involve our families. So we're going to Creagh next month to have one ceremony with Ionhar's kin and then on to Fahamore to have another with my family. The army is letting us each have a full month's leave."

Feth served slices of cake onto the china plates Sean's mother had given them and brought them to the table.

"So we'll have a big party for you when you get back."

Sean asked Ionhar, "what say Keegan and Derdre?"

Ionhar waited impatiently to dive into the cake.

"In the spring," he replied. "Derdre has always dreamed of a spring wedding when the flowers are blooming."

"Not too late in the spring, I hope," Feth said, then regretted it when she saw her friends catch her meaning.

Because if they wait too long Keegan may be fighting again. I always say too much when I drink ale !

"Early April I think," Ionhar rumbled with a smile. "Now for the cake."

Sean reached over and intercepted Ionhar's fork-wielding hand.

"Hold on just a moment, my storyteller friend."

Sean got up and went to a wall cabinet, from which he drew out a large bottle of wine. Bringing it to the table, he set it in front of Ionhar with a great flourish.

"To have with your dessert, fair sir!"

Ionhar gave Sean a puzzled look, then held up the bottle to catch the candlelight.

"What's this for? Sean, this is very expensive!"

"Worth every farthing for your services today."

"But I just told—"

"A story? Oh, it was a fine story and the children loved it. No, the wine is for what you said just before you left. From now on, all I have to do is threaten a misbehaver with not hearing your next story. You've saved me from spending half my day shouting for quiet!"

Another roar of laughter followed that Gwen joined but could not quite figure out. When he found his voice Sean related Ionhar's final message to his youthful charges. Feth hunted up the corkscrew and served the wine in rinsed-out ale glasses, regretting for just a moment that she didn't have proper wine glasses to hold the fine vintage.

An hour later, the friends adjourned to the great room's two small divans, which they slid near the hearth after moving the table and chairs to one side. Rascal had an especial liking for Ionhar and took up a place on his considerable lap. Feth waited until she was snuggled up against Sean with his arm around her shoulder before saying what she needed to say.

"I did get one bit of bad news today," she said. "I talked to Mor again about Derdre." She looked into Gwen's eyes. "I don't think she can fight with us again."

Gwen sighed and nodded. "I was pretty sure about it already, Feth. Ionhar and I talked about it last night. But look at it this way. If she can at least pull a target bow, a light one, and ride, she can work on the training program with Arvel. He'll be back soon with the replacement horses."

"I hadn't thought of that," Feth said, her mood brightening. "You think she'd want to do it?"

Gwen spread her hands wide. "What do you think?"

"Of course she will!"

Ionhar drew Gwen under his massive arm. "So, enough business for tonight! Sean, I want to hear a history story, something about really old times."

"Yes, Sean," Feth said, taking his hand in hers. "You were talking about the ancient Romans yesterday. Tell us about them."

"Tell you about the Romans?" Sean said, laughing. "The orchids will be blooming before I finish!" He stared at the flames for a long moment. "I have it. I'll tell you about Rome's greatest enemy in early times, before they conquered all of Europe. His name was Hannibal ... "

Two hours later, Gwen and Ionhar reluctantly took their leave. Feth cleaned up the remains of dinner and stored all the food in a mouse-proof cabinet while Sean made sure the fire was safe to let burn down for the night. Then they climbed into the chilly loft and quickly dove under the heavy goose down comforter. A moment later, Rascal burrowed his way underneath with them.

"Our vicious mouser," Feth said, stroking his head till he rattled with a loud purr. "I guess you can stay there for now, I'm too tired and full to play the barbarian queen tonight."

Sean wrapped her in his arms. "That's good, because my back needs till morning to recover from last night. Then I'll ravage you properly."

They kissed and said good night. Soon Sean's deep breathing signaled his descent into dreamland. Feth could not sleep just yet. She was too filled with love for the man holding her and for her friends who had so recently fought with her to save the Province from utter destruction. Before she drifted off herself, she heard the mouse skittering about the rafters.

"Rascal," she said sleepily. "Mouse."

He kept purring under the warmth of the covers.

She awoke once in a pitch-dark room. Sean was snoring lightly. It was the same dream again, the one that made her heart pound and her mouth dry as dust. She held the sword high and shouted, "Dragons, ready charge!" And then it was all a bloody maelstrom and Derdre lay dying.

Her trembling hand found Rascal, and with the help of his renewed purring, she slept on until the gray light of dawn.